# GOOD NEIGHBOURS

# GOOD NEIGHBOURS

BETH HERSANT

Copyright © 2015 Beth Hersant

The moral right of the author has been asserted.

Apart from any fair dealing for the purposes of research or private study, or criticism or review, as permitted under the Copyright, Designs and Patents Act 1988, this publication may only be reproduced, stored or transmitted, in any form or by any means, with the prior permission in writing of the publishers, or in the case of reprographic reproduction in accordance with the terms of licences issued by the Copyright Licensing Agency. Enquiries concerning reproduction outside those terms should be sent to the publishers.

Matador
9 Priory Business Park
Kibworth Beauchamp
Leicestershire LE8 0RX, UK
Tel: (+44) 116 279 2299
Fax: (+44) 116 279 2277
Email: books@troubador.co.uk
Web: www.troubador.co.uk/matador

ISBN 978 1784622 251

British Library Cataloguing in Publication Data.
A catalogue record for this book is available from the British Library.

Typeset in Adobe Garamond Pro by Troubador Publishing Ltd

**Matador** is an imprint of Troubador Publishing Ltd

*To Amelia and Matthew, for believing that I could do anything.*

*To Mom and Dad, for the tools to accomplish it.*

*To my Richard, for the chance. Thank you, my love.*

# CHAPTER 1

# EDEN

*"And the woman said unto the serpent, 'We may eat of the fruit of the trees of the garden, but of the fruit of the tree which is in the midst of the garden, God hath said: Ye shall not eat of it, neither shall ye touch it, lest ye die.'*

*"And the serpent said unto the woman, 'Ye shall not surely die. For God doth know that in the day ye eat thereof, then your eyes shall be opened, and ye shall be as gods.'"*

*Genesis 3:2-5*

Myrddin awoke. He lay in the animal skins that were his bed. It was early; there was not even a grey sliver of dawn in the sky; and it was cold.

His stomach ached. It was this which had awakened him – a persistent, gnawing hunger that made him too restless for sleep and too lethargic to get up and start the day. He looked at Nimue lying next to him. Her face was pale and her brow was furrowed even in slumber. Other mornings he had looked upon that face in the dim light and run gentle fingertips along the smooth line from temple to cheek to neck to breast. She would open her eyes and smile, and he would pull her to him in the drowsy heat of animal skins and soft flesh and the taste of her mouth.

On this day his mood could not be softened by the curve of hip or thigh. He was hungry – so very, very hungry. And what was worse: he was forsaken.

"Your problem, Myr, is that you are too proud." Even after many years, the words of the old medicine man stung him.

Proud! He laughed bitterly to himself and struggled stiffly to get up. A wave of nausea swept over him and he waited on hands and knees for it to pass. To think that his great transgression was to become too proud – it made his head hurt.

Born the last of his mother's six sons, it was clear that he was the runt. Later in mankind's history, a doctor may have identified the problem, the scrofulous taint that had left the child pale and small, narrow-chested and weak. But even without this diagnosis, it was clear to the tribe that this little one did not fatten up like the rest. He was not as quick or as agile as the others. In a world where a man's worth was measured by the strength of his arm in battle and the stealth of his step while hunting, he was backward and clumsy. And low, low down in every pecking order. Pride indeed!

While his brothers played at war and hunted birds for practise, he – red-faced from their teasing – would go off alone and sit for hours watching the creatures of the greenwood: the scuttling things and the birds and the four-legged ones.

And that is when it began … the voices.

At first he thought it was his mother calling him home, but when he looked for her among the lime and yew trees there was no one there. It made him afraid. He never told anyone, not even when, during the summer of his tenth year, the voices became insistent.

For him, there was something different about that summer. The very heat of it seemed to seep into his skin, making him restless. He went off his food. He could not sleep. He tossed and turned, fidgeted and pestered his mother, until his father got angry and sent him back to bed with a sharp smack on the rear. The child could not find the words to tell them that, as he lay in the darkness, the voices called and called his name.

Then came the fever and a headache of such blinding fury that his shrill cries hastened his father's steps to fetch the medicine man.

Old Garanhir looked grimly at the boy. "Does he take food?"

"No," replied his mother.

"Pass anything?"

"No."

Garanhir lit a fire and fed it with sacred herbs. Then he began to sing a prayer that the smoke would carry upward to The Elders. It was basic medicine, good ceremony, but even this had an alarming result. The child shrank from the light and clutched his head, whimpering in pain.

Garanhir stopped. He now knew what was wrong. The child would die. "I need stronger medicine," he told the anxious parents and left to gather plants that might offer the boy some relief.

When he returned, Myrddin was delirious. To the boy himself, it felt as if he were underwater. Every now and then, he would float to the surface and see his mother sitting next to him, urging him to drink the thin green liquid that the medicine man had given her.

During these moments he seemed to be standing outside himself – detached from the boy who had just wet the animal skins of his bed. He watched his own hands pluck restlessly at the soiled blankets. Then another wave seemed to roll over him and he sank once more…

## A Side Note

*Garanhir was treating an illness that would later be identified as tubercular meningitis, a disease characterised by high fever, delirium and the patient's inability to tolerate noise or light. Early doctors noted that children with scrofulous taint were more susceptible to contracting the disease, particularly if they lived in conditions where food and hygiene were poor. Death normally occurs within 2-3 weeks, but can come within a matter of days. Recovery is exceedingly rare but not entirely unknown, even in cases which present the full array of symptoms.*

"Come, little brother. It is time." A gentle voice roused him and Myrddin took a deep, easy breath. The pain was gone; a sense of exquisite relief filled him.

"Come," said the voice again and Myrddin realised that it came from an old man standing at the door of the tent. He did not know this man, but he had the dark eyes, prominent chin and long straight nose of the tribe. The boy felt instinctively that this stranger somehow *belonged*. Without fear or hesitation, he rose and took the man's hand, glancing over his shoulder as he left the tent. To his surprise, his mother did not seem to notice that he was leaving or indeed that he was well again. Instead, she sat crying by his bed. In another moment he realised why: his body still lay there as if dead. He was sorry to be leaving her, but he felt so healthy and peaceful that he followed the old man outside. The tribe was busy after a successful hunt. On a bed of leaves the men had piled large chunks of freshly butchered meat which the women were hanging on drying racks – long poles suspended between forked branches. Myrddin's stomach rumbled hungrily. There would be a good feast tonight and much laughter and singing.

But suddenly this happy scene was far away and below him. Myrddin and the old man were rising, rising into the air until they came to rest upon a field of clouds as solid beneath their feet as snow-covered earth. The old man pointed to the East. The rising sun seemed to reach out with golden hands to touch him and in that warm embrace he saw. Yes. The glowing orb of the sun changed before his eyes into a drum, the beat of which echoed his own heart. The drum became a circle of people, his tribe dancing, and in the middle of the circle stood Myrddin chanting and praying and listening with new ears to the voices of the ancient and nameless powers, the Elders.

"This is kelwel, the calling, little brother," the old man said. "Return to your people and serve."

### A Side Note

*Within tribal communities, it is not uncommon for a medicine man to be "called" during a terrible childhood illness. Black Elk (Hehaka Sapa, in his own tongue) was a revered Holy Man of the Oglala Sioux. He too heard voices and, while seriously ill, received a vision which led him into service as tribal shaman. Chambers Dictionary of the Unexplained defines this as "ecstatic phenomena" from the Greek ekstasis, "meaning 'to cause to stand outside'; in the ecstatic trance, the individual's spirit is (literally or metaphorically) taken 'outside their body'" to experience some epiphany.*[1]

Myrddin opened his eyes to find his mother and father next to him and Garanhir chanting quietly nearby. The old man stopped abruptly and stared open-mouthed at the boy.

"He is awake," he said incredulously. "Give him something to drink."

It was a miracle! It was the best of blessings! The boy who was all but dead was now quick and alive! News spread through the tribe like wildfire, and many people came to look upon the wonder of this.

Myrddin's father, near speechless with gratitude, gave Garanhir his best stone axe and fine animal skins to honour the medicine man who had saved his son. Garanhir accepted these gifts with reluctance. In fact, he had not saved the boy. As far as he knew, nothing could have saved the boy. Every child that had ever cried out and shrank from the light had died, no matter how much he prayed. It was the will of the Elders. Not this time, though. He looked at Myrddin with renewed interest. There is something different about you, he thought. Very different.

Days later Garanhir went to check on the boy, who was recovering quickly. He found him sitting by his parents' fire, but not sitting as he used to, as all children did. He did not slouch or fidget or rock back and forth or play with his toes or daydream. He sat perfectly erect and still with a look of intense concentration on his face. He held himself, Garanhir realised, with the tranquillity and poise that marked wise men and sages.

"Fatel yu genough-why? How are you, Myrddin?"

"Much better, thank you."

Garanhir sat opposite him. "That sickness should have killed you. Do you know that?"

"Yes."

"And yet it did not." He paused; his heart was suddenly beating faster, for now he felt certain that his suspicions were correct. "Myrddin, when you were asleep with the sickness, where did you go?"

"What?" The child looked warily at Garanhir. "Nowhere. I ... I was here."

"Oh, ok." The older man nodded. He changed the subject to more mundane things: the weather, the last big hunt and the feast that followed. "Of course, you missed the feast because you were ill. But it was a good and happy time. Did it look that way from above?"

Myrddin, put at his ease by the innocent conversation, answered without thinking, "Yes." And there it was again – the fear in his eyes as he realised his mistake. "Do you think I am crazy?" he whispered.

"No," Garanhir chuckled. "I think you are chosen to follow me."

And so, Myrddin, the thin and sickly youngest son, was identified as the tribe's next medhek[2] – medicine man. For the first time in his life, he saw himself as useful and worthwhile. No, it was more than that. Hunters were useful and the tribe had many of those. But there was only one medicine man, and now only one chosen successor. He was special.

And there, thought Myrddin, enters pride. Millennia before it was counted among the deadliest of sins, pride was recognised as a crippling illness by tribal shamans and medicine men.

"You must not forget," Garanhir had repeated again and again, "that the power you wield is not *your* power, but that of the Elders. You are like a hollow reed between their world and this one. And the power flows through that reed … that is, as long as you are worthy."[3]

By now Myrddin had managed to get out of bed without disturbing Nimue and was picking his way through the greenwood, uncertain where to go. The old man had been right. Myrddin had grown too proud. He liked his position in the tribe very much. He had respect now and authority second only to the chief. He liked, too, how Nimue looked at him with something like reverence in her dark eyes. Even now he marvelled at how easily he had won her from stronger, more violent men. His own brother had wanted her, but did not dare challenge him for fear of bad medicine.

Little by little he had become full of his own importance – a sticky black sap that clogged the reed. The power of the Elders could no longer flow through, and this was the result: starvation and a once mighty people brought low.

He tried so hard to reach out to the higher powers and beg their mercy. Three times he had painted himself in red ochre and worn the horns of deer upon his head. Three times he had danced and chanted to summon the prey. But the game trails had remained deserted, and no new tracks or scat could be found. It did not make sense. Although it was too early for honey, nuts or berries, there should have been an abundance of meat – of solitary bucks and herds of doe slowed by their pregnant bellies. In another month each would give birth to twin fawns and swell their numbers even more. Where were they?

The situation was now desperate. Myrddin was desperate. He had to put things right and save Nimue and the others from the slow, wasting death that now faced them. But how? He did not know, and the voices, now silent, offered no advice.

"Not feeling so special now, are you?" he said aloud, and that question sparked an idea.

Much, much later in mankind's history, the Catholic Church would prescribe the antidote for the sin of pride. It was simple: humility, a recognition that your talents come from your Creator and not from you. Myrddin did not have access to the theological scholarship of the church, but he did have an astute and logical mind. He reached this conclusion by himself.

Quickly he retraced his steps back to the camp and started singing loudly a prayer of atonement to the Elders. The noise awoke the tribe who, in their weakened state, emerged slowly from their tents to see what all the fuss was about.

Myrddin stripped off his fine animal skins and beads and feathers and all the physical marks of his office. He had thought himself so superior, but (idiot that he was!) he had forgotten that he was here to serve and help his people. He got down on his hands and knees and prostrated himself before them as they watched in astonished silence.

Tribal chief, Gwyn ap Nudd (translation: Gwyn, son of Nudd), thought the medicine man had lost his mind. "Myr, it is not right for you to behave in this way. Get up!"

Without a word Myrddin rose and prepared himself carefully, painting his body and face with a mixture of red ochre and charred ashes of the sacred herbs. He sat naked in a circle he had scratched into the dry earth and shivered. The cold bit into his flesh and seeped into the very bones of him. But the campfire, still fragrant with sage, seemed to reach a warm hand out to touch him. His heart leapt. *Even in disgrace the Elders comfort me!* And he looked up into the lightening sky with gladness.

He closed his eyes and filled his lungs with long deep breaths and, as he exhaled, he tried to empty himself of all doubts and distractions. He needed to become like a hollow reed again, ready to channel the power and the wisdom. He then rose and began to sing, stepping in time with his words. His chant went on and on, and slowly the confused tribe joined him. It was a colossal effort as he poured every bit of himself into his beseeching. Finally, after hours of this, his legs began to tingle and sting as if they were full of agitated bees. *Dalleth, it begins.* As the sensation rose up to his stomach and then his heart, he felt like a falling leaf making its slow, swinging descent. Dimly he was aware of the dull thud of his body as it hit the ground, but his eyes were cast upward, awaiting the vision that would tell him where the herds had gone.

*I am sorry,* he whispered. *Oh my Elders, I offer myself up for your use.*

All was darkness before his eyes. Then slowly, almost grudgingly, there appeared before him a green valley. Melting snow and the early spring rains had turned it into marshland, pungent with the smell of rotting vegetation and lit only by the yellow-green light that filtered through the trees. It seemed barren of all animal life except for one lone auroch, a bull with large forward-slanting horns. It pawed the ground restlessly and coughed out its low "hunh, hunh, hunh" grunt of alarm. At first Myrddin could not see what made the animal uneasy. Then he realised that its shadow, which stretched from the auroch's hooves back along the ground, had begun to move by itself. With the dry fluidity of a serpent, it began to snake its way up the animal's hind legs. Terrified, the bull tried to run, but finding its feet bound together it tripped and went down with a heavy thud. As the shadow coiled around torso, then neck, the beast panicked, thrashing and calling in high anguished shrieks. In another moment the shadow engulfed the auroch, completely hiding it from view, and the only sound Myrddin now heard was his own jagged breath.

Myrddin opened his eyes and slowly sat up. Many people crowded around him asking him what he had seen.

"It is killing the herds," he answered in a trembling voice.

"What is?" Gwyn leant forward anxiously.

But Myrddin could only shake his head. "I don't know."

The meaning of visions is never completely clear. It does not work that way. Yet each image is potent and carries its own message. The place was easy enough to identify. The boglands he saw were adjacent to Nankérvis, the valley of the deer, and half a day's hike from camp.

All right, so it hides on the hunting grounds, but what *it* was – he had no idea. That shadow had seemed so ... snake-like. Myrddin pondered this as Nimue put her cloak over his shoulders and started rubbing his numb hands between her own. He smiled gratefully at her.

"Nimue, the largest serpent you've seen – what was it like?"

She looked at him in surprise. "Husband, you know far more than I."

"No, I don't," he answered simply. "Tell me."

"It was quite small, harmless." She reconsidered this statement, then amended it. "Well, maybe not if it bit a baby, but to you or me, it is nothing."

Myrddin nodded. She had confirmed what he himself had been thinking.

The snakes that the tribe encountered – adders mostly – could not be thinning out the herds. So what was?

"My mother used to tell me, though, of other serpents that lived long, long ago," she continued absently. "They were said to be huge…"

"How big?"

"Like monsters," she shrugged. She shook her head in embarrassment. "But that is only a story."

"There's a lot of power in stories," he said quietly, and cast his eyes to Gwyn, who stood nearby waiting for the vision to be explained. "Send scouts out to Nankérvis."

Gwyn sent out his scouting party and the tribe waited anxiously for the news. It came the following day. Of the eight men dispatched to the moor, only one – Eiddyn – limped back to camp, badly injured.

Bending over to inspect the large gash that ran down the length of the man's calf, Myrddin recoiled from the rancid odour. He had seen poisoned wounds before, of course – enough times to know that when they start to smell of rotting meat, it's over. Already thin red lines had traced their way from the swollen cut upward, to meet at the man's groin which was painfully tender to the touch. His forehead burned with fever.

Septicaemia (from the Greek *sepo* meaning to putrefy and *haima* meaning the blood) is an awful way to die. The poison which was now in Eiddyn's bloodstream travelled the larger arteries to his to liver, kidneys, lungs and brain, while clogging up the smaller blood vessels and forming abscesses.

Laying a compassionate hand on the man's forehead, Myrddin told him that love and light awaited him. The Elders would receive him the way a mother takes her new-born into her arms. There was nothing to fear. But Eiddyn was not thinking of the afterlife. Through the insistent lethargy that weighted his limbs and dulled his mind, he tried to focus. He had something to tell Myrddin – something important – but his parched brown tongue struggled to form the words.

Myrddin bent low over him, the better to hear, and a change came over his face as he listened. Gone was the sadness. Gone was the tenderness. Instead, his features hardened and he turned grim eyes upon the people. "We go to war."

And so, while Eiddyn alternately sweated and shivered his way toward his grave, the tribe danced that night and painted their arms and faces with clay, until each face flashed grey in the moonlight. Watching these preparations, Gwyn tried to quiet the tremor in his stomach. Shortly he would be leading his half-starved people into battle, and he wondered if there would be any tribe left come morning. Through the crowd, he looked for Mora, his wife. Clutching their baby daughter to her chest, her anxiety had erased her normally smiling mouth and redrawn it in a grim downward arc. He wanted to go to her and stroke her hair and tell her that everything would be all right, but he did not trust himself to. He did not believe that this would end well and he was afraid that, if he touched her, it would feel like a goodbye and he would weep.

It is not fitting for a chief to cry in front of his people. The face he showed them must be one of determination, confidence, strength; and so he joined in the dancing with great ardour. When the dance reached fever pitch, Gwyn gave the signal and the war-party headed for the moor.

Nankérvis was big with many places to hide. It would be a waste of precious energy to search every ravine and beat every bush. No. It must be made to come to them. At a nod from Gwyn the warriors took up positions, crouching behind the sharp spikes of gorse and hiding amongst the bracken. A second nod from Gwyn sent Rhydderch trotting off into the gathering dawn. The men waited in silence.

It seemed an eternity before Rhydderch stumbled back, holding his side as if wounded, crying out in pain. So well did he play his part that the men who waited could not tell if he was really hurt or not. Either way, the bait proved irresistible. The earth now trembled with the footsteps of the coming beast. The warriors exchanged nervous glances and Gwyn barked the order to stand firm. An expectant hush fell over the clearing for one brief moment, as if nature herself held her breath. Then it happened – that explosion of movement and sound that is war.

Gwyn had seen many battles in his time: skirmishes with rival tribes, auroch hunts, and then the single combat he had waged to take his father's place as chief. But none of this prepared him for what emerged from the bracken.

It was a huge serpent. In our native tongue we had a name for them, although no one in living memory had ever seen one. We called them: "Dhragon" – "dragons." With grace almost beautiful, it plucked Rhydderch from the ground and bit through the man's chest. The warrior's lower half tumbled back to earth and lay, legs still twitching, in a pool of blood. Shouting in horror and fury, Gwyn leapt forward and his men closed in on every side.

The dragon was not impressed. Hunkering down to protect its vulnerable belly, it received the first onslaught of spears and arrows as if it was an insignificant swarm of gnats. The creature almost seemed to "smile" – an evil twisted grimace that the chief knew was a prelude to attack. He threw himself flat on the ground as the dragon spat venom into the faces of the men on Gwyn's left. It was as if they had been doused with a corrosive acid. They ran screaming until they could run no more and collapsed.

All was the yellow flame of torchlight and the red of blood and the rancid smell of the creature's breath. Ignoring this, Bucca and Barinthus jabbed at its face with long spears, aiming unsuccessfully for the eyes. Bucca quickly jumped clear, but Barinthus was caught by another cloud of venom as the creature tossed its head from side to side. Other warriors leapt at the beast, but their axes were no use against the serpent's thick black scales. Still, they harried the monster until Gwyn, grabbing a spear and making one quick prayer to the Elders, ran to face the dragon head on.

The dragon threw back its head and roared. Seizing his moment, Gwyn thrust the spear. *Get it in the mouth ... if I could just get in the mouth...*

Back at camp, Mora prayed and even tried to bargain with the Elders, promising them greater tribute and devotion if only Gwyn was spared. It brought her no real comfort for she felt sure that tomorrow she would be burying her husband.

Slowly though, the warriors returned singing songs of victory. They carried the bodies of the slain and the wounded, but there was no sign of Gwyn. Mora ran through the crowd looking from one face to another and still could not find him. Her heart pounded and she felt faint and sick.

Then suddenly there he was ... miraculously, wonderfully, alive. He smiled at her and she collapsed into his arms in a fit of weeping. In her imagination she had gone so far and seen too much: the death of her husband and the destruction of the people – a slow death by starvation or else enslavement to another, stronger tribe and the depths of grovelling and whoring to which she would sink just to stay alive. *It is a long way to travel and the only way back is through tears, plentifully shed.*

For the tribe, the moment was bittersweet. Great victory and honour had been bestowed upon us, but at the cost of many lives – many sons and fathers. Myrddin sang and danced through the night and the women wailed. Smooth riverstones the colour of flesh and blood[4] were anointed with saliva and herbs, and placed in each corpse's mouth to be removed just before burial. These were soul stones, the vessel which now carried that part of their spirits that would remain with the tribe forever. With the souls of the dead attended to, all that remained now was to bury the bodies. They were painted with red ochre and wrapped in fine skins, ornately sewn with shells and animal teeth. Into the grave went their weapons and tools.

Nearly ten thousand years later, archaeologists would excavate the site. They would clean and polish the tools once more and place them lovingly in glass cases. A nearby placard describing "Our Stone Age Ancestors" would feature a computer-generated face based on one of the skulls and eyes would again look upon Eiddyn. They would piece together the shattered pottery and note with tenderness the fact that someone had loved these men enough to place flowers in the grave. They would examine the remains in an attempt to discover the cause of death, and look for clues as to what event had caused so many men to die so violently together. In the end they would conclude that we had warred with a neighbouring tribe and lost. With no other logical explanation available, the mystery would be pronounced "solved".

The only question left hovering over the find would concern a small soapstone carving of a mythical creature. Some would point to the wings and declare it to be a bird; others would insist that the wavy "meander patterns" that ran down its body looked like the scales of a serpent. Ultimately they would decide that it was a tribal deity – The Great Mother, "goddess of water and air."[5] And they would be wrong. Myrddin had carved the dragon in stone. He felt that this reminder of their greatest triumph should accompany the fallen in death.

With the spiritually-charged night fading, a hungry people began to cast their eyes toward the nearest source of meat. Used to venison, they looked reluctantly upon the great dead reptile. It was, to put it mildly, grotesque. Long and snakelike with four clawed feet, its gleaming black scales made it look wet, slimy, and somehow poisonous. Worst of all was its mouth of jagged teeth still besmirched with the shredded flesh and blood of the slain.

Gwyn palely surveyed the carcass and his empty belly lurched. "Godhough lagha. You know the law," he said firmly to dispel this moment of squeamishness.

Indeed, the tribe knew the law well. It forbade waste, especially of food. Duly the dragon was butchered and eaten.

# A Side Note

*The type of dragon killed by the tribe was known in later folklore as the Knucker due to its habit of dwelling on marshy terrain, known in our tongue as "knúckey." The knucker is a long, snake-like dragon found throughout Great Britain and Western Europe. In old English it was called the nicker meaning "water monster" or sometimes just referred to as "Old Nick", marking its association with the devil. To the Anglo Saxons it was the worm or wyrm.*

*It kills by constriction, coiling its long body around its victims or by poisoning them with its venomous bite and lethal breath. A pamphlet circulating in 1614 described the effects of Knucker venom on humans with the discovery of "a man and a woman ... found dead, being poysoned and very much swelled, but not preyed upon."* [6]

*Found near its food source of deer and rabbit, its colouration helps it to hide. Knuckers are said to have black, green or brown scales and only vestigial wings which generally do not enable flight.*

*Our battle with the dragon echoes through later folklore, particularly in the tale of "The Linton Worm."* [7] *The story tells of a knucker who terrorised a village until the good knight, Sommerville of Lauriston, set out to defeat it. Uncertain how to slay the beast, he hid near its lair and observed it for a while. The worm soon caught his scent and approached, mouth open, tasting the air like a snake. "And that," Sommerville realised, "is the answer." He must spear the dragon in its gaping maw.*

The following morning, Gwyn awoke with a raging headache. He left his tent and walked to the edge of the camp to urinate, marvelling at the pounding in his head. It was as if the tribal drums were beating a war dance inside his skull: duh duh duh, duh duh duh. His stomach lurched and he fell to his knees, vomiting. Even when there was nothing left to bring up, he continued to dry heave. Still the pounding continued: duh duh duh.

Had he been somehow injured in the battle? If so, then why was he only feeling the pain now? And still the drumming: duh duh duh. 'Mine. Mine. Mine.'

Gwyn looked up in surprise. "Who said that?" It was early – not yet light and the tribe was still asleep.

'Mine. Mine!'

He jumped to his feet and searched for the voice. There was no one, not another soul with him at the edge of the camp. Then a flutter in the branches above caught his eye. A small bird marking its territory sang 'Mine!' and took to the air.

Certain now that he was very ill, Gwyn staggered to his tent and went back to sleep.

Hours later he awoke feeling much better. His head was tender but bearable, and he was already sure that his encounter with the bird had been a dream. His family, however, was in trouble. Mora sat with her head in her hands groaning softly. The children were crying and had been sick in their beds. The baby was screaming as if being tortured. Gwyn ran for the medicine man, only to find him unconscious. A quick round of the camp revealed that the whole tribe suffered from the same complaint and the only counsel he could give his people was to go back to sleep, it would be better when they awoke. Gwyn spent an anxious afternoon, comforting his children, wrapping his wife in warm animal skins, and cradling his baby daughter while she howled.

On one of his many trips to fetch water, he was stopped once again by a voice – a rapid high-pitched duh-dah, duh-dah, duh-dah. His eyes were once again drawn to the tree branches above. Again: duh-dah, duh-dah, duh-dah. 'Hun-gry, hun-gry, hun-gry.'

So not a dream then. He felt vaguely sick.

"Where are you?" he sighed, reaching up to pull a limb aside. There, in a hollow, a small bird busily arranged moss, grass and feathers into a nest. He did not have a name for her, but she was pleasing to look at with her black head, white cheeks, and wings of moss green.

Another bird arrived with a caterpillar in his beak which the female greedily devoured.

Duh-dah, duh-dah, duh-dah. 'Need-more, need-more, need-more,' the female chirped and returned to her nest-building while her mate went to fetch her more food.

### A Side Note

*Parus Major, otherwise known as the Great Tit, times its breeding to coincide with early spring and the caterpillar bloom on which they feed their chicks. The female builds the nest while the male sings to protect his territory and gathers food for her. At her every call (and there are sometimes fifty a day) he delivers a caterpillar. This is essential to keep up her strength. She carries twelve eggs – one to be laid each day on completion of the nest.*

"No wonder you are so hungry," Gwyn murmured as he noted that her bright yellow belly was swollen with eggs yet to be laid. The observation turned his mind to his own nest and his own children, still so painfully ill. He hurried back to camp.

Gwyn was not a philosophical man. He did not normally waste energy on the big imponderables of life, but he was asking questions now. What is happening? I can hear the birds! I know. I know what they are saying and what they are doing and why. Is this part of the illness? Is the whole tribe affected? Or am I just mad? Maybe I'm asleep. Or knocked out. Did I get hit on the head by that dragon?

He stopped short. The dragon. We ate of it –all of us. Has it cursed us somehow? Poisoned us? Managed, even in death, to kill us?

He was running now, though sick and exhausted. He ran straight to Myrddin's tent. "Old man!" he shouted. "The dragon! What is happening to us?"

But there was no getting any sense out of the medicine man yet. Trembling, Gwyn returned home and sat on the floor of his tent rocking his baby in his arms. He had only one question left unasked. "What have I done?" he whispered to the now unconscious child.

The following morning brought some semblance of order back to the camp. When the tribe finally rallied, they reached the general consensus that the dragon meat had done something to them. The people could understand the birds, they said. And the frogs by the stream and the crawling things that hid beneath leaves and fallen trees. It hurt, they said, all these voices speaking at once, a constant din.

At the tribal gathering, all eyes fell on Myrddin, hoping for an answer.

"No idea," the dazed medicine man shook his head.

It was all pretty much as Gwyn had expected: fear, confusion, anger, recriminations, and Gwyn watched his triumphant victory over the dragon transformed into a curse that had befallen the people ... who now blamed him. Predictably, the first on the offensive was Bucca.

"What have you done to us?" he hissed.

"I have done nothing but slay the dragon. It is ancient law that we do not waste food. What could I have done different?"

"Did you ever think that maybe that beast would be poison to us?"

"Did you?" retorted Gwyn. "I saw you, Bucca, elbowing the younger men out of the way to get your rightful share of meat."

The young man blushed but would not be silenced: "You have killed us all, you …"

At this moment Barinthus emerged from his tent. He was among those wounded by the knucker venom. His left leg from thigh to ankle had been black and swollen and Myrddin believed he would die of his wounds. Barinthus, however, was walking unaided. As he limped to the circle, Myr leapt forward and examined the leg. It was red and painfully blistered, but healing. Barinthus had somehow managed to slough off all of the dead skin and damaged tissue. "Praise the Elders," he muttered. "It is a miracle."

"So perhaps," Gwyn flashed Bucca a dangerous smile, "I have not killed us after all."

Soon all the ill and wounded, even the baby, were once more bright-eyed and rosy-cheeked. Soon our ears grew accustomed to the noise and could pick out individual voices among the many. And soon our minds grew accustomed to the new situation; after all, it is said that "the marvellous and the astonishing only surprise for a week."[8]

It was a blessing, surely, from the Elders! We felt health and strength course through us. And what is more, our power rapidly grew until we could hear every sound borne on the wind.

It sounds fantastic, I know, but the idea is not new. In fairy tales and folklore we see it again and again – whethel na-yller y grysy, incredible stories based on whispers of what happened to us…

### A Side Note

*Long, long ago, in the northern lands of ice and snow that you call Scandinavia, there lived a young man named Sigurd. He was fine and strong and worked as apprentice to his uncle Regin, a skilled blacksmith.*

*But a life of honest work and simple living was not enough for the uncle.*

*"We could have more, boy. So much more!"*

*"How, uncle?"*

*The blacksmith nodded grimly, "From my brother."*

*Regin's brother, Fafnir, had come into a large sum of money. He guarded it so jealously that he began to change. Imagine greed so complete that it spreads through the body like cancer, twisting first the mind and then the face. The limbs and spine follow and then the skin until Fafnir was no longer a man but an abomination, a dragon guarding his hoard.*

*"To get the treasure," said Regin, "we must simply kill the dragon."*

*"Oh, is that all?" Sigurd laughed.*

*"It is not so hard, so long as we are cunning."*

*Brawn would be required, yes, but brains also. Regin forged a mighty sword called Gram. The metal had been touched by the god Odin himself. They dug a pit near Fafnir's cave and Sigurd hid there until he heard the dragon pass overhead. With one swift movement he thrust the sword upward, piercing the beast's soft belly. Writhing and shrieking, Fafnir died.*

*But the story does not end there. To honour the victory, Regin cooked the dragon's heart for Sigurd to eat. Ingesting one drop of dragon blood was enough: Sigurd could understand the birds that called and chirped in the trees above.*

*They were talking about him and Regin.*

*They were talking about Regin's plan to kill Sigurd and keep the money for himself.*

*The sword, Gram, flashed for a second time that day and Regin lay dead at the hero's feet…*

*And so you see our experience echoes through your own culture. Even the Brothers Grimm, in their story "The White Snake," speak of a king of legendary knowledge and wisdom "as if news of the most secret things was brought to him through the air." The king had an odd little ritual that excited the curiosity of his servant. Every day the king, while quite alone, ate from a covered dish. Inevitably the servant peeked under the lid and found a white snake coiled on the plate. He too ate of it and was immediately granted the power to understand the birds and animals. Today, this phenomenon is known as clairaudience or the ability to hear things beyond the normal human auditory range.*

To eat of serpent flesh and receive knowledge beyond our wildest dreams – this was our fate. And like Sigurd and Grimm's wise king, it did not take our warriors long to exploit the advantage they had gained. To hear our enemies' plans before battle: how could we lose? We know all.

But knowing all, Myrddin realised, is a mixed blessing. Yes, you hear your enemies plotting. Yes, you can speak with the birds and animals and all of nature. But imagine also the lies and secrets revealed. Think on it: if your neighbours could hear all you say, what trouble and hard feeling would it bring?

Myrddin foresaw a time when the tribe would be thrown into chaos. Every secret would be exposed to daylight: every mutinous word, every piece of spiteful gossip, every illicit tryst, every harsh jest – all this and much more would echo in each ear until neighbour hated neighbour and husbands despised wives.

So he set the craftsmen to work hollowing out bits of bone and antler. Yes, we could hear everything borne on the wind, but words uttered through these tubes, could not drift to our ears. Again we would have privacy.

Privacy, he reasoned, begets dignity. And those who live with dignity can live in peace.

Peace was exactly what Mora craved. With her husband embroiled in tribal affairs and four lively children tugging her attention in different directions, she needed a moment of relative peace to think things through.

She had, perhaps, a more creative mind than her husband, which is why he valued her opinion so highly. Vivid minds, however, are prone to doubt. For Mora doubts were like the mimicking calls of ravens as they arrive in a black flutter and peck away at her strength and resolve. Were the children healthy? Would they make it through another harsh winter? Fryok, her third son, was clumsy and slow to learn the ways of the hunt. He was falling behind other boys of his age. What was wrong with him? And was it somehow her doing? And Gwyn … much had changed since dhragon nyth: the night of the dragon. And, yes, it did boggle the mind, but as usual the tribe expected him to have all the answers.

"And where is he to find them?" she muttered to herself. Even Myrddin did not understand what had happened, how that beast's flesh could endow us with the ability to hear all things.

And Bucca (a scowl twisted her features) continues to agitate. She knew his ambition would ultimately lead him to challenge Gwyn to single combat, a fight to the death to determine who will be chief. What if Bucca should win?

She kicked a fallen twig petulantly out of her way as she walked through the greenwood. What it came down to was that she hated being inside her own head. A battle always seemed to rage there between the need to get on with the business of life and the fears that made her want to crawl back into bed and hide. It was torment.

'I smell it…' The voice was not human, and Mora halted in her tracks scanning the woods around her.

"Show yourself!" she demanded. Her hand went instinctively to the knife she carried in her belt.

A grey she-wolf appeared silently in front of her. Mora recognised her as the dominant female of the local pack. "Beautiful," she murmured. But deadly. Mora hesitated, torn between the impulse to run and the equally strong desire to reach out and touch the soft fur on the animal's flank. She stood her ground.

"What were you saying?" she asked, trying to control the slight tremor in her voice.

'I can smell it … your fear.' The wolf inhaled deeply. 'It smells good.'

"Don't even think about it."

'I'm not hunting.' The animal yawned lazily and sat down in front of this human woman who had caught her interest. 'Fear is a wonderful thing … and terrible.'

Mora's curiosity was piqued. It had never occurred to her before to consider things from the perspective of any of the creatures of the greenwood. But now she wanted to grasp the complex nature of fear as understood by the wolf.

She could see, on the one hand, how it could be pleasurable. To smell the panic of the beleaguered stag only whets the appetite and brings the anticipation to a delicious climax before the denouement of the kill. On the other hand, there was no greater ill you could inflict upon an animal. A wolf afraid is in greater distress than a wolf in pain.

But there was something else – a third facet that acted less on that bit of the brain that feels and more on the part that thinks.

'Fear,' the wolf insisted, 'is a great tool.'

"How is that?"

'It tells us what is coming…'

# A Side Note

*There has been a lot of anecdotal evidence over the years to suggest that animals can predict the future. One widespread superstition is the belief that dogs can sense the approach of death. Steve Roud, in* The Penguin Guide to the Superstitions of Britain and Ireland, *notes that a dog's "behaviour can be interpreted to predict future luck, good or bad. A dog howling was one of the most widespread death omens."*[10] *Peter Haining in his book,* Superstitions, *concurs: "There is a school of thought that believes animals are psychic ... Aside from being man's best friend, the dog has much to tell us about the future, according to superstition. Most particularly, dogs are believed to be able to 'see death approaching a human being.'"*[11]

*But is that only a superstition? Oncologists in California have documented cases proving that dogs can detect cancer: "...both Labradors and Portuguese water dogs can detect lung and breast cancer with greater accuracy than state-of-the-art screening equipment ... The dogs correctly identified 99 per cent of lung cancer sufferers and 88 per cent of breast cancer patients simply by smelling their breath."*[12] *Furthermore, Temple Grandin and Catherine Johnson, in their book* Animals in Translation, *have cited examples where dogs have predicted that their owners are going to have a seizure thirty minutes before it hits.*[13] *So if a dog can sense an oncoming seizure and smell breast cancer, then surely, a major physiological event, like the onset of death itself, would not be lost on them.*

*Nor is the phenomenon limited only to diagnosing illness. Animals seem to know when a natural disaster is imminent. Throughout history we hear of cases of rodents evacuating the city, dogs howling, and animals heading for open ground prior to an earthquake. We saw it in Helike, Greece (373 BC), Messina, Sicily (1783), and in Talcahuano, Chile (1835).*[14] *An article in The Sunday Express, dated 10th December 1978, reported on a recent earthquake in the Italian village of Friuli. Prior to the tremors local animals began acting strangely – howling, barking, breaking out of their pens and, in some cases, literally evacuating the built-up areas of the town. For this reason stations monitoring seismic activity in China are equipped not only with modern instruments but also with herds of deer or broods of chickens, whose erratic behaviour warns of imminent tremors.*

*Likewise, in the aftermath of the giant tsunami of 26 December 2004, it was reported that Sri Lanka (which lost upwards of 22,000 people) had no animal casualties, "not even a dead hare or rabbit." And this despite the fact that Yala National Park Wildlife Reserve was badly hit by floodwaters.*[15]

*How? No human foresaw these events. Does this mean that animals are psychic? No. The ability is most likely rooted in their highly-developed senses and their sensitivity to ground tilting, fluctuations in humidity and air pressure and changes in electric and magnetic fields.*[16] *Professor Richard Wiseman, in his book* Quirkology, *notes that: "Many animals are sensitive to frequencies undetectable by the human ear, including both ultrasound (high frequency) and infrasound (low-frequency) sounds." He goes on to say that "infrasound is deeply strange. It can be produced naturally from ocean waves, earthquakes, tornadoes, and volcanoes."*[17] *Essentially, animals can hear disaster approach or feel it rumble through their bodies.*

*According to Grandin, smell (and the fear it inspires) also helps animals predict the future. Let's take her example of a common rat. Put in very simplified terms: the rat, when it comes across the recent scent of a cat, becomes afraid, even if the cat is no longer present. The rat knows that "most predators are territorial, where a cat has been in the past is an excellent indication of where it's going to be in the future."*[18] *The smell, coupled with the fear it evokes, warns the rat that caution is required here from now on. And voila! We have pseudo-fortune-telling rats. They know where they are likely to be attacked and can take steps to prevent it.*

Back in those early days in the greenwood, the she-wolf was trying to convey this idea to Mora.

The woman shook her head in exasperation. "I still don't understand. How can your nose tell you what's coming?"

Now bored with the discussion, the wolf rose. 'It tells us what has been and hence what is likely to be again.' And with this she disappeared into the forest.

Mora pondered this as she walked home. "What has been will be again," she murmured. She knew instinctively that there is truth in this. Is it like, she wondered, a great circle? All the experience of men happening again and again; each event coming back to us and not so very new? She looked at the trees and realised that this was true of all things. It was now summer and yet the trees thought of autumn. The seasons continue in their endless cycle and the trees knew this. She could sense it, all the preparations being made for the long winter sleep. They would not need their leaves much longer and already had begun to withdraw much of the goodness from them; all the life, all the green would be absorbed back into the tree to nourish it, and the leaves would blaze in yellow and red before dying and falling to earth. There the worms and scuttling things would break them down into rich, dark soil that would feed the tree next spring as buds burst forth once more in green. A perfect, elegant, ingenious circle, and hence the ability to know what is coming and be ready. It is, in fact, as if all of creation knows instinctively that: "What has been is what will be, and what has been done is what will be done; and there is nothing new under the sun."[19]

And so we began to learn things from the animals and plants, all sorts of things that were at once frightening and seductive in their power. For Mora, the she-wolf's lesson and a little dragon magic were a potent combination. Spurred on by her worries about the uncertainties of life, she gradually began to realise that once you knew enough of the past, it was indeed possible to know the future. The understanding came slowly, ineffably, but accompanied by a long-sought-after sense of control over her life and her destiny. How wonderful indeed.

Mora was not the only one who began to play with the gift. Uninterested by the prattle of birds and animals, Bucca sat gazing intently at the camp fire. The tribe, of course, had learnt how to make fire long ago. In his youth Bucca had learned the technique from his father. You sit on the ground with a foot over each end of the fire block (a three-inch stick with a notch in the middle). The pointed end of a second longer stick is fitted into the notch, and twirled between your hands until enough heat is generated to cause a spark and light the kindling. Bucca's hands were rough and thickly calloused from years of this. It had been a difficult skill to learn: day after day of practising, sweating not from any fire produced, but from the exertion. But practise does indeed make perfect, and he was now so adept that he carried his drill-stick in a quiver with his arrows and the fire block hung round his neck like a pendant, ready to ignite another fire when the tribe needed it.[20] It made him proud to know he was useful in this way for fire was life to the people and he could bestow it in moments. And yet…

He looked around him at the lime, oak and yew trees that stood like ancient pillars holding up a vaulted blue ceiling of sky. With one smouldering twig he could reduce it all to ash. Now that was power, and it was just the beginning. The dragon flesh had opened his eyes to possibilities he had never been aware of: the ability to read cinders and know the future, and the knowledge of mysterious vapours on marsh and moor that could self-ignite. And then, if he really applied himself, one day he might even learn how to walk through fire itself.

"Teach me," he murmured, gazing intently into the glow.

Hanyfer left the greenwood and weaved her way through the dense bracken to the cliffs overlooking the ocean. She had never given this wide expanse of blue much thought, not until she sat by the brook and listened to its babbling waters speak again and again of the sea. The sea: vast and primal, terrifying in its power, and yet still the cradle of all life on earth. 'It is home,' said the river. 'It is freedom.'

She had by now managed to pick her way down to the beach and the waves lapped gently at her ankles. The cold water, the sand between her toes, the briny air that filled her lungs – all made her feel intensely alive and strong, and suddenly aware.

After the battle with the dragon she had kissed her father's bloody cheek and held him as he died. One detail, forgotten in grief, now came back to her: the salty taste of blood on her lips. The sea, she realised, was as salty as human blood and it ebbed and flowed along a circulatory path like blood in the veins. But despite her new-found kindred feeling for the ocean, her first tentative steps into deeper water were met with a rebuff. A wave crashed into her legs, nudging her back to the beach.

Undeterred, she approached the water again. A trained eye would have noted the murk and foam of the water as it roughly retreated from the beach and would have been forewarned. But Hanyfer could not yet read the sea for signs of danger. When she reached thigh-deep water, the ground beneath her feet seemed to crumple and she was tugged under by a rip. Shocked by her sudden dunking, the girl clawed in the direction of the shore against the current. She could make no headway and began to panic as she was dragged roughly backward toward open water.

Perhaps it was a sudden clever idea; perhaps it was an insight born of dragon magic, or perhaps it stemmed from a lifetime of acquiescence to the stronger, more turbulent personality that was her father, but Hanyfer suddenly stopped her frantic scrabbling and let the rip carry her. The current released her just beyond the breakers and the girl worked her way back to shore. She had learnt her first lesson: never fight the sea.

For Danjy, on the other hand, life had become intolerable. While the rest of the tribe embraced the dragon magic and rejoiced, he alone found it irritating. He had, since early childhood, hated loud noises, a quirk that had never fully gone away. And now, with the sudden increased sensitivity of his ears, all the voices barged into his head unbidden, crowding out his thoughts, wrecking his peace and trying his patience. He was becoming more and more irritable, and apt to fly into a rage simply because someone spoke to him.

Desperate for an escape, Danjy took refuge in a cave not far from camp. Within its dark recesses, he at last discovered a place of quiet solitude … and he found something else. Deep within the cave, the walls were covered in paintings. A herd of deer (painted in red and yellow ochre) leapt across the wall, only to be met by a line of hunters with bows and spears at the ready. Next along was a series of symbols he did not understand. And then more deer, each more sloppily rendered than the last, as if the artist's hand was becoming increasingly unsteady. What did it mean?

Myrddin, he knew, often came here to pray, but the nature of this prayer seemed to be more elaborate than Danjy realised. The medicine man had not chronicled important events, but had created image after image of the tribe's main prey … to what end? *To summon it*, he decided. That is why there were so many pictures of deer wrought with a shaky hand: the medhek was starving when he painted them.

Danjy firmly rammed his torch into a fissure in the rock. In the flickering light he noticed a small pile of things on the ground. A strip of bark that Myrddin had used as a palette to mix the ochre with animal fat. A few shallow soapstone lamps, the animal fat all but burned away. And brushes made of crushed twigs bound together. Many of these were snapped in half … out of frustration?

"It must have been terrible for you, old man," Danjy murmured. "All this effort for nothing."

His own voice rang in the cave, and Danjy realised that Myrddin had chosen to paint where the acoustics were at their best, presumably to sing and chant to the Elders while he worked.[21]

Danjy liked it here among the colourful figures of deer and auroch. He could finally hear himself think. And the caves had real potential: flint for weapons and tin and precious stones. He could be useful here instead of sulking around camp, cantankerous and irritable. Yes, he nodded, here in silence and meditative darkness he could be at peace – a peace normally reserved for the dead.

And on it went, with each of us harkening to a different call, each grasping for some new and shining aspect of the Great Gift.

For the tribe as a whole, it brought us out of the Stone Age. The worms of the earth taught us of the raw, dark energy of the soil and how it gives life to seeds. We settled upon the land and became farmers, no longer living in animal-skin tents but in huts of mud and thatch. We learned how to roast and grind the grain to make bara (heavy bread).

Instead of following the herds' annual migration, we kept animals as domesticated beasts: cattle, sheep, goats, pigs, all belonging to the tribe. We could hear where the roe deer hid in the thicket and the fox had his lair, and the wild boar snuffled through loose earth for roots. These fell under our spears and filled our bellies.

Well-fed and prosperous and oh-so-mighty in war, we soon had many slaves from rival tribes to do the mule work for us, to pull the ard[22] and reap the grain.

Despite all this Gwyn was uneasy … and it really irritated him. He knew he should be ecstatically happy. The people of the Coranieid, his people, were healthy and powerful. We were feared by our neighbours and instructed in all kinds of magic by the creatures of the greenwood. We ate well and danced to the drum and adorned ourselves with copper and amber, fine skins and new clothing made from flax. So what was the problem? Why could he not sit back and enjoy it? *I am beginning to sound like Mora*; he smiled tenderly at the thought of his wife.

Optimistic by nature, Gwyn was not a worrier. He dealt with problems when they looked him in the eye; he did not waste time and energy creating things to fret over in the night when any sane man should be asleep. "So," he asked himself again, "what *is* the problem?"

Days later he was strolling through the greenwood with his son, Fryok. It was a hot day and they sought the shade of the trees for a bit of relief. Quickly bored, and neither of them great conversationalists, they decided to check the traps. It was a disappointing haul – two rabbits and a fox. The last trap, however, held only a bloody hind leg.

"Has someone stolen our game?" Fryok asked quietly.

"No," replied Gwyn, who had seen this before. The snare had misfired. Instead of closing around the fox's neck in a strangling hold, the loop managed only to snag a limb. Desperate to escape, the animal had gnawed off his own leg.

Fryok was at once fascinated and disgusted by the idea. "That would really hurt."

"It would be agony," his father nodded, clearing the trap and casting the limb into the bushes. "And it would take a while."

Gwyn looked around carefully. "Actually, this is a good opportunity for you to practise tracking."

"Oh, do I have to?" Fryok whined.

"Yes, you do," Gwyn answered firmly. "You hate hunting because you are not skilled at it. If you become good, you will see the pleasure in it."

Fryok looked at him dubiously. He was an exceedingly bad hunter, much to his father's chagrin. It was not for lack of trying. Unfortunately, the harder he tried the clumsier he became. And now, here was another humiliating lesson which would invariably end with Gwyn getting cross.

"Come on. You have a wounded animal that is bleeding badly and limping. He can't have gone far."

And so it began. As the child started to look, Gwyn resolved to be patient this time – but, alas, that resolve did not hold. Fryok first missed the tracks in the soft earth and then trampled them so that they could now tell him nothing. Gwyn started to fidget, but held his tongue. The boy then failed to see the rather blatant smear of blood on the leaves of the nearby bracken, and Gwyn gnawed on his lip to keep from swearing. But when the child walked within two feet of the dead three-legged animal and did not notice it, Gwyn could contain himself no longer. The forest erupted in a tirade of almost incoherent profanity that sent the birds fleeing with plaintive calls.

Fryok stood quietly and let it wash over him. Truly he looked pathetic, and this brought Gwyn's ranting to an abrupt halt.

"Let's go home," he said gruffly, feeling guilty now at his lack of patience, and more angry with himself than with the boy.

To make peace, he tried to make conversation. "Can you imagine how desperate the fox was to do that to himself?"

Despite his anger and hurt feelings, Fryok could never bring himself to reject any bone his father threw him. "Yeah," he answered hoarsely. "It's quite a price to pay for freedom."

The words resonated within Gwyn and he stopped abruptly and looked at his son. "That is it exactly."

Of course. Now Gwyn realised what was gnawing at him – why he was feeling so uneasy despite the tribe's prosperity. He had lived long enough to know that nothing was free. There was always a price to be paid. So what would be exacted from the tribe in return for all this abundance?

One day Nuadu, a slave tilling our fields, collapsed with fever and was carried to Myrddin's hut. Myrddin was unconcerned and when the man's face reddened with clusters of tiny pimples, he told Gwyn to expect an outbreak of measles, a disease that most of us had already had as children.

But the illness took an unexpected turn. The spots on the man's face grew into large blisters. His face, even his eyelids and ears, swelled painfully. Unable to swallow, he drooled, and when a wracking cough shook his body, Myrddin received a face-full of spit.

Gwyn was appalled. "What is it?"

"I really don't know."

"And the Elders…"

"Silent on the matter … which does not bode well."

Gwyn said no more and left the medicine man to his work. However, he seemed singularly incapable of settling to any work of his own. He knew he'd been getting paranoid lately – wondering not if, but *when* the tribe's luck would run out. But now he seemed to see impending calamity in all things.

*What does it matter, really*, he asked himself. *One sick slave?*

But Nuadu's face, swollen as if he had been badly beaten, and him lying there drooling like a dog – Gwyn had never seen anything like it.

But then, he told himself, you had never seen a dragon before you had to kill one.

He took a deep breath that puffed out his chest and set his jaw in determination. This illness, whatever it is, he would deal with it. The people of the Coranieid could not be wiped out by monsters, nor were they going to be threatened by pestilence.

"All will be well." Yet even as he spoke these words, he did not believe them.

### A Side Note

*Confluent Small-Pox is a highly contagious and usually fatal form of the small-pox virus. Edward Jenner, who first formulated a vaccine against the disease in 1796, described it as "the most dreadful scourge of the human species". Smallpox had an illustrious career before its eradication in 1979. It has scarred the faces of Lincoln, Mozart and Stalin and killed Pocahontas, Mary II, and Tsar Peter II of Russia. On a much wider and more horrifying scale, the disease led to the collapse of the Aztec and Incan Empires.*[23]

Myrddin, exhausted from praying and chanting, sat watching his patient. Nuadu's condition had worsened. While the swelling in his face had subsided, his hands and feet were now swollen masses of pustules and the man was delirious. The pustules ripened like grotesque fruit and began to weep a foul-smelling yellow matter. Unable to bear the stench, Myrddin had Nuadu moved to a tent away from his dwelling.

Another slave, and then another, was brought to him with fever. All were sent to the tent. All developed the same yellow blisters. Eventually each of them died, choked when their throats swelled shut or poisoned by the boils and abscesses formed by the ruptured blebs – more and more reeking bodies to be unceremoniously burned.

Gwyn, he knew, now had a problem. Not only were the Coranieid becoming increasingly afraid of the pestilence, but it was planting time on the farm and his workforce had been decimated.

The chief gathered the men together and went to raid for slaves among the neighbouring villages. Even before entering them, the harsh bark of coughing met their ears. It was the same everywhere: the dead rotted next to the dying who ranted and drooled, covered with oozing sores and burning with fever. Bucca vomited just from the smell and Myrddin, shocked and appalled by the conditions, tried to pray but couldn't somehow find the words.

Returning to our village, Gwyn finally broke the silence. "Myrddin…"

"Yes?"

"We're going to get it, aren't we?"

"I'm surprised we haven't already."

"What can we do?"

"Nothing."

"But..."

"I told you before," Myrddin snapped. "The Elders are silent."

Gwyn nodded.

"I guess we had better get planting," Barinthus said quietly.

Bucca snorted, "What's the point?"

"I'd rather stay busy just now," Gwyn murmured. "Wouldn't you?"

"What you say is wise," Myrddin nodded. "It is better to keep occupied then to sit and brood."

Truly that was easier said than done. And though no one would articulate it, we all waited for the first sign of what must be an inevitable downfall ... the fever.

We waited.

And waited...

And waited...

And nothing whatever happened.

Not even Myrddin (who had dealt directly with the afflicted) took ill. It was, in fact, the biggest anti-climax in our history.

Eventually, we stopped shambling around like dead-men-walking and began to realise that we were fine. The disease had not touched us. Out of all the tribes, we alone survived unscathed. It was another bennath, a blessing! A miracle! But what did it mean? We knew that the dragon flesh had given us extraordinary knowledge, and therefore power. But had it given us something else as well?

Look how Barinthus healed after the battle with the dragon! Look at this rotting pestilence that has laid all others low! Yet we stand tall and strong. Finally, inevitably, someone uttered the word "immortal," and it was as if a floodgate of certainty had been opened. The whole tribe was suddenly sure that we were invincible! Imagine the intoxicating realisation of all we had become: first omniscient, now immortal. Truly we were masters, nay, more than that: we were "dhew", gods who had dominion over every living thing upon the earth.[24]

## A Side Note

*The idea of a certain food bestowing godlike power is old and widespread.* Chambers Dictionary of the Unexplained *notes that "divine immortality is often conferred by a special food or drink reserved only for the gods: ambrosia in classical mythology, amrita in Hindu tradition and the golden apples tended by Freya in Norse myths," or in this case dragon flesh. The book goes on to say that recipients of this gift "are not subject to old age and may effectively live for ever unless they are killed."*[25] *We see one variation on this theme in the German myth "Nibelung" in which dragon blood makes the hero Siegfried invincible. However in the story he does not ingest the blood, but bathes in it and hence, "no weapon can hurt him."*[26]

Myrddin listened as the tribe talked of this. He warned them again and again not to make too many assumptions, not to get too proud. From bitter experience he knew how pride proceeds a fall, but they would not listen. In fact, they had begun to look upon him as a joke. All that ancient and sacred power that he once controlled was nothing compared to what we could do now. With the people hearing voices and privy to secret information, he was no longer unique. With wounds healing themselves, who needed a medicine man? What, then, was he good for? He was old-fashioned, outdated. Even Nimue looked at him differently. The distinguished husband she took to her bed was now a scrawny and unremarkable man. She felt as if she had somehow been cheated and no longer softened to his touch.

As distressing as all this was, Myrddin had something far greater to worry about: the people now thought they were better than the Elders. They had abandoned their faith and shunned their gods. Sooner or later, he knew, we would be punished.

Distraction – that was the answer. With all his advice falling on deaf ears, Myrddin needed something to distract his mind from the infuriating impotence of his situation. He knew exactly what would take his mind off things. The wind had carried it that morning – ow crya kepar ha ky, the thin low howl of wolves – not calling out a warning to rival packs, not lonely for a mate. No, today the news was joyous. The cubs had been born.

He approached their lair with caution, careful to step loudly on fallen twigs to announce his presence in advance. As he stepped into the clearing, every wolf was on its feet, hackles up, ears forward, ready to pounce. As they picked up his scent, he saw them all relax, tails wagging, and knew that he may approach.

As was custom, he went first to the alpha male (a large grey wolf he had named Masek) who briefly allowed him to run a hand down his flank before moving off to lie down alone. With the necessary protocol over, other wolves vied for Myrddin's attention, tails wagging in wide arcs. 'What have you brought us today? What have you to eat?' they asked as they licked and sniffed at the bag he carried.

Myrddin produced half a dozen rabbits and threw them to the waiting jaws of the pack, making certain, of course, that the biggest one went to their chief. They ate in a silence broken only by the crunch of bone.

'You know,' Masek gnawed happily on a bit of grizzle, 'I still don't understand why you don't eat rabbit.'

"My people believe that if we eat it, we will become timid like the rabbit."

'Humans and their notions,' the grey wolf snorted. 'Although, from what I hear, you don't think of yourselves as human anymore.'

Myrddin sighed wearily, "Why talk of that when you have such happy news?"

'Come,' Masek got to his feet and led the man to a den dug between tree roots and extending ten feet underground. Myrddin had to crouch on all fours to enter. There in the shadows four tiny cubs nursed on mothers' milk. The alpha female, he called her Kensa, gazed at him contentedly.

'Beautiful, aren't they?' she murmured quietly.

"Very," Myrddin nodded.

'Three boys and a girl…'

"They will be fine and strong and run with the pack on moonlit nights." His compliment pleased her and she gave his hand a gentle lick before settling down to sleep.

Over the next few weeks, Myrddin made many visits to the pack to check on the cubs' progress. They were indeed beautiful animals: two grey boys with big clumsy paws that tripped them up when they tried to run. These he named Brengy ("noble dog") and Arranz, for his silvery coat. The pack, as always, was perplexed by his need to name everything. They did not rely on names, only on scents as distinct and individual as fingerprints. Frankly, they could not see the point of names or the sentimentality that led Myrddin to call the one female cub Delennyk, "little petal." He had always liked it and would have named his own daughter Delennyk had he been blessed with one. That, however, was unlikely now that Nimue would no longer touch him.

But one of the cubs was strikingly different. Pure white fur, light skin and a pink nose — he was the most beautiful wolf that Myrddin had ever seen. At three months, when the eyes of the others turned yellow like the rest of the pack, the white cub's eyes remained a deep and sparkling blue.

"Gwynhelek," he murmured as he scratched the cub behind his ears. "That is what I shall call you. In my tongue it means 'white' and 'splendid,' like you."

'You have stayed long enough,' growled Kensa.

Surprised, Myrddin immediately rose and took his leave. He did not understand why Kensa should so suddenly evict him from the den, but he knew better than to question or argue.

With the human gone, Kensa sat watching her cubs. The white one, the one Myrddin favoured so much, had found a stick and was contentedly gnawing on the end of it to lessen the discomfort of teething. Never before in the history of the pack had a wolf been born so fair.

*He is so different.*

Instinctively, animals feel simultaneously intrigued and wary of anything new or odd, and so this cub made her feel uneasy and conflicted. The life of a wolf is, usually, stridently black and white. Things are good to eat or they are not. Actions are acceptable or they are not. Everything is firmly categorised and understood with no ambiguity. Take Myrddin, for instance (although she did not call him by name). Whenever her mind conjured up an image of the man, she remembered his scent – a mixture of burnt sage, earth, sweat and smoke from a cooking fire. He was a good human. Period. But she had no category in which to place her son. There was no precedent by which she could judge if he was "right" or not.

Cubs, of course, had been born different in the past. The pack had seen its share of defects: lame paws or small, frail pups who did not last long. So is that the answer? Do white fur and blue eyes constitute a defect? Is he alright? She sniffed the air trying to read the answer in his scent.

Probably not, she thought glumly. The fact remained that the best and strongest wolves came from ordinary stock: grey or brown with eyes of yellow. Those who differed tended to be ill … or trouble.

### A Side Note

*Albinism is a rare, naturally occurring condition in which the animal lacks melanin – the chemical responsible for skin pigmentation. Melanin is not only found in skin cells, but also in the brain where its absence can impact upon behaviour. Albino animals are prone to a range of problems including poor eyesight and aggressive tendencies.*[27]

Back at his hut, Myrddin was surprised to find Nimue there. He stood at the door watching her as she pinned her long dark hair up in a bronze comb. His heart ached at the sight of her. She was so beautiful.

"What?"

"You did not come home last night," he replied quietly.

"So?"

"So where were you?"

"Out."

"Where?"

"Just out."

Suddenly impatient with her monosyllabic responses, he shouted, "Who were you with?"

She stood up and smiled at him. "Handy things, those hollow tubes. So good for keeping secrets."

Rage and jealousy flashed white through his brain and his hand met her cheek in a sharp slap. Grabbing her roughly he spat the words into her face, "Do not forget who I am!"

"Who are you?" she laughed spitefully. "Medhek? Medicine man? Who needs you? Who in the tribe is sick? Who needs your prayers and chanting and ridiculous fainting visions? Tell me, has Gwyn asked your advice lately? Has anyone?"

Myrddin felt like he had been kicked in the stomach by an auroch. Unable to find his tongue, he merely stared at her, trembling.

"I didn't think so," she said as she turned on her heel and left the hut.

He sat for a while, head in his hands. He wanted to cry but was too weary even for that.

"What have I done to deserve this?" he directed the question upward. The whole tribe was prosperous and happy. Only he was bereft and lost. Only he was completely superfluous.

He had come full circle, right back to that awkward, useless child he used to be. The thought of it was unbearable. Surely life was supposed to be a straight line where you lived and learned and progressed and never, ever went back. Then he remembered his original vision. It was all about circles, was it not? The sun, the drum, the dancing tribe. Why was he so surprised to see that pattern repeated here?

There was, he supposed, one bright side to that idea. If indeed life took you in endless loops, then he was not yet finished. He had felt useless before, and the Elders had intervened and given him purpose. Might they not do it again? Had they not proven that they have use even for a runt? He had only to believe and wait for the time when someone would again call his name…

Years passed and our tribe of gods dominated the land, while hapless mortals offered tribute and raised great stones in our honour. It was like an endless summer of easy and abundant days. I remember one day my brother Fryok called our sheep from their night paddock to take them out to pasture.

"Be careful, my son," Mora said automatically. For all of our deathless years, she had never been able to break her habit of admonishing us to "take care." Those words were as quick to trip off her tongue as "I love you" and really, they meant one and the same thing. With a cheerful wave, he scampered off to the fields and mother returned to her weaving.

Fryok sat watching the flock through the long, drowsy afternoon. Eventually, the sun and the heat got the better of him and he fell asleep in the soft grass. Breathing softly and steadily, mind filled with dreams and nonsense, he did not notice the first lines of dusky colour that bled across the blue sky. Nor could he smell, as the sheep did, the wolf that came with the gathering night. Finally, their uneasy bleating awakened him and he sat up blinking in confusion. He jumped up with a start. It was late! Knowing that he should have had the sheep back to the village ages ago and that his father would be vexed, he quickly began to herd the animals back toward their paddock.

From the bushes nearby, blue eyes watched intently.

'Wolf! Wolf!' the sheep bleated to Fryok and the boy scanned the tree line until he spotted it: a beautiful animal with fur as white as snow. He was not afraid. The wolf pack and the people of the Coranieid had an understanding. The wolves did not attack our livestock and we did not make war with the pack. They showed us the proper respect and we rewarded them with gifts of food. There it is: everyone is happy.

Fryok shooed the flock along and was annoyed to find that the wolf followed. Still he was not afraid, only irritated. The wolf's presence upset the sheep and made them harder to control. In their panic a few of the lambs strayed from the flock and the wolf closed in.

He had had enough. Fryok spun around to face the wolf. Maybe a few sharp raps with his staff might teach the animal some manners. But something about its eyes, the way it looked at Fryok with such naked hunger, surprised and frightened the boy. Though we had subjugated the pack, though there had not been a death in the tribe for many years, though Fryok believed we were invulnerable, still some ancient, deeply-written instinct told him to run. And within the wolf, the sudden, rapid flight triggered something that was just as deeply etched: the impulse to pursue. Fryok sprinted down the hill but in moments the wolf was within pouncing distance. He dipped his head to keep his prey in focus and leapt. Fryok's screams were abruptly cut short as the powerful jaws clamped on his throat in a suffocating bite.

Any parent will tell you that there is a certain sound a child makes that is not fooling around nor an exaggerated bid for attention. It is the sound of genuine pain and fear and it slices through you like a blade. This is what Gwyn now heard back in the village. Grabbing an axe, he sprinted for the field with the rest of the tribe in tow. We arrived to find Fryok being dragged into the undergrowth at the edge of the clearing. At the sight of the tribe the wolf dropped his prey and disappeared into the deepening gloom. My mother raced to Fryok and cradled him in her arms. "It will be all right, my son, this will heal like all the rest."

But the boy did not stir.

"Fryok … wake up."

Nothing.

"Fryok!" She frantically shook the boy to rouse him. His head lolled to one side. Blank eyes stared skyward. She shook him harder, shouting and shouting his name.

"Mora … Stop." Gwyn was beside her now with a firm hand on her shoulder.

"No!" she screamed.

As he pulled his wife off the dead body of their son she began to beat furiously on his chest with her fists. "You said! You said we couldn't die!"

"I know, I'm sorry..." He held her to him and she collapsed into inconsolable weeping.

The tribe stood there in a stunned silence broken only by the muffled sobs of my mother. We were trying to take in the full meaning of what had just happened. We had been very, very wrong. We could die after all.

### A Side Note

*The story of Fryok's death was never forgotten and eventually reached Aesop's ears in 654 B.C. But for Aesop a tale of random tragedy was not sufficient; every story must have a moral, a lesson to be learned. And so the tale, though greatly changed, has been passed down to you as "The Shepherd's Boy and the Wolf":*

*The shepherd boy (now without a name) grows bored while watching his flock and decides to play a trick on the people of his village.*

*"Wolf! Wolf!" he cries and they come running with axes and pitchforks, only to be laughed at by the little churl.*

*It is, the boy decides, a good joke – one certainly worth repeating again and again.*

*Then one day a wolf really does attack the sheep. This time the villagers, tired of the child's pranks, do not come to his aid. He is devoured.*[28]

"Myrddin! Myrddin!" Gwyn cried hoarsely, as he staggered back home with his dead child in his arms.

Slowly, the medicine man emerged from his hut. Confronted with this sight, however, he immediately leapt forward, trying to examine the boy.

"Don't bother," Gwyn croaked, "he's dead."

Myrddin seemed less surprised by this than the rest of us. "Gallas ow holon pur glaf. I am sick at heart."

The chief looked uncertainly at his medicine man. He knew he had marginalised his friend in the time since the change. But surely Myrddin would help him now. He had to. "Will you perform the rites?"

"Of course," Myrddin answered gently and took the boy to begin preparations.

Gwyn, his throat too tight to say anymore, nodded his thanks. Then turning sharply on his heel, he headed back toward the woods.

Ignoring all of the accepted courtesies, he strode right into the clearing where the pack had its den. "Where is he?" he yelled.

The alpha male, stepped forward calmly. 'If I am not much mistaken, you have business with the one you call Gwynhelek?'

"Do not get in my way…"

'I don't intend to,' Masek snorted. 'He is there.' And with a nod toward a trembling white form on his left, he walked casually away.

Gwynhelek was in a state of panic. First he tried to cower closer to his pack, but they would have none of it. The Coranieid may be mortal, yes, but they were still the most powerful force in the greenwood. The wolf pack wasn't going to take them on – certainly not to defend this crazy, freak-of-nature that had been born into their midst. The only wolf to hesitate nearby was Kensa, his mother. But, at a low snarl from Masek, she backed away. She knew – they all recognised – the inevitability of what was about to happen.

With no support from his fellows, the white wolf crept submissively on his belly up to Gwyn. He rolled over to show his stomach and tried to lick the man's hand.

Gwyn shook his head. "No." He raised his axe.

Gwynhelek began crying, screaming in the high-pitched yelps of an animal in distress. 'No … no … please, wait.'

The axe fell again and again. Fryok was avenged.

That night Myrddin made Fryok's soul stone and we buried him the following day. Sunlight streamed through the trees in solid shafts of gold. It would be a beautiful day of blue skies and fleecy white clouds that promise fair weather. I could not get my mind around it: how the sun could shine so gloriously on such sadness. It was perverse.

"Oh, little one, it is a hard lesson, perhaps the hardest of all." Myrddin placed a gentle hand on my head.

"What is?"

"To learn that the universe is indifferent to our fate and heaven does not fall for fal-tha-rals."

"Trifles?" I spat the word back at him. "Fryok's dead. This is the first funeral I've ever been to – how is that a trifle?"

"Look," he pointed to smouldering yellow ball of the sun and then to the pale shadow of moon that still hung in the sky. "The sun and moon have been travelling since long before I was born, and they will continue on their way long after I am dead. To such titans we are merely ants scurrying about. And what is one ant more or less? They will not pause to mourn our passing, just as they did not pause to note that we had arrived. Look at the greenwood ... does it shrivel and die because we grieve? No. All things carry on and if you think on it, you will see that it must be so."

He was right, of course, the world does not stop for our little tragedies and life must go on. But for us it went on in altered form, twisted somehow by the event.

Gwyn watched as earth and stone covered the thin little body. The pain was like a solid lump in his stomach and chest, making him feel sick, making it hard to draw breath. And he was angry, so very angry. He was angry at Fryok for tarrying too long in the pasture. Even the knowledge that this was unfair did not help to quiet the raging inside his head. And he was furious with that fucking wolf and wished that he could kill it over and over again. Indeed he had tried to, he beat that thing with his axe long after it stopped screaming and long after it lay still. He beat it into a barely recognisable pulp. He wanted to beat it some more and keep striking it until he felt better. But that was never going to happen, was it? He would never feel right about this. He suddenly remembered all the times he had lost his temper with the boy, and he felt ashamed and certain that he was the worst of fathers. Too much, it is too much. He did not know how to deal with the tidal wave of grief and guilt that washed over him. He wanted to cry out but could not find his voice. All he could do was watch as the sun beamed down on the grave, and inwardly rage against life and all its cruelty.

Ironic, really, that Gwyn stormed and thundered and Mora should be so very calm. After her initial outburst, she had become still and quiet as a winter night. It was as if her grief was a fire that burned itself out leaving only cold ash and darkness.

"How did I not foresee it?" she asked of no one in particular.

"Even with the gift of prophecy," Myrddin answered. "You cannot expect to know all things. I knew that wolf from the day of its birth and I did not see that madness in him." He shook his head sadly.

"But we are as…"

"…gods?" The old man snorted. "Do you still believe that?"

"No."

"Look at your daughter."

"What about her?"

"She is growing up – much slower than a normal child, but she is insistently growing up."

"What of it?" she snapped.

"That means she is ageing. And so are we. We may have more years than other humans, but we are not infinite."

Mora sighed wearily. "Why do you tell me this now, old man?"

"Because you must understand that you are not a goddess who could have saved your son. You are extraordinary, yes; but you have limits. We all do."

"I know these things."

"You understand them with your head, not your heart."

"No." The mother looked upon her son's grave. "My heart will never understand this."

Numbly she walked off toward the greenwood, then stopped. What good was the gift of prophecy if you could not save the ones you love? The question fluttered around inside her like an agitated wasp and suddenly she felt restless, anxious, like she should be doing something but did not know what.

She turned abruptly on her heel and went to gather the washing, a big heap of which she carried to the nearby stream. Although the local populations had rebounded after the pestilence and we again had slaves aplenty, Mora had never stopped washing her family's clothes. It was peaceful work and she had always done some of her best thinking while kneeling by the stream, her hands in cold water.

She wet the clothes and added soap (a mixture of thistle ash and tallow), working it into a lather with her fingers. And she admitted to herself that, when it came to prognostication, her results had been inconsistent. One day she would receive a blindingly clear view of a future event, a vision that went through not only her mind, but her body like a bolt of lightning. The next day … nothing. It was an imprecise art and that should have been the first inkling, really, that we were not gods. But she had not been wise enough to see.

"I didn't want to see it," she murmured. What a price she had paid for her lack of vision. Was it even worth continuing her work?

She remembered again that sensation – the tingling electricity that arced through her whenever she saw the future – and realised that, for all its imperfections, she could not give it up. She had tasted the power and like any addictive drug, she wanted more.

So what if we are not gods, she thought. We are powerful. I am powerful and I will become more so. She decided to devote every waking moment to honing her talents until she could see Death approach and find a way to bar his path.

She pushed a loose strand of hair out of her eyes with the back of one wet hand and gazed into the clear brook to focus her thoughts.

"Show me," she whispered.

Every day after that would find her scrying, searching for some hint of our fate within the blue waters, while she washed and washed the clothes.

**A Side Note**

*A method used to see the future, often associated with crystal balls, is known as "scrying." Any reflective surface, however, can be used. Polished metal and pools of ink or water are said to focus the mind just as effectively. Therefore scrying falls under the category of crystallomancy, the art of looking for signs and portents within reflective surfaces. It is said that Nostradamus divined his famous prophesies in this way by staring into a brass bowl full of water.*

The following spring Tamara, one of our women, went to seek Mora's council. She found her in her usual spot along the riverbank.

"Mora…" Tamara hesitated, uncertain whether she should interrupt.

Mora (who hadn't genuinely smiled or laughed since Fryok's death) arranged her features in what she hoped was a friendly, welcoming look. "What can I do for you, Tam?"

The young woman was still hesitant. "How is it coming?" She nodded toward the stream.

"The scrying? Slowly, but I am making progress. Why?"

"I was hoping you could find out something for me."

"I will try. What is it?"

"Well, you see … Barinthus wants a son and we've been trying for a while and …"

Mora interrupted, "How long?"

"Too long. Years."

"I see."

Tamara's eyes filled with tears. "I started bleeding again this morning and I don't know what to do."

"Calm yourself," Mora said soothingly. "I will look."

She did look, day after day. Focusing her attention on the clear water, it showed her many things: a woman with sunken eyes and long blonde hair who carried herself with all the dignity of a queen, a dead fisherman lying on the sand with the incoming tide licking hungrily at his body, a hut on fire and the man within now silent. She saw all these things and more, but no babies. None within the tribe at all. When was the last child born? Then she realised: it was her own daughter born in the Time Before.

There was only one division in time acknowledged by the tribe. There was the Time Before (when we, the Coranieid, were ordinary men). Then there was the Time After – after the knucker and the change. She suddenly went very cold. There had been no babies born since the dragon. Not one.

She was on her feet and running, calling to her husband and Myrddin as she entered the camp.

"Oh god, oh god!"

"What is it, child?" Myrddin asked.

But Mora addressed her question to Gwyn. "Do you remember what you said to me after the change?"

"What?"

"You were worried. All of the gifts that had been heaped on us – you said there would be a price."

"Yes."

"Well look!" she gestured wildly at the huts around her.

"I don't understand what you mean," Myrddin said, already wondering if a mixture of chamomile, lavender and hops was needed to calm her down.

"Look! What don't you see? What don't you *hear*?"

Neither of the men had an answer, and neither was inclined to take the woman's hysterics seriously.

"No babies cry."

Chief and Medicine Man looked at her in stunned silence.

"That doesn't mean anything," Gwyn said uncertainly.

"There have been no births since the dragon!"

A grimace twisted her husband's features as if a sharp pain had just arced through his skull.

"Don't you see?" she whispered.

Gwyn went very pale, "The price for our good fortune and longevity…"

"…is our children," Mora finished the sentence for him. "And Fryok is dead and we are ageing and …"

"One day the tribe will be no more," Myrddin said grimly.

I watched the three of them as they stared helplessly at each other. There was nothing more to say. What will be will be and life, however altered and twisted, would go on.

It is possible now, after many years, to think back on that sickening realisation and be a little more philosophical about it. It is, I think, like one of your books about Adam and Eve in the garden. They ate fruit of the Tree of Knowledge and must have felt what we felt: wave after wave of understanding washing over them. But there is always a price to be paid.

"And the LORD God said, 'Behold the man is become as one of us, to know good and evil: and now, lest he put forth his hand, and take also of the tree of life, and eat, and live for ever' – Therefore the LORD God sent him forth from the garden of Eden" (Genesis 3:22-3). That is how it goes, right? And I look now at my empty arms that would have cradled children and I comprehend. We too had eaten of the Tree of Knowledge, and ultimately we too had been denied the fruit of the Tree of Life. For you see, I was that baby girl that wailed in Gwyn's arms. I was the last child of the tribe.

CHAPTER 2

# "PARADISE LOST"

*"Too well I see and rue the dire event*
*That with sad overthrow and foul defeat*
*Hath lost us Heaven, and all this mighty host*
*In horrible destruction laid thus low,*
*As far as gods and heavenly essences*
*Can perish: for the mind and spirit remains*
*Invincible, and vigour soon returns,*
*Though all our glory extinct, and happy state*
*Here swallowed up in endless misery."*

*John Milton, Paradise Lost, Book I, lines 134-42*

In the greenwood there grows a tree with tiny white flowers arrayed in umbrella-shaped clusters. With the coming of autumn, these are replaced by black berries from which we made wine. And in winter, the tree sprouts ears. It was this that attracted my attention to the tree for I felt it to be kindred to the tribe, to a people so reliant upon our miraculous ability to hear. In reality, the "ears" I observed were a type of fungus, but by the time I learned this, I had already come to love the tree and visit it often.

You can still catch a glimpse of the child that I was, hidden amongst the leaves of elder tree and then of book where Hans Christian Andersen wrote of "the little maiden ... with elder blossoms in her hair [who] sat up in the tree, and nodded ... my real name is Remembrance."[29]

As last and youngest child of the tribe, it was decided that I would be keeper of the tribe's memories, the soul stones and the stories. And so it is for me to write this and tell you of all that followed on from those early days in the greenwood. There is much to tell.

"Are you sure about all this?" Tamara asked.

"Not absolutely, no," Myrddin admitted. We were seated in a circle around the main village fire, discussing Mora's theory that the dragon magic had left us barren.

"So then there's still a chance," she replied.

"I've looked and looked, Tam. I can see no births in our future. None at all," Mora said gently.

"Like that means anything!" Barinthus snapped. "You couldn't even see Fryok…"

Gwyn was on his feet now and one belligerent look from the chief was enough to silence Barinthus before he said anymore.

"Maybe we're wrong. If so, wonderful!" Gwyn addressed his remarks to the group. "But if not, then…" he faltered for a moment, searching for the right words.

Myrddin came to his aid, "If not, we must find some way to accept our fate and carry on."

A bitter laugh rang out and Bucca rose to his feet. "Carry on," he sneered. "We have learned that we are mortal. We have realised that we are ageing. And now you tell us there will no more children born of the Coranieid. The tribe is doomed." He turned to Gwyn. "I was right! I told you that you had killed us, but no! You never make a mistake. You never lead us down the wrong path. And look where we are!"

"That's enough!"

"I'm just getting started. I…" But his words were cut short as Gwyn's axe flew at him and embedded itself in the ground at his feet.

"You are not fit to lead," Bucca continued quietly. "Y- torraf genough."

Translated, this means "I break with you." These words signal a challenge. Upon hearing them the chief has two options: abdicate his position or fight.

Gwyn was not at all surprised. He'd known that this was coming. He smiled sourly, "As you wish," and immediately launched at his rival with a blow to the face.

Bucca staggered backward, bleeding heavily from the nose, and pulled his knife from his belt. Gwyn threw up an arm to block the attack and cried out as the blade bit into flesh. Daunted by neither blood nor pain, he brought his knee up sharply into his opponent's groin. Grappling, the men lost balance and fell to the ground, rolling over and over in the dust.

Myrddin watched the proceedings calmly, but inwardly prayed that Gwyn would be the victor. Bucca, he knew, would make a terrible chief. He was hotheaded and selfish and not overly-intelligent. Gwyn, on the other hand, possessed the three qualities that Myrddin thought crucial for leadership. He knew the value of compassion and so the people loved him. He was willing to take advice and listen to reason. And finally, Myrddin smiled to himself, when required he could be an absolutely ruthless son-of-a-bitch.

Bucca was receiving a lesson on what the word "ruthless" truly means. Gwyn had the man by the hair and was pounding his face repeatedly against a rock. Bucca's broken left arm hung limply at his side and his right ear had been torn (or was it bitten?) to a bloody pulp.

"Enough!" he croaked at last. "You win!"

Gwyn released him and stood proudly over the moaning figure of his rival. "Anyone else?" he looked haughtily around the circle of wide-eyed faces.

No one spoke. Indeed no one would meet his gaze lest it be interpreted as a challenge.

"Right, then." Gwyn walked into the centre of the group. "Ha rak why dhe'm curuna (since I still lead) here is what we're going to do. Whether children come or not, we are *still* the Coranieid. We are mighty and the march of time has slowed for us. We can live many lifetimes and I say that we do so with power and with pride!"

These words stirred the tribe who rose to their feet shouting their agreement.

"There is just one thing," Myrddin raised a hand for silence. "The other tribes see us as gods. For that to continue, the truth must be kept hidden. Their numbers increase and should they stop believing…"

"Have you so little faith in our warriors?" Hanyfer asked.

Myrddin looked at her soberly. "It is not a question of faith. It is a matter of fact."

Myrddin went to Bucca and helped him to his feet. He knew that Gwyn was annoyed with him. The chief had had the people fired up and Myrddin's words had poured cold water on that. But the point had to be made. The tribe's single greatest task now was to protect our secret – to never let outsiders see that we were vulnerable. For if they did…

Ah well, no use dwelling on it. "Come on, Bucca," he said quietly. "I have quite a bit of work to do on you."

He led Bucca back to his hut and bade him sit. The man had received such a thorough beating it was difficult to know where to begin.

"First let's get you cleaned up." He rinsed the blood and dirt off of Bucca's face and cleansed his wounds. The young man's nose was clearly broken and he had two black eyes.

"You won't be looking too pretty for a while," he murmured, applying a mixture of red comfrey and witch hazel to the bruises.

"Doesn't matter what I look like. Slave girls don't say no." An idea struck him. "Hey, that's a point! Why don't we just breed with them?"

Myrddin shrugged his shoulders. "Our men have been using the slave girls for years. Have any of them fallen pregnant?"

"No," admitted Bucca.

"Exactly."

"This is all Gwyn's fault … ouch!"

"Sorry," Myrddin's tone was unconvincing as he applied an agrimony compress to Bucca's mangled ear. "Gwyn could not have foreseen any of this and you know it. What? Do you think you could have done better – you who couldn't even predict the beating you just volunteered for?"

Bucca did not answer and so Myrddin continued. "Frankly, I don't see why you'd want to be chief. This is really going to hurt." He yanked his patient's arm to realign the broken fragments of bone.

Swearing and panting loudly, Bucca managed to ask, "What do you mean?"

"It's a terrible responsibility."

"You talk too much, old man."

"Perhaps, but I'm right. There, all done. You'll heal quickly enough. We always do."

"Tell that to Fryok."

Fryok and the grim truth of our mortality was hidden away then, denied. It made it all the more painful somehow to impose such silence on our grief. We could no longer think on him as son or brother or friend, but as a symbol of our weakness that must be concealed as though it were shame. It was necessary though and, Myrddin noted with satisfaction, successful. The neighbouring tribes, the *gonys* (servants) as we called them, continued to believe that we were due offerings of food and treasure and fine young slaves to toil in the service of their gods. It was not difficult, really, for we knew these people. We had, once upon a time, been just like them, and hence knew how to manipulate their fears and their faith to our purpose.

Myrddin walked straight into one of their villages one night, flanked on either side by wolves. It was as if each of the gonys had suddenly been turned to stone. No one moved; they scarcely dared to breathe. With his features arranged into a look of malevolent superiority, Myrddin nodded to the wolves who fanned out and began to sniff each villager in turn. Passing from man to man, a quiet yip signalled that they had found health and strength – good slave material. Myrddin would beckon and the chosen would fall into line.

For the slaves themselves, it was an odd moment. One of the first things they had been taught was that it was an honour to serve the tribal gods. It distinguished you as being fine and strong in their sight. They knew they would be well treated and well fed. Perhaps they would even be honoured with a visitation when god or goddess would deign to join with a mere mortal. And yet to be called away meant an end to your old life and goodbye to home, family and friends forever. It was sad, but then sacrifices were required of the chosen.

Myrddin, satisfied that he had enough hands for the coming harvest, left without another word. Yes, he nodded to himself as he walked back to camp, they still believe.

All of these events took place on the island that was our home. Later, much later, we would call this place Enys Breten: the Island of Britain. If you know your history, you will know that Britain received many visitors throughout the years – most of them unwelcome. The first of these came from Gaul circa 600 B.C. Gaul (or Gallia as the Romans called it) extended from the Atlantic to the Alps, from the English Channel to the Mediterranean Sea, and was inhabited by three nations made up of smaller, autonomous tribes. Between the Sequana and Garumna Rivers (later known as the Seine and the Garonne) lived the nation of the Celtae – tall, fair warriors, great in number and mighty in battle. These were the iron men whose weapons were wrought from a new and superior metal to our stone and copper and bronze.

And here, history beguiles us. According to popular belief, these Celtic warriors invaded our island and swept its Stone Age inhabitants aside like we were little more than dry leaves. Not quite.

First of all, while they were of the Celtae nation, they never called themselves "Celts." That term was first used in 1792. The Helvetii, the Sequani, the Carnutes and Senones – these and other tribes made up the Celtae nation and they did not sweep down upon us like the wrath of God in one dynamic invasion to set the history books alight. No. They trickled down on us like rain. Through trade and migration and settlement the trickle became a rising flood of influence that gradually engulfed the island.

It happened slowly, surreptitiously. And then one day, it announced its arrival with the smell of burning flesh. The gonys were cremating their dead. This was unheard of. They, like us, had kept soul stones and buried the deceased in cairns – pits covered with heavy stones. That was how it was done: the soul was preserved and the body given back to the earth. It was a sacred obligation that even we felt compelled to observe.

"It is Hedrek's doing," Tamara said. "He lets that bitch lead him around by the nose."

Hedrek, the gonys chief, had recently taken a new wife, a Sequani woman named Derdriu. She was very beautiful with golden hair and eyes of green, full-bosomed and with a healthy blush to her skin. Tam was deeply jealous of the girl whose womb was already swelling with her first child.

"She tells him again and again that the soul stones are unnecessary. She says the Sequani know that the soul is reborn a hundred, a thousand times over and so death is not the end, but the beginning. It is just a gateway into a new body and a new life."

"And he believes that?" Gwyn asked incredulously.

"Yes," Tamara nodded. "But that's not the worst of it. Danjy, show him…"

Danjy stepped forward and held up a beautiful sword, the hilt of which was ornately fashioned out of bronze. The iron blade, however, had been bent rendering the weapon useless.

"What's this?"

"They cast offerings like this into pits."

"Offerings to who?"

Danjy snorted, "Not to us, that's for sure. There are bodies down there as well, animals and people, all with their throats slit."

"I saw her when I last looked in the water," Mora said.

"What did you see?" Myrddin asked.

And my mother's eyes glazed over the way they did when she recalled a prophesy and the words spilled from her in a monotone:

"Much damage, Derdriu, will follow....
through your fault, fatal woman....
Harsh, hideous deeds done...
And little graves everywhere."[30]

Gwyn was confused. "She demands blood tribute?"

"Not to her," Tamara shook her head. "To the Sequani dhew."

We bristled at the mention of the Sequani gods. Cernunnos (the lord of animals), Camulos (the god of war), and Sucellus (the god of weather and the harvest) – these were not merely stories to challenge our ideology, they were direct rivals to us, the Coranieid. All of our previous efforts had been toward one end: to convince outsiders that kepar ha Dew y-fedhen, that we were as gods. And now, behold, new gods were worshipped in the shady groves of the greenwood and offerings that would have lined our coffers were cast deep into pits, besmirched with the blood of the slain. It was as bent and twisted as the swords they ceremoniously ruined as an act of tribute.

Hedrek had made the Celtae holy men, the druids, welcome at his fire and Mora was incensed to learn that they considered themselves "the true seers". They claimed an intimate knowledge of the birds and animals and the ability to know the future.

"It's a farce," she ranted. "Oh they learn from the beasts all right – by slicing them open and pretending to read the future from a pile of steaming guts. These people are insane!"

"That may well be, but more and more of them are looking to settle here," Myrddin said quietly. "We have a problem."

"Yes," agreed Barinthus. "And the solution is?"

"War, obviously," answered Bucca. "We kill them and..."

"...risk getting killed ourselves?" asked Myrddin. "Risk revealing that we are mortal after all?"

Bucca went red in the face and fell silent.

"No. Open conflict is not the way," Myrddin was pacing now, thinking.

The tribe fell silent awaiting his judgement on the matter. You see, his kindness to Gwyn after Fryok's death had not gone unrewarded. Once again the chief looked to him for advice. Once again Myrddin held a prominent place within the tribal hierarchy. And once again, he noticed, Nimue's eyes held a certain softness when she looked at him. He tore his gaze away from her face and stared determinedly at his own feet as he considered the problem at hand.

He reached a decision. "It is a war, Bucca – not one of spears and arrows, but of ideas, of faith. We fight now for souls."

Gwyn sighed wearily, "Speak plainly, Myrddin."

"Two sets of gods vie for the gonys. We must convince them that we are gwyr dhew – the true gods."

"And how do we do that?"

Myrddin looked at Gwyn shrewdly. "Punish them for their sins."

In the middle of the night the wolf pack howled, an incessant ghostly moan, unceasing. We entered the gonys village on silent feet, faces painted grey, and Myrddin began to sing. Slowly, the confused people emerged from their huts, in thin shirts and with no weapons.

Pointing his staff of carved bone at Hedrek, Myrddin shouted, "Ty a nagh dhe fay ha gordhya fals dhew!" (You have denied your faith and worshipped the false gods!). This cannot go unpunished! I call down upon you the own-mollath! Fearful curses! Ken dhe ola why a-s-byth! You shall have cause to weep!" And with that we withdrew as the gonys stared after us in astonished silence.

Curses, from the Anglo-Saxon word cursien meaning "to invoke harm or evil upon"[31], have existed as long as mankind has walked the earth. After all, man swiftly learns to hate and envy man. We called it the mollath and had lived long enough to know how a good curse works.

First of all, the man has to know he has been cursed. It makes him uneasy and watchful for signs of ill-luck. It is well said in *Folklore, Myths and Legends of Britain* that the "curse was a devastating weapon; provided that the victim knew he was ill-wished, auto-suggestion could do much damage."[32] The victim would become fearful. He might find it hard to sleep and fatigue would make him accident-prone and more susceptible to illness (real and imagined). Most of all, every misfortune would be taken as proof that the curse was active. In short, the victim's mind does much of the required work.

But for us it did not stop with mere suggestion. The mollath, we knew, benefits from a little "help." Night after night Gwyn dragged a carcass to the wolves' den.

Edern, descendant of old Masek, would greet him, "Welcome once again, O Gwyn ap Nudd."

"Will you sing for us?"

"As always."

"Your payment." Gwyn dropped a deer in front of the drooling mouths of the pack. Excited by the smell of fresh meat, the wolves began to howl.

Back in the gonys village, Hedrek had just blown out his candle and now lay in the darkness listening to the eerie cry. The language of the wolves may be untranslatable, but it spoke to him nonetheless of loneliness and a world wholly indifferent to his fate.

He glanced uneasily at the sleeping figure of his wife and wondered yet again if he had been foolish to listen to her stories of the Celtae gods. But her people were so prosperous. They did not live in subjugation. They did not see the best and strongest of their tribe carted off as slaves. They did not cripple themselves by paying endless tribute. Surely, such a people had powerful gods indeed. But were they powerful enough? he wondered.

He knew full well that these thoughts were blasphemous and therefore dangerous. He had learned at his mother's knee that the Coranieid were kind gods who had stopped the endless feuding among local tribes.

"Because of them we prosper, my son," Kerra had said, "and we need have no fear of attack. Such gods," she argued, "deserve our love and devotion."

But when Hedrek was small, the only object of undying love for him was Kerra. She fed and clothed him, cleaned the blood off his skinned knees and tucked him into bed at night. She was his world.

And then they took her.

Late one night one of the Coranieid – the one with grey eyes and grey beard – entered the camp flanked by wolves. Hedrek, awestruck at the sudden appearance of a god in their midst, hid behind the folds of his mother's skirt. The wolves fanned out, sniffing each villager in turn. They would yip at the scent of a man or woman and the god would beckon them to come.

Hedrek was afraid and wound the fabric of Kerra's skirt up in his little fists. His heart was racing as a large grey wolf approached and sniffed his mother's hand. It uttered a short bark.

Hedrek screamed and clung to his mother.

"I must," she said, trying to free herself. "I must."

There were tears in her eyes and this only caused him to struggle harder, to shriek louder, "Na-garaf, mam, plekya! No, mum, please!"

His father intervened now and pried his fingers open, releasing Kerra's skirt. He struggled in his father's arms, kicking and flailing, his hoarse cries of "Na-garaf! No! No!" the only sound to break the heavy silence.

And then she was gone forever.

Even now as a grown man and chief, the recollection of that night made his eyes sting and his chest feel tight. If we had worshipped the Sequani dhew, he thought, then she would never have been taken.

Still, were the Celtae gods stronger than the Coranieid? He thought they were. He had been prepared to bet everything on that belief. But now, lying in the darkness listening to the thin lupine voices, his resolve began to waver. And Derdriu was not helping. It turns out that the Sequani are deathly afraid of curses. Perfect. She had seen her own holy men, the druids, cast many. They would stand on one leg and close one eye to focus all of their malevolent energy and direct it at their target. And it *worked*, she insisted. It could cover a man in boils or conjure up a violent storm to defeat an army. Even in bed, she wore a charm around her neck, a small leather pouch containing the tip of an ox tongue, to protect her and her unborn child against the evil eye.

Hedrek sighed. The inevitable question, then, is this: If Celtae gods were so powerful, why was Derdriu afraid? Why was she not confident of their protection?

But then, he reasoned, she had not been easy for some time. It was hardly surprising. She had left her tribe and her father and come to live among strangers and their strange ways. She had become a queen, a wife, a lover in one fell swoop, and now she carried her first child in her belly. It was a lot to get used to. Perhaps her anxiety had less to do with curses and more to do with all the newness in her life.

Yes. That must be it, he thought. But he, Hedrek, would not cower under his covers like a frightened woman. His hand reached automatically for the handle of his battle-axe, a beautiful weapon that he kept beside him as he slept. No. He would not lie awake, trembling in his bed. Resolutely he closed his eyes and eventually drifted off to sleep.

## A Side Note

*According to folklore, there were many things you could do to protect yourself from an ill-wish or curse. The most common response was to wear a charm: a pouch which often contained some very extraordinary items. These included the tip of an ox tongue, a bit of donkey's ear, earth, teeth, bones taken from a grave and later, a few words of scripture. What a donkey's ear was supposed to realistically achieve is unclear. One thing, however, is certain: the charm could restore a person's confidence and therefore negate many of the psychosomatic effects of the curse.*

Noisy nights were followed by quiet days ... too quiet. No birds sang and Hedrek's tribe grew increasingly uneasy. Many had started leaving tribute to the Coranieid again: fine weapons and jewellery, pottery and gifts of food arrayed on the ancient cairns. Hedrek felt vaguely sick. All his efforts to direct his tribe away from the Coranieid had only intensified their fervour. The more the unnatural silence of the day and the ghostly calling of the night unsettled them, the more devout they were in their prayers, the more desperately they sought forgiveness. After four nights of howling, everyone's nerves had begun to fray. His people looked pale and haggard. A burnt hand while cooking, a broken harness, a lost brooch, a sick baby – all were attributed to Coranieid magic. Despite the fact, Hedrek realised, that these things happened all the time. Usually his people would shrug their shoulders and say "That is life." But now, every mishap was imbued with a sinister air.

The next night Hedrek found it even harder to sleep. He had thought that all that incessant howling night after night was the most disturbing sound imaginable. But now the howling had ceased. Instead of curling up amidst the blessed silence, he grew anxious. It was as if all the world held its breath and waited ... for what? Indeed, what was he waiting for? What was he expecting to happen? The fact that he could not define it did not matter. Dawn found him, sitting outside, keeping watch over his village, unable to close his red and tired eyes.

Among our number there was one called Vixana. She did not like the cold of the sea-wave like Hanyfer nor the chill of the caves like Danjy, but was always happiest bent over her cooking, warming her gnarled, old fingers in the steam from the pot. For her the dragon magic had sharpened her once faltering mind and cleared the cataract fog from her eyes as if a strong, fresh breeze had blown the clouds away. And all at once her mind remembered its former inquisitiveness. Soon she grew bored with merely cooking her nightly stew.

One day, Gwyn came charging into her hut, demanding, "What on earth are you doing, woman?"

Vixana looked at him placidly. "Just trying something…" she smiled, throwing a handful of baneberry into her cauldron.

Gagging from the thick, black smoke that issued from the pot, Gwyn swore and hastily ducked outside. "I don't care what you're trying to do," he shouted back through the open door. "Your neighbours complain. They can't stand the stench."

"Well, what would you have me do?" Vixana asked, emerging into the open air.

"Move your … whatever-the-hell you call it …out of the village."

"To where?"

"Anywhere downwind so we're not plagued by the smeech."

Vixana re-entered her hut, clucking angrily to herself. Smeech, indeed! Her work did not smell that bad. Nevertheless, she took to making her concoctions out on the moor.

In retrospect, she had to admit that it was very pleasant there with heather underfoot and a wide, grey expanse of sky above. The air was fresh and cooled her sweating brow as she worked. And with each new discovery, her triumphant whoops were echoed by the gulls overhead.

One day, while stirring merrily and singing a jolly song to herself, she stopped abruptly. "It is not polite to sneak up on an old woman," she said without turning to face her visitor.

"I wasn't sneaking," Gwyn replied joining her at the cauldron. "How goes it?"

"Very well, indeed," Vixana smiled.

"Good, good… Things go well with the gonys. They grow more ragged by the day."

"Your curse is working then," she chuckled.

"Yep. It's time, I think, to give the blade another twist."

Vixana looked at him shrewdly. "What do you have in mind?"

The chief smiled down at her, "What have you got?"

With the coming of night, a thin mist snaked its way across the moor and through the nearby wood. Vixana stoked the fire under her cauldron and the mist began to thicken. It tumbled like fog into the valley where the gonys huts were huddled together in a ring. The old woman at her cauldron did not know it, but she had just made herself the stuff of legend. Two thousand years later, Hans Christian Andersen would write that when "the meadow was covered with vapour … the Moor-woman was at her brewing"[33] and weather folklore surviving into the twenty-first century would remember "the witch Vixana [who] conjured up mists to confuse and waylay travellers."[34] Unconscious of the fact that she had just taken her place in history, the Moor-woman chuckled quietly and threw another handful of herbs into the pot.

As the mist advanced, we moved with it, little more than ghosts in the fog. Hedrek and the rest of his tribe must have sensed our coming for they stirred uneasily in their beds.

The first to die were the village dogs, their throats slit to keep them from barking. Then our men set to work slaughtering the livestock. Edern's rout of wolves feasted as never before and when they were done, there was little meat left for the gonys to salvage.

In the meantime, the women of the Coranieid had been charged with a different task. "Gwytha tam na-guskens," Gwyn had said. "Take care they get no rest at all." And to this end we pressed our lips to their ears and began to weave the thin gossamer threads of dreams. As the spell took hold, we lay on each man's chest, running fingers through his hair and all the while whispering. Of monsters in the dark. Of jealous gods. Of us.

### A Side Note

*That feeling of a sinister night-time presence in the room and of a paralysing weight on the chest is well documented. Modern science has given it a name, "sleep paralysis," and explains it thus: at the onset of REM sleep, the brain immobilises the body to keep it from acting out any dreams. Sometimes people awaken before this paralysis has worn off and there they are – lying in the dark, unable to move or cry out. Suffers describe sensations of being crushed or choked and some have reported visual and auditory hallucinations of someone else being present in the room or in the bed.*

*That is logical enough, but in the absence of sleep clinics and specialists, early men identified another cause ... the Mara. The Mara were demons from teutonic folklore who, it was said, would lie on their sleeping victims, pinning them under their weight and hence conjuring terrible dreams of being crushed or suffocated. They were originally called "nightmaras" or alpdrucken (meaning "elf pressure")[35] and, when in a more impish mood, they would fiddle with their victims' hair, leaving it in a mess of tangles known as "elf locks."*

*Later, in medieval times, these dreams would be attributed to the incubi and succubi – carnal demons who would seduce and lie with humans in their sleep. Ruthless and intimate, the Mara are known to have haunted generations of men who, vulnerable in slumber, were condemned to "sleep in the affliction of these terrible dreams that shake us nightly ... in restless ecstasy."[36]*

In the morning Hedrek awoke feeling as if he had barely slept. He sat up and scratched his itching scalp to find his hair a matted mess. He cast a bleary eye around the room. In a dim sleepy way, he was aware that something was amiss. He could not, however, figure out what. Rubbing his eyes he turned a sharper gaze on his surroundings. What, he wondered, is wrong here? Then he realised ... his axe was gone. A search was made and the exhausted villagers found all that we had done and all that we had taken. Animals and bread and milk. Ornaments and weapons. But the not the axe, that lay beside Hedrek's dead horse, its blade stained red.

Watching from the cover of the trees, my father smiled as Hedrek went raging through the village. "I still don't think it was dramatic enough."

"It's fine," I whispered. "He's rattled."

"You don't think that bit with the horse lacked flare somehow?"

"You hacked the beast's head off, what more is needed?"

The slaughtered animals were merely a calling card to say that we had been. The true purpose of our visit, however, had yet to be discovered.

Days before the attack, Tamara had picked her way through the woods until she spotted the dark green leaves and purple bell-shaped flowers of the dwale plant. Dwale is an old name no longer in common usage. Now it is called Deadly Nightshade or Belladonna. Such a pretty name, belladonna, for such an ugly purpose. But this did not give Tamara pause, nor prick her conscience as she gathered the poisonous berries. She had come to harbour an almost irrational hatred for Derdriu with her beauty and her lies and her ripening belly. But all that was about to change.

"This," she murmured as she crushed the berries and collected their juice, "will still your lying tongue."

And so as Hedrek surveyed the damage we had done to his village, a shaken Derdriu steadied herself with a drink from the cup she kept by her bed. Returning to his hut, Hedrek found his wife slumped weakly on the floor.

"Your face is so red! Are you alright?"

"I'm so thirsty," she rasped.

Hedrek poured her more water from the nearby pitcher but this only made her cough and splutter. Despite her great thirst, she seemed unable to swallow. With his nerves at breaking point, the chief dashed from the hut shouting for his medicine man.

Salan arrived and surveyed Derdriu grimly.

"What ails her?" Hedrek asked.

"I don't know. Leave her to me."

The chief hesitated by his wife's side.

"Go on!" Salan admonished. "It is a bad day and the people need you."

Reluctantly, Hedrek left.

Belladonna poisoning presents an array of symptoms, each worse than the last. First the mouth goes painfully dry, accompanied by a terrible thirst. It becomes hard to swallow. The skin of the face flushes a bright red and pupils dilate, blurring vision. Then delirium sets in. The body is covered with a rash similar to scarlet fever. The patient becomes unable to pass water despite a desperate need to do so. Then comes the drowsiness, the laboured breathing, the painful convulsions and finally death.[37]

Salan watched all of this unfold without the slightest notion of how to stop it. Out of his depth, he summoned a Sequani medicine man, the druid called Gwydion.

Gwydion examined the girl in silence – an agonising silence through which Salan fidgeted nervously.

"Poison," the druid said at last.

"What can we do?"

Gwydion did not answer immediately. The time for an emetic had long passed. He could give her selago, a sort of cure-all that might stave off death; and he would call upon Nodens, the god of healing, and pray for his intervention.

"Leave her with me," he said quietly and got down to work.

Fidchell is an ancient form of chess played with stone-carved figures of kings, queens and warriors. It was reputed to have a strange, prophetic quality – the outcome of the game mirroring the course of fate itself. Personally, Ciarán had always doubted this. For the Sequani chieftain, it was merely an evening's amusement. And why should he not enjoy himself? Everything was going according to plan: trade with the locals had proved lucrative and his people were well-fed and richly adorned. A series of tactical alliances now guaranteed security for Sequani settlers in the area and he was expecting his first grandchild.

"Your move," Maeldun said.

Ciarán turned his attention back to the Fidchell board that rested between them. Maeldun was threatening his king. "Clever," he murmured as he contemplated his next move.

He spotted his chance and moved one stone warrior forward and to the left.

"That's careless," Maeldun replied. "I'll just take your queen." He removed the piece from the board.

"I lose my queen," Ciarán smiled, shifting another piece into place, "but win the battle."

"Dammit!" Maeldun laughed. "You win again."

At that moment Loeg appeared at the door. "You have a visitor."

"Who?"

"It is Gwydion come to see you."

"Excellent! Come in, come in!" Ciarán greeted the man warmly. "What news?" He paused then, taken aback by the man's appearance. Gwydion looked unusually pale and tired. Blue eyes that normally smiled in friendship upon the Sequani chief were now grim and troubled.

Ciarán's smile remained fixed, "What…"

"Derdriu."

"Go on, then," he said as casually as he could, "Tell me."

As he listened to the account of how his pregnant daughter died, his eyes rested on the stone figure of his fallen queen as it lay beside the Fidchell board.

When at last Gwydion fell silent, Ciarán had only one further question: "Who?"

As the druid launched into an account of the Coranieid and the curse, Ciarán's eyes roamed over the ranks of pale stone warriors that he had so skilfully manipulated to win the game.

At last he raised his eyes to Maeldun. "We go to Hedrek. I want to see these gods for myself."

After he had sent Gwydion on ahead to announce his coming, Ciarán broke the news to his wife, Olwen. Her keening – loud, racking wails like a damned banshee – grated on him. More than anything he just wanted to sit quietly in front of the fire and try to thaw the icy cold that had stiffened his limbs and numbed his brain. Finally Olwen cried herself to sleep and his friends went away (all offering their deepest sympathy) and he sat by the fire, trying to gather his scattered thoughts.

They were all of the past. He had sat just like this in front of the fire the night Derdriu was born. She had slept contentedly in his arms while he marvelled at her tiny perfection: her long eyelashes and little fingers and toes. In that moment, Ciarán realised how desperately he loved her ... and how vulnerable that made him. He remembered feeling a moment's panic and thinking, I have so much to lose.

He may have feared that this moment would come, but in truth he had had no concept of how bad it would be. The cold that permeated his limbs, the pain and inexplicable fear that made his breath tremble with each exhalation, these now educated him on the true nature of grief. It was as if Life was a physical being, a towering giant who had just beaten and ravished him and left him meek and broken upon the ground. He wept, his body wracked by sobs, his hands twisted into clawed fists as he sought to endure his pain.

When morning dawned a dismal and cloudy grey, Ciarán mounted his chariot. His face, stoic and impassive, betrayed none of his suffering to the curious eyes of his men. As they rode out towards Hedrek's village, he kept seeing over and over again an image of Derdriu when she was about three, in a little tunic and miniature torc that Olwen liked dressing her in. Her curly hair was bushy. "It needs to grow a bit before it will lie in waves," his wife had said, licking a cloth and wiping a smudge of dirt from the child's face. For some reason he could not fathom, that moment had stuck. It was as if Derdriu was frozen in time; in his mind he would always see her as three years old.

That, of course, made it difficult when it came time for her to marry. He had been reluctant to let her go; and now he bitterly wished he hadn't. Why did I say yes? he wondered. There were good reasons to be sure, but it took a moment to remember what they were.

It was all about alliances and trade. The Sequani were expanding further and further west. While he could fight the natives and take the land from them (a small, rowdy voice within him still insisted it would be fun to do so), he knew that peace was best for his people. It is better to form links through alliance and marriage, to mix the blood rather than spill it. "He who is chief, let him be a bridge,"[38] that is what Gwydion, Chief Druid of the Sequani, had said; and the tactician in Ciarán had agreed.

Still, if Derdriu had not favoured Hedrek, he would not have forced the union upon her. But she did like him … very much. She said he had courage which went beyond that required to swing an axe or lob a spear. He dared to ask questions that his people never asked. And he looked upon her as if she were a revelation. He never tired of listening to her talk about her life, her faith, her hopes for the future. He made her feel "gorthelyk" as he put it, beloved. So Ciarán acquiesced. His little girl became a married woman, soon with child, and still Ciarán saw her as a toddling three-year-old with big green eyes and bushy hair.

The initial passivity of his grief began to disperse to be replaced by anger and a hatred unlike anything he had ever known. Ciarán was, of course, capable of dreadful outbursts of temper. But this feeling of pure, cold loathing was new. Because it did not contain the heat of his former rages, he recognised that it had the necessary staying power. He could sustain this hatred forever – certainly for as long as it took to exact his revenge.

Ciarán's arrival at Hedrek's village caused its customary stir. The natives of Britain were a simple people, and the flamboyant appearance of the Sequani ruler left them in awe and not a little intimidated. He wore a heavy, golden torc, the sign of his high office. His body was painted, his shoulder-length hair was bleached, and he was covered in lavishings of gold – bracelets, armlets, rings, a jewel-encrusted brooch and a fine woollen cloak. Large, powerful hands gripped the reins of two fine horses that pulled his chariot. Every inch of the man screamed power and wealth and majesty.

As Ciarán dismounted, Hedrek braced himself, sure he was about to bear the brunt of the Sequani chief's outrage. To his surprise, the Celtae man embraced him like a brother.

"This loss weighs heavily on us both," Ciarán said quietly.

A Sequani funeral is a dramatic affair. In the old days, they would have exposed the body to the elements before burial, but you can imagine how unpleasant that became. And so fire, a quicker, cleaner way of disposing of the body, was favoured. Derdriu was arrayed on a sturdy pyre. Clothed in a fine woollen gown with her golden curls cascading over her shoulders, she was as beautiful in death as she had been in life.

Gwydion called upon Epona, goddess of fertility and the dead to watch over her and her unborn child. Then he lit the platform. The gathering smoke and rising waves of heat obscured the greyish tinge of Derdriu's face and Ciarán was suddenly seized by the irrational idea that she was not dead, but merely sleeping. Panic began to rise in his chest and just as he was about to leap forward and drag his daughter from the pyre, a strong hand grasped his arm.

"It is over," Gwydion said quietly. "Let her go."

Ciarán knew that he should be comforted by the knowledge that her soul would be reborn. He wasn't. Central to that belief was the idea that there was an unspecified period of time between one incarnation and another. Some said it was a time during which the soul learned so that it may live its next life more wisely. Some thought it was a time of punishment, when we atone for our sins. (Ciarán could not think of one thing in all of Derdriu's blameless life that would earn her punishment after death.) Others thought it was merely a period of waiting until the right body was growing in its mother's womb. In any case, he could well be dead by the time her soul looked again upon this world with human eyes. And even if she returned tomorrow, a babe in someone else's arms, how would he know her? For all the comfort offered by his faith, she was still utterly lost to him.

His eyes burned with fatigue. All he could see was yellow flame. All he could hear was the shrill keening of the Celtae women; and despite the intensity of the fire, he was so very cold. Ciarán plodded through the rest of the day in a haze. Derdriu's ashes were gathered and interred in a *cist*, a coffin of stone slabs covered by a mound of earth. Her golden torc, her jewellery and other grave goods were buried with her and it was truly a grave fit for a queen.

Turning away from it, he addressed Hedrek. "Now. Tell me about the Coranieid."

Later that evening, Ciarán and Maeldun sat together staring grimly at the camp fire. Maeldun looked uneasily at his friend. What a change had come over him!

Ciarán was by nature a highly demonstrative man. If he liked you, he radiated a warmth that was tangible. It was irresistible, that warmth, it bound you to him, inspired loyalty, called to you as a flame calls to a moth. His anger was equally luminescent – a ferocious blazing that made grown Sequani men cringe like errant children and his enemies grow pale with dread. Either way, as the analogy suggests, his personality was characterised by its passion, its fire.

But now there was something closed about the man. Of course Ciarán grieved for his daughter; but Maeldun had expected that grief to come as a great outpouring of emotion: tears, rages, drunkenness… not this silence, this cold composure which to Maeldun seemed almost eerie.

"So what do you think?" Ciarán's question startled Maeldun out of his reverie.

"I don't know what to think."

"I know the feeling."

"I mean, a tribe who are men one day and gods the next … how does that happen?"

"How, indeed."

"That is, of course, if Hedrek is telling the truth."

Ciarán raised his eyes from the fire to consider this. "He believes it to be true. I'm certain of that."

"But that doesn't make him right."

"No, which is why I want you to have a look. Are you game?"

Comforted by the fact that his friend was finally stirring into action, Maeldun smiled, "Always."

The next morning Maeldun and eight others set off to find the Coranieid village. Hedrek could only provide them with vague directions.

"They live in the depths of the greenwood, in an area that is forbidden to us," he explained, and so could only direct them across the moor, through the forest and to the edge of a lush glade – the border of Coranieid land.

"Don't worry," Maeldun assured Ciarán. "We'll find them."

As Maeldun reached the edge of our territory, however, his confidence wavered. The terrain was rough and wild with only the odd game trail cutting through the thick undergrowth. They tied their horses to trees and proceeded on foot.

Maeldun surveyed the forest around him with some measure of surprise.

He had expected it to be unusually dark and menacing, a fitting haunt for gods or demons or whatever the hell they were. But it was wholly unremarkable. Then Loeg, faithful servant to the chief, spotted them: the first footprints in the damp earth. Maeldun smiled to himself and pressed on, marking the trees so that he could remember the way when next he came with Ciarán and a full contingent of warriors. This was going to be easy.

Time passed and a thin wisp of fog began to seep through the forest. It thickened and spread until the party had to stop, unable to see clearly enough to follow the tracks. It pressed solidly against their mouths and noses, making them feel as if they might suffocate. Then in the dreadful gloom, Maeldun heard the first twang of a bowstring, the hiss of an arrow and Loeg, who stood at his shoulder, cried out in pain. Another twang, another hiss, another man cried out and Maeldun gave the order to retreat.

Nine men set out on recognisance, and Maeldun was surprised and delighted to see nine men emerge from the mist. They all had received only minor injuries and when he showed the tiny flint arrowheads to Ciarán, the chief laughed.

"Well, if that's the best they can do…"

Gwydion, however, knocked the arrowhead out of Ciarán's hand and retrieved it gingerly from the ground. "You shouldn't handle this so carelessly, my friend." Looking warily at Maeldun, he asked "How do you feel?"

"Fine," he shrugged. "I mean my mouth tingles a little, but that's probably from the smoke."

"Anything else?"

Maeldun looked at him uncomfortably. "My stomach feels sort of…" he searched for the right word, "warm."

Gwydion scowled. "Mar sin de go bhfuil sé[39] – so that's it."

"What?" Ciarán asked in alarm.

"Wolf's-bane. Come! I have work to do."

Wolf's-bane, also known as Aconite or Monkshood, is one of the most poisonous plants on earth. Nicholas Culpeper in his famous *Herbal*, warned that it will "inflame the heart, burn the inward parts, and destroy life itself."[40] Gwydion was well aware of this. He worked feverishly on the men with his tinctures and stimulants and prayers, but he could not halt the spread of that ominous tingling sensation as it worked its way through their bodies. He could not revive feeling to their numb skin, nor could he ease the violent retching nor restore their lost sight or hearing once it had gone. He could not stave off their convulsions, and finally, death claimed each man.

In the end Maeldun could not see the faces of his family nor hear their words of love and sorrow. But he could speak. For all its ravages, aconite left the mind untouched and aware.

"Is trua sin," Maeldun's voice was faint. "It is a pity that I go now. This promises to be one hell of a fight."

Ciarán grasped his hand.

The dying man became anxious, his groping hands caught at Ciarán's clothing. "They are taibhse – ghosts!"

And again, Ciarán felt the icy cold of his hatred roll through him like drifting snow.

The Sequani were rattled. While they could understand the trickery of poisoned arrows, they were unsettled by this unseen foe who moved silently through the mist. They even began to refer to the arrows as elf shot or fairy bolts.

For Ciarán the next move was clear – fortification; and hence, the gonys village was moved to the top of the nearest hill. Originally consisting of merely a knoll with a ditch at the bottom, the design of Celtae hill forts had evolved through the years into the formidable "glacis." A deep ditch was excavated all around the base of the mound and the rubble from the digging was piled around the outside of it to form a high rampart. Hence, an invader would have to climb the rampart, leap to the bottom of the ditch (a hazardous jump at the best of times) and then run up a steep incline all the while dodging a hail of spears and arrows. Once at the top, there was the added defence of two more walls to overcome before you lay hands upon one Sequani warrior.

The hill fort was completed in record time and defended both Sequani and gonys huts, granaries for storing food, a well and a blacksmith's. Furthermore, Gwydion and his druids passed the warning on to other Celtae settlements to reinforce their defences. The halcyon days when the Sequani went unchallenged were clearly over. For this reason, archaeologists would later note that the "greatest accumulation of hill-forts in Britain is located in south-western England"[41] – Coranieid territory.

Gwyn ap Nudd was unimpressed. They may pile the earth high and dig their ditches deep. They may line the only entrance to the hill fort with guard towers and barbicans, but they could not remain within those protective walls forever. Neither could their livestock.

"We wait," he told us as we gathered around the village fire. "After all, we've no shortage of time."

And sure enough, the sheep and cows were brought out to pasture. These were returned to their night paddock riddled with fairy bolts. The druids, who served as a cohesive influence, binding one settlement to the next, began to disappear while on their travels. The leafy groves, their sacred places of worship, were no longer safe.

And yet Ciarán remained unperturbed. He sat in his hut with the Fidchell board set up on the table in front of him. His eyes rested for a moment on the empty chair where Maeldun would have sat for a game. Ignoring the spasm of pain and loneliness that arced through him, he looked again at the board. A line of grey stone warriors faced his white ones. Picking up one of these pieces, he turned it over and over in his hand. It was cold and smooth, its grey face inscrutable.

"Nothing is invincible," he muttered.

He squeezed the figure in his fist, his strength having no effect on the stone surface. Yet it had once been part of a much larger rock. An artist had chiselled it down to size, rasped it into shape, compelled the limestone to bend to his will. Likewise, there had to be some way to chip away at the Coranieid. The old stories were full of heroes and villains, seemingly unbeatable warriors, who nonetheless had one vulnerability, one aspect that led to their downfall. Surely the Coranieid must have some weakness he could exploit. He knew this. He felt it in his bones. He just needed to find it.

**A Side Note**

*While a hero may seem invincible, they often have one fatal weakness. This is best illustrated in the story of Achilles. His mother, wishing to safeguard her infant son, dipped him in the River Styx, the black and murky depths that lie between the land of the living and the realms of the dead. Its waters conferred the gift of invulnerability and Achilles was later unstoppable as a man of war. However, in dunking the baby, his mother had held him by the heel – the one part of him not touched by the water, his only vulnerable spot. Therefore when Paris lodged an arrow in that heel during the Trojan War, Achilles fell.*

*This is not the only example of a chink within supernatural armour. For Samson, his strength resided in his hair. When Delilah cut it, he was quickly subdued by the Philistines who gouged out his eyes and imprisoned him. Returning again to the "Nibelung" and the story of Siegfried, we find that he bathed in the blood of a slain dragon which made him invulnerable. However, a leaf stuck to his shoulder, leaving one small patch of skin unprotected. Through this, he was later stabbed and murdered.*

And so the druid Gwydion was charged with the task of discovering the Coranieid's weakness, so Ciarán could go in for the kill.

The old druid chanted while the sheep was led to him. His mind was so concentrated upon the task at hand that it seemed that the only things in all the world were him, the sheep, and the knife. With one deft movement, he slit the beast's throat and continued to pray for the short time it took the animal to bleed to death. When it had stopped twitching and its eyes had glazed over, he got down to work.

Hepatoscopy is the practise of using animal entrails for divination. Gwydion was particularly interested in the liver from which, he believed, came the lifeblood of the animal. By interpreting any marks on the organ, he hoped to learn the will of the gods. Could the Sequani triumph over their enemies? How could this be accomplished? Unfortunately, the liver was clean of any blemish that might have instructed him.

Undeterred, he tried another method of augury: ornithomancy. At daybreak he sat on a nearby hill and again offered prayers up to the Sequani gods, asking them if the Coranieid could be vanquished. There was a break in the canopy of leaves above him, forming a ragged circle of blue sky. He watched this intently. Should an even number of birds appear, he would take the answer to be yes. An odd number meant no. He sat on that hill all day, growing stiff and hungry and not one bird appeared within the circle.

The druid was now annoyed. He even considered trying the ancient art of neldoracht – the interpretation of the shapes of clouds, but of course it turned out to be a beautiful day without a wisp in the sky.[42]

Gwydion had studied for twenty years to become a druid. He had mastered the power of the word and the arts of divination and healing. He had studied moral philosophy and worked for his people until his long beard had grown white and his wrinkled face read like a map of his many years. But now it all seemed to come to nothing.

He didn't know how the Coranieid had attained their powers, nor did he fully understand the nature of their strength, let alone where they might be vulnerable. And now, he thought, I have to pull that information out of thin air.

Then an idea struck him. The answer may not be available from thin air, but what about the other elements? Long, long ago he had been taught that there are four main elements: aer (air), tine (fire), uisce (water), cruinne (earth). Air would not record an imprint of the past, nor would the fluidity of water nor the brevity of fire. But earth was eternal. According to legend, the Coranieid had been men once and men invariably leave their mark upon the land. He began his search.

At the far edge of the moor there were two mounds of stone: one large and one quite small. The arrangement of rocks was not natural and bore the indelible mark of human organisation. Burial cairns. They were so far removed from the graves belonging to Hedrek's people that they excited Gwydion's curiosity.

Within Celtae philosophy, there was a belief that events left behind a kind of footprint that could be discerned even after centuries had elapsed.[43] But it would not be easy, nor comfortable. To delve into the cairns' history would require the dichetal do chennaib, divination through physical contact. In short, he must sleep upon these mounds of rocks and weeds and hope that his dreams would reveal past events. Gwydion sighed heavily. These campouts were very tiring for old bones. He was, however, out of options.

He prepared himself with the needed prayers and incantations, he chewed on animal flesh and as the sun set he waited to fall into what he hoped would be an enchanted sleep.

A clear day gave way to a clear and cloudless night. Even though it was spring, the evenings were cold. Gwydion noticed that he minded the cold more with each passing year.

"I'm getting too old for this," he muttered.

The stars overhead were like a multitude of flickering candles and the moon, now round and full, was bright. It was all very beautiful and tranquil and yet Gwydion was unmoved.

How surprised the Sequani would be if they could read his thoughts now.

As a druid, he was among the brightest and the best – a sage and healer of great wisdom. And somehow, the myth had grown that the waters of his mind always ran deep. Well, there were no profound thoughts keeping him awake on this night, only a profound boredom. He eventually nodded off and did not dream.

Next morning, he awoke stiff and cold and irritable. He had had enough. He had, after all, tried his best and Ciarán would just have to accept that.

He gathered up his blankets, his rations and his staff and started back toward the hill fort. Yet as he advanced across the moor, his steps began to slow. Gwydion knew that Ciarán and the others had absolute faith in him. In his mind he could picture the disappointment on every face when he admitted failure. He stopped walking. He could not bear it. Age had brought with it many things: wisdom and confidence and power. But it had not brought him freedom. He still cared what people thought and whether his good reputation should remain intact.

He sighed heavily and glanced back at the cairns, grey and inscrutable in the distance. "Cad atá tú chumhdaigh? What are you hiding?" He reached a decision: No, he would not give up. There was something there, he could feel it. He was going to find out what it was.

Another night asleep on the large cairn and Gwydion awoke with a sore throat and a headache. This, however, did not deter him. Sometimes, in fact, a little illness or fatigue was useful in divination. It was as if by dulling his conscious mind, he became more open to the world of intuitions and unseen things. A little valerian and lavender for his head and a decoction of oak bark for his throat and he was ready to try again.

Shivering beneath his blanket and now with a fever upon him, he fell asleep on the third night.

Men were shouting and waving spears and clubs. Men with grey faces and fearsome eyes. A black, serpentine shadow writhed at their feet and women cried over the torn limbs and unseeing eyes of the dead. A grave. A mass grave. And a voice, "You know the law." Cooking fires and a starving people feed at last. Yes. Full bellies at last. And more. Full minds and a world full of noise.

Gwydion sat up and blinked. How extraordinary. He was beginning to see, to understand. But a large part of the picture was still missing. He used yarrow and meadowsweet to nurse his fever during the day and settled down to dream again on the following night. Little did he know, as he curled up this time on the small cairn, that the little grave with its one little body would reveal the biggest secret of all.

Returning to Hedrek's camp, he was immediately inundated with questions from all sides. Have you learned anything? Are they gods or men or demons? Can we beat them?

Gwydion said nothing.

"Speak, friend," Ciarán insisted.

"A beaker of water, please," said Gwydion quietly.

This was brought to him, and then the druid did something quite odd. He poured the water onto the ground and angled the cup against a nearby rock. Extracting his knife, he began to saw away at the bottom of the cup until he was left with a thick ceramic tube.

He placed one end of the tube to Ciarán's ear and the other to his own mouth and began to whisper. At his words, Ciarán's eyes brightened and a cold smile played across his lips. "Fuair tú," he murmured. "Got you."

Hedrek walked quietly to a shady grove nearby. He led his finest horse, which was laden with many treasures: his great, beautifully crafted battle-axe which had been a wedding gift from Ciarán, his gold and precious stones, the finest pottery, as well as milk, grain and choice cuts of dried meat. He arrayed these on a low, flat rock known as mos dhew, "the table of the gods." Having tied his horse to a nearby tree, he knelt down and spoke these words aloud: "I know that I have sinned and strayed from the true faith. I know that my punishment for this was just. But I am just a man and men are so often wrong. I give to you, my gods, these gifts – the most precious things I own." And then in the ancient tongue of the Coranieid he asked, "Gaf dhym. Forgive me." He turned and, with bowed head and bent shoulders, walked slowly away.

Nearby, within the greenwood, my elder brother Maban and his best friend, Benesek, looked at each with raised eyebrows. Since we had learned to filter out a lot of the noise that met our ears, we found it necessary to post sentries to listen to the gonys and surmise their plans.

"Father will be pleased to hear this," smiled Maban.

"Too right. Let's go…" Benesek got up to leave.

"No, wait…" Maban at that moment had an image of himself walking into the village bearing not only glad tidings, but the treasure as well. He would cut quite a figure amongst the tribe – like a returning hero.

In Italy they have a saying: "Cursed is the young man of 100"[44] – basically unhappy is the old man who has not attained wisdom. This proverb encapsulates the flawed nature of Coranieid longevity. While Maban had lived for six millennia, he looked about twenty-five years of age and still had the hormones and arrogance of youth. Living as he did in his father's shadow, he still felt the need to somehow make his mark.

"Let's take it with us," he grinned, nodding at Hedrek's offering.

Mora had been at the stream all day. Her eyes were tired and her head ached. Hours of gazing into the water, while her hands busied themselves washing clothes, had come to nothing. It was not that she could not see future events; indeed, she could see so many things in the swirling water. But it was still too unpredictable. She wanted to be able to ask a question and get a specific answer. Instead, the images that came to her were so random as to be useless.

She sighed and stretched limbs stiff from kneeling on the riverbank. If she could just gain the necessary control, then all the future would be open to her. Frustrated and fatigued, she leaned back onto the soft grass and closed her eyes for a nap. Her dreams were fragmented with scattered images. She dreamt of grey stone and a black horse and jugs of warm milk.

Mora awoke with a start, dazed and feeling mildly sick. Her eyes glazed over and words of prophecy tumbled from her lips....

> "Mighty son
> don't venture out
> it is only asking
> to have your head
> knocked from your neck."[45]

Mora was on her feet and running.

"They don't look like much," Ciarán remarked. Two men were on their knees before him, their hands bound behind their backs.

Maban smiled up at him, "This is a big mistake."

Ciarán shrugged. "Don't care." He leaned forward until he was nose to nose with his captive. "I've heard a lot about you. They say that you are gods and all-powerful."

"That's right," interrupted Benesek.

"And," Ciarán continued, "I've been hearing that you are immortal." He paused. "Let's put it to the test."

He nodded and a garrotte was slipped over each man's head from behind. As a wooden peg was twisted tightening the leather thong, the two men began to choke and splutter as they fought for air.

At a nod from Ciarán, the garrotte was loosened and the chief waited patiently for his victims to stop gagging before he spoke. "Hurts, doesn't it? But then again you're gods, so this should not harm you."

He nodded and once again the loops were tightened.

Hedrek, standing at his shoulder, fidgeted nervously. If this didn't work, if Ciarán was wrong and these two survived, then they were all in a world of shit. Gwydion also had a moment's trepidation. He had been taught to trust his visions and certainly the dreams he had at the burial mounds had all the hallmarks of divine inspiration. But what if, asked a little voice within, those visions were more fever than fact? Well, we'll know in a few moments, he thought looking at the Coranieid men. Their faces were turning purple and their eyes bulged out of their sockets. This is the test.

Ciarán gave a signal and the loops were loosened once more. The men collapsed gasping in front of him and he lifted Maban's head up by the hair. The man's eyes were bloodshot, but he could read them as plain as day.

"Oh," Ciarán's brow creased with mock concern. "You're afraid. Now why would that be, oh god-immortal?" He snorted in contempt, "Finish it."

As the thong was tightened for a third and final time, the Sequani chief sat down to be entertained by his victims' death throes. Slowly suffocating with every twist of the leather, it took a further ten minutes for them to die.

In the heavy silence that followed, Ciarán spoke quietly to Hedrek. "There you are. What do you think of your gods now?"

Hedrek cautiously approached the bodies and nudged one with his foot. The one they called Benesek had, in his final moments, soiled himself. What an epiphany. So many thoughts and ideas leapt into his mind all at once; he felt dizzy. I had worshipped them! And so had my father and his father before him. Taught to kiss the hand you cannot bite, I had feared and appeased them! What an idiot, he thought bitterly. But then again, we are now free. A heady sense of liberation broke over him like a wave and he could have danced for joy. His eyes fell once again on the pathetic corpses at his feet, lying in their own filth with their bloated faces and protruding eyes. And he remembered how much he had lost to them: his mother, his wife, his child, his dignity. Anguish, anger and joy fought inside him for dominance and he took long, deep breaths to steady himself.

"Well?" Ciarán asked.

Hedrek looked upon the Celtae chief with shining eyes. "I say we kill them all."

Here's an interesting fact: the Celtae were head-hunters. They believed the soul resides in the skull and thus, by taking an enemy's head, you claimed his essence, his power. So it was that the bodies of Maban and Benesek were dragged outside and their necks severed. The brains were extracted and replaced with lime.

By the time we got to the gonys village, the two heads were positioned on the high wall of the fort's entrance. The Coranieid were struck dumb. Benesek's eyes were shut and his pale lips were drawn back against his teeth in an agonised grimace. Pain was etched into his face. Maban's waxen cheeks and mouth were slack and bore no particular expression. But his eyes – oh god, his eyes – stared down at us in horror. My brother, what was the last thing you saw before you died?

This was the ultimate desecration. We recovered their bodies from a nearby dung heap, but without the heads no soul stones could be made. Maban and Benesek were lost to the tribe forever, their souls obliterated.

I have often heard the phrase that someone "took leave of their senses," meaning I suppose that they acted foolishly and without common sense. But there is another, more literal interpretation of the old cliché that is only experienced by those in extreme shock. On that long, dreadful walk home, my eyes lost focus and I could only register a blur of colours – green, brown, and grey. Sound, too, was muffled as it would be underwater. The bodies must have reeked from the dung heap, but I can remember no smell. And my skin was insensible to touch. Despite the fact that I could negotiate my way through the greenwood with my eyes shut, I stumbled over the uneven ground and fell amongst the nettles. I had, quite literally, taken leave of my senses or more to the point, they had taken leave of me. Only my taste buds were left intact. I remember the sting of bile at the back of my throat and how my mouth watered before I was violently ill.

"Did you hear what that old druid was saying?" Tamara asked.

I made an effort to focus on her voice.

"Yeah," Bucca answered. "Something about how the heads will protect the fort."

"They believe a human skull is so powerful that it acts as a safeguard. Can even be used in divination," Myrddin's voice was a monotone.

"Of course it can. I'm getting a vision of the future right now," muttered Gwyn. "We go to war."

War indeed had been declared and both sides prepared accordingly.

Gwyn automatically walked through the old, familiar process of organising his warriors. It helped, having lots of little tasks to perform. It kept his thinking at a low, practical level so that he did not have to confront the deeper issues surrounding the loss of another child. He did not have to contemplate the dim oblivion that engulfed Maban and Benesek now that their souls were lost to us. Nor did he have to think too much about Mora who, catatonic with grief, would not get out of bed.

I too occupied my mind and hands with practical things in order to stave off the descent into grief and horror that I knew would eventually come. My fingers ached. For much of the day, I had sat with the others in the hanter, the central meeting place of the tribe, knapping arrows. It was fiddly work, honing the bits of flint into the correct shape and size, but soon I had a nice pile of arrowheads and could start binding them to smooth shafts of elm wood. Then would come the tedious business of fletching the arrows (securing specially-cut wood pigeon feathers to the shaft: three feathers 120° apart while taking care that the cock feather was perpendicular to the string-slot at the bottom of the arrow).

"Do not look so grim, Bucca." Gwyn, who had been working quietly by my side, finally broke the silence.

"We will be outnumbered," Bucca answered quietly.

"But our warriors are more skilled."

"It's true," said Myrddin. "The Sequani fight like idiot children."

"How so?" I asked, eager to finally hear some encouraging news.

"The Celtae are hell-bent on showing off their martial prowess and so they tend to be reckless and disorganised."

According to the Greek historian Strabo, when the Celts are antagonised "they gather in their bands for battle, openly and without planning, so that they are easily managed by those who wish to outwit them."[46] Some of them fought naked so that clothes would not impede their movements (nor provide them with any protection). They hacked away with long swords – beautiful weapons ornately crafted, but impractical. All you had to do was hem them in so they didn't have room to swing the blades with any force.

"So we keep to the forest," Gwyn was saying. "Use the elm bows. They'll inflict more damage at close range and, if you have to fight hand to hand, get right up close and take them out with your daggers."

Again, the tribe lapsed into silence, every one of us determined to concentrate on the work at hand and think of little else.

Hanyfer, however, could not ignore the trembling of her hands which seemed to vibrate in time with questions that buzzed through her head. She felt she had to talk or she would go mad. "They are a new breed, these Sequani."

No one rose to it. She tried again.

"They are demons," Hanyfer said.

Gwyn snorted with contempt. "That's a bit of an exaggeration, don't you think?"

"But look what they've done."

"It is terrible, yes," Myrddin said gently. "But take care what you call them, Hanyfer. Do not raise them too much in your imagination. They are men. And to us, men are cattle."

"The gonys are cattle," Barinthus remarked. "But the Celtae…"

"Are not even that useful," Gwyn interrupted. "They are bugs that have infested the tribe land. And bugs can be squashed."

"It is true," I nodded. I did not normally speak at the hanter, but I'd had an insight that I thought was worth sharing. "They are as mayflies: alive and on the wing for a single day before dying. Compared to them we are ancient as the oak."

The hint of a smile played across my father's lips. "That's right. It'll be as easy as swatting flies."

Ciarán smiled at the men and women assembled around him. "Once, long ago, my people were terrorised by a creature – a huge, black snake that came from the sea. Upon waking it would yawn and swallow cattle, ships, and people. When angered, it would flick its great forked tongue and level whole villages to the ground. The only way to appease the beast was to feed it: seven virgins every seven days.

"The creature was a stoorworm. A sea dragon, evil to the core. And this particular serpent was the biggest of them all; and so my ancestors called it Mester Stoorworm[47] – the master of all his kind." Ciarán paused and looked at the gonys. From their faces he could tell they were hooked. They wanted to hear more about this man-eater who still survived in Celtae memory through stories and dim childhood fears.

"Now I ask you: are the stoorworm and the Coranieid not alike?" This question was met with furrowed brows. They did not see his point yet.

"The serpent took property and livestock. The Coranieid took endless tribute. The serpent used its forked tongue to devastate whole villages; the Coranieid's lies have blighted your existence and the lives of your fathers before you. The serpent demanded the youngest, the finest as sacrifice. The Coranieid take the strongest as slaves." There were murmurs amongst the crowd as the parallels became clear.

Ciarán smiled at them. "And what became of Mester Stoorworm?" He paused for effect. "There was a young man named Assipattle; he said he would kill the dragon and everybody laughed. 'Who are you to claim such a thing?' they asked. 'You, the youngest of your mother's sons, who know nothing of the world and can boast of no great deeds. You are not a skilled fighter. The beast will have you for a meal.'

"Now I ask you: are you and Assipattle not alike?" The disgruntled looks on the faces of the gonys men told Ciarán that the insult had struck home. He shrugged. "That is what the Coranieid think. They do not fear you. You did not know enough about the world to recognise their lies. You have no great victories to make them think twice about interfering with you. No. They see you as children to be told what to believe and what to do."

There were angry comments from the listeners and so Ciarán hastened on. "Yes, you are like Assipattle – totally underestimated. Do you want to know what he did?"

"Yes!" said the crowd.

"He took a boat, filled it with peat and rowed out to meet the monster. The creature awoke and yawned," Ciarán feigned a massive yawn (he was getting into this now), "and in doing so, he inhaled the little boat with the boy still in it." There was a gasp from a woman on his left. Ciarán crouched down and mimed the actions needed to start a fire. "In total darkness, within the gullet of the beast, Assipattle threw the peat overboard and set it alight. The fire raged in the serpent's throat, making it writhe and shriek in agony. In its death throes, Mester Stoorworm coughed up the little boat and Assipattle rowed back to shore." There were cheers and applause at this.

"Once home, the king offered the boy his daughter's hand in marriage and made him heir to the throne. Now I ask you: are you and Assipattle not alike?"

"Yes!" they cried.

Ciarán nodded, satisfied. "I knew it. Then join with us, brothers, and we'll will ram the Coranieid's lies right back down their throats!"

Ciarán left the gonys to their enthusiastic preparations for battle and sought the solitude of his own hut. He was shaking a little. That was lucky. The Sequani desperately wanted war, but he needed to muster Hedrek's tribe as well. They would be useful if only as fodder to minimise Sequani casualties.

Problem: centuries of servitude had taken the fight right out of them, and he feared that nothing he could say would induce them to take up arms. In fact, he had not known what to say. What words could erase the habits of generations? So he had made a prayer to Ogham, the god of eloquence; and he was rewarded with a flash of inspiration. The fantastic visions that Gwydion received on the mounds reminded him of an old wives' tale about another dragon. And it fit. Perfectly. That, and a few dramatic twists in the telling, and Ciarán had led the sheep into the desired pasture. They were even now sharpening swords and fletching arrows, each hungry for Coranieid blood.

There was a tap on the door.

"Enter."

Gwydion ducked under the low door frame. He was impressed by Ciarán's speech. It was persuasive and well-crafted. Nevertheless, he was concerned. "So your plan is to ... what? Throw everything you have at the Coranieid village?"

"Pretty much."

"That is lunacy."

Ciarán looked at him sharply, but said nothing.

Gwydion continued. "They have the tactical advantage in the woods. They have the mist and the fairy bolts and plenty of cover to ambush our warriors and then melt back into the forest like ghosts. It will be a slaughter and you still won't get anywhere near their camp."

Hovering over his response, Ciarán silently regarded the druid. He was annoyed by Gwydion's challenge, but respect for Sequani holy men had been ingrained in him since birth. Furthermore, his respect for this particular man was great. Gwydion was his friend and counsellor and Ciarán did not wish to alienate him. On the other hand, Ciarán wanted this war so badly he could taste it. He wanted to sweep down upon the Coranieid and kill every last one, burn their village, erase all trace of them from the land.

"I understand your desire for vengeance," Gwydion said quietly. This was not the first time the druid seemed to know what Ciarán was thinking.

"Then why do say these things?"

Gwydion knew the Sequani chief well enough. Ciarán would not be diverted from his ultimate goal, but perhaps with a little diplomacy he would consent to a different, more sensible path to the same end.

"As I said, to hunt the Coranieid in their own territory is suicide. But there are other ways…"

"Such as?"

Gwydion held up the hollowed tube he had fashioned from a beaker. "Let's talk in private."

Lowthas tramped reluctantly through the greenwood. Hedrek's orders were clear: to take a message to the Coranieid. On the face of it, it seemed a simple enough instruction, but it was very probably a death sentence. So he had decided that, once near Coranieid land, he would deliver his message, rely upon them to hear and then get the hell out of there as fast as his legs could carry him.

This is close enough, he decided and said loudly in the Coranieid's ancient tongue. "Yma genef newodhow. I have news." He paused expecting some form of attack. Emboldened by the lack of hostility, he continued. "Ciarán challenges Gwyn ap Nudd to ún cas – single combat. If we win, you will leave the gonys and the Sequani in peace. If you win, the gonys are yours and the Sequani will withdrawal back to the homelands." He paused again and listened. The forest was totally silent. "Ciarán will be at Nanscáwen at sunrise tomorrow."

He turned and fled, racing through the greenwood in the direction of the moor. He was young and agile, untroubled by the uneven ground and the roots and brambles that snagged at his feet. He could see light through a break in the trees ahead. Just a little farther and he would be out of this world of green shades and ancient, malevolent gods. He smiled. I'm going to make it, he thought. He burst out of the wood and stood, hands on knees, panting in the sunlight. Yes!

He started back toward the village and then suddenly stopped, his right hand scratching at his left shoulder. He had been stung by some insect. As he resumed his journey home, he failed to notice – lying in the grass – the little scrap of flint that he had brushed from his skin. By the time he reached his hut, his mouth was tingling and his stomach felt oddly warm.

"So those are your options," Myrddin was saying. "A straight fight between two armies or single combat between two chiefs." He paused while Gwyn considered.

"If I win, do you really think they'll withdraw?"

"We haven't heard anything to suggest otherwise."

Gwyn nodded. "Then so be it."

"Are you sure?"

"Myrddin, I have one son left. I do not want to send him into battle."

Myrddin tactfully looked away as Gwyn wiped his eyes. "Then you'd better prepare yourself for tomorrow."

"Have the people armed and ready…just in case."

Mora lay in her bed. Even the news that her husband would fight Ciarán in the morning did not induce her to leave her hut. Sorrow was a weight on her mind making her thoughts dull, and on her limbs making them feel painful and heavy. The very act of rising and walking out into the sunlight felt like too much effort, let alone having to speak to anyone she might meet. No. Better to stay in the dark, dozing, waking, and dozing again. And while she slept she saw a field where elder branches nodded in the breeze and all was green. Then the flap of black wings broke the silence: ravens, dozens of them, with beaks dipped in blood.

Bucca was restless. Frankly he was disappointed. He had been all geared up to fight, but now that plan had gone by the wayside and he didn't know quite what to do with himself. He studied Gwyn, sitting at the hanter with his daughter and sighed. He did not like Gwyn. He tried to tell himself that he resented the man's frailties and mistakes. Or perhaps it was because of Gwyn's high and mighty attitude. But really it was because Gwyn was everything Bucca wanted to be and could not achieve. He was beloved of the tribe, where Bucca was tolerated. He was an excellent warrior, where Bucca was proficient. He was a wise leader, where Bucca lacked judgement and was doomed always to follow. No, he really did not like Gwyn. However he admitted to himself (grudgingly) that he cared about his chief; and with that admission came another realisation: he was worried about tomorrow. "Ciarán" – the Sequani word for dark. Gwyn – the Coranieid word for white. Tomorrow's battle, Bucca felt, was more than single combat of one man against another. It was more than a dispute between two tribes. It was a battle of white versus black, good versus evil, light and order versus darkness and chaos.

He rose, went to his hut and lit a fire. One of the talents Bucca was cultivating was fire-gazing. You could, with practise, see a myriad of things within the yellow glow. For instance, if the fire smoulders and then suddenly bursts into roaring flame, that indicates that a stranger will call. A round clump of ash is known as a purse and means that riches will soon come your way. And if the pile of burning wood should collapse to form two separate heaps, then it is a sign that you will soon part company with a friend.

Bucca, however, was looking for different information. He took a twig and fished a cinder out the fire and spat on it. It did not crackle and sizzle as it should have done. "Dammit," he muttered. It was an omen of death.

Sunrise the next day found two groups facing each other across the meadow at Nanscáwen, the Valley of the Elder Trees. The Coranieid, in flaxen breeches and hide tunics, had taken up position a short distance from the tree line. Across the field, the pale gonys looked on with wary eyes. Beside them stood the Sequani – naked painted warriors with torcs of gold around their necks. Hedrek marvelled again at the flamboyant appearance of the Celtae compared to the quiet subtlety of the Coranieid and wondered how he had ever believed in us as gods.

The Sequani postured and roared, brandishing long swords. How do I convey to you the nature of that sound? Celtic war cries were legendary in their ferocity. In the Irish epic *Táin Bó Cuailnge*, the hero Cúchulainn "gave the warrior's scream from his throat, so that demons and devils and goblins of the glen and fiends of the air replied, so hideous was the call he uttered on high."[48] It was just such a cry: a shriek to summon forth darkness and death. It stung our sensitive ears and a ripple of unease ran down our line.

My eldest brother stood at my side. I said, "Owain…"

"Pay no heed," he muttered.

"They are like stag beetles," Myrddin commented. "All show, and no bite."

## A Side Note

*The stag beetle is the largest beetle in Britain, growing up to five centimetres. The males have large, antler-like mandibles. If threatened he will rear up and open his jaws wide. This intimidating display is a mere bluff as its mouthparts are not strong enough to inflict much of a bite. In fact, the mandibles are primarily used to hold the female during mating.*

The gaesatae, the Celtae spearmen, fell silent and Gwydion stepped forward. Raising both hands to the heavens, he called on Camulos, his war-god, to visit his wrath upon us. His prayer became a rant so incoherent with rage that none of us could make out the exact details of the curses he heaped upon us. The Coranieid watched with bemused smiles.

Gwyn grew impatient and walked out to the middle of the field. When the tirade ended, he spoke in a resounding voice. "Tell me: do you Sequani bluster all day or do you actually get around to fighting?"

Ciarán stepped forward to meet him. The Celtae chieftain towered over my father. In his war paint and golden neck and arm bands he looked like an uncouth savage compared to the calm, sturdy man who stood before him.

When Gwyn accepted the challenge of single combat, I was not afraid. Such was my faith in my father that I believed that he could overcome anything. Everything within me knew that he would put things right. He would drive these barbarians back to the pit they crawled out of. He would make them return the heads of my brother and Benesek so they could be made whole again and I would safeguard their soul stones as decreed by the tribe. He would again see the gonys bow before him as they should. But at Nanscáwen, to see Gwyn dwarfed by the hulking frame of the Sequani chief, I felt the first flicker of doubt.

The fight began.

Ciarán's long sword to Gwyn's spear – the blows fell in a blur of motion that was difficult to follow. It was mesmerising in its way: that fluidity of parry, dodge and thrust. While Ciarán was stronger, my father was more agile. Several quick jabs of his spear had already found their mark. While none of the wounds looked fatal to my eye, the Sequani chief was bleeding freely; red blood smeared into the blue woad of his war paint, the result a sickly purple that made him look even more surreal.

And then I spotted something out of the corner of my eye. Gwydion had turned his back on the fight and stood facing the assembled forces of gonys and Sequani with his hand raised in the air.

"Owain…"

"What?"

"Something's wrong. They…"

The end of my sentence was never heard. At a signal from the druid, the enemy produced dozens of bronze horns, some straight, some curved – carnyxes, they called them – which blared in unison and echoed through the valley. The din seared through my head like fire. They knew. Somehow the Sequani knew the source of our power and had turned it against us. The tumult was like a screaming in my head that would not cease and I felt I might go mad. As I desperately clamped my hands over my ears, I saw many of our number stagger and fall to their knees, brought down by vertigo that left some of them retching on the grass.

A break in the sound and I heard my father's voice: "To the trees!" Those of us still on our feet grabbed our fallen tribesmen and pulled them toward the cover of the forest.

I was aware that the screech of battle trumpets had lessened, but a new sound had joined the tumult – a sound like many waters and loud thunder.[49] Hooves. The Celtae cavalry charged across the field and the little distance we had to run to reach the greenwood was suddenly too far. We could not drag our friends and reach the safety of the trees before the horsemen closed the gap. So we turned and fought. Our elm bows were powerful at close range and we loosed a volley of arrows into the faces of the oncoming cavalry. My arrow knocked one savage to the ground, and Bucca managed to drive his through a warrior's leg and into his horse's flank, pinning the man to his mount.

I strung another arrow, fighting the nausea and dizziness, the ringing in my battered ears. My second shot hit a Sequani in the chest, but not before his airborne spear impaled Bryluen, who fell beside me. A third arrow and another enemy down, but we were out of time. They were upon us and we now fought hand to hand. Indeed they were constrained by the crush of bodies as the two sides clashed. But this did not give us the advantage we anticipated. Our weapons of bronze and flint were no match for the iron blades of their swords. Outnumbered, reeling from the assault on our ears and with inferior weapons, we were forced to retreat.

Another blast from the carnyxes and I was on my knees, aware that to stumble meant death. But then a strong hand gripped my arm and hauled me to my feet. Owain was shouting something to me, although I could not hear it over the din. Together we fled into the forest. The trumpets ceased their blaring to be replaced by the triumphant yells of our enemy … and the screams of those we had to leave behind.

I fought my way through the thick vegetation of the greenwood. It had always been my home and protector, but now it seemed to turn against me, impeding my every step. Low branches lashed at my face and roots snagged at my feet. I sobbed as I ran and kept falling down. All my life I had known only Coranieid strength and power and pride. To have that stripped from us so suddenly, so violently felt like rape. I sank to my knees and wept. Then a strong arm was around my waist, lifting me to my feet, half-carrying, half-dragging me through the forest toward home.

One hundred and eighty-nine Coranieid went to Nanscáwen that morning. Eighty-seven limped home.
　　Among the dead …
　　Cadreth and Bryluen, Benesek's parents,
　　Kenal, the one among us who always greeted you with a smile and a joke,
　　Gennys, the skilled craftsmen,
　　Breok, the fisherman,
　　Hebasca, whose name meant 'solace',
　　Crewenna, with the lovely voice who remembered all the old songs,
　　Nessa, second daughter of Pawlyn,
　　Richow, who loved pretty things,
　　Enoder, the shy man who never told Richow how he loved her,
　　Wylmet, a tomboy in her youth and one of our best archers,
　　Nerth, known for his great strength and tender heart
　　…and the list goes on and on.
　　It seemed impossible, like the stars of heaven had fallen to earth.[50] My father, shoulders hunched and head bowed, led the bloodied survivors home

and threw down his spear in defeat. I tried to speak to him as he sat staring into the camp fire. He would not respond. He raised his head to look at me and I recoiled from him for in that moment he did not know me.

Myrddin busied himself tending to the wounded, and Mother (finally joining us) helped him. Owain comforted Hanyfer who sobbed uncontrollably in his arms. Bucca lit a fire for Sithny who had lost his entire family in the battle and sat trembling from the shock. Tamara and Barinthus had disappeared into their hut, and Danjy washed the blood from his hands and kept scrubbing them even after they were clean.

I knew at that moment the Celtae and gonys would be stripping our dead of their weapons, fine clothes and ornaments. They would then gather in the grim harvest of severed heads to line the walls of their fort. Gwydion would speak: a spontaneous outpouring of druidic verse in which he would lay claim to the land in the name of the Sequani.

I could not bear the thought of it. It was *deweth an bys*, the end of the world. I longed for sleep, for some oblivion in which to escape from all the horror and so I went to Myrddin's hut. In a clay jar he kept a mixture of equal parts henbane, darnel, black poppy and bryony root – sleeping powder.[51] Dissolved in water it works quickly and soon I closed my eyes upon that evil day.

Night fell and Ciarán retired to his hut.

Olwen wrapped her arms around his neck. "You did well today, my husband."

He didn't reply and so she slipped out of her dress and let it fall to the floor. "You deserve a hero's welcome."

This was not met with the enthusiasm she had anticipated.

Francis Bacon once said that a man who "studieth revenge keeps his own wounds green, which otherwise would heal and do well." Olwen did not know it, but the man she led to her bed was still in the throes of just such a fever. He offered her no kisses, no soft caresses or playful tickles to bring her to readiness – just his weight upon her and a rough hand that turned her face to the side and held it there so she could not see his eyes. His thrusts were those of a man who clearly still seethed from battle and they hurt her. For the first time in their marriage she hated him, cursed him for using her in this way – as something to vent his anger upon. But she said nothing, just waited till it was over, turned her back on him and eventually went to sleep.

In the darkness, Ciarán lay awake. He had thought that revenge was the cure not the illness, and thus was surprised to find that he did not feel any better. Beating the Coranieid had not brought Derdriu back, nor Maeldun. It had not restored to him his balance of mind. His brain still churned with anger and sorrow. Killing had not brought him peace. Nor had sex. Indeed, would anything? He groaned and marvelled at the fact that, despite his great victory, he remained somehow the loser.

Morning found Gwyn still sitting by the central village fire, which was now only cold ash. Bucca approached him. Gwyn knew that insults and recriminations were forthcoming, but he no longer cared.

"Y-fynsen ow bos marow – I would that I were dead."

"I am very glad you are not," Bucca replied. He smiled at Gwyn's surprise and relit the fire in front of his chief.

"I realise now," Bucca continued, "that it is just a little bit crazy to want your job. I'm very glad it's you and not me."

"Thanks," Gwyn muttered.

"I mean it. We need a good man to lead us, and that's you."

Gwyn's eyes welled up and he clenched his teeth in an effort to stifle a sob. He nodded his thanks to Bucca, who walked away, giving his chief time to compose himself.

"That was unexpected." Myrddin stood at the door of his hut. "I never thought he would come around."

"Wonders never cease." Gwyn sat in silence for a few moments then asked, "What can we do?"

"To re-establish the old ways? Nothing. The gonys know the truth now; they know their strength and they know we are vulnerable. They cannot be made to unlearn that fact. It's over."

"Then what do we do?"

"What everyone does when life gives them a good kicking: pick yourself up and keep going."

Gwyn chuckled, a mirthless laugh. "Don't know how."

"Oh, enough dramatics!" Myrddin snapped impatiently. "See to the wounded. See to the winter stores of food. Fix the holes in the thatched roofs before the autumn rains are upon us. And," he paused.

"What?"

"Reinstate the old faith."

"The Elders?" Gwyn frowned, perplexed. "What's the point?"

"We have had faith in nothing but our own superiority for far too long. After yesterday we're left with no faith at all."

"We don't need faith."

"Nothing else is going to fill the hole left by all of this."

Gwyn, who felt he did not deserve comfort after his failure, was not interested in consoling religion. He was struck by the sudden image of himself, shoulders and head bowed, standing humbly before the vague, dark forms of the Elders, begging forgiveness, begging to be allowed to come home. His pride, which had swelled considerably during his many years as a self-proclaimed god, recoiled from this. But pride was not the only obstacle, nor was it the biggest. His relationship with the Elders (in the time before the change) had been a deeply intimate one. He had shared his joys with them; he told them of his concerns, asked for their guidance, and when hurt, he would hold his pain up for them to see. Invariably they offered some balm for his wounds. Once, the day his father died, he had handed his grief over to them as he walked aimlessly through the greenwood. And the sun had shone in solid shafts of light through gaps in the leaves overhead and warmed him. A gust of wind buffeted a nearby lime tree, causing the petals of its flowers to sprinkle down upon him like green rain. It was a moment of such beauty and peace that he was comforted in his grief and remembered it even now.

But to acknowledge the pain that now seared through him, to hold it up and look at his failure, his grief, his horror – he could not do it. It was too much even for the mighty Gwyn ap Nudd. No, there would be no reconciliation between him and the Elders and hence no moment of truth. He was numb now and hollow. And that was good.

Myrddin was saying, "I know it is hard to go back…"

"Don't," the chief snapped. "Peddle your faith to the others if you want, but I don't think you'll have many takers. If the Elders exist they have utterly forsaken us."

"You can't really think that."

"Don't tell me what I think."

"So what, then, do you intend to do?"

Gwyn did not reply.

"What about the tribe? Will you lead them?"

Still no answer.

"What about your children?"

I, who had been listening to the conversation, leant forward, expectantly. Surely that would rally him. He would fight on. For us.

"You have two left," Myrddin said quietly. "The girl is as old as the hills but she looks ... what? ... like she's barely out of her teens. Will you abandon her to hide in self-pity?"

Gwyn glared at him, his eyes once again wet. There was a pause – a long pause during which I bit nervously at my fingernails and awaited his answer.

Gwyn did not speak, just slowly, painfully rose to his feet.

"What are you going to do?" Myrddin asked again.

"Tend to the wounded, check on our food stores for winter, mend the holes in the roof." He walked away.

CHAPTER 3

# "BULRUSH BASKETS"

> *"...she took for him a basket made of bulrushes ... and she put the child in it and placed it among the reeds at the river's bank... Now the daughter of the Pharaoh came down to bathe at the river. She saw the basket among the reeds and ... when she opened it, she saw the child, and behold, the baby was crying. She took pity on him ... She named him Moses, 'Because,' she said, 'I drew him out of the water.'"*
>
> *Exodus 2:3, 5-6, 10*

Within the greenwood there was a sheltered clearing. It was a quiet place of birdsong and the occasional bleating of the soay sheep that grazed there. It was early spring. One ewe – distinguishable from the rest by the white markings on her face – was restless. It was as if she could not quite figure out what to do with herself. She lay down. That was not quite right. She stood up; no, that would not do either. She pawed the ground. Finally, she lay down again some distance from the others and began to strain. From her back end, a large watery sack appeared, and the ewe grunted with each contraction of the birth. Two feet and a nose appeared and slowly, quietly a lamb was born. The mother was weary. Greedily she ate the placenta and then licked her new-born clean. The lamb, a fluffy brown creature with a sharp snout, nuzzled up to the ewe's swollen udders and had his first drink of mother's milk.

It was the first birth to occur within the Coranieid village in over six millennia, but we were not there to witness it. The mud huts had collapsed and the fences had been knocked down. A new lamb nursed off his mother in the hanter where gods once gathered around the fire.

As I write this, I have on the table in front of me a stack of books. I run my finger down their spines and marvel at how the authors of these five volumes have, through research or intuition, managed to chronicle the story of our days after Nanscáwen ....

Book One. *The Country Life Book of the Natural History of the British Isles* notes that:

> Around 600 B.C. a decline can be seen in most of the forest trees. Tree pollen declines in proportion to an increase in herb and grass pollen, indicating the removal of woodland and its conversion to pasture for domestic animals. Further proof is given by a slight increase in the birch pollen, for birch is a resilient tree and rapidly colonises open land when agriculture is abandoned.[52]

After the massacre at Nanscáwen, more and more Celtae came to our shores, intermarrying with the locals until they became one people. Increased population requires more land; the trees of the greenwood fell as they cleared terrain for new villages and pastureland for their animals.

My cousin Elowen knew, long before the rest of us, that we would eventually have to leave the village and our farmlands behind. For her the signs were clear. You see, while Hanyfer was drawn to the sea and Bucca to fire, Elowen was drawn to the earth and the trees that had their roots there. She had learnt much about them and from them. She recognised that, while they did not have brains in the same way as humans and animals, they did possess a degree of sentience. They understood the cycle of the changing seasons and prepared accordingly. They fostered the growth of a fungus later called mycorrizae. Elowen knew that the mushrooms that were visible above ground were only a tiny part of the organism. Below, within the soil, the fungus had spread out millions of tiny threads (mycelium) and these had attached to and become one with the roots of the old oak trees. The oak encouraged this because the fungus reached far beyond its own root systems, greatly extending the area from which it could draw moisture and nutrients from the soil. In return the wise old oak fed its helper on sugars it produced. A large, well-fed fungus could grow to cover thousands of acres and merge with the roots of many trees. In this way, the trees of the greenwood were connected.[53]

Hence they knew their numbers were decreasing. Each blow of an axe sent a tremor down the trunk, through the roots and into the soil. They could feel the roots of each dying tree contract – a death spasm that registered seismically on the sensitive tendrils of the mycelium. And they suddenly became aware of less competition for resources and space. The trees responded to this in their customary way: with passive stoicism. If the loss of a neighbour triggered anything resembling an emotion, the trees could only express it through an electrical pulse that was felt and echoed by nearby plants – a silent distress call that spooked even the insects that crawled on leaf and bark. Elowen was distressed by this and so took action.

One day a Sequani man by the name of Ferdia entered the greenwood with an axe upon his shoulder. He was in high spirits, for his errand was a jolly one: to gather the materials needed to build a home for himself and his new bride. Reaching the crest of a thickly wooded hill, he quickly felled a small yew tree and began the more arduous task of removing the gnarled branches covered in needle-shaped leaves. The trunk was straight and strong – a dozen more of these, he thought, and he'd have enough poles for the frame. He'd use yew trunks for the posts and weave hazel branches into panels known as wattles. These he would insulate with animal hair and plaster with clay and dung. The house would be round with a thatched roof, and the door would face east to let more sunlight in. He'd build hurdles to divide the space into rooms and he and Niamh would be happy there, they…

A rustle in the undergrowth ahead interrupted his train of thought. Ferdia was instantly wary. The woods were home to boar and wolf and, it was said, other things.

There it was again, the dim rustle ahead.

He'd heard tales of fairies with poisoned arrows who attack then melt back into the shadows like ghosts. Fight or flee, he wondered. For all his bulk Ferdia was a swift runner, though not swift enough to outrun an arrow. A fight, then, he decided. Gripping his axe, he stepped forward. Was it his imagination or had the forest suddenly become colder? Gooseflesh appeared on his bare arms and he shivered. And then there arose a figure from the undergrowth. It was thin, so thin that Ferdia was left with the impression that its black robes covered only bones. Its hood concealed its face and for a fleeting moment the man felt certain that he was gazing upon the embodiment of death itself. From somewhere within that dark hood, the thing began to shriek – some obscene cross between laughter and tortured screaming.

Ferdia's resolve to stand and fight evaporated, but as he turned to run the thick undergrowth caught at his feet and sent him sprawling. The dark figure loomed over him and screamed and screamed and screamed. Panicking, the man thrashed and kicked to free himself. And then he was running back down that terrible hill toward the light and order and sanity of his village. The forest seemed to impede his every step. Tangled nettles caught at his feet and tree branches whipped at his face as he fled.

Syncope, from the Greek sunkopto, meaning "to knock to pieces" is the enfeebled action of the heart due to a sudden shock. Despite his exertion, Ferdia's skin blanched cold and white. His breathing became ragged, his vision blurred and upon reaching the village, he collapsed.

## A Side Note

*Nymphs of the woods (also known as dryads) are part of a mythology dating back to ancient Greece. Thought to be the daughters of Zeus, they were not immortal but were said to live a very long time. Many believed that their fates were intrinsically connected to the forests they inhabited. Should the trees perish, so too would the dryads. Therefore they were fiercely protective of the woodlands, resorting to all manner of tricks to frighten away anyone with an axe.*

*As a result, there are many legends of haunted forests and hills. One such place, Creech Hill near Bruton in Somerset, is believed to be inhabited by "a gruesome black shape." This apparition once chased a farmer "uttering a fearful screech." Later it accosted a gentleman foolish enough to cross the hummock at night. Simon Marsden, in his book* The Haunted Realm, *gives the following account:*

*"he became aware of a deadly coldness. Suddenly something tall and black rose out of the ground in front of him. He struck at it wildly with his staff, but the stick went straight through his tormentor and he found that he was transfixed to the spot. Peals of crazy laughter deafened him....[and] he fainted dead away."*[54]

Such theatrics as these were effective at repelling individuals, but ultimately they could not halt the march of progress. Likewise, eighty-seven Coranieid tribesmen could not stand against thousands of encroaching Celtae settlers;

eventually we were compelled to set the thatch roofs of our huts alight, gather our belongings and flee deeper into the forest.

Book Two. *Magic, Myths and Monsters* cites the following episode from Celtic mythology. The product of later generations, the myth transfers the action to Ireland and changes the names of the participants. The Celtae are referred to as the Milesians and the Coranieid are dubbed the Tuatha de Danaan. These discrepancies, however, surround a central kernel of truth:

> The human Milesians arrive ... and defeat the Tuatha. Most of the latter flee ... Those who remain ... take refuge in the hills ... as the daoine sidhe – 'the little people' or 'people of the mounds.'[55]

"We have eighty-seven mouths to feed," Myrddin was saying around the fire at our new camp. "In order to do this we must have land for crops and pastures to graze animals."

"Yes, and we have neither," Robin pointed out. Robin stood with his son, Bucca – the only two members of their family to survive Nanscáwen. Robin was usually quiet. It was odd to see him on his feet at the new hanter, challenging Myrddin.

Elowen, who had emerged from her tent to join the discussion, began, "We could lay claim to new land…"

"Where?" Robin interrupted. "Where can we go? The Sequani have said they will kill us on sight. Where is safe?"

"I take it, Robin, that you have another suggestion?" Gwyn asked quietly.

He nodded, "We leave."

"Leave?" Myrddin asked.

"Yes. We find a new home elsewhere."

A grumble of uncertainty, like the sound of distant thunder, rippled through the tribe.

"Think about it," Robin insisted. "We find a new, fertile land with new people. People who do not know our secret. People who could be made to serve."

"You would return to our old ways?" Myrddin asked.

"Why not?" Another man, Ust, joined in.

"Oh, I don't know," Owain shrugged. "Following the old ways has led to such happiness…"

"I'm not leaving the tribe land," Elowen's voice was quiet but firm.

"Well, I might," Bucca retorted.

"And me," added Robin.

"Enough." Gwyn stood up and faced the company. "How many are in favour of going?"

Gwyn stared numbly at the sea of hands raised in the air – forty-five of them in all. "You are not prisoners here," he sighed. "Go if you wish."

The Coranieid word for loss is "coll" – four letters to encapsulate so much anguish. Since the arrival of the Celtae, we had been stripped of our godhood and our lands. More than two-thirds of the tribe had been slaughtered, none of whom had received a proper burial. A further forty-five left our beloved home to travel far away.

On the day of their leaving, I bid friends and kinsmen goodbye and walked back to camp. Myrddin, who had not gone to see them off, was standing by a large oak tree, muttering. I realised he was not talking to thin air, but to something he held in his hand. To be polite, I waited until the conversation was finished and he had placed the small brown insect back onto the tree. He crouched down and began drawing in the dirt with a stick.

"What's this?" I asked.

"A rough plan for Annwyn."

"Annwyn?"

"Our new home. He gave me the idea," Myrddin nodded toward the *Lem hartha* or bark imp, a little bug no more than half a centimetre long with a brown body and head that looked like a weathered acorn. You know it as scolytus intricatus, the Oak Bark Beetle.

"How is it," Myrddin asked, "that the beetle is not eaten by birds? Because it hides! It keeps itself out of reach. That is how we will live."

"Go on." My father had appeared at my side.

"This race of men multiplies and spreads and we'll always be driven before them, brushed aside to make way for the incessant march of mankind."

"You're just trying to cheer me up," Gwyn replied.

"It's no joke. But what if we no longer live *on* the land?"

"Meaning?"

"The beetles know. They burrow tunnels in the bark of the oak tree to keep safely hidden. Here," he pointed to his drawing with the stick, "is the mother gallery. This is where the beetle lays its eggs. It is the starting point. And these," he indicated dozens of wiggling lines that emanated from it, "are the tunnels dug by the newly hatched grubs."

"Yes," said Gwyn sarcastically. "That is obviously the answer. Let's dig tunnels and live like moles."

"Danjy tells me of other earth dwellers – wights, knockers, gnomes."

"So?"

"So they possess their own magics. It is said that they can move 'through the earth like fish through water.'"[56]

Gwyn was unimpressed. "Good for them."

Myrddin was growing impatient. "Don't you see? We could have a home again, safe and concealed and..."

"...dark and filthy."

"A great hall and many rooms and passages that lead anywhere you like."

Gwyn looked at him sceptically. "You can do this?"

"No, but I'm sure Danjy knows someone who can."

Danjy entered the caves carrying a basket. In it was cooked meat, heavy bread, milk, currants and blackberries. He sat in the darkness (to which his eyes were now well-accustomed) and began to eat slowly.

Very few minutes passed before he heard a loud snuffling. A clear, high voice spoke out of the darkness, "Smells fine."

Danjy smiled. "Hungry?"

"Digging always builds an appetite."

"Here, take the lot," he said and laid the basket on the floor of the cave.

A little sprite approached him cautiously. He wore a leather jacket and breeches and a wide brimmed hat on which he had fixed a candle that burned with a flickering blue light. He looked exceptionally old, his face lined with deep wrinkles and his shoulders stooped from the labour of many years.

"Hello, Blue-cap," Danjy nodded.

"And to you, young 'un," the knocker replied through a mouthful of bread. "How goes it?"

Danjy looked at him sombrely. "Not well. You have heard of our troubles on the surface?"

"Aye, th' Celtae are too numerous. Many of your people go away."

"Yes."

"And yet you stay," Blue-cap took a swig of milk. "Why?"

"Ties to the land are hard to break."

"That they are," the little man nodded. "*I* should not want to leave."

"And yet to stay is problematic. Where can we live that is safe and concealed?" Danjy, in a less than subtle fashion, looked about him.

Blue-cap burst into hearty laughter. "I see. Your people wish to go to ground."

"Yes, they do."

"And they will be needing some help with that."

"Yes, they will."

Blue-cap said amiably. "You know I don't work for free."

"Name your price, friend."

"Food. Good food from the surface for as long as you stay here."

"Done!"

"Tell your chief. A bargain is struck."

## A Side Note

*Knockers (pronounced knackers) are Cornish mining fairies – little men said to live deep within the tunnels of abandoned tin mines. Miners would sometimes hear them tapping away at the rocks of hidden galleries or singing to themselves as they worked. Occasionally, a man would find a pick made of antler and fashioned too small to be used by human hands, but otherwise evidence of their existence is scant.*

*They are purported to be friendly to men. They sometimes warn miners of an impending cave-in or lead a favoured mortal to rich seams of ore. But these gestures of friendship must be duly rewarded with gifts of food or else the knockers become angry and malicious.*

*A man by the name of Barker was once said to have withheld food from a knocker. The enraged sprite threw a heavy pick at his leg, leaving him crippled for life. As a result the phrase, "'As stiff as Barker's knee' was once a common saying in Cornwall."*[57]

*One particularly revered knocker was old Blue-cap. Said to be "the miner's friend ... he would settle on the barrows in the shape of a little blue flame." Old timers always insisted that "if Blue-cap should do you a service ... be sure to leave him his wages. He can be main useful to you if you treat him friendly."*[58]

Old Blue-cap was as good as his word. In a surprisingly short period of time, the great underground hall was completed and work had commenced on the side chambers.

Book Three. In the story *Ninety-three* Victor Hugo wrote of just such a place:

> Nothing could be more secret, more silent, and more savage than those inextricable entanglements of thorns and branches; those vast thickets were the home of immobility and silence; no solitude could present an appearance more deathlike and sepulchral; yet if it had been possible to fell those trees at one blow, as by a flash of lightning, a swarm of men would have stood revealed in those shades. There were wells, round and narrow, masked by coverings of stones and branches, the interior at first vertical, then horizontal, spreading underground like tunnels, and ending in dark chambers… One of the wildest glades of the wood… perforated by galleries and cells amid which came and went a mysterious society, was called 'the great city.' Another glade, not less deserted above ground and not less inhabited beneath, was styled 'the palace royal.' This subterranean life had existed … from time immemorial. From the earliest days man had there hidden flying from man. Hence those hiding-places, like the dens of reptiles, hollowed out below the trees.[59]

The door to the cavern was humble enough: just moss and twigs and forest floor indistinguishable from its surroundings. But open it and follow a downward sloping tunnel and there lay a great hall lit by torchlight. Long wooden tables and benches lined three walls and two high-backed chairs on the fourth faced the assembled company. Low doorways led from the hall in all directions, some to candlelit bedchambers, some to storerooms, and some to tunnels leading to other portals dotted throughout the countryside – little highways that allowed us swift access to forts and villages, farms and pastures.

It was beautifully done. Old Blue-cap was not just a workman, he was an artist. He understood the rock, and used its natural shapes to fashion a grand arch leading to the main hall. The floor was polished granite and the walls were adorned with strange imprints of spiral-shaped creatures more ancient than even ourselves. This, then, was to be our new home, Annwyn.

Through the years it would become legendary – the name would be whispered among wide-eyed children, spoken of by the fireside and written about again and again. Geoffrey Ashe, in *Mythology of the British Isles*, described the great hall where Gwyn "sat on a golden chair surrounded by retainers and musicians and beautiful damsels."[60] Geoffrey of Monmouth envisioned a great "house....with seventy doors" located deep within the woods.[61] *Folklore, Myths and Legends of Britain* stated that we lived in "an underground country where the summer never ends."[62] Hamilton and Eddy saw it as "a place of timeless perfection that exists on another plane … a beautiful and happy land of feasting, hunting, and love-making … Fairieland … also known as the Land of Youth, a place where time passes slowly and so people remain young…deathless."[63] And Neil Philip, in *Mythology of the World*, described it as "a place of peace and plenty, the fortress of apples, [which] survives as the magical realm of Avalon in the stories of King Arthur."[64] The composite created by these accounts is a shining image in soft focus, an ideal, a fairytale. In reality, though Annwyn was magnificent in terms of sheer achievement, it was … when you came right down to it … dark.

Gwyn was very aware of it – the dark. He had professed himself satisfied with Blue-cap's efforts and rewarded the knocker with generous gifts not only of food, but precious stones as well. And he *was* satisfied with the craftsmanship. But he had spent his life with grass beneath his feet and the great pillars of the trees holding aloft a blue sky above him. He was used to wind in his long hair and the sun on his face. By contrast, Annwyn was cold and the air stale. The only light (torchlight, candlelight) flickered drowsily and numbed his brain and the walls seemed tight around him.

He looked at the great hall and sighed heavily. Surely, surely it would be better to be dead. His failure as chief was now complete. He had lost the most decisive battle in the tribe's history. He had been driven from his home, and half of the survivors had abandoned him. They had voted with their feet; an act that conveyed more eloquently than words that he was not worthy of their trust. And now here he was, interred in this beautiful tomb and yet condemned to live on and drink in full his allotted measure of bitterness. The old saying is true: "If you hate a man, let him live."[65]

There was nothing for it: he would just have to grit his teeth until he felt better. And perhaps he might have improved if it had not been for Annwyn. It is difficult to articulate what was wrong with that place. As I've already intimated it was dark and claustrophobic, yet that does not quite convey its essential malignancy. It was malignant because it was dark and claustrophobic and we were there. It puts me in mind of a white-coated scientist in his laboratory. In front of him rest two beakers with two different chemicals in them. Each chemical is stable and inert. Yet when they are combined in a third, larger beaker a violent reaction occurs.

That image is apt. Annwyn's shadows and our turmoil – our grief and rage confined within those tight corridors and dim chambers – was an explosive combination. It was, to paraphrase Exodus 10:21, a place where darkness could not only be seen, but felt. These shadows found their echo in our souls and fed the blackness there.

It came over Gwyn gradually, stealing over him like the advancing shades of night. He seemed to withdraw into himself and took no interest in tribal affairs and no pleasure from our company. Indeed he displayed an indifference to life around him that I had only ever seen in those near death. He did not laugh anymore. Nor would he sing with the tribe, nor dance to the drum, nor caress his wife nor smile upon me, his daughter. His initial lethargy did finally give way to activity, but this was merely a fidgeting agitation, a restless need to do something without any indication of what that something might be. Finally, he rose from his chair and called the tribe to him.

"We hunt," he said simply.

"Stag?" Barinthus asked.

"Men."

Myrddin was appalled. "You would start another war?"

Gwyn looked at his medicine man coldly. "Open warfare is unnecessary."

"What do you propose?" asked Mora quietly.

"There are a thousand ways to make them pay without ever setting foot on a battlefield."

That night the tribe embarked on its first wild hunt. Prowling through the greenwood, we came upon a man and a woman who had met in darkness for some secret tryst. Gwyn pried their naked bodies apart and ran the man through with his sword. The woman screamed in horror as her lover writhed on the ground, choking on his own blood. When he became still the Coranieid fell upon the terrified girl, stabbing all that bare white skin until, stained a dark red, it no longer shone in the moonlight.

Myrddin did not join in the attack. That was predictable enough: he was a prayer and a healer, not a warrior. He did not really have the stomach for such violence. What surprised me though was my own hesitation. I was not a warrior, but I was a good hunter and I had fought with the tribe at Nanscáwen. So why this sudden squeamishness?

My gut and chest contracted painfully ... out of pity of all things. I actually felt sorry for the human woman and was distressed by her fear. She was naked and defenceless and pathetic, and there was no honour in this kill.

"Daughter..." Gwyn noticed my reticence and was waiting for me to take part.

Not to draw my knife would be interpreted as a criticism, and I did not wish to criticise my father. For the first time in many days he was on his feet doing something. It was a bennath, a blessing to see him show any spark of life. And he was wrong if he thought he was no longer a god, for I worshipped him. I had faith that whatever he did was right. So to honour my father, I drew my knife and buried it hilt deep in the woman's chest.

Gwyn smiled. The sharp, coppery scent of blood filled his nostrils and he realised that that sensation marked the first moment of pleasure he had experienced since Maban died. As such he was reluctant to let it go. He removed his tunic and dipped the hood in blood.

We stole food from the nearby village and returned to Annwyn, laughing and joking as you would after a night of revelry.

**A Side Note**

*The legend of the Wild Hunt eventually spread throughout Europe. In Germany it was called the "Wilde Jagd"; it was known as the "Hoste Antiga" or old army in Galacian and the Welsh called it "Cŵn Annwn," the hounds of Annwyn. According to Wikipedia, the "fundamental premise in all instances is the same: a phantasmal group of huntsmen...in a mad pursuit across the skies or along the ground... Seeing the Wild Hunt was thought to presage...the death of the one who witnessed it."*[66]

*Judy Allen, in her* Fantasy Encyclopedia, *has this to add: "On winter nights of storm and fury ... the Wild and Savage Hunt can be heard.... The hooves of their phantom horses make the sound of thunder, their spectral hounds howl down the wind."*[67] *And* Chambers Dictionary of the Unexplained *notes that in "Wales and the West Country, the leader of the Hunt was said to be Gwyn ap Nudd, the fairy 'Lord of the Dead.'*[68] *Hence, through mankind's fertile imagination, a few nights of raiding grew in legend until we were a ghost army thundering across the sky and snatching people away.*

Back at Annwyn, amidst the revellers returning from the Hunt, Myrddin alone looked sombre.

"Oh stop it, old man," Gwyn laughed. "You spoil our fun."

"I don't like it," Myrddin replied quietly.

"What?" sneered Gwyn, "do you pity those wretches in the woods?"

Myrddin did, but knew better than to admit it. Compassion for the enemy, for man, was not a popular viewpoint among the Coranieid. "No, I just don't see the point of all this."

"Then let me enlighten you." Gwyn sat down in his chair and looked at the assembled company. "I have been troubled for quite some time by one question: What are we?"

Everyone remained silent, listening intently; so Gwyn continued. "I mean, we are more than men and yet we are less than gods. So where does that leave us?"

He paused and looked at Myrddin who said nothing.

"Oh come on, wise one," Gwyn shouted. "You have an answer for everything. What are we?!"

"The Coranieid," Myrddin answered.

"Fuck that. It's too vague. I'll tell you what we are. We're monsters." Gwyn drained a flagon of wine and marvelled at how good it tasted. He smiled as he refilled his cup. "They still fear us, you know. They still tell tales about people who melt into the greenwood like ghosts and shoot fairy bolts." Again, he downed his drink in one and wiped his mouth with the back of his hand. "So I say: if they want fairies, let's give them fairies."

Book Four. In *Mythology of the British Isles*, Geoffrey Ashe discusses the idea of "fairies" at some length. Wisely he notes: "The fairies may have begun specifically as a pre-iron age layer of the population, who lingered in out-of-the-way places and were seldom seen, yet disquietingly known to exist ... Perhaps an ill-defined Bronze Age people who would not ... have been Celticised."[69] Webster's World Encyclopedia concurs, theorising that fairies were in fact… "original (stone age) inhabitants of large parts of Britain. But when the Celts – a much taller race, equipped with better armour – came from Europe to invade their country (about 500 B.C.), the indigenous fairies were unwilling to submit. They withdrew into the dense forests." Embittered by this exile from their lands, these aboriginal people continually harassed the Celts until the newcomers became so afraid that they sought to pacify the fairies with gifts of food and ale: "To propitiate them was a wise counsel. Therefore even the names by which they were called were chosen with great caution, and attempted to flatter them. They became 'the good folk,' 'the hidden people,' and 'the good neighbours.'"[70]

Many years later an old man, Senchan, sat by the fire trying to get warm. He felt the cold more and more with each passing year and suspected that this might be his last winter. The thought did not trouble him greatly, because he knew better than to think on it too much. He could accept his death as a necessary part of his life as long as he did not imagine his body set alight for cremation. That idea had frightened him ever since he was a small boy. He somehow fancied that his soul would still be in residence, but powerless to animate his limbs and so he would burn in agony and terror, unable to move or scream.

No, it was not wise to indulge the imagination to that extent. It changed nothing and only made him fearful. And so, as an exercise in mental distraction, he sat each night by the Celtae fire and told stories to the children. He had quite a knack for storytelling and loved to watch the little ones clap when the hero prevailed or gasp and cover their mouths when the tale took a grim turn. On this night, he spoke of the hidden people…

"They move silently through the woods. They wear green and blend in so well with the leaves that they are invisible to us."

"Then why does mother call them red-caps?" Sheáin asked. Sheáin was an intelligent boy, perhaps the smartest of the bunch. He was the one who always asked questions.

"She calls them red-caps because they dye their hoods with the blood of their victims."

"Why would they do that?" Sheáin asked.

Senchan shrugged. "Why do snakes bite? Every creature simply does what it does. It is said that long ago our ancestors defeated them in battle and they were forced to retreat underground. Maybe so. But did the hidden ones ever really feel that the war was over? I don't think so. I was just a little older than you, Sheáin, when I was sent by my mother to draw water from the creek. It was a hot day and, wanting shade, I chose the wiggly path through the wood instead of the straight one across the meadow. And that's when I found it … the body."

Senchan paused feeling the eyes of each child upon him. How much should he tell them? Should he describe how days in the summer heat had left the body bloated and coloured the skin a purplish-green? Should he depict, as only a story-teller can, the thick, bloody liquid that seeped from the corpse's nose and mouth? That image haunted his nightmares even now and so he merely said, "the man had been stabbed to death and left to wither. I always believed it to be the work of the hidden ones."

"Is that why we leave food out for them … so they'll leave us alone?" Sheáin asked.

"Yes. Their wounded pride still stings and so we offer gifts to soften their anger and keep them as good neighbours."

"But they're not," insisted Sheáin. "Ma says they steal children away."

"So they do," Senchan nodded and he smiled wryly at Sheáin, "especially children who keep interrupting." The child went pale and the old man chuckled to himself as he went off to bed.

As he lay there and tried to get warm under the covers, he had to admit though that it was no laughing matter. Just last week there had been an incident. Young Síle's baby had started to squawk and cry all through the night. The poor parents could get no rest and consulted the druid Tuan. Tuan had examined the child and proclaimed that he was a changeling. The fairies, he said, would sometimes spirit away a human child and in its place leave one of their own squalling brats.

Síle was inconsolable. "Why would they do this?"

The druid had shrugged, "I believe that they need humans to vary their own breeding stock. My advice? Get rid of it," he nodded at the screeching bundle on her lap.

Síle had walked to the river's edge and unceremoniously cast the baby in.

### A Side Note

*Throughout history and across the globe, many cultures have believed in changelings. Babies that were ugly, deformed, extremely unsettled, sickly or dying were all thought, at one time or another, to be left by fairies or evil spirits. It is not difficult to perceive the cause of this phenomenon. The concept of the changeling tapped into mankind's most primal fear – that someone or something would snatch our children away; and this idea was later immortalised by William Butler Yeats in his poem, "The Stolen Child":*

> "Come away, O human child!
> To the waters and the wild
> With a faery, hand in hand.
> For the world's more full of weeping than you can understand."[71]

*The Coranieid may have been guilty of many things, but kidnapping was never among them. That is the power of reputation for you. You establish yourself as fierce and terrible in the minds of others, and your reputation becomes a living, breathing thing, adding crimes to your tab that you never even contemplated. However the real tragedy of the changeling myth was the cruelty it inspired among mortal parents. An ugly or deformed child, a sick baby or one that cried and fussed too much might be suspected of being a fairy brat. These little ones were in real danger. It was believed that torturing a changeling would compel its fairy-parents to come back and retrieve it: "one popular method was to place it on a shovel and hold it over a fire."[72] Incredibly, up until the late nineteenth century, some children suspected of being 'fairy-born' were killed by their parents.*

Book Five. *100 Best Poems for Children.* In it we find a poem by William Allingham entitled "The Fairies":

> "Up the airy mountain,
> Down the rushy glen,
> We daren't go a-hunting
> For fear of little men;
> Wee folk, good folk,
> Trooping all together;
> Green jacket, red cap
> And white owl's feather!
> …They stole little Bridget…

> Between the night and morrow,
> They thought that she was fast asleep,
> But she was dead with sorrow.
> They have kept her ever since
> Deep within the lake,
> On a bed of flag-leaves,
> Watching till she wake."[73]

Mother arrived back at Annwyn with a noisy bundle in her arms. The ears of every woman pricked up and in a moment they surrounded her.

"Mora!"

"A baby!"

"Where did you get it?"

"Oh let me hold him!"

"Look at those tiny fingers."

They all spoke at once.

I confess that I did not like the look of this, but wait: my father was on his feet.

"Where *did* you get it?" his tone was serious and brought the women's clucking to an abrupt halt.

"Down at the river. The parents think that we stole their precious, perfect child away and left him as a changeling."

"Why?"

"He cries all night. Just bad colic. If the idiots had given him a bit of fennel, it would have soothed him. Instead," Mora paused, "they cast him into the water."

This little speech, with its carefully timed pause for effect, evoked the desired response. My mother's friends exclaimed their outrage.

My father, rock hard as ever, was unmoved. "That's a shame. But how does it concern us?"

"It concerns us because I mean to keep him." She spoke with the sharp edge to her voice that her husband knew all too well.

Gwyn sighed. One lesson he had learned was to pick his battles and, as he didn't really care about the child one way or another, why fight? He picked up the child and held him at arm's length, appraising him. He nodded as if satisfied (all for show really) and said, "You may keep him."

Mother cocked a shrewd eyebrow at my father, but merely bowed her head gracefully and said, "Thank you, my chief." Taking the child from him, she called out to me, "Come and meet your new brother! I thought I'd call him Mariot."

I cringed. The name meant "wished for child," but she already had children. What about me and Owain? Or were we not good enough now that we were too big to cuddle?

As I approached, she looked at me in surprise. "Such storm clouds in your face! What ails you? Look, isn't he lovely?" She held the child out for me to hold and in that moment he peed on me.

Unfortunately, that set the precedent. From that moment onward, every time an unwanted child was cast aside or left to die in the greenwood or was orphaned, a woman of the tribe was swiftly there to save him.

I could not understand it: this madness that infected us. In all other facets of life, we were steadfastly separate, and far above, these pitiful humans. We did not intermix. And yet when it came to babies, suddenly the women of the tribe would go all broody and bring one of the squalling brats into our midst. Our men looked on wearily at first, dreading the crying and disrupted sleep. But they were not as disgruntled as they pretended to be. In time even they were worn down by the smooth skin and innocent eyes of the children. Even they were known to scoop these small bundles up and hug them. It was the sight of my father – a king! – playing peek-a-boo with one of these urchins that made me angriest of all. We were as gods, fallen gods perhaps, but still wielding an unrivalled omnipotence. We were above these weakling creatures with their frail bodies and truncated lives and yet look how my father gets down on all fours to play with them! It was disgusting.

I myself refused to play. Someone had to maintain their dignity. And so I carried on as if Mariot did not exist. I would not hold him, feed him or change him. If he fell and bumped his head, I ignored his cries and I was totally unmoved when, during the winter of his third year, he died of influenza. I attended the funeral with reluctance and was dismayed to find that he was granted the same rites and ceremonies as Fryok! I was so angered that I refused to keep his soul stone.

"He was not a true member of the tribe," I spoke these words to the hem of my mother's gown instead of looking at her tear-streaked face.

"Please…" her whisper was interrupted by a vice-like hand on my shoulder.

"You will accept that stone," my father hissed in my ear. I obediently took it and left my mother to her grief.

"You know, sometimes you can be a spoilt brat," Owain had caught up with me.

"Flattery will get you nowhere." I kept walking.

"Why don't you just admit it? You're jealous."

I spun to face him. "Of who?"

"Of the human children. They come and suddenly you are not the most precious, littlest member of the tribe anymore." He looked at me with mock sympathy, "Does your daddy love someone more than you? You … are … jealous."

"Am not!"

"You even argue like a baby!"

"Speaking of babies," I lowered my voice and adopted the same infuriatingly sly tone that Owain often used on me, "how is your brat, Daveth doing? Has he gotten sick yet? Or had a ickle accident? Or is it his fate just to grow old and fall to bits in front of your eyes?"

He reached an angry hand out to grab me by the collar, but I dodged it and danced away from him. "Have your fun, Owain. For as you can see," I nodded toward the weeping figure of my mother, "it doesn't last long."

I had definitely hit a nerve – a nerve that had the whole tribe smarting. It was all well and good to take these children on, but to keep on burying one after the other? It was torture. Slowly the numbers of adopted children began to dwindle and were not replaced with new. Slowly, a bit at a time, the tribe chose the easier path: if you do not love, you do not grieve.

Seated in her bedchamber, Mora saw the wisdom of abandoning her attempts at motherhood, but that wisdom brought little comfort. Long ago, before the dragon and the change, she was the queen of the tribe and she was proud of that fact. But she could live without the title and the privilege. It was like a golden necklace – shining and beautiful, but not essential. The day that she bore her first child, however, now that was different. She was so devoted, so desperately, painfully in love with her children that motherhood came to define all that she was and all that mattered. It was a warm, animal-skin cloak that kept out the chill. And now, she thought running a hand across her barren stomach, without that cloak life was very cold indeed. What good is it – all these extra days of life – if you could not fully live them?

Her eyes began to sting and she angrily wiped her tears away. If adopting children was not the answer, then what was?

An image of her mother-in-law came to her unbidden. Mora had always quietly resented Pasca because she was so damned superior. The older woman used to descend upon their tent in a whirlwind of activity, deftly silencing the crying babe, spooning a decoction of herbs into the mouth of the sick toddler, and putting the oldest child back in his place with a sharp smack on the backside. All this was helpful, and yet it was apt to make Mora, sleep-deprived and fretting as she was, feel like a failure.

These feelings festered away, unspoken, until Mora fell pregnant with her fourth and final child. The word "hormones" had not yet been coined to describe the change that took place within her mind and body. She knew only that as her belly grew, so too did the likelihood that she would burst into tears over nothing at all. But her fear that she was a bad mother – that was not nothing. That was a persistent doubt that needled her endlessly. One day when the child who had grizzled all afternoon, had stopped and smiled for grandma, Mora reached her limit. When Pasca asked what ailed her, she replied in choking sobs that all she ever wanted was to be a good mother and she wasn't; she was a wretched one.

Pasca's response had surprised her. The older woman laughed, "Why should you be any different from the rest of us?"

"What? But you are so good with them…"

"Yes," Pasca interrupted, "for a while. Then I get to give them back and go have a good night's sleep." She looked at her daughter-in-law with real affection. "You should have seen me when Gwyn was young, I was so damned tired, I kept tripping over things. I even dropped him on his head once."

Mora broke into sniffley laughter, "That would explain a lot."

"You're doing fine."

Remembering this exchange now, Mora had to admit that it would be lovely to be a grandparent – to have the fun, but not the responsibility, to be able to play and succour and yet not be obliged to clean up vomit and chastise wayward behaviour. But that, she sighed, can never be. Her daughter and remaining son were barren also.

She looked at her reflection in the glass and smiled sadly. She really had not changed that much since the days when all she wanted was to be a good mother. Then the first inkling of an idea made her pause so she could bring it into focus. A good mother … with all the fun, and no responsibility. Yes. She rose, triumphant. She could have that after all. They all could. And so the idea of the fairy godmother was born.

## A Side Note

*The idea of the fairy godmother evolved over many years through many cultures. We see the first hints of it in Greek and Roman myth: Three women known as the Fates would sometimes visit a new-born and foretell his future. Eventually the role of fairy godmothers grew: instead of just predicting the child's destiny, they helped shape it.*

*In a Spanish translation of "Sleeping Beauty," a witch curses the princess, promising that she will one day prick her finger on the spindle of a spinning wheel and die. Fortunately "las hadas madrinas"—the child's fairy godmother – intervenes, saying "Vuestra hija no morirá, sino que caerá en un profundo sueño del que vendrá un príncipe a despertarla." To translate: the child will not die, but will fall into a deep sleep until a prince awakens her.[74]*

*Fairy godmothers not only protected their charges, but bestowed gifts upon them as well. The same story of Sleeping Beauty reworked by Walt Disney tells us of three good fairies: "'We have very special gifts for the little princess,' said the first fairy. She waved her wand over the sleeping baby. 'Little princess,' she said. 'I give you the gift of beauty.'"*

*The godmothers gave beauty and kindness to Sleeping Beauty. They sent Cinderella to the ball to find true love. In Charles Perrault's fairytale "Donkey-skin," they saved the princess from the horror of being forced into an incestuous marriage. But of all the gifts given by fairy godmothers throughout the ages, none proved so dangerous as the gift of a single idea…*

CHAPTER 4

# "THE DIVINE SPARK"

*"Ideas ... spring from individuals. The divine spark leaps from the finger of God to the finger of Adam."*

A. Whitney Griswold

As a boy Lludd was fond of stories. His favourite one was about the Trojan War, although granted it did get off to a slow start. Alphonse Marie Louis de Lamartine would later note that "There is a woman at the beginning of all great things" and the Trojan War was no exception. It all begins with Helen (wife of the Spartan King, Menelaus) and her lover Paris of Troy. Although their story has been described as "the oldest of the love stories of the world,"[75] Lludd fidgeted with impatience during the account of their romance. Generally speaking, eight-year-old boys are not interested in stolen kisses, furtive glances and the passion and urgency of new love. From this less than promising introduction, however, the story swiftly descends into some rather satisfying violence. Enraged by the insult to his honour, Menelaus leads a vast army of Greeks to the gates of Troy. Gruesome battle commences.

There was a really neat bit when Achilles squares off against the Trojan prince Hector and skewers him through the throat with his spear. Then Achilles "cut behind the sinews of both Hector's feet from ankle to heel and strapt them together with leather thongs, and fastened them to his chariot, leaving the head to drag ... Away they flew: the dust rose as the body was dragged along."[76] Hector's father, King Priam, was beside himself with grief, all of Troy wailed in unison and the Queen fell to her knees sobbing and tearing her hair. Personally,

Lludd had never seen anyone upset enough to do this. Even on the night his sister died, when he had cried and cried, it had not occurred to him to grab fistfuls of his own hair and yank them out by the roots. Perhaps the raw pain of a torn scalp provides a needed distraction from the colder, emptier pain of grief.

Anyway, ten years of tit-for-tat skirmishing passed with the Greeks unable to conquer the besieged city. Finally they sailed away from the Anatolian shores leaving behind a curious dogwood structure fashioned in the shape of a giant horse. Unwisely the Trojans claimed it as a trophy and brought it within the city walls. That night a regiment of Greek soldiers emerged from their hiding place within the horse and opened the gates of Troy to Menelaus's waiting army. And then *briseann gach ifreann scaoilte* – all hell broke loose.

Yes, the story of Troy had all the elements that might appeal to a small boy. It had glorious battle and heroic warriors, a neat bit of trickery and lots of bloodshed. But the part he loved best came after the fall of Troy, for this was the part that directly pertained to him…

Asleep in his bed, Aeneas of Troy was dreaming. His cousin Hector – covered in dirt, his hair matted with dried blood – stood before him. Drawing breath to speak, air whistled through the gaping hole in his throat and his voice was little more than a death rattle.

"Fly!" he was saying. "'And get thee from the fire! The foes … are on the ramparts … All Troy is tumbling from her topmost spire'… And yet not all shall perish. Some shall live … 'Take them … And seek for them a home elsewhere.'"[77]

Hector screamed and Aeneas leapt from his bed. Exhausted and still a little drunk from celebrating, he myopically surveyed his dimly lit bedchamber. The phantasm of Hector had gone, but the screaming did not cease. Then he realised: it was coming from outside. Other sounds began to separate themselves from the general din – the clash of swords, a woman's voice ("Όχι, δεν! παρακαλώ! No, don't! Please!"), a baby's cry abruptly cut off; all was "war shout and wail … thickening on the ear."[78]

Grabbing his sword, Aeneas joined his comrades in the midst of the fray. They hewed a path through the Greeks toward the palace, their king to defend. Too late. Aeneas found Priam on his knees at the altar of Zeus. He was not praying, but screaming and clutching at the blood-soaked body of Polites, his son. Before Aeneas could intervene, the Greek butcher Pyrrhus grabbed the old king by his hair. Priam flailed and slipped on Polites' blood, but he was dragged to his feet nonetheless. Pyrrhus, wielding the blade that had killed the son, now stabbed the father and left the two corpses lying side by side.

His duty to king and country now at an end, Aeneas ran to his family: to his wife Creusa, his ageing father Anchises, his young son Ascanius. "Seek for them a home elsewhere" – Hector's words rang in his ears as he hoisted the frail Anchises onto his back, grasped Ascanius tightly to his side and bade his wife to follow.

Troy was in chaos. There were pockets of resistance throughout the city, but these were falling one by one before the onslaught of Greek soldiers. From every home they passed, smoked billowed out into the street and high-pitched screams rose above the crackling fires. Anchises was coughing, choking on the fumes. Aeneas, his hand on the back of his son's neck, pushed the boy's head down toward the cleaner air near the cobbles at their feet. The hero pressed on.

The Great Temple loomed to their left. It sat placidly above the carnage wrought by the Greeks in the temenos: the sacred district at the foot of the temple where many had sought refuge at the altars of their gods. To avoid that, Aeneas dove down a narrow side street and followed a wiggling route through alleys and deserted agoras until he reached the south gate of Troy. Along the way others joined him, drawn like moths to Aeneas's determined flame. They left the city and skirted around behind the skênê, a low building that backed upon the amphitheatre. From there they headed for the hills and did not stop until reaching the secluded temple of Demeter.

When Aeneas collapsed on his knees in front of the goddess's statue, it was not out of reverence, but from physical exhaustion. His chest burned as he rasped for breath; his leg muscles were knotted in spasm; he could not feel his arms. It was several minutes before he could speak. And then a sort of giddiness overcame him. They had made it! Against all the odds, he had dragged his family and other noble Trojans to safety. Now a proper sense of gratitude filled him and he gave thanks to Demeter whose marble statue looked down upon him with such benevolence.

"Creusa, come!" his voice was a tired rasp and he was suddenly aware of his great thirst.

When she did not join him, he stood and called again, "Creusa! Come give thanks…"

Surveying the sea of faces in front of him, he could not find her.

"Creusa?" He shoved his way through the crowd pulling the veil off of every woman present, but she was not there.

"Oh my god." He staggered backward. Somewhere in all of that mayhem, she had become separated from the group. He bumped into something cold and large. Wheeling around, he came face to face with Demeter's statue. Demeter – goddess of the harvest, fertility and motherhood – regarded him with marble eyes, but now they did not seem so benevolent. They looked blank and dead.

"Son…"

"I don't want to hear it," Aeneas snapped. "She's alive."

"How can you know that?" The old man gestured helplessly, "How *could* she have survived?"

"She would have gone back to the house. When we got separated she would have returned there to wait for me."

"It's suicide…"

Aeneas turned away and started down the hill. "Look after the boy," he said and then the shadows of the forest swallowed him.

Retracing his steps, the hero paused as he neared the amphitheatre. The air had suddenly gone cold. The inexplicable change made him wary; every muscle in his body tensed, ready for action. The stone seats for the audience were carved step-like into the slope of the hill ending in a flattened area at the bottom called the orchestra. This is where the actors perform and standing at centre stage was a pale figure. Unable to make out its features in the dim light, he gave it a wide berth, circling around toward the seats. There was something uncanny about it, something somehow wrong. His hand clenched tighter on the grip of his sword.

"Oh god, the voice of death. It's come, it's here,"[79] he whispered, then stopped short. The line, he remembered, was from the tragedy "Antigone." He had sat beside Creusa in these very seats and watched as the title character spoke those words. But why had *he* uttered them? Why this memory? Why now?

He was nearer now to the figure – a woman who stood in front of the backdrop of the skênê.

"What are you doing, Aeneas?"

It was his wife. But it was not his wife. Not the warm, rosy-cheeked woman whom he loved. This Creusa was grey and pale. A wound in her side was covered by a blackened crust of dried blood. Aeneas's skin blanched cold and white. Gooseflesh rose on his arms and the short hair at the nape of his neck rose in fright.

"What are you doing?" she asked again.

"Coming for you," he whispered.

"My husband," she smiled at him sadly, "you can't. The Fates have ordained that you must go without me."

"No," he shook his head. "That wound can be treated…"

"Aeneas," she interrupted. "It's done."

He stared at her helplessly as he watched his own tragedy unfold on this deserted stage. He found that nowhere in his reeling, chaotic mind, could he formulate even a sentence of comfort to utter and so she filled the space between them with her words.

"Do not weep, beloved. Troy's women begin a life of slavery tonight, but I am free." A tear rolled down a cheek so pale as to be almost translucent. "Look after our son."

As Virgil would later describe in *The Aeneid*: "lo, the shadowy spirit … dissolved in air, and in a moment fled … swift as winged wind or slumber of the night."[80] It was the second time that night that Aeneas had been visited by a dead kinsman and this time it drove him to his knees, retching. Sobbing and trembling, he returned to Demeter's shrine and the Trojan refugees. Steeling himself for the struggle ahead he led his ragged band of survivors into the mountains.

From there they migrated to Italy where his descendants would one day found the city of Rome. Though greatly altered, life goes on and new generations of Trojans were born. Aeneas's son Ascanius had a son of his own, Silvius. In turn Silvius fathered Lludd's revered ancestor, Brutus I…

Venustia stared out at the blue waters of the Mediterranean and absent-mindedly rubbed her swollen belly. The baby had been real to her almost from the moment she discovered she was pregnant. She dreamt of him (for she was sure it was a boy); she sang to him all the old lullabies she had learned at her mother's knee; she told him of all the things that he would see and taste and feel for the first time; and she prayed for his health and prosperity. But now…

Suddenly her enthusiasm toward the prospect of motherhood had cooled. Damn Ascanius! Interfering old buzzard! Her father-in-law had insisted that she visit the soothsayer. Wouldn't it be good to know something of the child's destiny? he said. But Venustia had not liked the idea. Man is not meant to know the future, but to live his days as they come to him. Silvius, however, had deferred to his father ... as always ... and off to Rania they went.

Rania, the soothsayer, was an old hag of a woman, bent and stooped. Her eyes were clouded with the thick film of age – ironic really that someone who could not see across the room was able to see the future. And how did she do this? By asking Venustia to light a candle. It burned for a few minutes and then the old woman dripped some of its molten wax into a bowl of water. The wax swiftly cooled and hardened into two tight coils. Rania gasped. In another moment, the two coils broke apart and the old woman nodded and muttered something to herself. Watching her, Venustia realised that this was why she had been so reluctant to come. She was afraid of bad news. And here it comes...

"Ypárchoun kalá néa kai kaká . There is good news and bad," Rania said finally.

"What's the bad?" Venustia's voice was suddenly hoarse.

Rania looked again at the bowl. "The coil shape is a clear symbol. It represents a winding sheet ... a shroud. There were two of them."

"What does that mean?" Silvius asked.

"The child will kill both of his parents," she answered quietly, and then added inadequately: "I am sorry."

Venustia felt like she'd been slapped. "But ... but that is ridiculous."

Rania knew the girl was distressed. Who wouldn't be? "That is what I saw," she replied gently.

"Then you're wrong."

"Venustia!" Silvius cried and then to the soothsayer, "Forgive my wife; she is upset."

"Of course I'm upset," Venustia was shouting now. She turned on Rania. "What are you trying to do? Poison me against my own baby?"

"I am not trying to *do* anything," the prophetess replied patiently. "You asked the child's destiny, and I answered." She placed a consoling hand on the girl's shoulder. "I do not make up cruel things to hurt you; I speak only the will of the gods."

Venustia swiped her hand away. "To hell with the gods!"

"Daughter!" Ascanius, who had been silently watching the proceedings, spoke up. "You blaspheme!"

"You said there was good news," Silvius prompted desperately.

"Yes," Rania took a deep breath to calm herself. "The wax did not hold its shape for long, but broke up into pieces. That alters the message. While tragedy will attend the early of life of this child, there will come a break in the storm clouds – a time of prosperity when he will rise to greatness."

"Well thanks," Venustia snapped sarcastically. "I'm sure that will be a great comfort to me as I lie dying." And without another word, without looking at any of them, she turned on her heel and marched out of the room.

Rania watched her go. Poor little one. She would pray for her and beg the gods' forgiveness for her disrespect. She did not mean it, after all. She spoke out of fear.

The baby will kill both of his parents. What malakíes! Bullshit! Venustia lay a protective arm over her belly and stared with burning eyes out at the cool blue of the Mediterranean. At first she began to mentally argue with Rania – insisting that her son would be well loved and taught right from wrong. He would be a good boy and surely would never harm his parents. But she stopped herself at this first rebuttal. To argue with the prophecy was to lend it credence, to tacitly admit that it carried weight and needed to be refuted. It did not need to be refuted. It needed to be disregarded entirely. That, she decided, was the only sane option. What other choice did she have? Should she fear her own child? Should she learn, perhaps, to hate him because of the ramblings of some old crone? Should she brood on death for Zeus-knows-how-many-years and drive herself mad with worry? What would be the point? What a waste of time and life! No. She would not torment herself. She would choose instead to foster her own peace of mind by steadfastly ignoring the prophecy. And whatever will be, will be...

### A Side Note

*Ceromancy from the Greek κερί meaning wax and Μαντεία meaning divination is the ancient practise of foretelling the future from shapes formed by melting wax. According to* Chambers Dictionary of the Unexplained, *a circle represents a reconciliation and a tree-shape indicates that now is a good time to undertake something new.[81] The omens, however, are not always positive. As Steve Roud notes in* The Penguin Guide to the

> *Superstitions of Britain and Ireland*, "*a little projection of wax or tallow which, as the candle burns, gradually lengthens and winds round upon itself*" *is known as a winding sheet or shroud and is taken as a clear death omen.*[82]

Venustia cried out as another contraction hit. She did not know that it was possible to hurt this much. It'll pass, her sister kept telling her, and then you'll have your beautiful baby to hold. Venustia, however, was past caring about anything except getting this pain to stop.

Lucina, the midwife, was tired. This was her second delivery in two days and it was taking an inordinately long time. The girl Venustia had writhed and struggled now for nearly twenty-four hours, and was so tired that she almost seemed to pass out between contractions. Lucina had tried every trick she could think of. She had opened every door and untied every knot in the house, for this was meant to facilitate birth. She had tied a sprig of agrimony to Venustia's thigh in the belief that it would hasten the outcome. And she called upon the aid of the Eileithyia (pronounced Ilithyia), the goddess of labour pains and childbirth.

Unbeknownst to anyone in the room, Eileithyia did come and stood by the maternity bed. She was a much beloved goddess to whom women prayed during the desperate and often dangerous hours of childbirth. As it is said in the old hymns of Orpheus:

> *When rack'd with nature's pangs and sore distress'd,*
> *The sex invoke thee, as the soul's sure rest;*
> *For thou alone can'st give relief to pain,*
> *Which art attempts to ease, but tries in vain;*
> *Assisting goddess, venerable pow'r,*
> *Who bring'st relief in labour's dreadful hour...*[83]

Indeed she was a kind goddess who had brought relief to many. But even she could not alter the will of the Fates. They were present also, unseen by the mortals, standing quietly by, watching the proceedings with their pale, impassive faces and cold eyes.

"Σας μπορεί να σας βοηθήσω? May I help her?" Eileithyia asked.

"Impede the birth," the one called Atropos replied.

Eileithyia sighed, "Very well." Suspending an invisible hand over Venustia's abdomen, she clenched her fingers into a fist.

The girl screamed. When she was again able to form words, she panted, "When will it end?"

"I don't know," Lucina shook her head. She was getting worried.

Eileithyia stood with her hand poised above the pregnant girl for hour upon hour, preventing delivery. Meanwhile, each of the three Fates idly ran a single long white thread through their fingers, unmoved by the agonised and frightened cries of the girl.

They may well be immune to human misery, but Eileithyia was not. As the labour dragged on and on, the goddess was becoming increasingly distressed and began to resent the cool detachment of the three white-robed creatures who commanded that this should be so.

Eileithyia looked at them uncertainly and then plucked up her courage. "Why must she suffer so?"

"You heard her," the one named Clotho replied. "Such blasphemy. Such unwillingness to accept the will of the gods." She shook her head. "There are consequences, you know."

Eileithyia fell silent. She did not dare to challenge them further. The Fates were so deeply frightening. Their power was unlimited – god and mortal alike were subject to their decrees. Even Zeus himself was compelled to obey their commands and his eyes betrayed his unease whenever they were near. You certainly did not cross the Fates – not if you wished to live.

Finally, the third Fate, Lachesis, spoke up. "All right, let the child come."

Venustia shrieked again as Eileithyia released her grip.

"I see it!" Lucina said. "There now, my girl, we're nearly done."

But this was not the case. The child was large and not only his head crowned, but a tiny fist also. Lucina groaned. The position of the baby would complicate matters and lacerate the mother with each push. Be that as it may, there was no going back now.

"Come on, Venustia. Bear down. You can do it."

The girl, weeping from pain and exhaustion, pushed. Eventually, Lucina was able to grasp the infant's shoulder and gently pull him free.

Eileithyia stepped forward, there was still work to be done.

"No!" the harsh voice of Atropos stayed her hand. "Leave the placenta where it is."

Lucina quickly cleared the child's mouth and throat and he gave a good hearty wail. The boy was strong. She cleaned him up and wrapped him in swaddling clothes and placed him in his mother's arms.

Venustia smiled weakly. "He's beautiful."

"Yes he is." Lucina did not return the smile. She was slowly becoming aware that her patient was not out of trouble yet. She was still bleeding and should have passed the afterbirth by now.

Unable to wait any longer, Lucina took the child and handed him to his grandmother. "Venustia ... I need to remove the afterbirth. If I don't, you could bleed to death."

The girl groaned.

"I'm sorry," Lucina muttered and began her work.

Venustia's screams echoed through the neighbourhood and Silvius, waiting with his father Ascanius, flew into a panic. Three men had to restrain him or he would have burst into the room.

By and by, the screaming stopped and Lucina appeared at the door way wiping her bloody hands. "She's haemorrhaging and I can't get all the placenta."

"What does that mean?" Silvius asked, his eyes red from weeping.

"It means you should come in ... and say goodbye."

Venustia drifted in and out of consciousness. At some point she was aware that Silvius was by her side and then she was only aware of the racing beat of her own heart. The image of Rania's face flitted through her mind and again she heard the words, "the child will kill both of his parents." *He has killed me*, she thought not in horror, but in the vaguely surprised way of someone who was already relinquishing her grip on life in this world.

And for a moment she dreamt. She dreamt of a young man, tall and strong, leading a band of people toward the west, toward a green and pleasant island with lush woods and sparkling streams. "Brutus," she said aloud.

"What?" Silvius asked.

"Name him Brutus." Venustia looked at her husband and smiled. "The old woman was right. He is destined for great things."

A movement to her left caught her attention. She turned her head and there were three pale women all in white. Funny how she had not noticed them before. Between them they held a long, luminous thread, surveying it as if they were measuring out a very specific length. Finally satisfied, the one on the end, the eldest, raised a pair of shears and cut the thread ... and Venustia died.

## A Side Note

*As I said before, the idea of the fairy godmother evolved over many years through the old stories of the Greek and Roman Fates and the Scandinavian Norns. But unlike the fairy godmothers of Walt Disney, these early examples were a whole different breed.*

*The Fates were also known as the Moirae – moira (μοῖρα) being the Greek word for part or portion. It was their role to give each man his portion of life. The first of the Fates, Clotho, was always seen holding a distaff from which she spun the thread of each life. The second of the Fates, Lachesis, measured out the allotted length of thread and hence the predestined number of years. And finally, in the end, Atropos chose the manner of each man's death and then with her shears, she would cut the thread.*

And so, Silvius realised with a shudder, the prophesy is true. Finally he released his grip on his wife's hand. Lucina approached him with a bundle in her arms. He looked at it coldly.

The woman frowned. This would not do. He must not blame the child for this tragedy. She firmly thrust the bundle into Silvius's arms.

"Look," she said gently, "he has his mother's eyes."

It was true. The baby's eyes were big and blue – just like Venustia's; and there was something else – an arch of brow, a curve of cheek that reminded him of his late wife. His expression softened. Yes, she was there in the child's face. Part of her still lived.

It was enough, anyway, for a beginning. Silvius could, he decided, love the child for that part of Venustia that lived on in him. And soon, in spite of his turmoil and grief, Silvius realised that he could love Brutus for himself. Parental love is the most intense, desperate, fiercely defensive love on earth. And when finally Silvius found himself in the grip of that love, he no longer cared about Rania's prophecy. It did not matter if this child was destined to destroy him. All that mattered was that Brutus was his son – a simple phrase that held within it a galaxy of hopes, dreams, prayers and fears, insecurity and frustration, warmth and joy unlike any he had ever known. He was a μπαμπάς ... a father.

Years passed and one day, when Brutus was fifteen, Silvius took him out hunting. Father and son and the others in their party fanned out and waited for the beaters to drive the game toward them. Nearby a twig snapped and Silvius peered through the verdant shadows. He did not expect to spot a stag so quickly – but who knows, he might get lucky. Another snap of brittle wood and Silvius veered to the left.

Atropos deftly picked her way through the tangled undergrowth, rustling leaves and snapping twigs between her long fingers as she went. Thinking he was on the trail of an animal, Silvius followed. Meanwhile Brutus stopped and listened hard. He could hear the beaters tramping noisily through the woods ahead. Their efforts were successful for he could hear the approach of something large. A stag! It must be. He fitted an arrow to his bow and stood ready.

Atropos reached her two sisters, who stood by placidly holding another length of thread. She extracted a pair of shears from a small leather pouch she wore.

Lachesis was carefully measuring out the luminous string. "Wait for it … wait for it … Now."

At that moment, Silvius burst from the undergrowth and Brutus fired his arrow.

It happened in slow motion. The arrow was loose and flying and Brutus realised a second too late that it was not a stag, but his father who emerged into the clearing. It seemed to take an eternity for the arrow to strike, but still not enough time for Silvius to dodge out of its way. The arrow hit him in the chest, killing him instantly, and simultaneously Brutus' world fell to pieces.

His kinsmen, who knew of the prophecy, were very decent to him. But their manner toward him had changed. It was not overtly tangible, this change; indeed their words were kind and their actions beneficent. It was their eyes that betrayed them: they looked at Brutus with frightened eyes, suspicious eyes and guarded expressions. He could not live under the scrutiny of those eyes, but then, did he deserve to live at all?

No, he decided; he did not.

That thought, like the eye of a storm, brought a moment's peace to his breast as it heaved with sobs. To die. It seemed the only way to pay for what he had done, to end his pain and to quiet the manic voices in his head that shrieked that he was a monster, a devil of some kind placed on earth merely to harm those he loved. Yes.

Standing on the Mediterranean shore (indeed not far from where Venustia used to sit) he looked out across the blue waters with burning eyes. He was not a strong swimmer. All he had to do was paddle out as far as he could and wait to tire. Maybe even the sharks would finish him. He stepped into the water.

Knee deep ... and he had the sudden recollection of walking along this beach with his father. He was a little boy and had trotted through the surf and amused himself looking for seashells.

Hip deep ... and he remembered the moment he overheard two servants talking about the prophecy. So horrified was he that he fled to his father and demanded to know the truth.

Chest deep ... and he remembered his father's response...

Silvius had sat down opposite him and looked him squarely in the eye. "We all have a destiny, my son. Your mother was destined to die in childbirth and that is not your fault."

Brutus had sniffled and wiped his eyes.

"Do you know what she said to me before she died?" Silvius asked.

Brutus shook his head.

"That you would be a great man. She saw something of the future, I'm sure of it. And it brought a smile to her face even as her life ebbed away." Silvius looked at his son tenderly. "Nothing alters the course of fate. It is not your fault if fate uses you as its instrument. But I tell you this: everything happens for a reason. Every tragedy in our lives is like..." he paused looking for the right analogy. "It's like a blacksmith. He heats the metal in a hot fire so that it can be recast. Then he hammers it into its new shape. Our trials are like that, blow after blow of the hammer. But it reshapes us. If I die then wait a bit, my son, and see what new thing you become as a result. And know always that I love you."

Chin deep ... Brutus stopped. "Alright, father," he said aloud. "I will do as you say. I will wait."

He left his village that day – numb, exhausted and so very cold. It seemed he could hear his own heartbeat, pulsing in his ears. Da dum, da dum, again and again, like the steady blows of a hammer pounding on steel.

Geoffrey of Monmouth describes what happened next:

He went therefore as an exile into Greece, and there fell in with the descendants of Helenus, the son of Priam, who at that time were held in bondage under the power of Pandrasus, King of the Greeks. For Pyrrhus, the son of Achilles, after the overthrow of Troy, had led away with him in fetters the foresaid Helenus and a great number of others besides, whom he commanded to be held in bondage... And when Brute understood that they were of the lineage of his former fellow-citizens, he sojourned amongst them... [and] he achieve[d] renown for his knighthood and prowess... For among the wise he was as wise as he was valiant among warriors... His fame was thus spread abroad among all nations, and the Trojans flocked unto him from all parts, beseeching him that he should be their King and deliver them from the slavery of the Greeks.[84]

As he grew and lived among the descendants of Helenus, something of his ancestor Aeneas emerged from within. Like Aeneas, he was excellent with sword and spear. Like Aeneas, he was noble of mind and stout of heart. Like Aeneas, who led survivors out of Troy's inferno, he too was a natural leader – brave and charismatic, the sort that men look to for guidance.

"He is exactly the sort of man we need," murmured Assaracus.

Assaracus, son of a Trojan concubine and a Greek noble, was a young man with a pronounced chip on his shoulder. Raised among the Greeks and favoured by his father, he had never thought of himself as anything but Greek. But when his father died and left him three fortresses, suddenly everything changed. His brother coveted his inheritance and brought the matter before King Pandrasus. That son of bitch, that kátharma, argued that Assaracus should not have that property because he was only a half-breed. Son of a Greek? Yes. But also the son of a Trojan whore. The land, his brother argued, should go to a pure-blooded Greek like himself. There was barely any debate – Assaracus was stripped of his lands. This left him impoverished and no better off than the Trojan slaves. Well, if the Greeks would shun him for his Trojan blood, then a Trojan he would be.

"Hello, Brutus!" he trotted over and fell into step with him.

"How are you, Assaracus?" Brutus asked.

"Fed up."

"Yes ... I heard the decision went against you."

"Has it ever occurred to you that we should do something about it?"

"Your inheritance?"

"No!" Assaracus said vehemently. "About all of this!" With a sweep of his arm he indicated the mud huts and wretched hovels that sprawled along the Akhéron river basin. "The Trojans were once proud and noble. Look at them now: living in squalor, enslaved to the race that killed Priam and Hector. And why? Are we not men? Is it really so impossible to seize our own destiny, to live free?"

Brutus looked at him coldly. "You are talking about starting a war, a war that pits slaves against the king's army … and for what? Your benefit?"

"What do you mean?"

"I think you're angry because the Greeks cheated you. And I think that if Pandrasus had granted you those castles, you would not feel so troubled by 'all this.'" He swept his arm toward the Trojan ghetto the way Assaracus had done.

"Yeah," Assaracus shrugged. He could not take offence at the mimicry – not if he wanted to get Brutus onside. "I am angry – I'm furious. And yes, I have a vested interest in this. But here's the thing: I don't want the castles back. I don't wish to live among the Greeks any more than I would share my bed with rats."

The two men, walking as they spoke, were passing a hut when Assaracus stopped at its door.

"I may have my own reasons for hating the Greeks. But then, so does everybody." He indicated the door with his hand and stood back to let Brutus enter.

In the dim light of the hovel, several women tended to a pregnant girl who lay on a bed of hay. She was whimpering.

"It is her time?" Brutus asked.

"To give birth? Not for another month." Assaracus picked up the lamp from its stand and held it up so that Brutus could see the girl clearly.

At first he wasn't sure what he was looking at. The young woman seemed be wearing an odd garment of white, brown and red. He realised with horror that this was not her clothing, but her skin. She had been horribly burnt. Her legs, her arms, her chest, her swollen belly were covered with weeping blisters and deeper leathery brown scorches.

"What happened?" Brutus whispered.

"She can't tell us," Assaracus answered. "But we know her master did this."

"He set her on fire?"

"Yes."

Brutus realised that the girl's agonised whimpers were in fact her attempts to scream. Of course she should scream – the pain must be horrific. But she did not have the strength. And more than anything, those weak cries told Brutus that she was dying.

Assaracus spoke, "Like I said, we all have our reasons for hating the Greeks."

The sight of those blisters, the black destroyed skin and the eschar, the smell of cooked meat and something undefinable that was sickly sweet, the horrible bleating cries of the dying woman – all overwhelmed him and Brutus quickly left the hut. He stood trembling outside with tears in his eyes.

Assaracus joined him.

"Why show me this?" Brutus struggled to form words.

"Because you can do something about it."

Brutus laughed bitterly.

"It's no joke. The Trojan slaves have had enough. They're ready to rebel. They just need a leader."

"And you think that I could…"

Assaracus interrupted him, "…I know you can. They love you," he gestured toward the cluster of huts. "They respect your skill and your honesty and," he reached up and roughly wiped a tear off of Brutus's cheek, "your compassion. They'd rally around you."

"I don't know." Brutus shook his head.

"I've heard your story … about your mother and father and the seer's prophecy. They say you are destined for greatness. Brutus, I don't believe in fairy tales. But I do believe that there is something in you – a light, a fire – that could lead your people out of this darkness. You can hide away if you want and pretend you're just like everybody else, *but*" he spat the word in Brutus's face and pointed angrily at the hut where the girl lay dying, "*that* sort of insanity will only continue … until someone stops it … someone like you." With that, Assaracus turned on his heel and walked away.

Brutus stood uncertainly on the banks of the river. After a moment's indecision, he poked his head into the girl's hut and asked, "Is there anything you need? Can I get her anything?"

The assembled women muttered their responses of "No, thank you," and "There is nothing else to be done," but Brutus wasn't really listening. He just stared at the girl who stared back at him with pleading eyes.

And that was the moment of his great epiphany: the hammer of fate had shaped him just like his father said. It had crafted him into a sword.

Like a latter-day Moses, Brutus sent a message to King Pandrasus asking him to "let my people go." It was eloquent, polite, and reasonable … and it hadn't a hope of success. But then diplomacy was not its true aim. The Trojans had already fled into the wilderness – a tactical retreat designed to look like cowardice. The letter provoked the expected response: King Pandrasus mobilised his army to pursue. There was almost a carnival atmosphere as the soldiers rode out that day. To corral a band of unarmed slaves was simplicity itself. Kill a few for sport, have a slave girl or two, and make an example of the one called Brutus – and that's another day's work done.

Again Geoffrey of Monmouth tells us what happened next…

> Brute issued forth with three thousand men, and suddenly attacked… The Trojans accordingly charged down upon them and attacked them stoutly, doing their best to overwhelm them with slaughter. The Greeks, moreover, suddenly taken aback, are scattered in all directions, and scamper off, the King at their head, to get across the river Akalon that runneth anigh. But in fording the stream they suffer sore jeopardy from the whirling currents of the flood. Whilst they are thus fleeing abroad, Brute overtaketh them, and smiteth down them that he overtaketh partly in the waters of the river and partly on the banks, and, hurrying hither and thither amongst them, rejoiceth greatly to inflict upon them a double death.[85]

The vast majority of the king's army were massacred upon the muddy banks of the river or else they fled into its waters and "went down to the depths like a stone."[86] In the end, Pandrasus was taken prisoner and forced to negotiate terms: ships and grain and all supplies needed for their exodus out of Greece, gold and silver and other riches, and, as a final mark of peace, the marriage of Brutus to the king's eldest daughter, Ignoge. Not bad for a young leader's first battle campaign.

Freedom is a fine thing, but it does lay a burden of choice upon your shoulders: where do you go and what do you do? Brutus was suddenly acutely aware of this. He had joined with these people and become their leader. He had freed them from the house of bondage. Now, where the hell was he going to take them?

Then upon their travels, the Trojans eventually came to a deserted city on the African coastline. There they found a temple dedicated to Artemis, goddess of the moon, the wild wood, and the hunt. At the urging of his fellows, Brutus went in to pray. Long hours passed and the weary hero fell asleep. Suddenly he was aware that he was standing in a grove of ancient oak trees. There was only the sound of birdsong and the trickling of a nearby, but unseen stream. Quietly a young maiden approached him. She had a quiver of arrows slung over one shoulder and carried a fine bow in her hand. At her heel sat a large hound that regarded him with wary eyes. The girl was tall and slim and very fair. A full, sensual mouth was counterbalanced by the cool grey intelligence of her eyes. She wore a short tunic that revealed shapely, muscular legs. Brutus, accustomed to seeing women in the traditional floor-length chiton, was unsettled by this.

"Artemis?" he asked almost timidly, for she closely resembled the statues he had seen in the temple.

A faint smile played across her lips and when she spoke it seemed less like the words were uttered aloud and more like they were whispered within his own head:

*"Brut, πέρα από τη ρύθμιση του ήλιου, του παρελθόντος της ευρείας σφαίρας της Γαλάτης, εκεί έγκειται ένα νησί στη θάλασσα άλατος. Είναι ο τόπος στέγασης των γιγάντων. Αλλά αυτές οι λίγες και θα εμπίπτουν τα πλήγματα από σπαθί σας. Και στη γη που θα δημιουργήσετε μια δεύτερη Troi και σπόρων προς σπορά μια γραμμή του ευγενές βασιλιάδες. Όλα αυτά οι μοίρες έχουν διατάγματα."* [87]

To translate…

"Brutus, toward the setting sun, past the wide realms of Gaul, there lies an island in the salt sea. It is the dwelling place of giants, but these are few and will fall under the blows of your sword. And in that land you will build a second Troy and seed a line of noble kings. All this the Fates have decreed."[88]

Brutus awoke in the temple, uncertain whether it was dream or vision that directed him toward some promised land in the west. What should he do? To ignore a vision sent from the gods could be fatal. And yet what if it was just a dream born out of wishful thinking? He could lead his people all the days of his life and still never find them a home. He looked speculatively up at the grey face of the Artemis statue. It gazed back at him impassively. He sighed. As a leader, he should be more decisive than this.

Walking to the entrance of the temple, he gazed out across the ruined city. Over the tops of the crumbling walls, he could see the mast of his ship, waiting in the harbour, the sail and rigging hanging slack, yet buffeted by a fitful breeze. He had an image in his head of a green island in the salt sea. He had a boat well stocked with provisions. He had a crew awaiting orders. To be afloat on such a full sea as this and not take the chance – it was incomprehensible, really. Of course, they would set sail.

Winding their way along the Mediterranean coast of Africa, they picked up more of the scattered descendants of Troy. Through the Straits of Gibraltar, around the Iberian Peninsula, and into the Bay of Biscay they sailed, stopping only to plunder an area that would later be known as Aquitaine for more supplies and treasure. And then finally, it came into view – an island like a green emerald set in a lapis lazuli sea. The woodlands were full of deer and wild boar. The forest canopies were alive with birdsong and the streams teemed with fish. Brutus recognised it as the island from his dream.

"We're home," he told his people.

Now the real work could begin. He set about dividing up the island between the best and most loyal of his warriors and he gave first choice to Ciaráneus. This man was, quite frankly, the best fighter Brutus had ever seen. During a skirmish in Aquitaine, he was reputed to have single-handedly killed 600 of the enemy. And yet, he was not merely a strong-armed brute. He was a clever military tactician and a fiercely devoted ally.

"Name your territory, friend," Brutus said to him.

The man shook his head. "I'll gladly accept whatever portion you offer, my chief."

"No. You above all have earned the right to choose."

Ciaráneus considered the matter for a while and finally decided upon the south-western corner of the island. It was a land of dense forests and granite cliffs that overlooked a churning sea; all that untamed wildness appealed to him.

Brutus was concerned. "But my friend, that is where *they* live."

"I know," Ciaráneus smiled. "I look forward to making their acquaintance."

"They" were a race of giants who inhabited the south-western tip of the island and used the aboriginal people there as slaves. Obviously they needed to be removed, to make way for the incomers. And so Brutus mustered his army and set about exterminating this race of monsters – a task he carried out with terrible efficiency. Finally, only one remained – the leader Gogmagog – and this one, Brutus spared.

"But why," he asked Ciaráneus, "do you ask me to keep this one alive?"

"I wish to fight him alone."

"Alone!" Brutus surveyed his friend in surprise. "That's madness!"

"You have seen me in battle…"

"True," nodded the chief. "You are the finest warrior among us. But still…"

"I want to try my strength against the brute."

A small, optimistic voice within Brutus insisted that Ciaráneus *could* win and he certainly would love to see it done. "All right," he consented. But, on the day of the wrestling match, he lined up his best archers to come to Ciaráneus' aid should he need it.

His friend bravely approached the monster, and soon the two were grappling in the dust. With his arms about Ciaráneus, the giant squeezed and there was a sickening crack as three of the hero's ribs broke. Undeterred by the injury (indeed enraged and spurred on by it) Ciaráneus charged at the brute, forcing him closer and closer to the edge of a steep and dreadful cliff.

"Go back to hell where you came from!" he bellowed and, with a mighty heave shoved Gogmagog over the side and onto the jagged rocks below. The sea churned red with the giant's blood and the surging waters beneath the cliff would forever be known as Hells Mouth for that was the place that Ciaráneus sent Gogmagog back to Hades where he belonged.

Once the land was clear of giants, Brutus built his capital city upon the River Thames and called it Troia Nova – New Troy. Then, Geoffrey of Monmouth records, "he presented it to the citizens by right of inheritance, and gave them a code of laws by which they might live peacefully together."[89]

### A Side Note

*Geoffrey of Monmouth wrote his famous* History of the Kings of Britain *sometime between 1129 and 1151, when he served as canon at the College of St. George in Oxford. By then, many of the events had been obscured by time and hence this account is not credited with great accuracy. Take for instance Brutus' loyal friend, Ciaráneus. When he arrived on our shores around 600 B.C, we knew him as Ciarán, the Sequani leader who defeated us in the Battle of Nanscáwen. By the time Lludd heard the story (circa 85 B.C.), he was called Ciaráneus and we were depicted not as a race of demigods, but of giants. Also the name Troia Nova had evolved into Trinovantum. Add another 1,215 years and the Romanization of Britain, and Ciaráneus becomes Corineus in Monmouth's account. He is depicted not as Celtae, but as Trojan, and Gogmagog, I suppose, represents Gwyn ap Nudd.*

*I have often wondered how we came to be depicted as giants within the old lore and finally, I think I have uncovered a clue. Genesis 6:4-5 states that "There were giants in the earth in those days... And GOD saw that the wickedness of man was great." There has been much debate among biblical scholars as to what is meant by that statement. Does it mean that, in ancient times, giants actually walked the earth? Or is it merely, as Hugh Latimer believed, a figurative expression? The wickedness of some men was so monumental that they were "'giants' for their cruelty, violence, and covetous oppression."[90] I cannot deny that the Coranieid had fostered just such a reputation in our bid to reign supreme.*

For Lludd, the story of Troy and Brutus was not just an entertaining diversion, but part of his own personal history. Brutus fathered Locrinus who sired Madden who begat Mempricius and on down the line to Lludd's own father, Heli. And so it was believed that royal blood, dating back to Aeneas of Troy, flowed through Lludd's veins.

Like Brutus, Lludd's mother had died in childbirth. He grew up having never known her and hence, not really missing her (the actual woman), but missing more the indistinct idea of a mother. She represented a void – an area of grey mist in his life that should have been filled by something solid. Usually he accepted this absence the way he accepted that rain was wet and winter was cold. It was all he knew and therefore normal. But there were moments when, in fear or in pain, he instinctively reached for something that was not there. Then he missed his mother bitterly, and wept not only for his present hardship but also for losses past.

One such time was during a bout of the "casachtach de chéad lá" or the Cough of 100 Days. Little did he realise, when he started with what appeared to be a mild cold, that his symptoms would develop into a cough of such ferocity that it racked his small body. He coughed until he threw up. He coughed until he burst the blood vessels in his eyes and the whites of his eyes turned a sickly red. He coughed and coughed and then struggled for breath in strange wheezing gasps. For eight weeks, he suffered thus and in that time he *really* wanted his mother, fixating on the idea that she would have been able to comfort him in a way that his nurse could not.

One night, while he cried for her (an unfortunate thing to do because it triggered another coughing jag), his father took the uncharacteristic step of dismissing the nurse. Heli scooped the child up in his strong arms and carried him to a nearby chair where he sat cradling the boy.

"You miss your mam."

Lludd sniffled and nodded his head.

"That's normal, especially when you're so sick."

"Why did she have to die?" the child asked the one question that has always plagued mankind.

"We all have to die. It is the one certain thing in life."

Lludd began to cry again, and again this precipitated another coughing fit.

Heli rocked him. "Shh. Don't upset yourself." Frowning in concentration, he idly stroked the boy's hair. "I think it's important when we lose things in this life – sometimes it's more important than what we gain."

"What do you mean?"

"Well, it's like your favourite story. If life had been easy and comfortable, Brutus would never have left home. The sons of Troy would have remained scattered and enslaved and Trinovantum, *New Troy*, would still be a wilderness of giants and demons. Instead here we are – Britons, a name we derive from his."

Heli gently lifted his son and carried him back to bed. "Maybe the loss you have suffered will spur you on to great things. But first, we must get you well." He kissed Lludd's forehead and soon the child was asleep.

### A Side Note

*The "cough of 100 days" was the vernacular name for Pertussis or Whooping Cough. While it begins with symptoms similar to the common cold, it swiftly develops into severe coughing fits followed by the stereotypical "whoop" of the child trying to draw breath. The paroxysms of choking coughs can be severe enough to burst the blood vessels of the eyes, cause a hernia, or even break ribs and this stage of the illness can last for an exhausting eight weeks. Slowly, however, the coughing subsides and most healthy children recover.*

It was a pale and tired boy who was eventually allowed out to play in the copse of old oak trees near home. The illness had taken its toll on him and so instead of running and climbing trees, he settled for the quieter activity of fashioning a bow out of a fallen branch. It was not going well, and he had been struggling with his project for some time.

"That won't work." A woman had appeared a few paces away.

Lludd was disconcerted. His normally sharp ears had failed to detect the stranger's approach. Indeed, she had materialised out of the forest like a ghost.

She was perhaps the most striking woman he had ever seen. She had large dark eyes, raven black hair and fair, unblemished skin. She wore a green dress, the skirt of which reached only to mid-calf, and had a quiver of arrows slung over one shoulder and a bow in her hand. In fact, she so closely matched the description of Artemis in the old stories that he stared at her open-mouthed.

"Your branch is too big." She cast a schooled eye around. "Here," she chose an elm branch three-quarters of an inch thick, "this will do nicely."

Kneeling beside him she extended an open palm. "May I?" and Lludd handed her the small knife his father had given him.

Anywhere in the world, at any point in history, you'd have to be a fool to hand your only weapon over to a stranger you just met in the woods. But to Lludd it did not feel crazy or foolish to trust this beautiful lady, who chatted to him in a silken voice as she whittled away at the branch, tapering the ends. Deft fingers cut string notches at each end of the stick.

"Ideally," she was saying, "we should have cut this branch while it was still green and left it to dry for a year, but I don't suppose you want to wait that long?"

When the boy didn't answer, she smiled wryly. "Do you have a tongue?"

The child nodded.

"Then why not use it?"

"No, bhean (his native word for 'lady'), I don't want to wait a year."

"The young never do," Mora chuckled. "Now … do you have a bowstring or do we need to make one?"

The child pulled one of woven horsehair from his pocket.

"That's good work – did you make this?"

Lludd shook his head. "My father did."

"Well, your father made a neat job of it." She strung the bow and handed it to the child.

He beamed at his new toy. "Thank you."

"You are very welcome. Now run along home before it gets dark."

Taught from an early age to obey the instructions of his elders, he rose without question and started home. But he did turn around once and caught a glimpse of the lady. A large grey wolf had appeared at her side. She absent-mindedly stroked its head and then both of them disappeared into the shadows.

"Artemis," Lludd gasped and ran all the way home.

Mora picked her way through the woods with the grey wolf at her side. She had happened upon the child while out hunting. Her initial intention had been to pass him by, but something about the boy had caught her attention. Truly he was a beautiful child with dark curls and shrewd, dark eyes that suggested a budding intelligence. Yet there was something else about him – an ineffable quality not stamped in his features, but present in their arrangement, in the expression he wore on his face as he sat absorbed by his work. It was, Mora realised, the same look of concentration she used to see on Maban's face. The thought of her dead son made her chest contract painfully in a spasm of grief. Maban. She felt compelled to approach the child.

"Still at it?" I asked. When Mother was late in returning to Annwyn, I went out to look for her.

"Yes, I haven't got a deer yet."

"I wasn't talking about the hunt."

"What then?" she asked.

"The boy." I fell into step beside her.

Mora did not answer.

"I thought after Mariot and the others that you were done with this nonsense."

"I won't adopt another child," she said heavily.

"So what were you doing?"

"Making a bow."

"Oh come on!" I hissed in exasperation. "Why do you insist…"

"He reminded me of Maban."

The mention of that name stabbed through me. I saw it all again, his severed head mounted on the wall of Ciarán's fort, the terrible look of fear and horror etched onto his waxen face.

"Caja," that was her little nickname for me and in our tongue it meant 'daisy.' "I just…"

"I get it," I interrupted. "You were looking for some small bit of Maban you could hold on to."

"So you do understand."

"I do not understand. That," I pointed in the direction the boy had gone, "is not Maban. He can't *be* Maban for you or for me or for anybody."

"I know that," she said tersely.

"Then why risk exposure? What happens when he runs home and tells Heli about the lady he met in the woods?"

"It'll sound like a fairy tale."

"And if it doesn't? What if Heli decides to watch his son and see this mystery woman for himself?"

"I'm not the child in this relationship, daughter," my mother hissed. "I can take care of myself."

"You are messing with a warrior chieftain's son. You could end up with your head on a wall."

"Enough!" Mora's eyes blazed and I took a step backward. "I am your mother and your queen and I'll do what I want. Now for your own sake get the hell out of my sight!"

There is no point arguing with my mother when she is that angry. I turned to go. "I just hope," I called back over my shoulder, "that this doesn't come back to bite you … or us."

Though by this point I looked about twenty years old, I was immature and still had the adversarial mentality of a teenager. Therefore, I had not yet come to grasp the concept of diplomacy. My advice may have been sound, but the delivery had so infuriated my mother that she was now determined not to heed it.

Lludd, in the meantime, was wrestling with a dilemma of his own. For a moment there in the forest he had been so sure that (like his ancestor Brutus) he had been befriended by a goddess. He ran home as fast as his legs could carry him, just bursting to tell his father all about it. But the sight of Heli, so calm and so normal, made the meeting in the woods seem distant and unreal. He realised how foolish it would all sound.

"What is it, son?" Heli asked.

Lludd thought fast. "Uh, I finished my bow." He handed it to his father for inspection.

"That is excellent work!" his father beamed. Then something must have struck him as odd, for he examined the bow more closely. "*Really* good work. I'm serious, Lludd…. *You* made this?"

The boy nodded and tried very hard to look truthful.

"Well, I'm very impressed." Heli handed it back.

Lludd went straight to his room and examined the bow closely. The Lady did exist, but whether she was human or something more, he did not know. There was, he decided, only one way to find out: go back to the woods and see.

Lludd spent most of the following day in the greenwood waiting for the Lady to appear, but mostly getting frustrated and bored. Patience, after all, is not a virtue of the young. As the day drew to a close, he sullenly grabbed his bow and started for home.

The forest was blanketed in a heavy quiet, broken only by the occasional cry of a distant wood pigeon. The shadows of late afternoon were stretching out their long fingers across the uneven ground. Then suddenly the gargling croak of a raven sliced through the dusky peace and made Lludd jump. A flap of wings betrayed the bird's position on a low branch just ahead.

The raven is a forbidding-looking bird because of its comprehensive darkness. Black beak, black eyes, black feathers and black feet. Not a hint of colour or light upon it, not even in its eyes which looked at him with supreme indifference. Lludd watched the creature uneasily. For one crazy moment, he found himself wondering if it was the Lady in a different form.

The raven croaked again and flapped off, leaving behind what appeared to be a few lighter coloured feathers. It struck the boy as odd and so he went in for a closer look. Arrows. Three beautifully crafted arrows for his new bow were tethered to the branch. Lludd's face beamed with delight. It was her.

Mora was concealed nearby and it was her disembodied voice that seemed to whisper through the rustling of the leaves: "Ár rúnda. Our secret." And the boy nodded fervently.

After he had gone, the raven swooped down to perch next to Mora. "Well done, my friend," she murmured. "Here you go." She tossed a vole to the waiting beak and the bird flew off to enjoy his meal.

Mora returned home feeling happy and vindicated. Her friendship with Lludd would cause no problem as long as she kept to a few sensible rules. Read some of the old stories and you begin to recognise a common thread that is spun throughout the tales of Fairy Godmothers. More to the point, you begin to notice three essential elements – three unspoken rules – that dictate the nature of the relationship. Take, for instance, Charles Perrault's fairytale, *Donkey-skin*. In it the fairy godmother is an ambiguous figure. She is described merely as wise and "in magic art …very skilled."[91] Her personality and the details of her life story are never revealed. She is not even identified by name. That is rule number one.

Mora had no intention of sharing her name with Lludd or telling him anything about her life. Their friendship would exist in a sort of bubble, separate from her world and his. And hence there would be no risk of exposure, no hint that she was queen of an exiled tribe that haunted the greenwood, extorted offerings of food from peasants, and killed anyone who ventured too near.

Rule number two: the child's real mother must be absent. This is significant, because there are few examples within the literature of a fairy godmother aiding a child still cared for by its mother. Why? Because, in most cases anyway, a child blessed with a living mother does not need a fairy. Besides, a mother is the world's best meddler. With a mother on the scene, it would be impossible to ensure the most important condition placed upon the relationship – that of secrecy (rule number three).

In *Donkey-skin* when the Princess seeks help, she finds the fairy in her dwelling, a place "set apart … in a distant grotto, filled with coral, pearls and shells."[92] The Fairy Godmother does not approach the castle, but engages in clandestine meetings in out-of-the-way places or else, in the case of Cinderella, only appears to the sobbing girl when all others have left. In return, the child never speaks of the fairy. To break this taboo would be the end of things. The fairy would disappear, never to be seen again. That is how Mora sought to conceal herself from Heli and, hence, keep her head firmly attached to her shoulders.

The meetings were infrequent. If he was playing alone in the greenwood, she would approach him. Otherwise, she would not draw near. But when they were together Mora could be exactly what she was meant to be … a mother. She cleaned and bandaged skinned knees and elbows. She'd sit for hours playing stones (an early form of marbles) or else entice Lludd into a game of Hood Man's Bluff. It was an early version of Blind Man's Bluff – a trifle for Mora, whose sharp ears could pick out the child's location no matter how quiet he tried to be. In order to prolong the game, she'd let him win.

She taught him things, too, about the greenwood and its creatures. She showed him the secret hiding places where the jays hid acorns for the winter and how a mess of woodpigeon feathers on the forest floor meant that the sparrow hawk had caught his supper. She taught him also to identify the chirrs of the male badger (the oily, vibrating purr he uses to call for a mate). And then she showed him how to find the sett where the cubs would be born.

"They mate all year round, but the cubs are always born in late winter … I have never understood why that is so."

### A Side Note

*While February marks the peak of badger mating season, they can and do mate throughout the year. Oddly, the cubs are usually born in February, no matter when mating occurred. This is due to delayed implantation, a reproductive quirk in which the fertilised eggs develop into a blastocyst (a tiny ball of cells) which remains in the uterus until late December, when it implants itself in the uterine wall and the cub finally begins to grow.*[93]

Mora picked her way to the edge of the wood. Beyond the tree-line lay a grassy field dotted with grazing soay sheep. "If you want to find an animal, then first find what it eats," she murmured.

"What? Sheep?" Lludd laughed.

"No, silly. That field gets good and churned up by the sheep as they graze. It's a good place to find earthworms."

"And the badgers eat the worms…"

"And so the badger sett will be within striking distance," Mora nodded. "Probably on a slope."

A small path worn along the field's edge gave them their first clue, and they followed this back into the woods. Just when Lludd was beginning to think that following the badger track was easy, it would all but disappear. It would then take the Lady a little while to pick it up again. How she could discern such a faint trail amongst all the tangles of the forest floor, the boy could not imagine, but he followed her eagerly.

Eventually they found a semi-circular hole in the side of a low hill. "And that," Mora pronounced triumphantly, "is the entrance to the sett."

"How do you know it's badgers and not rabbits or foxes?"

"That." She nodded at a mound of sandy dirt. "They never stop digging. That's debris they cleared from underground."

A badger sett, Mora explained, consists of an intricate series of tunnels opening onto larger underground chambers. This was only one entrance.

"How many are there?"

Mora shrugged, "Twenty, maybe more."

As interesting as all this was, another question hovered on the tip of Lludd's tongue. For weeks now, he had wondered where the Lady disappeared to after their meetings. She would see him most of the way home and then, almost in the blink of an eye, she would vanish. Where did she go? Where did she sleep at night? How was she able to almost melt into the forest like a green shadow that his eyes could never quite follow no matter how hard he tried?

He plucked up the courage. "Lady?"

"Mmm?"

"Where do you live? What is your home like?"

Mora sighed, thinking that her explanation of the badger sett also served as a pretty good description of Annwyn. She could not tell him that, of course. She would never reveal that much about herself. But it was more than that – more than just the keeping of her own rules. She could not bring herself to tell this innocent child the great price the tribe paid for its freedom – the loss of sunlight and fresh breezes, the loss of birdsong and, perhaps, even the loss of a little bit of her husband's sanity within Annwyn's dark chambers. No. Better to tell the beautiful lie.

"My home," she mused, "is a white castle among green mountains up where the air is thin and crisp. The entrance is through a sandstone gatehouse, flanked by two round towers and capped with a crow-stepped gable. Once inside, you will find the armoury on your right where the fighting men keep their weapons and train in the art of war. To the left is the bower where the ladies congregate to weave and gossip. And directly in front of you lies the Great Hall. It's five stories high and bends to follow the ridge of the mountain. It is crowned with innumerable towers and turrets that gleam when the sun strikes the limestone of their walls. And above the entrance to the Great Hall there is the image of a warrior upon a fine horse. At his feet there lies a coiled black dragon, impaled through the mouth by the man's spear."

She had been staring off into the distance, seeing her creation as her imagination built it. Now she looked down at Lludd and smiled. "It is said that long ago in the history of my people there was just such a creature – a sharp-toothed and poisonous dragon that brought the clan close to extinction. And it is said that one man finally killed it. We trace everything from that one moment."

Although the Lady was smiling, her brow darkened a little when she said this and Lludd was left with the vague impression that not everything that followed on from that event was as shining and good as she would have him believe.

"Anyway," Mora continued, "enough of this for now. It is time you headed home."

"Oh, do I have to?"

"Yes," she answered firmly. "I'll see you again."

And there were more meetings in the dappled green light of the wood. And the days of that summer seemed to stretch endlessly out ahead of them. But sadly nothing lasts forever, especially youth and the summer sun. Little boys grow into men, and in doing so walk a path that slowly winds away from mothers, even Fairy god-ones. If you had asked Lludd then "Will you remember this always?" he would have answered with an emphatic "*Yes.*" He would always remember what it was like to be eight or nine or ten years old; and the world of his childhood, revolving as it did around the Lady, would always be with him.

But those of you who have grown up know that this is not possible. An ever-widening ocean of years and experience pulls you in its current, further and further away till the land of your youth seems so distant that it might as well be a point on the other side of the globe. The child you were becomes a stranger (a wholly different person to who you are now). This is why generation after generation of children insists that their parents "just do not understand." And they vow that *they* will remember what it is like to be young. But they do not remember, because in the end, they can't – not really. Inevitably, their own children will one day make the same complaint and the same vow, and on and on it goes.

Although Mora had lived long enough to know that this is the natural order of things, she was saddened when, with each new summer, the boy came less frequently to the greenwood. When finally he stopped coming altogether, she sought him out. Her keen ears picked out his voice (now the deeper voice of a young man). It was barely a murmur, coming from a stable on the outskirts of Trinovantum. Nearing the stable, she realised that he was not alone. Lludd was breathing heavily and beneath the woodwind note of that sound there was the lighter pant of a girl. Her gasps increased in frequency and volume in time with his thrusts, a crescendo that peaked and then died away amidst satisfied moans and a staccato of kisses.

Mora's heart was pounding in her chest as she fled back into the greenwood. Why should the fact her boy now had a sex life disturb her so? Because. Because now he was all grown up and no longer wanted fairy tales. Because instead of needing a motherly bosom on which to lay his head for comfort, he wanted a firm, naked breast on a girl who would hitch her skirts up for him. Because she was old and familiar, and the girl was something new.

In Ethiopia they have a saying: "The marvellous and the astonishing only surprise for a week"[94] – meaning that no matter how beautiful and exotic a thing may be, we swiftly become used to it … and then just a little bored. A similar phrase, "familiarity breeds contempt," was first uttered in English around 1160; however it was a well-accepted premise long before then. In 570 B.C. Aesop wrote in his fable *The Camel*: "When the first men first set eyes on a camel, they were staggered … and ran away in fear. In time, seeing the beast seemed fairly mild … they used it with contempt."[95] It really doesn't matter, though, how old an idea is. When you experience it first hand, it throbs with the immediacy of a wasp sting. And when Mora realised that she had become like that camel, her vision blurred with a white-hot flash of rage that arced through her.

Worse yet was the snippet of pillow talk overheard as she made her retreat…

"How is your father today?"

"Worse. He looks like," Lludd paused to find the words, "like he's aged about twenty years in the last two months. And now his mind is going. A servant came in with some food and he thought she was my mother."

"My poor one." The girl kissed him again.

"Why is everything always such a fucking struggle?"

"I don't know."

They fell silent for a while.

"Anyway," Lludd's voice was hoarse with suppressed emotion. "Let's talk about something else."

"All right, tell me your plans again."

"Don't you tire of hearing them?"

"No, I love them. And I love how happy, how *paiseanta* [passionate] you are when you speak of them."

"Oh, you'd like a bit of paisean?" He kissed her neck.

She giggled, "Come on, tell me."

"First we get married."

"Of course."

"And then I get to work on Trinovantum. New Troy will be reborn into something magnificent – a shining city on a hill. The walls will be high and strong with a gatehouse flanked by two round towers."

"You can call it Lludd's gate," the girl said softly.

"Innumerable turrets that gleam in the sun and a statue downhill from the gate."

"A statue of what?"

"A great black dragon," he answered.

She laughed, "Where'd that come from?"

"Don't know – but I like the idea."

It was, Mora realised, her fabricated description of Annwyn. Not only had the boy forgotten her, forsaken her, but now he had stolen her fondest dream and presented it to some slut on her back in the hay.

When old Heli died, Lludd became king of the Britons. He married the girl and set his plans for New Troy in motion. That spark of inspiration from Mora, that shining vision of Annwyn, was translated into mortar and stone. According to Geoffrey of Monmouth, Lludd "re-built the walls of the town … and girded it round with innumerable towers."[96] He goes on to say that:

> He did likewise enjoin the citizens that they should build houses and stately fabrics therein, so as that no city in far-off kingdoms should contain fairer palaces… And, albeit that he had many cities in his dominion, yet this did he love above all others, and therein did he sojourn the greater part of the whole year, whence it was afterward named Kaerlud.[97]

The city was so beloved by its architect that it was indeed re-christened Kaerlud, a name which altered over time into Kaerlundein and then just London. It was surrounded by a high wall with a gate in the west known as Ludgate and the statue of a black heraldic dragon was erected at Temple Bar.

Mora sat idly snapping twigs between her long fingers and watched as stone was heaped upon stone. Gradually the gate began to take shape. Her features were composed into such a mask of frowning immobility that, had you been able to peel the mask away and look upon the spinning cogs of her mind, you would have been surprised and dismayed at the furious plans she was making. Even though her relationship with Lludd was platonic, she reacted to his betrayal like a woman scorned. Indeed she did feel used and cast aside.

"There are consequences, you know," she murmured.

Therefore, after a particularly heavy night on the drink, when the Coranieid tribe finally staggered out of their bedchambers in a dehydrated stupor, we found Mora collapsed in Annwyn's Great Hall, clutching at a bloody shoulder wound.

"What the hell happened?" Gwyn asked, shaking off his hangover and going to his wife's aid.

"Arrow," she gasped in pain.

The look on my father's face was murderous. "Who?" was all he managed to say.

In a choked sob, my mother replied, "Lludd."

Gwyn knelt beside his wife. "Pan vernans a-n-jevyth ef?" (What death shall he have?)

Mora did not answer. Indeed she could not as her love for the boy and her desire for retribution fought each other for supremacy.

"Cregy? Dybenna? Lesky?" (Hanged? Beheaded? Burnt?) Gwyn prompted.

"Bewa venjyans" she decided. Living vengeance.

That was the moment when, in spite of my concern, I took a closer look at my mother. She was going to let him live? A human attacks her and she opts for mercy? It made no sense in our world where mortals were killed for mere sport.

She must have felt my gaze, for she looked up at me and our eyes met. She quickly looked away, but in that instant I saw not pain nor fear nor anger, but guilt. Mora was lying.

I held my tongue while I considered this. Why would she lie? What could possibly have turned her devotion to Lludd into such hate? What had he done, really – for I was convinced that there had been no arrow. Or was it something he hadn't done? A flash of insight hit me like a bolt of lightning which seemed to illuminate everything with its white flare. I don't know how else to describe the sensation to you. It was hot and dazzlingly clear, and I had never known anything like it. Suddenly I found myself looking not *at* my mother, but *into* her. Her chest ached, but not from any physical wound. No, I heard her heart beating in my ears – a mother's heart, proprietary and proud. As Simone de Beauvoir would later write about such possessive motherhood, she is "contradictory: she would have him (her "son") of unlimited power, yet held in the palm of her hand; dominating the world, yet on his knees before her."[98] And that is precisely what he had failed to do. He did not recognise her kindness as a debt to be paid in homage. Children can be so ungrateful for all the time and attention and care lavished upon them, and then they leave the nest and the mother is no longer the centre of their universe. What a bereft and bitter emptiness filled that heart. She was a sun and her planet had escaped her gravitational pull and chosen to revolve around another.

It won't surprise you to learn that I had no sympathy for her plight. Her insistence on involving herself with mortal children had rankled from the beginning and now, finally, it had come back to bite her. Indeed it was about to take a chunk out of Lludd as well – an idea that pleased me. I kept my silence.

And so with Mora's little deception we, the Coranieid, made our first appearance in the written annals of men. Welsh Triad number 36 lists "Three oppressions that came to this Island … One of them (was) the people of the Coraniaid, who came here in the time of" Lludd.[99] *The Mabinogion*, a collection of Welsh stories based on pre-Christian Celtic mythology, picks up this thread and weaves it into a complete narrative. It states that …

> …three plagues fell on the Island of Britain, such as none in the islands had ever seen the like of. The first was a certain race that came, and was called the Coranians; and so great was their knowledge, that there was no discourse upon the face of the Island, however low it might be spoken, but that, if the wind met it, it was known to them. And through this they could not be injured. The second plague was a shriek … And this went through people's hearts, and so scared them, that the men lost their hue and their strength, and the women their children, and the young men and the maidens lost their senses, and all the animals and trees and the earth and the waters, were left barren. The third plague

was, that however much provisions and food might be prepared in the king's courts, were there even so much as a year's provision of meat and drink, none of it could ever be found, except what was consumed in the first night ... And thereupon King Lludd felt great sorrow and care, because that he knew not how he might be freed from these plagues.[100]

Spell it how you like (Coraniaid or Coranians); we had finally made the history books and this is how it was done...

With the coming of night, we waited in a claustrophobic burrow which branched off the main tunnel leading east from Annwyn. The burrow's entrance (concealed amidst woodland that would later be known as Battersea) was our nearest portal to Trinovantum.

"We get in, clean out the storehouses and get out. No," Gwyn looked pointedly at Owain, "improvising."

"Why do we have to haul all that food back to Annwyn?" Owain asked. "We're never going to eat it all."

"It's not for us." Gwyn's smile was enigmatic.

Owain shrugged and followed his chief out into the open night air.

Indeed, Lludd was prospering. His storehouses were full of cured meat, sacks of flour, loaves of bread and barrels of corma – a wheaten beer consumed with most meals. We took the lot and disappeared back into our warren of tunnels. The food, however, never made it back to Annwyn's Great Hall. Detouring down a side passage, we followed Gwyn through another hidden door and emerged in a glade deep within the greenwood. What I saw there made my stomach lurch.

There, bathed in the light of the full moon, stood a legion fresh from hell and all the nightmares of men. The Coranieid recoiled at the sight. Only Gwyn stood firm, nodding his head as if satisfied.

There were spriggans – tall, deathly pale and crusted over with mud as if they had just clawed their way out of some lonesome grave. Goblins loitered in the shadows picking dried blood out from under their long, claw-like fingernails. Imps, said to be offshoots of the devil himself, stared back at us with open malice. And Ghouls, reeking of carrion, gnawed on old bones. In short, every dark and soulless creature, everything that goes "bump" in the night awaited us in that glade.

"What they hell are you doing?" Myrddin hissed.

"What every great leader does," Gwyn answered. "delegating."

# A Side Note

*Human folklore is richly populated with a whole "parliament of monsters."[101] The reason for this is easy enough to ascertain. H.G. Wells noted that primordial man "feared the dark ... and thunderstorms, and big animals, and queer things ... [and] he did things to propitiate what he feared ... the imaginary powers in rock and beast and river."[102] But superstition did not die out with man's early ancestors. Peter Haining observes: "when civilisation dawned, and after it came the march of progress, nothing could shift the darkness of the unknown that was indelibly printed on the human psyche."[103] Hence, all manner of malevolent creatures were brought to life and nurtured by man's imagination. For example...*

*Spriggans are creatures roughly the size of a full-grown man. They inhabit chambers underneath old castles and burial cairns – damp, lightless places – and there they amass great wealth which they guard jealously. Soulless, eyeless creatures with pale translucent skin, they attack anyone who ventures into their catacombs. The survivors of these encounters are often so terrified that an illness comes upon them and they are left bedridden for days.[104]*

*Goblins, on the rare occasions when they are seen, look like diabolically ugly children. These are the mischief makers of the supernatural world. They spook herds of livestock, causing the cattle to stampede. They trip up the milkmaid so that she drops her full pail and they pinch the sleeping baby so that he awakens with a scream. While not murderous, they are malicious and their presence, while often unseen, is disquieting. When they are near, something inevitably feels wrong.*

*The oldest definition of the word "imp" was offspring or the offshoot of a plant or tree. Therefore within folklore imps are identified as the children of the devil himself. Specialising in creating fear and chaos, they have been responsible for many deaths. When a drowning man leaps upon his rescuer and pulls him under, they are nearby. Wherever angry people riot, they are present, stoking the fires. Whenever a woman was burned at the stake for witchcraft, they were there.*

*While the imps' vocation ends at death, the ghouls' job has just begun. Ghouls are said to haunt graveyards, disinterring and then feasting upon the dead. They prefer the bodies of those who were greatly mourned instead of what they call "unwept meat." Desecration of the beloved-departed seasons their meals and a broken or overturned headstone only adds to the flavour.*

We watched in mute horror as the creatures approached us and took the meat, bread and ale from our hands.

"You have kept up your end of the bargain," the death rattle of a spriggan's voice broke the silence.

"Just make sure you keep up yours," Gwyn answered.

"Gladly," a nearby imp laughed. And in almost the blink of an eye the whole unholy company had vanished.

Myrddin grabbed Gwyn by shoulder and roughly spun him around so that the two were standing nose to nose. "Explain."

"Don't get upset. Owain was right, we could never eat all that we've stolen … but *they* will." Gwyn nodded to the now empty clearing. "And in return they'll do our work for us."

"You mean against Lludd and the Britons."

"Yes. Really, after Nanscáwen, do you think I'd lead the few Coranieid who remain into open warfare? *Please.* But that merry band will wreak havoc and they'll do it with glee."

"But…" Mora interrupted.

"…how will Lludd know that the message comes from you?"

Mora nodded.

"One of these," Gwyn held up a raven's feather, "will be left at the scene of each crime."

"I love you," Mora laughed and kissed her husband on the mouth.

Lludd sat alone, brooding, in the dying candlelight of his great hall. On the wooden table in front of him sat a pile of raven feathers.

He picked one up. "The raid on the storehouses," he muttered.

He cast it aside and picked up another. "The fire in the stables."

Another feather. His brother Nynyaw a gibbering wreck. Frightened out of his senses by …what? What the hell could scare a grown man so much that he languished in bed and refused to take food?

Another feather. Graves dug up and the gnawed remains of the dead left scattered on the ground.

Another feather. A rash of disappearances and the people of Kaerlud afraid to venture out at night.

Another feather – this one found on his wife's pillow. She had screamed into the darkness. Lludd lit a candle and its flickering light revealed deep gouges all over her arms, chest and face as if some sharp-clawed animal had attacked her as she slept.

Lludd looked again at the feathers. At first he had not understood their significance; he knew only that there was something familiar about these little tokens left at the scene of every misfortune. Then he remembered … the lady with the shining black hair, the raven in the tree and the three arrows.

"Artemis," he whispered. He took a deep, calming breath. *All right. If I've managed to offend a goddess, what the hell can I do about it?*

Andras finished off the last of the corma and sighed discontentedly. No matter how much ale he knocked back, he could not attain that heady state of drunkenness that might bring him a moment's release.

As an imp or minor demon, the issue of happiness was complicated. There was too much bile and ice in his soul to allow for a moment of pure joy or even a little warm contentment. If there was anything that he hated and envied about the humans, it was their ability to take pleasure in simple things. They liked pretty flowers and the laughter of small children. They enjoyed the sensation of stroking the soft fur of a loyal dog. A few minutes rubbing up against each other brought them orgasm and a fresh breeze on a hot day was quite possibly the most satisfying thing in the world. For Andras this was not the case. Physical existence hung on him like an itchy coat and none of the body's senses could offer him any pleasure.

No, the only happiness to be had (if indeed you could call it that) was distraction from the tethers that bound him to this insipid world. In short, he sought refuge in his work. Problem was the work had become so … pedestrian. As the demon of discord, he had soured his share of marriages with suspicion, killed love as one might uproot a weed, ended friendships in bitter grudges, broken up alliances designed to keep the peace, and even started a war or two – but where's the novelty? What he needed now was an act of diabolical genius, something that would again give him that rush of sadistic pleasure that he ached for.

Harming the innocent was not only his lone source of fun, but it also reconnected him to the Master. As the victims of his plots cursed and cried and bled and died, it was as if he could feel another rejuvenating gust of hellfire from below. The heat of it made him feel clean and uncorrupted by nature. For nature, after all, was a sickening invention of God.

"Working hard, I see." It was the demon Orobas, the prophetic one.

"I am so fucking bored," drawled Andras.

"That's because you haven't spotted your opportunity yet."

Andras eyed him with a mixture of curiosity and caution. "What?"

"Dragons," Orobas grinned. "Mother and daughter."

"And you're suggesting a little bit of familial enmity."

Orobas shook his head in mock sadness. "The young always feel the need to rebel."

Andras sighed languorously, "Been there, done that."

"Not with dragons, you haven't."

Orobas surveyed his fellow demon. Look at him, he thought. It's like he's lost the will. This annoyed Orobas. Sloth may be one of the seven deadly sins, but it was not one that demons could indulge in. An all-out war was in progress upon the earth: good versus evil, and the powers of good would not sit idly by, content to be "fucking bored." To hide his irritation, he turned his back on Andras abruptly, taking care to flick his horsehair tail in Andras' face as he did so.

"Now that was uncalled for." Andras wiped his stinging eyes.

"You needed something to wake you up. Just think on it," Orobas' voice was suddenly full of enthusiasm. "A family feud between two dragons."

"So?"

"So … who do you think will get caught in the middle?"

And there it was: that spark of infernal inspiration in Andras' eyes. For truly, he could see it all – all the dreadful consequences spreading out in concentric circles the way a stone thrown in a pond sends ripples outward. He had but to throw the stone.

He rose to his feet. "Thanks for the tip. And Orobas…"

"Yes?"

"You are levelling with me, right?"

"You know I always tell the truth."

"You see, that's something I've never understood. An honest demon – it goes against the grain. Why do you bother?"

"Because," a cruel smile twisted Orobas' face, "more often than not, the truth hurts like hell."

## A Side Note

*From the texts of grimoires and books on demonology, there emerges a pantheon of demons said to populate the upper echelons of hell. Among them we find Andras and Orobas.*

*Andras is said to be a Great Marquis or Prince of hell. He has the body of a winged angel with the head of an owl or raven. Brandishing a sword or sabre, he is usually depicted riding a huge black wolf. His whole raison d'être is to sow discord and escalate conflicts. In his classic work on demonology,* Dictionnaire Infernal, *Collin de Plancy notes that Andras "teaches those whom he favours to kill their enemies [and] masters ... He stirs up trouble and dissension."*[105]

*Orobas is an altogether different demon. Normally depicted as a horse standing on its hind legs, he is able to assume human form when conjured. According to Johann Wier in his 1583 work* Pseudomonarchia daemonum: *"he giveth true answers of things present, past, and to come ... he deceiveth none."*[106]

After nightfall, when the candles of Trinovantum were extinguished, Hónglián Huā – Chinese for "red lotus" – crept from her cave on the hilltop and listened hard. No sound of human activity broke the animal rustlings of the night. She tasted the air with her tongue. No-one was near and yet the red dragon hesitated a moment longer, just to be sure. Finally she leapt. It was like watching a swan take flight: there was the web-footed run-up, the leap into nothingness, and her massive wings unfurled catching her in mid-air. A heady sense of freedom washed over her, but she did not pause to enjoy it. The night was short and she was hunting for two.

Hónglián's offspring – a white, adolescent female – curled up in the stuffy warmth of the cave. Her senses were sharp and so she heard the approach of the stranger long before he was within striking distance. Each rustle of leaf and snap of twig indicated that he was one step nearer. Therefore when Andras paused at the mouth of the cavern and cleared his throat to announce his presence, a white snout erupted out of the darkness. The young dragon bared her teeth and hissed a warning that she hoped sounded truly evil. But in her heart, she was afraid. Never before had anyone approached the cave and she was not certain what she should do about it.

Andras threw his hands up. "Whoa. I come in peace."

The young dragon Xiàngshù (which is Chinese for "oak") stared at the intruder in astonished silence. He had the body of a man, muscular, naked and pale, but with two wings sprouting from his shoulder blades. His head was that of a raven. She did not like it. The white flesh of his body shone in the moonlight, but his face (his eyes and his intentions) were permanently obscured by the comprehensive blackness of raven feathers.

"You are shocked by my appearance," he chuckled. "Ironic, really, when the sight of you would scare most humans to death."

"Who are you?"

"A neighbour. Another who, like you, must hide here in the shadows. Men are such barbarians when frightened."

"Everyone knows that," Xiàng shrugged. "So, neighbour, what do you want?"

"Just a little company. I get lonely out here."

"Are there no others of…" she paused, uncertain of what the hell he was, "your kind?"

"Oh yeah, there are lots like me wandering around – that's why you're looking at me like I'm some revolting new bug."

Embarrassed, Xiàngshù lowered her eyes. "I'm sorry."

"Don't be, I know I'm an acquired taste. So, what about you? Are you all alone out here?"

"No, I live with my mother."

"Excellent! May I come in and pay my respects?"

"She's off hunting right now."

"Of course," Andras nodded. "You're so young; you probably haven't learnt to fly yet."

The white dragon glared at him and unfurled her leathery wings.

Andras smiled. "Impressive. So you've been up?"

"I'm not allowed," Xiàngshù rolled her eyes as only an adolescent can.

"Why?"

"Like you said, humans are vicious when they get frightened."

"So you fly where they can't see you … out over the sea or a deserted moor."

"I told you I'm not allowed."

Andras took a seat beside her. "Do you always do as you're told?"

"Are you making fun of me?"

"No, I applaud you! Not many young dragons are as sensible as you. They get to an age when they feel restless, when all that raw power accumulating within just cries to be set free. Then Mummy tries to clip their wings and keep them home," he drawled, "and keep them safe. And they get soooo bored just sitting around listening to one proverb after another, swallowing nugget upon nugget of wisdom, when all they really want is one moment of delicious freedom to fly … to be … to live."

Xiàngshù listened and said nothing. He disturbed her, this stranger with his dark face and uncanny knowledge. It was like he was inside her head. She was so sick of the cave and the innumerable rules that hemmed her in just as she was beginning to feel the quickening of her power. She felt so strong and yet she might as well be dead, for her whole universe consisted of one dark cave and the star-lit glade outside.

When he spoke again, his voice was almost hypnotic. "It's hard, isn't it, to feel a light within yourself and have it smothered. Anyway," he jumped to his feet and returned to conversational tones, "I've taken up enough of your time, young one. Thanks for the company." Retreating into the shadows, he paused, "See you around."

Long after his departure, Xiàngshù was still thinking about her visitor. The fact that a stranger could walk into her life and voice her innermost thoughts was unsettling and intrusive. But then again, he understood her. He knew how strong she felt, and how stifled. He knew how she longed for a world bigger than the tiny monotony of cave and glade. He knew how her heart throbbed and her blood cried out for freedom and for flight.

Her mother did not understand. Oh sure, Hónglián Huā had listened to her daughter's pleas for more independence. Always the answer had been the same. Too many young dragons left the nest before they were ready. They were soon noticed and then hunted and killed. No, her mother had said time and time again, it was better to wait – to leave the cave a little later and to live a little longer.

What Hóngli had forgotten was this: when she was her daughter's age, she had felt immortal. Life had not yet come along and kicked her in the teeth and taught her of death and fear and pain. And without those lessons, Xiàngshù was just as ignorant. It was a dangerous ignorance for it bred impatience and overconfidence. Indeed, Xiàng viewed her mother's caution with contempt. Her mother was a magnificent, full-grown dragon; so why was she so afraid of the world? Surely the world should be afraid of her. Xiàngshù closed her eyes and imagined for a moment what it would all be like: skulking and hiding no longer, she would fling herself into the starry night and swoop boldly over the countryside. Men would see her and run from the terrifying grace and beauty that was a dragon in flight. She would hunt their livestock amongst the pastures and feed, not on the tepid slabs of meat that her mother brought home, but on the living animal. A dragon can hear the beat of a frightened heart and it would sound like a drum in her ears as she gave chase. She would finally understand the glory and solemnity of the kill, and feel the hot blood as it coursed from the soay's jugular over her clamped jaws. Indeed her own blood was hot with the desire to throw herself into a life that so far she could only imagine.

The muffled flap of leathery wings roused her from her contemplations. Hónglián Huā landed neatly in the clearing; she carried one sheep in her claws and another in her mouth.

"Dinnertime," she smiled.

Xiàngshù sat looking at her for a long time.

"Are you all right?" her mother asked.

"Yeah," Xiàng muttered and stepped forward for her share of the meal.

Mother and daughter ate in silence. Occasionally, Hóngli would look at her child uncertainly. She was so quiet and sullen. Probably hormones, she thought. These bouts of moodiness would plague the child until she reached maturity.

When finished, full and sleepy, she asked, "So what did you do tonight?"

"Huh?"

"What did you get up to while I was gone?"

"Nothing, mother. Nothing at all."

To watch a dragon feed is to watch the process of natural selection in operation. The Palaeozoic Era (600-250 million years ago) saw the emergence of the diapsids, the reptilian ancestors of the dinosaurs. Nature, constantly tinkering with the design of her creatures, crafted a reptile with two muscle holes on each side of the skull, back near the hinge of the jaw. These holes allowed for maximum jaw mobility, meaning that the beast could ingest large prey without shredding it first. Nature deemed this design to be a success and hence used it again and again: in dinosaurs, in snakes, in crocodiles, even in birds. And in dragons. A dragon contends with a large prey item, such as a sheep, by swallowing it whole in much the same way that a big python can eat a deer. The ligaments connecting the jaw bones far back in the skull are highly elastic and allow the jaw to stretch open wide. Furthermore, the lower jaw bones are not fused together at the chin. They can move apart to increase the gape of the maw.

Like its distant cousin the Black Komodo, a dragon will then become sleepy and lethargic for a few days while its stomach breaks the meal down. Finally, once every palatable morsel has been absorbed, the dragon regurgitates the indigestible parts of the soay (the bones, the skull, the horns, feet and hair) in the form of a compact pellet. Two brown pellets, rank in odour, deposited at the edge of the glade signalled to Hónglì that it was time to hunt again.

As soon as her mother left, Xiàngshù was at the mouth of the cave, waiting to see if her friend would return. Sure enough, with the familiar rustling of leaves and snapping of twigs, Andras appeared.

"Hello, young one," he greeted. "Will I have the pleasure of making your mother's acquaintance today?"

"No, she's hunting again." Xiàng eyed him shrewdly. "But you knew that, didn't you?"

Andras threw his hands up in mock surrender, "All right, you caught me. I'm here just to see you."

Xiàngshù grinned at him, "I'm glad."

"So, how is life in the dragon cave?"

"Dull."

"Did you talk to your mum about flying?"

"Won't do any good."

"Why not?"

"Because," Xiàng sighed, "we've been over it a hundred times already. I say I want to fly. She says it's too dangerous, that it would risk exposure."

"And I say that your mother's too strict. There's no harm in you flying – if you're discreet." Andras extended his own wings and flapped upward until he was a few feet above her. "So, do you want to learn to fly?"

"Oh yes."

It was harder than it looked. Xiàngshù did just what she had seen her mother do a hundred times: she crawled to the crest of the nearby hill, gave herself room for a good, long run-up, and then jerked her feet off the ground and spread her wings. She came down with an almighty thud. Her face hit the dirt and she spent several minutes sneezing from all the dust she had kicked up.

"It's not funny," she growled in response to Andras' laughter.

"You are very young," he chuckled.

"What's that supposed to mean?"

"The young always take themselves too seriously."

"Oh, and you don't, I suppose."

"No, I laugh at myself all the time. Did you know that the first time I tried to fly, I fell into a gorse bush?"

"You didn't," she giggled.

"Oh yes. I spent the better part of the next week, picking those spikey little needles out of my ass." He held out a hand and helped her up. "Come on; try again."

She stood again on top of the hill.

"Concentrate now," he warned, "or you'll end up in a heap."

Again the run-up, the leap and the wings – this time she flew maybe twenty metres before landing clumsily in the grass.

"That's better!" Andras clapped.

"Can I do it again?"

"I'm not your mother. You don't need my permission. Come on!" He flapped up the hill and waited for her to walk up and join him.

She was still panting from the exertion of her last attempt. "This is hard work."

"That's because you're making it harder than it needs to be. You don't need to flap so ferociously. Beat your wings a few times to get some height and then just glide." He demonstrated.

"Ok," she muttered to herself, concentrating hard. "Run, leap, flap, glide. Run, leap, flap, glide." She took off and beat her wings a few times and then caught an updraught.

"That's it!" Andras called from the air beside her. "Let that warm air current fill your wings like wind fills a sail… Yes, like *that*."

"I'm doing it!" There was genuine glee in her voice as she experienced for the first time the unbelievable freedom of flight.

Andras, confronted by pure happiness, flinched. He flew above her for a moment, so that she could not see his features twist into an expression of envy and loathing. He took a few deep breaths to regain his equilibrium, plastered a smile on his face and descended to fly next to her once more. "You've done really well," he crooned. "But we'd better stop now…"

"Why?" Xiàngshù whinged.

"I'll tell you why if you let me finish my sentence." Andras realised that he sounded too harsh and immediately tried to modulate his voice into a nicer tone. "I just don't want you to get into trouble, that's all. If your mother comes back…"

"I'm going to show her that I can do this."

"No, you're going to wait and practise some more. Then, when you're really good, you can show her that she's worrying over nothing."

Xiàng considered this for a moment. "I guess you're right."

"Of course I am. Right now, your mother could still argue that you are too inexperienced to be let loose. But if she sees you when you've become an expert flier, then what objection can she logically make?"

"None," Xiàngshù grinned. "None at all."

It was a whole different dragon that greeted Hónglián when she returned to the cave that night. Gone was the moody, sullen girl. Instead Xiàng was happy and talkative.

"What brought this on?" her mother smiled.

"I'm just glad to see you," her daughter lied.

"I love you, my little one. Here, have some food."

Once the complicated process of swallowing a large sheep whole was complete, the two dragons retired to their cave. Xiàngshù closed her eyes and dreamt of flight.

She was flying, really flying. During his third visit, Andras convinced her to leave the glade and accompany him to a cliff overlooking Colwyn Bay.

"Oh, I don't know about this," Xiàngshù surveyed the length of the drop and the waves crashing on the rocks far below.

"It is no different from flying in the glade," he insisted.

"No flying is flying, but if I fall here…"

"You won't. My friend, you are ready."

He had called her friend – she had never had a friend before and was suddenly overcome with love for him.

"Go on" he urged. "It's easy as picking an apple from a tree. Just leave yourself room for the run-up and then leap."

Xiàngshù took a deep breath. "All right."

Certain that he would not want to harm her, the young dragon ran and jumped off the cliff. For a moment, her lack of confidence made her falter and she began to fall. But then something miraculous happened: almost instinctively, she righted herself and rode a thermal upward.

In the poem *Beowulf,* a dragon's flight is described thus: it shall "mount the midnight air, gliding and coiling … flaunting his aspect."[107] While beautifully descriptive, this only hints at the sheer ecstasy experienced by a dragon on the wing. It is like jumping into the sea on a very hot day and feeling that cool relief in every cell of your body. It is like kissing the one you love – a feeling that this is something you are meant to do. It is destiny and at the same time it is freedom.

As Xiàngshù revelled in this, Andras flew a short distance away and watched. Well should he be content with his progress. In only three visits, he had managed to drive a wedge between mother and daughter. The young dragon was disobeying and keeping secrets and that was all to the good. But seeing her like this – so jubilant, so joyous – only left him with a bitter taste in his mouth and an unsettled feeling, comparable to the one you get when everyone understands the joke but you. He hated that feeling of always being on the outside of that laughter, and he hated Xiàng for her mirth.

They flew together for quite a while, Andras making certain they delayed an adequate length of time. Finally they returned to the glade with Xiàngshù still on a high from her adventure. And, sure enough, there sat Hónglián Huā, switching her long pointed tail like an angry cat.

"So you've been flying. I *told* you why…" she stopped abruptly when she spied Andras. "Now it all makes sense." She spat these words as she approached him.

Xiàngshù was taken aback. She had never heard the rasp of such bitterness in her mother's voice before. And she had never seen Hóngli look so … evil. That, she thought, is why mankind fears dragons.

"Demon," her mother hissed and leapt forward, landing so that she and Andras were nose to nose. Hóngli roared in his face. It was the nasal, high-pitched screech of a dumb, yet powerful animal – primitive, devoid at that moment of intelligence, filled with fear and hatred.

"Sordes!" she bellowed. "Tempus adepto a filia!" She saw him for what he was: filth, and told him to get the fuck away from her daughter.

Andras threw up his hands in capitulation. "Pacem! Peace, little mother!" He then leaned in close so that only Hóngli could hear. "My work here is done anyway."

Hónglián Huā lashed out at him. A dragon can kill an enemy with one blow of its strong, spine-tipped tail; and Hóngli was bent on destruction. The demon, however, was agile and managed to spring away so that Hóngli only landed a glancing blow. She swiped out a fore-claw and caught Andras on the shoulder.

Andras, while in pain, was not in any mortal danger. For a fleeting moment he wished he was. He wished that it was possible for him to die and therefore shrug off the physical existence he found so intolerable. But, alas, he was stuck on earth for the duration and no dragon could change that.

There was, however, one last brush stroke he could add to his masterpiece. He collapsed on the ground holding his wounded shoulder.

"Xiàngshù! Help me! She's gone mad!"

Xiàng hesitated. She was confused by this sudden eruption of violence within her peaceful glade and she felt that her mother had indeed taken leave of her senses. Andras was so small in comparison to Hónglián and he looked so vulnerable that she was moved to pity. She jumped in between them, shielding Andras with her body.

It was an ill-timed manoeuvre, for at that moment Hóngli lashed out at the demon again. This time her tail caught not Andras, but Xiàng in the belly – the one area on a dragon's body that is not armoured with protective scales. It was a superficial wound, but very painful and enough to rile Xiàngshù into action. Teeth bared, claws out, she charged at her mother.

Bloodlust is defined as a desire for extreme violence or bloodshed, often aroused in the heat of battle. Apt description and it is one of the greatest flaws of the species *draconis*. When the bloodlust is upon them, these otherwise intelligent creatures become vicious brutes without an ounce of common sense. And so the fight of dragon versus dragon was on. Geoffrey of Monmouth, although he gets the chronology wrong and depicts this event as happening decades later, describes the battle thus:

> ... forth issued the two dragons, whereof the one was white and the other red. And when the one had drawn anigh unto the other, they grappled together in baleful combat and breathed forth fire as they panted. But presently the white dragon did prevail... [the red dragon], grieving to be thus driven forth, fell fiercely again upon the white one, and forced him to draw back. [108]

It was a battle royal between two titans and, as Andras crept away unnoticed, it lay waste to the surrounding countryside. This, in and of itself, was no great problem. Hóngli, in a more lucid moment, had chosen a nesting site far away from human dwellings. In their rage and frustration, however, the dragons had thrown all caution to the winds. Their roars were heard. To the people of Lludd's kingdom, it sounded like the world was coming to an end. This had several consequences...

Cynon awoke, grabbed his sword, and rushed to the door of his roundhouse. Standing on the threshold, he stared about him in confusion. A terrible shrieking filled the night and seemed to come from everywhere and nowhere.

"Cynon?"

"Stay inside, Morfudd," he commanded and his wife obeyed.

"What's going on?" It was Heledd his neighbour, who stood in his doorway in a thin shirt, no trousers and with a sword in his hand.

"No idea." Cynon shook his head.

The roars of hidden monsters continued unabated. To that tumult another scream was added. Llyr, also known as "leath urlabhra" or "half-speech", had run out of his hut with his hands clamped over his ears and his eyes shut. Cynon was not surprised: since birth Llyr had been "Ní ceart go leor" – "not quite right." He managed to limp through life with his mother's help, but it was known in the village that this odd man with a child's brain could not tolerate change. Any disruption could provoke an almost childlike tantrum, and so most people left him alone.

From Llyr's point of view, the noise was all-encompassing. It could not be ignored or pushed to one side while his brain still functioned and thought. No, it washed over him in its full intensity, wave upon wave of sound, crowding everything else out of his head. He stumbled over the pile of firewood by his door and went sprawling. He did not even attempt to rise, but lay there on the ground, crying. His aged mother was soon beside him trying to gather him into an embrace.

And then, just before sunrise, the screeching stopped.

"It's over," Cynon murmured. "Isn't it?"

Heledd answered with raised eyebrows and a shrug.

A voice cried out, and at first Cynon thought it was the prelude to another uproar. In another moment he realised… "Morfudd?"

He darted back into the roundhouse and there saw his wife clutching her pregnant belly with bloody hands.

"It's too soon," she sobbed. Indeed it was. The baby was not due for another two and a half months.

"Dyfyr!" Cynon was at the door shouting for Heledd's wife.

Soon a portly woman entered. "Ó, tá tú droch-uan! You poor lamb!" she cried. "Come and lie down."

Ejected from the hut, Cynon didn't know what to do with himself.

"Come, neighbour," Heledd's voice was kind, "Dyfyr will look after her. Why don't we go and check on the livestock?"

"I should stay."

"You need to keep busy or you'll go mad… Come."

Reluctantly, Cynon followed. They walked in silence out to the pasture and the herd of soay belonging to the village.

"Oh no," Heledd muttered.

It was spring, lambing season, and in the night all of the ewes had dropped their lambs. They were only fourteen weeks into a twenty-one week gestation cycle and every lamb was still-born. The ewes had cleaned their babies and some were still "talking" to them in soft, low grunts.

"Cynon … Cynon!" Heledd was shaking him gently by the shoulders. "Come on, we have work to do. Two sheep are missing."

"That's no surprise – we've been losing the odd animal here and there for months."

"I know, but maybe these two just strayed… Cynon," Heledd planted himself in front of his friend and looked him in the eye. "Standing here wringing your hands will do you no good. Now I want you to go and look for those sheep."

"Yeah," Cynon nodded. "Ok." He began his search.

Meanwhile Heledd, with a swiftness you would not expect given his bulk, caught a ewe and held her fast. She had not quite managed to pass the placenta, which still hung from her rear end and dragged on the ground behind her. A shepherd all his life, he knew better than to remove it himself, and so he simply cut two inches off the end and resolved to let nature take its course. "Don't worry, you'll soon be rid of that." With a friendly pat on her rump, he let her go.

Cynon looked and looked, but could find no trace of the missing livestock. Finally, unable to stand it any longer, he hurried home. After seeing so many dead lambs, there was no real hope in his heart that he would find his baby healthy and well. But even though he knew this, even though he understood it on an intellectual level, a cold chill went through him when, as he approached the hut, he heard Morfudd crying. He paused to let the accompanying wave of nausea pass, and then entered.

Morfudd, lay clutching a small bundle to her chest, rocking it as she sobbed. Dyfyr, busy clearing away bloody rags, turned red-rimmed eyes to Cynon. "I'm so sorry," she whispered.

"Thank you, Dyfyr, for your help."

"I'll get out of the way, but I'll come by again later with some food." She turned to go.

"Dyfyr…"

"Yes?"

"What was it?"

"It was a boy."

It was the same everywhere. Still-born babies, still-born lambs and people haunted by the shrieking in the night. When news of these events reached Lludd, he sat for a long while with his head in his hands.

His wife sat with him until she could stand the silence no longer.

"Will you talk to me?" she whispered.

"I don't know what to say."

"What are you thinking?"

Her husband and king looked at her with haunted eyes. "I don't know what to do."

"Well then, we must find someone who does."

"Who?"

"What about Llevelys? You always said he was clever."

"Yeah, he got the brains in the family."

She wrapped her arms around him and kissed him gently. "Not all of them, my love. But he might just have an idea."

After the death of Lludd's mother, Heli eventually remarried and had three more sons – Caswallawn, Nynyaw, and Llevelys. With three older brothers in line for the throne ahead of him, Llevelys had sought his fortune on foreign shores. He married the daughter (and only child) of the recently-deceased king of Gaul and so came to rule over that country. It is said in *The Mabinogion* that "Lludd loved Llevelys best of all his brothers, because he was a wise and discreet man."[109]

That wisdom and discretion, Lludd thought hopefully as he set sail across the channel, may well help me now.

Upon meeting, the two brothers embraced and Lludd began to list all the evils that had befallen his kingdom in recent months. Llevelys, his face set in a look of grim concentration, sat quietly and listened.

"I don't know how they do it." Lludd shook his head. "We are besieged by an unseen enemy that comes, wreaks havoc and then disappears like … spirits."

"But the damage they cause is real."

"Very real."

"You have sought them out?"

"We have searched and searched," Lludd replied wearily. "I have warriors patrolling the streets of Kaerlud at all hours of the day and night. But they always seem to know our plans – where our forces will be and when. And then…"

"Stop, brother," Llevelys held up his hand abruptly. "No more talk of this just now."

"You won't help me."

Gaul's king smiled compassionately at the crestfallen look on his brother's face. "Of course I will help you. But let me attend to the necessary provisions first. We'll speak again tomorrow."

"But…" Lludd stammered, "can you give me no clue now?"

"Trust me, brother. By tomorrow I will tell you all."

Llevelys paced as he reasoned it out. "A race that can hear every word that is spoken…" he murmured. "Well of course. The first logical step would then be…". He never finished that sentence aloud. Instead, the Mabinogion tells us that he "caused a long horn to be made of brass."[110] It was hollow and there was an opening at each end.

"I feel really stupid talking to you through this," Lludd's voice, distorted and slightly magnified, reached his brother's ear.

Llevelys replied, "I believe your troubles are the work of the Coranians."

"Who?"

"The Coranians, the Coranieid. They are called by various names in the old stories. This group, this tribe of the netherworld, are said to hear everything borne on the wind; hence, this unorthodox way to communicate. If you are to defeat them, then your plans must be made in secret."

"I follow you," Lludd nodded.

Llevelys continued, "Men tend to view an invading enemy like an infestation that needs to be eradicated. Hence the old ones had certain magics to aid them in their cause. I know, brother, that you are not Asarlaí…"

"No, I'm no sorcerer, but I'll try anything."

"Very well." Llevelys nodded and handed him a sealed earthenware jar. "Do not open that jar now or it may cause you pain. Return home, and on the tenth day open the jar and mix its contents with salt water. You must utter the Seal ag laghdú over it before you deploy it against your enemy."

"What are the words of the spell?"

"Just this…

*Is féidir leat a chaitheamh mar ghual ar an teallach,*
*Is féidir leat crapadh mar aoiligh ar balla,*
*agus is féidir leat tirim suas mar uisce i buicéad.*
*Is féidir leat a bheith chomh beag mar gráin rois,*
*agus i bhfad níos lú ná an hipone de fíneog itch,*
*agus féadfaidh sé bheith ina yo chomh beag sin yu bheith rud ar bith.*

"Thank you, brother. I'll do just as you say."

"Wait," said Llevelys, "there's more…"

## A Side Note

*According to* The Mabinogion, *Llevelys gave Lludd insects which he "should take and bruise in water. And he assured him that it would have power to* destroy the race of the Coranians." This concoction, Llevelys insisted, would poison the enemy, but would not harm Lludd's own people.[111]

To this day I have been unable to discover what insects Lludd used in his bid against us. In fact there is nothing in legend or folklore about a bug that can poison one race and not another. The only clue I have come across is an ancient incantation used to "reduce your enemies to nothing." In English it translates into this:

> "May you be consumed as coal upon the hearth,
> May you shrink as dung upon a wall,
> and may you dry up as water in a pail.
> May you become as small as a linseed grain,
> and much smaller than the hipbone of an itch mite,
> and may you become so small that you become nothing."[112]

The mention of the itch mite here is curious for it is the only bug I have found in any of the old texts. It is known to modern science as sarcoptes scabiei; and in the 18th century, Italian biologist, Diacinto Cestoni proved that it was the organism responsible for the disease scabies.

While it was recognised by biological science some 1700 years after Lludd's reign, the itch mite was not unknown to early man. Not only was it used in the incantation above, but in the fourth century BC, Aristotle described "'lice' that 'escape from little pimples if they are pricked.'"[113] The earliest mention of the disease itself dates back to 1200 BC when the Book of Leviticus describes "the itching disease" and prescribes a course of treatment.[114]

Scabies is a highly contagious skin disease caused when female itch mites burrow into the epidermis and lay eggs in the host's skin. This causes itching on a monumental scale. In patients with a compromised immune system (such as the elderly and frail), scabies can develop into "crusted scabies" – a disease in which thick scales form on the skin.

Scales removed from one thus afflicted would provide thousands of mites to be used in the spell, but these must first be killed in order to prevent the disease from spreading to Lludd's own men. Hence, the material must be kept in a sealed vessel for ten days to two weeks, the period needed to starve the bugs to death.

I know it is conjecture ... but it constitutes my best guess. Fortunately, *the rest of Llevelys' advice is more specific. He also addressed those terrible shrieks heard by Cynon in the night. Said he:*

*"...behold it is a dragon. And another dragon of a foreign race is fighting with it, and striving to overcome it. And therefore does your dragon make a fearful outcry. And on this wise mayest thou come to know this ... cause the Island to be measured in its length and breadth, and in the place where thou dost find the exact central point, there cause a pit to be dug, and cause a cauldron full of the best mead ... to be put in the pit... After wearying themselves with fierce and furious fighting ...(the dragons) will drink up the whole of the mead; and after that they will sleep. Thereupon ... bury them ... and hide them in the earth."[115]*

Armed with this insight, Lludd set sail for home. Standing upon the deck of his ship, he chastised himself for not possessing Llevelys' brain or Heli's heart. And while he was in this flagellate mood, he chastened himself for something else... Was the Lady of the woods an embodiment of Artemis? He'd never know for sure. But goddess or not, she was something wholly extraordinary. Her presence in his life had been a gift, and then he had got bored and restless and moved on to new things and new people and She was forgotten. There was no doubt, he thought ruefully, that She was hurt and angry and had no interest in reconciliation. And so, he must now wage war in order to defend his people.

He suddenly felt very tired and very old. The same question that would crop up again and again in his life – Why is everything always such a struggle? – hung in the briny air before him.

And in that moment he remembered his father, and how he used to tell him stories of Brutus by candlelight. What had he said? That Brutus' losses were the making of him, that if life had been comfortable and easy, the hero never would have gone on to free his people, establish Troia Nova, and father a line of kings.

Well, the blood of his noble ancestor still flowed through Lludd's veins, and it was time he started acting like it. What else had Heli whispered to him as he drifted off to sleep? "Maybe the loss you have suffered will spur you on to great things." Lludd decided that it would. The hardships that so far plagued his reign would inspire him not to lie down and die, but to fight on to victory ... like Aeneas ... and like Brutus.

Upon his return, he calculated the island's geographic centre to be near Oxford. He chose a meadow edged round by woodland. In later years, it would be the sites of Cutteslowe Park and the suburb of Sunnymead, but at the time it was a quiet, secluded place – just the sort of place where dragons might try to conceal themselves. Now he had only to lay the trap.

"What have you got?" Lludd asked.

Mathgen, sorcerer of Kaerlud, sighed impatiently. He knew his king was anxious to begin preparations, but all this fidgeting in the background was distracting.

"Well?"

The sorcerer took a deep, calming breath and gathered his thoughts. "We have quite a few options…"

"Such as?"

"Such as a sleeping powder. It contains equal parts henbane seed, black poppy, darnel, and dried bryony root pounded into a fine powder and mixed in with the mead."[116]

Lludd nodded eagerly – so much so that Mathgen, with a start of realisation, finally perceived how distressed and harried his king had become. His own irritation evaporated and he added gently, "That's just for starters. If you want to be really sure, I can throw in other ingredients that hasten sleep … cleavers, lavender, valerian…"

"Use it all, and in great quantities. Once they're down, I want them to stay down."

"Consider it done."

Lludd turned to go, but paused at the doorway. "Mathgen," he said without turning around, "buíochas a ghabháil leat."

"You're very welcome."

The alchemist then turned his attention to the multitude of sealed jars and the herbs that hung drying from the ceiling in bunches. "All right," he muttered. "How much is it going to take to knock out two dragons?"

By nightfall all was ready. A huge cauldron filled with the finest mead and laced with every sleeping concoction known to man was wedged into a narrow pit in the field. Then Lludd's men retreated. For the trap to work, there must not be even a whiff of humanity nearby.

Hours later, the same terrible shriek sliced through the silence like a blade.

It sounded like a scream of inarticulate evil, but it was in fact two dragons arguing in their native tongue. In the air above, Xiàngshù was flying. Her mother was in pursuit.

Hónglián roared: "Get back to the cave *right now!*"

The white dragon spun around to face her mother. "I will not sit in that cave anymore!"

"Oh, so what will you do? Now that you have announced to the whole countryside what you are and where they can find you, what is your plan, oh wise one?"

Xiàngshù was infuriated by her mother's condescension, and purposefully flicked her sharp tail at Hóngli's tender belly, knowing full well the reaction it would produce. Enraged, Hónglián slammed into her daughter and the two grappled in the air.

For the young dragon the fight was going badly. No matter how hard she tried, she could not best her mother. Hóngli merely batted her attacks aside. Xiàng knew that she was in no real danger for her mother was actually being careful not to harm her, and that in itself was infuriating. She had begun to feel like a gnat that kept bashing its head against a bull as if to say, "Pay attention, dammit!"

Hónglián Huā always did this, always managed to make her feel like a baby – small and stupid and powerless. Would the bitch listen when Xiàng offered to show off her flying skills so that Hóngli wouldn't worry? No. Would she allow Xiàngshù to continue to see her one and only friend? No. In a cave filled with dragon hoard (gold and jewels and treasures from all over the world), the white dragon was bereft having lost something far more precious – the companionship of her best friend. Could her mother understand that? No. Hóngli just kept insisting that he was sordes, filth. But what had he done wrong, really? Sooner or later every dragon takes to the sky. He helped, that's all. He encouraged her and kept her safe. He talked with her and laughed with her and his friendship was the first and only thing in this life she could truly call her own. And in one petulant moment her mother had destroyed it forever.

Xiàngshù's impotence and rage welled up inside her until she gave vent with one vicious tail swipe to the side of her mother's face. Almost in slow motion, she saw Hónglián's head jolt violently to one side, causing her to hang unsteadily in the air shaking her head as if to clear it.

Sorry, but determined not to show it, Xiàng flapped down to a clearing to catch her breath. There she spied a huge cauldron. What it was doing out here in middle of nowhere was anybody's guess; but already the mead with its tang of honey-sweetness filled her nostrils. She was suddenly aware of how hot she was and how very thirsty. With one lithe bound she leapt to cauldron's edge and drank.

"Xiàng! Leave it!" Her mother landed in the clearing beside her.

"It's all right, Mum. It's lovely and…" the young dragon stopped as her vision blurred. Dazed, she looked around and watched in confusion as the landscape lurched diagonally to one side. "Mum… I… "

Alarmed, Hónglián approached the cauldron and sniffed it cautiously. Her well-trained nose detected something dark and bitter underneath the cloying sweetness of the mead. Her eyes narrowed malevolently as she scanned the surrounding tree line.

"It's a trap," she whispered. "Come on!" She took to the air and her daughter tried to follow, but the child stumbled in her run-up and landed on her nose in the grass.

Hóngli helped her to her feet and stayed beside her for a second attempt at a run-up. "That's it, now leap!" With her claws she jerked her offspring into the air to help her gain the needed height. Airborne, they made a beeline toward their cave miles away. Xiàngshù was flying erratically – in a graceless, drunken stagger across the sky. Her mother stayed close ready to grab her should she fall.

"I'm sorry, Mum…"

"It's not important."

The cave at Dinas Ffaraon Dandde was about 150 miles away as the crow flies – an easy jaunt for a sober dragon, but a hell of struggle for a doped one. Xiàngshù fought valiantly to stay in the air, but in the end she leaned more and more on her mother. Hóngli found her strength taxed to the limit, and her chest tightened in painful gasps from the exertion.

Finally, they spotted the twelve jagged peaks of Snowdonia and then the Glaslyn River. This they followed to Llyn Dinas, a shallow lake of about sixty acres in the valley below their cave.

Now, thought Hónglián, comes the hard part. The whole process by which a dragon arrests its forward momentum and eases back into a gentle, crouched landing is tricky enough at the best of times. With her now barely-conscious daughter in her claws, it was going to hurt … badly.

"Here goes," she muttered and began her descent. With Xiàngshù's added weight, Hóngli came in far too fast, and when she shifted backward to touch down, the pair over-balanced and landed in a crumbled heap with the elder dragon on the bottom.

As Hóngli struggled to her feet, she shrieked in agony. Trapped beneath her daughter's unconscious body, her left wing lay broken, twisted and useless. She dropped into a low crouch and stood there panting, trying to master the pain. It was then that she smelled them – men. Lots of men converging from all directions. Unable to fly and in no condition to take on an army, she had one option left. With an anguished scream, she yanked her crushed wing out from under her daughter and half-carried, half-dragged the child into the cave.

Positioning herself just inside the mouth of the cave, Hónglián tried to ignore the pain which coursed through her body in waves that felt like fire. She braced herself for battle. But they did not attack. They did not even approach the mouth of the cave. Instead a line of warriors cut off the only escape route and waited.

The red dragon's keen ears soon picked a faint, scratching sound coming not from the glade outside, but from above the cave's roof. Scratch, scratch, scratch and the grunt of men engaged in heavy work. Scratch, scratch, scratch and the muffled rattle of small stones down the hillside. Another heave, another grunt and the thud of heavy boulders rolling down toward the mouth of the cave.

"Oh, that is clever," she muttered as the avalanche blocked out the moonlight, sealing her in darkness.

Lludd stood staring at the sealed entrance to the cave when his brother, Caswallawn, joined him. "Do think it will hold?"

"Oh, yeah."

"How can you be so sure?"

"Because," Caswallawn replied, "I went in there myself. The entrance is to a long, narrow tunnel that leads down below ground. That tunnel is through solid rock as tight as a kistvaen. They have no room to manoeuvre to burrow their way out. Lludd," he smiled, "you've done it."

"I've taken care of one problem, perhaps," Lludd looked grim. "Now on to the next one."

The men dispersed and returned to their homes. Among them, Cynon and

Heledd walked side by side, stretching and rubbing the sore muscles in their backs and arms.

"Feel better?" Heledd asked.

"Go hiomlán. Absolutely, and I hope they rot in hell."

One down, one to go, thought Lludd. He now knew that it was these Coranieid (or Coranians or whatever-the-hell they were called) who were responsible for pilfering his supplies and wreaking havoc throughout his kingdom. And so, when two weeks had passed, he opened the jar that Llevelys had given him and mixed its contents with salt water. He armed each of his warriors with a quantity of this potion and stationed them at all of the larders where he stored food. Sooner or later, he knew, the enemy would strike again.

"And now, finally," he said to himself, "we are ready."

Two nights later, Owain returned to Annwyn in a terrible temper. He was wet, and gave off an odour of such foulness it made me retch.

"What happened to you?" I asked.

"Excellent question."

"All right," Gwyn said, "start from the beginning."

"I went to raid the storehouses again – you know, nick a little corma for the evening."

"Yeah, and…"

"…and someone was waiting for me. Not one of Lludd's men, but Lludd himself, fighting and cursing like a man possessed. Next thing I know, he throws this crap in my face!" Owain paused to wipe his eyes. "He did it with such a flourish that I was afraid for a minute that it was acid or something."

"What *is* it?"

"No idea."

"Does it hurt?" Mora asked.

"Not at all. It just smells like shit and is sticky as hell." He looked at Gwyn. "Please tell me we're going to give him a bollocking for this."

"That won't be necessary," Myrddin said quietly. "In fact, we don't need to fight Lludd anymore."

"Why not?" Mora and Owain asked in disgruntled unison.

"Because," Myrddin smiled benignly, "someone else will do it for us."

"I'm listening," Gwyn said.

"There's intrigue at the castle. Lludd's son, Afarwy, quarrels with his uncle, Caswallawn. The two are at such odds that Afarwy has taken steps to strengthen his position and ensure that Lludd's crown will be his."

"What steps?" Mora asked.

"He's summoned the Romans."

"Fucking hell," Owain muttered.

"And they'll come," Myrddin continued, "and annexe and conquer and threaten and negotiate and before you know it, Lludd will be paying tribute to Rome, and his government will be the mere puppet of fat men in togas." He paused and walked over to Mora. "Now tell me, my queen: need we do any more?"

When she did not answer, he spoke more sternly. "Every act of attrition against Lludd puts us at risk. Now, need we do any more?"

"No," Mora answered, tilting her chin up in a well-practised expression of dignity. "I care not for prolonging the grudge. Let the Romans do it for us."

And indeed they did – to such an extent that number 51 of *The Welsh Triads* lists "Three Dishonoured Men who were in the Island of Britain." First on the list is "Afarwy son of Lludd… He first summoned Julius Caesar and the men of Rome to this Island, and he caused the payment of three thousand pounds in money as tribute from this Island every year, because of a quarrel with Caswallawn his uncle."[117]

…Which reminds me of another story: the tale of the second 'Dishonoured Man' and ultimately, what he taught me.

CHAPTER 5

# "LAMENTATIONS"

*"... behold and see our disgrace!*
*Our inheritance has been turned over to strangers,*
*our homes to aliens...*
*Slaves rule over us;*
*there is none to deliver us from their hand.*
*We get our bread at the peril of our lives,*
*because of the sword in the wilderness...*
*The joy of our hearts has ceased;*
*our dancing has been turned to mourning.*
*The crown has fallen from our head;*
*woe to us, for we have sinned!*
*For this our heart has become sick,*
*for these things our eyes have grown dim,*
*for Mount Zion which lies desolate;*
*foxes prowl over it."*

*Lamentations 5:1-2, 8-9, 15-18*

"It is a strange desire to seek power and to lose liberty; or to seek power over others, and to lose power over a man's self." These words, uttered by Francis Bacon in the sixteenth century, epitomise Afarwy's mistake. In a bid to strengthen his position as Lludd's successor, he summoned Julius Caesar to our shores. However, the man who would one day 'bestride the world like a Colossus'[118] had no interest in Afarwy's ambitions. To Caesar, Enys Breten was an opportunity, a land of rich abundance ripe for the picking. He plucked the first fruit by forcing Britain to pay an annual tribute to Rome of roughly 10,000 aureus. That was the equivalent of 250,000 quarts of wheat or 750,000 quarts of barley or a day's wage for the labour of a quarter of a million men. It was such an obscenely exorbitant amount that Afarwy's name was mud forever after.

Twenty-three stab wounds on one Ides of March prevented Caesar from returning to fully subjugate the Island, but the future was no longer in doubt. The Roman Empire now knew of Enys Breten and its riches; they would return. It took almost a hundred years, but the Coranieid could wait. Thus far we had survived seven millennia and so a mere century was "but as yesterday ... or as a watch in the night"[119] – an inconsequential span to await the opening act of the drama that was about to unfold. Finally in A.D. 43, the curtain rose. Forty thousand legion and auxiliary troops under the Roman Emperor Claudius entered from stage right. The invasion had begun.

It was joyous. Those descendants of the Celtae who had spread like a plague across our lands now faced their own Nanscáwen – no, a hundred Nanscáwens, as defeat piled upon defeat. There was a really neat episode when the Iceni and their allies squared off against the Romans across a field near Lactodorum along the ancient track known as Watling Street. Concealed amidst the trees above the deep gorge where the Roman army stood in battle formation, the Coranieid eagerly waited for the show to begin. We'd brought a picnic.

"They can't possibly win," Tamara murmured.

"Who?" Barinthus asked, idly stroking her thigh.

"The Romans, I mean," she gestured at the amassed Celtae forces, "look at all of them."

"No, the Romans know what they're doing," Gwyn's eyes ranged over the field assessing its strategic merit. "Their troops are protected by the steep walls of the gorge so they can't be outflanked. The forest at their backs is dense, so there can be no surprise attack from the rear..."

I shook my head. "But they're outnumbered ten to one."

"Just watch," he nodded, smiling. "This is going to be great."

A hush had fallen over the Britons and now Boudicca of the flaming red hair mounted her chariot and spoke...

"I stand before you not as a noblewoman nor as your leader, but as one of the people avenging my lost freedom and..." her voice caught as she looked at her two daughters who stood in the chariot beside her.

And there it was again: that white flash of insight, that uncanny feeling I'd experienced when I looked at my mother and saw not her face, but her thoughts. This time it happened when I looked at Boudicca. I saw a memory play out within her head.

To teach her her place, the Romans had tied her to a post and tore her dress away exposing the white freckled flesh of her back. With a hiss and a crack the whip left its first stripe, and the queen cried out although she did not want to. She clenched her teeth as the whip sang in the air again and managed this time to limit her response to a low moan.

Her youngest daughter Tasca was weeping in the arms of a Roman soldier. He gripped the girl by her hair, angling her head so that she must watch. It took two Romans to subdue her eldest, Camorra, and they held a knife to her throat ... Ut 'eam. Oculos aperiat ...That's it. Eyes open.

By twenty lashes, the flesh of Boudicca's back was torn to bloody ribbons. By twenty-five a warm trickle of urine snaked down her legs and by thirty, all of her strength left her. She hung like an old rag doll from the post and briefly lost consciousness. She awoke on the ground. They had cut her down and thrown cold water in her face to revive her.

Tasca was on the ground, a Roman brute between her legs. She was crying so hard. The man, nearing climax, moaned and clung to her ever tighter rending a guttural cry of pain and horror from the child.

Camorra was proving more of a challenge. She kicked and bit and swore, but finally two of the brutes pinned her shoulders to the ground while a third thrust his way into her. And she stopped. She lay there, eyes closed, enduring. The last thing Boudicca remembered before she again lost consciousness was the sight of a single tear rolling down Camorra's cheek.

She was still speaking to her troops. "They will not sustain even the din and the shout of so many thousands, much less our charge and our blows. If you weigh well the strength of the armies, and the causes of the war, you will see that in this battle you must conquer or die. This is a woman's resolve; as for men, they may live and be slaves."[120]

They cheered maniacally for her and gathered into their tribal groups. Cheering turned to war cry, and a ripple of unease went through the Coranieid high up on the ridge. It reminded us of Nanscáwen. But that did not bother me. I remained fixated on the woman in the chariot and felt pity. And I felt something else ... recognition. All that pain and humiliation, all the horror and self-loathing because she wasn't strong enough to rise from the ground and save her girls – it was somehow familiar. Then I saw. Her pain, my father's pain after our defeat, they were the same.

A part of my mind detached itself from the emotion and marvelled at this bizarre turn of events. We hated the Britons, just as we had hated their ancestors, the Sequani. We had every reason, for they had taken everything from us and yet, as I looked upon this Celtae woman, there were tears in my eyes.

"What ails you, daughter?" Gwyn asked sharply.

I sniffled, "Dust. Or pollen."

He took a damp cloth and gently wiped my eyes. "Better?"

I nodded and clasped his hand as it cupped my cheek. I brought it to my mouth and kissed it, ashamed of my own disloyalty. But, it seems, not ashamed enough. For now I wanted Boudicca to win.

I saw her whole army tense up, the way a wolf tenses before it leaps upon its prey.

Don't do it, I silently pleaded. Don't charge.

Boudicca's command rang out and 100,000 Britons surged forward. As they sprinted across the open plain, Roman pila rained down on them. Hearty laughter rang from the Coranieid as the javelins found their targets. Men fell in droves, impaled through the chest, the stomach, the limbs. A second volley of pila, like a dark cloud, engulfed the British vanguard and those who followed now had to stumble over the bodies of their dead and wounded to continue their advance.

They funnelled into the bottleneck of the gorge. Within this cramped arena, the Britons did not have enough room to bring their long swords to bear. Clashing against the wall of Roman shields, they were cut down by the short swords which stabbed at them through the gaps in the shield wall. As this great Roman meat-grinder chewed its way through the British ranks, the Celtae turned and fled.

Amidst the crush of bodies, Cigmarw pushed forward. He was young, indeed this was his first time on the battlefield, and he was eager to prove himself to his Iceni clansmen. He had whipped himself up into a fury and could not wait to make his first kill. Then someone slammed into him hard, knocking him to the ground. Afraid he would be trampled by the multitudes advancing behind him, he quickly regained his feet and spun around to watch the man running away in a frenzy.

Cigmarw sneered in contempt. Coward, he thought. He did not utter the word aloud, but I heard him. His hatred of the Romans honed to a fine edge, he again advanced toward the shouts and clash of metal; the fighting was near. As he approached, another man ran past him out the gorge, and then another and another. He was hit again and again – on the right shoulder, in the left side, in the shins – by retreating Britons. His resolve wavered. Why would so many run? One or two, he could understand, but the men in front of him were fleeing in droves. Cigmarw stopped. I watched his eagerness wrestle with his growing uncertainty. Then a man in front pirouetted awkwardly around to face him. He wore a look not of battle fury, nor pain, nor even fear, but of surprise. Slowly, his hands futilely trying to gather up his spilling guts, the man sank to his knees and fell face-first onto Cigmarw's boots.

Eagerness and uncertainty were both silenced by the lightning bolt of fear and adrenalin that surged through the young Iceni. Cigmarw turned and ran. He ran blindly, ploughing into his own kinsmen and knocking them down. He briefly registered faces that he knew and loved gaping at him from the ground, but he could not pause to help them up. Not now. Panic eclipsed everything: he knew only that he must run. After what seemed like an eternity, he burst from the crowd and was again out on the plain. Just ahead he could see the line of waggons that carried their supplies and the British camp followers (their wives, their children). Cigmarw stopped in his tracks. The waggons blocked the way to safety and a wave of fleeing Britons hit them, tipping them over, and sending debris flying. Cigmarw threw himself into the fray but found his way barred at every turn. He trampled men under foot as he fought to reach the tree line in the distance, but there was no escape. The advancing Roman line was a ravenous beast that chewed up everything in its path. Warriors, women, babies – all disappeared down its maw. Unable to find a way through the chaos to the safe haven of the trees, Cigmarw turned just in time to see the legionnaire approaching. His mind erupted in a cacophony of pleas and protests. I don't want to die. Oh god, WAIT! PLEASE WAIT! But, as tears rolled down his face, all he managed to articulate was "Please." A sword flashed in the sunlight and blood cascaded from Cigmarw's throat. He tried to stem the flow with his hands. Coughing and spluttering, he sank to the ground.

I could hear his heartbeat pulsing deep in my own ears. I saw the world blur through his eyes as the din of the massacre became blunt and murky like sounds heard underwater. I felt him relinquish his grip on life and then I felt nothing … a profound nothing … emptiness. Cigmarw was dead.

Seated amongst the tribe, I clasped my trembling hands together in an effort to steady them and took deep breaths until the wave of nausea passed. Cigmarw, a man I had never seen before that day, was dead. And I had died with him. That's what it felt like. He was so scared – I had felt that too. And then I had felt that terrible void left behind when he was gone.

"What's happening to me?" I murmured.

"What?" Owain asked.

"Nothing."

He nodded at the carnage below, "It's brilliant, isn't it?"

"Yes," I said, hollowly. "It's great."

As the merry band of Coranieid made their way back to Annwyn, I slipped away. It was a stupid thing to do. The Romans, still murderous, were butchering any survivors they could find. The Britons were desperate and therefore just as dangerous, but I needed to walk. Sometimes when you twist an ankle, it is necessary to walk on it and prove to yourself that you haven't done real damage. That is how I felt: I would walk until I was certain I was all right. I would walk until that terrible sense of emptiness left me. I would walk until…

A muffled sob nearby gave me a moment's pause. I followed the sound to a clearing in the woods and there she was, down on all fours, retching violently: Boudicca of the red hair and flaming eyes and fierce vengeance.

"Who are you?" she rasped.

I looked at her for a long moment. "A friend," I decided.

She sat down heavily and rested her head in her hands. "Friend or foe … doesn't really matter. I'm past all harm."

"What did you take?"

"Yew."

I winced. "That'll do it."

Bartholomaeus Anglicus, in his 1240 work *On the Properties of Things*, warned that the yew is "a tree with venim and poison."[121] It induces vomiting, convulsions and heart failure. I bent over her. Her pupils were dilated and her fair complexion had blanched a sickly white. If I had got there earlier, a salt water emetic might have purged the toxin from her system. But what would be the use? Should she survive, what fate awaited her at the hands of the Romans? Rape? Torture? Crucifixion?

When Vercingetorix united Gaul in a rebellion against Julius Caesar's forces, he was eventually compelled to surrender, left to rot in prison for five years, humiliated by being put on public display and then executed by slow strangulation. But that would not be Boudicca's fate. "In this battle you must conquer or die. This is a woman's resolve" – those were her words and she was adhering to them. I sat beside her and when she toppled over I cradled her head on my lap.

"I used to do this when I was little … fall asleep with my head on my mother's lap," she murmured.

I stroked her hair. "Me too."

It was over quickly. In the distance I could still hear the Romans beating the bushes for survivors and in that instant I made an unprecedented decision. I secreted her body away, hiding it in a tunnel long abandoned by the knockers. No one else saw her die. No one would find her body. There would be no grave for her people to visit or for the Romans to defile. Inevitably some would begin to whisper that she had not died at all. Her story would be told again and again and, with just enough mystery at its end to keep it tantalising, generations hence would know her name. Boudicca was already a hero to her people. Now she was the stuff of legend.

Back at Annwyn the party was in full swing. Hans Christen Andersen once imagined what a fairy celebration would be like:

> The elf girls were already dancing on the elf-hill, and they danced with shawls which were woven of mist and moonshine … below the elf-hill, the great hall was splendidly decorated … In the kitchen, plenty of frogs were turning on the spit, snail-skins with children's fingers in them and salads of mushroom spawn, damp mouse muzzles, and hemlock; beer brewed by the marsh witch, gleaming saltpeter wine from grave cellars; everything very grand.[122]

Again, it proves my point that men insisted on endowing us with greater magic and greater evil than we actually possessed. Yes, the celebration that night included music and dancing. But it was fuelled by such copious amounts of alcohol that many passed out in the Great Hall, while others remained conscious just long enough to sneak off for some rather truncated and disappointing sex.

"Not joining in the revels, I see." Myrddin was standing in the doorway to my chamber.

"No."

"What's that?" he nodded toward the glinting strands I clasped in both hands.

"A torque. It was hers."

"Boudicca's?"

I nodded.

Myrddin took it from me and held it up to my neck. "It is a cumbersome piece. Too bulky for such a delicate neck."

"I don't intend to wear it."

"Then why take it?"

A long silence stretched out. Myrddin waited patiently for me to fill it. I shrugged, "I just wanted it, that's all."

His brow furrowed. "You mean like a keepsake … something to remember her by?"

"What's happening to me?" I whispered and proceeded to tell him about everything that had happened that day. I told him about reliving Boudicca's memories and experiencing Cigmarw's death as though it were my own. Throughout my soliloquy Myrddin, thoughtful and silent, sat on a low bench and listened.

"So," I concluded, "what does it all mean?"

He shook his head and scratched his long beard. "I don't know, Caja. I honestly don't know."

Days passed – I don't know how many – and I never strayed from the isolation of Annwyn. I did not want to overhear people's conversations or set eyes upon men; to do so would risk another connection, another insight into their lives, their pain, their deaths. Since I could not become physically ill, I reasoned that I must be insane. Therefore I retreated to my bedchamber and lay staring at the ceiling, trying not to contemplate the prospect of an eternity of madness.

Finally, there was a knock on the door. Myrddin entered without waiting for an invitation and sat beside me. "You look terrible."

"Flattery will get you nowhere."

"How are you, Caja?"

I took a while to answer that. Lying there, day after day, in the dim light of my room, my mind had grown slow and muzzy. "Um, what's-his-name…"

"Who?"

"…Aristotle … he once said that melancholia plagued men who were really, really smart. It was the price they paid for all that insight and intelligence." I balled my hands into fists and rubbed my eyes. "So … good news! Apparently I'm a fucking genius."

"You have spent entirely too much time in this room. Come on." He extended a hand to me.

I did not move. "I don't wanna go outside."

"Do you want help with your problem or not?"

I nodded.

"Then come on."

I followed Myrddin through a maze of tunnels. It seems my mind was not the only thing that had become slow. My limbs lacked strength and felt cumbersome and heavy. I was vaguely dizzy. Finally we emerged out onto the moor. It was a clear, warm night and Myrddin paused and looked intently at the sky.

"See that?" He pointed upward at the stars.

"Which one?"

"The brightest one, there in the west."

"I see it."

"The ancient Greeks named that Hesperus, the evening star. By sunrise it will have moved to the east. For centuries man thought that the light in the east was different from the light in the west; and then about five hundred years ago Pythagoras realised that they are one and the same: the planet Venus."

I sighed dramatically. "That is all very interesting Myrddin, but I don't see how it applies to my problem."

"The question is: Why do I know that? Or, more to the point, why did I bother to learn it? It's because I love this." He gestured grandly at the sky. "I love the planets and the stars and the signs and portents that are there just waiting to be deciphered."

"And?"

"What about your mother? She spends every day gazing into the water to catch a glimpse of the future."

I looked at him blankly.

"Bucca looked to fire for the same thing, while Elowen tends her trees."

"Myrddin," I was becoming exasperated. "Just standing here talking to you is an effort. Will you get to the point?"

The old medhek continued. "I'm talking about the four elements, child. Bucca harkened to fire, your mother to water, Elowen's interests are rooted in the earth and I am obsessed with the sky, with…"

"…air."

He nodded, smiling at me. "We have all chosen our paths, or perhaps our paths have chosen us, but one way or another we have evolved into *elementals*."

"So?"

"So what is your element?"

I considered this and my stomach lurched. "I don't have one."

## A Side Note

*The notion of four "roots" from which all things grow was first proposed in the 5th century B.C. by the Greek philosopher Empedocles. Not only did he classify the four as earth, air, fire and water, but he identified each with a deity – Hades, Hera, Zeus, and Nestis. Later, in 48 B.C., Plato renamed these roots, calling them "elements."*[123] *The four classical elements were believed to be "the fundamental components of all things."*[124]

*Mankind's understanding of the elements slowly grew and expanded into the Periodic Table known to modern science. However, the original link between the roots and individual deities lingered on in Western thought for centuries. Hence, the concept of elementals evolved. Elementals are defined as "spirits of the individual elements"*[125] *and within folklore there are many different types.*

*Earth elementals range from Dryads and other wood nymphs to those beings that live and work underground like Knockers and dwarves. Brownies, who live in fireplaces and help with chores, are benevolent fire spirits. Conversely, Will-o'-the-Wisps use their flames to entice night-time travellers away from the road and into treacherous swamps. Nereids are nymphs of the salt sea, while Naiads are spirits of rivers and streams. And the air, too, hosts its own elementals in the form of sylphs, winged creatures who nest in the high mountains and combine to brew storms.*

"So now I'm a freak?" I asked.

"No," Myrddin shook his head. "You are different – but perhaps not as different as you appear. Aristotle suggested that there was a fifth element which he called quintessence."

"Which is?"

"Spirit."

"So with Boudicca and Cigmarw…"

"You caught a glimpse of their hearts, minds … souls. Has it happened to you before?"

I nodded mutely. I had seen my mother's lie when she instigated the feud with Lludd. That was an obvious example. But there had been others. I knew of Ciarán's grieving by the fireside and how lost Myrddin felt when Nimue strayed. But how? They had never spoken of those things. I knew of Xiàngshù's loneliness and of the mother wolf's unease because her son was so white, so different. All of these things – and so much more – had come to me naturally. It had never occurred to me that it was odd to know them, and so I accepted them as self-evident facts, as obvious as blue sky and yellow sun.

Myrddin placed a hand on my shoulder. "When I was young and received the calling to be shaman, I found it difficult to talk about all I'd seen in my visions. I thought I must be mad. But it isn't madness, child. It's a gift."

"It doesn't feel like a gift."

"Perhaps it will when you have gained mastery over it."

"And how do I do that?"

He shrugged. "Practise."

Since that conversation with Myrddin, I have wondered, through all the centuries of my life, why I was different. I do have one theory. When the Coranieid killed and fed on the knucker, I was an infant, the only baby under one year of age in the tribe. Something in that dragon flesh was potent enough to change us dramatically; and I received it through mother's milk. The first year of life, so modern science tells us, is marked by a continuation of foetal brain growth. The infant brain will, in that time, produce billions of cells and forge innumerable connections between those cells. With so much growth and development taking place over such a short period of time, babies are "enthusiastic learners and their brains are maximally malleable in the first year."[126] Into this lightning storm of synaptical firing comes a bit of magic, a bit of the uncanny; and the product was ... what? A gift, Myrddin said. Yet in those early days in the greenwood it was more like torment.

"I hate this," I muttered rubbing my temples. My head throbbed in time with my heartbeat, and was painful enough to make me feel sick.

Cathno looked at me expectantly and I tossed him another scrap of meat. The wolf caught it in mid-air and swallowed it down.

"You'd probably enjoy that more if you chewed it a bit first."

Cathno, who had been orphaned as a cub and raised by Myrddin as a pet, ignored this advice and sat down in front of me awaiting his next treat.

Over the course of three centuries, Myrddin had set me a series of tasks to help me explore the nature of this "fifth element." First it was reading spiders and insects, then fish and frogs, then birds, and now Cathno. The mind of each new creature was initially like a darkened cave that I must grope through until I could again perceive that flash of light that is quintessence, the soul.

Thus far I had made one great discovery: we are one. The substance of the brain, what scientists would later call neural tissue, is the same in the spider as it is in the bird. It is the same in the wolf as it is in me. Steven Pinker, in his book *How the Mind Works*, put it this way:

> There are birds that migrate by the stars, bats that echolocate...spiders that spin webs, humans that speak ... There are millions of animal species on earth, each with a different set of cognitive programs. *The same basic neural tissue embodies all of these programs....* [but] even if all neural activity is the expression of a uniform process at the cellular level, it is the arrangement of neurons – into bird song templates or web-spinning programs that matter.[127]

The building blocks are the same, but there are an infinite number of ways to stack them to create different structures.

Take Cathno. I looked intently at the wolf for a moment. He was a beautiful animal, deep grey with a shock of white fur extending inward from his jowls, and downward from his eyes. A quirky patch of brown fur along the bridge of his snout made him look like he'd just had his nose down a rabbit hole. And his eyes, contemplative and intelligent, were deep set and dramatically outlined in black. I looked deeper into those eyes and began to discern the mind of the animal. He had mechanisms (later called neurons) to perceive sounds, sights, smells and tastes – just like me. He had neurons responsible for propulsion, for walking and running – just like me. I detected all the automatic functions of respiration and metabolism, a low background hum beneath the louder workings of the forebrain: the part of the mind that thinks, that receives information from the environment, makes decisions based on that data and causes the body to act – again, just like me. But Cathno did not see the world as I did.

I sat in the greenwood – a green and brown backdrop for my forays into the mind of the wolf. Cathno, however, sat in a very specific location, frequented by a variety of animals. His nose could tell him what individual animals had passed this way, when they were here, what they had been eating, the general health of each creature and whether they claimed this patch of earth as their own territory or whether they were just meandering through. The leaves rustled overhead and he homed in on the sound. His nose told him "squirrel" – an electrical pulse of information that travelled from his olfactory neurons via the telegraph wires of axons into the synaptical receptors of the neurons that dictated motor function. Cathno tensed and watched the squirrel make its leap from one branch to another. Squirrels were fun to chase and good to eat, and the wolf waited to see if it would mistime its jump and fall within range. It did not. The ramped-up hum of Cathno's motor neurons fell silent; the wolf relaxed and turned its full attention back to me, or more specifically, to the scrap of meat I held. I tossed it to him and held my hands up to signify "All gone." The wolf began to wander around, listening and sniffing, the world an overwhelming tapestry of details too numerous for a human mind to process. It made my head throb harder and I broke contact.

"That is the difference between us," I murmured. "I see the forest, you see the trees – every single damn one of them."

Interestingly, for all of the innumerable details available to the wolf, his value system was refreshingly simple. Out of curiosity I looked at myself through his eyes. I smelled of Annwyn, of torch smoke and earth. Myrddin, his beloved friend, smelled of these things too. However Myrddin smelled older than this one, and … easier. The old man was easy in his mind, relaxed. There was no pheromone stink of anxiety or stress. But this one was not so comfortable in her own skin. Still there was the meat. The raw red meat. And that was a very good smell that still clung to her fingertips. This one brought meat and scratched his belly and never threatened harm and so, Cathno decided, of all the two-leggeds, this was a friend; she was good. That was his pronouncement on the matter and it could never be followed by a "but". I could say, "I love my father, BUT he has hardened in ways that frighten me." For Cathno there was only "I love..." No "but." No "if." No "except." As Temple Grandin would later observe, "humans have mixed emotions. A human can love and hate the same person. Animals don't do that. Their emotions are simpler and cleaner, because categories like love and hate stay separate in their brains."[128]

I got to my feet and whistled for Cathno. On my way back to Annwyn, unsure of what mood my father was in today, I could see the benefits of traversing the simpler emotional landscape of the wolf as opposed the muddle and murk of life with Gwyn ap Nudd.

Cathno sneezed. The human female was anxious again, unsettled. Nonetheless, he fell into step with her and strode toward Annwyn.

"I see blood and hear the endless clash of swords. They'll be like wolves fighting over a piece of meat – each with their teeth sunk into the flesh, tugging at it, ripping it," Myrddin paused and looked solemnly at Gwyn. "They'll tear the island apart around us."

"Uh, what did I miss?" I asked as Cathno went to Myrddin, tail wagging.

"Signs and portents. Apparently there's lots of doom and gloom written in the stars," Gwyn said dryly.

Mora's voice was sharp. "Do you doubt portents?"

Realising that he was dangerously close to another confrontation with the wife, Gwyn back-pedalled. "Of course not, it's just…" He looked at me for help in finishing his sentence.

I took a stab at it: "…a lot to take in?"

"Yes!" Gwyn pounced on the phrase. "It is so very much to take in."

Myrddin's prophecy is recorded in Geoffrey of Monmouth's *Vita Merlini*:

…wandering … he would look at the stars while he prophesied things … he knew were going to come to pass… 'Long discord shall hold the Scots … Wales shall rejoice in the shedding of blood… The city of Dumbarton shall be destroyed… Segontium and its towers and mighty palaces shall lament in ruin… Saxon kings shall expel the citizens and shall hold cities, country, and houses for a long time… Two hundred monks shall perish in Leicester and the Saxon shall drive out her ruler and leave vacant her walls … the Angles shall wear the diadem of

Brutus... The Danes shall come upon [us] with their fleet and after subduing the people shall reign.'[129]

"I just don't see it," Gwyn insisted. "This island has belonged to Rome now for 350 years. That's 350 years of stability, my friend. They simply would not allow the... the..."

"Orgy of violence?" Owain chimed in.

"Yes," he nodded. "The orgy of violence that you describe. I mean, according to your vision, this place is going to turn into a bloody free-for-all."

"Precisely," Myrddin nodded.

Cathno, disappointed that Myrddin had not welcomed him, nudged his master's hand impatiently; he wanted a petting.

Gwyn sat back in his chair. "And what exactly do you want me to do about it?"

"Nothing, my king, other than to be warned." The old shaman turned to the assembled company. "There are dangerous times ahead."

Tamara snorted and, grinning at Barinthus, crossed her eyes.

Myrddin was clearly irritated but said nothing more. He turned on his heel and strode from the Great Hall. I caught up with him outside his bedchamber.

"Myrddin, wait..."

He spun around to face me. "I saw it all last night. It's coming, Caja, and when it does the Coranieid will not go unscathed."

That pronouncement brought me up short. I had trouble articulating the question: "Who do we lose?"

"I don't know," he shook his head sadly. "But before all is said and done, you'll have three new soul stones to keep."

I gaped at him as he stepped into his room and quietly shut the door. Cathno, who'd followed Myrddin inside, sneezed. The scent of anxiety was strong on the old man. It smelled sweetly metallic, like a gathering storm.

Aesop, in his fable "The Lion, the Bear and the Fox", recounts a terrible battle between a lion and a bear who both seized a young goat at the same moment. According to the old sage, the fight was brutal and both combatants were quickly bloodied and exhausted. Each collapsed. At that moment a fox, who had been lurking nearby, dashed in and seized the goat. Unable to prevent this, the lion said to the bear: "Here we've been mauling each other all this while, and no one the better for it except the Fox!"[130]

The collapse of the Roman Empire, circa A.D. 410, saw Roman power in Enys Breten ebb away like a withdrawing tide. When the tide next came in, it brought enemies surging in from every side, fighting over Britain like the goat's kid in Aesop's story. From north of the Forth and Clyde Rivers came the Picts or "painted ones" – Celtae warriors who had not been Romanised. From the west came the Irish to plunder and seize territory; and marauding pirates from the continent harried the Eastern shores. Into this fray of ravening bears stepped a lion, Constantine, brother of the Breton King Aldroenus. With an army two thousand strong, he quickly restored order and the grateful Britons handed him the crown. He reigned in peace for over a decade and, with three strong male heirs – Constans who joined a monastery, Aurelius Ambrosius and Uther – the royal line seemed secure.

Then into the court of Constantine, a fox came creeping. His given name was Gwrtheyrn and fortune seemed to smile upon him. He was well connected and therefore made an advantageous marriage to Severa, whose grandfather Octavius was lord of the prosperous Gewissei clan. And then, as if ordained by the gods, the obstacles between him and political power began to fall. Old Octavius died, followed by his son Magnus in A.D. 388. Severa's brothers Ennodius and Victor also perished, leaving Gwrtheyrn the only surviving male heir to the title "Vortigern," Overlord of the Gewissei.

The old English word gewisse meant "reliable" and this is precisely the image that Vortigern Gwrtheyrn projected at court. He proved himself a staunch ally to the king by making his men-at-arms available for Constantine's use and providing monetary support for the crown. Because of this he was trusted, and Constantine counted him among his friends.

Then one day Óengus, a Pict informer in Constantine's employ, requested a private audience with the king. A short time later, Aurelius Ambrosius found his father lying in a spreading pool of his own blood. Constantine had been stabbed again and again – in the chest, in the stomach, in the arms he had flung forward to ward off the blows. The child followed the gaze of his father's dead eyes off to the left, but there was nothing there now. Then it hit him – the coppery smell of blood and something else, a rank odour from Constantine's perforated bowel set the child to heaving. Gagging dissolved into sobbing and sobs crescendoed into screams.

Roused by the boy's cries, Vortigern appeared and clasped Aurelius to his chest. It was this meeting of son and friend in common grief that first caught my attention. Something was amiss. The child was easy enough to read: his grief and horror broke over him in cold waves that wracked his small body as he wept. He cried so hard it felt like a hand gripped him by the throat, choking him. He could not catch his breath, and for one terrifying moment he thought he was suffocating. Finally his muscles relaxed enough to draw air. As he sank to his knees gasping, there was no real conscious thought, only the lightning storm of fear and pain and revulsion that thundered and flashed through his brain.

I did not expect Vortigern to reach that level of incapacity, but I did expect horror, grief, anger, *something* as he stood over the body of his friend and king. Instead the canvas of his emotions was blank. He comforted and soothed the child, but the words did not correspond to any feeling. I was taken aback. I knew who Constantine was, but he was not my kin or king. He was not my friend. And yet I was repulsed by the mutilation. Even I was moved by the child's distress.

"Why so cold, Gwrtheyrn?" I murmured, as I watched him scoop the child up and carry him to his nurse. And I resolved to follow this man until I could explain the empty place where his heart should be.

It did not take long for the bickering over succession to begin. Vortigern swiftly put an end to it when he hastened to fetch Constantine's first-born, Constans, from his monastery. Steady, reliable Vortigern secured Constans on the throne as the king's rightful heir and stayed on to advise the inexperienced, young monk in the ways of politics and governance. In short, Vortigern Gwrtheyrn did everything right.

"I learned nothing in the monastery to prepare me for this…" Constans sat in his private chamber with his head in his hands. His father's crown rested on the table beside him.

Vortigern had drawn a chair up close and now spoke softly to the new king. "I disagree, sire. We need a righteous man on the throne."

Constans smiled tiredly, "It will take more than good intentions to be king. You need wisdom … experience."

"'Where there is no guidance, a people falls, but in an abundance of counsellors there is safety.'"

"Proverbs, chapter eleven, verse fourteen," the king nodded. "You know your Bible well."

Constans studied Vortigern for a long moment. The man had been his father's faithful supporter. Upon Constantine's death, Gwrtheyrn acted swiftly to ensure Constans' right of succession and then graciously offered his services as advisor. And he had asked for nothing in return. The new king's heart swelled with affection.

"All right," he said at last. "What would you advise?"

A small smile twitched at the corners of Vortigern's mouth. "First we make you safe."

"The assassin has been killed…"

"…yes, but someone close to your father arranged that private interview, effectively giving Óengus the opportunity to strike."

"Who?"

"I don't know," Vortigern shook his head. "But how many people started jostling for power the moment your father hit the ground?"

Constans was silent for a long time while he absorbed that fact. "It could have been any one of them."

"Yes."

"So…"

"…so," Vortigern continued, "you appoint your own advisors to all key positions."

The new king sighed heavily and ran a hand through his thick mane of hair. "I wouldn't know who to appoint."

"I know, which is why I've taken the liberty of compiling a list of names for your perusal." Gwrtheyrn handed him a small piece of parchment.

Studying the inscribed names Constans asked, "And you trust these men?"

"Implicitly – I count each one a friend."

"And you choose your friends wisely?"

"My king, your father was my friend." A look of deep pain crossed Vortigern's face. He took a deep, steadying breath.

Constans rested a hand on Vortigern's shoulder. "You grieve for him too."

Gwrtheyrn could only nod.

Constans made his decision. "Fine. Summon them here." He handed the parchment back.

Now, with his composure intact, Vortigern said, "That is step one: surrounding you with advisors you can trust."

"And step two is…"

"… I want to install a stronger contingent here at the castle to act as your personal guard." He paused. "We'd be foolish not to learn from recent events."

"Your men-at-arms?"

"My men have homes and families and farms to see to. I was thinking of professional soldiers who will have one job only."

"Who did you have in mind?"

"Talorgan's men."

Constans shook his head. "Isn't he a Pict?"

Vortigern nodded. "Your father's war with the Picts was not a straightforward affair. It was not merely us against them. The Picts themselves are fractured into clans that fight each other. Some of those clans opposed Constantine. Some came to his aid."

"And this Talorgan?"

"Was a staunch ally and was richly rewarded for his efforts."

"And so..."

"... he responds well to a generous patron. With his group here, no one could touch you."

"All right," Constans rose. "Pay them whatever they ask. Just get them here."

Vortigern was taken aback. "You would allow me access to the treasury, my lord?"

"Yes, my friend. You are my right arm in this."

With new advisors installed and Talorgan and his men on guard, Constans settled into life at court. It was a difficult transition. The young king may have physically left his monastery, but his heart had not. Even without eight rings of the church bell, he was up at midnight to begin his day with the Matins service. But there was no one at the castle to chant the psalms with him. His studies and prayers were constantly interrupted with every single trivial matter of state. He could not even enjoy his meals in peace. Back home, for that is how he referred to his monastery, the monks would sing grace and then lapse into thoughtful silence while they ate and listened as one of the brethren read from the Bible. Here dinner was held in the great hall and accompanied by endless, mindless chattering and raucous laughter. Used to a life of quiet contemplation, he was now perpetually surrounded by people with the ironic result that Constans had never felt so alone.

Vortigern, God bless him, devised a solution. One day he arrived with three monks in tow.

"Who is this?" Constans rose from his throne, smiling.

"I spoke to the Prior of the local abbey, sire. He concedes that the transition from monastic life to the life of a king must be a difficult one. And so he recommended that for a while you walk with one foot in each world. These," Gwrtheyrn gestured to the monks, "will live with you as spiritual brothers. When you are not engaged in affairs of state, you can resume the pattern of life you followed at the monastery. He prays that this may help you remember God in all of your decisions as king."

"That is a wonderful idea." Constans' eyes were shining. He embraced Vortigern warmly.

"I thought it right, sire, to thank the prior for his help with a donation to the abbey."

"Of course, of course…" the king's attention was now upon the three monks. "Whatever you feel is appropriate," he cast over his shoulder as he went to clasp each of his new brothers by the hand.

Vortigern was well pleased with his plan, and left the king's chamber smiling.

"We're not going to live like monks, you know."

"Talorgan, hello! What makes you think you've got to live like a monk?"

"That." The Pict gestured to the closed door of the king's chamber.

"That," Vortigern said, nodding in the same direction, "is what Constans needs. I think I understand what you need."

"Really," Talorgan cocked an eyebrow.

"Constans will retire after his nine o'clock Compline service. I'd like you and your men to meet me in the Great Hall then."

When the band of assembled Pict guardsmen entered the Great Hall that night, the room was aglow with candlelight and a great fire roared in the hearth. The tables groaned under the weight of silver platters heaped with mutton, pork, beef and fish. There was chicken, duck, capon and eels. Fruit from the orchards tumbled from immense silver bowls and there was fresh bread by the plateful. Pitchers of wine, mead and ale were so plentifully distributed along the tables that a man could not reach for meat for fear of tipping one over.

The food, it seems, was not the only thing on the menu. Women, large of breast and slim of waist, flitted from man to man filling up empty tankards. They'd lean provocatively over the tables, displaying a wealth of cleavage, to pass plates of delicacies.

As hours passed and his men were made content by food and jolly by alcohol, Talorgan leaned close to Vortigern so that his words could be heard over the din. "So Constans is all right, after all."

"What do you mean?" Vortigern slurred back.

"All this," the Pict swept an arm to indicate the fine room and all of its abundance.

Gwrtheyrn laughed. "You think that Saint Constans arranged for a night of gluttony and whoring?"

"Then…" Talorgan paused. "This is all you?"

"Of course."

"Then you have my thanks."

"What's in the blood will out, my friend. Constans needs his prayers and books. You and I need some of this!" he made a playful grab for the nearest female. She giggled and came to him. He pushed his high-backed chair, Constans' chair, back from the table so she could sit on his lap.

Talorgan's brother Giric was already four sheets to the wind and rose to dance to music that only he could hear. He began to sing…

"My Mistress is a mine of gold, would that it were her pleasure
To let me dig within her mould and roll among her treasure."

He seized a buxom lass and danced with her as the men clapped out the beat.

"As under the moss the mould doth lye, and under the mould is mony
So under her waste her belly is placed, and under that her cuny."[131]

On the last word, the girl grabbed a great handful of her skirts and pulled them high to give the fellows a little taste. This was met with raucous laughter and thundering applause.

"I've got one!" Vortigern shouted once the furore had died down.

The assembled company hushed and looked at him expectantly.

He stood and with an air of utmost seriousness, Gwrtheyrn began to sing…

"Oh say, gentle maiden, may I be your lover
Condemn me no longer to moan and to weep
Struck down like a hawk, I lie wounded and bleeding…"

The Picts stared back at him in surprise. They had not known he possessed such a sweet singing voice. But then a wickedly lascivious grin crossed his face as he finished the stanza:

"Oh let down your drawbridge, I'll enter your keep!"[132]

This was met with a howl of laughter and Talorgan clapped him roughly on the back. Vortigern swept the girl at his side up into his arms and carried her off. At the other end of the castle, the distant noise filtered into Constans' dreams and he shifted uneasily in his sleep.

These parties became a regular fixture at the castle, laid on by Vortigern whenever he was at court. Before long, Talorgan and his friends began to praise the man for his generosity, his largesse. He was a kindred spirit, they felt, and wise too. It was no secret around the palace that Gwrtheyrn was the brains behind the throne.

One night in the midst of their revels, Vortigern made an announcement. A hush fell over the room.

"My dear friends – how I have enjoyed these hours spent with you…"

Talorgan, although his mind was already fogged with ale, picked up on Vortigern's tone. "There will many more," he said. He had meant it as a statement, but it sounded more like a question.

Gwrtheyrn shook his head. "Alas no, brother. I don't have the funds to continue this indefinitely."

"But…" Giric began.

Vortigern cut him off. "It is not through lack of desire. If I could … if I were as rich as the king … we would do this every night of our lives."

The men's high spirits were dampened considerably by this news. Even the local whores, who realised they'd just lost a steady gig, looked sullen.

Vortigern shrugged. "I guess we better make the most of tonight." And with that the hall erupted into a frenzy of merry-making made all the sweeter by the knowledge that time ran short.

As the weeks passed, a sombre mood fell over the Pictish guard. All of those feasts, all of the free alcohol and women had raised their expectations. Instead of viewing those riotous evenings as a treat, they had come to see them as proper payment for services rendered. And now they felt cheated.

"It is not Vortigern's fault," Talorgan commented. "He would continue if he could."

"Perhaps Constans…" Giric began and stopped because the suggestion was ridiculous. "Never mind."

Talorgan was quiet for a long while. "'If I were as rich as the king…'" he murmured.

"What?" Giric asked.

"Gwrtheyrn said: 'If I were as rich as the king, we would do this every night of our lives.'"

"Yeah, well, he's not the king."

"No," Uuredach chimed in. "But he should be."

The group was inching out onto thin ice and they knew it. They sat silently for a moment.

"He does all the king's work anyway," Talorgan stated and then nothing more was said.

But that comment of Vortigern's ("If I were as rich as the king, we would do this every night") tugged at them. I could see the brilliance of it: spoil them, get them used to a fine life and then withdraw it. And then throw out that one little phrase to imply that yes, you can have it all again if…

It was deviously subtle, a little twitch of the puppet strings.

That night Constans was hacked to death in his bed.

Upon hearing the news, the guardians of Aurelius and Uther fled with their charges across the channel to Brittany. Clearly they were no longer safe in England. And with all legitimate heirs to Constantine's throne out of the way, Vortigern stood poised to seize the crown.

There was one final loose thread to snip from the fabric. Gwrtheyrn could not risk being implicated in Constans' murder. And so he grieved and wailed over the death of the young king and swore vengeance upon his assassins. Talorgan, Giric and Uuredach were arrested and found payment for their services at the end of a hangman's rope.

As the crown, the diadem of Brutus, was placed upon Gwrtheyrn's head, I reflected on how many people would have had to die for this man to achieve ultimate power. Octavius, Magnus, Ennodius and Victor – his kinsmen by Severa – all perished before he could become Vortigern, overlord of the Gewissei. How had they died? I hadn't been paying attention then. Although mortality rates were high, wasn't that just a little too convenient?

Someone close to Constantine, had arranged that private interview with Óengus. Who? And why was Óengus dispatched before he could be questioned? Again, why did I not listen? Then there was Constans; his government was an extended exercise in puppetry, with Vortigern pulling the strings. And then, of course, we come to Talorgan, Giric and Uuredach – so easily manipulated, so easily disposed of.

Long ago, my mother uttered a prophecy about Derdriu and her words came back to me because they seemed to fit:

> "Much damage ... will follow...
> through your fault ...
> Harsh, hideous deeds done ...
> And little graves everywhere".[133]

For centuries a fundamental dichotomy was thought to exist within the human mind: the passions versus logic, desires versus reason, and Virginia Woolf's "red light of emotion" versus "the white light of truth."[134] This paradigm was eventually extended to include immorality versus righteousness. During the Enlightenment, many scholars believed that moral action depended upon the suppression of the emotions. Immanuel Kant, for instance, believed that "morality requires us to separate our rationality from our nature and act solely on the basis of logical principles."[135] The Church concurred, saying in the Book of Isaiah:

> "Come now, let us reason together, says the LORD:
> though your sins are like scarlet,
> they shall be as white as snow;
> though they are red like crimson,
> they shall become as wool."[136]

How are the sins of man purified? Through reason ... Come now, let us reason together. Anger and lust are emotions of heat, of red bloodshed and scarlet desire, while reason, hallowed reason, is a cool, white, illuminating light.

And yet ... when I looked into the mind of Vortigern – a psychopathic mind that had devised the deaths of ten people – I saw *only* reason. The mass just behind his forehead (later identified as the frontal lobes) buzzed with incessant activity. This is the region of the brain that is responsible for planning and thought. It speaks the language of rationales and logistics. It is the seat of hallowed reason. And Gwrtheyrn's capacity for logic was impressive. He was an extremely intelligent man. So if Goya is correct in saying that the "sleep of reason breeds monsters," then why was Vortigern not a paragon of virtue?

I delved deeper and noticed an anomaly. While his brain was lit up with a veritable firework display of electrical activity, two almond-shaped masses were conspicuously dim. These were the amygdalae which "colour our experiences with emotions… [sending] signals to virtually every other part of the brain, including the decision-making circuitry of the frontal lobes."[137] This was the source of the cold detachment I sensed as Vortigern stood over Constantine's body, comforting the murdered king's son. And yet I could not grasp how a lack of emotion could make him so brutal.

I had seen hideous deeds done in anger and fear. I remembered Tamara assuaging her jealousy of Derdriu by picking belladonna to poison her and her unborn child. I remembered the look of satisfaction upon my father's face as he dipped his cap in the blood of his victims during our first Wild Hunt. I remembered the snowy coat of the wolf, Gwynhelek, stained red after Gwyn beat him to death in vengeance. All of these acts had been committed in a red haze of emotion.

Constantine was murdered in the white light of reason. And yet it was a wrongful death. How had I known that? How had I, who had witnessed death after death until it seemed almost meaningless, known that killing Constantine was an evil act? I cast my mind back, trying to recapture the moment: the coppery smell of blood, the tang of dung from the king's serrated bowel, the tempestuous sobbing of the child. I could see it. Standing there the first thing that occurred to me was not a thought, but a feeling, nauseous and cold. Before I knew it was wrong, I felt it was wrong. Then my brain, my logical frontal lobes, began to enumerate the reasons why it was wrong: Constantine was not only the rightful king, but a good one who had brought peace to chaos; he had a young family; he was betrayed by those he trusted; I liked him. All of these reasons were perfectly valid, but none seemed as strong as that initial flood of revulsion.

So is it emotion that keeps us honest? In their article on psychopathy, Derek Mitchell and James Blair note that psychopathic behaviour results from a lack of emotion, particularly empathy. They argue that:

> ...most social animals terminate their aggressive attacks when a member of the same species displays a submissive posture or cue. I suggest that sad, and perhaps fearful, expressions may serve a similar purpose in humans. Moreover, because they are emotionally unpleasant stimuli they act as punishments, thereby making the actions that caused them ... less likely in the future.[138]

Within the animal kingdom, submission is a primal cue that prompts an aggressor to call off the attack. Within the human world, fear and pain are primal cues that play on our empathy and initiate feelings of guilt. These "gut feelings" limit our aggressive behaviour and hence form the foundation for our moral decisions. The psychopathic mind, which for a variety of reasons cannot generate feelings of empathy, lacks the emotional filter that directs its decisions toward a moral end. Which part of the brain generates these emotions? The amygdalae – the part of Vortigern's mind that lay in darkness.

A crucial part of him was broken. He could not feel fear and hence, could not feel pity for the fear of others, nor could he look upon pain as anything but a by-product of the actions needed to achieve his goal. G.K. Chesterton had it right when he wrote: "A madman is not someone who has lost his reason, but someone who has lost everything but his reason." This raised an uncomfortable question regarding the ten people Vortigern had sent to early, unquiet graves: if he was broken, if his mind was incapable of pity or remorse, if he physically did not possess the ability to feel and hence make moral judgements based on those feelings, then was he truly responsible for his actions? Was he fashioned that way by nature or the Catholic Church's God? If so, why?

Such very big questions. Ironically, I was able to glean answers to them from a very small child. Huctia was a beautiful girl who lived with her family in a nearby village. The child had dark curly hair, striking blue eyes and strong pudgy legs. One day while playing, she tripped over an exposed tree root and went sprawling along the ground. Little stones tore at the flesh on her right knee and her hands, flung forward to break her fall, were raw and bloody. Dirt had been ground into her wounds. A squeal, first of shock then of pain, brought her father hence and he scooped the child up in his arms and kissed her.

Her amygdalae were on fire from the pain, but when she was gathered into her father's arms, I noticed a bright flash – a neural connection was being reinforced: I like comfort when I'm hurt; comfort the hurt. Her mother was with her a moment later, wiping her tears and speaking in soothing tones … more connections firing and reinforcing the knowledge of comfort, sympathy, kindness. The wonderful Jonah Lehrer would later pinpoint the nature of this process:

> The capacity for making moral decisions … requires the right kind of experience in order to develop… a potent set of sympathetic instincts… However, if something goes amiss during the developmental process – the circuits that underlie moral decisions never mature – the effects can be profound…. The developing brain can be permanently damaged… [through] child abuse. When children are … unloved … their emotional brains are warped….the biological program that allows human beings to sympathise with the feelings of others is turned off. Cruelty makes us cruel.[139]

I looked with greater interest at Vortigern's past. Sifting through his memories I saw…
    …Gwrtheyrn as a boy with a skinned knee reaching out to Vitalis, his father. The old man barked at him to stop crying and gave him a hard scuff for his clumsiness.
    …Gwrtheyrn huddled in a corner, his father standing over him, reeking of ale, shouting, hitting, kicking.
    …Gwrtheyrn kicking one of his father's dogs in anger, breaking its ribs. Each yelp, each sickening snap of bone making him feel better, calmer, more at peace. The animal had had to be put down.
    Vortigern's emotional neurons which were never fired by kindness, sympathy or comfort, had become shrouded in an ever-thickening dark cloud. He was not born a monster. He was made one – his insanity foisted upon him by Vitalis who, most likely, had his own father Vitalinus to thank for the sad legacy. And this was the outcome; I looked upon the graves of the ten, the victims he could not love nor pity, just as he could not fear that his actions might have catastrophic consequences for himself … and for the nation.

Leaving a trail of bodies like so many stepping stones behind him was bound to make enemies – most notably Talorgan's men, who were furious at Vortigern's betrayal. They managed to stir up enough of the old enmities to plunge the Picts back into war with the Britons. Vortigern was unperturbed. Talorgan's men were tools, merely tools that he had required in order to complete a specific task. Now that the job was done, now that he was king, he could discard those tools or, if necessary, break them.

The Picts, however, had other ideas. In fact, they did "their utmost to take revenge upon Vortigern. As day followed day, the king was therefore much concerned to see the casualties of his army in battle."[140] This would not do. And Vortigern predictably shone the fierce spotlight of his reason upon the problem. When faced with military defeat, you need to strengthen your army. How? With more men. Alas, each defeat at the hands of the Picts whittled away at his forces. He needed fresh blood, new soldiers from... That was the rub. From where?

The answer presented itself in the form of three cyuls or long boats that landed in Kent in 449 A.D.

"Why have you come?" Vortigern surveyed the strangers, a little awestruck. They were mountains – huge men with fiery eyes and arms like oak branches.

Horsa, who led them with his brother Hengist, spoke: "Most noble king, we hail from Saxony." He paused as the Britons silently recoiled. The Saxons were reputed to be a savage race. Horsa smiled benignly at them, "We have outgrown our homeland, my lord. There is no land, no work for us there. And so we come here to seek a living."

"How so?"

"My men are fine warriors. Surely we can be of some assistance?"

"You know of our problems with the Picts," Vortigern said blandly.

"We have heard," Hengist nodded.

Gwrtheyrn contemplated them for a moment. "Tell you what: tomorrow we take the fight to the Picts. Come along. If you prove your worth in battle, you'll be rewarded. If you don't..." Vortigern let the statement dangle there, unfinished.

Unphased, Horsa smiled. "It will be our pleasure."

In *The History of the Kings of Britain*, Geoffrey of Monmouth recounts the battle:

> the Picts... mustered a huge army to ravage the northern parts of the island... Vortigern called his men together and marched forth to meet

them... but little need had they of the country to do much of the fighting, for the Saxons did battle in such gallant fashion that the enemies... were put to flight, hot foot, without delay.[141]

Satisfied with the performance of the Saxons in the battle, Vortigern rewarded with them with land (Thanet) in which they might settle down. He even allowed Horsa to build a fortress there. These Saxons, Vortigern thought, who took their name from the Germanic word seax meaning "sword", would be his foederati – a concept employed by the Romans at the height of their power. Essentially, the foederati were mercenaries who were paid to fight for someone else's cause.

However, the wheels were not only turning in Vortigern's head, but in Horsa's as well. One day, he approached Gwrtheyrn solemnly.

"Why so sad, friend?" the king asked.

"I must take my leave of you, sire," Horsa replied.

The king was taken aback. "Why so?"

"He pines for his family," Hengist explained.

Vortigern burst out laughing. "Is that all? Bring them here!"

"You would allow this?" Hengist asked.

"Of course!"

"I don't know how to express my gratitude," Horsa paused and an idea seemed to come to him. "Actually I do. The Saxons here are of good warrior stock, but our numbers are limited."

"And?"

"Just think how much safer you would be with a Saxon army to command. No one could challenge you. Nothing could stop you."

Yes, Vortigern thought, an army of Saxons, each one a weapon I can deploy. Vortigern looked upon Horsa and his men the way a craftsmen admires a fine set of tools.

"Do it," he smiled. And with those two words he damned us all.

Welsh Triad 59 lists "Three Unfortunate Counsels of the Island of Britain." Number one was Afarwy's mistake in summoning Julius Caesar. Number two was "to allow Horsa and Hengist and Rhonwen (Renwein) into this Island."[142] When Vortigern allowed the two Saxon brothers to summon their kin hither, he essentially opened a sluice-gate through which more and more of their kind flooded.

In *De Excidio Brittaniae et Conquestu*, St. Gildas the Wise describes the event:

> ... wild Saxons, of accursed name, hated by God and men, admitted into the island, like wolves into folds [they] first fixed their dreadful talons in the eastern part of the island, as men intending to fight for the country, but more truly to assail it. To these the mother of the brood, finding that success had attended the first contingent, sends out also... accomplices and curs... to their bastard comrades. From that source... the root of bitterness grows as a poisonous plant.[143]

As a mighty oak grows from an acorn, great evil often springs from a humble source. Horsa and Hengist brought their families over as well as a company warriors "all for the king's use." Upon their arrival Hengist hosted a great banquet at the newly built Saxon fortress at Thanet. Vortigern arrived to find a bull chained to a heavy wooden stake outside the keep.

"Lay your bets!" A tall man, well over six feet, bellowed. A throng of people crowded round.

"What do they bet on?" the king asked Horsa.

"How many dogs that big bastard," he nodded at the bull, "can kill before the pack takes him down. Care to make a wager?"

"No thank you," Vortigern replied as he watched the revellers retreat to a safe distance. Then they released the dogs – vicious, slathering things that made straight for the bull. A yelp, a thud, and a cheer signalled the first kill as a well-timed kick of the bull's hind legs broke the cur's back and left it twitching upon the ground. A small twitch of a smile played over Vortigern's lips.

Another yelp, another whine – this time as a dog was gored by the bullock's great horns. Seizing their opportunity the rest of the pack moved in, attacking the bull's hind legs, trying to bring it down. The bloody spectacle elicited more cheers from the crowd as Vortigern and Horsa headed toward the great hall, or (as the Saxons called it) the Mead Hall.

The huge wooden structure sported a high, vaulted ceiling and on its walls hung ornate shields and many fine tapestries. The wooden tables groaned under the weight of the food heaped upon them: bread and honey, beef and salmon, cheese and butter and cask after cask of ale, all in great abundance. And while they ate, they were entertained by a minstrel whose bell-like voice was magnified by the acoustics of the room...

> "O where hae ye been, Lord Randal, my son?
> Where hae ye been, my handsome young man?"
> "I hae been to the wildwood; mother, make my bed soon,
> For I'm weary wi' hunting and fain wald lie down..."

She was tall and her fair hair hung down her back in a long plait. Her ankle-length, loose fitting dress did not mask the voluptuous curve of her breasts that fell away into the flat lands of her belly or the foothills of her hips. Gwrtheyrn watched her approach.

> "Where gat ye your dinner, Lord Randal, my son?
> Where gat ye your dinner, my handsome young man?"
> "I dined wi' my true love; mother make my bed soon,
> For I'm weary wi' hunting, and fain wald lie down..."

"Was hail!" she said as she handed him a large goblet of wine.

"Was...what?" Vortigern enquired.

The girl laughed. "I'm sorry. This place reminds me so much of home, I forget I'm in Britain. I said, 'Was hail' – it's a toast. You would say 'Drinc hail' in return."

"Then Drinc hail, pretty one!" Gwrtheyrn toasted her and drank deeply.

> "O I fear you are poisoned, Lord Randal, my son!
> O I fear you are poisoned, my handsome young man!"
> "Oh yes, I am poisoned; mother make my bed soon,
> For I'm sick at the heart, and I fain wald lie down."[144]

The girl flitted off and Vortigern's eyes followed her progress around the hall.

"I see you've met my daughter." Hengist had appeared at his shoulder.

Startled, Vortigern asked, "She's yours?"

Hengist nodded proudly.

"What's her name?"

"Renwein, my king."

He watched her. The girl moved with an easy, sensuous grace. Like a wolf. There was something wild, almost animalistic about the Saxons. He'd noticed it on the battlefield when they defeated the Picts and he noticed it now in the way she cocked her head to listen to the woman standing beside her. He noticed it in her impassive gaze as her grey eyes surveyed the occupants of the hall. He noticed it in the little lick of her lips as she seized a goblet of wine and drank.

Automatically, he compared her to Severa – the wife who'd given him a title and four sons and then died. Pale, insipid Severa with her flat chest and boyish figure. No curves. No meat on the bone. No fire. He cringed with distaste at the recollection of his late wife lying, cadaver-like, in their bed, eyes closed, teeth clamped shut as she endured him. It was hard to believe, really, that such tepid, nondescript sex could result in four strong boys. Renwein wouldn't be like that, he decided. That one would writhe and moan in ecstasy. She'd claw his back like a wild thing.

Vortigern remained at Thanet for another week and everyday he and Renwein would walk along a nearby stream. One day she slipped on a muddy patch and the king shot out a hand to catch her before she fell. The pouch that hung from her belt bounced against her thigh, its contents rattling.

"What do you keep in there?" he laughed, reluctant to release her.

Laughing, she wriggled from his grasp. "Runes."

"What?"

"They're…" she paused. "It's easier to show you, then to explain it. Come." She took his hand and led him back to the fortress.

Once seated in the now deserted Mead Hall, she upended the pouch, spilling a number of smooth green stones on the table. Each stone was flecked with dark red spots the colour of dried blood and each stone bore a strange symbol.

"And what is their purpose?"

"Each of the characters is a letter in the futhark … the runic alphabet. We use them to write messages or record events."

"I still don't understand the need for the stones, though."

"Each of the runes is also symbolic. You can ask a question and then pull runes from the pouch to receive an answer. It can even reveal the future."

Vortigern laughed.

"It is a very serious business," Renwein admonished him. She scooped the runes up and deposited them back in her bag.

Gwrtheyrn felt as if an invisible door was closing. That was not what he wanted. Oh, let down your drawbridge, I'll enter your keep, he thought.

He clasped her hands. "I'm sorry. I shouldn't laugh at things I don't understand." He paused. "Can you read my future in the runes?"

"I can try," she smiled. "Is there a specific question you wish to ask?"

"No, just what the future holds."

"All right."

Renwein closed her eyes and her features settled into a look of intense concentration. She pulled a tile from the pouch: an upside-down Uruz (∩) signifying weakness – you allow the wrong people to influence your decisions.

Next came an inverted Ehwaz (ꟽ). Combined with Uruz it predicts a change for the worse. You will be presented with an opportunity. Don't take it.

Gebo (X), a chance for love and marriage.

Inverted Laguz (⌐). Trouble rides on the skirts of a woman.

Reversed Wunjo (⌐). Treachery.[145]

Vortigern watched her in fascination. The smooth, olive skin of her face, her eyes, large and deep, her full, red mouth that frowned in concentration – everything about her was exotic and sensual.

"Well?" he asked.

She beamed at him. "It is an auspicious reading. Great opportunity awaits you with the aid of true friends. And this," she pushed the tile marked with an X forward with one long finger. "This suggests new love." She arched an eyebrow at him.

Gwrtheyrn had showed a great deal of restraint. Used to having what and who he wanted, when he wanted it, he had kept his desires in check for the sake of his alliance with Hengist.

But now, as she looked at him expectantly, the dam of his resolve broke. He seized her and kissed her hard on the mouth. She gripped him tightly as his hands roamed over her body, cupped a breast and tugged to lift the hem of her dress. As his fingers inched up her thigh, she caught his hand and held it firmly.

"Wait," she breathed.

"What?" his voice was hoarse and a battle royal waged inside him. He did not want to wait. He wanted to rend the wool from her body, to seize that long braid of hair and hold it like a leash as he dove into her. But as always, reason held sway. The alliance. Too important right now. Stop. He loosened his grip.

"Do you want me?" she whispered.

"Yes."

"I mean always. Every day and … night." She gently nibbled his ear.

He nodded mutely.

"Then speak to my father." She hastily gathered her runes from the table and was gone.

He did speak to Hengist, though not immediately. He was too worked up and would attend to that first. A random servant girl bore the brunt of his frustrated passion and then her thin, quivering frame was discarded, dropped unceremoniously on the floor like chicken bones after a feast.

Satisfied and with his brain now ready to negotiate a political marriage, Vortigern summoned Hengist. A short while later the deal was struck: Gwrtheyrn would have Renwein and in return Hengist was given all of Kent.

The first days of Gwrtheyrn's marriage to Renwein passed in a red haze of desire. And with his attention thus diverted, he did not see the scales of power begin to tip. More and more Saxons flooded in, and all of them expected the same deal given to Horsa and Hengist after they defeated the Picts – namely, they expected to be lavishly supplied with all needed provisions.

Vortigern sat on his throne and listened to the seemingly endless list of their demands. The Saxons had come in such great numbers to join "his" army, his foederati, that he now could not afford to pay them all.

"I'm sorry," he informed Horsa and Hengist. "What you ask … it's impossible."

"My people came here in good faith…" Hengist began.

Vortigern cut him off. "Don't you mean *our* people? We are family now, Hengist. Your daughter is my queen and *you*," he spat, "now have even greater reason to defend this realm."

The room went deadly silent.

Finally, Horsa said quietly, "Of course, highness. Forgive our impertinence." And with that they left.

St. Gildas, in his typically colourful way, describes the Saxon response:

Lamentable to behold, in the midst of the streets lay the tops of lofty towers, tumbled to the ground, stones of high walls, holy alters, fragments of human bodies, covered with livid clots of coagulated blood, looking as if they had been squeezed together in a press, and with no chance of being buried, save in the ruins of houses, or in the ravening bellies of wild beasts… Some … of the miserable remnant … were murdered in great numbers; others constrained by famine, came and yielded themselves to be slaves … some others passed beyond the seas with loud lamentations.[146]

For unleashing such destruction upon the land, Vortigern became known (in Welsh Triad 51) as the "Second Dishonoured Man in the Island of Britain."

"You are very quiet, my husband." Renwein rubbed Gwrtheyrn's shoulders.

"Don't feign ignorance," he said wearily. "Your father…"

"…my father is as trapped by circumstances as you."

Vortigern snorted.

"It's true!" she came around to face him and knelt in front of his chair. "He invited a select group from Saxony, never this many. And now he struggles to control them."

The king stared impassively down into her big, doe-like eyes and said nothing.

"But he *is* your friend," she said emphatically. "He wants to negotiate a new treaty…"

"I know."

"Isn't that proof?" She rose slightly and hugged him, frowning when he did not soften to her embrace.

"This is not like you," she murmured, hitching up her skirt to straddle him in his chair.

He did not want to respond to her. He had an inkling that she was the honey that had baited the trap he was in, but she was moving now, slowly against him. Involuntarily his body reacted. In another moment he was fumbling to free himself of his clothing, to seek again her warmth, to hear her moans rise until she called out his name as her back arched in climax. He couldn't stop himself.

Afterward, the pair lay naked in front of the fire.

"You really think I can broker a treaty with your people?" he asked.

"I know you can." She rose and sifted through her clothing that lay heaped on the floor. She returned carrying her leather pouch and snuggled down next to him.

"What are those for?" he nodded at the bag of runes.

"Tomorrow you and the British nobles will meet with the Saxon people. I wish to know the outcome, my love."

He sighed. "Oh what the hell … go on." He lay back and closed his eyes.

She drew a stone: inverted Raidho (ᚱ), a warning. *Now is not the time to enter into negotiations.*

*Because of …* Wunjo (ᚹ) *and* Algiz (ᛉ) [both upside-down] *deception and treachery.*

*Probable result …* reversed Othala (ᛟ) … *you will stand alone.*

"You will lay your troubles to rest," she lied. "These indicate shrewd dealings and success." She kissed him. "Rest, my husband, for tomorrow you will triumph."

She pulled a wolf-skin blanket, a wedding gift from her father, over them both and soon they slept.

The conference at Amesbury was a crowded affair, with three hundred British nobles and as many Saxons in attendance. Vortigern rose and the room fell silent.

"I come here today to broker a lasting peace between Britain and the people of Saxony and to avoid any future…," he smiled wryly, "…misunderstanding."

"Hear, hear!" Horsa interjected.

Vortigern continued. "Our initial agreement was never intended to include the services of so many Saxons. Indeed I never authorised a mass migration."

"And yet they are here," Hengist said quietly. His face was a blank mask and the king could not discern what thoughts lay behind those words.

"Yes, so we propose to handpick your finest soldiers to comprise our armies. These will receive payment as per our old agreement. We will also allocate farmland for the soldiers' families. The rest of you…," he paused, "…will return to Saxony."

A silence – complete, sepulchral – fell upon the hall. The king did not expect his opponents to agree to deportation. It was merely the opening salvo of the negotiation and now it was their turn….

"Do you have a counter-proposal?" he asked.

"Only this," Hengist plucked a dagger from his boot and drove it into the chest of the nearest Briton. The signal given, every Saxon present suddenly had a knife in his hand.

Vortigern, whose brain could not generate feelings of horror or sympathy, watched in fascination as arterial blood pumped steadily from the severed carotid of the man on his right. Another Briton, pinned to the floor under the weight of a huge Saxon, screamed as blow after blow of the knife struck him in the gut with a dull thud that sounded more like punches. Blood welled up from the cuts like water from a newly-dug well, and puddled on the floor around him. Like Constantine, the king thought. Another noble, a blade thrust up through his chin and into his hard palate, fell choking to the ground.

On and on it went. Finally the war cries ceased as did the victims' screams, and Vortigern alone stood facing a room of bloodied, murderous Saxons.

"I propose that we bring *more* of our people here and settle them on our new land." Hengist, still panting from the exertion of butchery, reopened the negotiations.

"New land?" Vortigern asked.

"Sussex and Essex."

The king did not reply.

"Gwrtheyrn, you can always join your friends…"

"Fine."

"See?" Hengist clapped him on the back with a gory hand. "I knew if we put our heads together we could come up with a new arrangement."

Ironic, Gwrtheyrn thought dispassionately, to have gained dominion over men, to have become king, and yet in doing so, to have made myself a prisoner.

"You heard?" Pascent asked.

Vortigern's four sons by the dead Severa met in secret.

The eldest, Vortimer, nodded. "He gave them Essex and Sussex."

"It doesn't stop there," Pascent sighed. "The Saxons have also occupied London, York, Lincoln and Winchester."

"Fuck."

"That's one way of putting it," Cattigern murmured.

Young Faustus spoke. "Father will muster an army, surely."

"Will he?" Vortimer snorted. "And if he did, who would rally round him at this point?"

Pascent looked at his older brother. "They might rally round you."

"What?"

"Vortimer, you have to try."

According to the history books Vortimer's forces did make some headway, and in one great push forced the Saxons back into Kent, killing Horsa in the process. He then rode to tell his father the good news, but not all of Vortigern's court rejoiced. As Renwein wept for her uncle, she was struck by an image of her father, prostrate with grief, chewing on the word revenge the way a man will bite on a leather strap to keep from screaming while his arm is amputated. His right arm. His brother.

She left the castle and quickly made for the nearby wood. Once there she began her search. She was sure she had seen it during one of her walks and there it was, low to the ground, the light purple flowers of the autumn crocus. What was its other name? Ah yes, "the naked lady." She chuckled to herself. Those can be very dangerous indeed.

That evening Vortigern and his son dined together privately, still deep in their plans of how to deal with the Saxons. Renwein herself brought their dinner.

"Here you go," she handed a plate heaped with food to her husband. "It's capon tonight ... nicely stuffed." She laid the final dish in front of Vortimer and left quietly.

The leaves of colchicum autumnale, or autumn crocus, are extremely poisonous, and once ingested quickly went to work on Vortimer's throat, stomach and bowels. Vortigern watched the poison progress through its full range of symptoms: the terrible thirst, the crippling stomach cramps, the vomiting and purging. His mind was ticking away. Of course, Vortimer had been poisoned. He was the only real challenge to Saxon dominion left. Which meant, of course, that the poison selected would be lethal. The aim was not to make him sick, but to eliminate him entirely. *Oh I fear you are poisoned, Lord Randal, my son...*

His firstborn lay weak and twitching as the king's physicians bustled around him. They could do nothing, really, save clean the vomit from his chin and the filth from his legs.

Then finally: "He's gone, sire."

Vortigern did not register who said it. He was already heading for the door. He found Renwein in their bedchamber.

"How is he?" she looked pale and anxious.

"Dead."

"Oh my poor one!" In three quick strides she had crossed the room to embrace him. "I am so sorry."

"Are you?" he asked, standing tree-trunk stiff in her embrace.

"You know I am. I'm sorry for you. No man should have to bury his son."

"I'm curious, Renwein," he said stepping away from her. "What do you think his death means to me?"

"Why," she faltered, "a terrible grief, such pain…"

The blow when it came was wholly unexpected. As his fist connected with her chin, white flashes of pain seemed to dance in front of Renwein's eyes. She fell backward and had barely hit the floor when Gwrtheyrn grabbed a fistful of her hair and dragged her to the table. With his free hand he tipped it over, and before the dazed girl could clear her head enough to act, he bound her hands and feet, each to a table leg.

"What are you doing?" she shrieked.

He stood over her, looking at her dispassionately until she quieted down.

"'A terrible grief,' you said. 'Such pain.' Haven't you realised yet, wife, that I don't grieve. It's odd really. I never have. Never felt the need."

He lay on top of her and spoke softly. "You see, I am very blessed. I don't feel sadness or fear or…," he lightly ran a finger along her cheek, "…pity."

"That's not true," she spluttered. "I know you love me."

Vortigern laughed, low and mirthlessly. He sat up and produced a dagger. "I like this blade because it is sharp enough and strong enough to get the job done. But I don't love this blade. If I should lose it, I'd procure another. It is just a tool. That's what your father was: a means to an end." He looked down at her. "That's what you are."

"No…"

"You were a good lay, Renwein, and a fun diversion; but we're done now."

The woman's shrieks echoed throughout the castle. Servants stopped uncertainly in the hall, but no one dared to enter that room. Truly the cries were piteous as Vortigern dismantled the tool that had outlived her usefulness. Finally, covered in his wife's blood, Vortigern rose.

"It would appear your father isn't the only one who carries a dagger in his boot," he said to the mutilated corpse.

He poured himself a fresh basin of water, then washed and changed clothes. As he left his bedchamber, a knot of assembled servants scurried off in an effort to look busy. He grabbed one by the shirt.

"There's a mess in there," he nodded towards his door. "Clean it up."

Trembling, the servant entered the room. As the sounds of violent retching echoed down the hall, Vortigern Gwrtheyrn walked calmly away.

"And so the plot thickens…" Elowen murmured.

She was concealed in a nearby copse of trees, not far from where Renwein had picked the poisonous leaves.

"And I thought our family was peculiar." My brother Owain gave me a playful nudge.

"Well, it looks like the excitement's over," Tamara added. "Let's go; I could use a drink."

"Wait!" I said.

A pale woman had emerged from the castle. She walked straight to the rubbish heap and, shivering, deposited a pile of bloody rags.

"Boring," Tamara intoned in a sing-song.

"I wonder…" I said.

"What?" Owain asked.

"Drink! Now!" Tamara tugged at his arm.

"You go on," I said. "I'll catch you up…"

"Are you sure?"

"Yes. Go and have fun." And with that Elowen, Tamara and my brother departed.

I sat concealed in the copse as dusk fell and a chilly silence settled upon Castle Vortigern. At last, when no one stirred nearby, I crept to the rubbish heap.

A virulent stench hung tangibly in the air and I clamped a kerchief over my mouth and nose in a vain attempt to filter out the smeech. The tatters of Renwein's long, grey dress were stained a reddish-brown and were just visible in the failing light. Gingerly I picked through them until my fingers closed upon a leather strap. I worked it free of the bloody cloth until I held the rune pouch in my hand.

I had watched her mind as she had read the tiles for Vortigern and I knew: the runes had spoken true even if Renwein had not. They did indeed possess an insight into the nature of things and, therefore, might be of use. With my prize tied firmly to my belt I went in search of Owain and the others.

Picking my way through the wildwood, I heard a scream in the distance, followed by laughter. Then a male voice – "Fuck you!" – Owain's voice. I started to run. It took me some time to find them, the sound was muffled by the foliage and difficult to track. Finally I came to the edge of a clearing. Owain and Tamara were backed against a large oak tree with eight Saxons advancing upon them, the brutes towering over the smaller Coranieid.

A quick look into Owain's mind clarified for me just how the hell this could have happened. They had started drinking without me. They drank too much, too quickly – certainly enough to dim their senses, to erode their attention so that the approach of the Saxons had gone unnoticed. And now they were in trouble.

I scanned the ground around me looking for an ally, any creature who could take a message to Annwyn. But the forest creatures are wise and make themselves invisible when trouble is near. I did not see anything I could use. I did, however, notice a pale gleam amongst the scrub. Elowen. She lay there, eyes open, covered in so much blood I couldn't tell how she had been killed. Her mouth hung open; hers was the scream that I had heard from afar.

"This is a big mistake," Owain growled as the men advanced upon him.

Those had been Maban's last words. I cast around desperately for something, anything I could use to defend my one remaining brother. There was nothing but the knife I wore in my belt. It would have to do.

However, before I could launch an attack, Owain launched his. A quick stab to the right and a Saxon hit the ground. He did not get up. A slash to the left sliced another assailant across the cheek, but not before the man drove his sword into Owain's gut. I ran at them screaming but it was too late – a third brute wielding a long-handled axe brought it down swiftly opening up Owain's back, severing his spine. I felt again the abrupt nothing as the hum of my brother's brain fell silent. The sudden nothingness hit me like a physical blow, but I slashed at the man nearest Tamara until he fell.

The nearest door, I thought as I ran, dragging a sobbing Tamara behind me. The nearest door…to the LEFT! We veered sharply in that direction. Crashing through the trees behind us, I could hear our pursuers drawing near. There were five, my ears calculated from the sound, and one shambling further behind clasping his lacerated cheek. Then another sound I didn't immediately recognise, like a great exhalation of air. What makes that noise? Tamara cried out and fell, her hand wrenched from my grip. A spear had punched through her back and out the other side. I touched her mind. It was silent as the grave.

Another spear landed at my feet. I turned and ran. Thousands of years old and I felt like a helpless child again. Running for home. Running to my father.

> "Sisters and brothers, little maid,
> How many may you be?"
> *"How many? Seven in all,"* she said,
> And wondering looked at me…
>
> *"Two of us in the church-yard lie,
> My sister and my brother;
> And, in the church-yard cottage, I
> Dwell near them with my mother."*…
>
> "You run about, my little maid,
> Your limbs they are alive;
> If two are in the church-yard laid,
> Then ye are only five."…
>
> "How many are you then," said I,
> If they two are in heaven?"
> Quick was the little maid's reply,
> *"O Master! We are seven."*[147]

It would be another 1200 years before Wordsworth wrote that poem … 1200 years before someone would distil my thoughts into inked letters on a page. If I were to write it…

> "Sisters and brothers, little maid,
> How many may you be?"
> *"How many, sir? Why, we are four."*
> "Then where's the other three?"
>
> *"Three in the churchyard lie:
> A wolf's jaws sharp and keen
> Severed little Fryok's thread…"*
> "Which left, then, only three."

> *"Maban died by Sequani hands,*
> *His head placed on a wall."*
> "Then with brother Maban and Fryok dead,
> That leaves two in all."
>
> *"Owain was slain by Saxon brutes."*
> "That left you all alone;
> With all three brothers dead, my dear,
> Then you are only one."
>
> "How many are you then" said he,
> "If three are now no more?"
> Quick was the little maid's reply,
> *"O Master, we are four!"*

Owain's soul stone rests with the others in a box in my room. I had delivered my news that night to my horrified tribe, and then walked away and left them to their grieving. I just couldn't. I couldn't watch my mother sink to her knees while her terrible, keening sobs echoed through Annwyn. I had no interest in listening to Danjy bluster on about revenge, or in watching as it took five men to hold Barinthus back so that he would not go after Tamara and rush headlong into the Saxon raiding party. Hanyfer's quiet sobs for my brother – another image I did not need.

Most of all, I could not look upon my father. He was bad before; what the hell would he become with this latest tragedy heaped atop the rest? I didn't want to watch it happen – to look inside the shell of his skull and watch the madness take an even firmer hold. No. I sought quiet, darkness, solitude.

We buried our dead; I took the fucking soul stones and committed a story about each one of them to memory. *My real name is Remembrance.*

I remember falling at Nanscáwen, the noise of the great Sequani carnyxes driving me to my knees. That's it, you're dead, I thought and then a strong hand, Owain's hand, pulled me to my feet and led me back to our fire. My brother ... my hero.

I remembered Tamara, a water-nymph by nature. The great river that runs through our old tribe lands was named for her: The Tamar.

And I remember Elowen – little waif-like Elowen, scaring the shit out of some big beefy Sequani man (Ferdia was his name) because he tried to chop down her trees.

Unfortunately Elowen's solution would not work now. The Saxons would not be frightened away by some bogeyman from the woods. No, the problem of how to deal with the "Saxon menace" was a particularly thorny one. Gwyn made a case for the total annihilation of the enemy.

"Kill all of the Saxons?" Danjy laughed. "How?"

"They massacred three hundred British nobles and made pretty short work of it," Hanyfer added. "And we are only forty-two...," she paused, looking stricken, "I mean thirty-nine."

"Could we handle it the same way we handled the feud with Lludd: get someone else to do the fighting?" Mora asked.

"Who?" Barinthus asked.

"What do you have there, Caja?" Myrddin was looking at me. Now everyone else was too.

"What the hell are you doing?" Gwyn snapped. "Instead of joining in and helping us find a solution, you sit there fiddling with pebbles."

"They're runes. They were hers," I said quietly.

"Whose?" Myrddin asked.

"Renwein's."

"And that's relevant, why?" Danjy asked.

"They work," I shrugged. "I was just thinking: wouldn't it be deliciously ironic if the cure for the Saxon plague was to be found in these?" I held up the blood-stained pouch.

"It would be," Mora nodded. "But do you know how to use them?"

"Yes."

My father looked at me sceptically. I shrugged, "I've watched her do it enough times."

"Then try it," Myrddin urged.

"What? Now?"

"Do you have something better to be doing?" Gwyn asked.

"Fine." Suddenly very self-conscious, I closed my eyes.

Barely a minute had passed when Danjy asked, "Anything yet?"

"Danjy, shut the hell up."

Finally all fell silent. I'd watched Renwein do this a hundred times, not as an outsider observes, but from within. It was surprisingly easy to replicate her frame of mind. I imagined that I was sitting in a pool of bright light beyond which darkness obscured everything. The room could have been cavernous or no bigger than my bedchamber – it was impossible to know. Silently, I asked a question: how can we challenge the Saxons? I concentrated hard on my query, focused on it until my head hurt and then drew five runes. I opened my eyes.

Ansuz (ᚨ), Raidho, (ᚱ), Tiwaz (ᛏ), Othala (ᛟ), Sowilo (ᛋ) lay on the table in front of me.

"What do they say?" Mora asked quietly.

I stared at the tiles for a moment until I saw it clearly: "With ... Ansuz, which means wise counsel and Raidho," I looked at the gathered Coranieid, "that's a travel rune, it means mobility ... a great warrior (Tiwaz) will ... Othala, retake possession of the land and be ... Sowilo – victorious."

I spotted something else. "These two runes appearing together," I pointed to Tiwaz and Sowilo, "indicate that the warrior will be damn-near invincible."

"So," Gwyn said, "with wise counsel and mobility, a great warrior will retake the land and reign victorious. It's a little vague, isn't it?"

"Hang on," Myrddin said. "These stones are symbolic, right?"

I nodded.

"But they also comprise an alphabet. Each rune is a letter, right?"

"Right."

"So what does it spell?"

"That's easy," I looked at the tiles. "Ansuz, Raidho, Tiwaz, Othala, Sowilo. A, R, T, O, S. Artos."

"What's an 'artos'?" Hanyfer asked.

"Not what," Myrddin replied. "Who."

"Ok," Barinthus said, "who is Artos?"

Myrddin looked at Mora. "That's what we better find out."

Vortigern felt like a fox being hunted down by a pack of ravening hounds. Hengist had sworn vengeance for the murder of Renwein, and to make matters worse the two remaining sons of Constantine – Aurelius Ambrosius and Uther, now grown to manhood – were coming to take back what was rightfully theirs.

"Build a newer, stronger fortress," his magicians advised. They had divined that its location should be in Snowdonia.

Willing to grasp at any straw now, Vortigern complied and construction on his stronghold began. Stone piled upon stone and the walls began to rise.

Then one day Vortigern arrived at the site to check on the building's progress. He found a demolished pile of rocks.

"What happened?" he asked calmly.

"I don't know, my lord. I don't know what could have done this." The project's overseer was visibly shaken.

"Never mind," Gwrtheyrn replied and with one deft movement, produced a dagger and buried it in the man's chest. He twisted the blade to release the suction and withdrew it as the man fell.

"You," he pointed at the overseer's assistant. "You're up. Fix it." He turned and strode away.

The walls were rebuilt and again they toppled. Another man lay dead. This pattern – build, fall, die – was repeated twice more, as Vortigern pondered the conundrum. The builders can't be fucking with me, he thought. They're too scared. So if it isn't sabotage, then what the hell is going on?

Here the story takes a curious turn. According to folklore, he consulted magicians who made the rather bizarre pronouncement that Vortigern must find and sacrifice a fatherless child and anoint the castle's foundations with his blood. A search of the local countryside revealed the existence of a small boy whose his mother swore that she had never had sexual congress with any man. The child, she claimed, had been sired by an incubus. Ergo he had no (human) father. Vortigern spoke to the boy and realised that, due to his unusual paternity, the youth had an uncanny knowledge of hidden things. He knew why the walls of the king's fortress would not stand. Gwrtheyrn released the child unharmed and some believe that he grew up to be Merlin, of King Arthur fame.

This episode never happened, but we knew what the problem was (and in the story, so did the child). Gwrtheyrn was trying to build a castle on top of the subterranean cave where the dragons Hónglián Huā and Xiàngshù had been trapped by King Lludd so long ago. The mother dragon's efforts to break free sent seismic tremors through the ground, shaking the newly erected walls, reducing them to rubble.

One day, when the tremors shook Annwyn itself, Hónglián finally broke through. Mankind always tries to imbue events with meaning. So when the dragons vaulted into the air with a loud shriek, witnesses saw it as a metaphor for the turmoil that had engulfed the island. The white dragon, they said, represented the Saxons; the red, the Britons. As the two dragons clung together for mutual support (their wings had grown weak in captivity), men thought they were locked in combat, just as the Britons and Saxons were.

I sat with Myrddin as we watched the dragons flap away.

"You look deep in thought," I said.

"There's something about this that niggles me. I just can't put my finger on it."

"It'll come," I said and rested my head on his shoulder.

It bugged him royally. Myrddin stood out on the moor, staring up into the night sky. He was missing something important, something to do with the dragons he'd seen in flight. He looked speculatively at the constellation "Draco." He stared at it till his head hurt, and was about to give up when finally he saw it written in the stars. Aurelius Ambrosius will come as will his brother Uther, Uther Pendragon, father of Artos.

Myrddin stared open-mouthed at the message etched in the starlight. "Brilliant," he murmured. "But they're going to need our help."

Later, standing before Gwyn ap Nudd in Annwyn's Great Hall, Myrddin related the news.

"Wait a minute," Gwyn said, the fingers of his right hand pinched the bridge of his nose as if he suffered from a bad headache. "You're telling me that the saviour of our tribe lands is this Artos, but he's going to need our help."

"Yes."

"And this Artos will be the son of Uther?"

"Yes."

"And Uther, though the son of a Breton, is a descendant of the Celtae."

Myrddin suddenly felt as if he was standing on a frozen lake and the ice beneath his feet was beginning to crack. "That's right," he said softly.

"Our ancient enemies were of the Celtae. So we're helping them now?"

"The enemy of my enemy is my friend."

"Oh," Gwyn's voice was low, but he had a face like thunder. "So now the Sequani are our friends?"

Mora recognised the signs. Gwyn was about to blow and she could not abide it. She was too raw after Owain's death. "Friends or not," she said matter-of-factly, "this is the only possible solution. I've seen it too … in the water."

"We'll need to plan this carefully," Danjy added.

And as the group gathered to discuss logistics, they turned their backs on Gwyn ap Nudd. The chief of the Coranieid found himself overruled, ignored.

Aurelius Ambrosius and Uther came forth, and their arrival marked the beginning of the end of a long, painful chapter of British history. They caught up with Vortigern at Genoreu and set his fort alight. The wooden structure caught quickly and from my vantage point on a nearby hill, I could see Gwrtheyrn clearly, standing at a high window, calmly awaiting death.

He deserved to die, I did not doubt that. But at the same time, I could not shake the image of him as a child, cowering before his raging father. Every punch, each kick was like the resounding strike of a blacksmith's hammer, casting him into the man he would become, making him a monster. I pitied him. I understood that he could not have been anything other than what he was. I fitted an arrow to the string of my bow and let it loose. It struck Gwrtheyrn in the chest, ending his life before the flames could reach him. In my infantile philosophy, I had just learned something from Britain's second dishonoured man … I had learned mercy.

# CHAPTER 6

# "PECULIAR GRACE"

> *"Now, whether it were by peculiar grace,*
> *A leading from above, a something given,*
> *Yet it befell, that, in this lonely place,*
> *When I with untoward thoughts had striven,*
> *Beside a pool, bare to the eyes of heaven*
> *I saw...."*
>
> William Wordsworth, "Resolution and Independence"[148]

The battle raged along the banks of the River Cray until the mud, wet with the blood of the slain and churned by horses' hooves, caught at the feet of the Britons as they tried to advance. The din was incoherent: all war-cry and wound-cry, the clash of swords and the whinnying screams of injured horses. The coppery smell of blood infused the air, and ravens perched on high tree branches, waiting. Tonight they would feast upon cold flesh and the tender, unblinking eyes of the dead.

The year was 457 A.D. and the Britons under Aurelius and Uther had pursued the Saxons into Crecganford (latter-day Crayford) in Kent. We were there too. For days and days the runes had given the same reading over and over again:

Uruz (ᚢ) .... Thurisaz (ᚦ) .... Ehwaz (ᛗ) .... Raidho (ᚱ)
 U             TH              E              R

Uther. The fifth stone was always Tiwaz, which would wobble uncertainly on the table before coming to rest with the arrow pointing down. Tiwaz was the warrior symbol and an upright arrow (↑) meant victory in battle. The runes did not promise this. Uther, they said, may fall.

This did not suit our plans and so the Coranieid were positioned at strategic points along the river. Whenever Uther found himself surrounded by the enemy, a hail of arrows would clear a path for him to safety. Whenever a Saxon tried to strike at him from behind, Uther would hear a sharp cry and turn quickly to see another attacker fall dead in the mud. I watched as a sort of exuberance gripped him. At every turn in the battle he prevailed. He felt invincible, unstoppable. He felt fey. That word is no longer in use, but in my day fey was defined as the high spirits and overconfidence of one about to die. In a reckless charge, Uther pitched forward, the long sweeps of his sword scything the enemy down as if he was harvesting wheat.

He did not see it coming. From within the hectic fray a spear, six feet long and capped with a lethal iron tip, thrust upward, piercing Uther's shoulder and knocking him from his horse. As the Saxons moved in to finish him off, our arrows fell like rain and when the way was clear, Danjy and Barinthus darted forward to drag Uther from the field.

By then we had tunnels running beneath all the South of England, and the Coranieid, with Uther in tow, disappeared down the nearest portal. We did not get far before we were obliged to stop, so Myrddin could staunch the bleeding from Uther's wound. Danjy and Barinthus lay the injured man on the damp tunnel floor. The walls were tight around us and Myrddin motioned them back so he had room to work.

"Caja…"

"Here," I stepped forward, holding up a lantern.

The old medhek extracted a pad of dried sphagnum moss from his pouch and pressed the pale green leaves into Uther's wound. Sphagnum moss is wonderful stuff. When applied to a cut, it can absorb twenty times its own weight of blood as it swells to plug the gash. We would later discover that it also contains an antibiotic fungus to help prevent infection.

With the bleeding under control, we hastened back to Annwyn. It is one of the unexplainable quirks of knocker tunnels that the distance underground does not correspond to distances on the surface. A hundred miles above can be crossed on foot in an hour below in those tunnels and we were soon back in Myrddin's chamber. He swept everything off the long rectangular table that lined the wall opposite his bed. A silver cup and plate clattered loudly to the floor, as did a mortar and pestle and a bundle of dried herbs. We laid Uther out on the table.

"You can go." Myrddin, putting a pot of water over the fire to boil, dismissed his helpers.

Danjy shrugged at me and we made for the door.

"Not you, Caja."

"Tough luck. You almost made it." Barinthus wrinkled his nose at me and was gone.

I sighed heavily. "What do you need?"

"An extra set of hands."

"Barinthus has hands, Danjy has hands."

"Will you help me, please? He's starting to creem."

That is another phrase that has fallen into disuse: "to creem" – to tremble with pain or fear or, as modern science would put it, to go into shock.

"You're right," I stared down at Uther's face. His skin was a pasty white and his lips were tinged blue. "Rak galsa glan dyworto y wos," I said ('His blood has gone clean from him').

We removed his wet, muddy clothes and bathed him with warm water and towelled him dry, careful of course not to disturb the moss dressing on his shoulder. We tucked him into Myrddin's bed and covered him with wolf-skin blankets.

"I'll be right back," Myrddin announced.

I looked at him in alarm. "Where are you going?"

"I won't be long. If he wakes up give him a little warm water and honey to sip – sip, mind you. If he drinks it down too fast, he'll be sick."

"You still haven't answered my question."

"I need to talk to your father." Myrddin sighed and left, quietly closing the door behind him.

"Fuck," I muttered.

That conversation would not go well. The tribe chose to save Uther so that he may go on to father our champion against the Saxons, Artos. We had ignored Gwyn's protests on the matter and pretended not to perceive the ominous silence that had befallen our chief. He was angry, so very angry and yet could do nothing. There had been challenges to his power in the past – direct challenges that could be met with a fist. But this time the tribe had unanimously decided to act against his will. How do you counter people's indifference? Angry outbursts would not avail him; in fact they would make him ridiculous, like a child raging against the sanctions of his parents. And he could not violently re-establish the pecking order like he had when he pounded Bucca back into submission. There was no one person to fight. Until now, of course. Myrddin had not only saved Uther, but had brought him back to Annwyn!

"Fuck," I muttered again.

"Huh?" Uther's voice was a dry rasp.

"Here, take a sip of this." I supported his head with one hand while I tipped the cup to his lips with the other.

The man coughed weakly and I pulled the cup away.

"Where am I?"

"Shh, you're safe," I murmured. He heard my words but did not have time to register their meaning before he slipped, once again, into unconsciousness.

After what seemed like the passing of an age, Myrddin returned looking pale and shaken.

"How did it go?"

He smiled sadly at me. "Do you really want to know?"

"But..."

"Suffice it to say that Uther will stay where he is for now. Did he wake?"

"Briefly. He asked where he was, took a little drink and then passed out again. Should we get to work on that wound?"

Myrddin shook his head, "Not yet."

"Why on earth not?"

"Sometimes a badly wounded man will creem and the creeming is a sickness. He turns cold and pale and loses his wits. Operating on that wound before he stabilises will only make it worse. It could kill him."

"So what do we do?"

"We wait and let him settle down a bit." He pulled a chair up beside the bed where Uther lay, and sank wearily into it. "I'll stitch him up tomorrow." He rested his head in his hands. "You can go now, if you want."

I looked at this man who been like a kindly grandfather to me my whole life. He suddenly looked old and small ... and infinitely alone. He had just defied his chief in an ugly confrontation that would likely damage their friendship forever. A peek into Myrddin's recollections showed how Gwyn had to be restrained by Danjy and Barinthus or else he would have openly attacked the old man. On the other hand, Myrddin feared for Uther. The man had lost a lot of blood and was very weak. What if he died? What if all the turmoil was for nothing and the Saxons continued to rampage unchecked across our island?

"Right," I said decisively. "Come on, get up."

"Why?"

"I'll sit up with him tonight and you go get some sleep. You can take my bed."

"Don't be foolish."

"I'm not." I'd spoken too loudly and Uther stirred. I lowered my voice. "You're the one who has to patch him up tomorrow. So get some rest. I'll call you if anything happens."

"Are you sure?"

"Yes. Now go."

"Keep him warm and calm and give him drink."

"Why are you still here?" I asked, settling into the chair Myrddin had vacated.

"Thank you, Caja." Myrddin quietly closed the door behind him.

For many hours Uther did not stir. I checked many times to make sure that he was warm, but not overheating. And then, with little else to do, I watched him sleep. So … this was Uther, one day to be known as Uther Pendragon, father of Artos. For his sake, the Coranieid had once again entered into battle. For his sake, Myrddin had risked the wrath of Gwyn ap Nudd. And yet, he was a singularly unremarkable man. Yes, he was handsome in a rugged sort of way, but I saw no indication in face, in body, or in mind of the importance of this one life.

"So what is it about you?" I murmured.

His stirring, later on, woke me up. I had no idea how long I'd been asleep – not long enough, for I was shaky and felt sick.

"What is it?" I whispered, kneeling beside him.

"Hurts."

"I know. Hang on."

I mixed one of Myrddin's concoctions up with some honey and spoon-fed it to Uther.

"What is it?"

"It'll help with the pain."

He took about half and then weakly shook his head. "No more. Feel sick."

"Rest then." I sat beside him and held his hand. He stared glassy eyed at the stone ceiling of the chamber, squeezing my hand as pain throbbed through his shoulder with every heartbeat.

"The battle?"

"I don't know."

He tried to rise. "I've got to get back. My brother…"

With one firm hand on his chest, I was able to impede him. "You're not fit to go anywhere. Now sleep."

The following morning, Myrddin was happy that Uther was no longer in danger from the shock. We dosed Uther up with a strong solution of henbane, darnel, black poppy, dried bryony root, borage … the list of ingredients seemed endless and all were designed to make him sleep and keep him still. Barinthus and Danjy helped carry him to the table and then beat a hasty retreat, both hoping they wouldn't be called upon to assist. Myrddin laid all he would need out so that everything was to hand. Then we plunged our hands into a basin filled with another of his concoctions – oak bark, heartsease, thyme and garlic, an astringent mixture that made my skin sting.

My job was to remove the old dressing and plug the wound with a fresh clump of sphagnum so that Myrddin could clean around the gash while not pushing any dirt into the wound itself. This done, I removed the moss and got out of Myrddin's way. While I scrubbed my hands for a second time, the old man grabbed a handful of moss soaked in a solution of comfrey, garlic, and thyme and held it over Uther's shoulder, squeezing it like a sponge, irrigating the wound. With the injury now clean, he patted it dry and stitched it up with a bone needle and animal tendon as thread. I then applied another dressing of moss. We secured it in place with a cloth bandage and put Uther back to bed.

### A Side Note

*Back then all medicines came from nature. The astringent quality of oak bark combined with thyme (which contains thymol, a strong antiseptic used in surgery) cleansed our hands before we touched the wound. Myrddin irrigated the laceration with comfrey which "has a long history of use in traditional herbal medicine, especially for healing wounds...(It) contains allantonin, a naturally occurring chemical that stimulates cell proliferation and regeneration. It is used mainly to promote ... the proper development of scar tissue."*[149] *And garlic is one of the most effective antiseptics occurring in nature. The bulbs can be squeezed for their juice, which is then diluted in water and applied to clean sphagnum moss and used as a dressing for wounds.*[150]

*Needles made of bone have been used since three thousand years before the birth of Christ to stitch up lacerations with animal tendons. The tendons themselves are remarkably useful: they are strong and contain natural adhesives. All this combined with herbs for pain relief (such as viper's bugloss, meadowsweet and valerian) and a poultice mixed with spider webs (a natural source of penicillin) combined to make early surgical practises surprisingly effective.*

Uther slept most of the day, partly because of the injury, but mostly because we kept him well and truly doped. While he rested I crept off to my bed to snatch a few hours' sleep before I again took the night-shift. On the way to my room, I passed Gwyn in the hall.

"So..."

"Yes, father?"

"How's our guest?" His jaw was rigid with tension, his eyes steely.

I cringed beneath that gaze. "He lives. I don't really know how it all will come out in the end."

"That is the question, isn't it?" He turned and walked away.

How will it all come out in the end? That was the question. We had single-mindedly worked toward the fulfilment of the prophecy and had ignored all else. All right, if Uther lived, then Artos would be born. Artos would beat back the Saxons and our island would again know peace. But would Annwyn be as fortunate? Our chief felt belittled and betrayed and so very, very angry. And I was helping Uther. I saw the word "traitor" pass through my father's mind before he turned his back on me and walked away.

Later on, as I sat by Uther's bedside keeping my midnight vigil, I consulted the runes. There were so many questions buzzing in my head, but the stones do not work unless you pose one specific question. So I chose a selfish one: in this saga of Uther, Artos and the Saxons, what would become of me?

I drew one stone from the pouch and without looking laid it on my lap ...

inverted Othala (ᛟ) ... you will stand alone. I did not like that answer and so cast the rune back into its bag, shook the pouch and drew again. Again ᛟ. In exasperation, I tried a third time, fishing around in the pouch for a stone of a different shape or size. But no, the answer was the same.

"Perfect," I said to the rune. "Essentially you're saying that, when all is said and done, no matter what I do, no matter what my intentions, I'll end up alone." I swore loudly.

"Huh, did you say something?" Uther muttered.

"No," I answered. "How do you feel?"

"Like I've been run over by a horse cart."

"I'll get you something for the pain," I said, rising.

"No," he said, grasping my hand. "I want to be awake for a while. I need answers."

"Actually what you need is to drink. You have to keep your fluids up."

He shook his head.

"How about this: for every sip you take, I'll answer one question. Do we have a deal?"

He nodded. "Now the battle…"

"Drink first."

He grudgingly took a sip.

"Proceed," I smiled at him.

"How did we do?"

"It went badly. We reckon somewhere in the region of four thousand British casualties."

"And my brother?"

I held the cup to his lips compelling him to take another drink. "Safe back in London."

"Oh, thank God. Does he know where I am?"

I held out the cup.

"You know, this is getting irritating."

"And yet if you don't drink enough you'll die."

"Fair enough." He took another swig.

"We haven't contacted him yet."

"I need to get word to him."

I paused, mulling over my answer so much that I forgot to make him drink. "I can get a message to him. Let him know you're alive…"

"...he could come and fetch me from..." He looked around. "Where am I?"

"Uther, it isn't safe to move you yet."

"You didn't answer my question."

"And you haven't taken another drink."

"Damn it, woman, where am I? And who are you? And..." the man was too exhausted for a proper tirade.

"And why would we help you?"

"Well, yes."

I looked at him for a long moment, wondering just how much to say. "Those are complicated questions. Tell me, Uther, do you really want a long explanation right now?"

"No," he sighed. "I feel sick again."

I rose and grabbed a clay jar filled with a mixture of chamomile, meadowsweet and charlock. Dissolving the herbs in water, I said, "Suffice it to say that you are safe and among friends." I gave him the solution to drink. "This will settle your stomach."

He winced at the taste, but drank it down. "Ok, friend, what is your name?"

"You can call me Caja."

"That's a pretty name."

"It's a nickname, it means daisy." I sat back down in my chair. "You look like you can barely keep your eyes open. Do you want to sleep for a while?"

He nodded and nestled back down in his blankets. "Won't you tell me your real name?"

When I did not respond, he reached up and gently touched my cheek, "All right, Caja it is."

He closed his eyes and as he drifted off, his fingers roamed over his covers until he found my hand. He gripped it tightly and fell asleep.

The following day, after Uther had taken some food, he sat propped up in bed awaiting answers.

"My brother..."

"Knows you're alive."

"Then why hasn't he sent for me?"

I paused, "He doesn't know where you are."

Uther's eyes took on a guarded, suspicious expression. "Now why is that, I wonder? Are you Saxon?"

I looked at Myrddin. He pulled another chair up and sat down.

"We hate the Saxons," he said simply.

"Any particular reason?"

"Three reasons, actually. They killed three of our tribe."

"Your tribe?"

"The Coranieid."

Uther looked from me to Myrddin and back again, then burst out laughing. This sent waves of pain through his injured shoulder that brought his laughter to a stuttering halt. He took a few deep breaths to compose himself. "The Coranieid? Really?"

Myrddin nodded.

"The wee fairy folk," he started to giggle again and clasped his bandage. "Don't make jokes; it hurts to laugh."

"We are the people of the Coranieid, and you are in Annwyn," Myrddin said.

Uther looked at me. "Will you not tell me the truth?"

"It is the truth, Uther."

"I'll believe none of it."

"We saw your name," Myrddin continued, "in a prophecy. It has been foretold that you will one day father a child named Artos, and he will be a great king of the Britons. He will halt the Saxon advance."

"I'll say it again, old man: I don't believe you."

"Caja..." Myrddin looked meaningfully at me.

I nodded. I had already retrieved the information he wanted.

"Uther," I said quietly, "when you were a child, your father and older brother were murdered and your guardians spirited you away to Brittany."

"That is common knowledge."

I nodded. "There you had a nurse named Rozenn. You were sad and frightened by events you could barely understand. It was not so bad during the day when you could play with Aurelius and the other children. But at night you became fretful, and Rozenn would sing you to sleep."

"Anyone could have made that guess. Children fret when their fathers are murdered. Nurses sing lullabies. So?"

"I began to sing...

> "Sleep, my baby, close your eyes.
> It's time for dreams and lullabies.

May this world greet you with all that's bright and new,
And know that my heart beats for the love of you."

Uther looked at me in surprise. "Who told you that?"

I shook my head. "No one. I know you loved her, better than the mother who died when you were a baby, better even than Constantine." I paused. "But you would lose her too. Consumption. She got sick, then she seemed to get better. Then it hit her again and again, each time worse than the last. And then she started hacking up yellow stuff streaked with blood and you knew – you were fourteen and you knew – that she was dying. And she smelled strange; you didn't like her new smell. And still she kept trying to comfort you. She tried to sing to you, but her voice was so hoarse and it made her cough. And so you sang to her instead. What verse of that lullaby did you sing to her the night she died?"

Uther's eyes were wet with the recollection. "You tell me."

"You were alone with her at the end, half-singing, half-whispering in her ear. You changed the words of the lullaby, Uther…

"Sleep, my mother, close your eyes.
God's own angels drawing nigh.
I've loved every moment though they were too few.
And know that my heart beats for the love of you."

"How did you know?" he whispered.

"We fairy folk know things. Just as we know that you will have a son and he will be king."

"But Aurelius…"

"Will die without issue."

Uther stared into space for a long moment. Then he said to Myrddin, "Can I just … rest for a while?"

"Certainly," Myrddin said, and we both rose to go.

But Uther clutched at my hand. "Please stay."

"Of course."

We did not talk much. I removed the blankets folded behind him so that once again he could lie flat. I gave him a drink and sat by his bedside. He seemed always to reach for my hand when I sat near him.

"You have a pretty voice."

"Thank you," I murmured. "But you should try to sleep now."

"Will you sing it again?"

I was taken aback. "Do you really want me to? It was an intrusion to recount that memory…"

"I wouldn't have believed you otherwise."

"Close your eyes, then." And I sang Rozenn's lullaby through to the end, although Uther was asleep by the end of the third verse.

As his breathing came slow and deep, I pulled the stone out of its pouch. My fingers found it automatically now … reversed Othala (ᛟ) … you will stand alone.

Whether it was a need to flout destiny or whether it was the sudden realisation that I wanted something more than just to hold Uther's hand, I leaned over him and kissed him gently on the lips. It was an impulse – and not one that I intended to have any lasting consequence, but as I pulled away, Uther opened his eyes, ran a hand through my hair and kissed me back.

In the days that followed, I changed bandages and fed my patient while his shoulder slowly healed. We talked a lot, Uther and I. He assumed that I automatically knew everything about him, but I had not pried to that extent and so he offered information freely. He told me of his childhood in Saint-Malo, a fortified island where the English Channel kisses the mouth of the Rance River. From the fort, he could make out the thin, grey line of the British coast and was told from early childhood that that land was rightfully his, but it had been stolen. He was supposed to feel angered by this, he knew. But in truth there was nothing in that strip of rocky shoreline that spoke to him of ownership or belonging or home. Indeed, he felt nothing when he looked upon England.

The only enticement was Vortigern. Vortigern had spilled the blood of Constantine and then Constans. That same blood flowed through Uther's veins and pulled him with the inexorable force of a spring tide toward England and vengeance. Alen Coran once said that to have a "grievance is to have a purpose in life." But when that grievance is avenged and one's purpose is fulfilled – what then? That, for Uther, was the puzzle. Yes, the Saxons needed to be dealt with and his brother needed to be established as the rightful king. But Uther had found his appetite for war sated when he set light to a wooden fortress in Genoreu, trapping Vortigern inside. In his heart all he wanted now was a quiet life on his own bit of land with his own crops and animals, a gaggle of children and a wife to cling to when nights are cold and rain taps upon the roof.

"Of course, I could never say that … not to Aurelius, not to anyone."

"You told me," I smiled.

"I felt I could. Do you ever feel that way, though? Like what you're expected to be and what you want to be are two different things?"

An image came to mind of two naked bodies covered in stab wounds – the grim work of Gwyn's first Wild Hunt. I remembered kneeling by the murdered woman to dip the hood of my cloak in her blood, because that was what I was expected to do.

I had felt sickened and empty. There was no sense of satisfaction or victory in the killing – those two star-crossed lovers had been as easy to overcome as newborn lambs. There was only a cold sense of disconnection, as if some invisible thread binding me to the tribe had snapped. I continued to live within Annwyn, but since that night, I had the growing impression that I was outside the group, a secret infidel that masked mutinous thought with smiling compliance.

"I can see by the look on your face that you know exactly what I mean," Uther said quietly.

I sighed. "It's a disturbing feeling, isn't it?"

He nodded, "Surrounded by people who don't – or can't – understand you."

"A freak."

"Alone.

We looked at each other for a long moment.

"Do you think that's why we kissed?" he asked. "Because we're two lonely souls?"

"I don't know."

Uther's smile faded. "I wish you'd tell me your name."

"I can't."

"Why not?"

"It is an old, old superstition among my people. To learn the true name of something is to gain power over it."

"How?"

"Have you never heard of witches invoking a spirit's name to harness it? To use it?"

"But you're not a spirit."

"We are fay."

"Fairy folk?"

I nodded. "The hidden people. That's how we survive…"

"…by hiding." He finished my sentence for me.

"Yes."

"And that's why Annwyn's underground?"

His questioning had made me uncomfortable and so my answer was sharper than I intended. "Actually, that's because of you."

"What?"

"Well, your people…"

"The Britons?"

I shook my head. "Go further back."

"The Celtae?"

"Centuries ago, the Celtae drove us from the surface. We lost our lands, our dominion, everything."

"And yet you helped me…"

I shrugged, "It is an old grudge. A very old grudge. The Sequani who drove us out are less than dust and we have more immediate problems."

"The Saxons."

I nodded, "The Saxons. We lost three Coranieid because of them."

Uther was silent. I could see the thought formulating in his head. The Britons had just lost 4,000 men in the Battle of Crecganford, and here we had lost a paltry three.

"One of them was my brother," I said quietly.

That was enough to tip the scales in his mind. To him Aurelius was worth a million men.

"I will make them pay, Caja."

"I know you will, and your son even more so."

"Ah, yes," he smiled. "I've been wanting to ask: who is the mother of this great Artos?" He cocked an eyebrow at me. "You, perhaps?"

I sighed, "And yet again the conversation returns to that kiss."

"It was a good kiss."

"Yes, it was."

"So you could be the woman in the prophecy."

I shook my head. "I can't have children, Uther. I'm not the one."

"And so we circle back to that one damnable problem of living as others would have us live."

"What choice is there?"

He shrugged, "We do what we want."

I laughed mirthlessly. "Oh, is that all?"

I rose from my chair and stood at the table, gathering soiled bandages to take away. With my back to him, I asked, "All right. If you were free to choose, what would you do right now?"

"I'd kiss you again." With difficulty, he rose to his feet. "If I kissed you now, would you kiss me back?"

I was flustered by how near he'd come. "That's – that's irrelevant. You're not free, Uther, and neither am I. There is someone out there, the future mother of Artos and…"

"She will give birth to the saviour of all Britain, I know. Now answer my question."

I stood there awkwardly.

He leaned in. "All you have to do is say 'no.'"

I didn't.

Soon Uther was well enough to leave Annwyn. Myrddin, under the false protective name of Merlin, accompanied him back to his world and stayed on to advise him. I remained in Annwyn and slipped into a melancholy unlike any I'd ever known. Unable to sleep in my own chamber I curled up in Myrddin's bed, for the covers still held the musky scent of Uther's sweat. It had been hot under the wolf-skin blankets and we had kicked them to the floor as we clung to each other. I could still feel him in my skin and in the way my stomach fluttered at recollection of his touch. I ached for him.

It has been said that to love "is to receive a glimpse of heaven"[151] and that is true. I had been shown heaven and then the iron gate of responsibility and obligation descended, barring me from it forever. The Italians call it "malato d'amore"; in Germany it is liebeskrank and in my native tongue it is known as the "hyreth," the longing. Lovesickness. But my pain, while huge to me, was yet another fal-tha-ral – a trifle in the grand scheme of things. While I languished in Annwyn, the fight between Briton and Saxon raged on the surface. British folklore picks up the thread of the story from here.

> … it befell that Aurelius was [eventually] slain by poison at Winchester…
> At the same time came forth a comet of amazing size and brightness …
> at the end whereof was a cloud of fire shaped like a dragon… Then

> Merlin ... cried, with a loud voice: 'O mighty loss! ... Alas! ... Aurelius Ambrosius is dead.... Haste, therefore, noble Uther, to destroy the enemy; the victory shall be thine, and thou shalt be king of all Britain. For the star with the fiery dragon signifies thyself; and ... portends that thou shalt have a son, most mighty.'[152]

Uther, the new King of Britain, sat alone, head in his hands and wept. With Aurelius gone, he had no family left. He was alone. He would never admit it to another, but it made him afraid for now there was no one on this earth to love him – no one to be always on his side.

"...except me."

Uther looked up, startled. "H-how did you get here?"

"We have ways," I said.

"I'm so glad you're here." He rose to embrace me and began to sob in earnest. His knees buckled and under his weight we both fell to the floor while I held him.

I had watched this man grit his teeth in stoical silence while the agony of his wound was upon him, so to see him weeping on the floor hit me like a physical blow. I soothed him and kissed him, and in his sorrow he kissed me back. His grief was cold, a grey and barren landscape; and so he sought me for warmth, for comfort. I wrapped myself around him like a blanket. Other parts of his mind were firing now with desire, with love – a golden light in the greyness as he hitched my skirts aside and pulled me to him. He clung to me and in all my long life I had never felt so precious, so needed. His movements became more urgent and I could not seem to pull him close enough to me as I ached and strained against him.

He went rigid, gripping me hard, his breath coming in sharp gasps with an emphatic, "I love you."

We lay tangled upon the floor, panting.

"I do you, know ... love you," he said.

"Then I will never leave."

Later that night I slipped out of Uther's bed. Myrddin had called in low tones that only a Coranieid could perceive.

"Then I'll never leave?" Wide-eyed, he repeated my words back to me.

"It's not polite to eavesdrop."

"I'm Coranieid!" he shouted. "How can I not eavesdrop?"

He took a deep breath in an effort to calm down. "All right," he said, rubbing his temples to relieve the building migraine. "Forget for a moment that with those words you thwart the prophecy that we've pinned our hopes on. Forget that he will age in front of your eyes and die while you still look like a girl. And forget that you cannot give him an heir. Have you forgotten about your father?"

True. I had not been thinking of Gwyn ap Nudd.

Myrddin continued, "He almost ripped my head off for letting Uther sleep in my bed. What the hell do you think he'll do if he finds out you've taken him into yours?"

"Then he better not find out," I said quietly.

He snorted. "And so I become your accomplice?"

"My father won't so much as look at me because I became yours."

He stopped short. "Why didn't you tell me?"

"You already have enough to worry about."

He nodded. "All right, we'll make this work somehow, but Caja, make sure that ... uh," he waved his hand vaguely in the direction of the king's chamber.

"Uther?"

"Yes, Uther. Make sure he understands: he can never so much as speak of your affair. Your life may depend on it."

### A Side Note

*It has long been a feature of most fairy stories that, when a fay loves a mortal, there is some prohibition, some forbidden act that, if committed, would bring the affair to a swift and bitter end. In* The Lais of Marie de France *(a collection of medieval romances), we find the story of "Lanval." In it the hero meets and falls in love with a beautiful and mysterious woman. Together they are happy, but when Lanval must return to his lord's court, she warns him...*

> *"Love ... I admonish you now,*
> *I command and beg you,*
> *do not let any man know about this.*
> *I shall tell you why:*
> *you would lose me for good*
> *if this love were known;*
> *you would never see me again".*[153]

*In their notes on "Lanval," Robert Hanning and Joan Ferrante point out that "Lanval's love comes to him ... whenever he needs her, but she remains invisible to everyone else, as though she were the creation of his fantasy... As in so many of Marie's lais ... once the love is known to others it is lost, as though it can only exist as the private possession of the lovers."[154]*

*This idea is not unique to medieval romances. In* A Thousand and One Arabian Nights, *we find the story of "The Man Who Never Laughed." In it a poor young man is transported to a splendid kingdom where the queen consents to marry him. The man experiences unparalleled bliss as king of a peaceful, prosperous nation with a beautiful queen at his side. She tells him: "Everything I own is now yours... But one thing I must deny you. Do not open this door, or you will bring misfortune and ruin upon yourself."[155] Of course, as the years pass he grows curious to know what lies behind the forbidden door. Finally he succumbs and opens it. Stepping over the threshold he hears the door slam behind him and is transported back to his old life of poverty without his queen and far, far away from her kingdom. The moral of the story is: Never break the rules.*

"I don't understand," Uther shook his head. "Why so many secrets? I can't know your name. I can't know how to find Annwyn. And now I can't tell anyone about us?"

Uther and I were whispering through a clay beaker with its base removed. "Please. You can never speak of it."

"But why?"

"It's dangerous."

"How?"

"You remember I told you of your ancestors, the Celtae, and their war with my people?"

"Yes, but you said that was an old grudge, forgotten now that we have united against the Saxons."

"It's forgotten by me and Myr ... Merlin, but not by all."

"Who bears me a grudge over something that happened hundreds of years ago?"

I fell silent.

"Caja..."

"My father ... our chief. The King of Annwyn."

Uther, who had been leaning forward ready to passionately defend his point, sat back heavily. "He still hates us?"

"More than you know."

"And, therefore, if he were to find out that his daughter was in love with a Celtae…"

"… I don't know what he'd do."

He looked at me for a long moment. "You're afraid of him."

Flustered by that comment, I dropped the beaker. I scooped it up again in a huff and pressed it to Uther's ear. "Enough. Either you can protect this secret or you can't."

"All right, all right ... I'll keep silent. I promise."

I gave him a quick kiss and turned to go. If I stayed away from Annwyn for too long, the tribe would begin to ask questions. As I walked away, I overheard a snippet of conversation between Uther and Myrddin.

"You gave her your promise?" Myrddin asked.

"Yes, but I still don't understand the need for it."

"It's simple, Uther. If this becomes known, he'll kill her."

And so Uther and I met in secret. Just like in the fairytales, the relationship existed, could only exist, in a world removed from his real life and mine. I came to realise however that love, described by Shakespeare as steady and constant as the stars, has one great limitation: it cannot escape the vicissitudes of real life. If love is a cliff, then life is a sea that batters against it with tempests, worries, and temptations that can erode and weaken it if it is not strong. And the worst storm was yet to come, gathering when, one Eastertide, Uther held a feast at his castle and Myrddin recognised, among the faces of all those present, the future mother of Artos.

Her name was Ygerna, wife of Gorlois (the Duke of Cornwall) and described by Geoffrey of Monmouth as "the most beautiful woman in Britain."[156] Uther did not even notice her; he was missing me and, although surrounded by a great number of people, he felt entirely alone. Myrddin whispered something in his ear and he went very pale. His jaw set obstinately, he seized the old man by the elbow and ushered him into a room where they might speak privately.

"I won't do it," Uther said simply. "I'm a man, not a horse you hire out for stud."

"Think about Caja…"

"I *am* thinking of her."

"If you do not go through with the prophecy, the Coranieid will want to know why. They will look for a reason."

Uther blanched whiter still.

"If she is found to be that reason…"

"She could come to me; I'd protect her," Uther protested.

"For how long?" Myrddin asked flatly.

"As long as it takes!"

The old medicine man smiled at him sadly. "I know you would. You'd protect her as long as you live."

"Yes."

"And then she'll pay."

"What?"

"Before you're even in the ground."

Uther shook his head, "No."

"We are fay. We live a long time. Don't you understand that they can wait you out? And when you're out of the way, they will…"

"What's the woman's name again?" Uther interrupted.

Myrddin looked at him vaguely. "Umm … damn it! I keep forgetting things." He closed his eyes and in an effort of concentration found the name. "Ygerna."

"She's already married."

"And yet that does not alter the fact that she is the future mother of your child."

"What of Gorlois?"

"An obstacle."

"I'm not going to murder the man just so I can shag his wife!"

"Worry not, Uther. It won't be murder. Now go, speak to her."

Every marriage is different. The distillation of two unique human beings into "one," into a unified whole, creates some strange and wonderful concoctions. And it can also create some beastly ones. Michel Eyquem de Montaigne once said that "Marriage is like a cage. One sees the birds outside desperate to get in, and those inside equally desperate to get out." This is a fitting description of the marriage of Ygerna and Gorlois.

Gorlois was old and prosperous, with two strong fortresses, many fine horses and a pretty wife not even out of her teens. And while he was normally happy to display the symbols of his earthly success, he found himself becoming more and more possessive of Ygerna. Wherever she went, men's eyes slid over her body. He'd catch one staring at the neckline of her dress or watching the roll of her hips as she walked away. At home, his own men-at-arms would look upon her form with appreciation, and now the king himself was showing a particular interest in her. It made him feel threatened. He did not mind men looking at his horses, in fact he enjoyed the praise they heaped upon his harras and the wistful look they'd get that said, "I wish I had." However, he reasoned, a palfrey doesn't forsake its rider because the man is old and grey. But Ygerna, she can choose whom to smile upon, whom to lie with. And there were many to choose from – younger men, and handsome. While his gnarled hands loved the firmness of her thigh and the softness of her breasts, did she in turn love the feel of his hands? Or would she prefer the smoother hands of youth? Of all his possessions, the girl was the one thing that might slip from her bridle … at least when he was not looking.

Throughout the feast Gorlois' discomfort grew. The King spent much time speaking to Ygerna and she was lively and animated. Suddenly the two burst into laughter and Gorlois cringed in jealousy because he was on the outside of the joke. He wants her, he thought. That is not surprising; she is a beautiful woman after all. But she wants him also. He was sure of it and became equally sure that tonight, while he slept, she would slip away to Uther's bed and, like a thief in the night, the king would take what rightfully belonged to Gorlois. It would not stand. And at that moment, he decided that after the feast he and Ygerna would slip quietly away from Uther's castle. It was an affront, very rude to go without thanking his host. Be that as it may, they were leaving.

"They did what?" Uther asked his close friend, Ulfin of Ridcaradoch, again.
"They've gone … and without saying a word to anyone."
"Send a messenger on a swift horse to call them back."
"I already have, my king. I knew you'd be offended at such behaviour and hoped that if they came back in time, you wouldn't have to be troubled by this," Ulfin said quietly.
"What was Gorlois' response to the messenger?"
Ulfin hesitated.
"Well what?"
"Go to hell."

Uther began to pace the room. He was unbelievably angry: at the insult, yes, but more at the fact that he now had to fight Gorlois for something he didn't even want. He took a deep breath that did nothing to calm him, and said in a shaking voice, "Muster the troops."

Gorlois was not a total idiot. He knew, as soon as he had spoken in anger the words "Go to hell" to Uther's messenger, that he was in for a fight. It could not be otherwise, for a king cannot let a snub like that go and still command the respect of his subjects. Gorlois, himself, could not have acted otherwise. He was too proud. Uther was wrong to pay so much attention to a married woman, and the old man would be damned if he was going to be the one to apologise. And so the fight was on.

Gorlois, fed up to the back teeth with worrying about Ygerna's virtue, locked her in a tower at his fortress at Tintagel. On the western coast the high jagged cliffs of Britain towered over a churning sea; and in the midst of that sea there was a rough circle of land, almost an island, but connected to the mainland by a narrow bridge of soil and rock. There above the Atlantic stood Tintagel, an impenetrable fortress of thick walls and steep towers. A few well-trained men could repel an army on that land bridge, but Gorlois was taking no chances; he placed a company of men there to protect his wife and then hastened to his other fort at Dimilioc.

High in her tower, Ygerna sat staring dumbly at the wall.

"Unbelievable," she whispered.

She was not stupid. Her marriage to Gorlois was the seal on a political alliance brokered by her father. She'd had no illusions going into it. She did not hope to find love. Whenever the old man got that look in his eyes, she would dutifully undress, lie down, close her eyes and dream that the man on top of her was … different, a man who would talk to her and come to know her, and she would want to tell him things about her life and her thoughts. Gorlois did not know her at all. He thought he did. He thought that his rough fumblings in bed equated to true knowledge, and she often bristled when he said things like, "I know what you need" and would present her with another dress or brooch when she looked sad. She did not want another dress; she wanted to get the hell away from him for a while, take one of his fine palfreys and ride free. With Gorlois that was quite impossible – he would never allow his lady to go unguarded. *His* lady.

All of that was difficult enough, but now… she looked around the small room situated at the apex of Tintagel's highest tower. It was decorated with fine tapestries. Upon the table rested two silver place settings, beautiful gowns were neatly folded into an ornate oak chest and upon the bed rested blankets each more expensive than a warhorse. Gorlois had run his hand along them, proclaiming how soft and luxurious they felt.

"This can be our own little love nest, my dove," he had said. "Don't worry, I'll come to you often so that you are not lonely."

And then thankfully, he had left to make war on the King. The King! And why? Because Uther had spoken to her? No, she decided, because she had spoken back, had enjoyed the conversation of such a charming man, had laughed at his jokes. In some perverse way this was about *her* behaviour, not Uther's. And the result? She had become a bird in a very expensive, gilded cage.

She rose and examined the knives on the table. If they were sharp enough, she could open up her wrists, and as she bled to death she would make damn sure that she ruined those dresses, those soft blankets where she was supposed to lie while he used her body while leaving her soul to rot. Damn it. They were dull.

## A Side Note

*"I cannot praise a fugitive and cloistered virtue, unexercised and unbreathed, that never sallies out and sees her adversary, but slinks out of the race where that immortal garland is to be run for, not without dust and heat."*[157] *These words, uttered by John Milton, encapsulate the fallacy of locking Ygerna away "to protect her virtue." There is no virtue where there is no choice and no temptation. There is only servitude and imprisonment. Unfortunately "the lady in the tower" is a common theme in the old stories.*

*In Greek mythology Acrinus, King of Argos, receives a prophetic warning that one day his grandson will kill him. To thwart destiny he must ensure that his only child, a daughter named Danaë, does not procreate. And so he shuts her up "in a strong brass tower."*[158] *Did these measures ensure the girl's chastity? No, Zeus appeared to her in a shower of gold and by the end of the encounter, Danaë was pregnant with Perseus.*

*In the Jewish fairytale, "The Princess of the Tower", the king's daughter, Solima, rejects one noble suitor after another. Again, an oracle opens his mouth and proclaims that the girl will marry a pauper. In a rage, the king "swore he would imprison her in his fortress in the sea .... on a tiny island miles from land."[59] This too was a beautiful prison, much like Ygerna's.*

*Rapunzel was also shut away in a tower with no doors and no stairs. What incurs the wrath of her captor, the evil witch of the story? An act of free will: Rapunzel's choice to lower her long hair so that a man could climb into the tower and love her. The punishment for this is extremely cruel. Rapunzel is cast into the desert to live a life of poverty and misery. When her lover next comes to the tower, the witch is lying in wait: "'Aha!' she cried mockingly, 'you would fetch your dearest, but the beautiful bird sits no longer singing in the nest; the cat has got it, and will scratch out your eyes as well.'"[60] The young man is blinded and left to wander the world in helpless grief.*

While Uther and Gorlois faced off against each other at Dimilioc, Myrddin slipped away on an errand. He sought Vixana, the Moorwitch, and found her on a wind-swept heath far from the dwellings of men.

"Hulloo!" she called when she saw him approach.

"Hello, Vix!" he hailed her. "How are you?"

"Old."

Myrddin chuckled. "Me too, and growing forgetful."

"So what brings you? Let me guess, you need a favour."

"Yes."

"Go on then."

"I need a potion ... a spell."

"To accomplish what exactly?"

Myrddin hesitated. "I have found the mother of Artos, and Uther clears a path to her as we speak. But ... he does not love the lady."

"And that's a problem?"

"Yes."

"Most men I know would screw a snake if they could get hold of its ears." She laughed. "Why is love suddenly an impediment," she paused, "unless there is another?" She read it in Myrddin's face. "There is ... someone he does not wish to betray. Who is it?" she asked eagerly. "I'd love some good gossip."

Myrddin had his lie ready. "He does not like women, Vixana."

The old moor woman howled with laughter. "Really? I never would have pegged it."

"You see the problem."

"Indeed. And so we need something to make him more ... amenable to the experience."

"Yes."

Vixana tapped a long fingernail on her cauldron. "It will take some doing. Let me have a think."

This period of British history is a tug-of-war between legend and fact. According to legend, Uther, pining for Ygerna, slipped away from the battle and journeyed to the fortress where she was kept. The castle could not be penetrated by force, but perhaps it could by subterfuge. So Merlin devised a potion that would transform Uther into the exact likeness of Gorlois. In this guise, he was able to walk unimpeded into Tintagel, make love to Ygerna and safely leave.

It is certainly an interesting story, but it is untrue. Uther did not sneak away to seduce Ygerna through falsehood. He instead concentrated on Gorlois, with the inevitable outcome that the Duke of Cornwall was slain. The path to Ygerna was now clear – except, of course, for the obstacles in Uther's own head. These would be more difficult to shift. And so Myrddin had consulted Vixana. He did not need a potion to change Uther into the likeness of Gorlois. He needed to change Ygerna. It was a matter of perception. If Uther could pretend for a while that he held, not some strange woman who had been picked for him, but the woman he had chosen for himself ... then the prophecy could be fulfilled.

To that end, Vixana made her way to the fields where the peasants grew their wheat and rye. She was looking for something in particular and passed rows of healthy stalks as she slowly picked her way down to a marshy patch at the edge of the field. There, upon the sickly yellow feathers of bog-bound rye, she found them – little oblong particles of ergot, dark and hard. She gathered these and dissolved them in water in a bowl lined with moss.

She took the resulting extract and combined it with hobs and the grey-green leaves of sitherwood, an aphrodisiac also known as southernwood, lad's love or maid's ruin. Bringing the mix to a boil, she sneezed as its bitter, camphorous steam hit her in the face. Sniffling, she stooped and checked once more that the rowan twigs she had woven into a protective hoop were bound fast and completely encircled both her and the cauldron. She groaned as she straightened up and rubbed the spasming muscles of her lower back with old, gnarled fingers.

Vixana hesitated for a moment; she hated the next part, for she did not like to call upon demons. Fingering the small, holed stone that hung from her neck by a leather cord, she took a deep breath and said in a low, firm voice....

> "I, Moorwitch, call upon the One
> who walks in thunder, lightning and in rain."

An expectant hush fell. "Futur," she whispered, and a cold wind blew across the moor, making Vixana shiver. Lightning flashed in the distance and she counted until she heard a rumble of thunder. The "storm" was five miles distant. The wind whipped her hair wildly about her; another flash, another rumble – three miles now and the wind screeched like an animal in rage or in pain. When lightning and thunder flashed and spoke as one, she closed her eyes and began her chant, her voice rising to be heard above the wind...

> "Once the battle's lost and won,
> Great business must be wrought anon.
> Here boils a vaporous drop, profound,
> Procured from wet, infected ground,
> And here distilled by magic sleights
> To raise your false illusive sprites
> Before his eyes, so foul is fair ..."[161]

Vixana sliced open her palm and held it over the cauldron. "My offering to you!" she yelled, opening and closing her hand to keep the blood flowing freely. The spell was wound up, coiled like an adder, ready. She doused the flames beneath the cauldron with cold water and while she waited for the decoction to cool, she bandaged up her wounded hand. Slowly the wind died down and the ambient temperature began to rise. She bottled up the concoction but still did not step out of the circle of rowan. Finally, the creatures of the moor began to stir and Vixana sighed with relief. The birds, the bugs, the animals would not emerge until the demon had gone. It was now safe to leave. With the heel of her boot she snapped the protective hoop of rowan branches. The Moorwitch sang softly to herself as she limped away.

# A Side Note

*For centuries, witches and warlocks have called upon demons to lend their power to spells. According to Rosemary Ellen Guiley in* The Encyclopedia of Witches and Witchcraft, *"powerful words which, when rhythmically chanted ... from within a magic circle, effect the conjuration of spirits and demons or the achievement of spells. The names of power are the secret names of ... deities" and demons.[162] This old superstition lay behind the Coranieid's reticence to reveal our true names to outsiders; hence, Myrddin adopted the name Merlin in his dealings with Uther, and I was known only by a pet name, Caja.*

*The specific demon invoked by Vixana is Furtur (or Furfur), a name derived from the Latin "furcifer" or scoundrel.[163] The Lesser Key of Solomon defines him as the demon who ignites lust between man and woman and who raises "Lightnings and Thunders, Blasts, and Great Tempestuous Storms."[164] Vixana was therefore cautious in dealing with him. According to the old folklore, hoops of rowan and holed stones could be used as protection against evil spirits. The spell itself was a rhythmic chant in an attempt to produce the desired results. The perceptive genius of William Shakespeare would later echo those words in his Tragedy,* Macbeth, *in the spells of Hecate and the three witches.*

*Underlying all the poetry and myth and legend, there was a firm scientific foundation for Vixana's work. Ergot is a fungus that grows on rye under damp conditions. If harvested and placed on a growth medium (particular mosses will do), the chemical compounds in the ergot can be separated with the introduction of water to extract lysergic acid, a strong hallucinogen and the main component of modern-day LSD.*

*Lysergic acid triggers a number of perceptual changes within the minds of men. Their vision blurs; colours are more intense and light sparkles effervescently (the false "sprites" that Vixana spoke of in her spell). Solid objects appear fluid, with the ability to morph and change. Sounds are distorted, and a man under its influence begins to feel disconnected from himself. With his heart and soul held at bay and the drug shifting the images before his eyes, Uther would be more amenable to fathering a child by Ygerna and hence, the prophecy could be fulfilled.*

With Gorlois dead, Uther approached the guards at Tintagel and offered them safe conduct back to their homes, as well as full payment for the services they had rendered to the Duke. As the last of Gorlois' men left, Uther mounted the steep tower steps and, reaching the top, smashed the lock upon the heavy wooden door.

Inside, Ygerna backed into a corner, slid down the wall and sat on the floor hugging her knees. She was trembling, fully expecting that the door would be kicked inward and she would be ravaged. Therefore it came as quite a shock to her when the man outside knocked.

After a long pause, a muffled voice called, "Duchess? It is Uther, your king. May I come in?"

The lady sat there dumbstruck and after another pause, Uther said gently, "Ygerna, I only want to talk to you."

She rose, smoothed the skirt of her gown and opened the door.

"Hello," he said.

"Hello."

"I am sorry about your husband. Believe me, I did not want to fight him."

"I know."

She stood back and let him enter.

"If there is anything you need, anything you require, you have but to ask. Again, I am so sorry for the grief I have inflicted upon you." Uther fidgeted awkwardly. "I'll leave you now," he said abruptly and made for the door.

"I hated him." Her words stopped him in mid-stride.

He turned back to her, "Why?"

"He locked me in here, alone, because he was afraid that I liked you."

"And do you?"

Ygerna stared at him as a heady sense of freedom came over her. It felt a bit like she'd had too much wine. Gorlois was dead and she was free, free to do this... She went up on her tiptoes to kiss him.

"Ygerna, you don't have to..."

She silenced him with another kiss and pressed her body against his. "For once, I want to hold a man and have it be my choice."

"Wait."

Suddenly her cheeks flushed red with embarrassment. "I'm sorry! I thought you wanted..."

"Ygerna, just wait. I will be right back."

He left the chamber and in the cool, dim light of the stairwell, popped the cork off a bottle and downed the elixir in one swallow. When he began to feel its effects, he returned to the room and stood blinking, his eyes dazzled by the flickering light of so many candles. Nothing in the room seemed particularly solid, least of all the body of the girl on the bed. She was naked, and seemed to have the same ethereal quality of his beloved.

He whispered, "It's you," and the girl on the bed – his girl, his love – opened her arms to embrace him. He was with her in moments.

And as he whispered to her words of love that were meant for me, I ran for Annwyn. I needed a few tons of granite ceiling above me to block out his words and Ygerna's moans. As I ripped the twigs of the nearest portal aside, I could hear them moving together, breathing quick and shallow. She called his name and I flung myself into the tunnel, landing scraped and bruised on the rocky slope. I clamped a hand over my mouth to stifle my sobs; I could not be caught crying now – it would raise questions, and so I bit the fleshy pad at the base of my thumb until pain overrode sorrow. I wiped blood from the corners of my mouth, dusted myself off, and headed for home.

After that night, events moved swiftly. Mora had a vision: Artos had been conceived. To give him a legitimate claim to the throne, Uther and Ygerna were married. I stayed away. I could not watch it all happen.

One day Myrddin asked, "When are you going to stop feeling sorry for yourself and go to him?"

"I can't."

"I know you feel betrayed, but the only reason he went through with it was to protect your secret."

"I know."

"And he had to be drugged to do it."

"I know."

Myrddin rested a tender hand on my shoulder. "Knowing is one thing. Understanding it, feeling it, is another."

I nodded mutely, sniffling.

"Come, I want to show you something."

Myrddin led me down a small, cramped tunnel.

"I didn't even know this existed."

"It's new," he said, carefully picking his way over the uneven ground.

"Where are we going?"

"You'll see."

We seemed to walk for a long time. Every time I tried to straighten up to silence the spasms in my back, I would bump my head on the tunnel's low ceiling.

"It's not a comfortable walk, I know," Myrddin said.

"Why the hell didn't the knockers make it bigger?"

"They dug it in a hurry."

Finally we emerged into a little cavern, lit by candlelight. It was sparsely furnished with a table, a few chairs and a bed. On the edge of the bed sat Uther, fidgeting and looking anxious.

"Caja..."

"Where are we?"

"In a cave below Tintagel."

"Ygerna..."

"Is in the castle above us. I have enemies and this is the safest place for her and the child."

An awkward silence fell and Myrddin left discreetly.

Uther paced the room. "You hate me, don't you?"

"No, I hate her. She has everything in this world that I want. She's your wife. She gets to bear your child. She can walk with you in the daylight and grow old with you and..." I was crying too hard to continue.

Uther tried to hug me, to comfort me and I pushed him away. People say that when they are really angry, they see red. I don't. I see white: a white flash of rage before my eyes that never fails to surprise me with its intensity. I was so angry with him. Yes, he was trapped by circumstances; yes, from the beginning I knew it would come to this, but still...

Uther was trembling now. "Please, Caja, I'll do whatever you ask. I'll renounce Ygerna and her child. I'll abdicate the throne. We could go away from here ... we could go anywhere; it doesn't matter. Just tell me what to do."

And again it was the vulnerability of this strong man that gave me pause. I was jealous as all hell, but I was also in love. The battering of a sea of difficulties had not eroded that.

"What do you feel for her, Uther?"

"Responsibility."

"And me?"

"I love you," he said simply. "I can't do this without you."

I looked at him for a long moment and realised that my whole frame was leaning in his direction. It had always been thus. I had always felt that pull, that need to be near him. And in one moment of pure, clear insight I was able to distil my problem down to its essence which consisted of one question: Can I walk away? The answer from mind, body and soul was no. I could never turn my back on this man.

"Come here."

He swept me into his arms and we clung to each other desperately, and I could feel all of those larger forces of the outside world swirling around us: my father, the survival of Britain, the Saxon threat, the child. It felt as if a storm raged just outside and that tiny chamber was a little island of sanity in its midst.

## A Side Note

*Gale-force winds off the Atlantic whip Tintagel and send white-capped waves surging into "Merlin's Cave" – a cavern carved out of the rock by centuries of turbulent water. It runs beneath the castle itself and today, at low tide, tourists explore it. Yet as they pick their way through, slipping on the green slime of algae and seaweed, they are unaware that, just behind the back wall of the cave, another chamber is hidden. Carved by knockers and accessed through a hidden tunnel, it was the only safe place in the world where Uther and I could meet.*

Years passed and Artos grew; Uther and I continued to meet in our own little cavern sunk beneath Tintagel like a dungeon. Ironically, it was the one place in this world where we were free to be ourselves. We met there as often as we could. And it was there that I began to notice the cough. Whenever Uther would get worked up while making love or venting his frustrations over the Saxons, he would be gripped by a coughing fit. At first it was as if he had a tickle in his throat, but eventually it developed into a more violent hacking that hurt his chest. Rozenn. He had picked it up from her. Rozenn died of consumption (later identified as tuberculosis), but she did not have us, the Coranieid, and our thousands of years of experience working for her. Therefore I consulted Myrddin. Unfortunately, even thousands of years of experience, by that time, only amounted to the following:

A mustard poultice for inflammation of the lungs: take mustard seed steeped in tepid water, linseed soaked in boiling water and mix the two, allow it to cool and apply the resultant paste to the patient's chest. But the pungent aroma of the mustard only made it more difficult for Uther to breathe. I adjusted the ratio of linseed to mustard in an attempt to make it milder. Still, the poultice produced no noticeable improvement.

I tried instead smearing his chest and feet with goose grease – another home remedy that made no difference.

I treated his cough with white horsehound, elderflowers and thyme and still the hacking kept him awake all night.

Myrddin steeped dried marsh mallow root in cold water for hours and hours, added ale and strained the resulting mixture through muslin. I then stirred in copious amounts of honey and fed it to Uther four times a day, but still he coughed and spat up blood.

I tried snail broth and even, when a local man committed suicide, unearthed the body so that I could procure his hand. A dead man's hand (especially that of an executed criminal or a suicide) was thought to have miraculous healing powers. Passing it over the diseased area of the body seven times, would achieve "Transference of the disease … as the hand moulders, the affliction will disappear."[165]

But nothing worked. The tuberculosis continued to ravage his lungs, breaking them down, liquefying them into yellow matter streaked red with blood which he would spit up in ever-increasing quantities. He'd lie on his side in bed, knees hitched up from terrible stomach cramps. And when he gritted his teeth against the pain, I noticed a lurid reddish line where his teeth meet his gums.

"I'm so tired," he rasped. "I've been lying in bed all day, but I feel like I've run miles."

"It's the illness. Exhaustion is often the cause of…" I stopped short.

"I know I'm dying, Caja." He paused. "I wanted to talk to you about that, about how it will happen. I want you there … at the end."

"What about Ygerna, Artos, your men? They'll want to be with you."

His voice was hoarse and his sentences were punctuated by pants as if he could not quite catch his breath. "So much … in my life … has been dictated by duty to others. Now I'm going to have things the way *I* want. I want to die here … with you beside me." He became agitated. "Promise me…"

"I promise."

As usual, Myrddin was the one to devise a solution. Our lie is recorded in your history books: Uther, suffering from a lingering illness, retired to Veralum to drink from the medicinal spring therein. And while he was there, the treacherous Saxons poisoned the spring "and so, on the very next day, he was taken with the pains of death … before the villainy was discovered, and heaps of earth thrown over the well."[166]

That is the legend. In reality, Uther lay in our little chamber behind Merlin's Cave and I lay by his side and tried to warm him when chills made his body quake. I had never prayed before – my tribe had lost its religion when I was still very young – but I was praying now to some ill-defined god whom I did not know, nor understand. I begged him. I bargained with him, promising him everything that was in my power to give, if only Uther would recover. But the prayers of a faithless girl went unheeded. Uther's mind was growing dim; his pain and exhaustion were so big in his mind that he was losing the capacity to focus on other things – this life, this love, me. He was letting go, and the letting go made it easier to die. I knew this. And still I wept bitterly because love may not be forever, not if it can be crowded out of the mind by pain.

And then on his final day, he opened his eyes, looked at me and smiled. "I love you, Caja," he rasped and my heart leapt because, although he had let the rest of the world go, he still held on to us. I told him my real name then and I held him and sang that lullaby he learned in his youth in Brittany.

> "Sleep, my true love, close your eyes.
> God's own angels drawing nigh.
> I'll come to you, darling, when my life is through,
> And know that my heart beats for the love of you."

As he took his last breath, in his mind I caught a glimpse of something, something unfathomable to the living. And then his mind went dark.

Myrddin made him a soul stone and gave it to me before he turned the body over to Ygerna and Artos. He had chosen a small, smooth piece of grey agate with darker lines that described the shape of a spearhead if you held it one way and a heart if you turned it 180°. Very symbolic. But I stared at that stone for a long time, wondering for the first time in all these years what the hell was the point? The stone was supposed to be the vessel which now carried a part of his spirit that would remain with me forever. But it was cold to the touch – the way he had been cold when chills gripped his body. I rubbed the stone between my hands the way I had rubbed his fingers in an effort to warm him. But the stone did not retain heat, not unless I held it constantly, working it in my palms until my hands cramped up.

John Keats once wrote in a letter to Fanny Brawne, "I have so much of you in my heart."[167] But my heart was silent on the matter, numb. My skin, however, nearly drove me insane. I could still feel him, his flesh against mine; I could taste his kiss on my lips and the sensation made me ache. Until that tactile remnant faded, I did not have a moment's peace. And when it finally did fade, my heart awoke to a life without him … a long long life with no one in this world to love me like he did. The emptiness, the darkness, the grinding pain of those days was all.

And still time marched on and Artos succeeded his father as king. Any consideration of Artos' life leads back to that tug-of-war between legend and reality. The legend tells us that upon Uther's death, his son came upon a sword lodged in a block of marble. On the sword these words were engraved: "Whosoever pulls out this sword from … this stone is rightly the king of all England."[168] Many had tried to extract the sword and failed, for it lay waiting for the hand of the true king: Artos … Arthur.

King Arthur, through the telling and retelling of his story, would come to epitomise the ideal of manly perfection. He was chivalrous, brave, honest and faithful; he was wise and compassionate and good. As Christabel Coleridge once said, he towered "above his fellows in beauty, courage, and virtue as to catch upon his shoulders the sunbright mantle … sending his name down 'like a roaring voice through all time,' to encourage the growth of heroes."[169] That is all very stirring and romantic, but the reality was somewhat different. Historians now believe that our idea of King Arthur evolved from a real man named Artos, a Romanised Celt who led a successful cavalry campaign against the Saxons. This battle-hardened horseman did not charge into the fray in shining armour with a bejewelled crown upon his head. No, he was a rough figure clad in leather and iron – perfect attire for the business of killing Saxons.

By his side, to counsel and guide him, stood Merlin, reputed to be the most gifted wizard of all time. We knew him only as Myrddin, our medicine man. But as Terry Breverton notes, "Myrddin Emrys … is the Merlin of Arthurian legend… He became known as Merlin because the Latinised form of Myrddin would have been Merdinus."[170] It was Myrddin who provided Artos with a suitable weapon to battle the Saxons. Crafted in Annwyn and imbued with fairy magic it was called Caliburn, a name that would evolve through time into *Excalibur*.

Tennyson, in the *Idylls of the King*, recounts the event:

> The Lady of the Lake …
> Clothed in white samite, mystic and wonderful.
> She gave the King his huge cross-hilted sword,
> Whereby to drive the heathen: a mist
> Of incense curl'd about her, and her face
> Wellnigh was hidden in the minster gloom;
> But there was heard …
> A voice as of the waters, for she dwells
> Down in the deep… 'Excaliber'.[171]

Hanyfer, down in the cold still waters of the lake, waited and listened. She could hear the chop of oars as Artos rowed out. The moonlight filtering down through the water's surface dimmed as mist from Vixana's cauldron crept across the lake. Pushing off the bottom, she rose; arms at her side, feet together, her strong legs bending in waves, she swam like a fish or mermaid. Nearing the surface, she thrust an arm upward, pushing the sword into the air. She felt Artos grasp the blade and released her grip. The king watched her pale arm slide back into the depths.

Examining the sword, Artos fell immediately in love with it. It was a thing of beauty, a work of art, but its scabbard was more precious still. It was infused with a protective charm to stave off all injury in battle. It made Artos invincible.

And so the runic prophecy was correct:

| Ansuz | Raidho | Tiwaz | Othala | Sowilo |
|-------|--------|-------|--------|--------|
| ᚨ | ᚱ | ↑ | ᛟ | ᛋ |
| A | R | T | O | S |

With Ansuz or wise counsel from Myrddin, Artos deployed Raidho – the mobility of his cavalry against the Saxons to great effect. According to Vita

Merlini, Merlin also recommended a military alliance between Artos and his blood relative, King Hoel of Brittany: "With his help Arthur ... attacked the enemy whom at length he conquered and forced to return to their own country."[172] And so Tiwaz (an unbeatable warrior) reclaimed the land (Othala) and achieved Sowilo, a great victory. At Mount Badon in 516 A.D., Artos routed the Saxons who fled the island. This is why archaeologists now detect a "Saxon migration away from Britain back to their original homelands."[173]

With the prophecy fulfilled and the Saxons routed, Artos settled down at his headquarters near Sparkford to reign in peace. Legend has it that this stronghold called Camelot was built in one night by Merlin, and in it Arthur, his queen Guinevere, and the Knights of the Round Table established a society based on chivalry, virtue, and courage – a shining example of the human capacity for greatness.

If only that were true. Yes, Artos did settle at an earth-work fort later known as Cadbury Castle. Yes, he married Gwenhwyfar (called Guinevere in later stories) and yes, he kept a company of warriors with him. But these were rough, battle-hardened veterans and Artos was not the embodiment of perfection. In fact, he was poised to make a terrible mistake...

Artos sat on his throne drumming his fingers on the arm-rest. He was discontented. That, to be honest, made no earthly sense. He had ... well, everything: wealth, power, security, friendship, a beautiful wife, three gorgeous mistresses, the loyalty of his men. The list of his blessings went on and on. And now, finally, he'd exacted revenge on the Saxons for the murder of his father.

He still recalled the moment, perhaps the happiest of his life, when at Mount Badon, he killed a Saxon and turned, ready to battle the next. But there was no "next" – the battle had been won and he, covered in blood from head to foot, shouted, "We've done it! At last!" The elation of that moment was exquisite, but it had faded. The unbridled joy he'd felt was impossible to sustain.

In fact he was becoming quite philosophical on the nature of happiness. It seemed that it was not something you could procure and possess forever. It was not a destination to be reached. Instead, the quest for lasting joy was the pursuit of a ravenous beast. And you had to feed it perpetually, every coin added to your amassed wealth, every battle victory, every compliment you received, every orgasm, every delicious bite of a good meal – and it would swallow it all down and demand yet more if you wished it to stay. Henry George said it best: "Man is … the only animal that is never satisfied." And Artos, a man of action, a man born to win a war and hooked on the adrenalin rushes of a lifetime of battle, was now bored.

He therefore turned his gaze upon the most intriguing thing in his life: Merlin. He had inherited his advisor from Uther.

"But why," he had asked his father, "do you rely so heavily upon the counsel of one man?"

"Because he is not a man," Uther had replied. "He is of Annwyn."

"You mean…"

"He is of the wee folk. All the stories you've heard are true. Annwyn is real and the fay; and they know things."

"Such as?"

"Such as you will be the one to defeat the Saxons. They desire this and hence, they will help."

Artos had heard many tales about Annwyn. One source said it was a little chain of islands and upon each there was a mighty fortress. Another said it lay beneath the hills and its entrance was the door to hell. It was a Netherworld, an Otherworld, a Land of Youth where time stood still. It was also a land of treasure. The sword Caliburn had come from Annwyn and there was no finer weapon on earth. And he'd heard stories that, hidden in its depths, there was an enchanted war club that could kill nine men with a single blow; and then you could use its handle to restore them to life again. There was a harp fashioned from polished oak that, when played, could dictate the course of a battle. And there was a cauldron known as "Undry" for it never ran out of food and never left a man hungry.

Every time Artos broached the subject of Annwyn and its treasures, Merlin would become evasive and tell him nothing. Therefore Artos determined to find out the truth on his own. Annwyn, he decided, was a physical place. Uther himself had been there, and described the chamber he was in as dark with nary a window to let in sunlight. It was probably underground. Therefore, there must be an entrance and a tunnel. But where? And how could he find it?

Merlin seemed positively ancient and yet he was unbelievably spry, for whenever he took his leave of Artos, he seemed to vanish into thin air. It was a puzzle: how could he follow Merlin and discover the portal to Annwyn?

Artos was many things – a lover, a fighter, a king, and surprisingly, a man of letters. He had been well educated and read Latin, Greek and the runic alphabet. He was a bard who composed poetry and song. Thus he applied his knowledge to the problem. If Merlin was of the fairy folk and could disappear into the wildwood, then surely the task was to find some way to track the magician so that he might be followed. Artos had to find a way to the make the invisible, visible. He consulted the old alchemic texts and grimoires and after many months of fruitless searching found what he was looking for: a recipe entitled "If thou wouldst see fairies." This was followed by a list of ingredients: oyle, rose, hollyhock, marygolde, hazle, and thyme, and instructions on how to combine them and steep them in the sun for three days. The result was a foul-smelling, sickly green ointment that could be applied to the eyes.

With the ointment prepared, he resolved to try it on Samhain (later known as All Hallows Eve or Hallowe'en). It was a fitting day to make the attempt because Samhain was thought to be a good day to spot fairies. On Samhain the real world and the supernatural world overlap, allowing passage from one to the other. On Samhain it was said that poets could enter the Otherworld.

However when the moment arrived, Artos hesitated. The concoction he had made was untried and he feared that if he had made any error in its creation, it might damage his sight.

"One eye, then," he murmured, applying it to his weaker eye on the left.

"Fuck!" he swore and tried to wipe the stinging ointment out of his eye with his sleeve. This did little to alleviate the pain and his eyes watered and his nose ran as he ducked his head into a basin of cold water. After much cursing and rubbing, the stinging in his eye began to subside. It felt as if there was an extra lens covering the orb and through it, everything looked a bright green. Within that emerald field, the lines and patterns of the world around him stood out in sharp relief. In this way, he watched Merlin leave the castle and shift aside what looked like an unravelable thicket to reveal a dark hole in the ground. The old wizard shimmied in and pulled the ground-cover back over the entrance.

Artos waited for a while and then summoned a small group of reliable men.

"What task do you have for us tonight, my lord?" Bedwyr asked, trying not to stare at the greenish tinge of the king's left eye.

Artos grinned. "We're going on an adventure."

He led them to the thicket and with their help moved it aside. They hadn't even entered the tunnel yet, and they were bleeding from the brambles and thorns that tore at their skin. The king lowered himself into the tunnel and paused, looking up at his followers. They hesitated for a moment and then one by one joined him in the darkness.

Lighting a torch, Artos led the way through a long damp tunnel that spiralled downward into the cold earth. Eventually they came upon storerooms packed with bread and flour, casks of ale, venison and game birds hanging from the ceiling. Ahead of them the tunnel forked, and laughter echoed from the passage on the right. It sounded like a great gathering, and so Artos veered left. This tunnel led to another chamber in which nine fairy women gossiped and laughed as they wound each other's hair into intricate knots which they pinned carefully in place.

"Let me see," a raven-haired woman held the face of a girl in her hands. "Caja, you look so tired! You haven't been yourself lately."

The girl did not reply.

"How are you going to find a man if you mope around all day? Here…"

She tilted the girl's head back and, grabbing a small jar, let a few drops of liquid drip into her eyes.

"There, a little belladonna to make your eyes sparkle."

Indeed, her eyes did shine and the pupils dilated making them look big and doe-like.

Artos watched the girl with interest. The women were obviously preparing for some festive gathering and yet the girl looked so sad. What ails you? he wondered.

A short time later the women departed, and Artos and his men hid themselves in another storeroom to escape detection. When all was clear they emerged from their hiding place, and crept into the room where the women had dressed and brushed their hair. It was the bedchamber of the queen. Rich tapestries of birds, wolves, and mythical beasts hung from the walls. A wooden box, its lid engraved with an intricate leaf pattern, held golden brooches studded with emeralds, opals and rubies. A comb sporting a large sapphire glittered in the candlelight.

Cai, a man like a brother to Artos, reached for the box and the king slapped his hand away.

"That's not what we're here for," he whispered.

"What *are* we here for?"

"That," Artos pointed to a cauldron of beaten gold and rimmed with large pearls. It was so beautiful it must be "Undry", the cauldron of legend. It was surprisingly light and as Artos picked it up, a woman's voice, nearby, called irritably, "I said I'll get it!"

The girl with the sad eyes walked in on Artos and his men. She stopped short but, recovering quickly from her shock, she hissed, "You fool!" and punched Artos squarely in the eye.

Stumbling in on Artos and his band of thieves, I noticed the green film covering his left eye and knew in an instant how he had managed to find Annwyn. A well placed punch sent him falling backward, the cauldron clattering to the ground. The back of Cai's hand sent me sprawling and before I could stop them, Artos and his men grabbed the cauldron and ran.

"Gweres! Help!" I called, but Annwyn's walls were thick, purposely so, to give us privacy.

I picked myself up, stemming the flow of blood from my nose with a kerchief and headed towards the Great Hall to alert the others. But then I stopped. That was Artos – Uther's son. I pulled my lover's soul stone out of the pouch of runes that I wore at my waist and resolved to delay long enough to allow Artos a chance to escape.

Even with my delay, the fastest of our archers caught up with them and killed all but Artos and two others.

Back at the castle, Artos consulted pellars and monks for help, but none could restore sight to his left eye. My punch had driven the ointment deep into the socket, damaging lens and iris and cornea. Generations hence would still tell stories about people who rubbed green ointment into one eye so they could see the fairies. When the trick was discovered, invariably the fay would retaliate with "a well-directed blow from the elf's fist, which deprives them of the sight of that eye forever."[174]

But this loss was a minor consequence compared to what happened next. When I revealed the theft to the assembled Coranieid at Annwyn's Great Hall, my angry tribe plotted its revenge. The story of that vengeance consists of three separate threads that, when plaited together, would secure the king's downfall. The first thread was the story of Myrddin; the second, that of Gwyn and the third was of Mora. I will tell them in order.

# Myrddin

Myrddin was forbidden from offering any future help or advice to Artos. The old man, however, was soft-hearted. He had been a great friend to Uther and had rocked Artos as a baby. He would not stay away. In fact later that night, he crept along the tunnel leading to the king's castle. There, at the burrow's entrance, he found Nimue waiting for him.

"What are you doing here?" Myrddin was breathless from the long hike.

"Waiting for you. I wanted to see if you were all right."

"You don't care if I'm all right, Nimue."

"That's not true. We've had our ... problems," she said, "but I still care what happens to you."

The old man laughed, but without mirth.

"Don't you see? If you go to Artos, you face exile from Annwyn. Maybe even death."

Myrddin shrugged, "Well, I've lived a good life."

"Don't be flippant. You're risking everything and for what? A human who thanks us for our help by stealing from us! Caja is one of your favourites – he broke her nose. Where is your loyalty?"

"You are a fine one to speak to me of loyalty."

"I know and I'm sorry. But I'm here now. So please stop before you throw your life away."

"It's too late, Nimue."

She stood before him quaking with emotion. "I can't change your mind?"

"No."

"Then grant me one thing."

"What?"

"One last night."

"With you?" he asked sceptically.

She embraced him and whispered in his ear, "With me."

Myrddin stood ramrod straight and kept his arms at his sides. He did not believe that she truly wanted him and yet here she was pressed against him, kissing him. She was breathing heavier now as her hand slid down and slipped inside the front of his breeches. Myrddin's knees nearly buckled with the jolt of arousal that coursed through him. She led him back down the tunnel to Annwyn and veered off into a chamber he'd never seen before.

The room was not deep down and carved out of bedrock like the rest of Annwyn's chambers. While the walls were stone, it had a ceiling of hard-packed earth and a tangle of interwoven tree roots. She lit a torch and as Myrddin fumbled out of his clothes, she stepped out of the room. Nimue, the dryad, uttered these words, "Cref yu gwrydhyow an spedhes – ow dywla colm. Strong are the roots with which I bind thee!" Across the doorway of the chamber, thick roots shot down from the dirt ceiling to bar Myrddin's exit.

The medicine man scowled at her. "That won't hold me."

She gestured casually toward the bars of his cage. "Then be my guest."

Myrddin grabbed a thick root and, with considerable effort, tore it free. "Ha! I'm be out of here in no ti—"

Another root, thicker than the last, shot down from the ceiling.

"No you won't," Nimue said gently. "I'm sorry Myrddin, but this is for your own good."

As she turned to walk away, he shouted, "How long?"

"Just until we're done with Artos."

And so it came to pass that Merlin "was lost to Arthur"[175] because of the wiles of Nimue; "imprisoned by her magic … entangled … in a thorn bush."[176]

## Gwyn

According to folklore, Gwyn ap Nudd was known under various names. The Welsh called him Gwynwas. The Cornish knew him as Melwas, and the Latinised version of his name was Malvasius.[177] This said, it is possible to piece the next part of our story together from fragments of history and myth: Encarta Encyclopedia notes that "Guinevere was kidnapped by Melwas … whose stronghold was" Glastonbury Tor.[178] Glastonbury Tor was reputed to guard "the entrance to the underworld known as Annwyn."[179] Caradoc in "The Life of Gildas" recounts how "Glastonia … was besieged by the tyrant Arthur with a countless multitude on account of his wife Gwenhwyfar, whom … the wicked king (Melwas) had violated and carried off and brought there."[180] Gwenhwyfar was thus snatched away and brought, bound and blind-folded, into Annwyn.

Since Nanscáwen my father had become increasingly unhinged … cruel and quick to anger. This was never more apparent than in his treatment of Artos' wife. It was as if all Gwyn's fear and frustration, all his grief and loss and anger were unleashed upon this one Celtic queen. I know this, because I heard it. Hers were the inarticulate screams of the brutalised. Inarticulate, yes, but eloquent. They spoke of terror and torture and rape. These were not the modulated screams you hear in your movies in which the heroines want to sound tragic but pretty. These were the guttural cries of the helpless, the hopeless – harsh and shrill. A plea followed by no, No, NO! Then a cry of agony and then weeping and a hoarse "Why?"

The only answer she received to her question was more pain, punctuated by her own shrieks. While the rest of the Coranieid went resolutely about their business, pretending not to hear, I stood irresolute in the hallway. Her fear was infectious; I began to shake and my heart thudded painfully in my chest.

"No, get … get off me!" followed by a moan of satisfaction from my father sent me running. I felt tangibly sullied by what I had heard and made for the river. I had some vague idea that I could wash this feeling off of me.

Standing thigh-deep in the cold water, my breath came in ragged gasps. "He is a king, a god … he is entitled to work his will," I wept. But those words rang hollow.

Really, what was the use of it – of all this life – if we were going to live as the pettiest of tyrants, the smallest and meanest of men? We were like the gods of Greek mythology – frivolous, petty gods who needed to assert our authority again and again. But surely true power is self-evident – it does not require demonstration upon the weak. At that moment I was struck by a new idea – a concept so dangerous, so traitorous that it brought tears to my eyes: we deserved Nanscáwen. We deserved to lose our dominion over the land and its people because we were too proud, too filled with our importance, too corrupt. Nanscáwen wasn't an unwarranted tragedy that befell my people, it was a needed lesson in humility. And clearly, we still had not gotten the message.

But if we were being taught a lesson, then who was the teacher? My eyes instinctively looked skyward. In the summer heat, the clouds had piled themselves high until they looked like a great anvil suspended in the air. Surely it cannot be true that over all this chaos presides … something. Not gods with a little "g" like the Coranieid, but a God.

"Then why haven't you shown yourself?" I demanded of the clouds above. "Why haven't you spoken out?"

"Shh," whispered the reeds at the river's edge.

I looked at them. They speak without mouths or words, but through rustling movement. It was an interesting concept: to speak through movement ... or events? Fryok's death, the battle lost to the Sequani, a woman's cries that drove me to stand in cool waters and shout at the sky – were these messages? Was God speaking? I looked around. We, "the gods," did not make this world. So who did? It was too intricate, too perfectly balanced to be some fluke, some accident of nature. The Catholic Church believes that the world itself indicates "a higher intelligence... Rather than being mere chance, life on earth is no mistake ... it follows a plan."[181] And in the words of Colin Tudge, "in the face of wonders that are not of our making," reverence "is our only proper response."[182] These thoughts were radical and dangerous, and yet they settled quietly upon me and felt like truth.

Druids, like old Gwydion, called such a realisation an imbas, a moment of sudden illumination. All right. If there is a God and He speaks to us through events – what is the significance of Gwyn's assault on Gwenhwyfar? What is God trying to tell me? That such actions are wrong? I knew that already. I knew by my shaking hands and pounding heartbeat. But events such as these pose the uncomfortable question: What are you going to do about it?

"Fuck." I glared up at the sky. "Why is it my responsibility?"

The heavens were silent.

"Obviously because no one else will do a damn thing about it!" I yelled with all the petulance of an angry child. "Do you care at all what will happen to me if I intervene?"

Again, heaven had no answer.

To intervene would redirect the wrath of Gwyn ap Nudd from Gwenhwyfar onto me. Could I withstand it? I am one of the Old Ones, the Coranieid, who live long and heal fast. I had no doubt that I could bounce back a damn sight faster than Gwenhwyfar ever could.

The wind carried a murmur of activity from a distant village. Voices, the low of cattle and the metal ring of a blacksmith's hammer as it rose and fell. And I remembered the words that Silvius was reputed to have spoken to Brutus: hardship in our lives is like a blacksmith. Our metal is heated so that it can be recast, then it is hammered into a new shape. Our trials are like that: blow after blow of the hammer ... wait a bit and see what new thing you become.

"I understand," I whispered. As I waded back to the bank, I knew: God was hammering me into a shield.

By nightfall those high, towering clouds had unleashed their thunder and rain on us below. I returned soaking wet to my father's house with a heavily laden basket. My father and the others were in the great hall, and it was clear from the ring of his voice that he was in high spirits and had been on the mead. I quietly slipped past and headed for Gwenhwyfar's room. It was a pretty room fit for a captured queen, with a large canopied bed, lush bedclothes, a comfortable chair, a table and a warm fire. But now the bedclothes had been wrenched from the mattress and lay crumbled on the floor. The chair was broken, the table overturned, and Gwen lay on the floor in a naked, bloody heap. Her eyes were open but she did not see me. I spoke to her but she did not hear. It was only when I touched her that I got a reaction. She recoiled from me and pushed with her feet until her back met the wall. I took a firm hold of her and hauled her up to sit on the bed. She struggled weakly and slapped my face.

"I'd save my strength if I were you."

I hung a cauldron over the fire to bring water to the boil.

"What are you doing?" she rasped.

"Running you a bath. It's a restorative; I'd call it a cure-all, but I'm afraid that's too optimistic."

I boiled together hollyhock, damewort, mallow, hay riff, bugloss, wild flax and brown fennel, allowed it to cool below scalding temperature and had Gwenhwyfar soak in it while I washed her arms and feet. When she was warm and dry, I treated the cuts and bites on her thighs with agrimony, heartease and comfrey; I applied houseleek and witch hazel to the bruises on her face and chest.

She grabbed my hand, "Why are you helping me?"

For the first time since entering the room, I looked her in the eye. It was a mistake: my own eyes began to prick with unbidden tears. "You'll want to drink this," I pressed a cup into her hands. "It'll help you sleep."

"I don't want to sleep. He might come back…"

"He won't, I promise. Now drink while I make up your bed."

While Gwenhwyfar slept, I found an unbroken chair and sat at the table casting runes….

Inverted Kenaz ( 〉 ) … something important is ending. Yeah, no shit.

Because Sowilo ( ϟ ) and Algiz ( ᛉ ) … you bring light to darkness; you shield the weak. I noticed that the rune for protection, Algiz, looked like a stick figure with its arms raised to the heavens in supplication. How apt.

The result an inverted Berkana (ᛒ), you will alienate your people. Terrific.

Last rune: reversed Othala (ᛟ), you will stand alone. Yeah, I get that one a lot.

The door to the room creaked open. My father, reeking of ale, stared at me in surprise.

"No more," I said quietly. My voice sounded surprisingly calm and sure.

He left, slamming the door behind him, but not before I saw the look on his face.

"I am going to pay for that," I said, running a thumb over the Othala stone.

Before dawn, when Annwyn was silent and my people were breathing deeply in sleep, I awakened Gwenhwyfar, dressed her in one of my gowns and wrapped my cloak about her shoulders. Bidding her to be absolutely silent, I led her out of Annwyn and to the encampment where Artos rallied his men to fight for her.

"Your husband is camped just over that rise," I told her. "Go to him."

As I turned to leave, she grabbed my wrist, "What will happen to you?"

"I'll be fi—"

"No you won't. Not with him. Come with me."

"Go… And Gwenhwyfar, tell your husband to give back what he's taken." I walked away.

"Thank you!" she called after me.

I returned to Annwyn to await my punishment. I didn't have to wait long.

Back at Annwyn, the tribe was awake and gathered in the Great Hall. They were silent.

The calm before the storm, I thought. As I stepped over the threshold, they parted for me so that I could approach Gwyn's throne unimpeded. There sat my father.

"The sun has only just risen," he said calmly, "and already you've had such a busy day."

"Father…"

"First, you gave that bastard Vortigern an easy death. Then you sided with Myrddin to bring Uther into Annwyn, and now this." He smiled at me in such a way that my stomach lurched.

"Why is it that my only remaining child sees fit to betray me? Is it me,

Caja? Did I, in all these centuries of providing for you, do something to deserve this?"

I took a deep breath. "All this hatred for the Celtae, for mankind, for the world … I can't sustain it as long as you can… I don't want to. And your hatred for them is bigger than your love for me. You are set to prove that by whatever you have planned for me now."

He rose and swiftly descended the stone steps leading down from his throne.

"Please, father, it's not too late…"

He gripped me by the hair.

"…to show me you can still love me!" I shouted through gritted teeth as he dragged me from the Great Hall.

"Gwyn, please!" my mother wailed, following us.

Through the long, dark tunnels of Annwyn we moved. Every time I stumbled, I was hauled up and struck in the face or chest or given a humiliating kick to my rear or kidneys.

Dragged bleeding into the sunlight, I found a knife pressed to my throat. My mother was there. "Please stop this!" she wept. "She's all I have left!"

"Then I'll leave the decision to you," Gwyn snapped. "Exile or death?"

My mother was on her knees now weeping.

"Well, what's it to be?"

Mora took a few gasping breaths and struggled to her feet.

"I'll count to three," his blade broke the skin of my neck. "One … Two … Thr—"

"Exile!" my mother shrieked.

"Y-terryn genough! We break with you." He threw me to the ground.

And they were gone.

I lay, weeping in the dirt for a long while. And then I picked myself up and walked away from Annwyn and my tribe.

## Mora

She was calmer now. Calm enough to plan.

She'd been furious at first. That cauldron Artos stole – the one reputed to belong to the chief of Annwyn – was in fact hers. It had been a gift from Owain and she used it for scrying when the stream was frozen in winter or when the rain was pelting down. And Artos had taken it. Yes, she had been furious.

And then she had been distraught. Her daughter – her last remaining child – had been cast into exile all because of Artos and his wife.

But now she was no longer angry or distressed. Now her mind was clear and thinking. The Coranieid had made Artos and now they would break him. To this end, she crept into Artos' camp and stole the scabbard of the sword Caliburn. He was no longer invincible in battle; he could be hurt.

In legend this act was attributed to Morgan le Fay. The Fairy Morgan has an intricate history in the old stories. She was said to be Arthur's half-sister, a healer and a witch. She was a water elemental and the Breton word "morgan" meant water-nymph. She was depicted as both a web-footed hag and as a beautiful young woman – a temptress who "represents raw sexuality and the terror of the battlefield."[183] She was thought to be an embodiment of Modron, the goddess of fertility and motherhood.[184] She was also portrayed as the Morrighan – the ancient Celtic goddess of war. As such she was said to be "the goddess of divination and prophecy"[185] who knew in advance the outcome of any battle and the names of those who would be slain therein. From this root sprung the myth of "The Washer at the Ford," an entity "linked to the Morrighan and Morgan le Fay … [who] brings portent of death from the Otherworld."[186] Legend has it that the Washer at the Ford "wanders near deserted streams where she washes the blood from the grave-clothes of those who are about to die."[187]

Mora did not need to go scrying to know that the king's time on this earth was coming to an end. She would see to it. Now that Artos was as vulnerable as anyone else on the battlefield, she had only to ignite a conflict. She chose Medrawd (the king's illegitimate son by his mistress Garwen) as her catalyst.

While out hunting, Medrawd had chased a deer deep into the greenwood; on a powerful steed (a gift from his father) he outpaced his companions and found himself lost and alone. He paused, looking about him uncertainly and there between the trees, he caught a glimpse of a woman all in green.

"Hey! Hello!" he called, but she did not acknowledge him. Instead she picked her way down the steep side of a ravine. Unable to follow her – the slope was too sharp and tangled for his horse – he cut around in a wide arc, that brought him to a stream that trickled along the base of the chasm. There the woman knelt washing clothes in the chilly water.

She looked up at him and smiled. "Greetings, your majesty."

Medrawd laughed. "I'm not king. I am, however, lost. Do you know the way to the road on the plain?"

"Of course. Let me guide you."

She stood and approached him. She was a beautiful creature with dark, deep eyes and raven black hair. Medrawd was surprised by her boldness when she extended a hand and allowed him to pull her up to sit behind him in the saddle. What manner of woman would go so willingly with a stranger she met in the woods? he wondered. But then she wrapped her arms about his waist and pressed tight against his back. Medrawd was aroused by the feel of her breasts against him.

"What ... what is your name?"

"Call me Morgan."

"All right. So Morgan, which way?"

She directed him as they picked their way through the dense foliage. Finally, they emerged onto the plain with the road in sight.

"Thank you, lady," he said.

She hopped down. "You are very welcome, highness."

"Why do you keep calling me that?"

"Because one day soon you will be king."

"On what do you base that assertion?"

Morgan raised her hands and shouted, "Düs omma, fleghes!"

Medrawd did not understand her words, but moments later a raven swooped down and landed on her arm like a trained hawk. Then a great, grey wolf emerged from the woodland and lay at her feet.

"I know many things," she said quietly. "I can look upon the scattered seeds and know which will grow and bear fruit and which will not. And I tell you: you will grow to be an oak, a king, mighty and strong. But first you must chop away the old dead wood that crowds you out."

"Who are you?" he whispered.

"One who would see you reach your full height." She turned to leave.

"Wait!" he called, but the lady was gone. She seemed to melt back into the forest.

As he rode home, Medrawd (also called Medraut or Mordred in the old stories) was greatly troubled by his encounter with the lady in the woods. She said he would be king – a fine notion, but first he must cut away the "old dead wood" that stood in his way: Artos. She was suggesting that he commit treason and patricide. But that was absurd. Yes, he hoped to one day be king, and could be, if Artos and Gwenhwyfar did not produce a legitimate heir. And the queen after all was missing, maybe even dead. In which case, he need only wait.

As he entered the great hall, Medrawd stopped short. There, seated upon their thrones, sat Artos and Gwenhwyfar.

"Father! You're back! And you've found her! Welcome home, my queen!" He bowed low before Gwen, although in his heart he was dismayed.

"Thank you, Medrawd," Artos said tiredly. "Have you seen Merlin? Has he come back?"

"Not since your raid on Annwyn."

Artos nodded grimly. "I feared as much. Listen, I need you to do something for me."

"Name it."

"I need you to take the cauldron back."

"What?"

"You heard me."

"Father, you were lucky to get out of those tunnels alive. It would be foolhardy to…"

"Just take it to the entrance…"

"That entrance is now sealed."

"Just leave it there," Artos snapped. "They'll find it."

Medrawd gritted his teeth. The king had gotten himself embroiled in a conflict with the fay. By the looks of things Gwenhwyfar has paid dearly for it, he thought surveying the cuts and bruises on her face, her blackened eyes and split lip. And now he, Medrawd, would have to risk his life to take the damn cauldron back. All the while Artos sits there unscathed.

"As you wish, father," he said tersely and left.

With a contingent of men, Medrawd entered the forest and placed the cauldron by the thicket that had once been an entrance to Annwyn.

"Here it is … your cauldron … back." Initially he felt stupid talking to empty woodland, but when an arrow struck the man on his right, he realised it was not empty. Soon a hail of missiles from unseen bowmen found their targets as one by one his men fell. Medrawd turned and fled. He arrived back at his father's castle with an arrow impaled through his sword arm and the bitter knowledge that he was the lucky one – the rest of his men had perished in the wood.

It was a long painful night for him. The court physicians had to break the arrowhead off so that they could pull the shaft out of his arm, a procedure that made him shriek with pain. The wound was cleaned and bandaged and Medrawd was left to lie in his bed, staring at the ceiling while pain coursed through his arm clear up to his shoulder, his neck, and his jaw. At some point he must have dozed off because when he next opened his eyes, sunlight streamed in through the window where his father stood.

The king turned a haggard face to his son. "How do you feel?"

"Like hell."

"The rest of your men are dead."

"I know."

Artos fell silent for a long while. "Did they take the cauldron back? Did they say anything?"

"No," Medrawd rasped. "They just fired arrows at us."

"But will it appease them?"

Medrawd was surprised to see fear in his father's eyes. It made him angry. "How the hell should I know?" he snapped. "I was too busy to stop and chat. Maybe next time *you* should go and deal with them rather than letting everyone else pay for your mistakes!"

"That's enough!" And with that Artos stormed out.

Medrawd lay on the bed, his body rigid, his arm throbbing. "My thoughts exactly," he murmured.

In the days that followed, Medrawd often went out riding through the greenwood until he again found the stream that ran along the ravine.

"I wondered when you'd be back." The lady in green looked up from her washing. "I see your arm is healing nicely."

He held it up. "Your people?"

She nodded and went back to her scrubbing. "I told them to let you live."

"Why?"

"As I keep saying, you are destined to be king. Besides, I like you."

"I don't understand, Morgan. Why do you care if I'm king or not?"

Mora dropped the garment she'd been washing and sat back, brushing hair out of her eyes with the back of a wet hand. "Your father is king because we made him king. We introduced his father to his mother. We protected him as a child. We gave him a weapon that made him invincible and put our wisest counsellor at his side …"

"Merlin?"

"Merlin. We did all this for one reason: to wreak vengeance on the Saxons."

"Which he did."

"Yes," she nodded. "But then he got ambitious, and stupid." She laughed bitterly. "To steal from Annwyn ... that was a declaration of war. And already there are casualties," she looked meaningfully at his arm.

Mora rose and approached him. "You have a decision to make, Medrawd," she whispered.

"What?" he asked, his heartbeat quickening.

Mora pulled an amber comb from her hair, and her raven black locks fell around her face in ringlets. Coyly she twirled a strand of hair around one finger. "We made Artos king. We could do the same for Medrawd."

She was shimmying out of her dress now. The man could not believe his luck. This is actually happening, he thought.

"But that is up to you," Mora continued. In nothing but a thin shift, she moved in close to him. "Are you going to fight to keep that spoilt child on the throne? Or are you going to step forward and be the king Britain needs?"

She kissed him then, and his hands of their own volition slid around her waist. He pulled her close and they tumbled to the ground, entwined.

"What must I do?" he gasped as she straddled him.

"Assemble your forces," she panted. "Quietly."

"And Artos?" He bit his lip and thrust harder.

"To him ... you must appear innocent. All innocence on the surface." She smiled at him wantonly. Medrawd groaned and pulled at her hips. Her voice was husky in his ear, "But be a snake, ready to strike."

In that moment she moved so expertly on top of him that he felt as if he was floating.

"Can you do that?"

"Yes."

"Can you?" she gasped.

"Yes!"

In his life he had known passion and pleasure, but nothing like the lightning bolt of ecstasy that arced through him now. Mora, unmoved by the proceedings, strained against him until she wrung the name "Morgan" from his lips. Afterwards he clung to her with such ardour, showered her with such tender kisses that she knew she had him.

"I'll make you king," she murmured.

He panted, "What do you want me to do?"

Gradually, quietly, Medrawd garnered support from old opponents of Uther Pendragon, from Gorlois' extended family, and from Henin's clan – his mother's people. Then he waited.

He did not have long to wait. News reached the king that Rome once again demanded tribute from Britain. Artos responsed by taking his best warriors to the continent to challenge the Roman emperor Lucius. He was victorious, but at great cost: the cream of his army was lost in the effort. Upon hearing this, Medrawd seized power. For this reason, Medrawd (later known as Mordred) was forever remembered as the Third Dishonoured Man in the Island of Britain.

As the two forces – the king's depleted ranks and his son's swelling army – squared off at Camlan, Mora visited Artos in the night. It had been a long time since she had played the role of the mara, the thing that comes to weave unquiet dreams, but she had not lost her touch. In *Morte D'Arthur*, Sir Thomas Mallory describes the dream. Artos beheld a chair held fast to a giant wheel and "thereupon sat the king in his richest clothes." His chair was at the top of the wheel, far above an inky black lake that writhed with serpents. He was relieved to be out of their reach; but the wheel began to turn, moving him downward, down until he was in amongst the serpents that fastened on each of his limbs.[188]

The meaning of this dream was hardly ambiguous: fortune's great wheel had exulted him to great heights and now it would cast him down. Mora chuckled as she made her way back to the greenwood. Let him chew upon that for a while.

She was in very high spirits. Her plan had thus far worked perfectly. In fact James Wilhelm pegged it when he called her "the presiding genius of the story."[189]

But despite all that cleverness, I was concerned. "Have you forgotten the Saxons?" I asked.

Mora spun around in surprise. "Caja?" She embraced me. "How did I not hear you?"

"Well, I am trying to lay low."

She nodded. "Are you well?"

"What do you think?"

"I'm sorry. I am working on your father. He will relent."

I shrugged. "Mum, when you take out Artos, the Saxons will come back with a vengeance."

She paused to consider this, then shrugged. "Saxons, Picts, Romans, Celts – I'm starting to think that it makes no damn difference."

"Perhaps. But you could keep the Saxons at bay a little longer. If you're willing to resort to a few theatrics."

"I'm listening…"

It is said that at Camlan Artos asked for a parlay with Medrawd. So scant were the king's forces, he wanted time to garner support so that he could make a fair fight of it. Father and son met on the open field and Artos charged his men not to draw their swords unless threatened. According to the old ballad, "King Arthur's Death," that was when tragedy struck:

> "An adder crept forth of a bush,
> Stung one o' the king's knights on the knee…
> When the knight found him wounded sore
> And saw the wild-worm hanging there,
> His sword he from his scabbard drew …
> When the two hosts saw the sword,
> They joinèd in battàyle instantly."[190]

It is a fanciful bit of writing, but untrue. The only snake present at the conference was Medrawd. "Look like an innocent flower, but be the serpent beneath" – Mora had admonished him thus and Medrawd sat down to parlay with a dagger in his boot. The king had scarcely begun to speak when his son plunged the dagger into Cai's chest. The battle had begun.

What followed can only be described as a blood bath with Medrawd's superior numbers wiping out the king's men…

> "And when the king beheld his knights,
> All dead and scattered on the mould;
> The tears fast trickled down his face:
> That manly face in fight so bold….
> 'But see the traitor's yet alive,
> Lo, where he stalks among the dead!

> Now bitterly he shall abyde,
> And vengeance fall upon his head.'"[191]

Mounting his horse, Artos seized a lance and charged at Medrawd. Medrawd, knee-deep in the bodies of the slain, knew he could not run. He grabbed a spear that impaled a nearby corpse and yanked it free. Father and son met and Artos drove his spear through Medrawd's chest.

He looked up at Artos in shock. "But she said I'd be king." And then he died in all the time it takes to snuff out a candle or sever a thread. Mora's pawn was dead, but he had done his job. He had thrust his own spear upward into the king's belly.

Upon a lonely hill overlooking the carnage at Camlan, Artos handed the sword Caliburn to Bedwyr, his friend. "I need you to take this sword and throw it into yonder lake."

"My king," Bedwyr blustered, "I'm not going to throw your sword away."

"Do it!"

"This should be kept for generations to revere. They will look upon this and know the name of Artos."

"Dammit, listen to me!" Artos groaned, clutching his wound. "That sword belongs to the fay. If you keep it, they will haunt you all the days of your life."

"You jest."

"Do I look like I fucking jest?" Artos shouted. "I stole from them," he panted, "and since that day everything in my life has conspired to bring me to this." He showed Bedwyr his gory palms. "Now if you want to live, give back what is theirs."

Bedwyr, a young warrior in the king's service, was now sufficiently spooked. He ran down the hill to the lake at the edge of the battlefield. A thick mist tumbled along its surface and from within it he heard the sound of oars breaking water. He raised the sword to throw it.

"I'll take that."

A boat emerged from the mist and beached at the water's edge. A young woman held out her hand. Bedwyr turned the sword and offered her its grip.

There were three women in the boat: Hanyfer, who now held the sword, Nimue and Mora, who stepped forward and spoke: "Your king is gravely injured?"

"Yes."

"Fetch him. Now."

She spoke with such authority that Bedwyr ran scrambling up the hill. He returned a few moments later with Artos slung over his shoulder.

"Put him in the boat," Nimue said.

"Where are you taking him?"

Mora's voice was melodious, soothing, "To the Otherworld. There we will make him well and he will return to fight anyone who threatens this island. Spread the word, Bedwyr, he once was king and shall be again."

The bark slid back into the water and the mist and, weeping, Bedwyr turned away.

Once out of sight, Mora knelt down and clamped a hand over Artos' mouth. Without a word, she slit his throat.

As was the case with Boudicca, it was impossible for people to confirm the death of Artos without a body. Some said he was taken by Morgan le Fay to the Island of Avalon to be healed. Some said that he sleeps in a deep cave and will awaken when Britain needs him. Some even believed that he was magically transformed into a bird that still flies today. The point is that the Saxons remained wary and in this way the ghost of Artos "for a time at least delayed Britain's descent into the chaos known as the Dark Ages."[192]

CHAPTER 7

# "SEASONS OF MIST AND MELLOW FRUITFULNESS"

*"Seasons of mist and mellow fruitfulness*
*Close bosom-friend of the maturing sun;*
*Conspiring with him how to load and bless*
*With fruit the vines that round the thatch-eaves run…"*[193]

*John Keats, "To Autumn"*

First, the Coranieid ruled these lands.
Then the Celtae.
Then the Romans.
Then the Saxons.
Then the Normans.
It is always the same. The cycle of war, victory, dominion and dissolution repeats again and again throughout our history. We see it circling in the fates of individuals and nations. Artos saw it clearly in his last dream: the Wheel of Fortune had raised him to the top, to the pinnacle of wealth and power and esteem, and then the merciless, unceasing wheel turned again, casting him down.

Men imagined that a goddess – Fortuna – turned the wheel of men's fate. Dante called her the "Lady of Permutations":

> "…in changeless change through every turning year.
> No mortal power may stay her spinning wheel.
> The nations rise and fall by her decree."[194]

It is a grim view of life because, within its construct, the prince who awakens sleeping beauty with a kiss does not go on to live "happily ever after." There is no happily ever after, only good luck followed by bad, ascension followed by degradation, life followed by death.

The only way to escape this cycle is not to climb onto the wheel in the first place. The Roman philosopher Boethius, while musing along the same lines as Artos on the fleeting nature of happiness, took the idea one crucial step further: you "cannot keep it from departing when it will. How manifestly wretched, then, is this bliss of earthly fortune, which lasts not forever."[195] Therefore, do not strive in the service of ambition; do not prize earthly things which, by nature, are temporary; do not seek to raise yourself above all others; instead harken to a higher calling, a faith in God who is immortal and hence above the whims of Fortune.

Looking back on my life, I could see the Wheel of Fortune dictating its course. I was born into a tribe of gods, daughter of their chief, coddled and spoilt. Then in one grinding revolution we were cast down, driven from the land and the light. But the wheel was not done turning and in a final catastrophic fall, I lost kith and kin and Annwyn. Cast into exile, I sheltered in the cavern where Uther and I used to meet, and there I took great comfort in the writings of Boethius. He understood. He too had enjoyed great earthly prosperity, only to have it ripped from his grasp. And yet he was not bitter. He had intelligence and a good heart; and in *The Consolation of Philosophy* he came to this conclusion: "The wise man ought not to take it ill, if ever he is involved in one of fortune's conflicts… The time of trial is the express opportunity … to perfect his wisdom. Hence, indeed, virtue gets its name, because … it yieldeth not to adversity."[196]

I came to realise that even our tragedies do not arrive empty-handed. They come bearing gifts – of experience, of strength, of wisdom. And I resolved to put those gifts to use. Among the villagers there was one called Demelza who was a wise woman and a healer. It was to her that I imparted everything that

Myrddin had taught me. I taught her how to use houseleek and yarrow to treat ague, and to employ betony in cases of lipsy. I showed her how to make a poultice out of hops to reduce inflammation, and instructed her in the beneficial properties of burdock in the treatment of gout. These were quiet, homely moments and hugely satisfying, for Demelza was kind, had a wry sense of humour, and the hours passed quickly in her company.

We developed a little system for contacting each other. In the wood, not far from her cottage, a fine, old oak tree stood. A lightning strike had exposed a patch of sapwood on its trunk and this had eroded to produce a cavity two fists in diameter. Everyday I'd check the tree hollow for a communication from Demelza. A twig bearing the small oval leaves of the blackthorn shrub, for instance, signified that Demelza was dealing with a difficult case and needed my help. A pale pink, frilled Dianthus blossom meant "make haste" – "I need your help urgently." And every time she used one of my remedies to cure a patient she would leave me a sprig of agrimony – "thank you."[197] These I took home with me and hung upside down to dry, their tiny yellow flowers bringing a bit of sun to the cave.

While I collected my little yellow flowers, larger events were in motion, driven by those who still chose to ride Fortune's Wheel. The year was 1066, and by the fourth of January Edward the Confessor was dead. Fortune turned her wheel and the Saxon Harold Godwinson (also known as Harold II) rose to be crowned king. The seeds of his downfall, however, were already being sown. A rival claimant to the throne, William I of Normandy, was building a fleet to invade England and take the crown by force. History was again in the making, but in the spring of that year I was more intrigued by the sudden and unexpected sounds of habitation coming from Merlin's Cave.

The chamber that Uther and I once shared lay behind its back wall. The wall was thin and sound carried. But who – or what – would choose to live in Merlin's cave? It opened onto a thin stretch of beach, at that time inaccessible by foot or boat. At every high tide, the cold waters of the Atlantic would surge in, leaving only the nether two-thirds of the cavern dry. It was dark and damp and wind-beaten and was not fit for man nor beast.

On the next day when the sun shone down on calm water, I took to the sea and approached Merlin's cave. Hanyfer would have made the swim easily, but I was not good in deep water and so arrived on the beach breathless and tired. As I stood, hands on knees, gasping, a strong pungent smell made me cough, until I gagged up some of the sea water I'd swallowed on my way in. Something – something big – had scent-marked that beach, laying an undeniable claim to it.

I noticed then odd markings in the sand. There were tracks of a large creature walking on all fours. Each footprint showed where the animal's three long claws sank in the sand, followed by a ghost of a heel print. Whatever it was, it walked balancing its weight on the balls of its feet. Despite its size it did not plod along, but walked almost on tiptoe for greater speed and agility. Strangest of all, a deep line wiggled between the footprints, as if a heavy snake had followed the creature into the water. I stayed crouched over the tracks, puzzling, until the penny finally dropped. Of course … there was only one thing in this part of the world that left tracks like that in the sand: a dragon, with four clawed feet and a long tail dragging behind.

"Brilliant," I murmured.

There had not been a dragon in Britain in over six hundred years. A sharp decline in their numbers, combined with loss of habitat as the human population grew, meant that a dragon was now a rare and wonderful thing to see. And see it I would. I took shelter behind a large rock near the cave's entrance and waited.

Finally a quiet splash heralded its approach. It crawled up onto the beach with a large, wriggling grouper pinned in its jaws. The dragon's scales, a luminous white like mother-of-pearl, flashed in the sunlight and I smiled in recognition. It was Xiàngshù, the young dragon who fled these lands with her mother during Vortigern's reign. And now she was all grown up, returning to our island in the spring along with the chiffchaffs from southern Europe and the swallows from Africa.

I was tempted to follow her into the cave to speak with her, but not even an immortal Coranieid would dare interrupt a dragon while it was feeding. Therefore I left quietly and resolved to return.

Over the next several weeks, I kept my distance, stayed downwind and watched her. She fished and hunted often and seemed particularly hungry for the nutritious brains and skin of the fish and the protein-rich fat of seal blubber. She shifted boulders – with more difficulty than I would have expected – so that her beach was hidden from the view of passing boats and the entrance to the cave was more sheltered. And she cleaned like a medieval reptilian Martha

Stewart. It was singularly odd to see such a majestic creature doing housework, sweeping out her cave with her tail instead of a broom. Finally, I realised the truth: she, as the locals liked to say, had jumped over the besom. In plain speech, she was pregnant and hence, like the chiffchaff and the swallow, she was nesting.

And yet the problem still remained: how do I approach her? Dragons are an interesting dichotomy. They are as intelligent and articulate as the brightest of humans, but they can be as dangerous and unpredictable as any creature in any jungle on earth. Making contact with them is to flip a coin. Will it be heads or tails? A reasoned, articulate welcome or the roar and claws of a beast? And then, of course, there was the issue of Andras. That demon was the last stranger to offer her friendship; and he had ignited such strife between her and her mother that they were discovered and imprisoned for half a millennium. If I were to walk up to the mouth of her cave as he had done, she may very well rip me to pieces. And so I decided that the safest option was to let her find me. She must be the one to say hello first.

Exiled and alone in volatile times, I lived a quiet, inconspicuous life. Now however, it was necessary to make some noise. In my own cave, I started small with little domestic sounds of cooking and cleaning, the shh-shh of the broom, the scrape of a chair, the odd dropped cup. In response I heard a low snuffling sound up and down and along the wall. She was trying to pick up my scent. After days of this, I finally tried my masterstroke: first humming, then singing Uther's lullaby to myself as I worked. A mother-to-be would be touched by its words, and sure enough, when I'd finished, there was a light tap-tap-tapping on the wall.

I answered her back, tap, tap, tap.

She responded with a different rhythm and I copied it. She rapped again and again in increasingly intricate patterns until they got so complicated that I messed them up and burst out laughing.

"Hello?" her voice was muffled.

"Hello."

"Who are you?"

"I'm of the Coranieid."

"The Coranieid live in Annwyn." Even through the rocky wall her voice sounded flat, annoyed. She was thinking that I was a liar and a threat. For the sake of her young, she'd have to move.

"I lived in Annwyn … until I angered my chief."

"You crossed Gwyn ap Nudd? Are you crazy?"

"Apparently so."

"So … you're alone?"

"Yes."

There was a long silence then, "Me too."

"Isn't that how dragons rear their young? Alone, I mean."

"I have no young."

"Yet."

There was another long pause. "How do you know that I'm a dragon?"

I opted for the truth. "I've seen you."

"Then you have me at a disadvantage, for I have not seen you."

"Yet."

When she didn't respond, I asked, "If you do see me, are you going to bite my head off?"

"I honestly haven't decided yet."

Another silence lapsed while Xiàngshù considered her options. Finally she said, "Hey, Coranieid."

There was no answer.

"Hello," she drawled but again nothing. "Huh," she grunted. "Maybe I scared her off."

"Not likely." The voice came not from behind the stone wall, but from the mouth of the cave.

Xiàngshù emerged into the sunlight to find me standing at the water's edge. Her cerebral cortex ignited with rapidly increased alertness. The memory of Andras twisted her face into a scowl. She tensed up, ready. Her cerebellum back near the brain stem prepared to coordinate movement for flight or, more probably, fight.

"You've been spying on me."

"Yes I have. I wanted to know who my new neighbour was."

"So what have you learned?"

"I know that you are Xiàngshù, daughter of Hónglián Huā – how is your mother, by the way?"

Xiàng looked a bit dumbstruck. "She's in China."

"I know that the two of you left the Island during the reign of Vortigern Gwrtheyrn. I watched you go."

Xiàngshù's face was inscrutable. "I take it you know the whole story?"

I shrugged. "I'm Coranieid."

"Then you know that I don't trust you at all."

"Yet." I smiled wryly at her.

She snorted. "I don't like … this."

"What exactly?"

"The one-sidedness of it. You seem to know everything about me and I know nothing about you."

"Then ask questions."

"Ok," she paused, and then looked at me slyly. "What did you do to anger Gwyn ap Nudd?"

I sighed. I knew that was coming. "King Artos stole something from us. Gwyn took his revenge through Gwenhwyfar. I smuggled her out of Annwyn to safety."

"How did he find out?"

"Gwyn? He was waiting for me when I got home that morning. He dragged me out of Annwyn by my hair. He threatened to cut my throat." I pulled the neckline of my dress aside to show her the scar left by Gwyn's blade.

"But surely your family … they would have intervened …"

"Gwyn ap Nudd is my father."

She looked at me, aghast. "I'm sorry."

I shrugged with a nonchalance I didn't feel. "It was a long time ago."

I saw her visibly relax. The hyper-alert firing of neurons quieted and dimmed. She sat down on the sand.

"Things can sting for a long time," she said.

"Andras?" I asked, sitting down next to her.

"Andras."

"We make quite a pair," I chuckled.

"Yeah, well, misery loves company."

"And so does joy. When are you due?"

"I won't see the eggs before Christmas. I've got a lot to do before then."

"Need any help?"

Xiàngshù chiselled a shallow pit big enough for her clutch out of the granite floor of the cave, and we lined it with leaves for insulation. Some of the leaves were still on the twig, but that did not matter. Dragon eggs have rock-hard shells and thus the hollow did not need to be soft. It did, however, need to be warm. And so we set about the mammoth task of collecting firewood – enough wood to keep a fire burning for a full four years while the baby dragons incubated in the shell.

"I have had it!" Xiàngshù dropped a load of kindling onto the floor and stalked out of the cave. On the way, she tripped over an errant branch and cursed loudly.

It was late August, her belly was round and heavy with eggs and she was really minding the heat. She plunged into the sea and made straight for the cloudy depths where the water is coolest. I sat in the shallows and waited, wondering (not for the first time) how dangerous a hormonal dragon could become.

When she emerged, she was calmer. "Sorry about that," she said as she stretched out on the warm sand to bask.

"Nothing to be sorry about." I stretched out beside her with an arm draped over my eyes, shielding them from the sun. "I'll tidy up that kindling in a moment."

"Please take a break. If you get up and work, I'll feel honour-bound to help and I really just want to lie here for a bit."

We lay in companionable silence, soaking up the sun for a long time.

"So tell me about China," I murmured, half asleep.

"It's beautiful. Big, white-capped mountains and lakes of pink water lilies, green valleys and grand temples… Do you know they worship dragons there?"

"What?"

"Yeah, they pray to dragon idols and ask for rain and sun for their crops."

I sat up and looked at her. "We were worshipped as gods once. It didn't do us one bit of good."

"No dragon in China really considers itself a god. It's more like…" she searched for the words to explain, "…people's expectations of us have come to shape our expectations of ourselves. They regard us so highly that we don't want to disappoint them; we don't want to be diminished in their eyes."

I thought again of Gwyn and the way he looked at me before he turned his back on me forever. I knew very well how it felt to be diminished in the eyes of others. I cleared my throat and plunged back into the conversation.

"Tell me more about these dragon-gods. There must be a story or two behind it all."

"You're the story-teller. How did you put it? Oh yeah, 'the keeper of the soul stones and the stories,'" she said grandly. "The perfect omniscient narrator."

I laughed. "Yes, so tell me a story and I'll keep it."

## A Side Note

*The Four Dragon Kings:*

*Once upon a time, the land of China was dry. There were no rivers and no lakes dotted with pale water lilies. There was only a great sea to the East. Within the cool depths of that sea lived four dragons: the Long Dragon, the Yellow Dragon, the Black Dragon and the Pearl Dragon.*

*Even though they were many hundreds of years old, they lived a life of childish simplicity: eating, sleeping while rocked by the waves, and playing amongst the seaweed of the ocean bed and the downy clouds of the sky. On one such flight amidst the clouds, the Pearl Dragon stopped short and hovered in place.*

*"Look at this," he said to the others.*

*There upon the earth were many people gathered together, leaving an offering of a little fruit and a little incense.*

*"That is a scant offering," said the Black Dragon.*

*"It's all they have," replied the Long Dragon. "Look how thin they are!"*

*The emaciated crowd bowed in prayer and the voice of a white-haired woman rose. "God in Heaven," she said, "please send us rain, for without it our crops will die and we will soon follow."*

*Indeed there had been no rain that season, and the fruit withered on the vine and the green valleys turned a brittle yellow. Looking upon the villagers, upon the dull, weary despair in the eyes of their children, the four dragons quit their game and went straight to the Jade Emperor to report the problem.*

*The Jade Emperor, also known as Father Heaven, was god of all that was on the earth or in the sea. They found him sitting on his throne, listening to the ethereal songs of nymphs.*

*"What?" he said without opening his eyes.*

*"Your majesty," the Long Dragon said, making a deep bow, "the people of the land pray to you for help. Their crops fail because there is no rain..."*

*"They are starving," the Black Dragon interrupted. The Long Dragon*

was given to long explanations which the Black Dragon hoped to curtail. The Jade Emperor, after all, was not known for his patience.

Still with his eyes shut, Father Heaven raised one hand and motioned them away.

"So you'll send rain?" the Yellow Dragon asked anxiously.

The music stopped. The Emperor's eyes slowly opened and the look in them caused all four dragons to take a step backward.

"Tomorrow." His eyes slid shut again. "Go." He snapped his fingers and the nymphs resumed their singing.

"Well, that's settled. He'll send the villagers rain tomorrow." The Pearl Dragon sounded less than confident as the four of them made their way home.

Seated in luxury and in plenty on his throne, the Jade Emperor forgot about the villagers' plight as soon as the dragons left. He did not send rain the next day. Or the next. Or the next. Soon it became clear he would not send rain at all.

"He's not going to help," the Black Dragon told the other three.

"Then it is up to us," said the Pearl Dragon.

"But what can we do?" the Yellow Dragon asked.

"I don't know," the Pearl Dragon answered. "It is ironic, isn't it? We have so much water here," he gestured at the sea around them, "and the village has none."

"That's it!" cried the Long Dragon. He pushed off from the ocean bed and darted for the surface.

"What?" called the Pearl Dragon, paddling behind.

"We share what we have!" And the Long Dragon took a great mouthful of water.

He flew toward the village and sprayed it upward. The water fell like raindrops upon the parched fields. The other dragons followed suit, making trip after trip from the sea to the sky above the village. The beating of their wings was like thunder, and below the people rejoiced.

Back in his palace the Jade Emperor listened as an advisor told him what the dragons had done. Though he cared nothing for the villagers, he cared very much for his own authority to decide their fate. Therefore he imprisoned the dragons, each alone under a different mountain so they could never escape.

"That's a bit like you and your mum – imprisoned in that cave all those years." I rose and brushed the sand off my skirt.

Xiàngshù stretched. "Yep, but that's not the end of the story."

"So what happened?"

"The four dragon kings, in a last act of defiance and compassion, turned themselves into the four great rivers of China so that the people would always have water. They are the Huanghe or Yellow River, the Yangtze or Long River, Heilongjian or Black River and the Zhujiang or Pearl River."[198]

While Xiàngshù and I swapped stories and busied ourselves with domestic tasks, Fortune's Wheel kept turning and the Saxon King Harold II found his dominion under threat. On 26th September he fought off a Viking Invasion at Stamford Bridge in Yorkshire; it was a decisive victory for the king. However his great rival, William I of Normandy, chose that moment to attack, landing near Hastings on September 28th. After a forced march of two hundred miles, Harold's exhausted forces met the Normans in battle on 14th October 1066.

A hail of Norman arrows bounced uselessly off the wall of Saxon shields, and William's cavalry was routed by Harold's axe-wielding infantry. The Normans turned and fled. At that moment, Fortune tugged at her wheel once more: "Several units of the English army broke ranks, contrary to Harold's orders, and pursued the retreating Normans. Other Norman troops quickly surrounded and annihilated these units."[199] This episode did not go unnoticed. William's mind was already planning and calculating. The apparent lack of discipline amongst the British ranks could be used to his advantage. Therefore he ordered another of his units to feign panic and retreat. Again a large contingent of Harold's men broke ranks to pursue the fleeing Norman forces. Harold watched in horror as these men were also cut off and butchered. He lost so many soldiers that the tide of the battle swiftly turned. The last thing King Harold Godwinson saw as Fate's Wheel came to a rest was an arrow headed straight for his face. Harold II was struck by that arrow in the eye and died on the battlefield, while his men were massacred around him. And on Christmas Day 1066, five days after Xiàngshù laid her two eggs, William I – William the Conqueror – was crowned King of England.

As if nature mimicked the state of men, the weather was tempestuous that winter. Violent storms swept in off the Atlantic, battering the coastal villages. Beside the turbulent enormity of the gale, men felt small and at the mercy of mammoth and indifferent forces. When this happens, the minds of men become fertile ground for the cultivation of myths and legends, of stories to explain events beyond their ken:

> The coasts of Britain, lashed by fierce storms and shrouded by frequent mists, form the setting for many old and curious legends... They vary from the imaginary to the semi-historical ... to traditions which almost certainly have some foundation in fact.[200]

One day as the local fishermen loaded their nets and prepared to cast off, a thick fog rolled in from the sea.

"Oh hell," said Gennys.

Pawly shrugged. "So, it's misty."

"Fog fishing is crap. We never take a good haul in it."

"I don't know. Old Talek said he took one of his best catches in fog. Isn't that right?"

They looked to Talek to settle the dispute.

"Yup," the old man said.

"Yeah, but sailing in this murk ..." Gennys complained.

"... is normal," Talek finished.

Then from within the fog bank came a low, mournful cry. The men stopped working and stared at the mist.

"What the hell was that?" Pawly asked.

"That is not normal," Talek murmured.

The fishermen stood dumbstruck as the forlorn call of "whoo-whoo" began again.

"It's a sign." And with that pronouncement, old Talek turned on his heel and walked away.

"A sign?" Gennys shouted after him. "Of what?"

Talek turned back to them and shrugged. "No fishing today." And whistling, he headed home.

The others stood looking at each other uncertainly and then, one by one, they returned to the village.

Xiàngshù crawled out of the water near her cave.

"Very effective," I said.

She smiled indulgently. "Fishermen are superstitious. They only needed a little encouragement."

"The mist was a good trick. How'd you manage it?"

She shrugged, "Just breathe fire on the water to make steam."

I followed her into the cave. "But why warn them at all? It's dangerous, Xi, to involve yourself with humans."

"Seen Demelza lately?"

"Touché."

Back in the village, as the storm battered the fishermen's cottages, the men told their wide-eyed children about the unnatural fog they had seen and the ghostly "whooping" sound that issued from it.

"Old Talek said it was a sign," Pawly told his son. "And look at it enting down. I'm glad I'm not out in it."

### A Side Note

*The Legend of the Hooper (part 1):*

*In* Folklore and Legends of Cornwall, *M.A. Courtney describes an entity known to haunt the beaches of Kernow: "A remarkable spirit called the Hooper – from the hooping, or hooting sounds it was accustomed to make. In old times, according to tradition, a compact cloud of mist often came in from over the sea … a dull light was … seen amidst the vapour, with sparks ascending as if a fire burned within it; at the same time hooping sounds were heard proceeding therefrom. People believed the misty cloud shrouded a spirit, which came to forewarn them of approaching storms…"*[201]

While the wind howled and the rain came down in sheets, I returned to my cavern grateful for the door that Blue-cap had knocked between Xiàng's cave and mine.

"Hello, Myrddin! I didn't know you'd come."

When he did not answer me, I stopped and took a closer look at the old medhek. He looked pale and shaken, a sheen of cold sweat on his brow.

"Are you all right?"

"Yes." His voice shook. "I just got lost … in the tunnels."

"How did you manage that?"

"I don't know."

Myrddin had visited the cavern beneath Tintagel hundreds of times. Even after my banishment he came bringing supplies and news of the tribe. He knew those tunnels like the back of his hand.

"Myrddin, what's wrong?"

"I am."

"What do you mean?"

"I'm wrong. I keep forgetting things and getting confused. Caja, what's happening to me?"

"I don't know."

"But you could look … in my mind."

"Yes, but…"

"Please."

"As you wish."

I made us both a cup of sweet tea and waited for him to calm down. I watched him for a moment. Yes, he knew those tunnels like the back of his hand, but his hands had changed. They were now old man's hands – gnarled and withered and covered with liver spots. Quietly I looked not at his mind – at its thoughts and memories – but at the brain, the physical, raw material of the mind. I wanted to see if, like his gnarled hands, his brain had aged in some meaningful way.

What I saw was horrific. The human brain is normally a substantial organ, as plump and as grooved as a ripe blackberry. But Myrddin's was diminished. In particular, the hippocampus – that part of the brain in charge of memory and navigation – had shrunk. Normally the size of fat sausages, Myrddin's two hippocampi had shrivelled to bony fingers. The cerebral cortex, too, was showing signs of wear and the structural integrity of the neurons themselves had been corrupted. They were bound in what looked like tangles of thread that disrupted communication between neurons, hindering the regular functioning of the brain. While I describe this to you now in modern neurological terms, at the time I was only aware of a pronounced sense of degradation and the knotted tangles of Myrddin's thoughts.

"So are you going to look?" he asked.

"I already have."

Myrddin did not look at me; his gaze remained fixed on the cup of tea he clasped in both hands. "What did you see?"

"Something has attacked parts of your brain … like the part that fires when you remember directions."

"What is it?"

"I don't know."

"Will it heal?"

"I don't know that either. I've never seen anything like it."

He looked at me in surprise. "Never?"

"Never. You know, it could just be a sign of old age."

"Maybe."

"Think about it: the average life expectancy today is what? Thirty ... thirty-five? And how long have you been alive? Maybe this is just part of growing older, and the reason that I haven't seen it before is that people don't grow old – not like us."

"Maybe."

"Myrddin, a little forgetfulness, the odd episode like you had today is not the end of the world. We can deal with it."

My voice was firm; my reasoning could not be refuted by any known facts. In convincing him, I sought to convince myself that my initial reaction of horror was too strong. The degradation I had sensed was not as bad as I assumed. Myrddin would be fine and all would be well. Even so I walked him back through the tunnels, as close to Annwyn as I dared to venture, just to be sure.

### A Side Note

*I would later realise, while reading the works of Alois Alzheimer in 1906 and those of the scientists who expanded upon his work, that Myrddin had Alzheimer's Disease. It attacks the cerebral cortex and the hippocampus in the brain, causing a pronounced loss of mass. Its symptoms include confusion, mood swings, emotional withdrawal from family and friends, and loss of the cognitive "map" that helps us physically navigate to familiar destinations. Short-term memory of recent events goes first, leaving long-term memories (from childhood for instance) intact for a while. It is a progressive disease, worsening until the patient is left bedridden and unable to communicate or perform basic tasks. Gradually, the body begins to shut down and cause of death is often the result of some external factor, like pneumonia or some other illness that the patient's compromised immune system cannot fight off.*

*The causes of Alzheimer's are as yet unknown, although there are several theories. One is that during that explosive neural growth of early childhood, there is a mechanism in the brain that "prunes neural connections," regulating the vital development that is taking place. It is thought that, for some unknown reason, that mechanism is reactivated in old age "to cause the neuronal withering of Alzheimer's disease."[202]*

*If that is true, then it represents the Wheel of Fortune at its most cruel. In bringing us full circle back to our childhood, our second childhood, the very processes that helped us develop prove to be our undoing. As Dr. J.M. Gregor Robertson notes, we become "silly, weak, childish... While ... the things of yesterday are entirely forgotten, the events of early life may throng up and the person lives in the past, as it were calling the persons around him by the names of those he knew in youth, who have been long dead or absent."[203] H.C. Covey, in his article "A Return to Infancy: Old Age and the Second Childhood in History," agrees: "Through Western history, scholars and writers have characterised old age as a period of second childhood and childish behaviour... Explanations for this stereotype were linked to ... perceived and actual dependency of older people for care (and the incidence of) dementia. The second childhood was also interpreted as a stage of life where the life cycle returned to its beginning."[204]*

*Another theory centres on the neurons themselves. Every neuron, every brain cell, whether it's in the cerebral cortex or the hippocampus, has a cytoskeleton which maintains its structural integrity. The cytoskeleton is made up of microtubules – little tubes that feed nutrients to all parts of the neuron – and the activity of these microtubules is regulated by a protein called "tau." In Alzheimer's Disease, this tau protein, for unknown reasons, undergoes a chemical change and begins to bind with other strands of tau, forming the tangled, knotted threads I observed in Myrddin. These tangles choke off the supply of nutrients throughout the neuron by obstructing its flow through the microtubules. As a result the neuron dies, as do thousands, millions like it within the brain.*

*Back in 1067 I did not understand all of this and even now my grasp on the material is tenuous. But the horror of that moment as I looked into Myrddin's mind was rooted in the unwelcome intuition that the long thread of Myrddin's life was coming to a tangled end.*

Robert Frost once said, "In three words I can sum up everything I've learned about life: it goes on." And so it does. Despite exile, despite Myrddin's illness, despite wars and conquests and the rise and fall of nations, day follows day, one after the other ad infinitum.

By autumn 1069 more storms swept in from the cold Atlantic. This kept Xiàngshù busy forewarning the local fishermen of approaching danger. Early one morning, Xiàngshù stood poised at the mouth of the cave.

"What's wrong?" I asked.

"Red sky."

"Oh yes. How does it go? 'Red sky at night, sailor's delight.'"

She nodded, "Red sky in morning, sailors take warning."

"I was just reading about that. 'When it is evening, ye say, it will be fair weather: for the sky is red. And in the morning, it will be foul weather today: for the sky is red and lowering. O ye hypocrites, ye can discern the face of the sky; but can ye not discern the signs of the times?'"

She cocked an eyebrow at me.

"Matthew, chapter sixteen, verses two and three," I shrugged.

"I went in for a swim this morning. The blackfish are schooling."

"Which means?"

"It's a sign of an approaching gale – a bad one…"

"How bad?"

"Sixty, sixty-five knots. I'd better go and catch them before they put to sea."

I admonished her, "Be careful, and Xi …"

"What?"

"Get back here before that storm hits."

"Yes, Mum." She grinned at me and was gone.

That morning Colum and his ten year old son, Jowan, made ready to cast off. For the fisherman it was the morning after the night before – a night of heavy drinking that had left him ornery and hung over. In all truth he did not want to spend the day in a rocking boat with the smell of fish making his tender stomach roil; but he had no choice. During a game of *Hazards* last night he had done fair, just about breaking even. Other players, however, raked in pot after pot, the jammy bastards. Colum began to feel that surely he was due for a bit of good luck and so, in a moment of drunken optimism, had bet all on the last roll.

"It's my turn," he mumbled as he shook the knuckle-bone dice in his hand and cast them onto the table. The dice seemed to tumble in slow motion before coming to a rest. He blinked at them stupidly. Unbelievable. He'd rolled a double one and a roll of two was the only fucking roll that meant an automatic loss. After much profanity and a few vivid threats of violence, he was ejected from the game and returned home with nothing in his pockets. But that was all right. A good catch today would bring in enough money so that he could hide his losses from the wife. If he caught nothing, he was in for an ugly scene which his throbbing head could not abide. And so he was not pleased when he saw an unearthly fog bank drifting toward the harbour. A low, ghostly "Whoo, whoo" sent an involuntary shiver down his spine.

"Father, isn't that the…"

"The Hooper," Colum said.

With a resigned sigh, the boy started to put the nets away.

"What are you doing?"

"Stowing the nets."

"Why?" Colum demanded.

The child looked at him in confusion. "Well, because of *that*," he gestured at the mist.

"Cast off."

"What?"

"I said, *CAST OFF!*" Colum yelled and the boy obeyed.

Grabbing the oars they rowed out, but as they approached the fog bank, Jowan dug his oar into the water, slowing their progress and causing the small vessel to tack off to the right. His reticence was met with a sharp clip on the earhole and he pulled once again on the oars. They entered the fog. They could see nothing but white mist and a dim glow up ahead. Suddenly the boat came to an abrupt halt, and something in the brume shunted the boat back toward shore. Colum rowed with all his strength, but could not halt the backward progress of the vessel.

"Damn your hide," he hissed, grabbed a threshal and tried to beat his way through the fog.

Initially the blows of the flail landed harmlessly on Xiàngshù's thick scales, but then one unlucky strike caught her on her soft, unprotected belly. With a roar the dragon jerked backwards in the water, instinctively lashing out with her tail. The small wooden craft shattered, sending father and son into the water. Xiàngshù made a frantic grab at the boy, hauling him out of the water. The child lay cradled in her hands, his eyes open and devoid of expression, his head lolling at an unnatural angle to one side. The dragon shrieked in horror and shook the boy as if to wake him.

"No, no, no, no, no..."

Jowan hung there limply, and the dragon thought that his dead eyes now regarded her with a silent accusation.

"Oh hell, the father..."

The boy was dead, but she still might be able to save the man. Again and again, she dove, searching for him in the murk, to no avail. Finally she found Colum caught in a deep undertow, drowned. She left him there for the sharks.

### A Side Note

*The Legend of the Hooper (part 2):*
*Courtney had this to add to the story: "People believed the misty cloud shrouded a spirit, which came to forewarn them of approaching storms, and that those who attempted to put to sea found an invisible force – seemingly in the mist – to resist them. A reckless fisherman and his son, however, disregarding the token, launched their boat and beat through the fog with a 'threshal' (flail); they passed the cloud of mist which followed them and neither the ... (fishermen) nor the Hooper were ever more seen."* [205]

*The cause of the tragedy was rooted in the physical nature of the dragon herself. Dragons are protected by a thick coat of armour that is fireproof and capable of deflecting spears, swords and flying projectiles. As it is said in the Book of Job:*

> *"Who can strip off his outer garment?*
> *Who can penetrate his double coat of mail?*
> *...His back is made of rows of shields*
> *Shut up closely as with a seal...*
> *They are joined to one another*
> *...and cannot be separated*
> *...Though the sword reached him, it does no avail;*
> *Nor the spear, the dart or the javelin...*
> *Upon earth there is not his like, a creature without fear."* [206]

*The only exposed patch of flesh is located on the dragon's stomach, and this is as tender and sensitive as a human baby's skin. In the old Legend of Sigurd, the hero manages to kill the dragon Fafnir by hiding in a covered pit. When Fafnir passed overhead, Sigurd thrust his sword up into the soft underbelly of the beast.*

*It is an extremely vulnerable point, a chink in the dragon's armour. Therefore when Colum's whip bit into the tender flesh of Xiàngshù's belly, she lashed out instinctively. This wounded-animal rage (that grips a dragon when in pain) is legendary. In* Beowulf *it is said the dragon, enraged by a wound from the hero's blade, "grew savage in mood,/ spat death-fire."*[207]

"How are you?"

Xiàngshù did not answer. She was curled up by her eggs, staring listlessly at the fire. We sat in silence for a long time.

Finally she said, "I didn't mean to…"

"I know." I paused, knowing that what I was about to say would only make her feel worse. "Xi, I've been listening to the villagers. You were spotted."

"What?"

"When you came out of the mist to lay the child's body on the beach, someone saw you."

"Great."

"You're not safe here anymore."

She shrugged, "I can't do anything about that."

"You could leave."

"I won't leave my children."

"Take them with you."

She shook her head. "If I move them now, they won't hatch."

"Then lay low. Only go out to hunt and only hunt at night."

I stayed with her during her enforced confinement. We talked and drank and played chess, but no distraction, no amusement could banish the spectre of the dead fisherman and his boy from her mind.

"Checkmate," she said dully. "What's the score?"

"Thirty-five to two in your favour. My humiliation continues." I took another swig of mead. "Play again?"

"No, I'm bored with chess." She got up and paced restlessly around the cave. "I wonder how they are," she said finally.

"Who?"

"The fisherman's family."

I sighed, "You have got to let this go." I could see my words were having no effect and got frustrated. "Damn it, Xi, Colum got what he deserved."

She opened her mouth to speak, but I plunged onward. "These people," I drunkenly waved a hand in the direction of the village, "were presented with something mysterious and wonderful that protected them. And so Colum attacks it? What a moron! Face it: he didn't die because you were wrong, he died because he was idiot enough to take on the unknown with a whip while standing in a tottering row boat!"

"The child was innocent."

"He was his father's responsibility. Colum knowingly, purposely put his son in harm's way."

"He didn't know there was a dragon in the mist."

"No, but he knew – from your warning – that a bad storm was brewing. He took Jowan out anyway. One way or another it was not going to end well for them."

I sat down by the fire with a thud. "Come on, you need more mead. Lots of it."

I poured out a generous amount into the concave basin worn into the rocky floor. She sat next to me and drank.

"You look tired."

"Drunk is more like," I said.

"Why don't you get some sleep?"

"I'll just rest my eyes for a minute." I closed them and leaned back against a smooth patch of rock. "Tell me a story," I murmured.

"Really?"

"Yeah, one of your dragon tales."

### A Side Note

*The Story of Apalala:*
*Buddhist legend tells us that long ago in India there was a dragon who lived in the Swat River. His name was Apalala. He was a "naga" – a dragon*

with no wings and a human head. Having lived a long time, he had seen much sadness in this world, and his head was full of many worries about the future and regrets about the past. Hence, he was very unhappy.

One day the Buddha came to see him.

"You regret past actions," the Buddha said. "Go back and change them."

"I cannot go back in time," said Apalala.

"You fear for the future," said the Buddha, "Go forward and fix it."

"I cannot do that either," said the naga.

"Then what are you left with?"

The dragon looked confused.

Patiently, the Enlightened One continued. "The past is out of reach. The future has not yet arrived. You can live in neither. All you have is today and today is a wonderful gift."

"How so?"

"It is a spotless, new day in which you could do anything. What will you do with your day, oh Naga?"

Inspired by these words, Apalala devoted each new day to protecting the local people from the malevolent dragons who would harm them. The people were grateful and offered him tribute, and Apalala was happy. But as it is said, "The marvellous and astonishing only surprise for a week,"[208] and soon the villagers began to take their guardian for granted. They forgot him in their prayers and stopped leaving offerings of thanks, and he began to feel unappreciated, invisible, alone.

Hurt and angry, Apalala decided instead to become man's enemy. He "prayed to become a poisonous dragon, causing storms and destroying the land."[209]

"And you think that's what happened here?" I asked when she finished her story.

"I was angry at his lack of respect," Xiàngshù said quietly.

"You were hit in the stomach with a whip and lashed out in an instant. You did not have the time to reason it through the way you are now. You reacted."

"It was the wrong reaction."

"It was instinct. I know that you want to pattern your life after the four dragons in that story who turned themselves into the four great, life-giving rivers of China, but do you really think that any of them would have made that sacrifice if they'd been smacked in the face by the people they were trying to save?"

"I don't know."

"He hurt you; you defended yourself. It's as simple as that."

"But I didn't need to defend myself!" she snapped. "Compared to me and my size, he was a bug, an insect."

"His size has nothing to do with it. Bed bugs can kill an invalid by sucking him dry."

"No they can't."

"Yes they can. It happened in the village. A man in poor health died from blood loss, not from any wound, but by being fed on, night after night by bed bugs. His cottage was crawling with them."

"But…"

"Swarms of blackflies have been known to kill livestock – sometimes whole herds – by exsanguination."

"I just…"

"Cockroaches spread disease, and don't even get me started on tapeworms. There is nothing on this earth more dangerous than man, I don't care how much smaller he is in comparison to you. How can you doubt that after what Lludd did to you and your mother?"

"Enough!" she snapped.

We sat in awkward silence for a while.

"I'm sorry," I said quietly.

"You've nothing to be sorry for. Everything you said is true."

"Convincing your head is one thing, convincing your heart is something else."

"Yes, it is."

In December 1069, Xiàngshù grew more and more restless. Her conscience was a wasp that kept stinging her again and again, until finally she had an idea. Like the Naga of the story, she could not go back and change the past. Her only true possession was today, this present moment, and she knew at last what she would write upon the blank page of this spotless day.

Back in the village of Port Isaac, Colum's widow Senara lay awake. She did not sleep well anymore. Truth be told, she did not mourn Colum. Marrying him had been the biggest mistake of her life, although she did miss the money he brought in even though it was inconsistent. Now she was a widow with four children, and despite the difficulty of feeding four, she would have sold her soul, given anything, to again have five young mouths to feed.

"My poor baby," she whispered.

Jowan. Her first-born. Her fine young son. He was everything that Colum was not: calm, intelligent, considerate; and from the moment of his birth he had been the true love of her life. And now he was gone. She lay weeping, trying not to disturb the four sleeping babes who lay dreaming nearby.

Then a noise out front made her jump. It was a dull thud. Most likely some night-time creature had knocked over the wooden pail she had left there. She rose and walked silently to the window. What she saw filled her with cold terror: a great, white dragon was creeping toward her cottage. Its mouth was studded with vicious teeth; its claws were as long as knives and it moved with the grotesque fluidity of a snake. Closer and closer it came.

Senara did not know whether to scream for help or stay quiet, hidden in the shadows. In that moment of her indecision, she saw the creature deposit a small pouch by her door and then turn and disappear back into the gloom. She waited there by the window for a long time. Finally, when she could contain her curiosity no longer, she quietly, cautiously opened the door a crack. All was still and so in one quick movement, she slipped out, grabbed the pouch and dove back inside throwing her whole weight against the door as she slammed it shut.

Her youngest stirred uneasily in his sleep. She soothed him and then lit a candle, opened the pouch, and dumped its contents onto the table. There before her lay two large emeralds; they were beautiful, flawless, and worth a staggering amount. If Colum had fished religiously every day for ten years, he could never have earned enough to buy these stones. She sat back in her chair and looked at the jewels.

"So the beast wishes to pay wergild," she murmured.

Wergild, also known as blood money, was an integral part of Anglo-Saxon justice. Within its construct, the guilty literally paid for their crimes in the form of monetary compensation to the victim or his family. If you caused the death of a freeman, either on purpose or by accident, you were required to make restitution to the tune of two hundred scillings. At that time two hundred scillings could purchase a flock of sheep two hundred strong. Senara guessed that these gems were worth far more than that, and more than compensated for the loss of Colum.

"Fair enough," she said. "Colum is paid for."

But no amount of money on earth could replace Jowan.

I was waiting in Xiàng's cave when she returned.

"What are you doing?" I asked.

"Well hello to you too."

"You can't buy your way out of this."

"I'm not trying to," she snapped. "Colum had a family – a family that is now without a provider. That token will feed them and make sure they prosper."

"Yes, and now that the widow has prosperity, she can concentrate on the only other thing she wants."

"Which is?"

"Revenge."

"No…"

"She doesn't know you. She knows only the pain you've caused her. And for that she wants you dead."

Xiàngshù looked like she'd just been slapped. She sat down heavily. I rose and went to her and she put her face in my hands.

"You are going to have to be so careful."

My emphatic words were met with a resigned nod.

"You're always telling me stories; now I've got one for you…"

### A Side Note

*The Fable of the Labourer and the Snake:*

*Old Aesop once told the tale of a labourer's son who spotted a snake in the grass. The child was too young to recognise the danger and reached for the snake which bit him. Later that day the boy died. The father, in his anger and his grief, took up an axe and waited outside the snake's hole, intent on killing it. Eventually, the snake emerged and the man swung his axe. However, he managed only to chop off the tip of the snake's tail before the serpent slithered back down into its hole.*

*Weeping bitterly at his failure to kill the snake, the man devised a new plan: he would lure the snake out by feigning forgiveness and friendly intent. To this the serpent replied, "I can never be your friend because of my lost tail, nor you mine because of your lost child."*[210]

I told my story and then tapped a cask of ale that we'd 'liberated' from the local tavern. Xiàngshù drank until she passed out.

While Senara nursed a broken heart and Xiàng nursed a guilty conscience, events on a national scale remained turbulent. It had been over three years since William the Conqueror had become king and still his throne was not secure. A series of revolts in the north and east were further exacerbated by the arrival of a large army from Denmark who'd come to support the rebellion. I admit I paid little attention to these developments. I'd seen it all before; only the armour and weaponry had changed. As Samuel Johnson would later say, "Wheresoe'ver I turn my view/ All is strange, yet nothing new."

Then one day in early spring, Nimue burst through the door to my room.

"Nimue! What on earth ... what's wrong?"

"It's Myrddin," she panted. "Come quick."

I raced with her back to Annwyn. Gwyn was waiting outside Myrddin's room. I stopped short; it was the first time I had laid eyes on my father since he banished me.

"Go on. Help him," he said curtly.

I nodded and entered the room. Myrddin lay unconscious on his table, a blood-soaked bandage on his abdomen. I stared stupidly at it. I had been prepared to deal with a further complication of the medhek's neurological condition, not a bloody stomach wound.

"What the hell happened?" I demanded.

By way of answer, Barinthus lifted the bandage to expose a terrible injury. A sword or spear had caught him in the gut and his small intestine protruded from the opening.

"Do something!" Nimue's shriek prodded me into action. I grabbed a bottle from the shelf and poured its contents into a basin, plunging my hands into the stinging liquid.

"Did he pass out or did you drug him?" I asked.

"We drugged him."

"How long ago?"

"About forty-five minutes."

"Good. Throw those bandages away." I brought everything I needed to the table. "Dad, raise his knees."

"How?"

"Put a fucking blanket under them," I snapped.

He quietly obeyed.

With a mixture of thyme and comfrey I rinsed the wound, and patted it dry with sphagnum moss. Then I took a deep breath, "Here we go," I murmured and began to gently push his intestines back into his abdomen. Nimue, who had been quietly sobbing in the corner, became hysterical.

"Get her out of here," I hissed.

There was so very much blood, the intestine was slimy under my fingers, and I had to grit my teeth against the bile that was rising in my throat. Finally it was in and with a few deep stitches, I closed the wound.

As Danjy and Barinthus put Myrddin to bed, Gwyn helped me mop up the blood that covered the table and spilled onto the floor.

"Will he recover?" he asked quietly.

"I doubt it."

So did Gwyn. For a brief moment I saw his thoughts quite clearly. He believed that Myrddin was a goner and still he had sent for me. It was a good excuse to have me back. My surprise must have registered on my face, because my father blushed and looked away.

"Look after him," he said as he made for the door.

"Who did this to him?"

"The Danes … they just sacked Peterborough."

"What the hell was he doing in Peterborough? Our tunnels don't reach that far north."

Gwyn shrugged, "They do now. Apparently he asked Blue-cap to extend the network."

"When was this?"

"Last month."

"I don't understand."

"Your mother foresaw the battle while scrying."

My face flushed hot and my stomach lurched. "Are you saying that he planned this – that he put himself in harm's way?"

Gwyn nodded sadly. "Yes," he said and turned to go. "Call if you need anything." He quietly closed the door behind him.

Myrddin awoke in terrible pain and I threw everything I had at it: meadowsweet, viper's bugloss, honeysuckle, valerian, lavender. Nothing helped. All I could do was sit helplessly by and hold his hand.

"Why?" I asked him.

"It's time."

"What?"

"I have lived over nine millennia – that's enough."

He writhed in pain and every groan, every sob struck me like a physical blow. He hitched his knees up and lay in a foetal position gasping for breath.

"It's *not* enough," I sobbed.

"Caja, my mind is going … more and more." A spasm went through him and he cried out. "I don't want to live like that …" he panted, "… as less than me."

Kneeling beside his bed, I clasped his hand in both of mine and kissed it.

"I t-taught you well," he stammered. "Tell me: how will this progress?"

I shook my head vehemently. "I don't know."

"Yes you do! Now tell me!"

"Umm … terrible, terrible pain."

"Then?"

"Your stomach will go hard. You'll be sick and that will hurt even more…"

"And?"

"Fever, chills."

"Then death," he rasped.

"Yes," I sobbed.

"How long will it take?"

"You know."

"Tell me." He wept as he writhed on the bed.

"Too long."

The spasm of pain seemed to ebb a bit and he lay still, panting. He looked me in the eye. "Don't let it."

I shook my head.

"Caja, please!"

I rose unsteadily and looked at a row of jars on the far shelf. These were heavy with dust; he had not touched them in a very long time. Each contained a poison that would do the job. But it would be slow. Monkshood kills in a few hours, so does Baneberry, Deadly Nightshade, and Mandrake. He would suffer terribly in the meantime. I could not allow that. In order to be merciful, death had to be swift.

"I'll be right back."

I walked numbly through Annwyn's halls. Back at my old room, I retrieved a bow and quiver. I'd killed Vortigern instantly with an arrow from that bow and Myrddin was far more deserving of mercy than he.

Back in Myrddin's room I kissed him on the forehead, the way he used to kiss me when I was a child.

"Aim for the heart," he whispered.

"I will." I backed off a few paces. "I love you."

"I love you too."

I let the arrow fly.

For a long time after, I knelt beside the low bed and buried my face in his neck and wept. I wept for loss and pain and especially for fear. After nine millennia I could not imagine life without him. Even lately when he'd visited less and less, I always took comfort in the knowledge that he was there. And now without him the world was darker, less substantial and yet somehow infinitely more frightening. *What am I going to do without you?*

"You ended it, then." My father was standing in the doorway

I nodded. "He was just going to suffer for hours before he died."

"I know."

I rubbed my eyes dry and struggled to my feet. I didn't meet his gaze. "Thank you for letting me say goodbye… I'll go now."

"Stay."

I looked at him, not daring to hope…

"It's obviously dangerous out there. Stay here in Annwyn where it's safe." And with that he turned and walked away.

Fresh tears blurred my vision, but these were not tears of grief; they were tears of awe. In the Bible it is said: "do not worry about your life… Look at the birds of the air, they do not sow or reap or store away in barns, and yet your heavenly Father feeds them. Are you not much more valuable than they?"[211] In short, God gives us what we need. I lost Myrddin; God gave me back my tribe.

"Thank you," I whispered. It was my first Christian prayer.

My second prayer was uttered at Myrddin's funeral. Although I was not medhek, it fell to me to make his soul stone and perform the burial rites. I have the stone sitting here in front of me now – a small bit of quartz, clear as glass with tiny lines and fissures running through it. It is not flawless, but like Myrddin it is beautiful and full of light. I have carried it with me for centuries.

While I grieved for Myrddin and spent time with my tribe in Annwyn, Xiàngshù reached a decision: she would try, one more time, to make peace with

Colum's widow. She returned to Senara's cottage with more wergild and a fervent prayer for forgiveness. There she was surprised to find a large bowl of milk set on the very spot where she had left the two emeralds months before. Xiàngshù was touched by this. Back in China, the locals left daily offerings of milk for Hóngli in gratitude because she protected their village and brought rain when there was drought.

Maybe, she thought, the widow bears me no grudge after all.

The white dragon left another pouch – this one filled with sapphires and diamonds – next to the milk and turned to leave.

"You insult me," Senara stepped from the shadows.

Xiàngshù spun around to face her.

The woman lit a candle and held it aloft. "Why won't you accept my offering?"

"It's a wonderful offering," the dragon replied. "But it pays to be cautious."

"Yes, and yet here I am speaking to the creature that killed my son."

When Xiàng did not answer, Senara knelt and picked up the new pouch. "This is meant to say … what?"

"That I am so sorry. I swear it was an accident. I never meant to harm anyone. I…"

"I believe you."

"Thank you," the dragon said earnestly.

"I am willing to make amends," Senara replied. "I am even willing to take the risk of approaching you. And yet you, who are so powerful, fear me?"

"Please do not take offence."

"But I do."

Xiàngshù looked at her for a long moment. Finally, with a bow of her head she walked over and drank the milk.

"There," Senara smiled. "Now we are friends." She turned to go. "Goodbye, friend."

Something in her tone made the dragon's hackles rise. She looked at the now empty bowl. "Not again," she breathed and hastened away.

Back in the sound-proof tunnels of Annwyn, I knew nothing of this until Barinthus entered the Great Hall and made a beeline to me.

"They're killing your dragon."

I gaped at him. "Don't joke about that."

But his face looked drawn and infinitely sad. It was no jest.

I grabbed my bow and darted from the Great Hall.

"Go with her," Gwyn instructed Danjy and Barinthus, but I did not stop to wait as they armed themselves.

I hastened for Port Isaac. There in a clearing Xiàngshù was surrounded by jeering, shouting men who wielded spears, pitchforks and torches. She roared, crouching low, keeping her vulnerable belly to the ground. The men did not advance, but they did not retreat either. They were waiting for something.

"Poison," I hissed and fit an arrow to my bow.

From my vantage point on a nearby wooded hill, I had a clear shot at her attackers. But as I drew the string back, Barinthus grabbed me from behind.

"They'll kill you," he rasped as I struggled in his grip.

"No!" I shrieked and wriggled free.

Danjy tackled me to the ground, "It's too late!" he cried, pinning me.

In my flailing and kicking, I managed to knee him in the groin; with a sharp cry he rolled off me. I scrambled to retrieve my bow and stood again to fire. Strong arms closed around me then, stronger than Barinthus and stronger than Danjy.

"It *is* too late, Caja," my father said gently. "Look…"

Xiàngshù's legs gave way and she fell heavily on her chin. She made one half-hearted attempt to rise, but even that effort exhausted her and she slumped over onto her side. The nearest man seized his chance and, to the delight of the cheering crowd, ran forward and thrust his spear into Xiàng's chest. The dragon moaned; her hind legs twitched spasmodically. In her brain, the areas that regulated involuntary functions went dark. I saw the medulla, which regulates breathing and heart-rate, shut down and knew that all was lost. Her cognitive faculties lasted a moment longer and Xiàngshù's final thought was "My children." And then, starved of oxygen, the last flame of thought flickered out.

The villagers closed in then. Boys threw stones and the ground around her was littered with rocks and arrows. Slowly they managed to prise off her alabaster scales to keep as charms and talismans. I shrugged my father off and retched violently on the ground. They burned her flayed body and the air all around was filled with a choking black smoke and the sweet, cloying scent of charred dragon flesh. My best friend was dead. Murdered. She was the most beautiful creature I had ever seen, and by morning they were parading her head through the village on a pike.

My father, who had stayed with me, said, "Man is the cruellest creature on earth."

I turned to leave.

"Where are you going?" he asked.

"Someone has to look after her eggs," I said and headed for Tintagel.

By the time I reached Merlin's cave, I was shaking uncontrollably and could not get warm even though I curled up with the eggs by the fire. Grief hit me this time not as an emotional storm, but as a physical illness. I sobbed and retched through that long day and into the night, unable to keep down even a little water. I felt so ill that I wanted Myrddin. And then I remembered that he too was gone and it was as if something in me gave way – some internal support that kept me upright snapped like a twig. I grew very calm then, and listened to the rush and fizz of water as it lapped at the beach.

I am not a good swimmer, I thought. I could just paddle out until I become too tired to swim back.

Like Myrddin I too had lived for nine millennia. Maybe it was time to just stop. What is life but loss piled upon loss, one battle after another ad infinitum. The faces of all who had died came to me then: Myrddin, Xiàngshù, Owain, Maban, Fryok … Uther. Then my mind lit upon Nanscáwen, and with a cry I rose and staggered to the mouth of the cave. There on the threshold I paused. Ahead of me the Atlantic ebbed and surged in the darkness. Behind me the fire crackled, keeping Xiàngshù's eggs warm. Those were my two choices: dark, cold oblivion or light and life.

Without me to tend it, the fire would go out. Deprived of warmth, the eggs would not hatch, or – worse still – the chicks might hatch into this world and find themselves alone. I remembered how alone, how abandoned, how afraid I'd felt when banished from Annwyn. Could I inflict that on someone else? Could I just leave them to die slowly of hunger, thirst, neglect?

"No," I said aloud and walked back into the cave and into the light.

Thankfully, caring for dragon's eggs is not a complicated endeavour requiring specialised skills. For over three years, I had helped my friend keep the fire lit and the cave warm. I had seen her, on countless occasions push more hay or moss or feathers down the insides of the nest, careful always to leave a large part of the eggs' surface uncovered. Looking closer at the tough shells, I could see why: they were dotted with small pores through which the chicks could breathe. Despite the simplicity of the task, I became obsessed with the idea that the young might die before hatching, and so I fussed and fretted over them by day and lay down next to the nest at night. Again and again I would awaken from unquiet dreams and place a hand on each egg, waiting for the chick inside to move and display some sign of life.

After weeks of unnecessary labour in the subterranean half-light of the cave, I felt so woolly-headed that I decided to get out and walk in the sunlight and fresh air again. My meandering steps took me through the greenwood and along to Reskelly, whose name means "ford by the copse." Sure enough, there knelt my mother, washing clothes in the stream.

"Come help me," she called and dutifully I knelt beside her and started scrubbing a green tunic belonging to my father.

"I have not seen you lately," she said quietly.

"I've been looking after the chicks."

"Have they hatched yet?"

"No."

She stopped her work and took a deep breath. "Caja, don't let them."

"What?"

"End it now before they're born and you fall in love with them."

"Why the hell would you say that?"

"It is this," she gestured toward the water.

"Your scrying?"

"Yes."

"So what do you think you've seen?"

She bristled inwardly at the implied insult, but did not rise to it. "There is a storm coming, and those dragons are at the centre of it," she said calmly.

I snorted, "What storm?"

"When the villagers butchered Xiàngshù – that was not the end of hostilities, but the beginning. There will be more bloodshed before all is done. Unless you stop it. Now."

"Don't ask that of me."

"It is for the best."

"I won't harm them."

Mora looked at me, her mouth turned down at the corners, her face set in that familiar expression of disapproval that I knew so well from my childhood.

She shrugged. "Then there will be much for me to wash: a rough tunic, a peasant dress, a monk's robe, a knight's surcoat…"

"Do not pull that 'Washer-at-the-Ford' shite with me!"

"You doubt?"

"Of course I do!"

"Caja, look." She nodded down at the water and I followed her gaze.

There in my hands was not the green tunic I had been washing, but a blue gown, beautifully stitched and of heavy, expensive material. I swore loudly, dropped it into the stream and scrambled back from the water's edge. Mora retrieved it and when she wrung it out, it was again my father's kelly green shirt.

"You saw, didn't you? The blue dress?"

I nodded.

"You can save its owner." Her voice was gentle, but firm.

Watching the brook tumble over the rocks in the shallow stream bed, I considered this. "You're right," I said finally. "I can save her. I can save all of them." I rose. "I'll just make damn sure that Xiàngshù's death is the end of it. Her children will never know how she died. Thanks for the warning, Mother."

As I walked away, my mother mumbled to herself, "As you wish."

I was angered by my mother's words. I would not say this to her but, damn it, if her prophecies were at all reliable, then Fryok would be alive. So would Maban and Owain. But no, I had their three soul stones, incontrovertible proof that she did not know and see all. There was, however, the dress – that fine blue dress that was there one minute and gone the next. Where had that come from? The thought of it raised gooseflesh on my arms although the day was warm. It could have been a trick of the light as it refracted off the surface of the water. Or, I reasoned, if it was an actual prophecy, then maybe it was a needed warning that would help me avert disaster and still protect Xiàngshù's children.

"What it comes down to," I said aloud as I entered the cave, "is can I do it? Can I kill them right now?"

I crouched down next to the nest, resting a hand on the smooth, mottled shell of the nearest egg. "No," I whispered, "I cannot."

On 22$^{nd}$ December 1070, it was the first day of winter and the longest night. A winter gale howled outside and lashed the tiny beach with wave after wave of frigid water. Inside the cave, however, it was as hot as Dante's hell as I continually fed the fire to keep the eggs warm. Made drowsy by the heat, I sat dozing with my chin on my chest. A short time later I was awakened by a noise – a soft, cracking sound in the nest. One of the eggs was rocking slightly. A small crack appeared in its surface, and began to divide and spread until a fragment fell away and I caught my first glimpse of the chick's snout. With a little more pushing, the tough shell loosened enough to allow the dragon to wriggle free. It was a boy. The remnant of what looked like an egg-tooth hung loosely from its upper jaw and I gently plucked it away. He had the luminous white scales of his mother, a short snout and big, big eyes.

"Hello, little one," I whispered.

The second egg began to rock and slowly a little female emerged. I looked at them together as they sat unsteadily, blinking in the light; and indeed I fell in love with them just as I was meant to. It is nature's way: in her wisdom she made babies cute – little and chubby with big eyes that, like their paws, the dragons needed to grow into. The female, with scales of deep green – the colour of moonstone – sneezed. It upset her precarious balance and she toppled over in the dust. I scooped her up. The boy reached for me and I gathered them to me and at last I understood. I had known love before – love of tribe, of kin, of home, of Uther. But this was different. This was the love that prompted the Coranieid women to adopt mortal children. This was the love that hammered at Mora when she lost Fryok, Maban and Owain. It is the most selfless and ennobling love possible. It is a love that reveals to you the looming spectres of all the dangers in this world that your child must face, and it makes you afraid. It is a terrible love, and wonderful. And from that first day, I was at its mercy.

Because of his opalescent scales, I named the boy Kenwyn, meaning "white or splendid chief." The girl I called Barenwyn ("fair branch") which I thought quite fitting since her mother's name, Xiàngshù, meant "oak tree" in the East.

As days passed, however, I became concerned that my little branches were not as strong as the mother tree. Both of my dragons seemed to be lame, their legs weak and underdeveloped. This to me did not make sense. With birds you see two types of chicks: the naked and the hale. Blackbirds spend only two weeks in the egg and therefore are born blind and bare and lame. Mallards, on the other hand, take much longer to hatch. Hence the ducklings are born clothed in feathers, mobile and with their eyes open. The dragons had been four years in the shell, long enough to develop fully. They had their full complement of scales and their eyes were bright and curious. Then why could they not stand and move about?

In a panic, I contacted Demelza by leaving a bit of dianthus in the tree hollow along with a bit of rhubarb ("Advice needed urgently.") As was our custom, I went to her after sundown and she made sure she was alone.

"This is unexpected!" she proclaimed as I let myself into her cottage.

"What is?"

"You consulting *me* for advice. It's always the other way around."

"Yeah, well, I have no experience with babies."

"Let me see."

I sat the large basket that I had hefted all the way from Tintagel down on the table and opened it to reveal Kenwyn and Barenwyn.

"Oh hell!" Demelza yipped and jumped backward.

I looked at her disparagingly. "What is the matter with you?"

"You said 'babies'!"

"They are babies!"

"Baby dragons!" Hand on her chest, she took a few deep breaths. "They gave me quite a turn." She took a moment to compose herself, cleared her throat and asked, "So what's the problem?"

I gently lifted them out of the basket and placed them on the table. "I think they're lame."

Demelza approached the table cautiously. She was worried they might bite. However the more she looked at them, the more fascinated she became; her intellectual curiosity crowding out her fear.

"Well, it's clear," she said.

"What?"

"I have no idea why their legs are so scrawny."

"Thanks a lot. This isn't a laughing matter, Demelza. I can care for them now, but if they can't hunt when they're full grown, I doubt I'll be able to catch enough to keep them alive."

"I'm sorry, but I know nothing about baby dragons. This, in fact, is the first time I've ever seen one… It is curious, though."

"What is?"

"They both have the same problem. It wouldn't be odd for one of the offspring to be born lame; there's a runt to every litter. But both? It makes me wonder if perhaps this is normal. Did they have much spare room in the egg?"

"No."

"No room to move," she said, gently manipulating Barenwyn's feet, "and hence, very weak legs." She stood with an air of finality. "It's only a guess, mind you, but I think they'll be fine."

"But what should I do?"

"Feed them up and get them to work those legs as much as you can."

It was astounding how much labour was encapsulated by the three monosyllabic words: "feed them up." New-born humans cry for milk every few hours, drink a little from the breast, sleep and then cry again. Baby dragons cry frequently for food too, but they are not satisfied by milk alone. They must have meat, freshly caught and prepared. Therefore my life became a constant repetition of thieving milk, snaring and butchering game, hand-feeding the chicks, exercising their legs and cleaning up after them. I did not have the image then, but now in retrospect, I think that early motherhood is much like those amusing toys people attach to pet rodent cages. In short it is like one huge hamster wheel of tasks that must be performed again and again and again. I seemed to always be running, but I never felt like I was getting anywhere.

I did not appreciate the effect this had on me until one day when I'd nipped back to Annwyn to collect a few things. I passed Barinthus in the hall and he stopped and did a double-take.

"What?" I snapped.

"I didn't recognise you at first."

"What's that supposed to mean?"

"Nothing, honestly." He began to back away. "See you later."

Back in my chamber, I surveyed myself in the mirror. I looked like I'd been pulled backward through a hedge. My hair, fuzzy and dry, had worked loose from its plait; my eyes (my best feature) were puffy and heavily underlined with dark circles and bags. Between the constant fatigue and the boredom of my repetitive tasks, I'd started eating more and the surplus was visible on my belly and hips. Under the auspices of giving me a cuddle, the dragons (both of which had colds) had taken to wiping their noses on my dress. There were so many snot-trails across the green fabric that I looked like I'd been attacked by an army of belligerent slugs. And I smelled bad because earlier Kenwyn had spit up on me a yellow mixture of regurgitated badger and sour milk.

Centuries later some smart ass would compose this clever little ditty:

> "See the mothers in the park,
> Ugly creatures chiefly;
> Someone must have loved them once –
> In the dark and briefly."[212]

The bastard hit the nail on the head for there, in front of my mirror, I was sure that no man – human or of Annwyn – would ever want me again. The thought of centuries without sex made me weep. Clearly I was sinking under the weight of the task I had been given and worst of all, I knew better than to ask for help. My mother was firm in her belief that the dragons would bring trouble and so she (and therefore the others) would not help me raise them. That just made me cry more.

Later I returned to the cave in a clean frock, with my hair pinned up out of the way, essentially looking like a peasant and in a royally foul mood. I threw two dead rabbits on the table and set about preparing dinner.

"Mama..." Barenwyn was vying for my attention again.

"I'm busy. You'll have to wait."

"But Mama..."

"Damn it, Wynnie! I said I'm busy!" I spun around to face two smiling chicks. "What?" I snapped.

"Look." And with that she took her first steps.

"Look at you!" I cried, wrapping my arms around her. "What a clever girl!" I looked up and held an arm out to Kenwyn. "Want to join the cuddle?"

I held my breath. You can do it ... you can do it... I silently willed him on.

He toddled over to me and I collapsed laughing beneath their weight. Finally we were getting somewhere. Instead of going in endless circles, we had taken a step forward. At the time, it felt like a miracle. Years later, when man had discovered and studied the dinosaurs, I realised that it was not so odd for the chicks to be born lame. For instance, they believe that Maiasaura chicks were too cramped within the shell for their legs to develop prior to hatching. Hence the mother stayed with them, protecting and feeding them. That is why she was given a name that means "good mother."

Dragon chicks, it turns out, go through the same stages as human children. They just do it on a grander scale. For instance, when a human child is teething, their cheeks go red, they seem a bit under the weather, and gumming a cold teething ring soothes them. Dragons also need to chew … and chew … and chew … preferably on red deer antlers and cow bones. These they grind into small sharp shards which they abandon on the floor for me to find (usually first thing in the morning, while barefoot). This continues until all of the needle-like puppy teeth are replaced by the curved, serrated knives that line the jaws of a mature dragon.

When a human child learns to walk, he uses furniture to steady himself until he topples over, usually onto a bottom thickly padded with a nappy. When dragons learn to walk, they use their tails as a counterbalance. Even at birth a dragon tail is tipped with a viciously sharp barb. Now imagine if you will a tottering animal that has little control over his feet, let alone the lethal weapon at the end of his tail. That is why I forever associate the transition from baby to toddler with lacerated shins and torn dresses.

But bloody shins and splintered feet did not matter. They were walking! Their legs were healthy and, with mobility and an adult set of teeth on the way, they would soon be able to hunt. I enjoyed imagining all the things I would do with them once I did not have to spend every waking moment on the procurement and preparation of food. First I would teach them how to survive in this world – how to hunt and fish and remain hidden. Then I could teach them other things: how to read and play chess, how to identify which plants help and which harm. I would tell them all of the stories that I remember so that from them they may grow wise. Yes, things would be so much easier now that they were mobile.

Then one day Barenwyn, impatient for her dinner, decided to help me. She climbed onto the wooden table to skin the rabbits and it collapsed under her weight, spilling two days' worth of pilfered milk and breaking all the eggs Demelza had given us. The dragon landed badly, right on her face, knocking out three teeth (baby fangs, thankfully) in the process. Her howls of anguish echoed in my sensitive ears like a claxon and I hurried to comfort the child. Without thinking, I tried to pick up a creature that now weighed as much as I did and threw out my back. I gave her a hug, dabbed her bleeding gums with the hem of my dress and set about mopping up, while unable to either bend fully to the floor or stand erect.

When Barenwyn's protests had subsided to a pitiful whimpering, I realised that something was missing – some sound that was part of the familiar ambient noise of the cave. Kenwyn. Where was Kenwyn?

I checked the cave and the chamber at its rear, but he'd gone. The roar of the turbulent ocean that lay right outside met my ears then.

"Oh hell." Still hunched over, I staggered out of the cave. "Kenwyn!" I called, scanning the white caps for any sign of my son. "Kenwyn, answer me!"

I tore my shoes off and raced to the water's edge. "KENWYN!" Any pretence of composure I'd had was now quite gone as my mind conjured up images of his drowning body sinking into the murky depths.

And then I heard it: the mischievous giggle from behind a boulder along down the beach. I stood in front of it, hands on hips.

"How odd – a laughing rock." Ignoring the shouts of pain from my lower back, I lunged behind the rock, grabbed Kenwyn by the ear and marched him back into the cave. "Don't you ever, *ever* do that to me again. It's early to bed for you tonight."

"Oh Mum," he whinged.

"Hush!" In that moment I took that last step toward parental insanity that eventually comes to us all: I started ranting … to myself.

"Day and night, night and day, working like a slave and what thanks do I get?!"

It took two hours to tidy up the mess, get them fed and bathed and put to bed and I bitched through most of it. But then, when they finally fell asleep, all curled up with their snoring noses nestled on their hind feet, I stopped and sat and watched them for a while and I calmed down.

"All that time I spent worrying that you'd never walk," I shook my head. "I'm an idiot."

As a parent there are moments when your child asks a question, and you know you must get the answer right. The future could well hinge on the next words out of your mouth. So you speak carefully, and after contemplation.

One night, while curled up by the fire, they asked the question, "How did our real mother die?"

This is it, I thought. Right here, right now I could prevent my mother's terrible prophecy from coming true.

"Well," I said, "she was a very old dragon. She fell pregnant late in life."

"And so she just died of old age?" Kenwyn asked.

"Yes. It was her heart."

"Where is she buried?" Barenwyn whispered.

"At sea."

The child sniffled and with a gentle hand I lifted her chin till she looked me in the eye. "She always thought it a waste of time to fear death, because she said it comes to us all and is as natural as being born."

"Is she in heaven?"

"I always believed that life determines afterlife. It's like any endeavour: if you build a fine, strong house, then you get to live in a fine strong house."

"Like the three little pigs?" Kenwyn asked. "The pig who built a house of stone was the only one that was safe from the wolf."

I nodded. "Likewise, if you live a good life, you have a good afterlife. It is cause and effect in its purest form. And so yes, I believe your mother is in heaven – that is where angels go."

"What is heaven like?" asked Kenwyn. "Do they have rabbits there?"

"I expect so."

Barenwyn chimed in, "And pretty stones to collect?"

"The best hoard ever."

And they snuggled down and went to sleep. I took a deep breath and let it out again. So far, so good, I thought. Within a few years, any of the villagers with first-hand knowledge of Xiàngshù's death will have died and the truth will die with them. The story will be remembered, of course, but layer upon layer of myth and embellishment will be added to it until it is impossible to recognise the sapling from the tree it has become. At that point, I can dismiss any shred of the truth as folklore and there will be no need to worry ... none at all.

## CHAPTER 8

# "DEMON"

*"Then – in my childhood – in the dawn*
*Of a most stormy life – was drawn...*
*From the thunder and the storm,*
*And the cloud that took the form*
*(When the rest of heaven was blue)*
*Of a demon in my view."*

*Edgar Allan Poe*[213]

In the beginning God created the heavens and the earth. He created day and night, land and sea, plant and animal and man. It is said that, in the midst of these events, there was a time of great conflict in heaven. According to the Book of Revelation,

> ...war arose in heaven, Michael and his angels fighting against the dragon; and the dragon and his angels fought but they were defeated and there was no longer any place for them in heaven. And the great dragon was thrown down, that ancient serpent, who is called the Devil or Satan, the deceiver of the whole world – he was thrown down to earth and his angels were thrown down with him... Rejoice then, O heaven and you that dwell therein! But woe to you, O earth and sea, for the devil has come down to you in great wrath...[214]

Why should such violence occur within God's realm? For the answer we look to the Qur'an. It tells us that, when God created man, He said to the angels

> "Bow down before Adam," and they did. But not Iblis: he was not one of those who bowed down. God said, "What prevented you from bowing down as I commanded you?" and he said, "I am better than him: You created me from fire and him from clay." God said, "Get down from here! This is no place for your arrogance. Get out! ..." but Iblis said ... "Because You have put me in the wrong, I will lie in wait for them (Adam and his sons) ... I will come at them – from their front and their back, from their right and their left – and you will find that most of them are ungrateful." God said, "Get out! You are disgraced and banished! I swear I shall fill Hell with you and all who follow you!"[215]

Within the Christian tradition, it is thought that one-third of all the angels sided with Lucifer and were cast out. Lucifer became the devil, and his followers became the demons of hell whose sole purpose is to pervert God's creation – man. It began in the Garden of Eden when the devil, disguised as a serpent, convinced Eve to eat the forbidden fruit of the Tree of Knowledge. This was the first sin and marked the end of man's innocence. Within Muslim tradition, the devil (Iblis) also has followers. He is defined as "a fallen angel of Islam, a powerful subversive spirit and the chief of the djinn."[216] The djinn or jinn (from which we get the word "genie") are on a mission to corrupt mankind. The Qur'an asks: "Shall I tell you who the djinn come down to? They come down to every lying sinner who readily lends an ear to them."[217] And so you see, the two faiths echo one another in their stories of how evil first came into the world.

In *Paradise Lost*, John Milton identifies these fallen angels (these jinn and demons) by name and marks out their spheres of influence. They dispersed:

> "till wand'ring o'er the earth ...
> By falsities and lies the greatest part
> Of mankind they corrupted to forsake
> God their creator ...
> [and] adorn'd ...
> gay religions full of pomp and gold,
> And Devils to adore for Deities."[218]

First there came Moloch. Over the green fields and winding streams of Rabba, Argob, Basan and Arnon, there hung a reeking black smoke as the Ammonites burned their children alive in Moloch's name. Next came Chemosh who unleashed within Moab ungoverned lust. Osiris, Horus and Isis in their animal guises took root in Egypt; and Baalim, Ashtaroth and Thammuz led the people to worship graven images and false gods.

In the midst of all this darkness there shone a light, and that was Jerusalem, and the flame within the beacon was its Temple which, when finished, would house the very name of God. The year was 968 B.C. and the great Temple of Jerusalem, which King Solomon had commissioned, was four years away from completion. A veritable army of workmen and architects swarmed over the site. From the hill where the demon stood watching, they looked like a colony of ants, always busy, never still. He yawned and turned to face Moloch.

"All right, what's this urgent business you spoke of?" he asked.

"I come with your instructions."

The demon snorted, "What? From you?"

"No, this comes from *him*."

The demon went a shade paler. "What does he want?"

"He is troubled by this," Moloch nodded toward the construction site. "This new temple that Solomon is building ... it is said that the very name of Yahweh will reside there. It will undermine our position here in the East."

"Probably, but what do you want me to do about it?"

"Destroy it."

The demon laughed, "Oh is that all?"

Moloch nodded.

"Why me? If you're so keen to protect your interests, you do it."

Moloch leaned in until they were standing nose to nose. "I'm busy," he hissed. "The burnt flesh of the Ammonite children pleases him. But you are at a loose end once again. And so it falls to you to destroy that fucking temple. And Belial, don't fail."

"Are you threatening me?"

Moloch stepped back, his hands raised in mock placation. "Not I. I give you only a friendly warning. But you know the price of failure..." He left the sentence open-ended for effect as he faded from view.

Belial's face clouded over. To the empty space where Moloch had stood, he answered, "Yes, I do."

The demon sat on the hill and weighed his options. An overt attack on the Temple would not work. That is the sort of heavy-handed approach that brutes like Moloch would employ. No. Belial knew the power of subtlety. The trick was not to *do* anything. Belial's talent was not in action, but in influencing others to act; and for that task he was beautifully endowed. Unlike Moloch, who had the head of a bull and sported a ridiculously phallic set of horns, Belial was quite pleasing to the human eye. John Milton would later describe him as...

> "... graceful and humane (in appearance);
> A fairer person lost not heav'n; he seem'd
> For dignity composed and high exploit:
> But all was false and hollow; though his tongue
> Dropp'd Manna, and could make the worse appear
> The better reason, to perplex and dash
> Maturest counsels; for his thoughts were low
> ...yet he pleased the ear."[219]

While no altar stood in his honour, he was perhaps more dangerous than the others because he could be anywhere, at any time, always talking so sweetly and reasonably. Hence, many had strayed from God upon his advice.

**A Side Note**

*The Bible charts Belial's illustrious career as a corrupter of men. There was that night in Gib'e-ah in 1100 B.C. A Levite man, travelling home with his concubine to E'phraim, stopped to spend the night in Gib'e-ah. An old man returning from his work in the fields came upon them by chance and, as was the custom, offered them a place to stay for the night.*

*The Book of Judges, chapter 19, verse 22 tells us what happened next: "behold, the men of the city, certain sons of Belial (those men who fell under his influence), beset the house round about, and beat at the door, and spake to the master of the house, the old man, saying, 'Bring forth the man that came into thine house, that we may know him.'" They meant to "know" him in the carnal sense – to rape, abuse, and rob him of his wealth, and the old man pleaded with them not to do such a vile thing. But the men would not be deterred, and so the Levite seized his woman and pushed her through the door into the arms of the waiting crowd. All through that long night the gang raped and tortured and beat her, and by morning she lay dead upon the doorstep. In his wrath the Levite summoned the leaders of all of the twelve tribes of Israel and told them of the atrocity; and the Israelites decided as one to destroy Gib'e-ah and the men that dwelled therein. Belial had, through his wickedness, led the entire city to its destruction.*

*Then Eli's sons, the priests Phin'ehas and Hophni, fell under his influence. They claimed the "choicest parts of every offering" made to God for themselves and "lay with women who served at the entrance to the tent of [holy] meeting."[220] And so it is said that "the sons of Eli were sons of Belial; they knew not the Lord."[221] In his anger, God withdrew his support when the Israelites fought the Philistines. Israel lost 34,000 men and the Ark of the Covenant was taken from them in the battle. Phin'ehas and Hophni were captured and killed.*

The Dead Sea scrolls list the "three nets of Belial" as wealth, fornication, and corruption of holy places. With these he snared the men of Gib'e-ah and damned Eli's sons, but he doubted that those methods would work here in Jerusalem. The Temple had not yet been consecrated, and no priest presided there who might be lured away from the faith. And what of sex and money? He shook his head. Solomon had chosen his architects wisely – from among the most devout of his people. For them the Temple was a labour of love, not of profit, and the demon did not think they would be tempted by gold or flesh to forsake their mission. So what to do?

The scholar Stephen Asma notes that the "major weapons of the demons are fear and temptation."[222] Temptation may suffice for the weak, but fear, Belial realised, works on everyone. Yes. The demon needed to find a target with something precious to lose, something to protect: in short, he needed to find someone with a family.

The sun was nearly below the horizon as Ben-hesed gathered up his plans and started for home. It had been a long and hot day of toil, but even at this hour there was a spring in his step. Life had never been so good. Thorough and meticulous in his work, he had been chosen as one of the chief structural engineers for the Great Temple. The job would take years to complete and, although it would not make him a rich man, it would pay well and ensure that his family prospered. Yes, I am blessed, he thought and he said a silent prayer of thanks, his smiling face tilted up to the red and orange of the twilit sky.

So absorbed was he in his own thoughts that he did not see the stranger who had appeared directly in his path until it was nearly too late. He halted quickly, his sandals skidding on the dry dust and gravel of the road.

"Sorry, friend," he laughed. "I didn't see you there."

"No, *friend*." Belial mouthed the word like it was sour. "It is I who should apologise to you. After all, I bring you good greetings from Moloch."

Ben-hesed gave him a wide berth and continued on his way.

"I said I bring you greetings from Moloch."

The man sighed. The stranger seemed intent upon drawing him into conversation. He turned to face him. "Moloch ... the god of the Ammonites?"

Belial nodded.

"With the bull's head and the big horns?" Ben-hesed threw his hands up to either side of his head to indicate their span.

"One and the same."

"Friend, I think you'd better go and sleep it off." He turned to go but the stranger fell into step beside him.

"He looks upon you with favour. Indeed to enjoy the blessings that Moloch can bestow, you must only pay him tribute. Your son ... what's his name? Geber, isn't it?"

Ben-hesed halted abruptly. "How do you know my son?"

"He is a good boy," nodded the demon, "strong and fair and affectionate toward his papa. He will make an excellent sacrifice."

Ben-hesed went very pale. "Get ... the hell ... away from me!" he hissed.

Belial's hand shot out, gripping Ben-hesed by the throat. The man gasped and struggled but could not break the demon's grip. Belial leaned in close and smiled sweetly. "You are an architect, so I'll put this in terms you can understand. The equation here is simple: give Moloch what he wants and he will reward you with the best this wretched world has to offer – success, riches, women."

The demon released Ben-hesed who fell to his knees coughing and spluttering. With preternatural strength, Belial pulled the man to his feet, straightened his abaya and began to brush him off.

"Deny him," he continued quietly, "and Moloch will kill everyone you ever loved … including the boy."

Ben-hesed staggered backward, batting the stranger's hands away.

Belial's voice was as placid as if he were commenting upon the weather. "You see, either way the boy dies." He shrugged, "You might as well take the money."

Ben-hesed turned and ran.

He came to a little stream where the women often knelt to wash clothes. It was deserted at this late hour and he sat down to catch his breath.

"The man's a drunkard," he mumbled. But there had been no smell of wine on his breath. "A lunatic then." He rubbed his sore neck. "A very strong lunatic."

He took a deep breath and let it out slowly. All right. Think about this logically. He seems to know something of my son; but is that so odd? Many people know me through my work and if they know me, then they know of my family. That stranger could have heard Geber's name from anyone. He pondered this awhile and listened to the musical waters of the stream, unconsciously grabbing handfuls of sand from the bank and sifting it through his fingers. But what was all that nonsense about Moloch?

Ben-hesed marvelled at the recklessness of even saying such things. The Israelites looked upon the cult of Moloch with particular revulsion. To set a living child alight: is there any sin greater than that? And for it there would be a reckoning. God Himself told Moses that anyone "that giveth any of his seed unto Molech; he shall surely be put to death: the people of the land shall stone him."[223] No, the folly of the Ammonites would not be tolerated here, not even in jest.

"I'll alert the priests," he nodded, "and have Bas'emath keep the boy close to home."

Thus comforted, and with the matter settled in his mind, he rose and headed home for dinner.

The next day, Ben-hesed awoke feeling groggy and uncertain if his disturbing encounter with the stranger had been real or a dream. Of a naturally cheerful disposition, he opted for the latter, and kissed wife and child before heading off to work. Today they were erecting the great stone walls of the Temple. They had been shaped and prepared at the quarry, and only needed to be winched into place. "Only winched into place," he chuckled to himself. Each stone weighed more than forty tons – there would be nothing easy about manoeuvring them into position. The first of the slabs had already been moved, and rested at the edge of a deep trench that it would slot into as the stone was raised to a 90° angle with the ground. Wooden trusses would then support the walls until the roof could be lowered onto the structure.

Once onsite, Ben-hesed had the workmen line the sides of the first trench with wooden stakes so that the stone could slide in more easily. He hoped to keep the hole from collapsing in on itself under the pressure of the slab's weight as it shifted. Finally, when all was ready, he gave the order to raise the Temple's first wall. Many men and beasts pulled on the ropes. The wooden legs of the tripod that supported the pulley creaked but held, and slowly ... painfully slowly ... the wall began to rise.

At a rough inclination of 60°, the slab shifted forward and dropped into the trench. The earth beneath Ben-hesed's feet trembled with the impact.

"Come on ... come on ..." he whispered as the stone was finally winched into place.

"You did it!" Ahin'adab, Ben-hesed's oldest friend, appeared at his side.

Ben-hesed answered with a slightly giddy laugh.

"I told you not to worry. Now it's my turn."

Ahin'adab carried out his inspection and, when certain that the wall was secured to the trusses, led his team to the base of the stone to fill in the gaps in the trench with rock and earth. Ben-hesed began marshalling men into line, ready to pull the next slab into place, when someone shouted, "Look out!"

The wall had begun to sway. In another moment, the taut plucking snap of breaking rope reached his ears, and he watched as the stone fell almost in slow motion.

"Ahin! Ratz! Run!" he screamed.

Ahin'adab was already moving, dragging the man nearest him along behind. But the toe of his sandal caught in the churned earth of the site and sent him sprawling on his belly. Then he was gone. The great stone landed with a crash and broke into three pieces. Ben-hesed ran towards it.

"Ahin! Ahin! Oh God!" he screamed as he scrabbled with his bare hands at the loose dirt at the slab's edge.

The foreman, a big, burly, red-faced man, grabbed him from behind and pulled him away.

"No!" Ben shrieked, struggling to break free. "Ahin!"

"Hu hayan met!" The foreman rasped. "He's dead, Ben. I'm so sorry."

Ben-hesed arrived home. He didn't remember walking there. His wife Bas'emath saw him approach, saw that he wept and that his tears carved clean tracks down his dusty cheeks. She ran to him.

He buried his face in her neck and cried, "My fault … my fault…"

Bas'emath was a mother, and mothers know how to cope with tears. She led her husband inside and bade him sit. She gave him sheep's milk to drink, and gently wiped the dust off his face with a damp rag. When he was calmer, she sat opposite him at the table. "Now tell me what happened."

Ben-hesed outlined the details of the accident. Bas'emath felt sick and light-headed when she heard how Ahin'adab died.

"Oh my love, I'm so sorry," she whispered through her own tears. But her husband needed her now and so she gathered herself together. "I don't understand … how is that your fault?"

Ben-hesed hesitated.

"Talk to me."

He nodded toward his cup. "Can I have something stronger, please?"

She rose and brought him wine.

"You'd better have some yourself," he said and she poured out a second cup.

"Last night, on my way home, I met a stranger on the road."

"That is why you were late?"

Ben-hesed nodded. "He said he came with a message from Moloch."

"What?"

"He said that Moloch favoured me for some reason and that in order to receive his blessings I must pay tribute."

"Tribute…" Bas'emath said uncertainly.

"Geber."

His wife leaned back in her chair, her face looked as if it was set in stone. "You told him to go to Sheol."

"I told him to get the hell away from me. And he said that if I did not do Moloch's bidding that he would kill everyone I ever loved."

"And you think Ahin'adab…"

"Yes."

Bas'emath rose and wrapped her arms around him. "That is nonsense."

"But…"

"Listen to me," she knelt before him and looked up into his face. "That stranger was crazy – probably some poor soul with an addled mind and no one to look after him."

"But Ahin…"

"…was an accident. My love, how heavy was that stone?"

"Forty tons."

"It is dangerous work and the men labour all day in the heat. They get tired, a mistake is made, something is overlooked and then…"

"The stone falls."

She nodded.

Ben-hesed leaned forward and rested his head on her shoulder.

"What worries me," she continued, "is that stranger seems to have gotten into your head. You must put him out."

Ben-hesed embraced his wife and thanked God for Bas'emath, the gentlest and wisest of women.

The coming weeks, though sad, were uneventful. Ahin'adab was laid to rest, and Ben-hesed threw himself into his work with renewed fervour. He sensed, although never inwardly articulated, that the best way to achieve final peace for Ahin'adab, and himself, was to see the Temple completed.

Returning home one evening, his wife met him at the door with red eyes. Wrapping his arms around her, he asked, "What is it, my love? Why do you cry?"

"Your father…" she whispered.

Ben-hesed looked at her in horror for a moment and then ran down the street to his father's home. It was not far and the sound of his mother weeping greeted him before he reached the door.

"I don't know what happened," she cried to her son as he stood on the threshold and took in the scene. His father lay on his back on the floor, eyes open but no longer seeing, the pain he felt at the moment of his death still distorting his features. His mother sat beside the body, cradling her husband's head.

Ben-hesed knelt and shut his father's eyes and then gathered his mother into his arms and helped her to a chair. It took two cups of wine to steady the old woman enough to speak.

"When I left to fetch water, he was fine. He was happy. You know your father, how he jokes. I left him laughing…"

When all the right and proper things had been done, when Bas'emath had helped her mother-in-law to wash the body and prepare it for burial, when Ben-hesed had visited the priests and arranged the ceremony, then finally husband and wife were able to put their child to bed and talk privately.

Before Ben-hesed could begin, his wife cut him off. "It means nothing."

"How can you be so sure?"

"Because your father was old…"

"He was so full of life."

"How many times have we seen this, Ben? Just last year there was old Hirah. He seemed in perfect health and then went out one day to tend his flock and just dropped."

"But…"

"Your sandals are old and worn because you have walked miles in them. Our bodies are the same. We wear them for many years and many miles and eventually they wear out."

Ben-hesed nodded. "That is true."

She kissed him. "I'll tell you what is also true: you will drive yourself mad if you see every misfortune in life as part of some curse."

They say that time heals every wound and they say that because it is true. It takes a while, of course, for a grieving heart to pass a day without dwelling on its troubles, but rest assured, friends, that day inevitably comes. And so it did for Ben-hesed.

Belial waited for that: allowed Ben-hesed to heal after each tragedy, allowed the unfortunate man to finally struggle his way back to equilibrium only to hit him again.

One day while at the building site, Ben-hesed's son came running to him, calling his name. Thinking that the child was simply here to visit his papa, Ben-hesed scooped the boy up in a happy embrace. But the boy struggled free and tugged at his father's clothing. "Papa, come quick. It's mother…"

A chill ran through Ben-hesed as if his chest was filling up with cold water and he ran with the boy back toward his house. He found Bas'emath, leaning over a basin, being violently sick. He rushed to her side. When, at last, she was able to speak, she said, "Have Geber wait outside."

The child protested and refused to leave his mother, until – his patience at an end – Ben-hesed grabbed him by the back of his shirt and marched him out of the house. He returned to kneel beside his wife.

"I have been a fool," she croaked, "not to believe your story."

"No," Ben-hesed said firmly, "you have caught an illness and the doctors will heal you. It is like you said – it's just life."

"It's Belial."

"What?"

"The demon was here, he told me it's typhoid fever."

"No."

"He told me you must make tribute or I'll die."

For Ben-hesed the room was spinning. He toppled off his knees onto his rump and waited for it to stop. But it did not stop – instead his mouth started to water and he feared he would be sick too. He was brought back to his senses by Bas'emath.

"This is my final word," she gasped, "no one harms my son. No matter what."

They say that angels can take different forms when they interact with humans. The same can be said for fallen angels. The Second Book of Corinthians notes that the devil can disguise himself as an angel of light. King James thought demons could assume the likeness of departed friends; and Carol and Dinah Mack maintain that they "can appear as smoke, as temptresses, animals, grains of sand, flickering lights, blades of grass or neighbours."[224]

In order to finally break Ben-hesed, Belial assumed the form of a simple cockroach. As one of the oldest insect species on earth, roaches have long been a plague to man, infesting human settlements and spreading disease. Amy Stewart would later comment upon their role in the transmission of illness: they scuttle between people's food, refuse and sewage, carrying "any number of pathogens around with them, including *E. coli.*, salmonella … typhoid, dysentery, plague" and so on.[225] In this form Belial alighted on Bas'emath's food and she became ill. He later told the suffering woman that it was typhoid, but that was not true. He did not plan to kill Bas'emath, but only to make her sick enough to frighten her husband. Therefore he gave her a nonlethal case of food poisoning, the early symptoms of which could be mistaken for the onset of typhoid. Then he could dangle the possibility of his wife's recovery in front of Ben-hesed – if, of course, he was willing to make a deal.

As Ben-hesed hastened through the crowded streets of Jerusalem to fetch a doctor, Belial fell into step beside him.

"Your wife is very brave," he said.

Ben-hesed launched himself at the demon and grabbed him by the throat. Nimbly, Belial broke his grip and stood laughing at him.

"Yes, she is brave ... but misguided."

"Leave me alone." Ben hurried on, but Belial's words, "Her death won't save the boy," stopped him in his tracks.

It was now too much. Ben-hesed felt as if a swarm of bees had invaded his body, buzzing in his head until he could no longer think. Belial grabbed the unsteady man and ushered him down a nearby alley that was shaded and quiet. Ben-hesed fell to his knees and wept.

"My, such torment," Belial said. "I actually feel sorry for you. You know, there is one other way to please Moloch without harming Geber."

Ben-hesed seized at these words the way a drowning man will grab at anything that will keep his head above water. "What? I'll do anything ... what is it?" He wept, clinging to the demon's robe.

Belial bent down and caressed Ben-hesed's hair to soothe him. "Shhh. All this is not necessary. I will help you, but first you must help me."

The man raised a tear-stained face to his tormentor, "What must I do?"

Belial smiled. "Get your plans. You're going to show me how to undermine the temple."

Seated on his throne in his temporary palace, King Solomon massaged his temples with his fingertips. This did nothing, however, to soothe the pounding in his head.

"What happened exactly?" he asked.

Asif bin Barkhiya, his vizier, stepped forward. "The four walls of the Temple collapsed under the weight of the roof."

"Any deaths?"

"No, sheli 'melekh (my king)."

"Good." The king directed his next question to Hiram Abiff, the chief architect of the Temple. "What caused the collapse?"

"Honestly, sir, I don't know. The walls were secure and properly buttressed. They should have held."

"Well, you're obviously doing something wrong," Benai'ah, commander of the army spoke up. "This is the second time the roof has caved in, and there have been endless delays."

Hiram looked at him calmly. "If you're suggesting that our calculations were wrong, you are incorrect. Those walls should have held."

"Then how do you explain it?"

"I can't," Hiram shook his head.

"All right," Solomon cut in. "Let's assume that you are right, Hiram, and that human error is not responsible. What about human interference?"

"What do you mean?" Asif asked.

"I mean sabotage," Solomon answered. "Gentlemen, there appears to be a fly in the ointment. Hiram, I want the names of everyone who was working on the Temple when the problems arose."

"Yes, `melekh," he answered and hurried upon his errand.

"Do you really think its sabotage?" Benai'ah asked.

"Who would do that?" Asif interjected. "Who would undermine God's Temple?"

Solomon leaned back in his chair. "Who, indeed."

King Solomon surveyed the man who stood in front of him. He did not look at all well. His bloodshot eyes darted from Solomon to Benai'ah and back again. They were tired eyes, underscored with dark circles. He stood as a man cowed – shoulders hunched and head bowed, his neck stiff as if anticipating a blow. His trembling hands fidgeted nervously.

Solomon had compared the lists provided by Hiram and one name was common to them all.

"So you are Ben-hesed," he said.

The man nodded.

"My advisors have told me about you. They use words like 'gifted' and 'intelligent,' 'hard-working and conscientious.'"

Ben-hesed stared silently at the ground before Solomon's feet, engaged in the colossal effort of keeping his emotions under control.

"Abi'athar, the priest, talked to me about you too," Solomon continued as he rose and began to walk casually around, looking at one splendid object, lightly touching another. "He used words like 'pious' and 'faithful.' So I ask myself, why would someone of such good reputation sabotage the Temple?"

The trembling in Ben-hesed's hands began to spread. The man, Solomon realised, was blinking back tears and this moved the king to pity. Solomon walked to a gilded cage that held a large bird. He released it and threw it a handful of seeds.

"Have you ever seen a creature so beautiful as this?" he asked.

Ben-hesed shook his head.

"It is a peacock. It is thought to be symbolic – that, like that beautiful tail, God's teachings adorn the righteous man 'with the grace and splendour of many virtues.'"[226] He nodded, "There are many virtues, Ben-hesed. One that I prize above all others is honesty. Now tell me, *why?*"

Ben-hesed finally spoke. "You would not believe me," he whispered.

Flashing him a wry smile, Solomon replied, "You would be surprised at what I would believe."

Ben-hesed looked at his king and could discern no anger in his face. A small glimmer of hope ignited within him. Perhaps. Perhaps he could tell the story and be believed ... and be forgiven. He began to speak, haltingly at first, then quicker until all he had suffered these last months came tumbling out of him.

Solomon listened, his face becoming increasingly grave. When at last the man was silent, the king spoke mildly, "Thank you, friend. You have been a great help."

Ben-hesed looked at him, dumbstruck. "You ... you are not going to punish me?"

"Why should I?" Solomon stooped to pick up a fallen peacock feather from the floor. "You are the victim of the crime, not the perpetrator," he said, handing the feather to Ben-hesed. To Asif he said, "See that this man is restored to his post."

When all was prepared, King Solomon slipped a ring from his finger and held it up. It was wholly unremarkable in appearance: a dull grey band of pewter with no markings or adornments, and yet Benai'ah looked upon it in wonder. It was said that the Archangel Michael had given Solomon that ring so that he may control demons, djinn and unseen spirits.

Solomon spoke quietly. "Come ye then, Belial, from your hiding places. Come and behold the power of God whom all creatures obey."

The flames of the many lanterns in the king's throne room flickered as if from a gust of wind. Their light dimmed momentarily and, when once again they burned steady and bright, the demon was among them.

"You called?" he asked.

Solomon regarded him coldly. "That was quite a mess you made of the Temple."

Belial shrugged. "You may be able to summon me here," he said in a low voice, "but I don't take my orders from you. What do you hope to accomplish by all this? You can't keep me here indefinitely. That little trinket," he nodded at the ring, "doesn't give you that kind of power."

"No," Solomon answered, "it doesn't. But it allows me to do this: Belial, I charge you with the murders of Ahin'adab and Nepheg, father of Ben-hesed, with the torture of Ben-hesed and his family and with the sabotage of God's most holy Temple. And therefore I call upon the God of Justice to descend and cast ye, unclean spirit, into the depths, bound in flame!"

Benai'ah stepped forward and doused Belial in lamp oil. The oil had been blessed and burned even before Abi'athar the priest set it alight. The demon shrieked.

"Know the suffering of the blazing flame[227] and know that this vessel," Solomon pointed to a brass jar, "will be your prison from this day forward."

As the fire increased in intensity, Belial's screams echoed through Jerusalem. In his home, as he hugged his wife and child and thanked God for his narrow escape, Ben-hesed's prayer was interrupted by the demon's cries of anguish. For the first time in months, he smiled.

When the demon had been reduced to dust, his ashes were carefully collected and placed within the jar. The lid was fastened on tightly and upon it was engraved Solomon's seal, a six-pointed star which bore his name. Upon the vessel were these words of warning:

לעילב ךותב
Belial, within.

Solomon then gave the order for Benai'ah to personally take the jar to Ashdod and cast it into the sea.

While Solomon first waxed then waned as King of the Israelites, a small copper jar drifted aimlessly in the Mediterranean Sea. From the coast of Israel, it was taken slowly, slowly by the current past the city of El Iskandarīya, past the Island of Heraklion, and around the toe of Italy's boot. And while it drifted, Belial languished in his prison. No one could have guessed that the quietly drifting urn contained such torment. Indeed it is one of the Proverbs of Hell that "the busy bee has no time for sorrow."²²⁸ But left alone inside his own head, deprived of all activity and distraction, the demon found that his greed and anger and hatred – with no external target – now turned back upon himself. So desperate was he to be free, he promised to bestow great wealth and prosperity on whosoever should open the jar.

The years cycled by and onward he drifted past the southern shores of the Franks, through the narrow gap now known as the Strait of Gibraltar and out into the cold waters of the Atlantic. Belial was growing impatient and in his grudge decided only to grant his saviour three wishes instead of the boundless wealth he first promised. And yet no one came to his rescue. Currents nudged the jar northward until one day, at last, it was snagged in a fisherman's net.

### A Side Note

*In the* Tales from the Arabian Nights, *we read of "The Fisherman and the Afreet." It tells the story of a poor fisherman who went down to the beach to cast his nets. In them he snagged a heavy copper jar "sealed with a strange and ancient seal." Thinking that the urn must contain something very valuable, he prised off the lid and a "thin thread of smoke floated from the mouth of the jar ... growing thicker and thicker ... the smoke spread blotting out the sun and the sky, then became solid ... a monstrous demon – head, body, legs, arms and all!"²²⁹ The demon said that he was an afreet, a type of jinn imprisoned by Solomon long ago.*

*Similarly in "The Spirit in the Bottle" by the Brothers Grimm, a boy finds a sealed bottle in the woods and uncorks it: "Immediately a spirit ascended from it and began to grow, and ... in a very few moments he stood ... a terrible fellow as big as half the tree. 'Do you know ... what your reward is for having let me out?... Do you think that I was shut up there for such a long time as a favour? No, it was a punishment for me.'"²³⁰*

*In both stories the spirit, embittered by its long captivity, threatens its saviour with death. In both stories the outcome is the same. The frightened human says to the spirit, "I cannot believe you fit into that jar." Insulted, the afreet dissolves into smoke once again, gathers itself up and returns to the bottle to prove its magical power. The wily man quickly reseals the vessel, trapping the demon inside. Realising its mistake, the spirit begs to be released once more, promising in return not death, but wealth and prosperity.*

And so it was in the year 1066 that a fisherman named Casek set out in his small boat to fish off the coast of Cornwall. It was October and the water, churned up by strong winds, was biting cold. He doubted very much that he could land a decent haul in these conditions, but the thought of hungry mouths at home compelled him to try. He waited a moment for the net to sink and then pulled it in hoping for a good catch. Instead he found, among the broken shells and seaweed, a copper urn, finely etched with strange markings.

Elated at his luck to pull something so shining and beautiful from the sea, he quickly rowed home and, once on the beach, pried the seal off the jar expecting to find treasure within. Instead, a thin wisp of black smoke issued from the vessel, slowly at first and then with gathering speed. The formless cloud darkened and thickened as the terrified man dropped the urn and cowered on the ground. It was as if he had unleashed darkness itself into the world. The sun disappeared from view behind a cloud as dark and fluid as squid's ink. Then slowly each writhing tentacle of smoke seemed to gather itself into definite form – the legs, arms and torso of a tall man. The stranger's face was handsome and pleasing to the eye and yet every instinct, every heartbeat within Casek's chest thudded a nameless warning. Unsteadily he rose to his feet.

The apparition looked down upon the man and grinned; yet this brought Casek no comfort, for the stranger's eyes regarded him coldly. The eyes speak true, he thought, and the smile lies.

"Tell me your name," it said in a voice surprisingly sweet. Casek realised that even the seagulls had fled. Without their incessant calling, the lonely beach was unnaturally quiet.

"My name is Casek." The man was dismayed to find that his voice came only in a whisper.

"Casek," the spirit seemed to roll the name around on his tongue, "what place is this?"

"Dumnonia, sir," the man said with more strength. Yes, that is better, Casek, take heart.

The stranger sighed wearily, "A wretched backwater then. It figures." He looked desolately around him for a moment and then, remembering the frightened man who stood before him, he leaned forward until he and the fisherman were eye to eye. "Sadly, you are too late, Casek."

"Too late?"

"Yes," that sweet, melodious voice droned on. "Many, many years have I been trapped in that urn praying for deliverance. At first I swore that I would make the man who rescued me a king, rich and powerful, and I would shower him with all good gifts. And yet no one released me. To float in such darkness, such nothingness does something to you; did you know that? It twists even your best intentions and alters your most fervent vows until in my bitterness I decided at last that I would grant my saviour only one wish…"

"Yes?"

"How do you wish to die?"

The question struck Casek like a slap to the face. It was enough of a shock to finally rouse his anger. But he was not an idiot. The air around this stranger fairly bristled with magic, and no amount of fighting and raging would prevail against one such as this. No … but cunning might.

"Before I die, I wish to know one thing," he said as calmly as he could manage.

"What is that?"

"Did you, a proud and powerful demon, really come out of that tiny jar?"

"Indeed."

Casek shook his head stubbornly, "I don't believe it."

"It is the truth."

"What use have I for words? I only believe what I can see with my own eyes. I doubt you could do it."

Sadly this was the moment when Casek's story diverged from the fairy tales. Instead of obligingly gathering himself back into the bottle, Belial seized the urn and cast it far out to sea. "Anything else?" his tone was dangerous now.

The colour drained from Casek's face. "A quick and painless death."

"Done," spoke the demon and the man fell where he stood.

That was 1066: the year when the dragon Xiàngshù arrived on our shores, the year of the Norman Invasion, the year that the Saxon King Harold took an arrow in the eye at Hastings, and the year in which William the Conqueror was crowned Britain's king. Amidst such historic events, the death of a lowly fisherman passed by unnoticed by all except those who loved him. And us.

By nature, the Coranieid dislike demons. It is not because we considered ourselves to be such paragons of virtue that we were offended by their lack of a moral compass. Quite the opposite. We knew we were bad, but demons were infinitely worse. We were novice sinners compared to demons – the master craftsmen who could create a thing of evil so perfect in its malignancy that it frightened even the likes of us. That is why I was bewildered when Belial seemed to limit himself to the commission of relatively pedestrian sins: seducing buxom peasant girls, conning travelling merchants out of their money, the odd spot of recreational murder. Generally, though, he lived quietly, anonymously.

My attention was soon taken up first by Myrddin's death and then Xiàng's. Then her eggs hatched and I seemed to spend every waking moment procuring food for the young dragons. It was on one such hunt that I came upon Belial. He emerged from the local river wearing not a stitch, and grabbed a shirt that hung from a nearby branch, slipping it on so that it clung to his wet skin. I decided in that moment to abandon the snare I was setting on the muddy bank where the animals came down to drink. I rose and turned to leave.

"Interesting," he said.

I ignored him.

"I didn't think the Coranieid were afraid of anything."

I turned to face him.

"Yes," he smiled at me, "I know who you are."

He crouched down, grabbed a stick and drew a rough shape in the dirt: a six-pointed star. ✡

"Do you know what this is?" he asked.

"A hexagram. King Solomon's seal." I cocked a wry eyebrow at him. "Wasn't that on your jar?"

"Yes," he rose and brushed the dirt off his hands. "I thought you might be interested in it."

"Why would I be?"

He shrugged. "Like your tribe, King Solomon knew the speech of the birds and animals and insects.[231] It was a source of great knowledge for him, as it is for you."

"And?"

"And this symbol," he poked at the hexagram with a bare toe, "his seal, combines the alchemic signs for all four elements." He picked up a longer stick. "Here is earth," he traced over the ▽̄ part of the design. "Here is air." Again he traced a shape: △̄ And then we have fire (△) and water (▽). His whole philosophy was based on the harmonious union of the elements or, as it is embodied by your tribe ... elementals."

"That's very profound," I said flatly and turned to leave.

"The whole design is the alchemic symbol for quintessence."

I stopped short.

The demon pressed on. "He could see it … just like you can."

I stared at him wide-eyed. "How do you know that?"

"They call it intellectus. Angels have it, even fallen ones, and it is very useful indeed. It shows us the truth of things."

"Is there a point to all this?"

"When you look at me, what do you see?"

A plethora of insults couched in the crudest terms flooded my brain, but I opted for "a waste of my time," and turned again to leave.

In an instant he was in front of me, a vice-like grip on my arm that I could not break.

"Let go of me," I hissed.

"What do you see?"

I realised with horror that I could not escape him. So I arranged my features into what I hoped was an expression of boredom and sighed, "Fine."

Inwardly I cringed. I had looked into the hearts and minds of men for centuries – all were like open books to be read. But the mind of a demon, now that was something to be reckoned with. I stared at him intently.

Before I could address his mind, however, I had to get past his face. He was a dazzlingly handsome creature with a strong jaw and eyes like sapphires of Kashmir blue. I know that is ridiculously poetic, but he was like poetry, of smooth and unbroken lines that moved with a rhythm that stirred something within me. Those peasant girls never stood a chance. And even I could not look upon him without feeling my pulse quicken and my skin cry out to be touched. I tore my eyes from him with difficulty and shook what felt like a thickening net of cobwebs loose from my brain. So that is your game, demon, to dull the mind and bewitch the senses till people are like clay in your hands. It took a while to discipline myself not to be distracted by that face and those strong arms. His beauty did not reflect what was within; this I knew, but it was a long time before I could feel the truth of it. Such is the power of demons.

Once past those magnetic eyes, I hit another obstacle. Despite his painful grip on my arm, he looked totally relaxed, singing a ballad to himself while he waited. His voice was husky and mellow as the lute, and did it not play a pretty tune? Such a soothing voice telling such sweet, sweet lies. Again my head would fill with cobwebs and my heart would cry, "I believe you!" And again, I would fight not to be caught by the cloying beauty of his honeyed words.

"Oh, you are good, aren't you?" I murmured.

Finally immune to the charms of both voice and face, I could delve deeper into the mind of the thing. At first it felt like it usually did, like my own mind was moving freely through air, groping for something solid, the grooved and textured wall of his mind that I could run my hands over, the way the blind now read Braille. I could certainly hear his heartbeat in my head and I awaited that flash of light that is thought, that is self, that is soul. But the light never shone. All was darkness and emptiness and cold. All was silence…except, wait. The faint sound of something scuttling in the dark. I groped for it. But the ethereal, and yet tangible soul that I reached for was not there. There was only dark, gaping, hungry space and the arachnidan mind of the creature – so very clever and so cruel.

I was trembling violently now.

"What do you see?" he repeated.

"A yawning chasm where your soul should be … and within it, your mind."

He squeezed my arm harder and I yipped in pain.

"Now you know what you're dealing with. Don't forget it."

I felt like my arm was about to break and this roused my anger. I looked deeper, searching for a weakness. I found it.

"Yes, your mind," I continued, "so pitiless, mirthless … and afraid." I smiled at him malevolently. "What are you afraid of?"

"Nothing."

"Now it all makes sense," I drawled. "I know why you're keeping your head down and your crimes humble: you're hiding, aren't you. From him. From your master," my lips twisted into a sneer. "The last thing he made you do resulted in imprisonment. So many years spent inside your own head. What torture … what madness."

With a flick of his wrist he threw me violently to the ground. I landed badly, but as I rubbed my throbbing arm, I laughed. "That's why you're trying to scare me off. I remind you too much of Solomon. Oh," I cooed in a pouting baby voice, "are you afraid I'm going to put you in a jar?"

"Shut up bitch, or I'll…"

"What?" I spat. "You can't take me on without attracting too much attention." I rose to my feet and advanced on him as I spoke. "So go on and hide. Hide, you cur. But be a good boy, because I know what you're hiding from…"

It found him in 1071; Belial was summoned back East. 1071. That was the year that the Seljuk Turks captured Jerusalem and smashed the Byzantine Imperial Army in the Battle of Manzikert. I found a book the other day that actually, incredibly, states what happened: it tells us that Belial was "the Devil's special envoy to the Turkish Sultan, helping him plan new outrages against the innocent Christians of Europe."[232] It is only one short sentence and buried in a self-professed volume of tall tales, but it is the one whisper that all other history books ignore. For sure enough, when the demon arrived in the court of Sultan Alp Arslan things changed.

For centuries the Fatimids, an Islamic caliphate and the direct descendants of Fatima (daughter of the Prophet Muhammad), had held Jerusalem and there was peace. According to scholar Mike Paine, "the Christians there ... enjoyed reasonable treatment under the Muslims. The latter were prepared to allow Christian and Jewish practise to go on as recognition of the status of these two religions as ahl al-kitab, People of the Book. Indeed all three religions were connected."[233] Under the Fatimids, the Christians of Jerusalem were allowed to keep their Church of the Holy Sepulchre. Yet when Jerusalem fell to the Seljuks (new and fanatical converts to Islam), the church was desecrated and Belial danced through Solomon's city, delighting in posthumous revenge. Christian pilgrims, who had been welcomed into the Holy City for centuries, were now either killed on the road or arrested and sold into slavery. Some had been disembowelled as Turkish marauders sought any gold coins they may have swallowed in an effort to hide their money. And more was to follow. In a letter written to Count Robert of Flanders in 1093, the Byzantine Emperor, Alexius Comnenus writes:

> ...the enemy has the habit of circumcising young Christians and babies above the baptismal font...Then they are forced to urinate into the font...Those who refuse are tortured and put to death. They carry off noble matrons and their daughters and abuse them like animals... Then, too, the Turks shamelessly commit the sin of sodomy on our men of all ages and all ranks ... and, O misery, something that has never been seen or heard before, on bishops...[234]

He finished with an impassioned plea for help in staving off the Saracens. And so, on 18th November 1095, Pope Urban II proclaimed the First Crusade. The demon had helped to start a war.

But it must, thought Belial, be a most splendid war. He was on the move again and with no small purpose. He had been told to create trouble the way dark witches mix their brews. Ingredient number one, provocation, had already been obtained. The Seljuks, in the name of jihad, had burnt the Church of the Holy Sepulchre to the ground and defiled countless others. Even the baptismal fonts, the source of purification and acceptance into God's church, were smeared red with the blood of their forcibly circumcised captives. There is a sure way to get people's attention, he mused as he traversed the green and rolling hills of Saarland, on his way south and west. Murder, sodomy, forced circumcision, rape – these acts were not enough in and of themselves – but to do them in a church, to hang your helmet on the cross so you can bend the priest over his altar and give him one up the ass, he chuckled to himself, that'll do it. The Pope must be apoplectic. And now, he paused overlooking a picturesque village nestled into a green valley, for the second ingredient: stupidity.

In a monk's habit, he strode to the village, past the fields of ripening barley and rye, past the blacksmith's and the town well and up to the very porch of the church. He did not attempt to enter, knowing from painful experience how hallowed ground charred and blistered the soles of his feet. With one last glare of resentment cast upon the church door, he turned and began to preach:

"My friends, ye have heard of the terrible deeds of the Saracen and of the noble army – God's army! – that readies itself for battle." His voice, strong and melodious, echoed through the village.

In the pale early morning light, the first drowsy heads peeped from doorways and windows at the beautiful stranger who addressed them so familiarly. They gathered around him.

"And his Excellency, Pope Urban, has promised each member of that fearsome host a place at God's table in Heaven, as reward for joining the Crusade." He dropped his voice and looked sadly about him. "And that is good for the lords and knights rich enough to buy their armour. That is good for the soldiers and the priests who travel with them. But what of you, my friends? What of the humble farmer who forces his plough through the frozen earth in hour upon hour of back-breaking labour in order to coax God's abundance from the land … what about you? Where is your promise of salvation? Does it seem unjust to you, my friends, that the rich and powerful – those who have the best of this world – are now guaranteed the eternal splendour of heaven as well? Meanwhile, you toil away in the hope that, in that final reckoning, your virtue will outweigh your sin and all your mistakes." He paused a moment to allow them to think on their sins, and he could feel their stomachs contract as they made the mental leap from sin to fiery consequence. They would, he knew, have heard many brimstone sermons. "But fear not, my friends, for I have the answer. In the Book of Luke, our Lord tells us the parable of the lost lamb and of the shepherd who would leave ninety-nine sheep unguarded in the wilderness to search for the one who is lost." He swept an arm toward the paddock where the sheep were penned for the night. "To God, each one of you is like that one lamb, precious, important. And so to you He extends the same grace that he gives to kings: a place on the Crusade! Pope Urban himself calls on men 'of all ranks, knights and foot soldiers, rich and poor, to hurry to wipe out this evil race' who holds Jerusalem in thrall. Who among you is so godless as to say 'nay' when the Lord, your God, has offered you sure salvation? Who could? As for myself, I will grab this chance with eager hands … who will join me? Who will march with God's army and reserve his place in Heaven?!" Every arm was in the air and every voice was raised in unified assent. The demon smiled upon them … yes, you will do very well indeed.

The history books tell us what happened next. The People's Crusade, a ragtag band of peasants twenty thousand strong, marched toward Constantinople while the professional soldiers were still at home, making preparations. In their ignorance and zeal, they did not take the provisions necessary for such a quest, believing that the good Lord would provide. And provide He did. Were there not farms and flocks along the way? This first wave of God's army saw these as gifts for the taking, and descended like a plague of locusts on every village in their path.

Finally, upon reaching the Holy Land, the inevitable happened. The mob was forced to fight not peasants with trowels, but the highly fanatical and heavily armed Turks. Belial, still in the robes of a Catholic priest and calling himself "Peter the Hermit," had accompanied them as their spiritual leader, for it is said: "even Satan disguises himself as an angel of light. So it is not strange if his servants also disguise themselves as servants of righteousness."[235]

Outside the town of Civetot, he blessed them and said unto them: "Be strong in the Lord and in the strength of His might. Put on the whole Armour of God that you may be able to stand against the wiles of the devil."[236] And with that he sent them into battle. The vast majority were armed only with farming implements and sling-shots, and their protection (the metaphysical armour of their faith) did nothing to shield them from the spears, arrows and swords of the Turks. The result was unsurprising: most were slaughtered and those who survived were enslaved. And what of the man who sent them on this suicide mission? History tells us that Peter the Hermit returned to Constantinople having "been instrumental in leading tens of thousands to their deaths."[237]

After the slaughter Belial, now sans his monk's name and monk's habit, waited in Constantinople for the real Crusader army to arrive. This he joined and, in 1097, rode out in his splendid armour to lay siege to the city of Nicaea.

The day had been long and hot, but ultimately amusing. Encircling the walls of Nicaea, the Crusader army had been attacked by a Turkish force bent on breaking the siege. The Turks were defeated, and Belial sat on a hillside looking appreciatively across a battlefield strewn with bodies of Christian and Saracen alike. From nearby tents, the agonised cries of the wounded and, more ominously, the feeble moans of the dying, mixed with the buzzing of innumerable flies. A sharp wooden thwack, followed by laughter and a cheer, drew his gaze to the catapults, where men were hurling the severed heads of the Turks over the walls and into the city. A messenger had just arrived with news of reinforcements on the way and that, he mused, would be the final nail in the coffin for Nicaea. Their surrender was expected imminently.

But despite all this he was dissatisfied. Simple carnage was not enough. He should be able to make more of the situation. But what?

"What, indeed?" he murmured as he lay back and dosed, lulled to sleep by the repetitive dull thudding that heralded the flight of yet another severed head.

A change in the ambient noise roused him from sleep. The catapults were now still and silent and the mortally wounded had finally ceased their moaning and died. These sounds were replaced by grumbling voices.

"Here we have sat, in this wretched heat, battling for our lives and what do they do? They hand the city over to Alexius?"

"He only just got here..."

"I know. And because he wants his city pristine, he's asked Count Raymond to forbid looting."

"All this and no reward?"

"That's it."

Booty – money or valuables obtained as the victors looted a conquered city or the body of a dead enemy – was a major incentive amongst soldiers. They were often poorly and irregularly paid for their work and so, once victory was achieved, the cry of "A bonne usance!" (For my good use!) would be heard as the victors claimed the wealth of the vanquished. This did not happen at Nicaea. While Alexius had his city and the leaders of the crusade received their reward in Byzantine gold, the soldiers were given only an extra ration of food.

Belial smiled. He had found another ingredient for the witch's brew: discontent.

Discontent is a vine, he reasoned as he kept his horse in line with the rank and file that now marched toward Antioch. If it is to grow, it must be fed and watered. And what better place to nurture an army's dissatisfaction than another long siege outside the walls of another city?

The siege at Antioch lasted for seven gruelling months. The Crusader army, having exhausted all supplies available locally, had to range farther and farther afield in search of food. Troops from the city harried the Crusaders with nightly raids, and the promised reinforcements and supplies from Alexius never arrived. With the coming of winter, the food shortage became desperate. The sky never stopped pelting them with freezing rain, and the area was hit by an earthquake. Antioch had a large Christian population which surely would help the Crusaders from within … right? When even that failed to materialise, it was another, particularly sharp slap in the face. Morale plummeted.

And all the while Belial talked. He talked of the hardships of Nicaea and of the comrades they had lost on the bloody fields outside the city walls. And for what? An extra food ration and a pat on the head? Was it really going to be any different here?

"The nobles took an oath to turn Antioch over to Alexius as well. And where is that bastard and all his promised help?"

Walking through the Crusader camp, he muttered a word here and a phrase there – anything to keep feeding that vine of discontent as it snaked its way through the ranks.

To the pious he asked, "Why, if we are so favoured by God, does He punish us with starvation and earthquakes?"

To the materialistic he wondered, "How warm and snug the Christians of Antioch must be right now, sitting in their dry houses with full bellies!"

On and on he went and the vine grew strong. Arriving back at his own tent, however, Belial realised he had done his job almost too well. He had managed to depress himself. Looking dismally around at the rain and the mud and all these reeking human beings … he could not tolerate such squalor any longer. He turned a covetous gaze upon the city with its surplus provisions and sturdy roofs.

The decision made itself. I can, the demon reasoned, still do the job without unduly compromising my own comfort. And so, he stole a pike from outside a foot soldier's tent and waited for nightfall and the next raiding party from the city.

Sure enough they came, and with the practised ease of an experienced killer, Belial impaled a Turk as he rode past. The force of the blow vaulted the man off his horse. Quickly, already dreaming of hot food and a dry bed, he swapped armour and rumbled demonic threats at the dead man's steed until it was sufficiently cowed to allow him to mount. He joined the raiding party as it raced back to the city.

Belial passed a cosy winter within Antioch, pausing each day to smile down from the city walls upon the Crusaders in their squalid camp.

Spring brought better weather, but still no reinforcements – indeed these would never come. The Crusader Stephen of Blois, fed up with the siege, decided to take his troops and go home. On the way he met Alexius, who was bringing the long-awaited relief. Stephen painted such a bleak picture of the situation that the Byzantine Emperor was ultimately convinced of the futility of joining the Crusaders at Antioch. He too went home.

Within Antioch, Belial (now calling himself Firouz) seemed to be a talented soldier and a pious Muslim. By the end of May, Belial had gained enough favour to be entrusted with the command of three towers along the city's curtain wall. That is how a demon works. They do much damage, but only after we let them in. John Michael Greer would later note that: "Demons cannot force their way into the human mind … uninvited, for despite all their powers and unnerving forms, we are stronger than they are – at least potentially. They must seduce, flatter, wheedle, and cajole their way in, for they can only enter with our permission."[238] And once Belial had wheedled his way into Antioch's defensive force, he was perfectly placed to cause more mischief. One night he slipped from the city, unseen.

"Firouz," a man whispered emerging from the shadows.

Belial answered, "Yes?"

"Bohemond wants a word."

In his loose Turkish robes, the demon allowed himself to be led through the Crusader camp to the large and comfortable tent of Bohemond of Otranto – one of the five leaders of the Crusade. He accepted the wine that was offered him and stood calmly under the appraising eye of Bohemond.

"You say you were once a Christian?" the commander said quietly.

Belial bowed his head in assent. "Yes, my lord. I was forced to convert to Islam long ago."

"Tragic," replied Bohemond indifferently. "And I suppose that long separation from the true faith has been a torment to you?"

Belial looked shrewdly upon the portly man in his fine tent with his fine wine and answered, "As much as it would be for you, my liege."

Bohemond chuckled. It was, he knew, no secret that he was cut from a different cloth than Counts Raymond and Godfrey and the rest of those flaccid idiots who were here to 'fight the good fight'. No. He was here to acquire land and to fill his coffers with as much Turkish gold as he could lay hands on. Instinct told him that, likewise, this man Firouz cared not a stitch for converting back to Christianity. What he wanted was to be duly compensated for his services. Fair enough.

"How much?"

Belial raised his eyebrows innocently, "For what?"

"For access to your three towers. Name your price."

The demon's smile beamed like the smile of angels. "Oh, my lord, you are too kind, too kind indeed…"

On 3rd June 1098, in the dead of night and with a king's ransom safely tucked away, Belial smiled pleasantly upon the Crusaders as they clambered up ladders and took possession of his three towers. In all sixty men scaled the wall that night and quietly made their way to the main gates of the city, slitting the throats of sentries as they went. They threw open the gate to a waiting army that poured into the city like a raging flood, engulfing everything in its path.

Walking nonchalantly through the streets, Belial hummed softly to himself. Nearby a woman screamed as she was dragged into a house by a knight in splendid armour.

"Good luck wriggling out of your chain mail before she legs it," the demon laughed, but then was brought up short when he stepped on something soft. He looked down to realise that he was standing on a human hand that lacked an owner. "Damn," he muttered, "and my best sandals too." He continued on, scuffing the soles along the ground to scrape off the gore.

Further down the street, he came upon Imru. Belial had spent many a night standing on one of the towers, keeping watch. The long and monotonous winter nights were the worst – that is until Imru was assigned to the same post. He was a weaver of stories and would begin each shift with the words, "I remember, when I was a boy, how my grandfather used to say…" And so he would begin spinning out thread after thread of colour and detail, of thought and feeling, until Belial had quite forgot not only where he was, but, miraculously, what he was. He became so engrossed in these stories that he forgot to plan, to plot, to hate. And then there was the sun casting its first rays low on the horizon and the watch was over.

Now Imru lay in the street staring up at the demon with unseeing eyes. Briefly, Belial thought he saw in them a silent accusation.

"Don't be stupid," he muttered, stepping over the body. He did not make it more than three steps, however, before something tugged at him making him stop. He returned to the corpse and cast a knowledgeable eye over it. One wound to the gut, probably from a broadsword. He shook his head, stomach wounds are the worst. Belial's chest contracted painfully, though he did not understand what that meant. Nor did he understand why he felt compelled to kneel beside the body and close the man's eyes. "I'm sorry," he muttered and then, cursing his own folly, rose and walked on.

Up ahead lay the inner citadel of Antioch (still very much in Muslim control) and, Belial knew, reinforcements under the command of Kerbogha of Mosul would arrive shortly. The Crusaders would be trapped between the two. Trapped, indeed, in the summer heat with the rotting dead.

Death paints itself on a body in white and green and scurrying black. First, within hours of the last breath, the eyes glaze over a milky white. To the blowflies the body is a gift, a nest for their eggs and a ready supply of flesh for the new maggots. In a couple of days the belly turns a sickly green that radiates outwards till it finally reaches the fingers and toes. More flies and now beetles move in and the stomach bloats. Next the ants and cockroaches revel in the moist and sticky feast that has been left for them. Then the springtails arrive to help return the body to the dust from which it came.

*Imru.* His stomach lurched at the thought. For some insane reason he did not want to leave Imru to rot.

"Now why the hell does it matter?" he demanded aloud of no-one in particular. No answer was forthcoming; but it did matter. Suddenly it mattered very much.

Half walking, half running, he picked his way through the streets to the house where his gold lay hidden – gold that would buy burial for Imru and some words to be said over him, although he could not fathom why those words should be important. But not, he thought, clutching the bag of riches to his chest, all the gold. He still needed some of it, because tonight he was going to get laid and drink himself into a stupor so that again he might know what bliss it is to forget.

Meanwhile, the flies gathered and, with them, disease came creeping on silent feet.

The next few days passed in a drunken blur. Belial was dimly aware that events had followed their predicted course. The Crusader army was indeed pinned between the besieged enemy in the citadel and the fresh army that howled at the gates. The air reeked of decay, and sickness was rife. In fact it was a rumour of disease that finally cleared his pickled brain. Adhemar of Monteil, Bishop of Le Puy and Pope Urban's representative, was sick with fever. Now that was interesting. If any man stood in Belial's way, it was Adhemar. He was not only intensely moral, but very intelligent, a voice of reason in the chaos that was the Crusade.

Still reeking of stale wine, he made his way to Adhemar's bedside to pay his respects. The sound of vomiting told him, before he had even crossed the threshold, that he had come to the right place. The noble Bishop fell weakly back on his pillow, trembling violently. A woman, looking overly pale herself, carried the reeking basin outside and emptied it in the street.

"How are you, Adhemar?" the demon enquired, with just the right note of concern in his voice.

The bishop mumbled incoherently, and Belial raised his eyebrows in an unspoken question to the woman.

"His fever's so high, he doesn't know where he is."

Nodding grimly, he left – waiting, of course, until he was down the street and around the corner to smile and walk again with a spring in his step. "And that is ingredient number four added to the pot: the silencing of reason."

Now how can I use it to best effect? He looked about him at the downtrodden Christian faces. They were tired, scared and demoralised by a fight that simply would not end. They were losing hope, and in that lethargy would be useless to him. He needed a spur, something that would goad them into action.

"Please, Lord, please do not forsake me…" This one line of prayer reached his ears as he walked. He paused and looked about him the way one looks for the source of an unpleasant smell. There in the shade, his cheeks flushed and his forehead wet with fever, sat a young page. "If you could just give me a sign," he continued, unaware that he was being observed.

Belial snorted in disgust at these grovelling humans with their hands constantly raised in supplication. "Always pleading for help or a sign." This last word he spat with particular venom. Then he stopped. A sign. Yes. That just might work.

In peasant's garb, Belial waited impatiently outside the chapel. The eleven o'clock High Mass was nearly over, and he meant to speak to the priest once he set foot off consecrated ground. He did not have to wait long. For someone who had just extolled the glory of God to his congregation, the priest's countenance was very grim indeed.

"Father!" Belial rushed to him. "I must speak with you. Please, it's important."

Doubting that very much, Brother Paul reluctantly asked, "What is it, my son?"

"I was at my work and I fell upon the ground…"

"If you are ill…" Paul took a step backward.

"…No, it was not fever. It was," the demon paused and pretended to search for the word, "like a kind of dream." Entering wholeheartedly into the little drama, his eyes glazed over and he said in a low monotone, "'In a trance I saw a vision, something descending, like a great sheet, let down from heaven by four corners; and it came down to me.' Looking at it closely I saw an image of Christ on the cross, with a spear piercing his side. Then I saw that spear in the earth with stone upon stone laid above it." He appeared to snap out of it and asked, "What does it mean, Father?"

Paul was staring at him. His clothes were the rags of the humblest peasant, and his hands were rough and filthy from toil. And yet this man had just quoted

Peter's vision in the Book of Acts almost verbatim (Acts 11:5-6). Right up until that bit about Christ and the spear. That was new. Indeed, what does it mean?

"You said you saw the spear that pierced Christ's side buried in the earth?"

"Yes."

"It is interesting, that." Paul nodded.

"I saw a great stone building, and over the door a man holding keys in his hand."

Now it was Paul's turn to stare vacantly before him. "'I tell you, you are Peter, and on this rock I will build my church and the powers of death shall not prevail against it. I will give you the keys of the kingdom of heaven,'" he muttered.

"What?"

"Matthew 16, verses 18 and 19 about St. Peter. No … it can't be."

"What?" repeated Belial as he watched the holy man swallow the lie whole.

"St. Peter's Cathedral," Paul muttered as he turned and walked away, still deep in thought. "But surely it cannot be…"

Later that day, under the ruined walls of St. Peter's Cathedral, they found an old wooden spear, the tip of which was dark brown, the colour of dried blood. Paul grasped the holy relic in trembling hands and thought he could feel the power emanating from it in waves. It was a profound moment. And he was so filled with awe and gratitude that he wept.

The lance was taken to Adhemar. He was less than inspired. The bishop was lucid once again, certainly lucid enough not to fall for yet another spear that supposedly pierced the side of Christ. Indeed, this is not the first one I've seen, he thought, recalling one in Constantinople that was detailed in gold. No, I must caution them not to believe in it and certainly not to fight in the hope that this stick will protect them. At that moment, however, his body was wracked with coughing so violent that he was sick again. A bout of diarrhoea and vomiting was more than enough to induce Count Hugh and Duke Robert to leave him with hasty wishes of "Rest, brother, and feel better soon."

But no, I have something to tell you, thought Adhemar. His fever spiked again and he couldn't remember what he had wanted to say. And so Belial added a fifth ingredient to his witch's brew: unquestioning fanaticism. With the Holy Lance in their midst, the Crusaders rode out and confronted Kerbogha's army. Whipped into an ecstatic frenzy, they were like men possessed. Their attack on the left flank was so ferocious that the Turks there turned and ran hell for leather. With the line broken, others began to panic and were slaughtered as they fled.

Watching from the wall, Belial couldn't breathe he was laughing so hard. *They won! They fucking won! Unbelievable! Well, they say faith can move mountains…*

Faith had certainly moved an army, and kept the conflict alive. The citadel of Antioch quickly surrendered to Bohemond, who declared himself Prince and claimed the city as his own. It had been promised to Alexius, but fuck him. Having procured his own little kingdom, Bohemond remained at Antioch while the Crusaders, still feeling invincible, marched on toward Jerusalem.

Jerusalem herself had recently undergone great changes. The Seljuk Turks, who had sparked the Crusades with their violence and intolerance, had been defeated by the Fatimids who retook the city shortly after Antioch fell. The status quo that allowed Christians, Muslims and Jews to peacefully coexist had been restored, and under the guidance of its governor, Iftikhar al-Daula, Jerusalem stood poised to once again become a nexus of worldly prosperity and ardent faith in God.

Unfortunately the Crusaders' desire, their need to take Jerusalem, was as strong as any deep and fast-flowing river. Such a thing cannot easily change its course. From the very beginning, when Pope Urban preached the crusade, he admonished them to "fight for the deliverance of the holy places."[239] Jerusalem was the shining jewel of these. In fact, it was their main reason for being in the Holy Land – all their work at Nicaea and Antioch had merely laid the foundations for this one great quest.

Also, in their ignorance, they did not recognise the distinction between Seljuk and Fatimid … both were of Islam. Therefore, as they approached, Governor Iftikhar prepared for a siege. He expelled every Christian from the city so that there would be no treachery from within, no one to help the enemy over the walls. Jerusalem's wells would provide ample water for the city's remaining inhabitants, and enough food had been stockpiled for a lengthy siege. This, he admitted, was a sign of his tendency to be overly cautious. The siege would not be a long one. Even now, a Fatimid army was winging its way here from Egypt. They would drive the enemy away, and then things could finally return to normal. He sighed longingly at the thought of that golden day when he might settle down to govern in peace. *Allah, may it be soon.*

In the summer of 1099, the Crusaders arrived at Jerusalem and Iftikhar was further heartened by what he saw: they were a ragged bunch indeed. Their great destrier warhorses, which the knights used in their devastating raids, had perished in the heat. The soldiers themselves had fared no better. The blistering heat, rotten food and unclean water had led to outbreaks of typhoid that thinned their numbers and left survivors in a weakened state. Nor was there any relief to be had outside Jerusalem's walls. Iftikhar's men had poisoned every local well and chopped down every tree that might have offered a patch of shade. The only respite from their suffering came from the Fountain of Siloam, which only gushed one day in every three. Raymond of Aguilera (chaplain to the Count of Toulouse) recorded what happened when Siloam's waters sprang forth:

> Those who were strong pushed and shoved their way in a deathly fashion through the pool, which was already choked with dead animals and men struggling for their lives ... those who were weaker sprawled on the ground ...with gaping mouths, their parched tongues making them speechless, while they stretched out their hands to beg water from the more fortunate ones.[240]

Yes, the thirst was terrible, but these were no longer green recruits who would lay down and die. They were God's army, His chosen ones, who carried the Holy Lance into battle and prevailed. Up and down the ranks, they felt it – "a sense of inevitability ... of destiny."[241] Jerusalem was God's city and He shall have it back. It shall be cleansed of the taint of the infidel, and shine again as a beacon of the one true faith. Amen.

Iftikhar watched anxiously from the city walls as the siege towers went up – surprisingly fast for an army hard-pressed by thirst. For the first time he began to doubt the wisdom of his actions. Other governors of other cities (Tripoli, Beirut, Acre) had decided to pay the Crusaders off rather than fight them. None of those cities were molested. Nick Yapp, in his work, *Life in the Age of Chivalry*, explains why: "The chivalric code ruled that, if a besieged town or castle surrendered before hostilities began, the garrison and inhabitants should be allowed to march away unhindered."[242] If, however, the city refused to capitulate, the invaders would attack its inhabitants without mercy, killing them all.

With reinforcements on the way, Iftikhar knew that defeat was unlikely. "But not impossible," he murmured as he watched the Franks constructing their towers, their ballistae and trebuchets.

Thirty thousand people now resided within Jerusalem's walls – thirty thousand individual lives that he was responsible for. He scanned the horizon, looking for any sign of the promised army led by Egypt's vizier; yet the horizon remained an unbroken line. Turning back to face the city, his city, he doubled the guard, and prayed.

The prophet Muhammad once said, "Do you know what is better than … prayer? It is keeping peace and good relations between people, as quarrels and bad feelings destroy mankind." Men lost sight of this wisdom during the crusades. We were once all People of the Book – united in our quest to better know God. We were all pilgrims (granted, travelling different roads) but seeking the same destination. Ignorance, intolerance and fanaticism destroyed that understanding. And when wisdom and compassion die, people are next.

On the fifteenth day of July, the Crusaders stormed Jerusalem.

Iftikhar's home was on a hillside with the city stretching out in front of it. It was here that he stood and watched. He had at one time thought himself a man of the world. He was not young or naïve and, he felt, that he had seen enough of life and men to no longer be surprised by anything.

"I stand corrected," he mumbled as he looked on in horrified disbelief. Even his years as a general in the Fatimid army had not prepared him for this.

In the streets below, his soldiers were beheaded and the civilians were rounded up, tortured and executed. He pressed his hands against his ears in a vain attempt to block out the screams. First it was the men who, in the agony of their suffering, shrieked like women, desperate and high-pitched. Then the women, who were already hoarse with weeping and crying out last declarations of love to their men and their children – pain helped them find their voices anew. Tears welled up in Iftikhar's eyes and his fingernails dug bloody gauges into the palms of his clenched fists. But even the screams of the women were as nothing when compared to the cries of the children. The poor man's heart was pounding so hard in distress and horror that he thought he might die, and wished to Allah that it would happen soon. He was trembling violently now as he looked upon his city and all the people – thirty thousand souls – who had looked to him for protection. A thin line of spit ran from the corner of his mouth; he seemed to have forgotten how to swallow. He was violently sick on his own shoes.

New, stronger howling caught his attention, and carried his eyes in the direction of the synagogue where the Jews had taken refuge. The Crusaders viewed them as collaborators with the enemy, and hence they barred the doors from the outside, trapping the people within. They set the building alight. The thick, black smoke that issued forth did not come in time to hide one last detail that would haunt him for the rest of his life. There, in the lower-lying parts of Jerusalem, the streets ran ankle-deep in blood.

A firm hand clapped him on the shoulder, and he turned to face Count Raymond of Toulouse – the man to whom Iftikhar had surrendered.

"I'm sure you and your family want to get out of here," the nobleman said. "But first there is the little matter of the ransom."

Iftikhar gave everything he had to ensure the safe passage of his family. He led them out of the city, escorted by Raymond's men, and did not look back at Jerusalem. Briefly, he wondered how you are supposed to live after something like that. But even these thoughts were muffled as his mind went numb.

Belial watched him go. He had been stoking the fires of religious fanaticism within the Crusader camp for weeks, even claiming to have another vision: this time of the dead bishop Adhemar urging the soldiers to cleanse God's city in Saracen blood. Yet even he was surprised at how well his efforts had paid off. He had seen death before. He had seen slaughter. But this ... this was something special. He breathed in the metallic smell of blood and the acrid smell of burnt flesh. It was the aroma of the sixth ingredient he had added to the pot: loss of all humanity. Thanks to just enough illness and stress and exhaustion and thirst and rhetoric, the Crusaders were now worse than beasts. For surely, Belial had never seen an animal wrench a baby from its mother's arms to dash its brains against a wall.

For the demon it was an unmitigated success. Solomon's city was now a charnel house. Six months after the massacre, the city still reeked of decomposing flesh. As Fulcher of Chartres noted: "Oh what a stench there was around the walls, within and without, from the rotting bodies of the Saracens, lying wherever they had been hunted down."[243]

This fact was grotesque, but there were more far-reaching consequences than just the bad smell. Christianity and Islam were now locked in hostilities that would continue for another 173 years through a second crusade, a third, a fifth, an eighth. Animosity and distrust would linger between the two, well into the twenty-first century. Having been instrumental in stirring up this noxious state of affairs, Belial quit the dust and the heat of the Holy Land. The demon was once again on the move.

CHAPTER 9

# "DUMB WITNESS"

*"See you ... it is a pot that boils and seethes and every now and then a significant fact comes to the surface and can be seen. There is something in the depths there – yes, there is something! I swear it..."*

Agatha Christie, Dumb Witness[244]

George was a knight. He had fine chainmail armour, a strong sword arm, and a swift horse. He had an impeccable sense of duty and a pious soul. And George had fleas. To say this, especially in 1258, was not a criticism: everybody had fleas, from the poorest serf to the king himself. Later, when scientific names became the vogue, these evil little bloodsuckers would be christened *pulex irritans* and ways would be devised to kill them. However, at this early date, people accepted them as an inevitable part of life.

Unfortunately on this particular day, the fleas were under George's armour, hopping and biting with gay abandon. When one of the little bastards got into his helmet, underneath his arming cap, and started nipping him behind the ear, it distracted his attention at just the wrong moment. Seizing the opportunity, Edwin de Loire swung his mace. The blow connected with George's left shoulder and almost unseated him from his horse. Regaining his balance, he struck Loire's head with the flat side of his broad sword, sending his opponent toppling to the ground. When the dust cleared, the first sight to meet Edwin's eyes was the tip of George's sword, inches away from the nasal bar of his helmet.

"Reddition? (Surrender?)"

Edwin nodded reluctantly, "Oui."

And so George added another opponent's armour, weapons and horse to his growing wealth. He helped Edwin to his feet – the fight was for sport after all – and returned to the melée. When the tournament was over, George accompanied his lord, Sir Ralph Arundell, back to the fortified manor at Lanherne, removing his helmet and scratching frantically at his ear as he rode.

They were greeted at the gate by a young woman, and George instinctively sat straighter in the saddle. She was beautiful, with pale unblemished skin and brown hair that had lightened in the summer sun to reveal a hint of reddish gold. Her eyes, large and blue, conveyed intelligence but, he noticed, did not echo the smile that played across her lips. On tiptoe, she tilted her face upward to kiss Ralph on the cheek, and then turned an appraising eye on George.

"I was watching the melée … what happened to you out there? Sir Edwin almost had you."

Ralph laughed and clapped George on the back. "He's quite literally had a flea in his ear. I've had it happen; you can't concentrate at all till you get the bugger out."

Hawisa nodded, "Redigan will have something for that."

"Do not trouble yourself, lady," George said hastily.

"It's no trouble. She's here now." The girl walked away and George watched her go.

His horse shifted impatiently beneath him. The beast was tired and hot and needed tending. George dismounted and with a nod to Sir Ralph walked his mount to the stable. His armiger appeared, helped him out of his armour and then reached for the horse's reins, but George shook his head. After the dust and clamour of the melée, he wanted a few quiet moments alone. He unsaddled the horse, hung the bridle nearby, and began to dry the beast down with handfuls of fresh straw.

He always found this calming. The animal might be a dumb brute but his company was soothing, and George needed to be soothed. He was becoming increasingly perturbed by the girl – desperate to be near her and ashamed of the desire at the same time. She was, after all, Hawisa Arundell, daughter of Sir Ralph, his liege, and betrothed to Hammond de Valletort who was currently in the Holy Land. The marriage would unite the two great families of Cornwall: the Arundells and the Valletorts. Therefore Isa was out of reach. Any attempt … it was not even an option.

Since the age of seven, when George's father sent him to Lanherne, Sir Ralph had been everything – teacher, father, friend. Hell, he worshipped the man, and Sir Ralph was the embodiment of everything he wanted to be. He was an excellent chevalier and strong enough to cleave an enemy from the top of his helmet down to his breastbone in one stroke. Great was his renown. Great, too, was his largesse; he generously rewarded the loyalty of his vassals, each one of which would ride beside him through the very gates of hell. George himself had nearly died in Ralph's defence and had been given this horse, a courser, the best warhorse that money could buy, in return for his service.[245] And yet here he was pining for the man's engaged daughter.

"I'm an awful person," he muttered to the horse.

And yet his feelings for the girl were as persistent as that damned flea, distracting him, demanding to be addressed.

"And why?" he asked aloud.

Was he simply one of those fools who always wanted what he cannot have? The girl becomes unattainable, so now he wants her with a fervour bordering on desperation? Or was it really love?

He remembered how one day, when he was armiger to Sir Ralph, he had given in to temptation and tried on his master's armour. Ralph caught him in the act, but instead of giving George a sharp scuff for his transgression, he merely asked, "How does it feel, boy?"

Embarrassed, George had replied, "Very uncomfortable."

Sir Ralph had laughed, "That is because it was not made for you. When you wear armour that fits, you'll feel the difference."

And that, he realised, was the problem with Hawisa: we fit.

Redigan, the local pellar or wise woman, was in the Great Hall patching up those hurt in the tournament. As Hawisa made her way there, the smile disappeared from her face. She hated melées and only watched them because her own imagination conjured up worse images than what was actually taking place. But oh how her stomach had lurched when George took that blow from Sir Edwin. "Ils sont imbéciles," she muttered to herself.

She knew that she was supposed to be impressed with today's display of military prowess, but Hawisa seldom felt how she was meant to feel. There was something in her that all too often seemed to fall out of step with the world. However, she was smart enough now to conceal this.

She had not always been that shrewd. As befitting a lady of her station, she had been taught to read by Brother Simplicianus, who presided over the parish church. Once, when she was twelve, he asked her to read 2 Samuel, chapter six in which David is moving the Ark of the Covenant: "'And they set the ark of God upon a new cart, and brought it out of the house of Abinadab that was in Gibeah: and drave the new cart.'"

"Very good, Hawisa. Your Latin is improving. Continue," the aged monk nodded.

The girl resumed. "'And David and all the house of Israel played before the LORD on all manner of instruments … And when they came to Nachon's threshing floor, Uzzah put forth his hand to the ark of God, and took hold of it; for the oxen shook it. And the anger of the LORD was kindled against Uzzah; and God smote him there for his error; and there he died by the ark of God.' … Why?"

"Why what, child?"

"Why did God smite Uzzah?"

"Because he presumed to lay hands upon the Ark of the Covenant," Simplicianus replied as if to say, "Isn't it obvious?"

But to Hawisa, it was not obvious at all. "The oxen stumbled and the Ark was unbalanced – it might have fallen from the cart."

"Ah yes, but why was it on the cart in the first place? In Numbers chapter four, God specified that the Ark should be carried by poles upon the shoulders of the Levites. It was not to be thrown on the back of a cart like a bale of hay. Uzzah should not even have laid eyes upon the Ark; it should have been covered by the priests."

Such a sense of injustice filled her that Hawisa could not let the matter drop. "But was that Uzzah's fault?"

Simplicianus looked at her perplexed. "How do you mean?"

The girl sighed impatiently, "David was the king. Should he not have ordered that the Ark be covered and carried by poles upon men's shoulders?"

"Yes, the whole company was at fault."

Hawisa shook her head. "David was most at fault, for he did not command that God's will be obeyed."

"David did not touch the Ark."

"No. Uzzah did – to keep it from falling into the dirt."

Simplicianus had had enough. "The Ark was filled with the divine presence of God Himself!" he snapped. "It was a most sacred and holy object and they treated it a little too casually. So it became unbalanced! Do you think that God would allow His own sacred vessel to fall at men's feet? Where was Uzzah's faith in the power of his God? Where was his proper humility?"

An instinct told her to stop talking, but she ignored it. "It happened in an instant, father. Did he even have time to think of all those things? He tried to preserve the Ark of God and he was killed for it."

"Are you saying that God's punishment was unjust?" The monk's tone was low and dangerous.

Hawisa hesitated, and then managed a less than convincing "no." This was met with a sharp smack across the knuckles with a palmer.

"Do not lie. And do not think that such blasphemies go unpunished."

Hawisa sat there, fingers stinging, blinking back tears of surprise and shame. "I'm sorry."

The man looked upon the face of his favourite pupil, and was moved to pity. "I take no relish in chastising you, Hawisa. But what you're saying is blasphemy. Now, do you repent this folly?"

"Yes."

"Good, although this is one for your next confession." He sat back in his chair and considered her for a moment. She was intelligent – no doubt about it. And she had faith, real faith. For Hawisa, religion was not a duty to be trudged through, but something she embraced. All the more reason, he said to himself, to handle this issue with a bit of compassion.

He finally spoke: "The faith can be challenging, can it not?"

"Yes."

"And I know that difficult questions arise for which there seem no satisfactory answers. But that is what faith is for: not to provide us with all the answers, but to help us endure without them."

"Yes, Father."

The lesson over, he sent her on her way.

Hawisa cursed herself not for harbouring such an opinion, but for being foolish (and overconfident of her relationship with the monk) enough to voice it. The opinion itself was valid.

If I were Uzzah and saw the Ark tip, she thought to herself, I would have done the same thing. I could not have done otherwise, because when something is important you protect it. And if God still thought he should be killed… Oh, just forget it.

That day, as she was escorted home by one of her father's men, they took the usual shortcut through the churchyard with its yew trees and slippery jack toadstools. Despite the fact that she was always in the company of others, at that moment she felt like the loneliest human on the planet. Her ideas were not only at odds with her teacher (and probably everyone else around her), but they were at odds with her God.

Certain that she was an awful person (and perhaps even damned by her own stubbornness) she passed a long line of gravestones. Maybe it was her heightened state of emotion or maybe it was just because it was so apt, but in her young brain the analogy stuck. All these doubts needed to be boxed up and buried. And her thoughts on the story of Uzzah were not the only things to be firmly put back in the box. When she found herself promised to Hammond, she firmly put away her anxiety about marrying a stranger. When a knight was brought in bleeding from the ears after a melée, she shoved her horror and disgust aside and congratulated her father on his success. How very ironic that she, who was so good at executing her duties, was inwardly somehow wrong – a misfit, la boutade, a freak.

At the recollection of all this she paused and smoothed her gown, along with the lines of anxiety that creased the corners of her frowning eyes and mouth.

"Isa, mon chou! How good to see you!" Redigan had spotted her as she hesitated on the threshold of the great hall.

Hawisa beamed at her. The old pellar was of Celtic stock, but had learned a bit of Norman French out of affection for the girl.

"Salut, Redigan."

"And what can I do for you today?"

"You're busy; I'll come back," Hawisa nodded toward the young knight who sat before Redigan holding a bloody cloth to his cheek.

"No I'm finished here." And with an order to rest, she dismissed the young man. "So, what do you need?"

"Something for fleas."

"That's easy enough." Redigan fished through her basket and extracted a small pouch. "Bog myrtle, southernwood and rue. Sprinkle a bit of this on your clothes and that'll see 'em off."

"It's not for me; it's for one of the knights."

"Oh," Redigan nodded. "I wonder who…" she smiled impishly.

Hawisa blushed. "I'd better go. But thanks."

She hurried off to find Jory (her nickname for George since he came to Lanherne when she was five). As she walked calmly through the halls of the manor, certain buried thoughts rattled the hinges of their box.

Medieval society was divided in two: the spear side and the distaff side. The spear side quite obviously referred to the male sphere and not just because a spear is such a blatant phallic symbol. It is the side of war, of defence, of conquest, and prowess. The distaff side therefore denotes the female sphere of influence – a distaff being a tool used to spin yarn before the introduction of the spinning wheel.

It was an evening in late August. The bread harvest was in, and the grain had already been ground into flour at the watermill. The Harvest Home Festival and the melée to celebrate this were now over. The last of the blackberries had been picked, and the pigs were not due for slaughter until September. Likewise, the orchard crop was not yet ripe.

Hawisa, whose mother Eva was in poor health, was responsible for running the kitchen at Lanherne, and juggled all of these things in her mind. For some reason she felt quite restless that night, and fidgeted for something to do. So she called her ladies to her to while away a few hours of late sunlight at spinning, weaving and embroidery. They may still be languishing in summer heat, but the colder months were not far away and she wanted to replenish the castle's stock of blankets and warm clothing for winter. It was tedious work and so Hawisa was not surprised when Constance, a girl of eight sent to her by the Fitz Turold family, asked for a story.

Hawisa had an excellent memory for stories. She liked how they allowed her to step outside herself for a while. It was as if she could see the story unfold in front of her, and so vivid were her descriptions that she could bring the scene to life for others as well. Many a long hour of needle and thread had swiftly passed while she recited the tales of Roland, Tristan and Isolde, Guigemar and Equitan.

"How about the story of Lanval," she suggested.

"I was hoping you'd tell of Guinevere again."

Hawisa knew the child was still very homesick, and only wanted to hear her favourite story. Still, for some reason Hawisa had never liked the story of Lancelot and Guinevere. She cringed inwardly, but smiled at the girl and began…

"Of all the knights of Arthur's round table, none was more noble than Lancelot. The son of King Ban of Benoic, the foster child of the Lady of the Lake, he was the best of knights. Is it any wonder, then, that Arthur loved him?..."

Outside, reclining in the balmy air of the August night, and half drunk on wine, Hanyfer and I listened to the story.

"And yet, there among all the shining towers of Camelot, despite all the assembled strength of the Round Table, we find the seed of Arthur's destruction. For when the bright threads of that world startled to unravel, it was not because of sword or spear. It came in the pretty form of a woman.

"Queen Guinevere had eyes like emeralds and hair like golden flax and Arthur loved her...."

Hanyfer sat up, "Queen who?"

"She means Gwenhwyfar," I mumbled drowsily. "They say her name differently now."

"And Arthur is meant to be Artos, right?"

"Yep."

"Then who is Lancelot?"

"Never existed. He's been added to make the tale more interesting."

"Honestly," Hanyfer sighed in exasperation. "I don't recognise the story anymore, and I was there! What's all this about a round table?"

"You know Wace?"

"The poet?"

"He added it."

"Why?"

"Apparently, so that all of Arthur's knights would feel they had an equal place at court," I snorted.

Hanyfer laughed, "The Artos I remember didn't care a fig whether his vassals all felt equally valued and anyone who complained would have gotten a kick in the ass."

"Too right."

"I still don't understand why they must make all these changes. Why not speak of the thing as it was?"

"They can't comprehend the thing as it was. Too much time has passed and, in these modern days, they cannot understand what it was like back then. Take Guinevere. The Gwenhwyfar we knew was of Celtic stock. Do you remember what a queen was to the Celts? A leader and a warrior and an equal to any king. She could have had a hundred lovers and no one would have batted an eyelash. Compare that to a Norman lady – all fine gowns and domestic duty and Catholicism. How can one comprehend the other? And so Gwenhwyfar must change. She is made into Guinevere, the lady, and any hint of congress with other men is used as a moral lesson. Yes, she found true love, but look," I said dramatically, "at the terrible cost! It is the beginning of the end of Arthur's noble court. And all because she was selfish enough to choose love over duty."

"Noble court?" Hanyfer laughed again. "They were a rugged bunch."

"And now they are very gentile. Human beings can rarely see beyond their own times."

Constance's voice interrupted the flow of Hawisa's narrative. "Why couldn't Lancelot and Guinevere stay away from each other?"

"Love exerts a strong pull on people and … ouch!" Hawisa had pricked her finger with her needle, and instinctively stuck it into her mouth to stop the bleeding. "It's no excuse, though. They were not animals in rut. They had responsibilities and they had a choice." She let out a heavy sigh. "It is getting late. Off to bed now."

Hanyfer yawned and stretched. "Good idea… You coming?"

"I'll be along in a minute."

Hawisa came to the window and stared at the last oranges and pinks of the sun as it dipped below the sea on the horizon. And she thought about Guinevere. The thought of bringing such disgrace upon herself horrified her, and yet she understood Arthur's queen. To love someone that you cannot touch or kiss is a terrible thing. Its leaves a hole inside you, a hollow that you are meant to fill with devoir, with duty. She sighed wearily and felt the full and monumental weight of her obligations to her family, her father, her God. Her duty to them, which loomed above her as big as a cathedral, was still not enough to fill that hole in her heart, and watching her, I knew it never would be. And I ached for her because I knew only too well what it felt like – the loneliness, the isolation of living as a secret infidel among those who could never understand.

Six hundred and seventy-two years later Sigmund Freud, in his seminal book *Civilization and Its Discontents*, would encapsulate Hawisa's problem perfectly: "The liberty of the individual is not a benefit of culture… Liberty has undergone restrictions through the evolution of civilisation, and justice demands that these restrictions shall apply to all… (However man) will always, one imagines, defend his claim to individual freedom against the will of the multitude." He goes on to say that "It does not seem as if man could be brought by any sort of influence to change his nature into that of ants."[246] And yet we try to be obedient members of our group and, within Hawisa's colony, she was fated to be a worker. She sighed and muttered, "Retour dans votre boîte … Back in your box," and resumed her weaving by candlelight.

I headed toward Merlin's Cave. As much as I sympathised with Isa, I was (ironically) now the one in authority. I thought of my two charges: the dragons Kenwyn and Barenwyn. It was now my job to make them obey rules that restricted their choices, to make them comply and do things they didn't want to do. They were now 187 years old, mere teenagers, but swiftly approaching the age when they must make their journey east.

Back at the cave, I broached the subject again.

"I still don't understand why we have to go on that stupid trip," Barenwyn said with an angry flick of her tail.

"To complete your education."

"But surely you can do that, Mum."

I half-believed that was true. When Xiàngshù was forced East by her mother, she was a wayward teenager in need of firm guidance. She was a danger to others, and hence others would soon be a danger to her. Her mother had little choice but to remove her to a place of calming influence and ancient knowledge. But with my dragons this was not the case. They were so good, and I – more ancient and wise than any monk in China – was their teacher. Could they not stay and learn from me? Then, of course, I would not have to part with them; I would not have to let them go.

Xiàngshù, however, had made her wishes very clear. Often she had spoken of her time in the East and how it had been the making of her. She wished her children to have the same opportunity. She spoke of it as the best gift she could ever give them.

But Xiàng was no longer here. I was raising and protecting the chicks now. Was I also obliged to honour all her wishes? I saw her face again – the best friend I had ever had – and realised that yes, I was thus obliged for she would have done the same for me.

"We'll talk about it later," I said. "You may both find that, when the time comes, you are more than ready to leave the nest."

"Never," Barenwyn rested her head in my lap.

I smiled down on her. "Never say 'never', little one. When you are older, you may well want a bit more than this cave and me and the greenwood."

"What more is there?"

"Oh, the world holds such wonder and colour. You have yet to see mountains capped with snow even in summer and hear the music of foreign tongues. You have yet to look upon people and marvel at their lives – so different from yours and yet to them so ordinary. You have yet to smell the spices of the East and the sharp scent of Northern pine. You have yet to taste kir in France and olives in Italy and decide whether you like them." I paused. I had just answered my own question. Of course the dragons must go. To keep them with me and deny them the world: it was too selfish. My throat suddenly felt very tight.

"It sounds wonderful," Kenwyn said.

"It is," I whispered. Yes, they must go. But not yet. We still had time.

With evening now closing in, the dragons would soon go out to hunt and fish, and then with full bellies they would return to the warmth of the cave and sleep. I kissed them goodnight and told them to be good and warned them away from men and their villages. They fidgeted – impatient at having to listen to the same lecture again and again. But, I reasoned, if I said these things often enough, perhaps they would become ingrained.

My last task of the evening was to walk the hidden paths of the greenwood and leave offerings – mice for the owls, berries for the hares, a few nice fat woodpigeons for the foxes – payment for those creatures awake and watchful in the night. In return for these gifts, I had an army of chaperones who would watch over the dragons and be swift to peck or scratch at the doors of Annwyn if there was any sign of trouble.

There was no trouble. The creatures of the greenwood were unanimous: Kenwyn and Wynnie were two beautifully behaved dragons. Good, sensible kids. And so by mid-October I decided it was time for their next lesson. Arriving at the cave I announced, "I have a surprise for you."

Like children the world over, they were on their feet, anxious to see what mother had brought them.

"This," I said, proudly holding up two flint stones.

It was amusing to watch their reactions. They were clearly disappointed with the unremarkable, dull grey stones, but wanted out of courtesy to look pleased.

"They don't look like much, do they?" I asked.

"Well, no," answered Kenwyn with a guilty laugh.

"And yet these two stones are more precious than any jewel in any dragon's horde."

"How so?" Wynnie asked.

"With these ... you'll breathe fire."

### A Side Note

*According to the book* Dragonology *there is, within a dragon's lower jaw, a pouch in which he keeps iron pyrite granules and a flint stone. To breathe fire, a dragon expels flammable venom through two hollow fangs in its upper jaw while simultaneously jerking its head to produce a spark from the friction of flint dashed against pyrite. This ignites the venom which can then be spat at any potential threat. The resulting stream of flame is lethal, burning at 1,000° Celsius[247] and is described in the epic poem* Beowulf *as "blood smoke" and "the hot war-breath of venom and fire."[248]*

*Crucial to this process is a simple piece of flint. As Christina Rossetti would later write:*

> *"An emerald is as green as grass*
> *A ruby red as blood;*
> *A sapphire shines as blue as heaven;*
> *A flint lies in the mud.*
>
> *"A diamond is a brilliant stone,*
> *To catch the world's desire;*
> *An opal holds a fiery spark;*
> *But a flint holds fire."[249]*

And so in October, while leaves of yellow and red fell in the greenwood, there was warmth and brilliant light beneath Tintagel as my dragons harnessed the power of fire. Yes, I thought with pride and sorrow, they are growing up.

November came and the golden, temperate days of early autumn gave way to the first frosts and the coming winter gales. Frost is the most insidious killer I've ever known. It creeps up in the night and freezes the water within plants; typically the younger, more tender shoots are most vulnerable. Ice crystals form inside the plant and expand until they rupture its cells. By midday, with the sun in the sky, the ice melts and the plant itself may look fine. Sooner or later, however, it will begin to show signs of the irreparable damage that has occurred within.

While this silent killer glistens at sunrise, the days themselves grow shorter as darkness claims hours that once belonged to the light. In the greenwood the wrens – birds who prefer a solitary roost – now huddle together in the cold of the long night. And within the human world, November is known as the "blood month," a time to slaughter livestock and salt the meat or hang it in the chimney to cure. Great fires are ritualistically lit to ensure the renewal of life in the soil and, as the darkness and cold draw in, it is thought that demons walk the earth.

On the second of the month we see the advent of All Souls' Day, when special requiem masses were held to pray for the souls of the dead so that they may pass from purgatory into heaven. All Souls' Day has always been painful. The longer I live, the more people I outlive: Myrddin, Uther, Xiàngshù, Owain, Maban, Fryok, Tamara, Elowen, all of those lost at Nanscáwen – the list goes on and on and on. In churches on this day, the priest reads from the Book of Luke chapter 22 in which Christ, soon to die upon the cross, addresses His disciples as "those who have continued with me in my trials." I looked upon my growing collection of soul stones and realised that that is how I view my dead. I carry them with me, and at times they are very heavy indeed.

Suddenly restless, I quit the shadows of Annwyn to walk among men, to hear their prayers mingle with the crackle of bonfires and the laughter of children as they dashed from door to door begging soul cakes. In time each of those children would age and die. But that isn't really the point, is it? One day they will die, but before that there will be thousands of days in which they will live. Surely that counts for more than the dying. Surely that tips the scales in favour of life. Why then does the day of Myrddin's death loom larger in my mind than all the years in which he drew breath?

"I've got it wrong," I murmured as I left the village and took to the solitary paths of the greenwood.

My dead, "those who have continued with me in my trials," should be cherished not because they died, but because they lived. And I began to list all of the wonderful things of their living: Myrddin's acceptance, Uther's tenderness, Owain's strength... I was so preoccupied with these thoughts that I did not hear the stag until it was too late.

It crashed through the thicket and barrelled onto the path. I caught a momentary glimpse of quintessence, of the animal's mind. I saw that it was in the grip of great fear and panic before I fell, tangled beneath its hooves. And then it was gone. I lay upon the path, gasping and trembling. Sound returned to the forest, and I called to the noisy starlings in their roost: "Gwere-vy! Help me!" The last thing I saw before I passed out was the flock, a thousand strong, take to the air. In the moonlight it looked like a great cloud of smoke.

I awoke in my old bed in Annwyn. The room was filled with people. At first their words were unintelligible, a murmured gibberish that I couldn't understand. But, slowly, details of the room and the people in it became clear and the gibberish resolved into words.

"What do we do?" My father's voice.

"Well, normally I would ask her how to treat such injuries." It was Mora.

"She's not in any condition to help herself," Gwyn snapped.

The shock ebbed away and pain flooded into its place. Then there was no more talk in the room, only my screaming and a tussle as Danjy and Barinthus struggled to keep me still. Gwyn, his face a deathly white, left the room.

Thumbing through my medical books now, I realise that I was lucky. While the stag had broken my back, the break occurred below the second lumbar vertebra. A few inches higher and I would have lost the use of my legs and probably would have died in about a week. A few inches above that and I would have been paralysed from the neck down and dead within forty-eight hours. Higher still would have meant instant death. But, with the break lower down, there was no paralysis and there was the possibility of recovery: if, of course, I could hang on through the tortured hours that were to follow.

We have many words for pain. My thesaurus lists seventy-two synonyms for it ranging from ache to torment, and twinge to misery. Not one adequately describes how I felt. Medical science would define my condition as "nociceptive somatic pain" which results "from injury to part of the body such as bones... It is usually well localised, and is often described as sharp ... or gnawing."[250] That's closer. I felt as if I was in the jaws of some great beast, its bottom teeth impaling me through my lower back as it chewed. Aeschylus once said, "O Death ... scorn thou not ... to come to me... Pain lays not its touch upon a corpse." Too right. In short, I wanted to die.

I had all the standard analgesics: viper's bugloss, meadowsweet, honeysuckle, lavender – nothing made a dent. The pain was too strong, and its teeth were too sharp. And then my father in a fit of desperation approached a knight newly returned from the Holy Land. He gave the man a king's ransom in gold and jewels in return for a large quantity of yellow powder and it made the pain-beast be still. Imagine that: take a little yellow powder and all is well.

### A Side Note

*The use of opium, also known as lachrymal papaveris or poppy's tears, dates back to Neolithic times and was widely used in Egypt and the Arab Empires as a potent form of pain relief. It contains both codeine and morphine which lull the user into a dream-like state in which there is no pain, no distress, only warmth and a profound sense of well-being. It's associated dangers? Well, they don't become apparent until later.*

Even without the opium, long-term incapacitation does something to you. It does more than immobilise your body and blunt your mind with pain and fatigue. It removes you from the world, which quite happily goes on without you. The dragons kept on growing (I had Hanyfer keep an eye on them for me). The people of the village continued to work and laugh and cry and make love. And I lay still, counting the cracks in the ceiling – present but not. Therefore eight days after the accident, I started a diary. I wanted to maintain some connection to the march of time...

10 Du (November) 1258

Today is St. Martin's Eve in honour of Martin of Tours, a Roman soldier who converted to Christianity and refused to fight. For this he was imprisoned. When later released, he became a monk and was credited with many miracles.

It is said that he cured a leper with a kiss and prayed three corpses back to life. It is also said, quite bizarrely, that he is the patron saint of wine growers, tavern keepers and drunkards. Therefore he is a fitting saint to honour today.

In the village they will be done slaughtering their livestock. Most of the meat will be salted or smoked for later use, but some will be eaten today – the first fresh meat many have tasted in months. And so it is a time of feasting and merry-making when minstrels sing chansons de geste and chansons d'amour (songs of war and songs of love) and games of dice are played. I told Hanyfer to warn my dragons to remain home tonight lest they are spotted by some reveller rolling home from the pub in the wee small hours.

Yes, it is a day to make merry … and it all sounds thoroughly exhausting. Better to stay here in the warm, sipping tea made from the yellow powder which I believe to be as much of a miracle as any performed by the saint.

11 Du 1258

Sad tidings from the village today. A local man, Myghal (pronounced Ma-hail), was found at the bottom of a ravine, his neck broken. He had been celebrating (probably a little too much) at the tavern and lost his footing on the coastal path on his way home. Hanyfer says that they've taken him home so that his wife Enor can clean the body and prepare it for burial.

Kervardhu (December) 1258

Winter has arrived. Although I have not seen it, I know what's happening in the lands above Annwyn. The greenwood is no longer green, but a tangle of grey and brown branches, seemingly lifeless. And yet much is happening. While red squirrels search for nuts hidden earlier by the jays, a few acorns will remain undiscovered under the fallen leaves. These will sprout roots and thread them into the earth. Winter moths mate; the hatching of their young will coincide with the first bloom of tender young leaves in spring. All this transpires quietly, unseen.

In contrast, the birds of the wood are locked in a fierce struggle for their lives. Their main task now is to procure enough food during the day to fuel them through the bitter cold of the night. If they don't eat enough, they'll be dead by morning. And so the daylight hours are filled with a flurry of activity. The rowan berries are stripped from the trees and any patch of earth that isn't frozen is mined for worms and insects. Some birds are adaptable: the blackbird, for instance, expands its menu to include newts, frogs and even tiny mice. Others just become more aggressive, bullying smaller birds away from the available food. Theft is rife. I once saw a robin snatch a worm right out of a mole's chops – plucky little bastard.

Kenwyn and Barenwyn will likewise start to feel the winter's pinch. The cold will thin the herds of deer, and so they must rely more on fishing the frigid waters of the Atlantic and stalking the elusive wild boar. I have asked Hanyfer to top up their larder when possible.

Through all this scrambling for food and seeking for warmth, the ancient oak trees simply mark time. In fall and winter they produce a dark ring of bark that separates the lighter wood grown last summer from the new wood they'll grow next spring. If you were to cut the tree down, you could count the dark rings to determine its age. It is significant, I think, that trees measure time not in the linear fashion of men, but in ever-increasing concentric circles. The trees know that time does not necessarily proceed in a straight line as men conventionally believe, but in a cyclical fashion, repeating the same patterns again and again. There are variations, of course. Within the rings of the trees, these result from fluctuations in the weather as each ring is formed. In human affairs, the variations reflect the current progress of man's understanding: his fads, fashions and inventions. But whatever is new about the details, the underlying story is the same.

"I think you need to lay off that tea," my father said, glancing down at the words I've just written.

"Why?" I asked.

"You get too philosophical when you drink it."

13 Kervardhu 1258

Within medieval storytelling there is a common theme of forbidden love that is rendered again and again in various incarnations. King Arthur's queen, Guinevere, loved Sir Lancelot. King Mark's wife, Yseult, loved his nephew Tristan. Sadly this occurrence is not confined to fairy tales. Noble marriages are intended to produce heirs, cement political alliances or add to someone's wealth and landholdings, and hence love and marriage seldom go hand in hand. Therefore I was surprised today to hear a new twist in the old tale.

Word reached Lanherne that Hawisa's fiancé, Hammond de Valletort, is dead. He died last June in the Holy Land while serving under Philip de

Montfort as they tried to recapture Acre in the Battle of Saint Sabas; typically it's taken six months for word to reach England. After delivering the news to their daughter, Ralph and Eva discussed the matter privately.

"It's a sad thing," Sir Ralph said. "I thought her reaction would be stronger."

"Hawisa only met him once."

"He was going to be her husband."

"And yet they were strangers," Eva replied. "For heaven's sake, Ralph, she's had longer and more affectionate relationships with your hunting dogs." Seeing the deflated look upon her husband's face, she placed a hand on his shoulder. "What's really troubling you?" she asked.

He sighed. "I was relieved to find Hammond. Married to him, Isa would never have known hunger or want. She'd be safe at Saint Germans and…"

"And?"

"He was a good man. Decent, you know? He would have been kind to her; our grandchildren would have wanted for nothing and now…"

"And now we have to find another man for her. It won't be difficult."

"Eva, I know lots of good men – good, honest and poor. And I know lots of wealthy idiots who would make her miserable. But finding a husband for her who has it all…"

Eva laughed.

"It's not funny."

"Can it be that you really don't know?"

"Know what?" he asked.

"That there is a knight here at Lanherne who is honourable, who is amassing great wealth and who worships your daughter."

Sir Ralph looked dazed. "Who?"

"George."

There was a long silence followed by "And how does Hawisa feel about him?"

"Smitten."

Ralph's face was stern. "What have they been up to?"

"Nothing," his wife soothed. "They have, however, done an admirable job of pining for each other."

Placated, Ralph relaxed. "George…"

Eva nodded. "He'll wait awhile, of course. It wouldn't be decent to ask right away."

"No, it wouldn't."

Eva watched her husband's face carefully. She could see his mind grow accustomed to the idea. Finally he said, "That settles it then."

"Can you believe it?" Hanyfer gushed. "It's like a chanson d'amour!"

"It is good," I said. "Speaking of amour, how is Barinthus?"

Hanyfer blushed. "Very good indeed. I'm meeting him later."

"Will you…?"

"Check on the dragons first, I know." She refilled my cup. "Don't worry; they're fine."

28 Kervardhu 1258

Barinthus visited today with a report on the dragons (they are well) and also with news from the village: Morenwyn, one of the local beauties, is dead … stabbed.

"Not just stabbed," he shook his head, "disembowelled."

"What? Who did it?"

"I think it was Omfra … the man who's been courting her."

"What do you mean think? Don't you know?"

Barinthus shrugged. "I wasn't really paying attention."

I sighed. "What else?"

He looked at me blankly.

"What are the details surrounding the murder? Did they have a quarrel? Was she leaving him for someone else? Did he go mad?"

"I don't know."

I gave him a withering look. "You are a terrible gossip."

Hanyfer came later with more details. When the murder was discovered, the hue and cry went up. None of the peasants were at work (it is currently a workers' holiday) and so the village mobilised quickly, apprehending Omfra before he could claim sanctuary in the church.

"He was like a man possessed," Hanyfer said. "Screaming over and over that he didn't do it."

"That's to be expected." A twinge arced across my lower back. Hanyfer saw the shudder of pain run through me and handed me a cup of my tea. I took a long gulp and lay breathing heavily, waiting for the moment to pass. "So," I panted, trying to focus my mind on something other than the gnawing, "do any of our people know the truth of the matter?"

"No," she shook her head. "We were all in Annwyn when the girl was killed. Of course, the sheriff said he'll try for a confession."

"He'll get it."

Many methods are commonly used to obtain a confession within the Anglo-Norman legal system. Thumbscrews are popular, as is yanking out a criminal's fingernails with a pair of pliers. Iron shoes slowly crush a man's feet. And there is always the trial by water in which the suspect must plunge his hands, up to the elbows, into boiling water to retrieve a stone. Yes, the sheriff will get his confession; of that I have no doubt.

As Morenwyn was a young woman of child-bearing age, her family can demand two hundred livres in compensation for her death. Omfra will not be able to pay such an amount. Therefore he is doomed.

2 Genver (January) 1259

Sir Ralph Arundell has been appointed as the new sheriff. His first duty will be to execute Omfra for murder. The execution is scheduled to coincide with the twelfth night celebrations on the sixth of January. Barinthus came just now to tell me of my dragons, but I drifted off. I'm sure they are fine.

6 Genver 1259

Twelfth night and the Epiphany. Today is a glittering day in the human world and although I was not there to see it, I know well how the day will have progressed. It will have begun with a church service marking the Epiphany, the manifestation of Christ to the magi. The clergy themselves dress up as the three wise men and a giant, gilded star will have been hung from the church rafters.

Tomorrow will mark the start of the new agricultural year, when everyone will return to work after the long Christmas holiday. Today, however, there will be celebrations and feasting with gateaux des rois (also known as Twelfth Cakes) taking pride of place on the tables of Lanherne. But first, and quite unique to the celebrations this year, there was a rather festive public execution (always a crowd-pleaser). Omfra, being of low birth, died by the rope. Hanyfer said he protested his innocence right to the end.

23 Genver 1259

A bad day today. The pain in my back is worse, and I grow impatient for my next dose of the yellow powder.

"Will you hurry up and make that damned tea?" I snapped.

"It's coming," Hanyfer replied, ignoring my irritability. "Did you hear what I just said? Hawisa and George are engaged."

"Hanyfer…"

"Here you go!" she said, handing me the cup. "God, you're crabby today."

25 Genver 1259

Feast of the Conversion of St. Paul, who was baptised on this day by Ananius of Damascus. It is widely considered to be a day for prognostication. An old, old poem interprets the signs…

> If Paul's day be fair and clear,
> Then we shall have a happy year;
> But if high winds aloft should blow
> Then trouble and dissent are sown.
> Add to it a little rain
> For war, for grief, for death, for pain.

Mother just came to me to talk of the weather. It is whipping up a gale outside. I handed my empty cup to her – a silent request for more.

26 Genver 1259

More news from Hanyfer. Another tragedy.

Last night Sir Ralph and all his company were at dinner in the Great Hall at Lanherne when a harried-looking Sir Aubrey burst into the room and made straight for his liege. Quietly he informed Ralph and his family that Brother Simplicianus was dead. Amidst the inarticulate expressions of shock and all the questions of how and when and why, Hawisa Arundell, pale as a ghost but utterly composed, rose and said, "Take me to him."

Ralph laid a hand on her arm. "I'll deal with this."

"Take me to him!" she said louder and with more force than she intended. Several people who had been laughing and talking at another table stopped, and looked at her curiously.

Jory was at her side in a moment. "What's wrong?"

"Come. I'll explain on the way."

The body had been taken to an unoccupied chamber at the back of the manor. The room, with no fire lit, was cold enough for Hawisa to see her breath. She shivered and held her lantern aloft to look upon her teacher. His face bore no marks, but there was a trickle of blood at the corner of his mouth.

"What caused this?" Ralph asked.

Sir Aubrey shook his head. "I don't know."

Hawisa handed the lantern to her father and gently placed a thumb in the corpse's open mouth, pulling the lower jaw down.

"Isa, leave him."

She shook off her father's hand. "Do you want to know what happened to him or not?" After a moment's pause she murmured, "He hasn't bitten his tongue, so why is there blood in his mouth? ... Jory, do you have your dagger?"

"Yes."

"Cut the fabric away from his chest."

George looked to Ralph, eyebrows raised in a question.

"Do it."

The priest's torso was a mass of deep purple bruises and it was misshapen somehow. Hawisa pressed gently on his chest and recoiled. "His ribs are broken."

"Not just broken," Sir Ralph observed. "Crushed."

Hawisa was now looking at Sir Aubrey. "Did something fall on him? Was he pinned beneath a rock or a branch?"

"No. There was nothing like that. He was just lying on the path."

"What could have done this then?" asked George.

"An accident with a horse perhaps." Hawisa shook her head, bewildered.

"Was he murdered?" Ralph asked.

"Who would kill like this?" Jory pulled the cloth back over Simplicianus' chest. "There is no wound from a weapon."

"An unfortunate accident then," nodded Ralph. "I'll have him cleaned up and…"

"I'll do it," Hawisa said.

"There are others to do that job…"

"I want to."

Sirs Ralph and Aubrey left, but George remained.

"You should go," she told him as she gathered all the needed things.

He shook his head. "You'll need help ... lifting him, getting him changed."

The two of them worked in silence. They washed Brother Simplicianus' body and clothed him in fresh vestments. Hawisa lit candles and placed them around the body and George left, returning with a dish of salt which he placed on the priest's shattered chest. These were measures to protect the soul of the departed and ward off evil spirits and, though not strictly part of Catholic doctrine, they were commonly observed. Then Jory drew two chairs up to the body and they settled down to keep vigil.

"You don't have to stay," she murmured.

"I'm not going anywhere."

And, as the girl wept quietly, the knight reached over and took hold of her hand.

27 Genver 1259

Brother Simplicianus was buried today. Brother Gabriel presided. Amidst the standard prayers of "I am the resurrection and the life," and "the Lord giveth and the Lord taketh away," he paused to reflect upon the burden of grief.

"I found, among Simplicianus' possessions, a book with this page marked," he said. He opened the volume and began to read. "'The divine dispensation uses everything around us for its own purposes,'[251] and I believe this applies even to our grief. When I was a child and fell and skinned my knees, I would run crying to my father and he would wrap his arms around me and kiss the top of my head. Well, God is our Father and as His children we can turn to Him in our sorrow and expect the same comforting embrace. Therefore God manages to take even our trials and use them for His own good ends: to bind us closer to Him in His love. Let us pray..."

After they laid Simplicianus to rest and those closest to him threw a few sprigs of rosemary into the grave (rosemary for remembrance), the mourners filed away. Brother Gabriel caught up with Hawisa.

"What is it, Father?" she asked.

"He was very fond of you," the priest said quietly. "I think he would have wanted you to have this." He held out the book he had read from at the service.

Hawisa took it. It was beautiful – a work of art, but even more intriguing was its contents. It was a Bestiary, a volume examining all of the creatures God made. She opened the book to a random page. On it was a drawing of a bird with tail-feathers spread out behind it like a great fan. She read: 'Solomon brought a peacock from distant lands, with varied colours in its feathers; it signifies the ... grace and the splendour of many virtues.'[252]

"Thank you, Father." And clutching the book to her chest, she walked slowly away.

2 Whevrer (February) 1259

It is a time of fire and light. The first of Whevrer is Imbolc, one of the four great Celtic fire festivals and today is Candlemas when new mothers come to the church carrying lighted candles. And I care about none of it. Another fire – one within – consumes all of my attention. I must have a great fever, for I lie here drenched in sweat. I feel sick and anxious beyond measure, but there is no more yellow powder to soothe the symptoms of my injuries. I begged Father to go and trade for more. If he does not return with some soon, I feel certain that I will die.

3 Whevrer 1259

I have just awakened from a peaceful night's sleep. Father managed to procure more of the miraculous yellow powder and it immediately made me feel well. Oh such incredible relief.

He told me last night that there has been another incident in the village. The blacksmith's shop has burned to the ground ... with the blacksmith still in it.

"It's terrible," Gwyn shook his head, "I keep thinking about that old drinking game: you know the one where you float a lighted candle on a tankard of ale and drink? The rhyme that goes with that ... I can't get it out of my head...."

As the drug began to take effect, I murmured:

> "Tom Toddy es come hoam, come hoam,
> Tom Toddy es come hoam.
> Weth es eyes burnt, and his naws burnt
> And es eye-lids burnt also."

15 Merth (March) 1259

For the second time since the "accident," I want to die. The last two days have been the most wretched of my life. And things are about to get worse.

It started yesterday morning. I can walk now, so when Gwyn checked in on me, I was on my feet.

"It's good to see you up," he said.

"Still hurts like a son-of-a-bitch," I mumbled. "I need more of that painkiller."

"There is no more," he said matter-of-factly.

I looked at him in alarm. "Well … get some. We can trade…"

"No."

"Why on earth not?"

"Caja," he said hesitantly, "you haven't been the same since you started taking it."

"I have had a broken back."

He shook his head, "No, it's not your back. It's your head. You're not … here anymore."

"What the hell does that mean?"

"It's like you're dead. Your body's here but your mind's gone someplace else."

"Don't be ridiculous. Of course I'm here. And might I remind you that the reason why I'm still here is because that drug pulled me through."

"I'm not so sure about that. Your injuries have healed, but you look worse today than you did the night of the accident."

"What's wrong with the way I look?"

"You don't brush your hair or change your clothes. You don't eat. Look at how thin you are! And look at your eyes." He held up a looking glass in front of me.

I was startled by the gaunt face I saw there. My eyes were red and tired – old woman's eyes. And there was something else: a vacancy to them. They looked like the windows of an empty cottage.

"The drug is making you ill," he said quietly.

"Father, please!"

He shook his head and walked away, but paused on the threshold and asked, "How are your adoptive children?"

"They're … they're fine."

"How do know? You haven't asked about them in weeks."

I cried like a baby for a while until the need overrode the tantrum and my mind began to calculate. Who would have some? Redigan might. I had taught generations of wise women their craft and Redigan, being the most recent in the line, owed me more favours than I could count. For the first time since the accident, I left Annwyn.

She looked at me wide-eyed. "Good God! I didn't even recognise you! You look terrible!"

"So everyone keeps telling me."

"What's happened?" She ushered me in the door. "I have been trying to contact you for months."

"Accident. Long story."

"What do you need?"

"Poppy's tears."

Redigan looked about her, searching for the jar. "I have a little..."

"I'll take all you've got."

She looked at me sharply. "How much of that stuff have you had?"

I forced a laugh. "Today or since November?"

"Maybe you shouldn't."

Instantly I went on the offensive. "Cut the bullshit, Redigan. I've suffered a terrible injury. That yellow powder controls the pain. You owe me a hundred favours – more! So what the fuck is the problem?"

The woman was taken aback, but nodded obediently and handed me the jar. Greedily I snatched the lid off and then stared at the contents in dismay. One dose, one day's worth – that was all she had. Well, I thought shakily, I'll just have to find more tomorrow.

I shoved the jar back into her hands. "Prepare it."

It was only after I'd drunk the decoction she'd made that I realised how rude I'd been. "I'm sorry," I said quietly.

"It's all right."

She wrapped me in a blanket and I was floating away to a place of warmth and safety, to a place where there was no pain or fear. I'd never felt better in my life.

I have a vague recollection of there being some commotion at Redigan's cottage, an anxious man jabbering about ... something. And then Redigan was gone. I took no real interest in this, and slid into a fitful sleep.

I awoke the next morning to find Redigan sitting beside me. Her face was ashen.

"We need to talk," she said quietly.

"Well, good morning to you too."

"You know Sir Aubrey?"

I looked at her blankly.

"One of Ralph Arundell's men," she prompted.

I shook my head to clear it. "Vaguely."

"He's dead. He was attacked last night."

I knew she expected me to feel something about this. I really didn't. "And?"

"And while I was trying to stop the bleeding, he told me what attacked him. It was a dragon."

"What?"

"You heard me."

"Well if you think it was one of mine, you're crazy. They'd never do that."

"I know of no other dragons that are here."

"That's ridiculous. Aubrey must have been delirious, hallucinating as he died!"

"That's irrelevant."

"Why do you say that?"

"Because," she looked at me gravely, "I'm not the only one who heard him speak."

My blood ran cold. Lanherne. Every knight at Lanherne would be hunting for dragons ... for my dragons. I was on my feet and out the door without another word.

I took shortcuts through Annwyn's tunnels and soon arrived at the chamber beneath Tintagel that Uther and I once shared. I was relieved to hear their voices – Kenwyn and Wynnie were next door in Merlin's Cave.

Thank God you're home.

I paused for a moment, letting the pain in my back subside – too much exertion, too soon. And that's when I heard it.

"I didn't like the taste, though," Kenwyn was saying. "Too lean and not enough meat on the bone."

"Just be glad you caught him when he wasn't wearing his armour. You'd be picking chainmail out of your teeth for weeks."

My legs gave way and I was left, tottering on all fours, waiting for the wave of nausea to pass. When it did I rose, gathered myself together, and walked calmly into the dragons' cave.

"So what have I missed?"

My children looked at me aghast.

Barenwyn stammered, "D-did you…"

"Hear? Of course I did!" I was shaking with fury. "You were discussing the knight you killed. Well, here's something that might amuse you: he talked."

"What?" Kenwyn asked.

"He talked and now every knight at Lanherne will be out looking for you."

The pair sat in stunned silence.

"How many more?" I asked.

"How many more what?" Kenwyn asked.

"People! HOW MANY MORE?"

Barenwyn shook her head, "None."

"Liar!" I saw other faces flash across her mind – a priest, a maiden, a drunkard.

"No, you are the liar," Kenwyn snarled.

"How dare you!"

"You told us that our mother died because she was old. But that's not true. She was killed by the villagers here!"

"Who told you that?"

Barenwyn cut in. "It doesn't matter."

But I saw the image flit through the young dragon's mind: the handsome face, the beautiful eyes, the strong jaw. "Belial?" I choked. "He's here?"

"He's been here a while," Kenwyn said quietly.

How? How did that bastard arrive on these shores without the Coranieid knowing? When I next spoke, my voice was shaking. "Don't listen to him. Ever. His words are full of poison."

"His words are full of truth," Barenwyn countered.

"You would trust him over your own mother?"

"You're not my mother!" Kenwyn's hackles were up and he was bearing his teeth.

I took a menacing step toward him. "Do not forget yourself, Kenwyn. Or more to the point do not forget who I am."

The dragon backed down. "Do you deny it then?" he asked.

There was no point sticking to my story now. "Now you know the truth, do you feel better?"

"No."

"Exactly. What good has the truth done you?"

"Bugs! Insects!" Barenwyn ranted. "That's what humans are to us – nothing more than a pestering swarm of ants. And they killed her! Did you think we wouldn't want revenge?"

"I knew you would," I said quietly, "which is precisely why I hid the truth from you."

"To protect your precious little pets," Kenwyn sneered.

"No, to protect you. You may laugh and call them insects, but make no mistake: human beings are the deadliest creatures this planet has ever seen. And if you stay here to fight, you will die." I continued on, my voice breaking. "I couldn't bear it. I watched your mother die and, damn it, I will not see you butchered. And for what? Will it make things right? Will it bring her back?" I paused and angrily rubbed the tears from my cheeks. "You have to go away. Go east…"

"No," Barenwyn's voice was low. "We don't have to listen to you. I'll say it again: you're not my mother."

"So you keep reminding me. But if she was here, she'd be ashamed."

I was stalking through the greenwood looking for Belial, but I paused and demanded of the birds, "Why?! Why didn't you tell me?"

Silence.

"Answer me, damn you!"

One tiny wren spoke up, 'We couldn't.'

"Why?"

'The demon … he said he'd set the greenwood alight!'

"Where's Belial now?"

More silence.

"I'm going to set the fucking woods alight right now if you don't tell me!"

Resigned, a magpie flapped down and landed at my feet. 'Come,' he said.

I followed and as I picked my way through the forest I couldn't get the old children's rhyme out of my head. It predicted the future based on the number of magpies you saw:

> One for sorrow
> Two for joy.
> Three for a girl, and
> Four for a boy.
> Five for silver,

> Six for gold,
> Seven for a secret that's never been told.
> Eight for Heaven,
> Nine for hell,
> Ten and you'll see the devil himself…

We came to an isolated cottage and my guide beat a hasty retreat. Peering in the window, I found Belial asleep, a naked woman lying dead on the floor near his bed. For the second time I looked into the demon's mind. It was still harrowing.

"Let's see what bubbles to the surface," I murmured as I picked through the charnel house of his memories. Then I found it.

In September Belial crept back into England, quietly, unnoticed. On the fourteenth, he waited until I was in Annwyn before introducing himself to the dragons. It was a fitting day to choose, because the fourteenth of September is called "the devil's nutting day." To go a-nutting is a euphemism for conquest, seduction, sex. And he was out to seduce the dragons, not into his bed, but into hell. My mind harkened back to Xiàngshù's friendship with the demon Andras and I realised that history was again repeating itself. A demon's sole purpose is to sow discord and destroy innocence, and now Belial had the perfect opportunity to do just that. He knew the whole story (had been here when Xiàngshù was killed) and had only to wait until her children were old enough, powerful enough to exact revenge.

He kept the contact light at first, casual; and then on the thirty-first of October he let the truth slip. He mentioned that he knew their mother – their real mother – and both dragons' ears pricked up at this.

"I always thought that was such a shame," he said.

"Well," said Barenwyn, "she was very old."

"Old?" Belial looked at them quizzically. "Who told you she was old? Xiàngshù was in her prime when she was killed."

"What do you mean, killed?" Kenwyn asked.

Belial held up his hands in placation. "I'm sorry. I shouldn't have said anything. It's none of my business."

There was a dragon on either side of him now, barring his path.

"Speak," Kenwyn commanded.

And he told them the whole terrible truth: about how Xiàng (as the

Hooper) sought to protect the local fishermen. He told them about Colum and Jowan, of Xiàngshù's attempts to atone for their deaths and of how she was betrayed by the ungrateful Senara. Then he described their mother's death in gruesome, heart-breaking detail.

When he'd finished, Barenwyn backed away from him. "No, I don't believe it; I can't believe that."

Belial looked upon her with such compassion in his eyes that it made my stomach churn. "There is proof," he said quietly.

After a long silence, Kenwyn asked, "Where?"

He led them to the outskirts of the village. They waited there, concealed in the bracken.

"I don't know where your mother's bones lie," he told them.

"Then why have you brought us here?" Kenwyn asked.

"To show you that."

A man emerged from a cottage, picked up his axe and started splitting firewood. I recognised him as Myghal.

Barenwyn muttered, "I don't understand…"

"Human beings are afraid," Belial explained. "They fear so many things: sickness, death, the devil, monsters, the list is endless. So they try to protect themselves with amulets and charms to ward off evil. Do you know what the charm is to ward off dragons?"

My two children shook their heads.

"To sew a dragon's scale onto your clothing. Like that one."

The dragons looked closer and saw that, stitched onto Myghal's cloak, was a shimmering white scale.

Barenwyn gasped, "Oh my God, Ken, that scale looks exactly like …"

"Mine," he said heavily.

Belial continued on quietly. "Your mother had beautiful white scales just like you, Kenwyn. And her murderers peeled them off her body and kept them as mementos and good luck charms. Xiàngshù's scales – parts of her body – have been passed down through the local families, each generation lapping up the wonderful story of how she was butchered."

Having planted the seed, he left them. However, seeds need room to grow, and there was one obstacle in the way – the Coranieid bitch. A shudder went through me. The second of November – the accident. Of course. He crept up on the stag and jumped out at it from the bushes. Animals are perceptive, they know a demon when confronted with one, and so the terrified deer took off in the opposite direction: through the thicket, onto the path and into me. And then, while I lay screaming in Annwyn, that bastard went to Merlin's cave to comfort the dragons.

"I came as soon as I heard," he gushed. "How is she?"

"They've taken her to Annwyn," Barenwyn wept. "It's bad."

That is how the demon achieved unfettered access to my children.

The knowledge of how their mother died ate away at Kenwyn and Barenwyn until, on the tenth of November, the demon persuaded them to seek a little vengeance. Initially the dragons were reluctant, but Belial – knowing that the road to hell is traversed in little steps – reassured them: "We're not going to hurt anyone, just give 'em a little scare."

And so they lay in wait along the coastal path until Myghal came along, staggering slightly, and singing drunkenly to himself. At that moment Kenwyn leapt at him from the trees. The startled man shrieked and turned to run back the way he'd come, only to be met by Barenwyn, snapping a vicious set of jaws in his face. He staggered off the path, lost his footing and fell down the ravine. The dragons looked at each other in alarm.

Belial emerged from the trees, laughing. "Oh come now, don't look so worried."

"But what if he's hurt?" Barenwyn asked, peering over the edge into the darkness.

"He's fine." The demon sighed, "Look, if it will make you feel better, I'll go down and see to him myself."

"Would you?" Kenwyn asked nervously.

"Of course. Wait here."

He picked his way carefully down the sharp incline. Indeed, the fall had only knocked the wind out of the peasant and left him stunned. With strong and practised hands, Belial reached down and snapped the man's neck. He looked at the corpse in distaste. He always thought it base and vulgar to have to do the job himself. It was far better to get others to do it for you. That way their souls were indelibly marked, and his immaculate apparel remained clean. He grunted in irritation at his cloak, the fur matted with mud from his descent down the slope. Even his houppelande[253] was filthy at the hem and the cuffs. Still, he consoled himself, this should give those imbecile dragons the needed push. Killing is always easier the second time around and so, if they believe they've killed once…

When he regained the path on the ridge, he was out of breath and his face was carefully arranged into a look of surprise and consternation. "He's dead."

"What?" Kenwyn barked.

"No…" Barenwyn backed away, shaking her head.

"He is," the demon calmly replied.

The dragons stared at him in stunned silence. Finally Wynnie asked, "What are we going to do?"

"Why must you do anything?"

"The villagers…" Barenwyn began, but Belial cut her off.

"The villagers will think it was an accident. Did you not smell the ale on his breath?"

"They might be fooled, but Mum will not."

"How will she know? She lies injured in Annwyn."

"Yes," said Kenwyn, his voice shaking, "but the animals and birds will tell Hanyfer when she comes to check on us," he nodded his head toward the line of trees on the other side of the path.

"Oh dear, that is a problem…"

Barenwyn had begun to cry and Belial struggled to keep his face from twisting into a sneer of disgust. Instead he patted her snout gently and looked on her with compassionate eyes. "How about this: I'll make sure that no one tells."

"How can you?" the female dragon's voice quivered.

"I'll make it worth their while. Don't worry, my young friends. I'll take care of everything."

And he had. He made it clear to the birds and the badgers and the foxes and every living thing in the greenwood exactly what would happen if they told.

"Winter is coming," he shrugged casually, "It is a cruel time. Just staying alive is a hard job."

He was met by stony silence.

"All I'm saying," he continued innocently, "is that you don't need trouble right now. I mean, how would you survive if the forest was destroyed?"

'What's that supposed to mean?' growled the alpha male of the wolf pack.

"They are dragons," Belial answered simply. "Fire-breathing dragons. And, goodness, there is an awful lot of wood around here."

'You wouldn't…'

"I couldn't. But they can. All I'm saying is this: if you stay out of their way, they'll stay out of yours. Do unto others and all that."

The deal struck, he returned to the dragons' cave to find them sitting by the fire, looking morose.

"Why such long faces?" he asked cheerfully. "You look more like sheep than dragons." And again he felt an inward twist of disgust at their flaccid response to the night's events.

"Have you spoken to the creatures? Will they tell?" Kenwyn asked anxiously.

"Yes, I have and no, they won't. You're safe, my friends."

They poured such gratitude upon him and Wynnie even gave him a jewel from her mother's hoard – a huge, dark green jade from her time spent in the East.

"Well, it's late and you best get some sleep," he pretended to yawn. "I will say that I was impressed with you tonight."

"Why?" asked Kenwyn.

"There is nothing more majestic than a dragon displaying his prowess." He smiled and shook his head. "All that raw strength – didn't you feel it, boy? Didn't you feel the power within you that you have yet to tap? I caught a glimpse of it tonight and I tell you this: if you'd leave these artificially timid ways behind and embrace your true nature, you would be magnificent. Think on it. To be strong; to be feared. To wield the power of life and death like a god. To have these pitiful, stumbling humans – these insects who dared to kill a dragon – bow before you… Does it not light a fire in your loins, boy?"

"I'm not a boy."

"Then do not act like one." And with that he left, whistling merrily.

Belial returned to Merlin's cave the following day with a large quantity of wine. "I thought you might need this."

The two dragons smiled at him gratefully.

"How'd you sleep last night?" he enquired as he poured some into the stone basin so that they might drink.

"Not well," Barenwyn mumbled.

"I thought you'd have trouble," the demon nodded sagely. "Conscience is a bitch."

Belial shrugged off his pack and started rifling through it. "I was thinking about it last night, and came to the conclusion that there is something you should see. It'll make you feel better." He extracted a roll of parchment and, when he had unrolled it and weighted down its corners with stones, the dragons saw that it was a map of the ancient world.

"What's this for?" Kenwyn asked, gazing over the demon's shoulder.

"To illustrate a point."

"Which is?"

"It's time someone told you about the history of your kind. Knowledge of your ancestors will give you knowledge of yourself." He cleared his throat and began. "Dragons have been here since the beginning. Here," with a long finger he traced an arc stretching from the eastern shore of the Mediterranean to the Persian Gulf. "Mesopotamia. They have a story dating back to two thousand B.C. called the Enuma Elisha which tells of the creation of the earth. In it the goddess Tiamat, a dragon of the waters, is said to have led the hordes of chaos. In the same area, they worshipped a storm-god, a dragon named Zu."

"Here," Belial said, pointing now at Egypt. "Another dragon, the god Apophis, god of the darkness." He ran his finger up to Greece. "Here the dragon Typhon spews molten lava out of Etna and Scylla haunts the waterways. She was the serpent who devoured Odysseus' men. How did it go? She took 'the six stoutest and best' right off the deck of his ship and 'they were wrenched aloft screeching ... in voices made thin and high by agony,'" he intoned, quoting Homer.

"So we're not just forces of chaos, we're killers. How flattering," Barenwyn's tone was dangerous.

"Just hear me out," Belial pressed on, pointing again at the map. "Italy, where the giant boa devours whole herds in a single night. France and we see the serpent Tarasque, the terror of the River Rhone. The Celtae here," he jabbed at the map emphatically, "feared Master Stoorworm who could swallow a ship full of men whole. Scandinavia and we have legends of Fafnir and the fire-drake that killed Beowulf. They also speak fearfully of Nidhogg, the dragon who gnaws at the very roots of Yggdrasil, the tree that supports the whole world. And here..." Having traced a rough circle clockwise around the map, his hand came to rest on India. "Here we have Apalala, the naga who turned against mankind after his good deeds were met with ingratitude – just like your mother."

There was tense silence in the cave. Barenwyn was the one to break it. "Mother was kind, unlike them," she nodded towards the map.

"Yes," Belial answered, "she was beautiful and compassionate and she helped people and they killed her for it." He let that statement hang in the air for a moment and then shrugged casually. "If they had found you, they would have murdered you too … just for being dragons." The demon took a swig of wine and continued. "You know in the Orient, they worship your kind as gods and yet here you sit, skulking in the shadows, hiding from these puny creatures that you could swipe aside with a flick of your tail. It's perverse. Why are you so afraid to be what you are?"

"Evil?" Kenwyn muttered.

"Powerful."

"Our mother…"

"Was killed … oh!" Belial paused when Kenwyn shook his head, "You mean your adoptive mother." He laughed. "Fine. Let's look at her. The Coranieid are a powerful and savage race and hence the perfect example for you. They used to hunt, not stag or boar, but people. They earned the nickname red-caps because they'd dye their hoods in their victims' blood."

"She doesn't do that!" Barenwyn shouted.

"Not anymore, perhaps. But given her past, she is hardly in any position to tell you to sit still and behave."

He was stirring up another cauldron of trouble, and had obtained all the right ingredients: the provocation of Xiàngshù's murder, historical precedent, their adoptive mother's hypocrisy, and now for the most important – fear.

"Whether you want to hear it or not, men despise you just for being born. They fear you and hate what they fear, and if they learn of your existence they will come with swords and spears and pitchforks and torches – just like they did for Xiàngshù. And for that reason man and dragon are forever locked in a battle to the death."

Belial was growing increasingly frustrated. It had been weeks since the peasant's death and while he was moulding their ideas, he had been unable to convince them to take that final step into wilful murder. And then he hit upon an idea. One night after a few drinks at the cave he said, "I want to show you something."

He led them to a cottage that overlooked the sea. Two people were inside, and while Belial and his companions couldn't make out exactly what they were saying, it was clear they were engaged in a quarrel. In another moment, a man stormed out and slammed the door behind him.

"Wait here," Belial said, and he nonchalantly approached the cottage and knocked on the door.

It was answered abruptly by a woman. She glared angrily at her visitor, her expression quickly changing to surprise when she realised that it was not her man back for more argument, but a stranger – the most handsome man she had ever seen.

He raised the lantern he was carrying. "I'm sorry to trouble you, lady." Belial's voice was melodious. "I was passing by and heard the row. Are you all right?"

"Oh yes." She waved a hand dismissively. "That was just Omfra – he's always so jealous."

"If I had a beautiful woman like you, I'd be jealous too."

She smiled at the compliment. "I haven't seen you before … in the village I mean."

"I've only just arrived. I always hate this part of travel: arriving alone and friendless in a new place."

"Well then, let me welcome you." She retreated into the little house to pour two cups of wine. "Come in," she said.

"Come out," said he.

She sauntered to the door, a cup in each hand. "Why do you want to be outside on such a cold night?"

"For this." He placed his hand lightly on her arm and guided her out into the night.

Belial heard it, that little intake of breath when he touched her and knew that she was responding to him, like every other stupid whore on this island. After all, his face and voice were beguiling. His clothes were the fine garments that came with wealth and breeding. And he looked upon her with such rapt attention, such naked pleasure in his eyes that she felt beautiful, and special. They all thought they were special.

He manoeuvred her to the edge of the treeline and stood beside her gazing up at a full moon in a cloudless sky.

"It's beautiful," she murmured.

"Worth stepping outside for on a cold night," he nodded. "Do you know what they call it in Italy?"

"What?"

"La luna del cacciatore."

She giggled. "What does that mean?"

"Hunter's moon."

In one swift movement, he dropped his wine and shot his hand out to grasp the girl by the throat. She choked and struggled in his vice-like grip, unable to cry out.

"Kenwyn, Barenwyn," he hung his lantern on a nearby branch and, with a hand now free, tugged off her shawl and held it to the light. "Look," he said.

A shimmering white dragon scale had been sewn to the fabric.

A low growl rumbled like thunder as two dragons emerged from the trees. The panicked woman clawed at Belial's hand, but could not break free.

And still they hesitated. What the fuck is wrong with these dragons? Belial thought, exasperated. "Remember when I told you that if men knew you existed they'd come for you with swords and torches? Well, she's seen you now!" the demon hissed, snatching up the lantern and holding it aloft to give her a good look. "You can't let her live."

A pathetic, mewling sound issued from the girl.

Belial addressed his next comment to Kenwyn. Young males always had more aggressive energy and hence he was the best candidate for violence. "Why are you so afraid of seizing the power that is rightfully yours? Don't you see: with one act, your eyes will be opened and you will be like God! Kenwyn," he thrust the woman forward. "I give you a direct descendant of Colum and Senara!"

Kenwyn struck. The barb at the end of his tail sliced the woman across her midriff. Morenwyn, daughter of a farmer and no relation of Colum's, groped vainly at her stomach. As her intestines slithered wetly out of her gut, Belial released her and she died where she fell.

For days and days afterward, Barenwyn sat at home by the fire and could not be persuaded to leave the cave.

Meanwhile, Kenwyn got on with the business of vengeance. It was the twenty-fifth of January and Brother Simplicianus locked the church of St. Columb and headed back to the cloister where all the monks of the brotherhood slept. It was a short walk along the dark path – a good thing because the wind was bitter cold and chilled the aged priest to his bones.

"The Lord called me from the womb, from the body of my mother he named my name…"

Brother Simplicianus stopped short. "Hello? Who's there?"

The disembodied voice continued, quoting from Isaiah 49. The priest had read that very passage today at mass, but now the words frightened him, causing him to quicken his pace.

"He made my mouth like a sharp sword, in the shadow of his hand he hid me … until now…"

Kenwyn burst from the shadows and leapt upon him. There was a sickening crack as his ribs snapped beneath the dragon's weight. Sharp shards of bone, now loose in his chest cavity, tore through muscle and tissue, lacerated the heart, punctured a lung. He was dead almost instantly but Kenwyn, remaining on top of him, gazed down at the man's wizened face. "People are such ugly creatures," he said.

Belial was waiting nearby. "Indeed they are."

The dragon hopped off his victim. "Squashed like a bug," he said and without another word they disappeared into the night.

And still Barenwyn would not leave the cave. Then one night (right around Candlemas) while Kenwyn was out, Belial arrived, pale and out of breath, at Merlin's cave.

"It's Kenwyn," he gasped.

Barenwyn was on her feet. "What happened?"

"He's been spotted." The demon looked absolutely stricken.

"What?!"

"You have to stop him before he alerts the whole village."

"Stop who?"

"The blacksmith."

Belial doubled over and clasped his side as if he had a stitch. Yet as Barenwyn scrambled out of the cave and took to the air, the demon straightened up, dropped his pretence of hurry and alarm, and smiled.

"It's just too easy," he muttered.

Barenwyn reached her destination in minutes, and was relieved to find the village quiet and the blacksmith still in his shop. For her brother, for Kenwyn, she used the flint stone I gave her to set the shop alight. The man inside fought his way out, but he took the fire with him on his clothes and in his hair, and he ran screaming as if he could escape the flames that seared through layer upon layer of his flesh. Finally he fell silent and fell to the ground and burned.

She was amazed at the minimal effort required to take a human life and how, once it had been accomplished, no lightning bolt descended from heaven to punish her for her sin. Nor, in fact, did retribution come from within. Her conscience did not roar and rage at her; no heavy yoke of guilt weighed on her shoulders; she felt nothing for the man she just killed. Indeed she realised in that moment how very much she hated them all.

Then later, on March 15th, while I lay passed out at Redigan's cottage, Sir Aubrey took his new horse out for a ride. Kenwyn ambushed him in the greenwood. The dragon's head darted forward with all the speed of a snake when it strikes, his teeth fastening on Sir Aubrey's right thigh. As the serpent's head recoiled his teeth shredded muscle and tissue, lacerating the leg from hip to knee, exposing the bone. Blood poured from the wound and Sir Aubrey, clinging desperately to his mount, fled to Lanherne where he would later die from shock and blood loss ... but not before telling Sir Ralph about his attacker.

If I'd had anything in my stomach, I would have thrown up. Instead I just stood there at the window, staring at Belial as he slept. I didn't just want to kill him, I wanted to grab my father's axe and keep striking at him until I made that bastard understand, until I had adequately communicated my pain to him, until he felt the way I felt as I stood there trembling. I was reaching for the door latch when my eyes fell again upon the dead woman on the floor. I realised I wasn't strong enough to take him on ... not then, when my craving for the yellow powder was becoming more and more insistent. And so I turned resolutely away. There was much to do.

Sir Ralph's men were already beating the bushes looking for a dragon, and so I ordered my children to stay in the cave. Next I had a few quiet words with Vixana before I found Nimue and begged her help.

"Are you sure about this?" she asked.

Looking around the sparsely-furnished room (the same room she imprisoned Myrddin in), I nodded. "Remember: food and water only. Nothing else. No medicine no matter what I say to you. Got it?"

"Yes."

"Seal it up."

Nimue's incantation was the same as before: "Cref yu gwrydhyow an spedhes – ow dywla colm!" Branches as strong as iron bars grew over the doorway.

And now I will sit here and wait. Once upon a time, I did not need the yellow powder. I will wait until once again I do not need it. And then I will settle accounts with Belial.

Already I grow anxious and it feels like my guts are tying themselves into painful knots. And so I have scrawled one word on a wall in my room – one word to focus on:

## ᚠᛖᛜᚷᛖᚨᛜᚲᛖ
## VENGEANCE

The word "addiction" has a long and varied history. In Rome it signified a legally-recognised debt or being compelled by court order to surrender money or chattels to another person. In 1599 Shakespeare used the word in the play *Henry V* to denote an "inclination." It was not until 1906 that the term was applied to opium use, and while drug rehabilitation was hotly debated among physicians, no codified detox programme existed until 1939 – precisely 680 years too late to help me. I never realised when I started taking that painkiller what would lay in store for me when I tried to stop.

First came the illness. The Coranieid never get sick, but I was suddenly suffering from flu-like symptoms as well as crippling nausea, vomiting and diarrhoea. And worse was yet to come. I soon realised that forsaking opium was the equivalent of volunteering to be a victim of torture. The rack could not have inflicted more pain on my muscles and joints. My skin burned as if I was strapped to an iron chair perched above a raging fire. And I got about as much sleep as someone with a heretic's fork strapped under his chin. Indeed by day five, I would have sold my soul for the yellow powder and I begged Nimue to get some. On my knees, clutching at the bars I told her I would die without it. She said no and I cried and raged long after she walked away. By day six I wanted to kill myself, but there was nothing in the sparse room that would do the job.

Then, slowly, the pain began to ease and the tremors lessened. I spent less time devising ways to procure the drug and stopped, finally, contemplating suicide. With my mind clearer, my eyes once again fell upon the word etched into the wall: VENGEANCE. I fixated on it, used it as a needed distraction and formulated my plan.

Weeks after locking myself in that room, I was ready to leave. I called to Nimue and Hanyfer. "You can let me out now."

"What for?" Hanyfer asked.

"A bath and then some food."

They looked at each other uncertainly.

"Would you like some yellow tea?" Nimue asked.

"Offer it to me and I'll break your arm."

That convinced her, and with a word she bade the roots and branches to withdraw. I was free. It took a long while to get clean and comb all the tangles out of my hair, but when done and smelling of mother's rose water, I felt and looked a lot better. Yes, there were still bags under my eyes and yes, I had grown painfully thin, but when I looked in the glass, I recognised the person I saw there, and this brought a faint smile to my lips (the first smile in weeks). I ate a good meal, curled up in my own bed and reviewed my plan again and again until I finally drifted off to sleep.

The next morning I consulted with Vixana.

"Here you go," she said, handing me a burlap bag. "That's everything you'll need."

"Thank you."

"Caja..."

"Yes?"

She stood there wringing her hands. "Maybe I should go with you? You're still weak and ..."

"I'll be fine. This is the strongest I've been in months."

"That's not saying much."

I turned to go.

She followed, clucking after me, "There are rowan twigs in the bag. Don't forget to weave them into a hoop, and once the spell's begun don't..."

"Venture outside of the circle, I know," I called back over my shoulder.

"Caja!" She grabbed my arm. "If you give him any chance, he'll kill you."

I hugged her and kissed her cheek. "I'll see you tonight at dinner."

"Wait."

"What?" I snapped, getting frustrated.

She took off her necklace, slipped its leather cord over my head and let the heavy, holed stone fall against my chest. "It's protection against evil spirits," she said and hurried away.

I left Annwyn and selected a place about twenty-five miles as the crow flies from Lanherne. There on the banks of a supposedly bottomless lake, I sat down, extracted the rowan twigs from the sack and started to weave them into a hoop that would hopefully keep Belial off me while the spell was being cast. It was soothing work, completing a simple task with my hands, while listening to the shrill cry of the curlew and the splash of ducks landing on the pond.

The hoop was no sooner completed when I was hit with another flush of hot, then cold that made me sweat and shiver by turns. I may have won my first battle with addiction but I had not yet won the war, and so I sat hugging myself and rocking while I waited for the feeling to pass. "I should have brought warmer clothing," I mumbled to the ducks as I shivered.

Clothing. I stared out at the water and suddenly had an image of my mother kneeling by the stream, scrubbing clothes as the Washer at the Ford. She had asked me to kill the dragons when they were in the shell and I had refused.

"Then there will be much for me to wash," she had said.

A rough tunic (that was Myghal), a peasant dress (Morenwyn), the monk's robe of Brother Simplicianus and the surcoat of a knight – Sir Aubrey. And that was when I remembered the dress – the beautiful, blue gown of the fifth and final victim. Who the hell is she? I had sifted through Belial's memories and there had been no reference to a lady in blue.

She must still be alive then!

I scrambled onto my knees and detached the bag of runes from my belt. "Who?" I asked and plunged my hand into the pouch to extract one stone. I stared at it in horror. The stone was marked with this symbol: |. It was the runic letter "isa." I set off at a run.

It was the first of May, and back at Lanherne the community prepared for the Mayday celebrations that would welcome spring with music, dancing and games. But it was still early and so Hawisa decided to tick one more chore off her list before the revelries began. Tomorrow in the village they would shear the sheep and boil the wool, skimming the oily "yolk" from the surface of the water when this was done. This grease would be combined with wood ash to make soap – soap that smelled of animal fat. C'est dégoûtant, she thought, wrinkling her nose. It was therefore necessary to sweeten it with flowers. And so on this bright morning, she took Constance with her to the edge of the ploughed fields, where cultivated land met the wildwood.

"What are we looking for again?" Constance trotted along beside her.

"Woodruff – we can use it not only in the soap, but to scent the linen as well."

The girl looked at her uncertainly, "Do we need to go deep into the woods?"

"Are you worried about the attack on Sir Aubrey?"

The girl nodded.

Hawisa crouched down so that she could look the child in the eye. "You know that book I showed you ... The Bestiary?"

Constance nodded. She liked looking at the pictures.

"It speaks with great authority on dragons. According to it, the creatures only come out at night."

"Really?"

"Really. It says that dragons are the embodiment of evil, and evil grows in the dark, and then it quotes the Book of Job." She searched her memory for the passage and then paraphrased it for the child. "They rebel against the light and stray from its paths. They watch for the dusk; deep darkness is their morning and they ally themselves with the terrors of the night.[254] That," she tickled the girl's sides, "is why we go now, in the morning when the dragons hide from daylight."

She took the girl by the hand and continued walking. "Besides, woodruff doesn't like a lot of shade. It grows at the very edge of the woodland ... and here it is." She stooped and picked a light green stalk with small white flowers.

Once she had been shown what to look for, Constance quickly gathered a basketful while Hawisa collected ransoms (wild garlic) that grew nearby. Their work completed, they turned to head back to the manor.

"Going so soon?"

Startled, Hawisa spun around, looking for the man who spoke. She squinted into the gloom of the woods, but could see no one. "Who's there?"

"Only me." And with these words the verdant shadows of the forest seemed to come alive. What she thought was a fallen tree, green with moss, twitched and rose until it towered above her. A great head with a mouthful of jagged teeth emerged into the sunlight and Hawisa realised that it was not green, but a shimmering white, like mother-of-pearl that caught and reflected the colours around it. The dragon had hidden camouflaged nearby while they worked.

"Oh no," she whispered.

"Out gathering woodruff," the dragon murmured casually, closing his eyes and enjoying the warmth of the sunlight on his face. "Nice day for it."

"We were just leaving." In one swift movement Hawisa tossed her basket into the dragon's face, grabbed Constance by the wrist and ran. But the dragon moved like lightning, and with a flap of its wings barred their path to the road. A quick flick and its sharp tail spike gouged the ground in front of Hawisa, bringing her to a clumsy halt.

"Leaving? I think not."

Hawisa quickly scanned the farmers' fields nearby, but they were uncharacteristically empty. Of course, the May Day celebrations. There was no one to raise the alarm or to come to their aid.

She felt a tug on her skirt and saw that Constance's little fingers gripped it in terror. All colour had drained from the child's face and she was visibly trembling. A flash of anger shot through Hawisa, along with adrenalin. My God, she thought, I brought her here. And I'm going to get her out.

"I have read about you," Hawisa said, trying to keep the nervous quaver out of her voice.

"Indeed?"

"Yes, in a Bestiary. It said that you are the most noble and intelligent of serpents." In fact, it did not say that at all, but Hawisa did not think that now was the time for insults.

"What else did this illustrious book say about me?"

"That you like to prove just how clever you are. You ... you enjoy an intellectual challenge. And that if a man should beat you, you would set him free."

"And do you think you could beat me?" he asked, clearly amused.

"Do I have any choice but to try?"

"Not if you want to live." The creature's mouth twisted into a ghastly smile, and every muscle in the lady's body contracted in a spasm of fear. She wrapped her arms around herself, her shoulders curved inward and down, as if every sinew in her was tightening up. She took a deep breath and tried to relax her shoulders. Don't panic, don't panic.

The creature was saying, "And what form, pray tell, would this intellectual challenge take?"

"How about a riddle contest?" she heard herself answer.

The dragon considered this for a moment and then shrugged, "What the hell ... could be fun."

"So if I win, the girl and I go free..."

"...and if I win, I eat you both," his head shot forward and he snapped his jaws in Isa's face. His breath was hot and foetid.

There was a muffled sob from Constance, and Hawisa squeezed her hand. "Shall I go first?"

Settling himself down comfortably to bask in the sun, he murmured, "Go on then."

Hawisa paused and took a deep breath to focus her mind. She had always liked riddles and knew quite a few, but which would stump the beast?

"I'm waiting..."

She reached a decision, "All right...

> "Mademoiselle Etticoat
> In a white petticoat,
> And a red nose;
> The longer she stands,
> The shorter she grows.
> What is she?"

The dragon's brows creased in concentration. "A white petticoat," he murmured, "and a red nose." He tapped his clawed fingers distractedly on the ground. "Growing shorter... Oh, I see it. She's a candle, I presume?"

Hawisa's heart fell, "Yes. Your turn."

As Constance drew a trembling breath, the dragon considered. "OK," he nodded, "try this one...

> "Thirty white coursers upon a red hill
> They tramp and they champ, and then they stand still.'"

Hawisa's mind went blank. Think, she urged herself, because if you don't solve this, you're dead. Normally applying her mind to problems gave her no difficulty, but with the stakes so high she faltered. She could not seem to take her eyes off the crooked teeth that lined the creature's jaws. The sight made her want to weep. Perhaps this thing could be moved to pity or bargained with somehow? But no, she saw no compassion in its eyes. And all she could focus on were those horrible teeth.

Then a glimmer of an idea occurred to her. Thirty white coursers – she had originally pictured war horses, but had she not that very morning told the cooks what four courses to serve at dinner? Coursers tramping and champing, Mon Dieu! Teeth! The answer had literally been staring her in the face.

Her answer given, she gave him another riddle…

"What makes bitter food sweet?"

"Too easy," the dragon snorted in contempt. "Hunger. How deep is the ocean?"

Hawisa smiled; she had heard that one before. "A stone's throw. Try this…

> "I play on the ocean and dance on the sea –
> Neither boats, nor birds can ever catch me."

The dragon seemed to have more trouble with this one and pondered for a while. Finally, a grimace of uncertainty twisting his fanged mouth, he asked, "Sunlight?"

"Yes."

Sighing in relief, he fixed her with a determined look.

> "As I was going to St. Ives,
> I met a man with seven wives.
> Every wife had seven sacks,
> And every sack had seven cats,
> And every cat had seven kits.
> Kits, cats, sacks wives –
> How many were going to St. Ives?"

Hawisa's confidence was growing. She routinely handled the castle's accounts and was good at maths. Right, there are 7 cats each with 7 kits. That is 49 kittens per sack, plus the 7 cats themselves is 56. Each wife had seven sacks, so 7 times 56 is …392. But there are also 7 wives, so that is 7 times 392 or (she struggled momentarily and then double checked the answer) 2,744. But don't forget to add the 7 wives which is 2,751. And also the man with all these wives which makes the answer 2,752. Hawisa paused and noticed that the dragon was watching her with satisfaction while she calculated the answer. Why are you looking so smug? she wondered. And then it occurred to her. She had been tricked. The man and his entourage of wives and felines were not going to St. Ives, "I" was. "The answer is one."

The dragon looked annoyed. "Your turn."

But Hawisa could not think of any more riddles, and her courage faltered. If only Jory were here now, she would not be afraid. An image of him, smiling and strong, riding through the gate at Lanherne after the melée last August danced before her eyes. And it gave her her next riddle.

"They say when Homer travelled the Greek Isles as an old man, he met some boys on their way home after a day of fishing. He asked what they caught and they, who had no fish to show for their efforts replied, 'What we caught we threw away, and what we didn't catch we keep.' To what were they referring?"

The dragon looked at her blankly, "But that's nonsense."

"Not when you know the answer."

The dragon contemplated the riddle for a while. Then, becoming vexed, got up and paced back and forth trying to puzzle it out.

Hawisa waited patiently, not wanting to antagonise the beast by rushing it. Looking again at Constance, she noticed that the child was no longer trembling and the look on her face was one of hope. Hawisa felt it too: they might win!

The dragon petulantly kicked a large fallen branch aside and snarled, "All right, I give up. What is it?"

Hawisa smiled, "Fleas." There was a moment of breathless silence. Then Hawisa screwed up her courage and spoke once more. "So, according to our deal, we can go." With her hand on Constance's arm, she started slowly backing away in the direction of the castle.

"Of course," the dragon bowed his head courteously. He let her retreat a few more steps. "Oh, will you take a message back to Ralph for me?"

"What is it?"

"Simply this…" and with that, he struck.

Hawisa had just enough time to shove Constance out of the way before the dragon's fangs sank into her flesh instead. Shock and pain robbed her of her voice.

Dropping to her knees, she managed to choke out the words, "Constance, run!"

The child did not need telling twice, but was off with all the quick agility of young legs. A glance back as she raced across the field told her that the dragon was not in pursuit. She was running now, not for her life, but to save her beloved Hawisa. The girl quickened her pace.

Reaching the church of St. Columb, Constance was met by Sir Ralph, Sir George and a host of others, noblemen and peasant, all armed. Indeed a villager had spotted the dragon and raised the alarm.

"By the oak at the edge of the field! Vite!" she cried and scampered out of the way as the group surged forward.

Back at the oak, Hawisa was on her knees gasping, "You said I could go."

"And so you can," the creature laughed. "Now toddle off home… Oh, and I'd hurry if I were you. That venom works fast."

Hawisa struggled to her feet and set off at a staggering run. Her left arm around the bite was in throbbing agony and had begun to swell. She cradled it to her as she ran. There was a chance that this might be mended, but she needed Redigan and she needed her quickly. In another moment, she spotted the advancing crowd, her father and Jory at the front, racing toward her. Out of breath and feeling sick, she stumbled and fell. Sir Ralph was off his horse, gathering her up in his arms.

"J'ai besoin de Redigan," she gasped.

"You'll be all right," Ralph murmured, handing her up to Jory seated on his horse. "Get her back to the manor. Now."

"What are you going to do?" the young knight asked.

"I'm going to kill that fucking dragon."

Jory, with Hawisa in his arms, hurried toward Lanherne. He spurred his courser on faster and faster to a pace that could very well have killed the horse, but it did not matter. Nothing mattered except getting Isa some help.

Back at the manor he slid out of the saddle, clutching her tightly to him, but she squirmed and asked to be put down. He obeyed and, collapsing on all fours, the girl was violently sick.

The scene before Hawisa's eyes seemed to blur and swim, as if nothing was solid anymore. She was dimly aware of being picked up again, and this made her stomach lurch. As she was carried to her chamber, she tried to focus her mind on something else. But what? And then it occurred to her what she should do. A perfect act of contrition, a confession of sins and a showing of remorse for her shortcomings, all this was open to her even now as things began to feel hopeless. Yes, if she died today she could still do so in a state of grace. She tried to make her prayer silently, but her mind was becoming addled and kept drifting off. So she spoke the words aloud: "O my God, I am heartily sorry for having offended Thee. I detest all my sins, because I dread the loss of heaven and ... and..."

She lost first the thread of her prayer and then she lost consciousness. When she came to, she was lying on her own bed.

Back at the edge of the greenwood, Kenwyn was presented with the age-old choice: fight or flee. He was so confident in his prowess as a mighty dragon that initially he stood his ground. But he underestimated Sir Ralph. The dragon opened his maw to spray a plume of fire into the faces of his enemy, and everyone dove aside – everyone except Ralph Arundell. The knight pitched forward in one suicidal charge that rammed his lance down the dragon's throat. Kenwyn fell backward, his talons clawing at the spear to dislodge it. Bleeding profusely, he took to the air.

As I neared Lanherne, I heard the beat of Kenwyn's wings and called to him. We met in a secluded glade. Coming in for a landing, his knees buckled and he landed on his side. I ran to my son. He was bleeding heavily from the mouth; Sir Ralph's lance still protruded from his soft palette.

"Mum..." He was choking on his own blood.

"I'm here."

"I'm scared ... don't leave..."

"I'm not going anywhere."

Eva lent over her daughter, smiling, telling Isa that all would be well and that Redigan was on the way. But where is Jory? the girl wondered, and raised her head to look for him. She needed to see him with a desperation that sent another violent wave of nausea through her.

Having thrown up again, she felt mildly better and her vision seemed to clear. There he is, she thought with relief. George stood behind Eva, looking impossibly pale and pacing the room like a trapped animal, not able to help, not able to leave, and not knowing what to do with himself.

A maidservant tore open the bulging sleeve of Hawisa's blue dress, and she shrieked. Around the bite her skin was black and purple and grotesquely swollen. A tourniquet was applied to her arm above the wound, and she shrieked again. A second was applied four inches above the first, and a third was tightened above that.

Redigan was there now, telling her not to worry, that she would be all right. She had a knife in her hand, "I'm sorry, child, this will hurt." Swiftly the old woman cut a quarter inch deep incision across the two puncture marks and squeezed and rubbed the arm to get the blood flowing freely.

The pain was like nothing Hawisa had ever imagined, and her limbs jerked to free themselves from the hands that held her down. She opened her mouth to scream again, but only managed a hoarse whisper. She tried to speak, to beg them to stop, but it was as if her voice had been stolen from her. As the venom continued to paralyse her throat and larynx, it became not only difficult to talk, but hard to breathe – each inhalation was now a weak and shrill gasp. The last audible thing she managed to whisper was, "Can't see."

The blindness had snuck up on her. At first she thought it was just the lights in her room that were dim after the bright sunshine outside. But it kept getting darker and darker, until she was immersed in blackness.

Meanwhile Redigan was trying every herbal remedy she knew for poison. She tipped a cup to the girl's lips. But the tincture of ransoms, juniper and nettle, only caused the girl to choke and splutter. She was now incapable of swallowing.

The bedclothes were drenched with sweat, and she instructed the maidservants to remove the girl's outer corset, bliaut, and tunic, stripping her down to a long undershirt of yellow linen. With her hair unpinned and her thin legs left uncovered by the shapeless undershirt, she looked very young indeed. Jory was reminded of the child he met when he arrived here twelve years ago, and he clenched his teeth against the cry of anguish that burned his throat and pricked at his eyes.

Next Redigan rubbed a strong mustard poultice onto the girl's stomach and chest. She had mixed agrimony, alexanders, balm, borage, southernwood and mugwort into it for extra potency, but Hawisa lapsed into unconsciousness.

"Loosen the tourniquet," Redigan was saying.

Jory, who had first held Isa down so they could treat her and then gently stroked her hair when she had passed out, now jerked into violent action.

"No you will not!"

Redigan tried to explain, "We have to…"

"The poison!" he shouted, "you'll let more of the poison into her system!" Jory, red-faced and shaking, looked as if he might strike the old woman.

Eva placed a hand on his chest. "Just listen to her for a minute." She took a deep breath. "Why is that necessary?" she asked Redigan.

"The arm will die if I don't. One minute without the tourniquet will save it, and then I'll put it right back on. But if we don't do this," the wise woman looked at George, "you might as well cut her arm off right now."

"And the poison?"

"We've bled most of that out. The wound needs a hot iron now, then I'll bandage it up."

Redigan's instructions were followed. The tourniquet was loosened to re-establish blood flow to the limb, and then tightened again for another half an hour. An iron was placed in the fire, and as the wound was cauterised George flinched, expecting again to hear Hawisa scream. But even the pain of branding did not rouse her. He had calmed down for a moment, but now he felt panic rising in him once more. She should have felt that. She should have cried out – a strong, healthy bellow. But Isa lay still, as if dead.

He knelt beside her, hands clasped on her good arm, his head resting on the bed. Occasionally, he would caress her arm with his cheek and kiss her hand. But she did not stir.

Redigan watched the girl for some sign that she might rally, and the women of the castle sat quietly waiting.

The figure on the bed stirred.

Jory's heart leapt. Oh thank you! Thank you! She is young and strong and she will beat this.

But he soon realised that it was not the gentle stirrings of awakening consciousness that moved Hawisa's limbs. It was the increasingly violent twitch of convulsion.

"Hold her!" Redigan sprang to her feet and shoved a leather strap into Hawisa's mouth so that she would not bite her tongue. George pinned her shoulders to the bed, while the women held her feet.

When the fit subsided, Redigan bent over her patient and looked at her intently. The girl's breathing had slowed and become even more laboured. Her face, normally with a healthy blush to her cheeks, now wore a grey pallor. The wise woman knew only too well what she was seeing, and had to grip the bedclothes to steady herself. Silently she went to her satchel and rummaged through it.

Redigan returned with a small candle. She collected these. Every Candlemas the local priest would allow her to take the stubs of the blessed candles they had burnt for the service. These were thought to be powerfully good. They could banish the devil, protect against disease and, if placed in the hands of a dying person, safeguard their soul. She shoved the stub into Hawisa's hand. "You'd better go and fetch a priest," she murmured.

George gaped at her in horror.

"Go!"

And with that he was on his feet and moving. As fast as his legs could carry him, he fetched Father Gabriel. The shocked and bewildered man had just enough time to grab the essentials before he was half-marched, half-dragged to Hawisa's room.

Father Gabriel, short of breath from running, entered the room and stared in disbelief at Hawisa. He'd seen death a thousand times, but this was different. This was brutal murder. And while he believed that the body that lay before him was inconsequential compared to her soul, the girl's face was etched with lines of such terrible suffering that it moved him to tears. He swallowed hard and tried to focus on his duty.

It was clear that he could not administer the viaticum (or last communion) and likewise, she would be unable to confess her sins. So he sprinkled the room and the girl with Holy Water, leant over her and, with the oleum infirmorum on his thumb, anointed her forehead. He spoke gently. "Through this holy anointing may the Lord in His love and mercy help you with the grace of the Holy Spirit." He anointed the palms of her hands, grimacing at how swollen and purple her left one was and, steadying his voice, continued. "May the Lord who frees you from your sins, save you and raise you up." Thus absolved of sin and with God at her side, no more could be done but loosen the tourniquets every half hour and pray.

I sat in the greenwood, cradling my son's head in my lap.

"Is she really there, waiting?" he murmured.

"Who?"

"My mother."

"Yes."

He tried to be brave, to laugh. "And do they have rabbits there to eat?"

"Yes, they have rabbits."

In the emotionally tortured atmosphere of her room, Hawisa now felt no pain and no fear. In fact, she was dreaming. She was walking barefoot through tall grass and out of the corner of her eye, she glimpsed someone walking beside her – someone that she could not fully lay eyes upon, but who was there, for her. She was not alone. And all was green grass and blue sky and yellow sunlight and a basket of sweet-smelling woodruff hung from her left arm.

As she breathed her last, George's eyes fell upon the table beside her bed. Hawisa's Bible lay open upon it, as if she would return to it to continue her reading. Opened to Matthew 5, the Beatitudes, it said: "Blessed are the pure in heart, for they shall see God."

The sharp ears of the Coranieid pricked up and listened. They heard Eva sobbing in Hawisa's room. They heard Sir George as he grabbed Isa by the shoulders and shook her, begging her to wake up. And they heard a cry of anguish issue from the greenwood. They recognised the voice as mine, and every Coranieid woman who had ever adopted and lost a mortal child bowed her head in sympathy.

I don't know how long I lay there, but it was Barenwyn who brought me back to my senses. She came to me sobbing. I raised my arms to embrace her but, remembering the danger, pushed her away instead.

"Are you crazy? Get back to the cave before you're seen!"

"But Mum…"

"Go!" I shrieked.

I listened as she fled back to our home. She was repeatedly and violently sick along the way.

In my experience there comes a point when, under terrible duress, something in the mind gives. The thinking or reasoning part of the brain, overwhelmed by the influx of pain and fear and rage, seems to temporarily sever its ties to the parts that generate emotion. And suddenly, inexplicably, I go numb.

And so I rose and slowly, deliberately brushed the grass from my dress and walked steadily back to the bottomless lake and the burlap sack. Along the way

I pondered my new state of mind. As Vortigern so eloquently proved, if you take emotion out of a brain, you banish morality as well.

"Good," I murmured. I did not want pity or compassion to lessen what I was about to inflict.

I remembered Gwyn ap Nudd's first Wild Hunt – the two lovers we killed in the woods and how he bade us dye our hoods in their blood; for the first time the recollection made me smile. I am my father's daughter. What is in him is in me.

I had arrived at Dozmary Pool. I sat inside the circle of rowan branches at the very edge of the water, and arranged the contents of the bag around me. First I picked up the doll, otherwise known as a corp criadhach or body of clay, and with my knife etched the name on its chest: Belial.

Vixana had asked mice to sneak into the demon's cottage and steal a bit of hair from his comb. This I tacked upon the poppet's head. "I have made you," I murmured. "You are Belial."

Without the benefit of Solomon's ring to summon the demon, Vixana had suggested a spell. I tied the end of a long piece of black thread around the doll's neck, and proceeded to loop the rest of the string around the poppet and my left hand until we were joined.

"My gelwel ty. Belial, I call you." Repeating these words, I fell into a rhythm that was oddly familiar. And then I remembered: it was the drum beat of tribal ceremony, and I saw once again Myrddin stepping to the beat of the drum while the tribe swayed around him. In that moment, as I chanted, I felt the power of the old ways and my incantation intensified, building to a climax that ended abruptly with the appearance of the demon.

His face was like thunder, and that made me glad.

"Dus omma, dyawl (Come here, devil)," I said and slipped my bound hand out of the loops of string. I pulled the black thread tight around the poppet and tied it off in a series of knots.

"By knot of one, the spell's begun. By knot of two, I now hold you. By knot of three, I punish thee."

Unable to walk away, Belial flew into a rage. He threatened and cursed, and soon hit upon the idea that the only way to save himself was to kill me and to do it quickly. But he could not enter the circle. Failing in his human form, he tried again and again – as a raging bull, a tusked boar, a fanged adder. Exhausted and afraid, he finally collapsed onto his knees.

I smiled at him serenely and showed him a clay bottle.

"You can imprison me, but I'll get out – sooner or later – and I'll come for you," he hissed.

"I know." My voice was happy and light. "That's why I'm not going to make the same mistake Solomon did. You see," I began to mix myrrh with sea salt, oak moss and black powdered iron, "the bottle isn't for you. It's for the spell. And when it's cast, I will hide this bottle where no man nor demon could ever find it. No one will ever release you, not by mistake nor intent. You're done, bastard." I poured the mixture into the vessel.

Next I scribbled a few words on a small piece of parchment.

Growing desperate, the demon began to bargain. "You don't have to do this. I can give you anything…"

"Anything?" I looked up from my work.

"Name it."

"All right, lastedhes" (our word for filth, scum, vermin). "I want my children's innocence back. I want Hawisa to live and marry George. I want my son back from the dead. Can you do that, lastedhes?"

A tear rolled down Belial's dusty cheek. "No."

I shrugged, "Then I guess you're out of luck." I took up my knife and drove it into the poppet's chest. Belial screeched in pain.

Rolling up the paper, I tied the scroll with black thread and said "My fasta an colmennow. I fasten the knots. Ow dywla colm … my hands bind thee … to solitude … to torment … to slavery."

I dropped the scroll into the bottle and, as Belial wept, placed the stopper on the jar and sealed it with wax.

Belial's voice shook when he spoke. "What did it say?"

"It details the task you will perform again and again forever and ever. But first, I bind you here, unseen, knowing neither comfort nor rest." I worked as I talked, placing the doll in a bowl carved from oak. I set the wood alight.

Belial screamed and writhed and I set the bowl on the lake and gave it a little push. The water, of course, put out the fire – but not before the waxen poppet had melted. As the bowl sank, the molten wax dispersed in the pool. The demon was bound.

Belial stood knee-deep in its waters. "What's the task?" he asked hollowly.

"Empty the lake … with this." I tossed him a tiny limpet shell with a hole in it.

Unable to resist, Belial knelt and scooped up a shellful of water, plugging the hole with his finger. He walked a few steps onto dry land and emptied the few drops of moisture onto the ground.

I threw all of my paraphernalia back into the bag and broke the rowan hoop with my boot. Belial's head snapped back in my direction. He was desperate to make a grab for me, but his limbs would not comply. Instead his legs carried him back to the pool and to his task.

As he bent to fill his little shell again, I patted him on the head. "There," I said warmly, "that should keep you occupied. After all, we don't want the devil making work for idle hands."

CHAPTER 10

# "THE ROAD FORWARD"

"The bright road seems dark,
The road forward seems to retreat,
The level road seems rough."

*Lao Tzu, Tao Te Ching*[255]

George stood in Hawisa's bedchamber, alone. The room bore no signs of what had transpired there. The soiled sheets, the bloody bandages, the basin filled with emesis, and finally the body had been removed. The signs of death were wholly absent, but not the signs of life. Her clothing, her comb, her Bible were neatly stowed in their places, as if she would soon return to use them.

Briefly George wondered if he could sit in her room, and indulge in the fantasy that at any minute she could walk through the door. But it was impossible. His grief for her made him shake with exhaustion and a vague, half-formed fear of what life will be without her. It made his head throb and his stomach churn.

"George?"

Jory jumped and swore. "Oh! Lady Eva! Forgive me! I..."

"You were lost in thought and I startled you. I'm sorry," she said quietly.

Eva, due to ill health, had always been pale, but now in her black mourning clothes, her skin was the colour of bleached bone and she was skeletally thin. Sir Ralph, Jory thought, may soon have another loss to mourn.

"Ralph tells me that you're going to the Holy Land," she said.

"Yes."

"I can understand that. Every time I walk into a room here at Lanherne I expect to see her at her embroidery or bent over the accounts … or mooning over you." Her laugh was low and mirthless, and reminded George of fallen leaves set tumbling by the wind. "Yes, I can understand your desire to leave."

They stood in silence for a moment, and their gazes were drawn to the bed. It was an inanimate piece of furniture, but it was the most potent object either had ever encountered, for it was impossible to look upon it and not see Hawisa writhing there. Eva shook herself to banish the image.

"Anyway," she cleared her throat, "I wanted to give you this." She offered him a leather-bound volume, the Bestiary that Isa had inherited from Simplicianus.

"I couldn't possibly take this. It's too valuable…"

But the lady pressed it into his hands. "To remember her by." And she was gone.

I found Barenwyn in Merlin's Cave, curled up in her bed, looking pitiful. Silently I pulled up a chair and sat facing her.

"I got sick," she said.

"I know."

"I managed to lose my flint stone."

When I did not respond, she asked in a small, timid voice, "Will you get me another?"

"No."

"Why not?"

"Have you forgotten the blacksmith?"

Her eyes welled up with tears. "Mum…"

I laughed bitterly. "So now you acknowledge that I'm your mother. Lovely. That means … what? You're going to listen to me now?"

She nodded.

"Good, because I'm telling you to leave."

"What?"

"You haven't left yourself any other option. You've whipped the people here up into a frenzy. They'd kill you on sight."

My girl began to weep and her tears infuriated me, but I was too tired to rant and wanted the yellow powder more than ever.

"I hate them" – her words startled me from a daydream of amber-coloured tea.

"Pardon?"

"People… I hate them for all they've done to my family."

"Well, you're just going to have to get over it."

She gaped at me.

"I'm serious." I leaned forward in my chair. "Do you think you're the only soul ever wronged? Look at the Coranieid: the Celtae took everything from my people. We were gods and they stripped us of our power, decimated our numbers, drove us off the land and forced us to live in the shadows. And yet I do not make war on the descendants of the Sequani."

"Why not?"

"Sustaining that hatred takes too much energy, and it gives you nothing in return."

"It gives vengeance."

I snorted. "I took vengeance on Belial for everything he's done here, and I don't feel any better. Do I look happy?"

"No."

"Wynnie, like me you are going to live a long time. Do you really want to waste all those years feeling like this?"

She did not answer, but for the first time I saw doubt creep into her eyes.

"You know," I continued, "when I finally let go of the grudge, I found I had room in my life for other things. I fell in love with Uther. I found a kindred spirit in Hawisa and counted the great, the noble Xiàngshù as my best friend. And, despite the fact that I'm barren, I became a mother." I touched her face. "And as your mother I'm telling you: it is time to go east."

"But I don't know the way," she whispered.

"Yes, you do. You know it just as the birds know to fly south in the winter. Seek the Dragons' Gate, but Wynnie, keep to the remote trails that are shunned by men. To stay hidden is to stay alive."

According to Xiàngshù, the Dragons' Gate Caves (or Lóngmen Róndòng) lie on Dragons' Gate Mountain in Shanxi Province, China. It is a trek of 5,260 miles as the crow flies, but Barenwyn, in her need for concealment, would take a more circuitous route that would add many miles to her trip. She left at night. The first leg of her journey was a three hundred and twenty-five mile flight north and east. In the small hours of the morning she touched down in Sneaton forest, North Yorkshire. There she could quench her thirst at the Falling Foss, a waterfall hid deep in the wood. She then pressed on to the coast.

An hour before sunrise she arrived at a deserted stretch of rugged shoreline. Later it would be known as "Robin Hood's Bay," not after the Robin Hood who robbed from the rich to give to the poor, but after Robin, Bucca's father who led forty-five Coranieid to settle there so long ago. Their village, we knew, had been hit by pirates – a fierce band out of Norway who slaughtered the forty-five and then, fearing pirates themselves, settled further inland at Raw. It was this old Coranieid outpost that Barenwyn now sought, in particular a certain cave where she could hide when the sun came up.

### A Side Note

*Webster's World Dictionary suggests that Robin Hood was in fact a member of a fairy race. This view is based on a series of parallels drawn between Robin's merry men and the fairyfolk. They both lived in the woods and wore green as a form of camouflage. Both groups were excellent archers and even the "hood" of Robin's name may refer to the pixie caps that fairies wear.*[256] *The tourist website for Robin Hood's Bay concurs with this theory. It claims that there "is not a scrap of evidence to suggest that Robin Hood of Sherwood Forest folklore visited the Bay. The name is more likely to have grown from legends with local origins... Robin Hood was the name of an ancient forest spirit ... and the use of the name for such an elf or spirit was widespread in the country. Many natural features were named after these local folk of legend."*[257]

*One such feature was a cave carved out of the rock by centuries of rough water and high tides. It was known as the Boggle Hole. Boggles were said to be of the wee folk who stole food from the locals and caused great mischief on their farms. Every time someone went missing in the woods, it was believed that a boggle had got him. It was also said that boggles crawl "into people's beds at night ... (to place) a clammy hand on their faces" and bring them nightmares.*[258] *Known also as a boggart and the bogeyman, the boggle is known far and wide – as the Boggelman in Germany, Bocan in Ireland, Puca to the Saxons and Bucca to us.*

It was very different from Merlin's Cave. There was no warm fire to fill the cavern with yellow light. There was no soft hay in the corner on which she might sleep. There was no larder stocked with game and milk and wine. And there was no woman there to listen to her worries, to touch her face, to love her no matter what. Barenwyn passed a cold and lonely day, among the cave paintings and bits of broken pottery left by the dead forty-five.

At sunset the dragon once again took to the air, first to dive for fish and eels and then to begin a five hundred mile trek across the North Sea. As a thick fog rolled in with the night, Barenwyn was surprised to discover that she did indeed know the route by instinct. She did not need to navigate by the stars, only to heed the certainty in her own blood that this was the way. And so she finally came to rest on Mount Solfonn, in Norway, an inland peak away from and high above the men in their villages that lay clustered along the Norwegian coast.

Barenwyn had never seen a mountain before, and was surprised to find snow on Solfonn's peak even though it was May. She did not like it. All was white snow and grey rock and barrenness. Down below in the valley lay a forest of deciduous trees, very like the greenwood of home. She longed to be there amidst the bronze bark of hazel trees and the light grey branches of ash, hid by the serrated ovals of elm leaves to rest and lean upon the sturdy girth of an ancient oak. But she dared not venture down into the springtime forest, for fear of happening upon the dwellings of men, or meeting a hunter with a bow or a woodsman with an axe.

And so she kept to the heights, following the Kjolen Mountain range north and east. From Galdhøpiggen to Shøhetta to Borge she flew from peak to peak, finally coming to rest on the aptly named Frostisen, a glacier of dirty ice in Nordland. Barenwyn stood at the glacier's edge and looked out over Skjomen fjord. Evergreen forests ran along the mountainside down to the water's glassy surface that mirrored back the hills, the tree-lined slope, the vault of clear blue sky. Words like "beautiful" and "majestic" sprang into her mind to describe the view, but at that moment words paled in comparison to feelings.

The scene before her made her feel calm and quiet. After the months of building rage, after indulging her instinct for violence, after the grief and horror of losing Kenwyn and the sickening isolation of her exile, finally, finally she felt calm. God – the God her mother had often spoken of – seemed to be showing her a bit of mercy. He seemed to be saying that in a world of swords and axes, where they carved up a dragon and sewed her beautiful scales into their clothing, there was also this: sunlight on water, blue skies and green forests. There was beauty, and a moment's respite. In short, there was mercy. She stood for a long time looking at that scene, until the sunset told her it was time to be on her way.

The night, however, was short and she did not get far. In fact the days lengthened until the sun did not set at all. She had entered the Land Med Midnattssol, the Land of the Midnight Sun, where from mid-May to the end of July the sun never set. This posed a severe problem for the dragon, who could no longer conceal her movements under the cover of night. The mountain peaks, once a sanctuary and a guide, now left her feeling exposed, conspicuous, and she fled to the valleys and the evergreens. Obliged now to walk rather than fly, to advance with caution instead of speed, her progress grew painfully slow, and all the time the sun shone.

It is hard to sleep when there is no night. Barenwyn expected her insomnia to sap her strength. Oddly, it did not. On the contrary, she felt energised.

### A Side Note

*A difficulty experienced especially by newcomers to the northernmost climes is hypomania, a condition brought on by day after day of unfailing sunlight. Sleep deprivation combined with excessive daylight can trigger feelings of euphoria, boundless energy, and overconfidence. These feelings often result in unnecessarily risky behaviour.*

Barenwyn was flying in broad daylight, and in full view of the villages that dotted Russia's taiga, a green belt of pine, larch and spruce that lay south of the more sparsely populated – and hence safer – tundra. She had been flying for days, stopping only to drink from a stream or to feed on deer and elk, an exercise that seemed almost redundant for she was fuelled by the everlasting sun. She travelled east from Norway to the Yenisei River in Siberia, where she turned and headed due south to the Kunlun Mountain Range. She hoped to follow it almost to the edge of Shanxi Province in China. It was in Shanxi that she would find the Dragons' Gate.

Kunlun means "the mountains of blinding darkness," but there on the long plateau running along the southern face of the range, was the glint of sunlight on water. A lake. Barenwyn, her throat parched after an epic flight, descended to drink. She landed roughly, and struggled through marshland to the water's edge where she drank deep. Her stomach, however, rejected the fluid and she was sick almost immediately. Salt water. Confused, Barenwyn looked up from the brackish lake and studied her surroundings for the first time. Aside from the reeds and mossy grass at the water's edge, there was little vegetation: only brown scrub plants and no trees. Unlike the rich, dark earth of home, the ground here was the beige colour of sand. No crops would be coaxed from this soil, and in the absence of crops and decent pastureland there were no people. That, at least, was a blessing.

She struggled out of the marsh and felt the full weight of her long journey and lack of sleep descend upon her, like a heavy yoke across her withers, her head and her neck. Her front legs trembled. She should be on her way, but she was too depleted to fly. And with no water and apparently no food, she did not know how she would replenish her strength.

The Chang Tang Plateau is a six hundred and twenty mile stretch of wasteland just south of the Kunlun range. It has been described as "the most inhospitable area in the world."[259] Later on in history, intrepid explorers with more testosterone than sense would explore the Chang Tang, and they would all reach the same verdict. Rick Ridgeway, who famously climbed Everest and K2, said, "I have climbed the highest mountains on earth, but the Chang Tang sucks me dry of all energy."[260] And Swedish topographer Sven Hedin described it thus: "Pouring rain, marshy ground, quicksand! Detestable!"[261] It lies fifteen thousand feet above sea level, and even in the summer months the night-time temperature drops to -25°C. Blizzards howl across the plain all year round and there is not a single cave or tree to provide shelter.

As night fell, the temperature plummeted and the wind picked up, battering the dragon with icy snow as she huddled on the open plain. Barenwyn had never been so cold. With no shelter available, she fashioned her own, draping her leathery wings over her body like a makeshift tent. To warm her numb hands she opened her mouth to breathe a small plum of flame, but nothing happened.

"Damn it," she muttered, only now remembering that she had lost her flint stone. There would be no fire, no warmth and no light. Exhaustion overtook her and finally she slept.

When she awoke, she lay still and took stock of the state of her body and its fitness for travel. She was desperately hungry, but at least could quench her thirst with the newly fallen snow. And while she did not feel hearty and hale, she felt she had the energy to fly. Her wings were numb from the cold but not painful, and she was surprised when she stood and shook off the snow to find that they had reddened and blistered. No matter. The wings were still functional, though stiff and less responsive when she took to the air. She decided to fly low.

With the storm past and the sun high in the sky, the temperature on the plateau climbed to 20°C and with the warmth came the pain. The dragon landed and lay down waiting for the throbbing in her wings to pass. It did not pass. It seemed to pulse through her wings and up into her shoulders with every heartbeat, and was so intense that it would not allow her to lie still. She got up and paced. Afraid to spend another night on the plateau, she forced herself into the air again, and flew until she could bear the pain no longer. Then she would land and pace. Fly, land and pace; fly, land and pace. By sunset she had not covered much ground, and as the temperature dropped she folded her wings in an effort to shield them from the cold.

But now she was presented with a bigger problem: without the canvased shelter of her wing flaps, her core temperature dived and she began to shake uncontrollably. She feared that she would freeze to death, and so reluctantly unfurled her wings and curled up beneath them. By morning they were black.

Frostbite occurs due to the formation of ice crystals within the skin cells and deeper tissues of its victims, usually in temperatures below -12°C. The skin reddens and blisters, eventually turning black as clots form and inhibit blood supply to the affected area. The cells begin to die. There is a real danger that this necrotic flesh will develop gangrene. And so it was that Barenwyn lost the use of both her wings. As she walked the barren plateau, she watched them die, and knew that her only chance of survival was their removal.

They would need to be amputated right up at the fleshy bit below her shoulders. At least, she knew, she would not bleed to death. Like a gecko's tail, the vertebrae at the base of her wings were etched with fracture planes, allowing the wing to be removed without further injury to the main body of the beast. This did not mean, however, that biting her own wings off was painless. Indeed the dragon's shrieks echoed across the plain and when the deed was done, she lay down and wept.

She would have to walk all the way to Shanxi now – no small feat for an injured, starving animal. Once she spotted a bizarre creature with two great horns and long, shaggy hair that hung from its back like a frayed, woollen blanket. She gave chase, but was so weakened by hunger that it easily eluded her, and stood at a distance regarding her with curiosity.

"How the hell do you survive here?" she wept.

The yak blinked at her and trotted off.

Onward she trudged, growing thinner and weaker and finally tired of this accursed thing we call life until, in the very shadow of Dragons' Gate Mountain, she collapsed.

George's journey was much more straightforward and much less arduous. Once in France, he took the same route as Louis IX's forces when they embarked on the Seventh Crusade. He paid passage on a ship departing from the port of Aigues-Mortes. The vessel took him east into the Mediterranean, past the northern coast of the Almohade Empire, south of the islands of Sicily and Crete to land at Cyprus.

His journey may have been logistically easier, but it was still fraught with suffering. His dreams were plagued by images of Hawisa shrieking, tormented, her arm swelling hideously as she died. His worst dream, however, was the one in which she came back. It had been his wish, his deepest desire, to have her back in his life, but in the nightmare she stood before him, her cheeks devoid of colour, her bloodied arm hanging in tatters at her side. Her face spoke of such suffering that his impulse to embrace the girl quickly flipped to revulsion: a body that damaged should not persist. Hawisa – this Hawisa which was a walking testament to her death – was grotesque … and monstrous. And George, a knight who had never flinched in battle, screamed and screamed. Such were his nights. His days were hazy with fatigue and loneliness and he wondered at times if he would not be better off just flinging himself overboard. Perhaps then he would find some peace. And so it was a ragged, exhausted man who arrived at the Principality of Antioch.

Since the day when Iftikhar led his family away from the massacre at Jerusalem, the Holy Land had been in a state of flux. Hostilities between Christian and Muslim forces continued to bloody the soil – indeed, Louis IX's losses in Egypt in 1248 were so great that they brought the Seventh Crusade to an abrupt end. Likewise, conflict between the different Muslim factions and infighting amongst the Christian barons ensured that neither side knew any peace. Jerusalem herself – the jewel, the prize – had passed from Catholic to Islamic control and back again, until finally the Crusaders lost the city to Ayub of Egypt in 1244. Destabilising the situation even further, the Mongols invaded from the east, attacking rival Muslims and Christians alike, laying siege to their cities and issuing the following ultimatum: surrender and pay homage or face the consequences. The consequences were vividly defined when the Prince of Mayyafaraqin refused to surrender. The Mongols sacked his city, and their leader Hulagu had the prince executed by making him eat his own flesh as it was carved off his bones. Truly it was a turbulent, brutal world that greeted Jory when he landed at Alexandretta late that summer.

It is said that Jonah, after three days in the belly of a whale, finally relented to God's will, saying "What I have vowed I will pay. Salvation belongs to the Lord!"[262] And then the great fish vomited him up on the very coast where George now stood. Still feeling nauseous from the voyage and battered and bruised by life, Jory thought he knew how the old prophet must have felt.

It was very hot and very bright. A punishing August sun cast diamonds of light onto the bay and glared off the pale walls of the dwellings that crowded the plain. Strange trees clustered near the shoreline, bizarre things that looked like round bushes with large, bright green leaves stuck atop wooden poles. Palm trees. Further inland mountains of brown rock and parched, sun-baked scrub rose, their peaks smudged and indistinct in a bank of low-lying cloud. All very different from the green undulating hills of Britain. And the place smelled funny. Underneath the familiar scents of livestock and humanity, there was the aroma of meat unlike any he'd ever put to his lips. A pungent mixture of cumin and mint, allspice, parsley and garlic left the weary man uncertain whether he felt sick or famished. The chatter of foreign words formed a nonsensical din around him.

George's plan, formulated on the boat-ride over, was to commit to military service in the Holy Land. There was no current crusade he could join, no waiting army hungry for recruits, but there were Crusader strongholds from Baghras stretching down the coast to Chateau Pélérin. Surely one of these would welcome a man with a good sword arm. But first he had planned to go on pilgrimage. Aboard the ship he'd had the vague, half-formed idea that seeing the hallowed places – those most meaningful to his faith – would comfort him somehow, would spark something within him to counter the pain and grief and anger that dominated his thoughts. And so he had planned first to visit Antioch.

Antioch is known as the "cradle of Christianity." Its early Jewish population was evangelised by Simon Peter and the apostle Paul, and they became the first converts to call themselves "Christian."[263] Christ was born in Bethlehem, baptised in the River Jordan and crucified at Calvary; yet it was in humble Antioch that His story grew into a faith that would move nations.

And yet now, with his feet on dry land, George was uncertain about going there. The idea of seeing the little town should leave him feeling stirred, he knew, and expectant. It was a tangible link to his faith – a gift, really, to be able to walk in the footsteps of the prophets. Surely it should make him feel … what? Blessed? Beloved of God? But George did not feel that God loved him. Indeed God had shoved a knife into his gut and given it a good twist. For the first time, the knight admitted to himself that he harboured an anger toward God bordering on hatred. God could have spared Hawisa. God did not. It is said that God forgives our iniquity, but that was irrelevant. George did not forgive God. How the hell could a loving God allow someone as devout and gentle as Hawisa to suffer so? In a world full of self-interested bastards and maniacs, why would the Lord call her away? Was it greed? Did God collect the wheat for Himself and leave the chaff here to plague the earth? No, he would never understand it and he would never forgive.

This raised an uncomfortable question: if he was not here to be reconciled with Christ, then why was he in the Holy Land at all? He was too jaded and too fatigued to search for an answer. The depressing fact remained that he had time on his hands and nothing whatsoever to do. He felt more adrift now than he had on the boat. And so he would stick to the original plan, travel in this country, and get a sense of things before signing on to fight.

After a few days rest in Epiphaneia, he packed his horse with supplies and set out for Antioch. Unsure of the way, he joined a caravan of pilgrims led by two Templar Knights, on a route that would take him through the Nur Mountains. As they picked their way through the foothills, their horses skidding on the loose gravel of the path, Jory kept to himself. He had no desire for comradery, and followed the main body of the group at some distance behind. Every attempt to engage him in conversation was met with a courteous but monosyllabic response. George did not want to know these people.

However, when they reached the Belen Pass – a bottleneck in the road – they were ambushed by bandits. Still lost in his own misery, Jory had lagged so far behind that he could not even see his group. But he heard the shouts, and when a woman screamed, he spurred his horse forward and launched himself into the fray. George had trained himself to block out all distractions, all the blur and noise of battle, to breathe deeply and focus. Identify a target. There, a man in Turkish robes on horseback. Swing your blade. Down he goes. Find another … a Turk on foot dragging a woman by her hair. Lean low in the saddle, swing and down he goes. A third falls and a fourth. His blade was a scythe mowing down the chaff that God had allowed to remain here on earth. It was good, satisfying work and when he was done, he had an impressive harvest of dead opponents.

He looked around for another adversary upon whom to vent his anger, but there were none. Instead, his gaze fell upon the woman he had saved as she sat sobbing in the dust. He did not know this woman and yet, despite his resolve not to care, he was moved to pity. He bent, scooped her up in his arms and carried her to the man he knew to be her husband. One of the Templars caught his eye. A nod – thanks for your help – and Jory bent to clean his sword on the robes of one of his victims.

That night when they made camp, George did not withdraw but came and sat by their fire. They all smiled at him gratefully, and the husband of the woman he saved gave him extra food and a fine warm blanket before retreating back to his wife's side. Jory watched the pair as he ate. The husband, well aware that he had nearly lost his wife, was fawning over her. He fussed over her comfort and kissed and caressed her often. He clearly loved the woman, and thanks not to God but to George, she lived and the man remained whole.

"That was a brilliant display of swordsmanship today," one of the Templars had taken a seat beside him. "Damase," he said, extending his hand.

Jory shook it. "George."

"Good to meet you."

"We've already met."

"No, you grunted a few words in my general direction when you joined the caravan," Damase chuckled. "That's hardly a meeting. But I got to know you today. Where did you learn to fight like that?"

"Lanherne, England."

"Well, George of Lanherne, you were a great help. Thank you." Damase rose to leave, thought better of it and sat down again. "What are your plans here? I mean, you'll go to Antioch and then what?"

"No idea."

"I find that hard to believe."

"Why?"

"Because you are a very long way from Lanherne; you must have some purpose in coming here."

When George did not respond, Damase continued. "Laurent," he nodded at the other Templar, "and I had a bet about you. I wagered that you are ill, dying perhaps, and here to make this pilgrimage while you still have the strength."

Jory cocked an eyebrow at him.

"Well, you looked terrible – pale and thin and morose. But that sword of yours was not in the hands of an ailing man today."

"So you lost your bet."

"Laurent is very smug about it," Damase sighed. "Git."

They sat in silence, staring at the crackling fire.

"If it's not illness, then it must be upset. Something has left you raw," the Templar said quietly.

"Are you finished?" George asked sharply.

Undeterred, the Templar continued. "People do it all the time. They get hurt, badly, and they come here seeking some salve for their wounds. I guess I was wondering if you found yours today."

"My what?"

"Your cure. You were a shadow when you joined us, as cold as old ashes; and then a woman screams and you come alive. I've never seen so swift a change in a man. I think you needed something to fight and," he nodded toward the woman, "something to fight for... Just a thought." Damase rose, clapped a hand on George's shoulder and walked away.

In due course the little group reached Antioch, and George barely looked at the town. He did, however, look upon the Templars with renewed interest. The Poor Knights of the Temple of Solomon had been providing armed escort for pilgrims since the time of the Seljuks and had built their headquarters upon the Temple Mount, the site of Solomon's fallen Temple (hence their name). As warrior monks, they were known for piety, poverty and chastity. As it is said in their laws: "O you venerable brothers ... God is with you, if you promise to despise the deceitful world in perpetual love of God, and scorn the temptations of your body: sustained by the food of God and watered and instructed in the commandments of Our Lord."²⁶⁴ But this is not what attracted Jory's attention. The Templars were also known for their ferocity in battle. Saladin had called them "the firebrands of the Franks," an enemy so lethal that he had them executed immediately upon capture. Now that, for George, had potential.

Damase was right. Jory had come alive during that fight at the Belen Pass, and since then something within him had changed, had eased a little. He had been so angry for so long; that skirmish in the mountains had allowed him to syphon off some of his rage. And now he knew the answer to the question: why was he in the Holy Land? Quite simply, he was here to fight. He never got to fight the dragon that killed Hawisa. And he was unable to battle the poison that coursed through her veins. As a man of action it was intolerable to feel so impotent, and so he came to the one place on earth where he could find constant and sustained conflict: the Holy Land. And the Templars were in the thick of it.

"Question…" he said as he approached Damase. "If someone wishes to aid the Templars in their cause, but does not want to take monastic vows, how would you accommodate him?"

"We'd make him a sergeant."

"Which entails?"

"The man would live with us, train and work with us, but he would not be bound by the sterner rules of monastic life. He could keep his possessions, for instance, and would not make a vow of chastity." Damase paused and studied him. "You interested?"

George nodded. "Oh yes."

Barenwyn awoke in a cave dimly lit by candlelight. She was, she realised, lying on a bed of soft hay. Beside her, curled up on a straw mat was a plump, full-bosomed, round-faced woman, who was fast asleep and snoring. The dragon retreated from the sleeping figure back into her mound of hay, until her back pressed against the cool rock wall behind her. Her scrabbling woke the woman.

"Nǐ hǎo," the stranger nodded and rose to kneel on her mat. "That means 'hello.'" She smiled broadly at the dragon.

"Who are you?" Barenwyn's voice was a dry rasp.

"Guan. And you are called Barenwyn."

It was odd to hear her name pronounced with a Chinese accent, a little too much emphasis on the "b," a muddle over the "r" and an almost absent "n."

"How do you know my name?"

"We were told of your coming."

"By who?"

"By the gods." The woman shrugged.

*"What?"*

"Shh, you must rest now."

But Barenwyn shook her head. "Where am I?"

"Dragon Gate Caves," Guan beamed at her. "This cave is Yaofangdong," she nodded at the space around her, "Medical Prescription Cave."

She gestured with her hands: the universal sign for wait, stay put, and then rose to her feet. Picking up a lantern, Guan held it up to the nearest wall to illuminate dozens of inscriptions – thousands of intricate Chinese characters carved into the rock.

"See? Hǎo yào. Instructions for good medicine." She looked at the dragon and her expression changed. She still smiled, but there was a sadness, a sympathy in her eyes now. "You have been very ill."

She approached Barenwyn and gently touched her snout. This time the dragon did not recoil. "You get better," Guan nodded encouragingly, "Wǒ bǎozhèng. I promise. You rest now."

"But…"

"Xiūxí," the woman said firmly, and looked pointedly at the hay.

Barenwyn laid her head down and sighed. She was very tired. It would be good to sleep. The smiling woman curled up on her mat. In a moment she was snoring again.

"Well," Barenwyn whispered to the sleeping figure, "I suppose if you meant me any harm, I'd be dead already."

The woman opened her eyes. "Míngxiǎn."

"What does that mean?"

"Obviously," Guan said dryly and recommenced her snoring.

Birds were singing and sunlight filtered in through the mouth of the cave, pulling Barenwyn out of the unconsciousness of sleep. She opened her eyes and looked drowsily around her.

"Zǎo ān, good morning." In the cave's entrance stood Guan, a dark silhouette against the morning sunlight. "How do you feel?"

"Like a rag doll."

"I not surprised. Let me see you." She approached and held the dragon's head gently in her hands. "Stick out your tongue."

"What? Why?"

"Please."

Barenwyn obeyed.

"Huh." The woman made a small exasperated noise and placed two fingers on the dragon's wrist.

"What's the matter with my tongue?"

"Shh," Guan said as she took her patient's pulse. At last she nodded and rose. "Still very weak. I have medicine for that."

She left the cave and returned a short while later with a bowl of steaming liquid.

"What's that?"

"Special tea," Guan smiled. "Ginseng to give you fire, ginkgo to raise your spirits, reishi to make you strong, Dong quai to enrich the blood. All good for you. Drink."

Barenwyn looked uncertainly at the pungent concoction and took a tentative sip. "Uh. That's terrible."

"Taste not matter," Guan admonished. "Health matter. Drink."

Barenwyn grimaced. "I'll make you a deal: I'll drink the whole bowl if you explain how you know me."

Guan must have found this arrangement acceptable, because she smiled and bowed her head in assent. "Have you heard of Kau Cim?"

"No."

"It is way to know the future. You shake the qian tong – a cup full of bamboo sticks – and when one falls out it has a message from the gods."

"A stick told you I was coming?" Barenwyn tried to keep the mockery out of her voice and failed.

Guan nodded and tapped the bowl lightly with her finger, a silent instruction to drink.

When Barenwyn complied, the woman continued. "The monks of the temple received word in this way that you come. Always the same stick again and again. Stick Wǔ shí liù: 'The hidden dagger is a dragon and it comes over thousands of li.'"[265]

"So you knew a dragon was coming. It doesn't explain how you know my name."

"A sage in the temple dream of Xiàngshù, a dragon who live here long ago. He dream of her death, her babies and your war with men."

Barenwyn's face was grave. "So you know you're giving refuge to a killer."

"Shì de," Guan nodded.

"Doesn't that worry you?"

The woman rose and collected the empty bowl. "You are too weak to hurt anyone."

"But you're trying to make me strong again."

Guan smiled at her. "Perhaps by then you change your mind." And with that she left.

The following day Guan fed her patient rice and a thin soup of chicken, garlic, spring onions and ginger. And then she said, "Time to get up."

Still feeling listless and weak, Barenwyn did not want to leave her comfortable bed of straw.

"If you wish to walk again, you must use legs. Come, just to the mouth of the cave."

Barenwyn struggled to her feet and tottered there for a moment. She looked uncertainly at Guan and the woman nodded encouragement. Every unsteady step was painful, and every muscle and joint in her ravaged body cried out to stop this folly and return to bed. In particular the bandaged stumps of her lost wings throbbed and felt as if they were burning. It made her feel sick and dizzy.

"You are doing well," Guan coaxed. "Come."

Eventually the dragon managed to shuffle to the cave's entrance, and what she saw there was a revelation. Before her wound the placid waters of the Yī River between the steep slopes of two limestone cliffs. These cliffs were riddled with caves, some deep with their interiors shrouded in darkness and some shallow, mere alcoves that housed statues of the Buddha.

The Lóngmén Grottoes are a monument to the faith of generations: 1,400 caves adorned with over 100,000 statues of Gautama Buddha. These statues range from one inch to nearly sixty feet high and there are thousands of stele, stone slabs bearing inscriptions, prayers.

"It's beautiful," Barenwyn whispered.

"Yes," Guan beamed at her. "Enough for now. Rest."

As the dragon hobbled back to her straw bed, she asked, "My mother spent time here?"

"Shì de," Guan nodded.

"What did she do here?"

"Learn."

"Learn what?"

"Lesson depend on pupil."

"So what lesson do you think you're going to teach me?"

Guan smiled at her and helped her into bed.

Barenwyn persisted. "When do these lessons start?"

The woman set a bowl of herbal tea within easy reach of the dragon's nest and turned to leave.

"I asked you a question!" Barenwyn shouted at her back.

Guan turned to face her and regarded her with that same placid look of benevolence that she always wore. "Lesson already begun."

Article sixty-seven of the Rule of the Poor Knighthood of the Temple allows for the existence of sergeants – warriors who wish to serve with the Templars for a fixed period of time. And article sixty-eight mandates that these men be given black robes to wear to differentiate them from the true Templars who wear white with a red cross upon their chests. And so it was that Jory came to be seated in the refectory at the Templar fortress of Saphet, his black-clad arm resting on the table next to Damase's white-clad one.

It was a Saturday so no meat was served with the meal, and George looked morosely upon the vegetable dishes in front of him. A light tapping on the table drew his eyes to Brother Guillaume. The man had wrapped all the fingers of his right hand around the smallest digit of his left and was pulling on it. Jory frowned at him. Because some apostle – he didn't know which one – had said "Manduca panem tuum cum silentio" (Eat your bread in silence), each mealtime seemed to degenerate into a bizarre spectacle of grown men flapping their hands about in a strange sign language.

As the knight across the table continued to pull insistently on his little finger, George leaned over to Damase and whispered, "Is he calling me a wanker?"

Damase choked loudly and showered Laurent with half-chewed cabbage. When he regained his composure, the knight whispered back, "That sign mimics the milking of a cow," he voice shook with barely suppressed laughter. "He wants you to pass the milk."

As Jory handed the pitcher to Guillaume, he caught Damase's eye. The man's shoulders were shaking and his hand was clamped tightly over his mouth. This set George off, and in another moment both men had lost all control.

"Brother Damase!" Simon de la Tour spoke sharply from the end of the table. "Maybe you should be the one reading this," he held up the Bible in his hands, "and I'll eat."

"No, a thousand pardons, brother. Please continue."

Brother Simon cleared his throat. "Entreat me not to leave or to turn back from following after you; For wherever you go, I will go…"[266]

George's earliest days among the Templars were fraught with many such teething problems, but after a few months he settled in quite well. He was used to the structured life of a knight in service, and so was able to don the routine of life at Saphet like a well-worn glove. But he partook in only minimal devotion. While the brothers were at Matins, he was asleep. When the bell rang at 6 a.m. for mass, he rose to tend to his horse and sharpen his blade. All this was permitted because he had not taken monastic vows, but even he was not allowed to miss the Nones and Vespers services in the afternoon.

The blank look on his face while he sat in Chapel told Damase all: George was there in body only. The Templar had met many impious Catholics in his time and they tended to fall into two categories. The first consisted of the indifferent, those who did not feel any of the faith's real power and so they went through the motions mainly because it suited their purpose to be seen as righteous. The second group was the angry impious, those who believed fervently and who had been disappointed. At some vital point in their lives they had thrown a prayer to heaven, beseeching God and His answer had been "No." Jory, Damase decided, was of this second group. He *was* raw and suffering, stoically and quietly behind the door he had shut on God. It pained the Templar to think on it, for George had swiftly become his best friend.

Then early that winter an outbreak of influenza worked its way through Saphet, and George became very ill. At the height of his fever he babbled, saying outlandish things about someone named Hawisa … and a dragon. It could, of course, be the fever talking. Yet as Damase mopped his friend's brow he suspected that there was some truth in the man's delirious monologue. It was so heavily laden with emotion.

When Jory's fever finally broke, Damase asked, "So who's Hawisa?"

George, still pale and weak, regarded him warily from where he lay on the bed.

"Your wife?" Damase prompted.

"Elle aurait été. (She would have been.)"

"What happened?"

Tears of fatigue and convalescence filled his eyes and George, depleted by his illness, found that he was not equal to the task of containing the terrible secret any longer. It poured from him like flood waters through a broken dam.

Damase listened in grim silence, then said, "I am so sorry, my friend."

Many thoughts crowded into the Templar's mind. He selected one. "It is a terrible thing, but I doubt that it is meaningless."

George shook from the strain of his confession. "How so?"

"I think in life we always end up where we're meant to be. Sometimes we are led there by sweetness, sometimes we are driven there by sorrow."

Jory snorted. "So this is all part of what? God's plan?"

"There is something He means for you to do here."

"But Damase, here's the thing: I don't give a damn what he wants me to do."

"Lesson already begun," Barenwyn said in a passable Chinese accent. "What the hell does that mean?"

As the days accumulated into weeks and months, Guan would not be drawn on the subject. She fed her patient, took her on increasingly long walks and sat at her bedside reading to her, to help wile away the long hours of convalescence. Her voice was soothing, melodious, and Barenwyn's thoughts drifted, half-waking, half-sleeping, on the tide of that voice. Sometimes she would go under, dozing off in her bed of hay, and when she rose to the surface again, words filtered through…

"Gù shèngrén yīzhí dào bāokuò cǎiqǔ rènhé ā kè dùn qìyuē
Hé zuòfǎ, bù shǐyòng yòngtú jiàoxué…"

Translation:
"Therefore the sage keeps to the deed that consists in taking no action
And practises the teaching that uses no uses."[267]

To the dragon these words made no sense … action and inaction, use and no use. And still the voice flowed on…

> "Blunt the sharp edges;
> Untangle the knots;
> Soften the glare;
> Let your wheels move only along old ruts."[268]

"Walking in old ruts," Barenwyn said. "Like history repeating itself?" She sat up in bed.

Guan nodded. "Always." Noticing the dubious look on the dragon's face, she asked, "You doubt?"

She rose and carried a heavy volume over to Barenwyn, and sat down next to her in the hay. "See? Same things again and again," she said, opening the book and pointing to an artist's crude rendering of a dragon. "The dragons come to Lóngmen Shíkū over many centuries. All are the same."

"No, not the same," Barenwyn shook her head. "That," she pointed at the picture, "is what my mother called an eastern dragon, a lung dragon. I am a wyvern … of the West."

Guan's brow furrowed. "What difference?"

"Well, a wyvern is the largest of dragons, sturdily-built with meat on our bones and great wings like the sails of a mighty ship. This dragon," she pointed to the picture, "this lung is thinner, more snakelike and has no wings."

"Mèimei," which is Chinese for little sister, "I drew this of you."

Barenwyn gaped at her. "That's not possible," she murmured and exited the cave.

Guan followed her to the edge of the Yī where the water was clean and clear. The dragon gazed at her own reflection, and gasped at her transformation. That long trudge across the Chang Tang with so little food had stripped the meat from her bones. Her body had grown thin and snakelike, and this made it look like it had grown in length. Her face too had thinned, leaving the whisker-like frills on her snout and jowls more pronounced. And, of course, she had no wings.

"It is such a hard journey to reach Dragon's Gate. It changes you."

"Why do so many do it?" Barenwyn whispered.

"They come when they have need … like you."

They headed back inside.

"And so," Barenwyn mused, "the Wyvern and the Lung are not two separate types of dragon, but two stages in the life of one creature."

"Shì de," the woman nodded.

"But what does it mean?"

"In China dragons are loved. The Four Dragon Kings brought water to the people in time of drought, and became the Four Great Rivers so that man would always have water. The serpent Huanlong taught us to write," she gestured at the many prescriptions engraved on the walls, "and Shen Lung brings good fortune with each new year…"

"So?"

"So every dragon we worship began life with wings and breathing fire."

"They were violent?"

"Some very much."

"But they changed."

"Shì de."

Saphet was located in the remote mountainous region of upper Galilee, a rugged, sparsely populated area between the coastal cities that lined the shore of the Mediterranean and the towns and villages that clustered along the Sea of Galilee and the River Jordan. In such a place it is easy to disappear. A shepherd tending his goats does not return home to his wife. A young child strays too far from his mother's door and is not seen again. An old woman, living alone, is not missed when she does not return to add more wood to her fire and it burns out. The Templars heard rumours of this, but could discover no cause until two of their own went missing. Brothers Adrienn and Robert failed to return after escorting a group of pilgrims to Capernaum. Enquiries were made. Yes, yes, they had gotten to the town safely with their charges. And yes, they were in excellent health when they departed for home. But they never made it.

Days later Brother Robert's blood-soaked mare trotted up to Saphet's gate. His pack was still tethered to the horse and his purse still held money from the trip. So not bandits then. As the Templars inspected the mount and its packs for any further clues, George's nose was assailed by the pungent odour of fish. It was a distinctive smell and strangely familiar. Then he remembered that room back in Lanherne, Isa writhing on the bed and old Redigan poised over her with a knife. The old woman had made an incision across the two bite-marks on Hawisa's arm and rubbed it vigorously to squeeze the venom out. As the viscous yellow liquid drained from the wound, a sharp fishy odour had filled the room. It smelled…

"Exactly like this," he murmured.

"What?" Damase asked. He glanced at George and was startled by what he saw. All the colour had drained from his friend's face and he was trembling. "George?" he asked quietly.

"Huh? Oh! Nothing. I'm fine." And with infinite calm, Jory turned and headed for the stables.

Damase got distracted then by all the furore around the riderless horse, and when he looked for Jory a little while later he was gone.

George was hunting. Up rocky, mountainous slopes and down again into steep valleys, he searched for tracks and scat. But mostly he let his mount guide the way. Sir Ralph had told him of how his horse panicked as they neared the dragon that killed Hawisa. In fact, the animal had been skittish well before they even saw the beast. It knew. And so whenever George's courser shied away from a path, he urged the animal onward in that very direction.

This was right. This is what he should have done back at Lanherne. When they brought Sir Aubrey in, already half-dead from blood loss, and the knight had uttered the word 'dragon,' George should have hunted it down and killed it immediately. If he had, Hawisa would still be alive. He would not make that mistake again. And so the hunt went on all that day and into the night.

In the end it was not his horse's instincts that led him to the beast, but a woman's screams. It was a terrible sound, half shriek and half sob, and it spurred George forward. Bursting into a clearing, he found her – a Muslim woman in the coils of a long, snake-like serpent. Nearby lay the body of a man in an expanding pool of blood. His throat had been ripped out.

George shouted to draw the dragon's attention away from the woman, but to no avail. Stronger measures were needed, so he swung his blade and brought it down with all his strength onto the creature's tail. The barbed point at the end of the tail rolled away into the dust and the dragon roared. It let go of the woman and turned to face Jory.

It was a hideous thing, the angry red colour of an infected wound with a long serpentine body, a mouth full of jagged teeth, and only two legs at the front, by which it dragged itself toward him. George hopped off his horse and slapped it on the rear, but in truth the animal needed no encouragement to flee. Its eyes were wild with panic as it charged away.

At that moment the dragon struck first with its teeth, then with its whole body. Its head darted forward and its mouth clamped tight onto Jory's shoulder. His armour kept his skin unbroken, but the pressure of that bite was immense. George cried out in pain. With a good grip on its victim, the serpent wound itself around George. He had just enough time to raise his sword before the coils began to constrict. This was fortunate for, with the sword held in front of him, the great wyrm could not tighten its grip without slicing its own flesh on the blade. With a flick of its bleeding stump of a tail, it cast Jory to the ground.

It came at him next with its teeth and claws, trying to prise the knight's armour away and strike at the flesh beneath. Unable to bring his sword to bear in such close combat, George hammered at the side of the creature's head with one chainmail-clad fist. One of his blows stunned the monster, and George rolled out from under it. He did not allow himself a moment's hesitation. He launched himself onto the wyrm's back, plunging his dagger again and again right at the base of its skull, attempting to sever its spinal cord and render it paralysed.

He stabbed and stabbed as the thing writhed beneath him. He stabbed even when it stopped moving. He continued to hack away, even when men's shouts filled the clearing and Damase gripped his arm. Indeed he only stopped when the lindworm's head rolled free of its body.

"George!" Damase had him by the shoulders now. "Are you all right?"

Exhausted, Jory collapsed.

He awoke in his bed at Saphet. Damase was seated nearby carving a series of hash marks into the stone wall with his dagger: 𝍧|||...

"What's all this?" Jory rasped. His throat was very dry.

"One hundred and twenty-five," Damase murmured. "That's the number of lives you've saved from raiders and bandits here in the Holy Land. And then today," he scratched two more deep marks on the wall, "you saved two more people from a dragon."

"Two?"

"The woman, Ada Nasrallah and her unborn child."

"A baby?" Jory whispered.

Damase smiled and nodded. "Now I'm going to tell you something, George. You don't want to hear it, but I'm going to say it anyway. I know why you're so angry. In your hour of need you feel that God failed you. But you're missing the point. He created this world, but He does not come down here to fix every problem with it. That is for us to do."

"But…"

Damase ignored the interruption. "You say He let Hawisa die. I say that He saves women like Hawisa everyday … through us. And at the Belen Pass He saved that woman through you. And today He saved Ada and her baby through you. That is how God works in this world: through the actions of good men."

George said flatly: "Your argument is flawed."

"How so?"

"It is based on the assumption that one life for one hundred and twenty-seven is preferable, that having lost Hawisa I can console myself with the continued existence of one hundred and twenty-seven strangers. I'm here to fight, Damase, not to rescue, and I would gladly sacrifice every life I've saved if it would bring her back."

"Bollocks."

"It's not bollocks."

"If you really didn't care about those people, you would have acted differently today."

"How so?"

"The woman told me what happened: you lured the dragon away from her and then you fought it. Your first priority was to save the girl. Otherwise you could have attacked the beast while she was still in its grip. It was distracted and would have been easier to overcome. She would have perished, but that dragon would have died more quickly than it did, and you would not be lying here with two broken ribs and a dislocated shoulder."

"Enough!"

"I'm only telling you the truth."

"You Templars are all alike. You want us all to become like you – some instrument of God."

"No," Damase rose to leave. "I'm not saying you should become an instrument of God. I'm saying that you already are." He turned to go but paused at the doorway. "The Muslim name Ada, by the way, means 'Grace.' I'll spell it out for you because you West Country boys aren't too bright," he smirked. "You spent the afternoon saving grace."

"All right," Barenwyn was saying. "Let's say that I want to change … like those other dragons did."

Guan beamed at her.

"But how?" the dragon cried. "I've learned nothing since I've come here! We've talked about everything but the fiasco back in England! We haven't done anything!"

"No," Guan shook her head. "We have done something very important."

"What?"

"We become friends."

"What the hell does that have to do with anything?" roared the dragon in frustration.

Unflustered, Guan rose and started rummaging through the box where she kept her herbs. "Everyone," she said, "who comes here thinks learning is all meditation and cryptic words from the sages. No. It is simple."

She rose. She had something small clasped in her right hand. Barenwyn could not see what it was.

"I show you," Guan said and stood tall in front of the dragon. "I am human. Humans killed your mother. You have made war on humans. Therefore we are enemies."

"No, those people were in England. You weren't responsible for any of that."

"People are the same – here, England, everywhere. We are all born fearing what we do not understand and hating what we fear. Mèimei, we are enemies. What do you do with an enemy?"

"You kill it," Barenwyn whispered.

"Shì de," Guan nodded. "Here."

The woman held out her hand. In it was a small piece of flint. She tossed it to the dragon who caught it in her mouth and jerked her head sharply to lodge it in place.

"Now you breathe fire," Guan said quietly. "I am your enemy. Kill me."

"What?"

"Why are you confused? It is simple. Do it."

"No."

"Why not?"

"Well," Barenwyn floundered, "we're friends, like you said."

"I am human. Humans are your sworn enemy."

"Not you," the dragon said quietly.

"Just me? The monks of the Temple, then," she gestured toward the cave's entrance. "They are human. Go kill them."

When the dragon did not respond, Guan said more forcefully, "Go! Do it!"

"I don't want to."

"Why not?"

Barenwyn paused to consider the question. "It doesn't feel right."

"How so?"

"The thought makes me feel cold. You have been nothing but kind to me and the monks ... they wouldn't hurt a fly."

"Shì de!" the woman said triumphantly. "That cold feeling, the reluctance, is the basis for all moral action. We are presented with opportunity to stray and the feeling speaks first. It says, 'No.' And then the thoughts write for us the reason why we feel the way we do. They justify and strengthen the feeling with logic. See? You have learned!"

They were silent for a long time. Guan held up her hands and Barenwyn gently placed her head in them.

"I did not tell you all," the woman whispered.

"About what?"

"The Kau Cim stick that foretold your coming had more to say... 'The hidden dagger is a dragon, and it comes over thousands of li. This can only be good. In the end, her...'" she paused looking for the word, "jiānxīn, her hardships, will raise her higher."[269]

"What does that mean?"

"You have crossed Chang Tang. You know what it is to be weak. To know weakness is to know human beings. You have known what it is to be afraid. The men who killed your mother were afraid. And when you killed men, you were afraid. See? We are the same. And now that you know this, you are free to be ... what *will* you be, mèimei?"

Barenwyn looked at her for a long moment. "Better," she said.

Guan left the cave and returned to the temple. A woman rose to greet her.

"Thank you," I said.

"You heard?"

"Yes."

"It is good." But a troubled look passed over Guan's face. "She can never know that I am like you."

"Agreed," I nodded. "It wasn't your immortality that turned her around, Guanyin. It was your humanity."

The woman beamed at me. "What now?"

"I'll go home."
"You wait for her? On your island?"
"Yes. She'll come when she's ready."

## A Side Note

*Chinese Buddhists revere the much loved Bodhisattva Guanshiyin, whose name means "one who hears the cries of the world." Hearing these cries Guanyin (as she is called) embraces all beings with compassion. For this she is known as the Mercy Goddess, and her purpose is to relieve the suffering of this world and to teach others how to find the path to peace and enlightenment. This was illustrated in the "Precious Scroll of Sudhana and Longnü" in a tale that may strike you as familiar.*

*In it a man named Sudhana is walking in the mountains when he hears a voice crying for help. Eventually he discovers that the source of these cries is a snake trapped in a bottle. The serpent begs him to release her and he does. Once free, however, the snake grows in size and becomes a hideous beast which threatens to eat the unlucky man. Sudhana is saved by a young girl (Guanyin in one of her many forms). The girl tells the snake that it can eat her as well if the creature can demonstrate how it fit into such a small bottle. The snake wriggled back into the vessel, and the girl trapped it by replacing the lid. The snake begged piteously to be set free again and Guan replied, "You can earn your freedom, if you find the Way." By "the Way" she meant the path to enlightenment and the snake, desperate to be free, worked studiously for seven years. It was a wiser and kinder creature after that. It cleansed itself of all venom and remained with Guanyin as a disciple.*

*I have always thought that Guanyin is very like the Coranieid. I confess that I do not know her origins, but she has our ears and our immortal nature. It is said in the Lotus Sutra that she can bind demons and in the Legend of Miaoshan, she is portrayed as a healer who can also communicate with animals. These things describe Guanyin. What defines her is this: her love for all creatures, even and especially for those who have sinned and need help regaining the right path.*

*So you see, in every culture, in every corner of the world, we all – at times – need saving with a little mercy and a little grace.*

George was a knight. He had fine chainmail armour, a strong sword arm and a swift horse. He had an impeccable sense of duty and a pious soul. And George wore a Templar's white robe with a red cross. He stood in his room at Saphet for the last time and counted the hash marks etched into the wall: 518. Five hundred and eighteen lives that he had saved since coming to the Holy Land. What had Damase said all those years ago? God works through the actions of good men.

Jory had found it hard at the time to accept that God was working through him. He was still so very angry that God took Hawisa away. But to be mad at God is to acknowledge His existence. To acknowledge His existence is to accept the concept of heaven, of a life for the soul after the death of the body. In his time as a soldier, Jory had watched many men die. At first, when he was young and inexperienced, he would often mistake an unconscious man for a dead one. But then he learned. Death does not look like insensibility and it does not look like slumber. Death is absence; a crucial spark within us departs, leaving behind only inconsequential matter – essentially decaying meat. That is why God plays the long game. Our bodies (which are so crucial to us) are, from God's perspective, only vessels that house something of extraordinary value and importance. Hence the Lord is concerned not with the body which is temporary, but with the soul which is eternal.

An image of Hawisa's body convulsing on the bed came to him unbidden. Damase suggested that for her, death had been a mercy. It had ended her suffering and released her soul. Despite all his grappling with God, George always fervently believed that Isa was in heaven. And therefore, if he wished to see her again, he had better get there himself. Hence the revival of his faith, the monastic vows he took when he joined the Templars, and the 518 hash marks on the wall.

He picked up Hawisa's *Bestiary* and, as was his habit, let it fall open to a random page and read: "The Lord looketh from heaven; He beholdeth all the sons of men... He fashioneth their hearts alike; He considereth all their works."[270] He closed the book, gently ran his hand over its worn leather cover and placed it in his pack. It was time to go.

The year was 1266 and the Christian presence in Outremer was dwindling. And now the Mameluke Sultan Baybars besieged Saphet. Supplies within the fortress were exhausted, and the Templars' position had become untenable. Therefore Simon de la Tour had negotiated a truce. The knights would surrender the fortress in exchange for safe conduct to a port where they could catch a ship bound for home. George and Damase rode out side by side as the line of Templars exited through Saphet's main gate.

"I don't trust this," Jory said quietly.

"Me neither."

"We're in trouble, aren't we?"

Damase looked straight ahead as he rode. "Yep."

As the first whispers of swords leaving their sheaths met George's ears, he smiled. He and Hawisa would be together soon. "Salvation belongs to the Lord," he murmured and turned to face the enemy as they charged.

On that day in 1266, Baybars reneged on his promise of safe conduct and slaughtered every Templar garrisoned at Saphet. Although George of Lanherne was counted among the dead, his legend lived on.

The story of his fight with the dragon captured popular imagination and grew. It was such a bright and shining tale of chivalry and heroism that it was like the sun, its gravitational pull drawing other stories to cluster around it like the planets of a solar system. George's name became associated with George of Cappadocia, a legendary third century dragon slayer. And eventually he was muddled with the Catholic martyr, St. George, a Roman soldier who was tortured and killed in 303 A.D. for his Christian faith.

Even the story of his fight with the lindworm was greatly embellished. In the year 1275 Jacobus de Voragine, the Archbishop of Genoa, wrote that by the city of Silene there was a lake and in that lake there lived a dragon…

> And when he came nigh … he venomed the people with his breath, and therefore the people … gave to him every day two sheep for to feed him, (so that) he should do no harm … and when the sheep failed there was taken a man and a sheep. Then was an ordinance made … that there should be taken the children and young people … of the town by lot… (and) the lot fell upon the king's daughter … (and they) led her to the place where the dragon was.[271]

The peasant woman Ada was transformed into a princess, and that terrible, brutal fight to save her was made very gentile. According to legend, St. George impaled the dragon with his lance and then used the lady's belt as a leash to lead it back to her village. There he killed it, explaining that his faith in God gave him the supernatural strength he needed to defeat the beast. As a result tens of thousands converted to Christianity, and the story became a metaphor: the dragon was the devil, which was defeated by the power of the one true faith.

St. George/George of Cappadocia/our Jory was then credited with the defeat of other serpents such as the Brinsop Dragon and the Dragon of Uffington. And in 1350 King Edward III founded the Order of the Garter – the highest order of chivalry among knights – in George's name.

Epiphaneia, the little town in the Holy Land where George stayed before setting out for Antioch, is now said to be the birthplace of St. George, and the red cross on his white Templar robes is now on the flag of England. He is in fact our patron saint – another hero to take his place alongside Boudicca and Arthur and the other great legends of Britain.

Where there are heroes, there are also villains. To this day Belial remains bound at Dozmary Pool in Cornwall. It is said that on dark nights an anguished cry can be heard above the wind that sweeps across the moor. Unnerved by these strange nocturnal lamentations, the local people crafted their own story to explain it. For their protagonist they chose one of their own, a man named Jan Tregeagle. He was a wicked man who sold his soul to the devil, and married rich widows to kill them for the inheritance.

One day after his death, so the story goes, a dispute arose in the community regarding a financial transaction between two villagers. Jan Tregeagle had been the only other witness, and so when the case went to court, the defendant declared, "If Tregeagle ever saw it, I wish to God that Tregeagle may come into court and declare it."[272] It was a quintessential case of 'Be careful what you wish for,' because in that moment Tregeagle's spirit did appear in court to testify. The problem was that once the trial was over the restless ghost would not depart, and hence caused great anxiety among the people. A local parson and 'ghost-layer' bound Tregeagle's soul to Dozmary Pool, where he must forever toil to empty the lake with a holed limpet shell. Even now, "strange tales are told in that neighbourhood of his appearing to people, and of his dismal howls at not being able to fulfil his tasks."[273]

As for the Coranieid, we were doomed to extinction. We could die, but we could not give birth. Today, they call it negative population growth; we knew it only as fate and hence our numbers began to dwindle. The sad fact was, that as the centuries passed, my people grew tired. Ian Maclaren once said, "Be kind for everyone you meet is fighting a hard battle."[274] That is essentially life, what Glen Duncan called "the assault course of mundane cause and effect."[275] In his novel *The Last Werewolf*, Duncan's protagonist explains what it really means to live forever: "I'm immune to the news, *the* news, the breaking news, rolling news, news flashes. Live long enough and nothing is news … a hundred years go by and you realise that there are no new things, only deep structures and cycles that repeat themselves through different period details."[276] And without death, without a ticking clock, it all becomes meaningless repetition minus the impetus to do anything. Death is a gift, and not just because it provides a deliverance from physical pain. It is what gives our lives meaning. Knowing that life will end spurs us to truly live it, to imbue it with all of the content and significance that we can. People love and give birth and fight and weep and invent and destroy, all because life is brief and they have got to get on with it while there is time. If men are candles that will eventually burn out, then damn it, they will shine for as long as their length of wick allows.

Without that, what motivation is there to do anything? Anne Rice, in her novel *Interview with the Vampire*, asks: "How many vampires do you think have the stamina for immortality? … (it) becomes a penitential sentence in a madhouse of figures and forms that are hopelessly … without value. One evening a vampire rises and realises what he has feared, perhaps for decades, that he simply wants no more of life at any cost… And that vampire goes out to die."[277] So it was with us. We had a rash of "accidents," basically suicides either intentionally committed or achieved through reckless action.

Take Hanyfer, for instance. On 21st February 1811, a terrible gale was blowing in a stretch of water known as the Falmouth Roads. In zero visibility, the *HMS Franchise* collided with another ship in her convoy, the *John & Jane*. The *Franchise*, a forty-gun veteran of both the Napoleonic War and the Battle of Copenhagen, nearly sliced the smaller vessel in half. As somewhere between 224 and 269 people spilled into the tempestuous waters, Hanyfer went to help them. She never made it back to shore. Our water elemental drowned.

Barinthus, devastated by her loss, hung himself in her room in Annwyn three days later.

Danjy was killed on 25th June 1883. An earthquake with a magnitude of 4.2 hit the West Country. It was not exactly a grand display of the earth's power, and only caused a few items to fall from shelves in nearby houses. We knew from the animals that it was coming, and yet Danjy stationed himself in an ancient tunnel that had long been abandoned as unsafe. According to Blue-cap (who excavated the site afterward), Danjy had removed all the struts that supported the crumpling walls and must have just sat there, waiting for the cave-in.

And my father decided to take a stroll on the night of 20th March 1941 as the Luftwaffe dropped incendiary bombs on the streets of Plymouth. The following morning André Savignon described the scene: "in this town that was wasting away in reddish trails of smoke, only a few citizens wandered: the others were still in hiding; or lay, all distress ended, under the ruins."[278] Gwyn's body was never found.

Dutifully I kept their soul stones and their stories. You already know Gwyn's role in Arthurian legend, but did you know that Barinthus is remembered in folklore as a god of the sea who piloted the boat that took King Arthur to Avalon? Did you know that fake mermaids (cobbled together from bits of various animals and sea creatures) were put on display in sideshows, billed as "Jenny Hanivers"? Are you aware that Danjy became a cautionary tale? Local women would warn their children not to play in treacherous sea caves by telling them that, if they did, the good neighbours would spirit them away into "Dicky Danjy's Hole."

One by one we fell, and I collected stones and stories until only my mother and I remained. You may wonder why we hung on while everyone else around us was opting out. The answer is simple: Barenwyn. After a long stay in the East to allow her wings to grow back, she returned to Merlin's Cave; and there, like her mother before her, she built a nest and brought forth two perfect baby dragons. I was a grandmother, and Mora (now mellowed with age and with no dire prophecies to report) looked upon the fledglings as family. Indeed they breathed new life into us both. Amidst the drone of meaningless repetition, we felt again as if we had something to live for.

Then, on 29th April 1952, a patient from Broadmoor Hospital climbed the fence and escaped into the surrounding countryside. His name was John Straffen, and he'd been incarcerated there after killing two little girls the year before. Now free again, he came upon five-year-old Linda Bowyer as she rode her bike in the quiet village of Farley Hill. The child cried out once before Straffen's hands closed around her throat. Mora heard. The woman who drew unwanted babies from the water, who adopted discarded children, and who had invented the idea of the Fairy Godmother, once again rushed to a child's aid. In Merlin's Cave, surrounded by granite, I did not hear what transpired. I know only that when I found them later, the child was dead and my mum was barely breathing. Straffen had fractured her skull.

Back in Merlin's Cave, Barenwyn laid her out on the table while I cleaned my hands. I bent to examine Mora's head wound.

"Bloody hell," I murmured. "The bone's been smashed inward... If I can remove the fragments and prevent infection, she'll be all right."

"Mum," Barenwyn said.

"I know what you're gonna say, but we heal really fast. Now help me..."

"Mum, she's dead."

I glared at Barenwyn as if she had just uttered some blasphemy. "She'll be fine. Now stop wasting time and help me."

The dragon's voice shook. "She's not breathing."

"I'm not gonna say it again," I hissed through gritted teeth. "She'll be fine. Now we have work to do."

"Look, Mum. Just look. Do you see any life left in her?"

I looked then into Mora's mind. It was as dark and empty as an abandoned house. I swayed on my feet. The dragon chicks were crying now, and they each had attached themselves to one of my legs. I touched their heads with trembling hands.

"Let go," I whispered, disengaged myself from them, and slowly walked to the tunnel that would lead me back to Annwyn.

It was as dark and empty there as it had been within Mora's ravaged brain. No torches burned in the Great Hall, and the familiar sounds of voices raised in either laughter or anger were wholly absent. The storerooms were empty and the bedchambers vacant. Slowly over the years I had come to terms with our losses. I had wept for Hanyfer, and hated Barinthus for the weakness that led him to tie that noose. I had grieved for Danjy and tried to banish the image of him sitting there in the darkness waiting for the roof to fall in. Gwyn was the worst. My father, whom I so fervently loved and vehemently hated, had abandoned me again. He chose to walk off into an incandescent night of shell fragments and fire, and left me to face this world without his strength. I had also tried to accept that the tribe as a collective body was no more. I acknowledged that, without them, no physical place on this earth felt like home. There would never again be a meeting at the hanter or the people all in a circle dancing to the drum or any feeling that I belonged. I had wrestled with all of these things; and I had accepted them as unalterable fact. But this...

Odd really – regardless of how old you are, when you lose your mother you become a child again. I was a grandmother, for fuck's sake, and yet I felt orphaned and lost. Do you know the worst bit? I could feel her for days and days afterward, in my flesh and in my bones. It was her flesh after all. And it drove me half-mad. I would sit in my room at Annwyn and call desperately to her, and I sobbed as I called. At those moments I felt certain that I could call her back to life, because surely as a mother she could not ignore that distress. Surely that wretched sound would make her come as she used to run to me when I fell and hurt myself as a little girl. But she did not come. And then I knew, in my heart really knew, that she was dead.

John Straffen's trial for the murder of Linda Bowyer began on 21$^{st}$ July. I sat in the gallery and watched the first stuttering days of the trial as jury misconduct led to a dismissal of the "twelve good men and true." With another jury in place, we began again. I heard quite a bit about Straffen's diminished capacity, of how he had an I.Q. of sixty-four and a mental age of nine years and six months. Studying Straffen's gormless face as he slouched in the dock, I could believe it. There was not a whole hell of a lot going on in that brain: only a desire for self-preservation, the woolly ramblings of a truly stupid man and the dim stirrings of a truncated soul – perpetually angry, and mean.

While, in the end, I had been moved to pity Vortigern because of his mental state, because he had been crafted into a monster, I was wholly incapable of feeling sympathy for Straffen. I wanted the bastard to hang. Therefore I inwardly rejoiced when the lawyer for the prosecution, Solicitor-General Sir Reginald Manningham-Buller, introduced as evidence Straffen's previous convictions for the murders of five-year-old Brenda Goddard and nine-year-old Cicely Batstone in 1951. The defence moved for dismissal of these facts on the grounds that they were prejudicial. Judge Cassels overruled and the jury began to see exactly what Straffen was. In the end, it took them only one hour of deliberation to find John Straffen guilty of murder. Judge Cassels ruled that he would be hung by the neck until dead and the execution date was set for 4$^{th}$ September.

Over the years I had softened quite a bit. That epiphany I had in the time of Artos and Gwenhwyfar – that fate had crafted me into a shield – was something I'd taken very seriously. Aside from my final confrontation with Belial, I had endeavoured to live in peace. And so with Straffen set to pay for his crimes, I returned to Barenwyn and her children and resolved to let British criminal law have its way. But it couldn't be that simple, could it? All I wanted after that last, devastating loss, was something straightforward and uncomplicated: try him, convict him and hang him. But no. On 29th August, Straffen was granted a reprieve. He would not face the gallows after all. And in that moment, it felt like everything had been undone: all the years of progress, of self-control, of compassion and work and worship were swept away, leaving me with the painted savage I had been.

Straffen, I knew, was being transferred to Wandsworth Prison in London. If I wanted to get him, I'd have to do so while he was in transit, before he disappeared into the prison and its thick stone walls which were designed to protect people from him, served to protect him from me. I rose early, while Barenwyn and the children were still asleep, and picked up my old bow, a weapon that had spilled so much blood in the past. It was time to go.

As I left the cave, I paused and looked one last time at Barenwyn and the little ones. They were so angelic in sleep, so peaceful. It was, I realised, a peace that I was about to shatter. My hands began to shake. I acknowledged to myself that I was afraid – but of what? I was not, I decided, afraid of going into battle or of planting an arrow in a murderer's chest or of dying in the attempt. Then why did I tremble so? Because courtroom justice and backwoods revenge may accomplish many things, but they cannot restore what we've lost. My mother was dead; I was now the last of my tribe; and I was afraid to go on without them. The one thing that I had steadfastly ignored since Mora's death descended on me in all its terrible enormity. I was the last. I was alone. And I was petrified. That terror was the wellspring of my anger, and the anger demanded retribution.

I saw then that it is always the same. Gwyn feared the race that defeated us at Nanscáwen and so he established "The Wild Hunt." The villagers feared dragons and they slaughtered Xiàngshù. Kenwyn and Barenwyn feared the malice of humans and so they declared war and I feared the loneliness and isolation that I knew was to come. But, I realised, I feared something even more.

My eyes fell again on the chicks nestled against their mother, sleeping peacefully. I feared for their future and the damage I could inflict upon it. If I were to kill Straffen, I would be teaching my grandchildren the old ways. Fear, hate, kill, fear, hate, kill. And this is usually followed by: be killed in your turn. At some point surely it had to stop, and I reckoned that it must stop with me before yet another generation was corrupted and destroyed by it. Truly, in the great and ongoing war between good and evil, we don't need Andras or Belial whispering in our ears to lead us astray. We need only listen to the darkness within ourselves, to the mandates of our own ignorance and fear.

In every life there comes a moment of truth, a moment when we decide who we truly are. Mine had arrived. I looked at my bow. It was beautiful, a work of art and centuries old, and I snapped it in half. That was the last time I picked up a weapon.

And then there was one. The youngest child of the Coranieid tribe, the keeper of the soul stones and the stories, I walk among you now. I am the woman seated across from you on the tube or queuing behind you at the supermarket till. You've bumped into me on a crowded sidewalk. You've caught a glimpse of me as I sat in a restaurant window watching the people pass by – so many of them and each like a separate instrument of an orchestra playing the same melodies that we have sung since the dawn of man. The question that I would ask you, if we should ever share a bottle of wine and in the mellowness of the grape fall to discussing the big, philosophical questions of life, is this:

What are you an instrument of – good or evil?

# END NOTES

1. Una McGovern, ed., *Chambers Dictionary of the Unexplained* (Edinburgh: Chamber Harrap, 2007) 193. For further details see: John G. Neihardt, *Black Elk Speaks* (Lincoln: University of Nebraska Press, 1988) 18-47. Another similar account of the life of a medicine man is: Thomas E. Mails, *Fools Crow: Wisdom and Power* (Tulsa: Council Oak Books, 1991) 39.
2. The tribe speaks an early and imperfectly formed version of the tongue native to the area (later identified as Cornwall, England). Many of the words and phrases can be found in two excellent volumes:
   A) A.S.D. Smith (Caradar), *Cornish Simplified* (Redruth: Dyllansow Truran, 1994), and
   B) *Names for the Cornish* (Redruth: Dyllansow Truran, 1984).
3. Neihardt 204-5 and Mails 51.
4. The stone was potash feldspar and granite.
5. Neil Philip, *Mythology of the World* (London: Kingfisher, 2004) 28.
6. As cited on www2.prestel.co.uk.
7. "The Linton Worm," www.mysteriousbritain.co.uk.
8. Stephen Arnott, *Peculiar Proverbs: Weird Words of Wisdom from around the World* (Chichester: Summersdale Publishers Ltd., 2007) 84.
9. Jacob and Wilhelm Grimm, "The White Snake," *Grimm: The Complete Fairy Tales* (London: Routledge, 2002) 76.
10. Steve Roud, *The Penguin Guide to the Superstitions of Britain and Ireland* (London: Penguin, 2003) 147.
11. Peter Haining, *Superstitions* (London: Treasure Press, 1990) 82-3.
12. John Mitchinson and John Lloyd, *The Book of Animal Ignorance* (London: Faber and Faber, 2007) 55.
13. Temple Grandin and Catherine Johnson, *Animals in Translation: the Woman Who Thinks Like a Cow* (London: Bloomsbury, 2006) 288.
14. Joel Levy, *Freaky Phenomena: Over 1,500 Amazing and Bizarre Facts* (London: Elwin Street Productions, 2007) 68.

15. Karen Shanor and Jagmeet Kanwal, *Bats Sing, Mice Giggle: The Surprising Science of Animals' Inner Lives.* (London: Icon Books, 2010; Kindle edition) 1.
16. Shanor and Kanwall 117.
17. Richard Wiseman, *Quirkology* (London: Macmillan, 2007) 120.
18. Grandin and Johnson 203.
19. Ecclesiastes 1:9.
20. Francis Galton, *The Art of Travel (1872)* (London: Phoenix Press, 2000) 177-8.
21. H.G. Wells, *The Outline of History: Being a Plain History of Life and Mankind* (London: Cassell and Company Ltd., 1925).
22. One of the earliest examples of the plough was called the "ard."
23. Mary Dobson, *Disease: The Extraordinary Stories Behind History's Deadliest Killers* (London: Quercus, 2007) 138.
24. Genesis 1:28.
25. McGovern 339.
26. W.S.W. Anson, ed., "The Nibelung," *Epics and Romances of the Middle Ages* (London: Routledge, 1917) 266.
27. Grandin and Johnson 78-9.
28. Aesop, "The Shepherd's Boy and the Wolf," *Aesop's Fables*, trans. V.S. Vernon (London: William Heinemann, 1949) 41.
29. Hans Christian Andersen, "The Elder Tree Mother," *The Complete Fairy Tales* (Ware: Wordsworth Editions, 1998) 302.
30. Thomas Kinsella, trans., *The Tain* (New York: Oxford University Press, 1969) 10-11.
31. Stuart Gordon, *The Book of Curses: True Tales of Voodoo, Hoodoo and Hex* (Ebbw Vale: Brockhamptom Press, 1997) 2.
32. *Folklore, Myths and Legends of Britain* (London: The Reader's Digest Association Ltd., 1973) 112.
33. Hans Christian Andersen, "'The Will-O'-the-Wisps are in the Town,' Says the Moor-Woman," *The Complete Fairy Tales* (Ware: Wordsworth Editions, 1998) 859.
34. Leslie Alan Horvitz, *The Essential Book of Weather Lore* (London: New Burlington Books, 2007) 97.
35. Judy Allen, *Fantasy Encyclopedia* (London: Kingfisher, 2005) 127.
36. William Shakespeare, *Macbeth*, III.ii.17-19, 22.

37 J.M. Gregor Robertson, *The Household Physician*, division IV (London: Blackie & Son, Ltd., 1890) 1027-8.
38 From the Welsh Epic "The Mabinogion" as quoted by Claire Hamilton and Steve Eddy, *Decoding the Celts: Revealing the Legacy of the Celtic Tradition* (Rochester: Grange Books, 2008) 75.
39 The Sequani speak an early form of Gaelic.
40 Nicholas Culpeper, *Culpeper's Complete Herbal* (London: Arcturus, 2009) 13.
41 Microsoft® Encarta® Encyclopedia 2002.
42 Hamilton and Eddy 87.
43 Hamilton and Eddy 21.
44 Arnott 136.
45 Kinsella 109.
46 From Strabo's *Geographia* IV.4.2 as quoted by Hamilton and Eddy, 63.
47 Jennifer Westwood and Sophia Kingshill, *The Lore of Scotland: A guide to Scottish Legends* (London: Random House Books, 2009) 415-7, and www.dragonorama.com
48 Kinsella 141.
49 Revelation 14:2.
50 Revelation 6:13.
51 Nick Yapp, *Journeys into the Past: Life in the Age of Chivalry* (London: The Reader's Digest Association Ltd, 1999) 132.
52 Pat Morris, ed., *The Country Life Book of the Natural History of the British Isles* (Godalming: Colour Library Books Ltd., 1992) 76.
53 Colin Tudge, *The Secret Life of Trees* (London: Penguin, 2006) 260-1.
54 Simon Marsden, *The Haunted Realm: Ghosts, Witches and Other Strange Tales* (Exeter: Webb and Bower, 1987) 75.
55 *Magic, Myths and Monsters: An Almanac of Extraordinary Fabled Creatures of Earth, Sea and Sky* (Singapore: Carroll and Brown Ltd, 2006) 160.
56 *Magic, Myths and Monsters* 167.
57 M.A. Courtney, *Folklore and Legends of Cornwall* (Exeter: Cornwall Books, 1989) 128.
58 Eileen Molony, *Folk Tales from the West* (London: Kaye and Ward Ltd., 1971) 54.
59 Victor Hugo, `Ninety-three* (London: T. Nelson & Sons) 213-4.
60 Geoffrey Ashe, *Mythology of the British Isles* (London: Methuen, 2002) 107.

61 Geoffrey of Monmouth, "Vita Merlini: The Life of Merlin," Trans. John Jay Perry (www.sacred-texts.com.) 8.
62 *Folklore, Myths and Legends of Britain* 121.
63 Hamilton and Eddy 89.
64 Philip 53.
65 Arnott 190.
66 "The Wild Hunt" www.en.wikipedia.org
67 Allen 134.
68 McGovern 735.
69 Ashe 107.
70 "Original Fairies," *Webster's World Encyclopedia* 2001.
71 William Butler Yeats, "The Stolen Child," lines 9-12 (www.en.wikipedia.org).
72 McGovern 105.
73 William Allingham, "The Fairies," *100 Best Poems for Children*, ed. Roger McGough (London: Puffin Books, 2002) 7-8.
74 *La Bella Durmiente* (Madrid: Susaeta Ediciones, S.A.) 2.
75 Andrew Lang, "Adventures Among Books," as featured on www.djmcadam.com.
76 Homer, *The Iliad*, Trans. W.H.D. Rouse (New York: Mentor Books) 263.
77 Virgil, *The Aeneid*, Trans. E. Fairfax Taylor, (London: J.M. Dent & Sons, 1947) 40.
78 Virgil 40.
79 Sophocles, "Antigone," *Three Theban Plays*, line 1025, Trans. Robert Fagles (New York: Penguin, 1984) 107.
80 Virgil 57.
81 McGovern 103.
82 Roud 61.
83 Thomas Taylor, trans. "I. To the Goddess Prothyræa," *The Hymns of Orpheus* (London: Penguin, 1792) as featured on www.sacred-texts.com.
84 Geoffrey of Monmouth, *The History of the Kings of Britain*, Trans. Sebastian Evans, Book I, Chapter III, p. 7-8. as featured on www.sacred-texts.com.
85 Geoffrey of Monmouth, *History* (Evans), Book I, Chapter V, p. 10-11.
86 Exodus 15:5.
87 Provided by Microsoft® Translator.
88 Paraphrased from Geoffrey of Monmouth, *History* (Evans).

89 Geoffrey of Monmouth, *The History of the Kings of Britain*, Trans. Lewis Thorpe (London: Penguin, 1988) 74.
90 Hugh Latimer, Commentary on Genesis 6:4-5, *The Holy Bible*, Ed. The Rev. George D'Oyly and The Rev. Richard Mant (Oxford: Clarendon Press, 1817).
91 Charles Perrault, "Donkey-skin," *The Complete Fairy Tales*, Trans. Christopher Betts (Oxford: Oxford University Press, 2009) 59.
92 Perrault 59.
93 www.badgers.org.uk
94 Arnott 84.
95 Linda and Roger Flavell, *Dictionary of Proverbs and their Origins* (London: Kyle-Cathie, 2004) 95.
96 Geoffrey of Monmouth, *History* (Thorpe) 106.
97 Geoffrey of Monmouth, *History* (Evans), Book III, Chapter XX, p. 81.
98 Simone de Beauvoir, *The Second Sex* (London: Picador, 1988) 532.
99 Rachel Bromwich, ed. and trans., *The Welsh Triads*, (www.mysticcrossroads.com), Triad 36.
100 Lady Charlotte Guest, trans., "Here is the Story of Lludd and Llevelys," *The Mabinogion*, (http://etext.library.adelaide.edu) 1-2.
101 William Wordsworth, "The Prelude," Book 7, line 718, *Wordsworth: Poetical Works*, Ed. Thomas Hutchinson (New York: Oxford University Press, 1989) 546.
102 Wells 67.
103 Haining 8.
104 Courtney 128.
105 "List of Demons in the Ars Goetia" www.en.wikipedia.org.
106 www.deliriumsrealsm.com.
107 Michael Alexander, trans., *Beowulf*, lines 2832-4 (New York: Penguin, 1973) 140.
108 Geoffrey of Monmouth, *History* (Evans), Book VII, Chapter III, p. 171-2.
109 Guest 1.
110 Guest 3.
111 Guest 3.
112 Yapp 140.
113 "Scabies" www.en.wikipedia.org.
114 Leviticus 13:31.
115 Guest 3.
116 Yapp 132.

117. Bromwich, Triad 51.
118. Paraphrased from William Shakespeare's *Julius Caesar*, Act 1, Scene 2.
119. Psalm 90:4.
120. Tacitus, *Annals*, as quoted in "Battle of Watling Street" on www.en.wikipedia.org.
121. Amy Stewart, *Wicked Plants: The A-Z of Plants that Kill, Maim, Intoxicate and Otherwise Offend* (London: Timber Press, 2010) 221.
122. Hans Christian Andersen, "The Elf-Hill," *The Complete Fairy Tales* (Ware: Wordsworth Editions, 1998) 317.
123. "Classical Elements" www.en.wikipedia.org
124. McGovern 200.
125. Allen 29.
126. www.livestrong.com
127. Steven Pinker, *How the Mind Works* (London: Penguin, 1997; Kindle edition) 26.
128. Grandin 55.
129. Geoffrey of Monmouth, "Vita Merlini" 9.
130. Aesop, "The Lion, the Bear, and the Fox," *Aesop's Fables*, Trans. V.S. Vernon (London: William Heinemann, 1949) 83-4.
131. "The Bee Hive" from www.traditionalmusic.co.uk.
132. "The Chastity Belt" from www.traditionalmusic.co.uk.
133. Kinsella 10-11.
134. Virginia Woolf, "A Room of One's Own," *A Room of One's Own and Three Guineas* (London: Penguin, 1993) 30.
135. www.sparknotes.com
136. Isaiah 1:18
137. Pinker 371.
138. Derek Mitchell and James Blair, "State of the art: Psychopathy," *The Psychologist*, vol. 13 number 7, page 358 on www.thepsychologist.org.uk.
139. Jonah Lehrer, *The Decisive Moment: How the Brain Makes Up its Mind* (London: Canongate; Kindle edition) 173-4.
140. Geoffrey of Monmouth, *History* (Thorpe) 155-6.
141. Geoffrey of Monmouth, *History* (Evans), Book VI, Chapter X, p. 153.
142. Bromwich, Triad 59.
143. Hugh Williams, ed. and trans., *Gildas, The Ruin of Britain &c. (1899), Cymmrodorion Record Series*, No. 3., as featured by Robert Vermaat on vortigernstudies.org.uk.

[144] Anon, "Lord Randal," *Early Ballads*, Ed. Robert Bell (London: George Bell and Sons, 1889) 210-11.

[145] Guidance on rune symbolism from:
Joanna Sandsmark, *Explore Your Destiny with Runes* (London: Godsfield Press, 2006).

[146] St. Gildas the Wise, De Excidio Brittaniae et Conquestu, Chapter II, verse 24-5, www.ancienttexts.org.

[147] William Wordsworth, "We are Seven," lines 13-16, 21-24, 33-33, 61-64, *Wordsworth: Poetical Works*, Ed. Thomas Hutchinson and Ernest De Selincourt (New York: Oxford University Press, 1989) 66.

[148] William Wordsworth, "Resolution and Independence," Stanza 8, lines 50-55, *Norton Anthology of English Literature*, vol.2, Ed. M.H. Abrams (New York: W.W. Norton and Co., 1986) 204.

[149] Gill Farrer-Halls, *Good Health Magic* (London: MQ Publications Ltd., 2003) 14.

[150] www.botanical.com , "A Modern Herbal," copyright 1995-2013.

[151] Karen Sunde.

[152] Sir James Knowles, *The Legends of King Arthur and His Knights* (London: Senate, 1997) 8.

[153] Marie de France, "Lanval," lines 143-9, *The Lais of Marie de France*, Ed. and Trans. Robert Hanning and Joan Ferrante (Durham, North Carolina: Labryrinth Press, 1982) 109.

[154] Robert Hanning and Joan Ferrante, ed. and trans., *The Lais of Marie de France* (Durham, North Carolina: Labryrinth Press, 1982) 123-4.

[155] "The Man Who Never Laughed," *Tenggren's Goldern Tales from the Arabian Nights: The Most Famous Stories from the Great Classic, A THOUSAND AND ONE NIGHTS,* Retold by Margaret Soifer and Irwin Shapiro (New York: Random House, 2003) 97.

[156] Geoffrey of Monmouth, *History* (Thorpe) 205.

[157] John Milton, *Areopagitica: A Speech for the Liberty of Unlicenced Printing to the Parliament of England* as featured on www.dartmouth.edu.

[158] Lilian Stoughton Hyde, *Favourite Greek Myths* (London: George S. Harrap, 1906) 60.

[159] "The Princess of the Tower," from www.sacred-texts.com.

[160] Jacob and Wilhelm Grimm, "Rapunzel," *Grimm: Complete Fairy Tales* (Abindon: Routledge, 2006) 56.

[161] Shakespeare, *Macbeth*, paraphrased from the spells of the three witches and Hecate.
[162] Rosemary Ellen Guiley, *The Encyclopedia of Witches and Witchcraft* (Oxford: Facts on File Ltd., 1989) 239.
[163] "Furfur" www.en.wikipedia.org.
[164] Samuel Liddell, MacGregor Mathers, and Aleister Crowley, trans., *The Lesser Key of Solomon*, Kindle edition, Location 289.
[165] Roud 138.
[166] Knowles 11.
[167] John Keats, "A Letter to Fanny Brawne, 8 July 1819," *Love Letters of Great Men*, Ed. Ursula Doyle (London: Macmillan, 2008) 69.
[168] Michael Foss, *The World of Camelot* (London: Michael O'Mara Books Ltd, 1995) 9.
[169] Christabel Coleridge, "King Arthur, as an English Ideal," www.lib.rochester.edu.
[170] Terry Breverton, *Breverton's Phantasmagoria: A Compendium of Monsters, Myths and Legends* (London: Quercus, 2011) 35.
[171] Alfred Lord Tennyson, *Idylls of the King in Twelve Books* (London: Macmillan, 1962) 11.
[172] Geoffrey of Monmouth, "Vita Merlini" 15.
[173] Daniel Mersey, *Arthur: King of the Britons* (Chichester: Summersdale Publishers Ltd., 2004) 45.
[174] Courtney 121.
[175] Ashe 227.
[176] McGovern 453.
[177] "The Decline and Fall of the Gods," www.sacred-texts.com.
[178] Microsoft Encarta Encyclopedia, 2002.
[179] www.mystical-www.co.uk.
[180] Caradoc, "The Life of Gildas," www.Fordham.edu.
[181] Rev. John Trigilio Jr. and Rev. Kenneth Brighenti, *Catholicism for Dummies* (Hoboken: Wiley Publishing, Inc., 2003) 63.
[182] Tudge 9.
[183] Chris Thompson, "The Washer at the Ford," www.freakyphenomena.com.
[184] "Morgan le Fay, Queen of 'Gore'," www.earlybritishkingdoms.com.
[185] www.timelessmyths.com.
[186] www.celticgrounds.com.

187. "Bean nighe" www.en.wikipedia.org.
188. Sir Thomas Mallory, "Morte D'Arthur," *Norton Anthology of English Literature*, vol.2, Ed. M.H. Abrams (New York: W.W. Norton and Co., 1986) 402-3.
189. www.haverford.edu.
190. Anon, "King Arthur's Death," *Early Ballads*, Ed. Robert Bell (London: George Bell and Sons, 1889) 112.
191. "King Arthur's Death" 112-3.
192. *Folklore, Myths and Legends of Britain* 491.
193. John J. Keats, "To Autumn," lines 1-4, *Selected Poems and Letters*, Ed. Douglas Bush (Boston: Houghon Mifflin Co., 1959) 247.
194. Dante Alighierie, *The Inferno*, VII, lines 81-83, Trans. John Ciardi (New York: Mentor, 1982) 74.
195. Anicius Manlius Severinus Boethius, *The Consolation of Philosophy*, Trans. by H.R. James, M.A., Kindle edition, 31.
196. Boethius 119.
197. For more on this type of communication see:
Margaret Pickston, *The Language of Flowers* (London: Michael Joseph Ltd, 1991), and, Mandy Kirkby, *The Language of Flowers, a Miscellany* (London: Macmillan, 2011).
198. "The Four Dragons: A Chinese Tale," www.crystalinks.com/chinadragons
199. Microsoft Encarta Encyclopedia, 2002.
200. *Folklore, Myths and Legends of Britain* 27.
201. Courtney 71.
202. "Alzheimer's Disease" www.en.wikipedia.org .
203. Robertson 109.
204. H.C. Covey, "A Return to Infancy: Old Age and the Second Childhood in History," www.ncbi.nlm.nih.
205. Courtney 71.
206. Job 41:13, 15, 17, 26, 33.
207. Alexander 132.
208. Arnott 84.
209. "The Naga Apalala," www.dragonorama.com.
210. Aesop, "The Labourer and the Snake," *Aesop's Fables*, Trans. V.S. Vernon (London: William Heinemann, 1949) 149.
211. Matthew 6:25-26.

212 Anon, *The Funniest Thing You Never Said*, Ed. Rosemarie Jarski (London: Ebury Press, 2004) 22.
213 Edgar Allan Poe, "Alone," lines 9-10 and 19-22, *Edgar Allan Poe: Complete Tales and Poems* (New York: Random House, Vintage Books, 1975) 1026.
214 Revelation 12:7-9, 12.
215 The Qur'an, Sura 7: 11-13, 16-18.
216 Carol K. Mack and Dinah Mack, *A Field Guide to Demons, Vampires, Fallen Angels and Other Subversive Spirits* (New York: Arcade Publishing, 2011; Kindle edition) location 2194.
217 The Qur'an, Sura 26: 221-223.
218 John Milton, "Paradise Lost," *The Poetical Works of John Milton* (London: Frederick Warne and Co., undated) 86.
219 Milton, "Paradise Lost," 102.
220 I Samuel 2.
221 I Samuel 2:12.
222 Stephen T. Asma, *On Monsters: An Unnatural History of Our Worst Fears* (Oxford: Oxford University Press, 2009; Kindle edition) 105.
223 Leviticus 20:2.
224 Mack and Mack, location 294.
225 Amy Stewart, *Wicked Bugs* (London: Timber Press, 2011) 87.
226 Richard Barber, trans., *Bestiary*, MS Bodley 764 (Woodbridge: Boydell Press, 1992) 170.
227 The Qur'an, Sura 34:12.
228 William Blake, "The Marriage of Heaven and Hell," *Blake's Poetry and Designs*, Ed. Mary Lynn Johnson (New York: Norton, 1979) 89.
229 "The Fisherman and the Afreet," *Tenggren's Goldern Tales from the Arabian Nights: The Most Famous Stories from the Great Classic, A THOUSAND AND ONE NIGHTS*, Retold by Margaret Soifer and Irwin Shapiro (New York: Random House, 2003) 59.
230 Jacob and Wilhelm Grimm, "The Spirit in the Bottle," *Grimm: Complete Fairy Tales* (Abindon: Routledge, 2006) 403.
231 The Qur'an, Sura 27:16.
232 Dana Fagaros and Michael Pauls, *Tall Tales and Tittle-Tattle* (London: Cadogan Guides, 2003) 142.
233 Mike Paine, *The Crusades* (Harpenden, Herts: Pocket Essentials, 2005) 24.

234 Andrea Hopkins, *A Chronicle History of Knights* (Wigston, Leicester: Silverdale Books, 2005). 81.
235 2 Corinthians 11:14-15.
236 Ephesians 6:10.
237 Paine 36.
238 John Michael Greer, *Monsters* (Woodbury: Llewellyn Publications, 2001) 169.
239 Hopkins 83.
240 Michael D. Hull, "First Crusade: Siege of Jerusalem" as featured on www.historynet.com
241 Paine 47.
242 Yapp 97.
243 Simon Sebag Montefiore, *Jerusalem: The Biography* (London: Weidenfeld and Nicholson, 2011) 213-14.
244 Agatha Christie, *Dumb Witness* (London: Harper Collins Publishers, 1994) 148.
245 At the time, a courser cost somewhere between £20 and £100. In modern terms, it is the equivalent of being given a Mercedes.
246 Sigmund Freud, *Civilization and Its Discontents* (Toronto: Dover Publications, 1994) 27.
247 *Dr. Ernest Drake's Dragonology: The Complete Book of Dragons* (Dorking, Surrey: Templar Publishing, 2003).
248 Alexander 135 and 130.
249 Christina Rossetti, "Flint," *100 Best Poems for Children*, Ed. Roger McGough (London: Penguin, 2001) 96.
250 Angela Morrow, RN, "What is Pain?," www.about.com .
251 Barber 27.
252 Barber 170.
253 An ornate, velvet robe with full sleeves, tight cuffs and belted at the waist.
254 Job 24:13, 15, 17.
255 Lao Tzu, *Tao Te Ching*, Trans. Stephen Addiss and Stanley Lombardo (Cambridge: Hackett Publishing Company, 1993) 41.
256 "Robin Hood," *Webster's World Encyclopedia*, 2001.
257 www.robin-hoods-bay.co.uk
258 "Boggart" en.wikipedia.org
259 www.summitpost.org

260 www.summitpost.org
261 www.summitpost.org
262 Jonah 2:9
263 "Antioch" en.wikipedia.org
264 Bernard de Clairvaux, *The Primitive Rule*, www.the-orb.net.
265 Paraphrased from Dr. See Kin, "Reading 64 Chinese Fortune Sticks," on www.scribd.com
266 Ruth 1:16
267 Lao Tzu, *Tao Te Ching* on web.cn.edu
268 Lao Tzu
269 Dr. See Kin
270 Psalm 33:13 and 15.
271 Jacobus de Voragine, "St. George," *The Golden Legend (Aurea Legenda)*, Medieval Sourcebook on www.fordham.edu.
272 Courtney 72.
273 Courtney 72-3.
274 "Ian Maclaren" www.en.wikipedia.org
275 Glen Duncan, *The Last Werewolf* (London: Canongate, 2011) 10.
276 Duncan 48.
277 Anne Rice, *Interview with the Vampire* (London: Sphere, 2010) 255-6.
278 "Plymouth Blitz" www.en.wikipedia.org

CPSIA information can be obtained at www.ICGtesting.com
Printed in the USA
BVOW05s0325010515

397957BV00003B/9/P